VICTOR HUGO

Les Misérables

TRANSLATED AND WITH AN INTRODUCTION BY
NORMAN DENNY

LITHOGRAPHS BY
CHARLES KEEPING

VOLUME II

LONDON
The Folio Press
1976

PRINTED IN GREAT BRITAIN
by Fletcher & Son Ltd, Norwich

CONTENTS

VOLUME II

*Part Four: The Idyll in the Rue Plumet and the
Epic of the Rue Saint-Denis*

Part Five: Jean Valjean

ILLUSTRATIONS

VOLUME II

v

The Idyll in the Rue Plumet and the Epic of the Rue Saint-Denis

BOOK ONE

A FEW PAGES OF HISTORY

I. *Well-tailored*

THE YEARS 1831 and 1832, immediately succeeding the July Revolution, are among the most singular and striking in our history. These two years, in the setting of those that preceded and those that followed them, are like two mountains displaying the heights of revolution and also its precipitous depths. The social masses which are the base of civilization, the solid structure of superimposed and related interests, the secular outlines of France's ancient culture, all these constantly appear and disappear amid the storm-clouds of systems, passions and theories. These appearances and disappearances have been termed movement and resistance. At intervals one may catch a gleam of Truth, that daylight of the human soul.

This remarkable period is sufficiently distinct, and now sufficiently remote from us, for its main outlines to be discernible. We shall seek to depict them.

The Bourbon restoration had been one of those intermediate phases, difficult of definition, in which exhaustion and rumour, mutterings, slumber and tumult all are mingled, and which in fact denote the arrival of a great nation at a staging-point. Such periods are deceptive and baffle the policies of those seeking to exploit them. At the beginning the nation asks for nothing but repose; it has only one desire, which is for peace, and one aspiration, which is to be insignificant. In other words, it longs for tranquillity. We have had enough of great happenings, great risks, great adventures, and more than enough, God save us, of great men. We would exchange Caesar for Prusias and Napoleon for the Roi d'Yvetot—'what a good little king he was', as Béranger sang. The march has gone on since dawn, and we are in the evening of a long, hard day. The first stage was with Mirabeau, the second with Robespierre and the third with Bonaparte. Now we are exhausted and each man seeks his bed.

What do they so urgently look for, the wearied devotions, the tired heroisms, the sated ambitions, the fortunes gained? They want a breathing-spell, and they have one. They take hold of peace, tranquillity, and leisure, and are content. Yet certain facts emerge and call for notice by hammering on the door. They are facts born of revolution and war, living and breathing facts entitled to become part of the fabric of society, and which do so. But for the most part they are the under-officers and outriders whose business is to prepare lodgings for the commanders.

It is now that the political philosophers appear on the scene, while the weary demand rest and new-found facts demand guarantees. Guarantees are to facts what rest is to men.

That is what England demanded of the Stuarts after the Protector and what France demanded of the Bourbons after the Empire.

These guarantees are a necessity of the time. They have to be conceded. The princes 'offer', but it is the force of events that gives. This is a profound truth, necessary to know, which the Stuarts did not appreciate in 1660 and of which the Bourbons had not an inkling in 1814.

The predestined family which returned to France after the collapse of Napoleon was sufficiently naïve to believe that it was giving, and that what it had given it might take back; that the House of Bourbon possessed divine rights and that France possessed none; that the political concessions granted in the charter of Louis XVIII were no more than blossomings of the Divine Right, plucked by the House of Bourbon and graciously bestowed on the people until such time as it might please the king to reclaim them. But its very reluctance to concede them should have warned the House of Bourbon that the gift was not its own.

The Royal House was acrimonious in the nineteenth century. It pulled a wry face at every advance of the nation. To use a trivial word—that is to say, a commonplace and true one—it jibbed. The people saw this.

The Bourbons believed that they were strong because the Empire had been swept away before them like the changing of a stage-set. They did not perceive that they had been brought back in the same fashion. They did not see that they too were in the hands that had removed Napoleon.

They believed they had roots because they represented the past. They were wrong. They were a part of the past, but the whole past was France. The roots of French society were not in the Bourbons but in the nation. Those deep and vigorous roots were not the rights of a single family but the history of a people. They were everywhere, except under the throne.

The House of Bourbon was the illustrious and blood-stained core of France's history, but it was no longer the principal element in her destiny or the essential basis of her policies. The Bourbons were dispensable, they had been dispensed with for twenty-two years, the

4

continuity had been broken. These were things they did not realize. How could they be expected to realize them, maintaining as they did that the events of 9 Thermidor had occured in the reign of Louis XVII, and Marengo in the reign of Louis XVIII? Never since the beginning of history have princes been so blind in the face of facts, so unaware of the portion of Divine Authority which those facts embraced and enacted. Never has the earthly pretension which is called the right of kings so flatly denied the Right which comes from above.

It was a fatal blunder which prompted this family to lay hands on the guarantees 'offered' in 1814—concessions, as they described them. A sad business. Those so-called concessions were our conquests, and what they called our encroachments were our rights.

When it thought the time was ripe, the Restoration, believing itself victorious over Bonaparte and enrooted in the nation—that is to say, believing itself to be both strong and deep—abruptly showed its face and chanced its arm. On a July morning it confronted France and, raising its voice, revoked both collective and individual rights, the sovereignty of the nation and the liberty of the citizen. In other words it denied to the nation that which made the nation, and to the citizen that which made the citizen.

This was the essence of those famous Acts which are called the *Ordonnances de juillet*.

The Restoration fell.

It was right that it should fall. Nevertheless it must be said that it had not been absolutely hostile to all forms of progress. Great things had been accomplished while the régime looked on.

Under the Restoration the nation had grown accustomed to calm discussion, which had not happened under the Republic, and to greatness in peace, which had not happened under the Empire. A free and strong France had provided a heartening example for the peoples of Europe. Revolution had spoken under Robespierre, and guns had spoken under Bonaparte: it was under Louis XVIII and Charles X that intellect made itself heard. The winds died down and the torch was re-lighted. The pure light of the spirit could be seen trembling on the serene heights, a glowing spectacle of use and delight. During a period of fifteen years great principles, long-familiar to the philosopher but novel to the statesman, were seen to be at work in peace and in the light of day: equality before the law, freedom of conscience, freedom of speech and of the press, careers open to all talents. So it was until 1830. The Bourbons were an instru-of civilization which broke in the hands of Providence.

The fall of the Bourbons was clothed with greatness, not on their side but on the side of the nation. They abandoned the throne solemnly but without authority. This descent into oblivion was not one of those grave occasions which linger as a sombre passage of history; it was enriched neither with the spectral calm of Charles I nor with the eagle-cry of Napoleon. They went away, and that was all. In putting off the crown they retained no lustre. They were dignified but not august, and in some degree they lacked the majesty of their misfortune. Charles X, causing a round table to be sawn square during the voyage from Cherbourg, seemed more concerned with the affront to etiquette than with the crumbling of the monarchy. This narrowness was saddening to the devoted men who loved their persons and the serious men who honoured their race. The people, on the other hand, were admirable. The nation, assailed with armed force by a sort of royal insurrection, was so conscious of its strength that it felt no anger. It defended its rights and, acting with restraint, put things in their proper place (the government within the law, the Bourbons, alas, in exile) and there it stopped. It removed the elderly king, Charles X, from under the canopy which had sheltered Louis XIV, and set him gently upon earth. It laid no hand on the royal persons except with sorrow and precaution. This was not the work of one man or of several men; it was the work of France, the whole of France; victorious France flushed with her victory who yet seemed to recall the words spoken by William of Vair after the day of the barricades in 1588: 'It is easy for those accustomed to hang upon the favours of the great, hopping, like birds on a tree, from evil to good fortune, to be bold in defying their prince in his adversity; but for myself, the fortunes of my kings will always be deserving of reverence, and especially in their affliction.'

The Bourbons took with them respect but not regret. As we have said, their misfortune was greater than themselves. They vanished from the scene.

The July Revolution at once found friends and enemies throughout the world. The former greeted it with enthusiasm and rejoicing, the latter averted their gaze, each according to his nature. The princes of Europe, like owls in the dawn, at first shut their eyes in wounded amazement, and opened them only to utter threats. Their fear was understandable, their wrath excusable. That strange revolution had been scarcely a conflict; it had not even done royalty the honour of treating it as an enemy and shedding its blood. In the eyes of despotism, always anxious for liberty to defame itself by its own acts, the grave defect of the July Revolution was that it was both formidable and gentle. And so nothing could be attempted or plotted against it. Even those who were most outraged, most wrathful, and most apprehensive, were obliged to salute it. However great our egotism and our anger, a mysterious respect is engendered

6

by events in which we feel the working of a power higher than man.

The July Revolution was the triumph of Right over Fact, a thing of splendour. Right overthrowing the accepted Fact. Hence the brilliance of the July Revolution, and its clemency. Right triumphant has no need of violence. Right is justice and truth.

It is the quality of Right that it remains eternally beautiful and unsullied. However necessary Fact may appear to be, however acquiesced in at a given time, if it exists as Fact alone, embodying too little Right or none at all, it must inevitably, with the passing of time, become distorted and unnatural, even monstrous. If we wish to measure the degree of ugliness by which Fact can be overtaken, seen in the perspective of centuries, we have only to consider Machiavelli. Machiavelli was not an evil genius, a demon, or a wretched and cowardly writer; he was simply Fact. And not merely Italian Fact but European Fact, sixteenth-century Fact. Nevertheless he appears hideous, and is so, in the light of nineteenth-century morality.

The conflict between Right and Fact goes back to the dawn of human society. To bring it to an end, uniting the pure thought with human reality, peacefully causing Right to pervade Fact and Fact to be embedded in Right, this is the task of wise men.

II. *Badly Stitched*

But the work of the wise is one thing and the work of the merely clever is another.

The revolution of 1830 soon came to a stop.

Directly a revolution has run aground the clever tear its wreckage apart.

The clever, in our century, have chosen to designate themselves statesmen, so much so that the word has come into common use. But we have to remember that where there is only cleverness there is necessarily narrowness. To say, 'the clever ones' is to say, 'the mediocrities'; and in the same way to talk of 'statesmen' is sometimes to talk of betrayers.

If we are to believe the clever ones, revolutions such as the July Revolution are like severed arteries requiring instant ligature. Rights too loudly proclaimed become unsettling; and so, once righteousness has prevailed, the State must be strengthened. Liberty being safeguarded, power must be consolidated. Thus far the Wise do not quarrel with the Clever, but they begin to have misgivings.

7

Two questions arise. In the first place, what is power? And secondly, where does it come from? The clever ones do not seem to hear these murmurs and continue their operations.

According to these politicians, who are apt at dissembling convenient myths under the guise of necessity, the first thing a nation needs after a revolution, if that nation forms part of a monarchic continent, is a ruling dynasty. Only then, they maintain, can peace be restored after a revolution—that is to say, time for the wounds to heal and the house to be repaired. The dynasty hides the scaffolding and affords cover for the ambulance.

But it is not always easy to create a dynasty. At a pinch any man of genius or even any soldier of fortune may be made into a king. Bonaparte is an instance of the first, and an instance of the second is Iturbide, the Mexican general who was proclaimed emperor in 1821, deposed in 1823, and shot the following year. But not any family can be established as a dynasty. For this some depth of ancestry is needed: the wrinkles of centuries cannot be improvised.

If we consider the matter from the point of view of a 'statesman' (making, of course, all due reservations), what are the characteristics of the king who is thrown up by a revolution? He may be, and it is desirable that he should be, himself a revolutionary—that is to say, a man who has played a part in the revolution and in so doing has committed or distinguished himself; a man who has himself wielded the axe or the sword.

But what are the characteristics needful for a dynasty? It must represent the nation in the sense that it is revolutionary at one remove, not from having committed any positive act, but from its acceptance of the idea. It must be informed with the past and thus historic, and also with the future and thus sympathetic.

This explains why the first revolutions were content to find a man, a Cromwell or a Napoleon, and why succeeding revolutions were obliged to find a family, a House of Brunswick or a House of Orléans. Royal houses are something like those Indian fig-trees whose branches droop down to the earth, take root and themselves become fig-trees: every branch may grow into a dynasty—provided always that it reaches down to the people.

Such is the theory of the clever ones.

So the great art is this: to endow success with something of the aspect of disaster, so that those who profit by it are also alarmed by it; to season advance with misgivings, widen the curve of transition to the point of slowing down progress, denounce and decry extremism, cut corners and finger-nails, cushion the triumph, damp down the assertion of rights, swaddle the giant mass of the people in blankets and put it hastily to bed, subject the superabundance of health to a restricted diet, treat Hercules like a convalescent, fetter principle with expediency, slake the thirst for the ideal with a soothing tisane and, in a word, put a screen round revolution to ensure that it does not succeed too well.

This was the theory applied in France in 1830, having been applied in England in 1688.

1830 was a revolution arrested in mid-course, half-way to achieving real progress, a mock-assertion of rights. But logic ignores the more-or-less as absolutely as the sun ignores candlelight.

And who is it who checks revolutions in mid-course? It is the bourgeoisie.

Why? Because the bourgeoisie represent satisfied demands. Yesterday there was appetite; today there is abundance; tomorrow there will be surfeit. The phenomenon of 1814 after Napoleon was repeated in 1830 after Charles X.

The attempt has been made, mistakenly, to treat the bourgeoisie as though they were a class. They are simply the satisfied section of the populace. The bourgeois is the man who now has leisure to take his ease; but an armchair is not a caste. By being in too much of a hurry to sit back, one may hinder the progress of the whole human race. This has often been the failing of the bourgeoisie. But they cannot be regarded as a class because of this failing. Self-interest is not confined to any one division of the social order.

To be just even to self-interest, the state of affairs aspired to after the shock of 1830 by that part of the nation known as the bourgeoisie was not one of total inertia, which is composed of indifference and indolence and contains an element of shame; it was not a state of slumber, presupposing forgetfulness, a world lost in dreams; it was simply a halt.

The word 'halt' has a twofold, almost contradictory meaning. An army on the march, that is to say, in movement, is ordered to halt, that is to say, to rest. The halt is to enable it to recover its energies. It is a state of armed, open-eyed rest, guarded by sentinels, a pause between the battle of yesterday and the battle of tomorrow. It is an in-between time, such as the period between 1830 and 1848, and for the word 'battle' we may substitute the word 'progress'.

So the bourgeoisie, like the statesmen, had need of a man who embodied the word 'halt'. A combination of 'although' and 'because'. A composite individual signifying both revolution and stability—in other words, affirming the present by formally reconciling the past with the future. And the man was there. He was Louis-Philippe of Orléans.

The vote of 221 deputies made Louis-Philippe king. Lafayette presided, extolling 'the best of republics'. The Paris Hôtel de Ville

9

replaced Rheims Cathedral. This substitution of a half-throne for an entire throne was 'the achievement of 1830'.

When the clever ones had finished their work, the huge weakness of their solution became apparent. It had all been done without regard to the basic rights of the people. Absolute right cried out in protest; but then, an ominous thing, it withdrew into the shadows.

III. *Louis-Philippe*

Revolutions have vigorous arms and shrewd hands; they deal heavy blows but choose well. Even when unfinished, bastardized and doctored, reduced to the state of minor revolutions, like that of 1830, they still nearly always retain sufficient redeeming sanity not to come wholly to grief. A revolution is never an abdication.

But we must not overdo our praises; revolutions can go wrong, and grave mistakes have been made.

To return to 1830, it started on the right lines. In the establishment which restored order after the truncated revolution, the king himself was worth more than the institution of royalty. Louis-Philippe was an exceptional man.

The son of a father for whom history will surely find excuses, he was as deserving of esteem as his father was of blame. He was endowed with all the private and many of the public virtues. He was careful of his health, his fortune, his person and his personal affairs, conscious of the cost of a minute but not always of the price of a year. He was sober, steadfast, peaceable and patient, a friendly man and a good prince who slept only with his wife and kept lackeys in his palace whose business it was to display the conjugal bed to visitors, a necessary precaution in view of the flagrant illegitimacies that had occurred in the senior branch of the family. He knew every European language and also, which is less common, the language of every sectional interest, and spoke them all. An admirable representative of the 'middle class', he nevertheless rose above it and was in all respects superior to it, having the good sense, while very conscious of the royal blood in his veins, to value himself at his true worth, and very particular in the matter of his descent, declaring himself to be an Orléans and not a Bourbon. He was the loftiest of princes in the days when he was no more than a Serene Highness but became a *franc bourgeois* on the day he assumed the title of Majesty. Flowery of speech in public but concise in private; reportedly parsimonious, but this was not proved, and in fact he was one of those prudent persons who easily grow lavish where fancy or duty is involved; well-read but not very appreciative of literature; a gentleman but not a cavalier, simple, calm and strong-minded, adored by his family and his household; a fascinating talker; a statesman without illusions, inwardly cold, dominated by immediate necessity and always ruling by expediency, incapable of rancour or of gratitude, ruthless in exercising superiority over mediocrity, clever at frustrating by parliamentary majorities those mysterious undercurrents of opinion that threaten thrones. He was expansive and sometimes rash in his expansiveness, but remarkably adroit in his rashness; fertile in expedients, in postures and disguises, causing France to go in awe of Europe and Europe to go in awe of France. He undoubtedly loved his country but still preferred his family. He prized rulership more than authority, and authority more than dignity: an attitude having the serious drawback, being intent upon success, that it admits of deception and does not absolutely exclude baseness, but which has the advantage of preserving politics from violent reversals, the State from disruption and society from disaster. He was meticulous, correct, watchful, shrewd and indefatigable, sometimes contradicting and capable of repudiating himself. He dealt boldly with Austria at Ancona and stubbornly with England in Spain, bombarded Antwerp and compensated Pritchard. He sang the *Marseillaise* with conviction. He was impervious to depression or lassitude, had no taste for beauty or idealism, no tendency to reckless generosity, utopianism, day-dreaming, anger, personal vanity or fear. Indeed, he displayed every form of personal courage, as a general at Valmy and a common soldier at Jemmapes; he emerged smiling from eight attempts at regicide, had the fortitude of a grenadier and the moral courage of a philosopher. Nothing dismayed him except the possibility of a European collapse, and he had no fondness for major political adventures, being always ready to risk his life but never his work. He concealed his aims with the use of persuasion, seeking to be obeyed as a man of reason rather than as a king. He was observant but without intuition, little concerned with sensibilities but having a knowledge of men—that is to say, needing to see for himself in order to judge. He possessed a ready and penetrating good sense, practical wisdom, fluency of speech and a prodigious memory, upon which he constantly drew, in this respect resembling Caesar, Alexander, and Napoleon. He knew facts, details, dates and proper names, but ignored tendencies, passions, the diverse genius of the masses, the buried aspirations and hidden turbulence of souls—in a word, everything that may be termed the sub-conscious. He was accepted on the surface, but had little contact with the depths of France, maintaining his position by adroitness, governing too much and ruling too little, always his own prime-minister, excelling in the use of trivialities as an obstruction to the growth of great ideas.

Mingled with his genuinely creative talent for civilization, order, and organization there was the spirit of pettifogging chicanery. The founder and advocate of a dynasty, he had in him something of a Charlemagne and something of an attorney. In short, as a lofty and original figure, a prince able to assert himself despite the misgivings of France, and to achieve power despite the jealousy of Europe, Louis-Philippe might be classed among the great men of his century and take his place among the great rulers of history if he had cared a little more for glory and had possessed as much feeling for grandeur as he had for expediency.

Louis-Philippe had been handsome as a young man and remained graceful in age. Although not always approved of by the nation as a whole, he was liked by the common people. He knew how to please, he had the gift of charm. Majesty was something that he lacked; the crown sat uneasily on him as king, and white hair did not suit him as an old man. His manners were those of the old régime, his behaviour that of the new, a blend of the aristocrat and the bourgeois that suited 1830. He was the embodiment of a period of transition, preserving the old forms of pronunciation and spelling in the service of new modes of thought. He wore the uniform of the Garde Nationale like Charles X and the sash of the Légion d'honneur like Napoleon.

He seldom went to chapel, and never hunted or went to the opera, being thus quite uninfluenced by clerics, masters-of-hounds and ballet-dancers, which had something to do with his bourgeois popularity. He kept no Court. He walked out with an umbrella under his arm, and this umbrella was for a long time a part of his image. He was interested in building, in gardening, and in medicine; he bled a postillion who had a fall from his horse, and would no more have been separated from his lancet than Henri III was from his dagger. The royalists laughed at this absurdity, saying that he was the first king who had ever shed blood in order to cure.

In the charges levelled by history against Louis-Philippe there is a distinction to be drawn. There were three types of charge, against royalty as such, against his reign, and against the king as an individual, and they belong in separate categories. The suppression of democratic rights, the sidetracking of progress, the violent repression of public demonstrations, the use of armed force to put down insurrection, the smothering of the real country by legal machinery and legality only half-enforced, with a privileged class of three hundred thousand—all these were the acts of royalty. The rejection of Belgium; the over-harsh conquest of Algeria, more barbarous than civilized, like the conquest of India by the English; the bad faith at Abd-el-Kadir and Blaye; the suborning of Deutz and compensation of Pritchard—these were acts of the reign. And family politics rather than a national policy were the acts of the king.

As we see, when the charges are thus classified, those against the king are diminished. His great fault was that he was overmodest in the name of France.

Why was this?

Louis-Philippe was too fatherly a king. His settled aim, with which nothing might be allowed to interfere, of nursing a family in order to hatch out a dynasty, made him wary of all else; it induced in him an excess of caution quite unsuited to a nation with 14 July in its civic tradition and Austerlitz in its military history.

Apart from this, and setting aside those public duties which must always take precedence, there was Louis-Philippe's profound personal devotion to his family, which was entirely deserved. They were an admirable domestic group in which virtue went hand-in-hand with talent. One of his daughters, Marie d'Orléans, made a name for herself as an artist, as Charles d'Orléans did as a poet. Her soul is manifest in the statue which she named Joan of Arc. Two others of his sons drew from Metternich the following rhetorical tribute: 'They are young men such as one seldom sees and princes such as one never sees.'

Without distortion or exaggeration, that is the truth about Louis-Philippe.

To be by nature the 'prince égalité', embodying in himself the contradiction between the Restoration and the Revolution; to possess those disturbing qualities of the revolutionary which in a ruler become reassuring—this was his good fortune in 1830. Never was the man more wholly suited to the event; the one partook of the other. Louis-Philippe was the mood of 1830 embodied in a man. Moreover he had this especial recommendation for the throne, that he was an exile. He had been persecuted, a wanderer and poor. He had lived by working. In Switzerland, that heir by appanage to the richest princedoms of France had sold an old horse to buy food. At Reichenau he had given lessons in mathematics while his sister Adelaide did embroidery and needlework. These things, in association with royal blood, won the hearts of the bourgeoisie. He had with his own hands destroyed the last iron cage at Mont Saint-Michel, built to the order of Louis XI and used by Louis XV. He was the comrade of Dumouriez and the friend of Lafayette; he had been a member of the Jacobin Club; Mirabeau had clapped him on the shoulder and Danton had addressed him as 'young man'. In 1793, when he was twenty-four, he had witnessed, from a back bench in the Convention, the trial of Louis XVI, so aptly named 'that poor tyrant'. The blind clairvoyance of the Revolution, shattering monarchy in the person of the king and the king with the institution of monarchy, almost unconscious of the living man crushed beneath the weight of the idea; the huge clamour of the tribunal-assembly; the harsh, questioning voice of public fury to which Capet could find no answer; the stupefied wagging of the royal head under that terrifying blast; the relative innocence of everyone involved in the catastrophe, those condemning no less than those condemned—he had seen all these things, he had witnessed that delirium. He had seen the centuries arraigned at the bar of the Convention, and behind the unhappy figure of Louis XVI, the chance-comer made scapegoat, he had seen the formidable shadow of the real accused, which was monarchy; and there lingered in his heart an awed respect for the huge justice of the people, nearly as impersonal as the justice of God.

The impression made on him by the Revolution was enormous. His memory was a living picture of those tremendous years, lived minute by minute. Once, in the presence of a witness whose word we cannot doubt, he recited from memory the names of all the members of the Constituent Assembly beginning with the letter A.

He was a king who believed in openness. During his reign the press was free and the law-courts were free, and there was freedom of conscience and of speech. The September laws were unequivocal. Though well aware of the destructive power of light shed upon the privileged, he allowed his throne to be fully exposed to public scrutiny, and posterity will credit him with this good faith.

Like all historic personages who have left the stage, Louis-Philippe now stands arraigned at the bar of public opinion, but his trial is still only that of the first instance. The time has not yet come when history, speaking freely and with a mature voice, will pass final judgement upon him. Even the austere and illustrious historian, Louis Blanc, has recently modified his first verdict. Louis-Philippe was elected by the approximation known as 'the 221' and the impulse of the year 1830—that is to say, by a demi-Parliament and a demi-revolution; and in any event, viewing him with the detachment proper to an historian, we may not pass judgement on him here without, as we have already seen, making certain reservations in the name of the absolute principle of democracy. By that absolute standard, and outside the two essential rights, in the first place that of the individual and in the second that of the people as a whole, all is usurpation. But what we can already say, subject to these reservations, is that all in all, and however we may view him, Louis-Philippe, judged as himself and in terms of human goodness, will be known, to adopt the language of ancient history, as one of the best princes who ever acceded to a throne.

What can be held against him except the throne itself? Dismissing the monarch, we are left with the man. And the man is good—good sometimes to the point of being admirable. Often, amid the heaviest perplexities, and after spending the day in battle with the diplomacy of a whole continent, he would return exhausted to his private apartments, and there, despite his fatigue, would sit up all night immersed in the details of a criminal trial, believing that, important though it was to hold his own against all Europe, it was still more important to save a solitary man from the executioner. He obstinately opposed his Keeper of the Seal and disputed every inch of the way the claims of the guillotine with the public prosecutors, those 'legal babblers' as he called them. The dossiers were sometimes piled high on his desk and he studied them all, finding it intolerable that he should neglect the case of any poor wretch condemned to death. On one occasion he said to the person we have already mentioned, 'I rescued seven last night.' During the early years of his reign the death-penalty was virtually abolished; the erection of a public scaffold was an outrage to the king. But, the execution-place of La Grève having vanished with the senior branch of his family, a bourgeois Grève was instituted under the name of the Barrière Saint-Jacques. The 'practical man' felt the need of a more-or-less legitimate guillotine, and this was one of the triumphs of Casimir Perier, who stood for the bigoted side of the bourgeoisie, over Louis-Philippe, who stood for their liberalism. He annotated the case of Beccaria with his own hand, and after the Fieschi plot he exclaimed, 'A pity I wasn't wounded! I could have pardoned him.' On another occasion, referring to the opposition of his ministers in the case of Barbès, one of the most noble figures of our time who was condemned to death in 1839 for his political activities, he wrote: 'Sa grace est accordée, il ne me reste plus qu'a l'obtenir.'*

For ourselves, in a tale wherein goodness is the pearl of rarest price, the man who was kind comes almost before the man who was great.

Since Louis-Philippe has been severely judged by some, and perhaps over-harshly by others, it is only proper that a man who knew him, and today is himself a ghost, should bear witness on his behalf at the bar of History. His testimony, such as it is, is clearly and above all else disinterested. An epitaph written by the dead is sincere; a shade can console another shade, and living in the same shadows has the right to praise. There is little risk that anyone will say of those two exiles, 'One flattered the other.'

* 'His pardon is granted, it only remains for me to secure it.' The words may have been written to Hugo himself, who had sent the king a short poem pleading for Barbès. It is worth recalling that Hugo was living in exile when, long afterwards, he wrote this book.

IV. *Flaws in the Structure*

At this moment, when our tale is about to plunge into the depths of one of those tragic clouds which obscure the beginning of Louis-Philippe's reign, there can be no equivocation; it is essential that this book should state its position in respect of the king.

Louis-Philippe had assumed the royal authority without violence, without any positive act on his part, through a revolutionary chance which clearly had little to do with the real aims of the revolution, and in which, as Duke of Orléans, he had taken no personal initiative. He had been born a prince and believed that he was elected king. He had not conferred the mandate on himself or attempted to seize it. It had been offered him and he had accepted it in the conviction, certainly mistaken, that the offer was in accordance with the law and that to accept it was his duty. He held it in good faith. In all conscience we must declare that Louis-Philippe did occupy the throne in good faith, that democracy assailed him in good faith, and that neither side is to blame for the violence engendered by the struggle. A clash of principles is like a clash of elements, ocean fighting on the side of water, tempest on the side of air. The king defended monarchy and democracy defended the people; what was relative, which is monarchy, resisted what was absolute, which is democracy. Society shed blood in the conflict, but the present sufferings of society may later become its salvation. In any event, it is not for us to attribute blame to those who did the fighting. The right in the matter was not a Colossus of Rhodes with a foot on either side, monarchist and republican; it was indivisible and wholly on one side; but those who erred did so sincerely. The blind can no more be blamed than the partisans of La Vendée can be dismissed as brigands. Violent as the tempest was, human irresponsibility had a share in it.

Let me complete this account.

The government of 1830 was in trouble from the start, born on one day and obliged on the morrow to do battle. Scarcely was it installed than it began to feel the undertow of dissident movements directed against the newly-erected and still insecure structure. Resistance was born the day after its installation, perhaps even the day before. Hostility increased month by month, and from being passive became active.

The July Revolution, little liked by the monarchs outside France, was in France subject to a variety of interpretations. God makes known His will to mankind through the event, an obscure text, written in cryptic language, which men instantly seek to decipher, producing hurried makeshift renderings filled with errors, gaps and

16

contradictions. Very few minds are capable of reading the divine language. The wisest, calmest and most far-sighted go slowly to work, but by the time they produce their rendering the job has long been done and twenty different versions are on sale in the market-place. Each interpretation gives birth to a political party, each contradiction to a political faction; and each party believes that it has the sole authentic gospel, each faction that it has its own light to shed.

Power itself is often no more than a faction. In all revolutions there are those who swim against the tide; they are the old political parties. To the old parties, wedded to the principle of heredity by Divine Right, it is legitimate to suppress revolution, since revolution is born of revolt. This is an error. The real party of revolt, in a democratic revolution, is not the people but the monarchy. Revolution is precisely the opposite of revolt. Every revolution, being a normal process, has its own legitimacy, sometimes dishonoured by false revolutionaries but which persists, even though sullied, and survives even though bloodstained. Revolutions are not born of chance but of necessity. A revolution is a return from the fictitious to the real. It happens because it had to happen.

Nevertheless the old legitimist parties assailed the 1830 revolution with all the venom engendered by false reasoning. Error provides excellent weapons. They attacked that revolution very shrewdly where it was most vulnerable, in the chink in its armour, its lack of logic; they attacked it for being monarchist. 'Revolution,' they cried to it, 'why this king?' Factions are blind men with a true aim.

The republicans uttered the same cry, but coming from them it was logical. What was blindness in the legitimists was clear-sightedness in the democrats. The 1830 revolution was bankrupt in the eyes of the people, and democracy bitterly reproached it with the fact. The July establishment was caught between two fires, that of the past and that of the future. It was the happening of a moment at grips with the centuries of monarchy on one side and enduring right on the other.

Moreover, in external affairs, being a revolution that had turned into a monarchy, the 1830 régime had to fall into line with the rest of Europe. Keeping the peace was an added complication. Harmony enforced for the wrong reasons may be more burdensome than war. Of this hidden conflict, always subdued but always stirring, was born a state of armed peace, that ruinous expedient of a civilization in itself suspect. The July monarchy chafed, while accepting it, at the harness of a cabinet on European lines. Metternich would gladly have put it in leading-strings. Driven by the spirit of progress in France, it in its turn drove the reactionary monarchies of Europe. Being towed it was also a tower.

Meanwhile the internal problems piled up—pauperism, the proletariat, wages, education, the penal system, prostitution, the condition of women, riches, poverty, production, consumption, distribution, exchange, currency, credit, the rights of capital and labour—a fearsome burden.

Outside the political parties, as such, another stir became apparent. The democratic ferment found its echo in a philosophical ferment. The élite were as unsettled as the masses, differently but as greatly. While the theorists meditated, the ground beneath their feet—that is to say, the people—traversed by revolutionary currents, convulsively trembled as though with epilepsy. The thinkers, some isolated, some forming groups that were almost communities, pondered the questions of the hour, pacifically but deeply—dispassionate miners calmly driving their galleries in the depths of a volcano, scarcely disturbed by the deep rumblings or by glimpses of the furnace.

Their quietude was not the least noble aspect of that turbulent period. They left the question of rights to the politicians and concerned themselves with the question of happiness; what they looked for in society was the well-being of man. They endowed material problems, those of agriculture, industry, and commerce, with almost the dignity of a religion. In civilization as it comes to be shaped, a little by God and a great deal by man, interests coalesce, merge and amalgamate in such a fashion as to form a core of solid rock, following a law of dynamics patiently studied by the economists, those geologists of the body-politic. These men, grouped under a variety of labels, but who may be classified under the general heading of socialists, sought to pierce this rock and allow the living water of human felicity to gush forth from it.

This work extended to every field, from the question of capital punishment to the question of war, and to the Rights of Man proclaimed by the French Revolution they added the rights of women and children. It will not surprise the reader that, for a variety of reasons, we do not here proceed to a profound theoretical examination of the questions propounded by socialism. We will simply indicate what they were.

Problem One: the production of wealth.

Problem Two: its distribution.

Problem One embraces the question of labour and Problem Two that of wages, the first dealing with the use made of manpower and the second with the sharing of the amenities this manpower produces.

A proper use of manpower creates a strong economy, and a

proper distribution of amenities leads to the happiness of the individual. Proper distribution does not imply an *equal* share but an *equitable* share. Equity is the essence of equality.

These two things combined—a strong economy and the happiness of the individual within it—lead to social prosperity, and social prosperity means a happy man, a free citizen, and a great nation.

England has solved the first of these problems. She is highly successful in creating wealth, but she distributes it badly. This half-solution brings her inevitably to the two extremes of monstrous wealth and monstrous poverty. All the amenities are enjoyed by the few and all the privations are suffered by the many, that is to say, the common people: privilege, favour, monopoly, feudalism, all these are produced by their labour. It is a false and dangerous state of affairs whereby the public wealth depends on private poverty and the greatness of the State is rooted in the sufferings of the individual: an ill-assorted greatness composed wholly of materialism, into which no moral element enters.

Communism and agrarian reform believe they offer the solution to the second of these problems. They are mistaken. Their method of distribution kills production: equal sharing abolishes competition and, in consequence, labour. It is distribution carried out by a butcher, who kills what he distributes. It is impossible to accept these specious solutions. To destroy wealth is not to share it.

The two problems must be solved together if they are to be properly solved, and the two solutions must form part of a single whole.

To solve the first problem alone is to be either a Venice or an England. You will have artificial power like that of Venice or material power like that of England. You will be the bad rich man, and you will end in violence, as did Venice, or in bankruptcy, as England will do. And the world will leave you to die, because the world leaves everything to die that is based solely on egotism, everything that in the eyes of mankind does not represent a virtue or an idea.

It must be understood that in using the words Venice and England we are not talking about peoples but about social structures, oligarchies imposed upon nations, not the nations themselves. For nations we have always respect and sympathy. Venice, the people, will revive. England the aristocracy will fall; but England the nation is immortal. Having said this we may proceed.

Solve these two problems—encourage the rich and protect the poor; abolish pauperdom; put an end to the unjust exploitation of the weak by the strong and a bridle on the innate jealousy of the man who is on his way for the man who has arrived; achieve a fair and brotherly relationship between work and wages; associate compulsory free education with the bringing-up of the young, and make knowledge the criterion of manhood; develop minds while finding work for hands; become both a powerful nation and a family of contented people; democratize private property not by abolishing it but by making it universal, so that every citizen without exception is an owner, which is easier than people think—in a word, learn how to produce wealth and how to divide it, and you will have accomplished the union of material and moral greatness; you will be worthy to call yourself France.

This, apart from the aberrations of a few particular sects, was the message of socialism; this was what it searched for amid the facts, the plan that it proposed to men's minds. An admirable attempt, and one that we must revere.

It was problems such as this which so painfully afflicted Louis-Philippe: clashes of doctrine and the unforeseen necessity for statesmen to take account of the conflicting tendencies of all philosophies; the need to evolve a policy in tune with the old world and not too much in conflict with the revolutionary ideal; intimations of progress apparent beneath the turmoil; the parliamentary establishment and the man in the street; the need to compose the rivalries by which he was surrounded; his own faith in the revolution, and perhaps, finally, a sense of resignation born of the vague acceptance of an ultimate and higher right: his resolve to remain true to his own kin, his family feeling, a sincere respect for the people and his own honesty—these matters tormented Louis-Philippe and, steadfast and courageous though he was, at times overwhelmed him with the difficulty of being king.

He had a strong sense of the structure crumbling beneath him, but it was not a crumbling into dust, since France was more than ever France.

There were ominous threats on the horizon. A strange creeping shadow was gradually enveloping men, affairs and ideas, a shadow born of anger and renewed convictions. Things that had been hurriedly suppressed were again astir and in ferment. There was unrest in the air, a mingling of truths and sophistries which caused honest men at times to catch their breath and spirits to tremble in the general unease like leaves fluttering at the approach of a storm. Such was the tension that any chance-comer, even an unknown, might at moments strike a spark; but then the dusky obscurity closed in again. At intervals deep, sullen rumblings testified to the charge of thunder in the gathering clouds.

Scarcely twenty months after the July Revolution the year 1832 opened with portents of imminent disaster. A distressed populace and underfed workers; the last Prince de Condé vanished into limbo; Brussels driving out the House of Nassau as Paris had driven out the Bourbons; Belgium offering herself to a French prince and handed over to an English prince; the Russian hatred of Czar Nicholas; at our backs two southern demons, Ferdinand in Spain and Miguel in Portugal; the earth shaking in Italy; Metternich reaching out for Bologna and France dealing roughly with the Austrians at Ancona; the sinister sound in the north of a hammer re-nailing Poland in her coffin; angry eyes watching France from every corner of Europe; England, that suspect ally, ready to give a push to whatever was tottering and to fling herself upon anything ready to fall; the peerage sheltering behind Beccaria to protect four heads from the law; the fleur-de-lys scratched off the royal coach, and the cross wrenched off Notre-Dame; Lafayette diminished, Laffitte ruined. Benjamin Constant dead in poverty, Casimir Perier dead of the exhaustion of power; political sickness and social sickness declaring themselves simultaneously in the two capitals of the king-dom, the capital of intellect and the capital of labour—civil war in Paris and servile war in Lyon, and in both cities the same furnace-glow; the red glare of the crater reflected in the scowls of the people; the south fanatical, the west in turmoil; the Duchesse de Berry in La Vendée; plots, conspiracies, upheavals and finally cholera, adding to the growling mutter of ideas the dark tumult of events.

V. *Facts making History which History ignores*

By the end of April the whole situation had worsened. The ferment was coming to the boil. Since 1830 there had been small, sporadic uprisings, rapidly suppressed, but which broke out again: symptoms of the huge underlying unrest. Something terrible was brewing, and there were portents, still unclear but vaguely to be discerned, of possible revolution. France was watching Paris and Paris was watching the Faubourg Saint-Antoine.

The Faubourg Saint-Antoine, surreptitiously heated, was begin-ning to boil over. The taverns in the Rue de Charonne, odd though the adjectives may sound when applied to such places, were at once sober and tempestuous.

In these places the government was openly under attack, and the question of 'to fight or do nothing' was publicly debated. There were back-rooms where workers were made to swear 'that they would come out on to the streets at the first sound of the alarm and would fight, no matter how numerous their enemies'. When they had pledged themselves a man seated in a corner of the room would proclaim in a ringing voice, 'You have taken the oath! You have sworn!' Sometimes the proceedings took place in an upstairs room behind closed doors, and here the ceremony was almost masonic. The initiate was required to swear 'that he would serve the cause as he would serve his own father'. This was the formula.

In the downstairs rooms 'subversive' pamphlets were read—'blackguarding the government', according to a secret report. Remarks such as the following were heard: 'I don't know the names of the leaders. We shall only be given two hours' notice on the day.' A workman said: 'There are three hundred of us. If we put in ten sous each that will be 150 francs for ball and powder.' Another said: 'I don't ask for six months or even two. We can be on level terms with the government in a fortnight. With 25,000 men we can stand up to them.' Another: 'I never get any sleep because I'm up all night making cartridges.' Now and then, 'well-dressed men, looking like bourgeois' appeared, causing 'some embarrassment' and 'seeming to be in positions of command'. They shook hands with 'the more important' and quickly departed, never staying longer than ten minutes. Significant remarks were exchanged in undertones. 'The plot is ripe, it's all prepared' . . . 'Everybody was muttering things like this', in the words of a man who was present. Such was the state of excitement that one day a workman cried aloud in a café, 'We haven't the weapons!', to which one of his comrades replied, 'But the military have!'—unconsciously parodying Bonaparte's proclamation to the army in Italy. 'When it came to something very secret,' another agent's report said, 'they did not divulge it in those places.' It is hard to imagine what more they had to conceal, when so much was said.

Some meetings were held at regular intervals, and certain of these were confined to eight or ten men, always the same. Other meetings were open to all comers, and the rooms were so crowded that many had to stand. There were men who came from enthusiasm for the cause, and others 'because it was on their way to work'. As in the Revolution, there were ardent women who embraced all newcomers.

Other revealing facts came to light. A man walked into a café, had a drink and walked out again, saying to the proprietor: 'The revolution will pay.' Revolutionary agents were elected by vote in a café off the Rue de Charonne, the votes being collected in caps. One group of workers met on the premises of a fencing-master in the Rue de Cotte. There was a trophy on the wall consisting of wooden two-handed swords (*espadons*), singlesticks, bludgeons, and foils. One day the buttons were taken off the foils. One of the men said, 'There are twenty-five of us, but they don't reckon I'm worth anything. I'm just a cog in the machine.' He was Quénisset, later to become famous.

Small, significant trifles acquired a strange notoriety. A woman sweeping her doorstep said to another woman, 'We've been doing hard labour for a long time, making cartridges.' Posters appeared in the open street, appeals addressed to the Garde Nationale in the *départements*. One of these was signed, 'Burtot, wine-merchant.'

One day a man with a black beard and an Italian accent stood on a boundary-stone outside the door of a wine-shop in the Marché Lenoir and read out a striking document that seemed to have emanated from a secret source. Groups of people gathered and applauded. The passages which most stirred them have been recorded. 'Our doctrines are suppressed, our proclamations torn up, our billposters hounded and imprisoned . . . The recent collapse of the textile industry has converted many moderates . . . The future of the people is taking shape in our secret ranks . . . This is the choice that confronts us: action or reaction, revolution or counter-revolution. For no one in these days believes any longer in neutralism or inertia. For the people or against the people, that is the question, and there is no other . . . On the day we no longer suit you, destroy us; but until then, help us in what we are doing.' This was read out in broad daylight.

Other still more startling occurrences were, because of their very audacity, viewed with suspicion by the people. On 4 April 1832 a man climbed on to the boundary-stone at the corner of the Rue Sainte-Marguerite and proclaimed, 'I am a Babouviste!'; but they fancied that behind Babeuf lurked Gisquet, the Prefect of Police.

This particular speaker said, among other things:

'Down with property! The left-wing opposition is cowardly and treacherous. They preach revolution for effect. They call themselves democrats so as not to be beaten and royalists so as not to have to fight. The republicans are wolves in sheep's clothing. Citizen workers, beware of the republicans!'

'Silence, citizen spy!' shouted a workman, and this brought the speech to an end.

There were strange episodes. One evening a workman near the canal met a 'well-dressed man' who said to him: 'Where are you going, citizen?' . . . 'Monsieur,' the workman replied, 'I have not the pleasure of your acquaintance.' . . . 'But I know you well,' the man said. And he went on: 'Don't be afraid. I'm an agent of the committee. You're suspected of not being reliable. Let me warn you, if you give anything away, that you're being watched.' He then shook the workman by the hand and left him, saying: 'We shall meet again.'

Police agents reported scraps of conversation overheard not only in the cafés but in the street.

'Get yourself signed on quickly,' a weaver said to a cabinet-maker.

'Why?'

'There's going to be shooting.'

Two ragged pedestrians exchanged remarks reminiscent of the *jacquerie*:

'Who governs us?'

'Why, Monsieur Philippe.'

'No, it's the bourgeoisie.'

It would be wrong to suppose that we use that word *jacquerie* in any pejorative sense. The 'Jacques' were the poor, and right is on the side of the hungry.

A man was heard to say to another: 'We have a fine plan of campaign.'

Four men seated in a ditch at the Barrière-du-Trône crossroads were holding a muttered conversation of which the following sentence was overheard:

'They'll do their best not to let him go for any more walks in Paris.'

Who was the 'he'? An ominous riddle.

'The principal leaders', as they were called in the Faubourg, kept aloof. They were believed to meet in a café near the Pointe Sainte-Eustache, and a certain Auguste, president of the Tailors' Benefit Society in the Rue Mondétour, was said to be the link between them and the workers of the Faubourg Saint-Antoine. However, the identity of these leaders was never finally established, and no positive fact emerged to invalidate the lofty reply made later by one of the accused on trial by the Court of Peers in answer to the question:

'Who was your chief?'

'I knew of no chief, and recognized none.'

But all these were no more than words, suggestive but inconclusive, fragments of hearsay, remarks often without context. There were other portents.

A carpenter engaged in the erection of a wooden fence round the site of a house under construction picked up on the site a fragment of a torn letter on which he read the following: 'The committee must take steps to prevent the enlistment in its sections of recruits for other associations . . .' And further: 'We have learned that there are rifles, to the number of five or six thousand, at an armourer's shop in the Rue du Faubourg-Poissonnière (No. 5 bis). That section has no arms.'

This so startled the carpenter that he showed it to his comrades, and they found near to it another torn sheet of paper which was even more revealing. We reproduce the exact format for the sake of the document's historic interest.

Q	C	D	E	*Learn this list by heart, then destroy it. All persons allowed to see it will do the same after you have given them their orders. Fraternal greetings.* L. *u og a fe*

The persons in the secret learned only later what the four capital letters stood for—Quinturians, Centurians, Decurians, Eclaireurs (scouts). The letters *u og a fe* were a coded date—15 April 1832. Under each of the capital letters were names with brief remarks appended. Thus: Q. Bannerel. 8 muskets. 83 cartridges. A safe man.— C. Boubière. 1 pistol. A pound of powder.—E. Teissier. 1 sabre. 1 ammunition pouch. Reliable.—Terreur. 8 muskets. Sturdy . . . And so on.

Finally a third sheet was found bearing, pencilled but still legible, a further and cryptic list of names. The loyal citizen into whose possession these documents came was familiar with their meaning. It seems that the names on the third list were the code-names (such as Kosciusko and Caius Gracchus) of all the sections of the *Société des Droits de l'Homme* in the fourth Paris *arrondissement*, with, in some cases, the name of the section-chief and an indication of his address. Today these hitherto unknown facts, which now are only a part of history, may be published. It may be added that this League of the Rights of Man appears to have been founded at a later date than that on which the pencilled list was found. At that stage, presumably, it was still in process of formation.

But on top of the spoken and written clues, concrete evidence was coming to light.

A raid on a second-hand dealer's shop in the Rue Popincourt unearthed, in the drawer of a commode, seven large sheets of grey paper, folded in four, containing twenty-six squares of similar paper folded in the form of cartridges, together with a card on which was written:

Saltpetre	12 ounces.
Sulphur	2 ounces.
Charcoal	$2\frac{1}{2}$ ounces.
Water	2 ounces.

The official report of the raid stated that the drawer had a strong smell of gunpowder.

A builder's labourer on his way home from work left, on a bench near the Pont d'Austerlitz, a small package which was handed in to the watch. It was found to contain two pamphlets signed Lahautière, a song entitled, 'Workers Unite' and a tin box filled with cartridges.

Children playing in the least frequented part of the boulevard between Père-Lachaise and the Barrière-du-Trône found in a ditch, under a pile of road-chippings and rubble, a bag containing a bullet-mould, a wooden form for making cartridges, a bowl in which there were grains of hunting-powder and a small metal cook-pot containing remnants of molten lead.

Police officers carrying out a surprise raid at five in the morning on the house of a man named Pardon (he later became head of the Barricade–Merry section, and was killed in the uprising of April 1834) found him standing by his bed making cartridges, one of which he had in his hand.

Two labourers were seen to meet after working hours outside a café in an alley near the Barrière Charenton. One passed the other a pistol, taking it from under his smock; but then, seeing that it was damp with sweat, he took it back and re-primed it. The men then separated.

A man named Gallais boasted of having a stock of 700 cartridges and 24 musket-flints.

The Government had word one day that firearms and 200,000 cartridges had been distributed in the faubourgs, and, a week later, a further 30,000 cartridges. The police, remarkably enough, were able to lay hands on none of this store. An intercepted letter contained the following passage: 'The day is not far distant when within four hours by the clock 80,000 citizens will be under arms.'

It was a state of open, one can almost say tranquil, ferment. The coming insurrection made its preparations calmly under the nose of the authorities. No singularity was lacking in this crisis that was still subterranean but already plainly manifest. Middle-class gentlemen discussed it amiably with work-people, inquiring after the progress of the uprising, much as they might have asked after the health of their wives.

A furniture-dealer in the Rue Moreau asked, 'Well, and when are you going to attack?', and another shopkeeper said: 'You'll be attacking soon. I know it. A month ago there were only 15,000 of you; today there are 25,000.' He offered his shotgun for sale, and his neighbour offered a small pistol at a price of seven francs.

The revolutionary fever was steadily rising, and no part of Paris, or of all France, was exempt. The tide was flowing everywhere.

Secret societies, like a cancer in the human body, were spreading throughout the country. Out of the Society of Friends of the People, which was both open and secret, sprang the League of the Rights of Man, which, dating one of its Orders of the day 'Pluviôse, in the Fortieth Year of the Republic', was destined to survive court orders decreeing its dissolution, and which made no bones about calling its sections by such suggestive names as 'The Pikes', 'The Alarm Gun' and 'The Phrygian Bonnet'.

The League of the Rights of Man in its turn gave birth to the League of Action, composed of eager spirits who broke away in order to progress faster. Other new associations sought to lure members from the parent bodies, and section-leaders complained of this. There were the *Société Gauloise* and the Committee for the Organization of the Municipalities, also societies advocating the Liberty of the Press, the Liberty of the Individual, Popular Education, and one which opposed indirect taxation. There was the Society of Egalitarian Workers, which divided into three branches, Egalitarians, Communists, and Reformists. There was the *Armée des Bastilles*, a fighting force organized on military lines—units of four men under a corporal, ten under a sergeant, twenty under a second-lieutenant, and forty under a lieutenant—in which never more than five men knew one another, a system combining caution with audacity which seems to have owed something to Venetian models: its Central Committee controlled two branches, the Action branch and the main body of the Armée. A legitimist society, the Chevaliers de la Fidelité, tried to establish itself among these republican bodies, but it was denounced and repudiated.

The Paris societies overflowed into the larger provincial cities. Lyons, Nantes, Lille, and Marseilles had their League of the Rights of Man, among others. Aix had a revolutionary society known as the Cougourde. We have already used that word.

In Paris there was scarcely less uproar in the Faubourg Saint-Marceau than in the Faubourg Saint-Antoine, and the university schools were as agitated as the workers' quarters. A café in the Rue Saint-Hyacinthe, and the Estaminet des Sept-Billards, in the Rue des Mathurins-Saint-Jacques, were the students' headquarters. The Society of the Friends of ABC, which was affiliated with the 'Mutualists' in Angers and the Cougourde in Aix, met, as we have seen, at the Café Musain, but the same group also gathered at the cabaret-restaurant near the Rue Mondétour called Corinth. These meetings were secret, but others were entirely public, as may be gathered from the following extract from the cross-examination of a witness in one of the subsequent trials: 'Where was this meeting held?' . . . 'In the Rue de la Paix.' . . . 'In whose house?' . . . 'In the

27

street.' . . . 'How many sections attended?' . . . 'Only one.' . . .
'Which one?' . . . 'The Manuel Section.' . . . 'Who was its leader?' . . .
'I was.' . . . 'You are too young to have taken the grave decision to
attack the Government. Where did your orders come from?' . . .
'From the Central Committee.'

The army was being subverted at the same time as the civil
population, as was later proved by the mutinies in Belfort, Lunéville,
and Épinal. The insurrectionists counted on the support of several
regiments of the line and on the Twentieth Light Infantry.

'Trees of liberty'—tall poles surmounted by a red bonnet—were
erected in Burgundy and in a number of towns in the south.

This, broadly, was the situation, and nowhere was it more acute,
or more openly manifest, than in the Faubourg Saint-Antoine,
which was, to say, its nerve centre. The ancient working-class
quarter, crowded as an ant-heap and laborious, courageous and
touchy as a hive of bees, simmered in the anticipation of a hoped-for
upheaval, although its state of commotion in no way affected its
daily work. It is hard to convey an impression of that lively and
lowering countenance. Desperate hardship is concealed beneath the
attic roofs of that quarter, and so are rare and ardent minds; and the
moment of danger occurs when these two extremes, of poverty and
intelligence, come together.

The Faubourg Saint-Antoine had other reasons for its feverish
state. It was particularly affected by the economic crises, bankruptcies, strikes, unemployment, that are inseparable from any time of
major political unrest. In a revolutionary period poverty is both a
cause and an effect, aggravated by the very blows it strikes. Those
proud, hard-working people, charged to the utmost with latent
energies and always prompt to explode, exasperated, deep-rooted,
undermined, seemed to be only awaiting the striking of a spark.
Whenever there is thunder in the air, borne on the wind of events,
we are bound to think of the Faubourg Saint-Antoine and the fateful
chance which has set this powder-mill of suffering and political
thought on the threshold of Paris.

The drinking-places of the quarter, so constantly referred to in
this brief account, have acquired an historic notoriety. In troubled
times their customers grow more drunk on words than on wine.
A prophetic sense pervades them, an intimation of the future, exalt-
ing hearts and minds. They resemble those taverns on Mount Aven-
tine built round the Sybil's cave and stirred by the sacred breath,
where the tables were virtually tripods and one drank what Annius
calls 'the Sybilline wine'.

The Faubourg Saint-Antoine is a people's stronghold. Times of
revolutionary upheaval cause breaches in its walls through which the

popular will, the sovereignty of the people, bursts out. That sovereignty may behave badly; it blunders, like all human action, but even in its blunderings, like the blind Cyclops, it remains great.

In 1793, according to whether the prevailing mood was good or evil, idealistic or fanatical, masses poured out of it which were heroic or simply barbarous. We must account for the latter word. What did they want, those violent men, ragged, bellowing and wild-eyed, who with clubs and pikes poured through the ancient streets of distracted Paris? They wanted to put an end to oppression, tyranny, and the sword; they wanted work for all men, education for their children, security for their wives, liberty, equality, fraternity, food enough to go round, freedom of thought, the Edenization of the world. In a word, they wanted Progress, that hallowed, good, and gentle thing, and they demanded it in a terrible fashion, with oaths on their lips and weapons in their hands. They were barbarous, yes; but barbarians in the cause of civilization.

They furiously proclaimed the right; they wanted to drive mankind into Paradise, even if it could only be done by terror. They looked like barbarians and were saviours. Wearing a mask of darkness, they clamoured for light.

And confronting these men, wild and terrible as we agree they were, but wild and terrible for good, there were men of quite another kind, smiling and adorned with ribbons and stars, silk-stockinged, yellow-gloved and with polished boots; men who, seated round a velvet table-cloth by a marble fireplace, gently insisted on the preservation of the past, of the middle-ages, of Divine Right, of bigotry, ignorance, enslavement, the death-penalty and war, and who, talking in polished undertones, glorified the sword and the executioner's block. For our part, if we had to choose between the barbarians of civilization and those civilized upholders of barbarism we would choose the former.

But there is, mercifully, another way. No desperate step is needed, whether forward or backward, neither despotism nor terrorism. What we seek is progress by gradual degrees.

God is looking to it. Gradualness is the whole policy of God.

VI. *Enjolras and his Lieutenants*

At about this time, Enjolras, with an eye to possible contingencies, made a tactful survey of policy among his followers. While they were holding counsel in the Café Musain, he said, interlarding his words with a few cryptic but meaningful metaphors:

'It's just as well to know where one stands and whom one can count on. If one wants active fighters one has to create them; no harm in possessing weapons. People trying to pass are always more likely to be gored if there are oxen in the street. So let's take stock of our manpower. How many of us are there? No point in putting it off. Revolutionaries should always be in a hurry; progress has no time to waste. We must be ready for the unexpected and not let ourselves be caught out. It's a matter of reviewing all the stitches we've sewn and seeing if they'll hold, and it needs to be done at once. Courfeyrac, you can call on the polytechnic students, it's their free day. Today's Wednesday, isn't it? Feuilly, you can call on the workers at the Glacière. Combeferre has said he'll go to Picpus, there are a lot of good men there. Prouvaire, the stone-masons show signs of cooling off, you'd better find out how things are at the lodge in the Rue de Grenelle-Saint-Honoré. Joly can look in at the Dupuytren hospital and take the pulse of the medical students, and Bossuet can do the same with the law students at the Palais de Justice. I'll do the Cougourde.'

'And that's the lot,' said Courfeyrac.

'No.'

'What else is there?'

'Something very important.'

'What's that?' asked Combeferre.

'The Barrière du Maine,' said Enjolras.

He was silent for a moment, seeming plunged in thought, and then said:

'There are marble-workers at the Barrière du Maine, and painters and workers in the sculptors' studios. They're keen, on the whole, but inclined to blow hot and cold. I don't know what's got into them recently. They seem to have lost interest, they spend their whole time playing dominoes. It's important for someone to go and talk to them, and talk bluntly. Their place is the Café Richefeu and they're always there between twelve and one. It needs a puff of air to brighten up those embers. I was going to ask that dreamy character, Marius, but he doesn't come here any more. So I need someone for the Barrière du Maine, and I've no one to send.'

'There's me,' said Grantaire. 'I'm here.'

'You?'

'Why not?'

'You'll go out and preach republicanism, rouse up the half-hearted in the name of principle?'

'Why shouldn't I?'

'Would you be any good at it?'

'I'd quite like to try,' said Grantaire.

'But you don't believe in anything?'

'I believe in you.'

'Grantaire, do you really want to do me a service?'

'Anything you like—I'd black your boots.'

'Then keep out of our affairs. Stick to your absinthe.'

'That's ungrateful of you, Enjolras.'

'You really think you're man enough to go to the Barrière du Maine? You'd be capable of it?'

'I'm quite capable of walking along the Rue des Grès, up the Rue Monsieur-le-Prince to the Rue de Vaugirard, along the Rue d'Assas, across the Boulevard du Montparnasse and through the Barrière to the Café Richefeu. My boots are good enough.'

'How well do you know that lot at the Richefeu?'

'Not very well, but we're quite friendly.'

'What would you say to them?'

'Well, I'd talk to them about Robespierre and Danton and the principles of the Revolution.'

'*You* would?'

'Yes, me. Nobody does me justice. When I really go for something I'm tremendous. I've read Prudhomme and the *Contrat Social* and I know the Constitution of the Year Two by heart. "The liberty of the citizen ends where that of another citizen begins." Do you think I'm an ignoramus? I have an old *assignat* in my drawer. The Rights of Man, the Sovereignty of the people, I know the lot. I'm even a bit of an Hébertist. I can hold forth sublimely—for six hours on end, if need be, by the clock.'

'Be serious,' said Enjolras.

'I'm madly serious.'

Enjolras considered for a few moments, then made a gesture of decision.

'Very well, Grantaire,' he said soberly. 'I'll give you a trial. You shall go to the Barrière du Maine.'

Grantaire was living in a furnished room very near the café. He went out and was back in five minutes wearing a Robespierre waistcoat.

'Red,' he said, looking meaningfully at Enjolras. Smoothing the red points of the waistcoat with a firm hand, he bent towards him. 'Don't worry,' he said, and putting on his hat marched resolutely to the door.

A quarter of an hour later the back-room at the Café Musain was empty. All the 'Friends of ABC' had departed on their respective tasks. Enjolras, who had reserved the Cougourde d'Aix for himself, was the last to leave.

Those members of the Cougourde d'Aix who were in Paris were

accustomed to meet in the Plaine d'Issy, in one of the abandoned quarries which are so numerous on that side of the city. While he was on his way there Enjolras reviewed the situation. The gravity of the times was apparent. When events which are the premonitory symptoms of social sickness stir ponderously into motion the least complication may impede them. It is a time of false starts and fresh beginnings. Enjolras had a sense of a splendid new dawn breaking through the clouds on the horizon. Who could tell? Perhaps the moment was very near when, inspiring thought, the people would assert their rights, and the Revolution, majestically regaining possession of France, would say to the world: 'More is to follow!' Enjolras was happy. The temperature was rising. He had, at that moment, a powder-train of friends scattered through Paris, and he was rehearsing in his mind an electrifying speech that would spark off the general explosion—a speech combining the depth and philosophic eloquence of Combeferre, the cosmopolitan ardours of Feuilly, the verve of Courfeyrac, the laughter of Bahorel, the melancholy of Jean Prouvaire, the knowledge of Joly, and the sarcasm of Bossuet. All of them working together. Surely the result must justify their labours. All was well. And this brought him to the thought of Grantaire. The Barrière du Maine was only a little off his way. Why should he not make a slight detour to look in at the Café Richefeu and see how he was getting on?

The clock-tower in the Rue de Vaugirard was striking when he thrust open the door of the café and, letting it swing to behind him, stood with folded arms in the doorway contemplating the crowded room filled with tables, men and tobacco-smoke.

Grantaire was seated opposite another man at a marble-topped table scattered with dominoes. He was banging on the marble with his fist, and this was what Enjolras overheard:

'Double six.'

'Four.'

'Blast! I can't go.'

'You'll have to pass. A two.'

'A six.'

And so on. Grantaire was wholly absorbed in the game.

BOOK TWO

ÉPONINE

I. *The Field of the Lark*

AFTER witnessing the unexpected outcome of the plot of which he
had warned Javert, and directly after Javert had left the building,
taking with him his prisoners in three fiacres, Marius himself slipped
out. It was still only nine o'clock. Marius went to Courfeyrac, who
was no longer the unshakeable inhabitant of the Latin Quarter but
'for political reasons' had gone to live in the Rue de la Verrerie, this
being one of the quarters favoured by the insurrectionists at that
time. 'I've come to lodge with you,' Marius said, and Courfeyrac
pulled one of the two mattresses off his bed, spread it on the floor
and said, 'You're welcome'.

At seven the next morning Marius returned to the tenement, paid
his rent and what he owed Ma'am Bougon, had his books, his bed,
his work-table, his chest of drawers, and his two chairs loaded on to a
handcart, and departed leaving no address, so that when Javert
came round during the morning to question him further about the
previous night's affair he found no one there but Ma'am Bougon,
who simply said, 'He's cleared out.'

Ma'am Bougon was convinced that Marius was in some way
hand-in-glove with the criminals. 'Who'd have thought it?' she said
to her friends in the quarter. 'A young man who looked as innocent
as a newborn babe!'

Marius had two reasons for this prompt removal. In the first
place, he now had a horror of that house in which he had encountered,
at such close quarters, and in its most noisome and ferocious aspects,
a form of social ugliness that was perhaps even more repulsive than
the evil rich: namely, the evil poor. The second reason was that he
did not want to be involved in the criminal proceedings which must
surely ensue, when he would have been obliged to testify against
Thénardier.

Javert assumed that the young man, whose name he had not
noted, had taken fright and bolted, or possibly had not even gone
back to his lodging at the time when the trap was sprung. He
nevertheless endeavoured to find him, but without success.

Two months passed. Marius was still lodging with Courfeyrac. He learned from a friend at the law-courts that Thénardier was in solitary confinement, and every Monday he sent the clerk of the prison of La Force five francs for his benefit. Being now entirely out of funds, he had to borrow the sum from Courfeyrac. It was the first time in his life he had ever borrowed money, and these weekly subscriptions were an enigma both to Courfeyrac, who supplied them, and to Thénardier, who received them. 'Who on earth is the money going to?' wondered Courfeyrac, and 'Where on earth is it coming from?' wondered Thénardier.

Marius was deeply unhappy, his whole world in confusion and nothing good in prospect that he could see—once more blindly groping in the mystery that entangled him. He had had a brief, shadowy glimpse of the girl with whom he had fallen in love and the elderly man whom he presumed to be her father, those two unknown beings who were his sole interest and hope in life; and at the moment when he had thought to draw near them a puff of wind had borne them away like shadows. Not a spark of certainty or truth had emerged from the dreadful shock he had sustained, no possible basis of conjecture. He no longer even knew the girl's name, which he thought he had discovered. Certainly it was not Ursula, and 'the Lark' was only a nickname. And what was he to make of the man? Was he really hiding from the police? Recalling the white-haired workman he had seen near the Invalides, Marius now felt tolerably sure that he and Monsieur Leblanc were the same. Was he in the habit of disguising himself? He was both heroic and two-faced— why had he not shouted for help? Why had he run away? Was he in fact the girl's father? And finally, was he really the man Thénardier claimed to have recognized? . . . A string of unanswerable questions which, however, did nothing to diminish the angelic charm of the girl he had seen in the Luxembourg. Marius was in utter despair, his heart aflame and his eyes blinded, driven and drawn but unable to move. Everything was lost to him except love itself, even the instinctive perceptions of love. Ordinarily that flame which consumes us brings with it a hint of divination, something for the mind to work on. But Marius had none of these obscure inklings. He could not say to himself, '—if I was to go there, or try that? . . .' She must be somewhere, the girl who was no longer Ursula, but there was nothing to tell Marius where to look. His life could be summed up in very few words: absolute uncertainty and impenetrable fog. To see her again was his constant longing, but he had lost hope.

And to crown it all he was again in the grip of penury. Drawn close to him, hard on his heels, he felt that icy breath. For a long time now, in his state of torment, he had ceased to work. Nothing is more dangerous than to stop working. It is a habit that can soon be lost, one that is easily neglected and hard to resume. A measure of day-dreaming is a good thing, like a drug prudently used; it allays the sometimes virulent fever of the over-active mind, like a cool wind blowing through the brain to smooth the harshness of untrammelled thought; it bridges here and there the gaps, brings things into proportion and blunts the sharper angles. But too much submerges and drowns. Woe to the intellectual worker who allows himself to lapse wholly from positive thinking into day-dreaming. He thinks he can easily change back, and tells himself that it is all one. He is wrong! Thought is the work of the intellect, reverie is its self-indulgence. To substitute day-dreaming for thought is to confuse a poison with a source of nourishment.

This, as we may recall, was how it had been with Marius at the beginning, before love had come to plunge him wholly into that world of aimless and meaningless fantasies. A world in which we leave home only to go on dreaming elsewhere, indolently astray in a tumultuous but stagnant void. And the less we work the more do our needs increase. That is a law. A man in that dream state is naturally prodigal and compliant; the slackened spirit cannot keep a firm hold on life. There is good as well as bad in this, for if the slackening is perilous, generosity of spirit is healthy and sound. But the poor man who does not work, generous and high-minded as he may be, is lost. His resources dwindle while his necessities increase.

It is a slippery slope on to which the most honourable and strong-willed man may be drawn, no less than the weakest and most vicious; and it ends in one of two things, suicide or crime. Marius was slowly descending it, his eyes fixed on a figure that he could no longer see. This may sound strange, but it is true. The memory of an absent person shines in the deepest recesses of the heart, shining the more brightly the more wholly its object has vanished: a light on the horizon of the despairing, darkened spirit; a star gleaming in our inward night. This vision wholly occupied the mind of Marius, so that he could think of nothing else. In a remote way he was conscious of the fact that his older suit was becoming unwearable and the new one growing old, that his shirts and hat and boots were all wearing out; that is to say, that his very life was wearing out, so that he said to himself: 'If I could see her only once more before I die!'

He had but one consolation, that she had loved him, that her eyes had told him so, that although she did not know his name she knew his heart, and that perhaps, wherever she now was, in what-ever undiscoverable place, she loved him still. Perhaps she even thought of him as constantly as he did of her. Sometimes, in those

35

unaccountable moments known to every lover, when the heart feels a strange stirring of delight although there is no cause for anything but grief, he reflected: 'It is her own thoughts that are reaching me! . . . And perhaps my thoughts are reaching her!'

Fancies such as these, which an instant later he brushed aside, nevertheless sufficed to kindle a glow in him which was something near to hope. Occasionally, and particularly in those night hours which most fill the dreamer with melancholy, he would write down in a notebook which he reserved wholly for that purpose the purest, most impersonal and loftiest of the meditations which love inspired in him. In this fashion he wrote to her.

But that is not to say that his reason was impaired. The reverse was true. He had lost the will to work and to pursue any positive aims, but he was more than ever clear-thinking and right-minded. He was calmly and realistically aware, if with a singular detachment, of what was going on around him, even of events and people for whom he cared nothing; he summed things up correctly, but with a sort of honest indifference, a frank lack of interest. His judgements, being almost absolved from hope, soared on a lofty plane.

Nothing escaped or deceived him in his present frame of mind; he saw into the depths of life, mankind and destiny. Happy is he, even though he suffers, whom God has endowed with a spirit worthy of both love and misfortune. Those for whom human affairs and the hearts of men have not been informed by this double light have seen and learned nothing. The state of the soul that loves and suffers is sublime.

So the days drifted by, bringing nothing new. It seemed to Marius only that the dark distance left for him to travel was rapidly growing shorter. He believed already that he could clearly see the threshold of the bottomless abyss. 'And shall I not see her even once more before I come to it?' he thought.

After walking up the Rue Saint-Jacques, by-passing the barrier and going some way along the former *boulevard intérieur*, one comes to the Rue de la Santé, then to the Glacière and finally, a little before the stream of Les Gobelins, to something like an open field which, in all the long, monotonous girdle of the outer boulevards of Paris, is the one place where Ruysdael might have cared to set up his easel. That indefinable something which we term charm is to be found there, in that green patch of grass strung with washing-lines and worn garments, in an old market-garden farmhouse built in the time of Louis XIII, with its tall roof eccentrically pierced with attic windows, and within the sound of laughter and women's voices. In the near distance are the Panthéon, the Tree of the Deaf Mutes, the Val-de-Grâce, black, squat, fantastical and magnificent; and somewhat lower, the staunch, square thrust of the towers of Notre-Dame. Because the place is worth seeing no one visits it; at the most a hand-cart or carter's waggon may pass by every quarter of an hour.

It happened, however, that Marius, in the course of one of his solitary walks, went that way, and that on this occasion there was a great rarity on the boulevard, another pedestrian. Vaguely struck by the picturesque look of the place, Marius turned to him and asked its name. 'It's called Lark's Field,' the stranger said; and he added: 'This is where Ulbach murdered the Ivry shepherdess.'

But after hearing the word 'lark' Marius had ceased to listen. In the state of dreaming there are sudden crystallizations that a word may suffice to bring about; the thoughts fix suddenly upon a single notion and nothing will dispel it. 'The lark' was the name which had replaced 'Ursula' in Marius's doleful musings. 'So this is her field,' he thought with the kind of irrational amazement proper to these fancies. 'Now I shall find out where she lives.'

It was absurd but irresistible. Every day thereafter he visited the field of the Lark.

II. *The Hatching of Crimes in the Incubator of Prison*

Javert's triumph in the Gorbeau tenement had seemed complete but was not. In the first place, and it was his chief vexation, he had not laid hands on the victim of the plot. The prospective victim who escapes is even more suspect than the prospective murderer, and it seemed likely that this person, if he represented so rich a haul for the band of ruffians, must have been no less valuable a capture for the authorities.

Montparnasse had also escaped. They would have to wait for another chance to lay hands on that 'devil's playmate'. Montparnasse had in fact run into Éponine when she was keeping watch under the trees of the boulevard and had gone off with her, deciding that he was more in a mood to amuse himself with the daughter than play hired assassin for the father. It was a fortunate impulse and he was still at large. As for Éponine, Javert had picked her up later and she had gone to join her sister in the Madelonnette prison.

And finally, while the band were being conveyed from the tenement to the prison of La Force, one of its leading members, Claquesous, had got away. None of the police escort could say how it happened. He had simply vanished like a puff of smoke, handcuffed though he was, and all that could be said was that when they reached the prison he was no longer with them. It sounded like a fairy-tale—or perhaps it was something more sinister. Had he really melted like a snowflake into the shadows, or had he been assisted? Was he in fact one of those double-agents, much employed by the police in that unruly time, with one foot in the world of crime and one on the other side of the fence? Javert did not approve of these stratagems and would have nothing to do with them; but there were other police-officers in his section, his subordinates in rank but possibly more in touch with the workings of high authority, and Claquesous was so notable a villain that he would make an excellent informer. The thing was by no means impossible. However this might be, Claquesous had vanished and was not to be found, and Javert was more enraged than surprised.

As for Marius, 'that little nincompoop of a lawyer who had probably been scared out of his wits', and whose name Javert had forgotten, he was of trifling importance. In any event, a lawyer was easy to lay hands on—if, that is to say, he really was a lawyer.

The investigation had begun. The examining magistrate had thought it expedient to release one of the Patron-Minette gang from close confinement, hoping that he would talk. The one in question was Brujon, the long-haired man whose conversation Marius had overheard in the Rue du Petit-Banquier. He had been quartered in one of the prison yards, the Cour Charlemagne, where the warders were keeping an eye on him.

The name of Brujon is still remembered in La Force. In the hideous courtyard of the New Building, officially the Cour Saint-Bernard but known to the criminal world as the 'lion's den', on one of the foul, gangrenous walls reaching to the roof of the building, close by a rusty iron door once that of the chapel of the ducal palace of La Force, which was later converted into a prisoners' dormitory, there was to be seen, as recently as twelve years ago, a crude drawing of a *bastille*, a prison-fortress, carved with a nail and bearing the name of the artist: BRUJON, 1811.

This Brujon of 1811 was the father of the Brujon of 1832.

The son, of whom we caught only a glimpse in the Gorbeau tenement, was an artful and decidedly capable young rogue whose general expression was one of innocent bewilderment. It was this look of innocence which had prompted the magistrate to release him from solitary, feeling that he might be of more value in the Cour Charlemagne than confined in a cell.

Criminals do not cease their activities because they have fallen into the hands of the law; they are not to be deterred by trifles. To be imprisoned for one crime does not prevent the planning of the next. They are like an artist with a picture hanging in the salon who nevertheless keeps busy in the studio.

Brujon seemed quite lost in prison. He was seen to stand about the courtyard for hours at a time, blankly contemplating the squalid list of canteen prices, which begins, 'Garlic, 62 centimes' and ends with 'Cigar, five centimes.' Or else he stood about shivering, with chattering teeth, saying that he had a fever and asking if any of the twenty-eight beds in the fever-ward was vacant.

But towards the end of February 1832, it transpired that the witless Brujon had despatched three missives by prison messengers, sending them out not under his own name but under those of three of his fellow-prisoners. The three missives had cost him a total of fifty sous, a lavish expenditure which attracted the notice of the prison governor.

The matter was inquired into, and by consulting the record of such services posted up in the prisoners' common-room it was found that the sum had been divided as follows: three letters, one to the Panthéon, costing ten sous, one to the Val-de-Grâce, costing fifteen, and one to the Barrière de Grenelle, costing twenty-five sous, this last being the most expensive commission on the list. But it so happened that the Panthéon, the Val-de-Grâce, and the Barrière de Grenelle were the pitches of three of the most formidable 'barrier-prowlers', namely, Kruideniers alias Bizarro, Glorieux, a released convict, and Barrecarrosse, all of whom thus came under police observation, the presumption being that they were connected with Patron-Minette, two of whose leaders, Babet and Gueulemer, were now in custody. The three missives had been delivered, not to addresses but to persons waiting for them in the street, and it was believed that they had to do with a criminal enterprise in process of being planned. There were other reasons for suspecting this; the three men were accordingly arrested and it was assumed that Brujon's operation, whatever it was, had been nipped in the bud.

But about a week later one of the night warders, going his rounds on the ground-floor of the New Building, peered through the peep-hole in the door of Brujon's dormitory while he was slipping his time-disc into the box, known as the *boîte à marrons*, which was fixed to the wall outside every dormitory for that purpose, the system being designed to ensure that the warders performed their duties faithfully. He saw Brujon sitting up in bed and writing something by the dim light of the wall-lamp. He went in and Brujon was sent back to solitary for a month, but they were not able to discover what he had been writing. The police outside could not help them.

What is certain is that the next day a '*postillon*' was flung from the Cour Charlemagne into the Lions' Den, clearing the intervening five-storey building. A *postillon* is convict slang for a carefully kneaded lump of bread which is flung 'into Ireland', that is to say, over a prison roof from one courtyard into another, the term being of English origin, meaning from one country into another. Whoever picks up the missile will find a message inside it. If it is picked up by a prisoner, he passes it on to the person it is intended for; if by a warder—or by one of those secretly bribed prisoners known as 'sheep' in ordinary places of detention and 'foxes' in hard-labour prisons—it is handed in at the office and passed on to the police. On this occasion the *postillon* was delivered to the right address, although the addressee was at the time in a solitary-confinement cell. He was none other than Babet, one of the four leading spirits of Patron-Minette.

The message contained in the lump of bread was as follows: 'Babet. There's a job in the Rue Plumet. Garden with a wrought-iron gate.' This was what Brujon had written the previous night.

Although he was under close surveillance, Babet contrived to get the message passed from the La Force prison to that of the Salpêtrière, where a 'lady friend' of his was confined. The woman passed it on to an acquaintance of hers, a woman called Magnon who was being closely watched by the police but had not yet been arrested. This Magnon, of whom the reader has already heard, had a particular connexion with the Thénardiers (to be described later) and by visiting Éponine could serve as a link between the Salpêtrière and Madelonnette prisons.

As it happened, the Thénardier daughters were released on the day she went to visit Éponine, the preliminary investigation into the affairs of their parents having disclosed insufficient evidence to warrant their detention. When Éponine came out, Magnon, who had been waiting at the prison gate, handed her Brujon's note and asked her to spy out the land. Éponine, accordingly, went to the Rue Plumet, located the wrought-iron gate and garden, and after a careful study of the house and its inhabitants called upon Magnon, who was living in the Rue Clocheperce. She gave her a 'biscuit', to be passed on to Babet's mistress in the Salpêtrière: the term, in the recondite jargon of the underworld, signifies 'no good'.

A few days later, when Babet and Brujon passed one another in a corridor of La Force, the one going to interrogation and the other coming away from it, Brujon asked, 'What about Rue P.?' and Babet answered, 'Biscuit'. Thus a criminal operation conceived by Brujon in the prison of La Force was still-born.

But the miscarriage, as we shall see, had results quite outside Brujon's intention. It happens often enough that, thinking to plan one event, we set in motion another.

Marius no longer called upon anyone, but it happened now and then that he saw Père Mabeuf. While he had been slowly descending that melancholy stairway which may be termed the steps to the underground, since it leads to that place of darkness where life can be heard passing over one's head, Père Mabeuf, in his own fashion, had been making the same descent.

The sales of *Flora of Cauteretz* had wholly ceased; nor had the attempt to develop a new strain of indigo been successful. Monsieur Mabeuf's small garden in Austerlitz had the wrong exposure: all he could grow in it were a few rare plants which flourished in damp and shade. Nevertheless he had persisted. He had acquired a plot of land in the Jardin des Plantes, where the conditions were more favourable, in order to continue his experiments at his own expense, having raised the money by pawning the plates of his *Flora*. His luncheon was restricted to two eggs, one of which went to his elderly housekeeper, whose wages he had not paid for fifteen months, and often this was his only meal in the day. He no longer laughed his childlike laugh; he had grown morose and did not receive visitors. Marius was wise in not attempting to call on him. Occasionally they passed one another on the Boulevard de l'Hôpital when the old man was on his way to the Jardin des Plantes. They did not speak, but merely exchanged gloomy nods. It is the sad fact about poverty that the moment comes when it destroys relationships. They had been friends but now were merely on nodding terms.

Royol, the bookseller, was dead. Monsieur Mabeuf now had nothing but his own books, his garden, and his indigo plants, all that remained to him of happiness, pleasure in life and hope for the future. They enabled him to go on living. He said to himself: 'When I have grown my blue berries I shall be rich. I'll get the plates out of pawn and make my *Flora* fashionable again by dressing it up with humbug, newspaper advertisements and so forth; and I'll buy myself a copy of Pietro de Medino's *Art of Navigation*, the 1559 edition, with woodcuts—I know where I can get one.' In the meantime he worked all day on his indigo plot, returning home in the evening to water his garden and read his books. At this time Monsieur Mabeuf was very nearly eighty.

One evening he had a startling visitation.

He had returned home while it was still light. His housekeeper, Mère Plutarque, whose health was failing, was ill in bed. After dining off a bone on which a few scraps of meat remained and a piece of bread which he found on the kitchen table, Monsieur Mabeuf had gone to sit in the garden, on the old, overturned boundary-stone which served him as a garden bench. Close by this was a tumbledown wooden building of the kind commonly found in old orchard-gardens, with rabbit hutches on the ground floor and fruit-racks on its upper storey. There were no rabbits in the hutches but there were still a few apples on the racks, the last of the autumn crop.

Wearing his spectacles, Monsieur Mabeuf sat turning over the pages and re-reading passages of two books which delighted him and, which was more important at his age, greatly occupied his mind. The first of these was the famous treatise by Pierre de Lancre on *The Inconstancy of Demons* and the other was the discourse of Mutor de la Rubaudière on *The Devils of Vauvers and the Goblins of La Bièvre*. The latter was especially interesting to him because his own garden was one of those places believed in former times to be haunted by goblins. The sunset was beginning to cast a light on the upper half of things while it buried the lower half in darkness. While he read, glancing from time to time over the top of his book, Père Mabeuf was appraising his plants, among them a very fine rhododendron which was one of the consolations of his present life. They had had four dry days, wind and sun but not a drop of rain, and everywhere stems were wilting and buds drooping; everything needed to be watered, and the rhododendron was looking particularly sorry for itself. For Père Mabeuf plants were living beings. He had been working all day on his indigo plot and was tired out, but he got up nonetheless, put down his books on the bench and walked shakily to the well. He found, however, such was his state of exhaustion, that he had not the strength to pull up the bucket, and so he stood back, gazing wretchedly up at a sky that was now filling with stars.

The evening was one of those whose serenity allays the sufferings of man with a melancholy but timeless delight. The night promised to be as parched as the day had been. 'Stars everywhere,' the old man thought. 'And nowhere a cloud, not even a teardrop of rain.' His head sank on his breast, but then he looked up again. 'A tear of sympathy!' he prayed. 'A drop of dew.' Again he tried to raise the bucket but could not.

And at this moment a voice said:

'Père Mabeuf, would you like me to water your garden?'

At the same time there came a rustling like that of an animal in the undergrowth, and from behind a shrub a tall, thin girl emerged who stood boldly confronting him, seeming less like a human being than a manifestation of the dusk.

Before Père Mabeuf, who as we know was timid by nature and easily alarmed, could say a word, this apparition, whose movements

42

in the half-light had a sort of eerie abruptness, had drawn up the bucket and filled the watering-can. He watched while, bare-footed and clad in a ragged skirt, she bent over the flower-beds showering them with life; and the sound of water falling on the thirsty leaves was an enchantment to his ears. He felt that now the rhododendron was happy.

Having emptied the first bucketful, she drew a second and a third. She watered the whole garden. The sight of her striding along the paths, blackly silhouetted against the darkening sky with lanky arms outstretched under a tattered shawl, made him think of a large bat. When she had finished Père Mabeuf went up to her with tears in his eyes and laid a hand on her forehead.

'God will reward you,' he said. 'You must be an angel since you care for flowers.'

'I'm no angel,' she replied. 'I'm the devil, but it's all the same to me.'

Without heeding her words he exclaimed:

'How wretched it is that I'm too poor to be able to do anything for you!'

'But there is something you can do,' she said.

'What is it?'

'You can tell me where Monsieur Marius is living.'

He did not at first understand and stood with dim eyes gazing blankly at her.

'What Monsieur Marius?'

'The young man who used to come here.'

And now Monsieur Mabeuf had searched his memory.

'Ah, yes. I know who you mean. Monsieur Marius . . . You mean the Baron Marius Pontmercy, of course. He lives . . . or rather, he doesn't live there any more . . . I really don't know.' He had bent down while speaking to straighten a branch of the rhododendron. Still in this bowed position, he went on: 'But I can tell you this. He very often goes along the boulevard to a place in the neighbourhood of the Glacière, the Lark's Field. If you go that way you should have no difficulty in meeting him.'

When eventually Monsieur Mabeuf straightened himself he found that he was alone. The girl had disappeared. He was then genuinely a little apprehensive.

'Really,' he reflected, 'if my garden hadn't been watered I should think it was a spirit.'

Later, when he was in bed and on the verge of sleep, in that hazy moment when thought, like the fabulous bird that changes into a fish in order to cross the sea, takes on the form of dreaming in order to cross into slumber, this notion returned to him and he murmured confusedly:

'After all, it was very like what La Rubaudière tells us about goblins. Was it a goblin, perhaps?'

IV. *The Goblin appears to Marius*

On a morning a few days after Monsieur Mabeuf received this strange visitation—it was a Monday, the day on which Marius was accustomed to borrow five francs from Courfeyrac for Thénardier— Marius, having put the money in his pocket, decided to 'go for a stroll' before leaving it at the prison, hoping that this would make him more disposed to settle down to work on his return. It was his invariable procedure. First thing in the morning he would seat himself at the writing-table contemplating a blank sheet of paper and the text he was supposed to be translating, which at that time was an account of the celebrated controversy between two German jurists, Gans and Savigny, on the subject of hereditary rights. He would read a few lines and struggle to write one of his own, and, finding himself unable to do so, seeing a sort of haze between himself and the paper, he would get up saying, 'I'll go for a stroll. Then I shall be more in the mood.' And he would go to the field of the Lark, where the haze would be more pronounced than ever and his interest in Gans and Savigny proportionately less.

He would return home and again fail to work, being unable to bring order to his distracted thoughts. He would say to himself, 'I won't go out tomorrow. It stops me working.' And the next day he would go out as usual. His dwelling-place was more the Lark's field than Courfeyrac's lodging. His real address should have been: Boulevard de la Santé, seventh tree after the Rue Croulebarbe.

On this particular morning he had deserted the seventh tree and was seated on a parapet overlooking the stream, the Rivière des Gobelins. Bright sunshine pierced the fresh, gleaming leaves of the trees. He sat thinking of *Her* until his thoughts, turning to reproaches, rebounded upon himself, concentrating painfully on the indolence and spiritual paralysis that now possessed him, and the darkness that seemed to be thickening around him so that he could no longer see the sun.

And yet, amid the distressing incoherence of his meditations, which were not even a conscious process of thought, so far had he lost the will to action and the active sense of his despair; amid his melancholy self-absorption the stir of the outside world still reached him. He could hear, from either side of the little river, the sound of the Gobelins washerwomen pounding their linen in the stream, and above his head he could hear the birds singing and their wings fluttering in the elms—overhead the sounds of freedom, heedless happiness, winged leisure, and around him the sounds of daily work: joyous sounds which penetrated his abstraction, prompting him almost to conscious thought.

And suddenly, breaking in upon his state of tired ecstasy, a voice spoke, a voice known to him.

'Ah! There he is!'

He looked up and recognized the unhappy girl who had called upon him one morning, the elder Thénardier daughter, Éponine, whose name he had subsequently learned. Strangely, she appeared at once more impoverished and more attractive, two things which he would not have thought her capable of. She had progressed in two directions, both upwards and downwards. She was still barefoot and ragged as she had been on the day when she had marched so resolutely into his room, except that her rags were two months older, dirtier, their tatters more evident. She had the same hoarse voice, the same chapped, weather-beaten skin, the same bold and shiftless gaze, and added to these the apprehensive, vaguely pitiable expression that a spell in prison lends to the face of ordinary poverty. She had wisps of straw in her hair, not because, like Ophelia, she had gone mad, but because she had spent the night in a stable-loft. And with it all she had grown beautiful! Such is the miracle of youth.

She was contemplating Marius with a look of pleasure on her pale face and something that was almost a smile. For some moments she seemed unable to speak.

'So at last I've found you!' she finally said. 'Père Mabeuf was right. If you only knew how I've been looking for you. Did you know I've been in jug? Only for a fortnight and then they had to let me go because they'd got nothing against me and anyway I'm not old enough to be held responsible—two months under age. But if you knew how I've been searching—for six whole weeks. You aren't living in the tenement any more?'

'No,' said Marius.

'Well, I can understand that. Because of what happened. It's not nice, that sort of thing. So you've moved. But why are you wearing that shabby old hat? A young man like you ought to be nicely dressed. You know, Monsieur Marius—Père Mabeuf called you Baron Marius Something-or-other, but that's not right, is it? You can't be a baron. Barons are old. They go and sit in the Luxembourg, on the sunny side of the château, and read the *Quotidienne* at a sou a copy. I once had to give a letter to a baron like that—he must have been at least a hundred. Where are you living now?'

Marius did not answer.

'You've got a hole in your shirt,' she said. 'I'll mend it for you.'
Her expression was changing. 'You don't seem very glad to see me.'

Marius still said nothing, and after a moment's pause she exclaimed:

'Well, I could make you look happy if I wanted to!'

'How?' said Marius. 'What do you mean?'

'You weren't so unfriendly last time.'

'I'm sorry. But what do you mean?'

She bit her lip and hesitated as though wrestling with some problem of her own. Finally she seemed to make up her mind.

'Oh well, it can't be helped. You look so miserable and I want you to be happy. But you must promise to smile. I want to hear you say, "Well done!" Poor Monsieur Marius! But you did promise, you know, that you'd give me anything I asked for.'

'Yes, yes! But tell me!'

She looked steadily at him.

'I've got the address.'

Marius had turned pale. His heart seemed to miss a beat.

'You mean—'

'The address you wanted me to find out. The young lady—you know . . .' She spoke the words with a deep sigh.

Marius jumped down from the parapet where he had been sitting and took her by the hand.

'You know it? You must take me there. You must tell me where it is. I'll give you anything you ask.'

'It's right on the other side of town. I shall have to take you. I don't know the number, but I know the house.' She withdrew her hand and said in a tone of sadness that would have wrung the heart of any beholder, but of which Marius in his flurry was quite unconscious: 'Oh, how excited you are!'

A thought had struck Marius and he frowned. He seized her by the arm.

'You must swear one thing.'

'Swear!' and she burst out laughing. 'You want *me* to swear!'

'Your father. You must promise—Éponine, you must swear to me that you'll never tell him where it is.'

She was gazing at him in astonishment.

'Éponine! How did you know that was my name?'

'Will you promise me?'

She seemed not to hear. 'But it's nice. I'm glad you've called me Éponine.'

He grasped her by both arms.

'For heaven's sake, will you answer! Listen to what I'm saying. Swear that you won't pass this address on to your father.'

'My father . . .' she repeated. 'Oh, him. You needn't worry about him, he's in solitary. Anyway, what do I care about my father.'

'But you still haven't promised.'

'Well, let me go,' she cried, laughing, 'instead of shaking me like that! All right, I promise. What difference does it make to me? I'll say it. I swear I won't tell my father the address. Will that do?'

'Or anyone else?'

'Or anyone else.'

'Good,' said Marius. 'Now take me there.'

'This minute?'

'Yes, this minute.'

'Well, come along. Heavens,' she said, 'how delighted you are!' But after they had gone a little way she paused. 'You're keeping too close to me, Monsieur Marius. Let me walk on ahead and you must follow as though you didn't know me. It wouldn't do for a respectable young man like you to be seen in company with a woman of my kind.'

No words can convey the pathos of that word 'woman', spoken by that child.

She walked a few paces and then stopped again. Marius caught up with her. She spoke out of the side of her mouth, not looking at him.

'By the way, you remember you promised me something?'

Marius felt in his pocket. All he had in the world was the five-franc piece intended for her father. He got it out and thrust it into her hand, and she opened her fingers and let the coin fall to the ground. She looked sombrely at him.

'I don't want your money,' she said.

BOOK THREE

THE HOUSE IN THE RUE PLUMET

I. *The Secret House*

ROUND about the middle of the last century a Judge of the High Court and member of the Parliament of Paris, having a mistress and preferring to conceal the fact—for in those days great aristocrats were accustomed to parade their mistresses, but lesser mortals kept quiet about them—built himself a small house in the Faubourg Saint-Germain, in the unfrequented Rue Blomet, now the Rue Plumet.

The house was a two-storey villa, with two reception rooms and a kitchen on the ground-floor, two bedrooms and a sitting-room on the first floor, an attic under the roof and in the front a garden with a wide wrought-iron gate to the street. The garden was about an acre in extent, and this was all that could be seen from the street; but behind the villa there was a narrow courtyard, with, on its far side, a two-room cottage with a cellar, designed, if the need arose, to harbour a nurse and child. This cottage communicated, by a concealed door, with a very long, narrow, winding passageway, enclosed in high walls and open to the sky, so skilfully hidden that it seemed lost in the tangle of small-holdings of which it followed the many twists and turns until eventually it emerged, by another concealed door, at the deserted end of the Rue de Babylone, in what was virtually another quarter, half-a-mile away.

This was the entrance used by the villa's original owner, so cunningly contrived that even had anyone troubled to follow him on his frequent visits to the Rue de Babylone, they could not have guessed that his ultimate destination was the Rue Blomet. By shrewd purchases of land the ingenious magistrate had gained possession of the whole area and was thus able to construct his secret passage without anyone being the wiser. When, later, he had divided up the land and sold it for vegetable-plots and the like, the new owners had supposed that their boundary-wall was also that of their neighbour on the other side, never suspecting that in fact there were two walls with a narrow, flagged footpath between them. Only the birds had observed this curiosity, which doubtless was the subject of much interested speculation among the sparrows and finches of a century ago.

The villa, built of stone in the style of Mansart and wainscoted and furnished in the manner of Watteau, rococo within and austere without, enclosed in a triple flowering-hedge, was a blend of discretion, coyness, and solemnity such as befitted an amorous diversion of the magistrature. Both it and its passage have now vanished, but it was still standing fifteen years ago. In 1793 it was bought by a speculator who intended to pull it down, but being unable to complete the purchase he was forced into bankruptcy, so that in a sense it was the house that pulled down the speculator. Thereafter it remained uninhabited, crumbling slowly to ruins as any house does that has no human occupants to keep it alive. But it still had its original furnishings and was still offered for sale or rent, as the very rare passers-by along the Rue Plumet were informed by the faded billboard fixed in 1810 to the garden gate. And towards the end of the Restoration these same observers might have noted that the billboard had been taken down and that the ground floor shutters were no longer closed. The house was again occupied, and the fact that there were double curtains in the windows suggested the presence of a woman.

In October 1829, a gentleman getting on in life had rented the property as it stood, including, of course, the cottage at the back of the villa and the passage leading to the Rue Babylone, and had restored the two concealed doorways. As we say, the villa was already more or less furnished. The new tenant, having made good certain deficiencies, and put in hand repairs to the stairs and parquet flooring, the windows and the square tiling of the yard, had quietly moved in with a young girl and an elderly servant, more in the manner of an interloper than a man taking possession of his own house. The event had occasioned no gossip among the neighbours for the excellent reason that there were no neighbours.

This unobtrusive tenant was Jean Valjean, and the girl was Cosette. The servant was an unmarried woman named Toussaint whom Jean Valjean had saved from the workhouse, and who was old and provincial and talked with a stammer, three attributes which had predisposed him in her favour. He had rented the property under the name of Monsieur Fauchelevent, of private means. In the events that have already been related the reader will no doubt have been even more quick to recognize Jean Valjean than was Thénardier.

But why had Jean Valjean left the Petit-Picpus convent? What had happened?

The answer is that nothing had happened.

49

Jean Valjean, as we know, was happy at the convent, so much so that in the end it troubled his conscience. Seeing Cosette every day, and with the sense of paternal responsibility growing in him, he brooded over her spiritual well-being, saying to himself that she was his and that nothing could take her from him, that certainly she would become a nun, being surrounded by soft inducements to do so; that the convent must henceforth be the whole world for both of them, where he would grow old while she grew into womanhood, until eventually he died and she grew old; and that, ecstatic thought, there would be no other separation between them. But as he thought about this he began to have misgivings, asking himself whether he was entitled to so much happiness, whether in fact it would not be gained at the expense of another person, a child, whereas he was already an old man; whether, in short, it was not an act of theft. He told himself that the child had a right to know something about the world before renouncing it; that to deny her in advance, without consulting her, all the joys of life on the pretext of sparing her its trials, to take advantage of her ignorance and isolated state to prompt her to adopt an artificial vocation, was to do outrage to a human being and tell a lie to God. It might be that eventually, realizing all this and finding that she regretted her vows, Cosette would come to hate him. It was this last thought, almost a selfish one and certainly less heroic than the others, that he found intolerable. He resolved to leave the convent.

He resolved upon it, recognizing with despair that it must be done. There was no serious obstacle. Five years of retreat and disappearance within those four walls had dispelled all cause for alarm, so that he could now return to the world of men with an easy mind. He had aged and everything had changed. Who would now recognize him? Moreover the risk, at the worst, was only to himself, and he had no right to condemn Cosette to imprisonment in the convent because he himself had incurred a life-sentence. What did the risk matter, anyway, compared with his duty? Finally, there was nothing to prevent him from being prudent and taking precautions. As for Cosette's education, it was now virtually complete.

Having made up his mind he awaited a favourable opportunity, and this soon came. Old Fauchelevent died.

Jean Valjean applied to the Prioress for an audience and told her that, his brother's death having brought him a modest legacy sufficient to enable him to live without working, he wished to leave the convent, taking his daughter with him; but since it was unjust that Cosette should have been brought up free of charge for five years without taking her vows, he begged the Reverend Mother to allow him to pay the community an indemnity of 5,000 francs. In this fashion he and Cosette departed from the Convent of the Perpetual Adoration.

When they did so he himself carried, not caring to entrust it to any other person, the small valise of which he had always kept the key in his possession. The little case had always intrigued Cosette because of the odour of embalming which emanated from it. We may add that thereafter Valjean was never separated from it. He kept it always in his bedroom, and it was the first and sometimes the only thing he took with him when he changed his abode. Cosette laughed at it, calling it 'the inseparable' and saying that it made her jealous.

For the rest, Valjean did not return to the outside world without profound apprehension. He discovered the house in the Rue Plumet and hid himself in it, going by the name of Ultime Fauchelevent. But at the same time he rented two apartments in Paris, partly so that he might not attract attention by always remaining in the same quarter, but also so as to have a place of retreat if he should need one and, above all, not be taken at a loss as he had been on the night when he had so miraculously escaped from Javert. Both apartments were modest and of poor appearance and were situated in widely separated parts of the town, one being in the Rue de l'Ouest and the other in the Rue de l'Homme-Armé.

Every now and then he would go to live in one or the other for a month or six weeks, taking Cosette with him but not their housekeeper, Toussaint. They were waited on by the porters of the two apartment-houses, and he let it be known that he was a gentleman of private means living outside Paris who found it convenient to keep a pied-à-terre for his use in the town. Thus this high-principled man had three homes in Paris for the purpose of evading the police.

II. *Jean Valjean*—Garde Nationale

Properly speaking, his home was in the Rue Plumet, and he had arranged matters as follows:

Cosette and the servant occupied the villa. The main bedroom with its painted pillars, the boudoir with its gilt mouldings, the late magistrate's salon hung with tapestries and furnished with huge armchairs—all these were hers; and she also had the garden. Valjean had installed in the bedroom a bed with a canopy of ancient damask in three colours and a very fine old Persian rug bought in the Rue du Figuier-Saint-Paul, but he had enlivened these austere antique splendours with gay and elegant furnishings suited to a young girl, a whatnot, a bookcase with gold-embossed volumes, a work-table inlaid with mother-of-pearl, a brightly decorated dressing-table, and a washstand of Japanese porcelain. Long damask curtains in three colours on a red background, matching the bed-canopy, draped the first-floor windows; and there were tapestry curtains on the ground floor. In winter Cosette's little house was heated from top to bottom. Valjean himself lived in the sort of porter's lodge across the yard, with a mattress on a truckle-bed, a plain wooden table, two rush-bottomed chairs, an earthenware water-jug, a few books on a shelf and never any fire. He dined with Cosette, and there was a loaf of black bread for him on the table. He had said to Toussaint when she first entered their employment, 'You must understand that Mademoiselle is the mistress of the house.' 'But w-what about you, Monsieur?' asked Toussaint in astonishment . . . 'I am something better than the master—I am the father.'

Cosette had been taught the rudiments of housekeeping at the convent and she had charge of the household budget, which was extremely modest. Jean Valjean took her for a walk every day, always to the Luxembourg garden and to its least frequented alley-way, and on Sundays they attended Mass, always at Saint-Jacques-du-Haut-Pas, since it was a long way from their home. That is a very poor neighbourhood and he was generous with alms, which made him well-known to the beggars haunting the church. This it was that had prompted Thénardier to address him as 'The benevolent gentleman of the Church of Saint-Jacques-du-Haut-Pas'. He liked to take Cosette with him when he visited the poor and the sick, but no visitor ever came to the house in the Rue Plumet. Toussaint did the shopping and Valjean himself fetched water from a nearby pump in the boulevard. Their store of wine and firewood was kept in a sort of semi-underground cellar near the Porte-de-Babylone door, of which the walls were carved in the semblance of a cave. It had served the late magistrate as a grotto: for without a grotto, in that time of follies and *Petites-Maisons*, no clandestine love-affair had been complete.

In the Rue de Babylone door there was a box designed for the reception of letters and newspapers; but since the present occupants of the villa were accustomed to receive neither, the only use of this former receptacle of *billets-doux* was for the reception of tax-demands and notices concerned with guard-duty. For Monsieur Fauchelevent, gentleman of private means, was a member of the Garde Nationale, not having been able to slip through the meshes of the census of 1831. The municipal inquiries undertaken at that time had penetrated even into the Petit-Picpus convent, a hallowed institution which had endowed Ultime Fauchelevent with an aura of respectability, so that when he left it he was considered worthy to join the Garde.

Accordingly, three or four times a year Jean Valjean donned his uniform and did his spell of duty—very readily, it may be said, because this was a trapping of orthodoxy which enabled him to mingle with the outside world without otherwise emerging from his solitude. Valjean had in fact just turned sixty, the age of legal exemption, but he did not look more than fifty and had no desire in any case to escape the sergeant-major or fail the Comte de Lobau. He had no standing in the community; he was concealing his true name and identity as well as his age; but, as we say, he was very willing to be a National Guard. His whole ambition was to appear like any other man who pays his taxes; his ideal was to be an angel in private and, in public, a respectable citizen.

One detail, however, must be noted. When Valjean went out with Cosette he dressed in the manner we have described and could easily be mistaken for a retired officer. But when he went out alone, which was generally at night, he always wore workman's clothes and a peaked cap which hid his face. Was this from caution or humility? It was from both. Cosette, accustomed by now to the strangeness of his life, scarcely noticed her father's eccentricities. As for Toussaint, she held him in veneration and approved of everything he did. When their butcher, having caught a glimpse of him, remarked, 'He's a queer customer, isn't he?' she answered, 'He's a s-saint.'

None of them ever used the door on the Rue de Babylone. Except for an occasional glimpse of them through the wrought-iron gate, it would have been difficult for anyone to guess that they lived in the Rue Plumet. That gate was always locked, and Valjean left the garden untended in order that it might not attract notice.

In this, perhaps, he was mistaken.

III. *Of Leaves and Branches*

This garden, left to its own devices for more than half a century, had become unusual and charming. Pedestrians of forty years ago stopped in the street to peer into it through the grille, having no notion of the secrets concealed behind its dense foliage. More than one dreamer in those days allowed his gaze and his thoughts to travel beyond the twisted bars of that ancient, padlocked gate hung between two moss-grown stone pillars and grotesquely crowned with a pattern of intricate arabesques.

There was an old stone bench in one corner, one or two lichen-covered statues, a few rotting remains of trellis-work that had blown off the wall; but there were no lawns or garden paths, and couch-grass grew everywhere. Gardeners had deserted it and Nature had taken charge, scattering it with an abundance of weeds, a fortunate thing to happen to any patch of poor soil. The gillyflowers in bloom were splendid. Nothing in that garden hindered the thrust of things towards life, and the sacred process of growth found itself undisturbed. The trees leaned down to the brambles, and the brambles rose up into the trees; plants had climbed and branches had bent; creepers spreading on the ground had risen to join flowers blossoming in the air, and things stirred by the wind had stooped to the level of things lingering in the moss. Trunks and branches, leaves, twigs, husks, and thorns had mingled, married and cross-bred; vegetation in a close and deep embrace had celebrated and performed, under the satisfied eye of the Creator, the holy mystery of its consanguinity, a symbol of human fraternity in that enclosure some three hundred feet square. It was no longer a garden but one huge thicket, that is to say, something as impenetrable as a forest and as populous as a town, quivering like a bird's nest, dark as a cathedral, scented as a bouquet, solitary as a tomb, and as living as a crowd.

In the spring this giant thicket, untrammelled behind its iron gate and four walls, went in heat in the universal labour of seeding and growth, trembled in the warmth of the rising sun like an animal which breathes the scent of cosmic love and feels the April sap rise turbulent in its veins, and, shaking its tangled green mane, sprinkles over the damp earth, the crumbling statues, the steps of the villa, and even the empty street outside, a star-shower of blossom, of dew-like pearls, fruitfulness, beauty, life, rapture and fragrance. At midday a host of white butterflies hovered about it, and their fluttering in its shadows, like flakes of summer snow, was a heavenly sight. Under that gay canopy of verdure a host of innocent voices was raised, and what the twitter of birds neglected to say the buzz of insects supplied. In the evening a dreamlike haze rose up from it and enveloped it, a shroud of mist, a calm, celestial sadness covered it, and the intoxicating scent of honeysuckle and columbine emanated from it like an exquisite and subtle poison. The last calls could be heard of pigeon and wagtail nesting in the branches, and that secret intimacy of bird and tree could be felt: by day the flutter of wings rejoiced the leaves, and by night the leaves sheltered the wings.

In winter the house could just be seen through the bare, shivering tangle of the thicket. Instead of blossom and dewdrops there were the long, silvery trails of slugs winding over the thick carpet of dead leaves; but in any event, in all its aspects and in every season, that little enclosure breathed out an air of melancholy and contemplation, solitude and liberty, the absence of man and the presence of God.

The rusty iron gate seemed to be saying: 'This garden belongs to me.'

It mattered little that the streets of Paris lay all around it, the classic, stately mansions of the Rue de Varenne no more than a stone's throw away, the dome of the Invalides very near and the Chamber of Deputies not far distant. Carriages might roll majestically along the Rue de Bourgogne and the Rue Saint-Dominique; yellow, brown, white and red omnibuses might pass at the nearby intersection; but the Rue Plumet remained deserted. The death of former house-owners, the passage of a revolution, the collapse of ancient fortunes, forty years of abandonment and neglect had restored to that favoured spot fern and hemlock, clover and foxglove, tall plants with pallid leaves, lizards, blindworms, beetles and all manner of insects, so that within those four walls there had risen from the depths of the earth an indescribable wildness and grandeur. Nature, which disdains the contrivances of men and gives her whole heart wherever she gives at all, whether in the ant-hill or the eagle's nest, had reproduced in this insignificant Paris garden the savage splendour of a virgin forest in the New World.

Nothing is truly small, as anyone knows who has peered into the secrets of Nature. Though philosophy may reach no final conclusion as to original cause or ultimate extent, the contemplative mind is moved to ecstasy by this merging of forces into unity. Everything works upon everything else.

The science of mathematics applies to the clouds; the radiance of starlight nourishes the rose; no thinker will dare to say that the scent of hawthorn is valueless to the constellations. Who can predict the course of a molecule? How do we know that the creation of worlds is not determined by the fall of grains of sand? Who can measure the action and counter-action between the infinitely great and the infinitely small, the play of causes in the depths of being, the cataclysms of creation? The cheese-mite has its worth; the smallest is large and the largest is small; everything balances within the laws of necessity, a terrifying vision for the mind. Between living things and objects there is a miraculous relationship; within that inexhaustible compass, from the sun to the grub, there is no room for disdain; each thing needs every other thing. Light does not carry the scents of earth into the upper air without knowing what it is doing with them; darkness confers the essence of the stars upon the sleeping flowers. Every bird that flies carries a shred of the infinite in its claws. The process of birth is the shedding of a meteorite or the peck of a hatching swallow on the shell of its egg; it is the coming of an earthworm or of Socrates, both equally important to the scheme of things. Where the telescope ends the microscope begins, and which has the wider vision? You may choose. A patch of mould is a galaxy of blossom; a nebula is an ant-heap of stars. There is the same affinity, if still more inconceivable, between the things of the mind and material things. Elements and principles are intermingled; they combine and marry and each increases and completes the other, so that the material and the moral world both are finally manifest. The phenomenon perpetually folds in upon itself. In the vast cosmic changes universal life comes and goes in unknown quantities, borne by the mysterious flow of invisible currents, making use of everything, wasting not a single sleeper's dream, sowing an animalcule here and shattering a star there, swaying and writhing, turning light into a force and thought into an element, disseminated yet indivisible, dissolving all things except that geometrical point, the self; reducing all things to the core which is the soul, and causing all things to flower into God; all activities from the highest to the humblest—harnessing the movements of the earth and the flight of an insect—to the secret workings of an illimitable mechanism; perhaps—who can say?—governing, if only by the universality of the law, the evolution of a comet in the heavens by the circling of infusoria in a drop of water. A machine made of spirit. A huge meshing of years of which the first motive force is the gnat and the largest wheel the zodiac.

IV. *The Changed Grille*

It seemed that this garden, having been first created for the concealment of libertine mysteries, had deliberately transformed itself so as to render it suited to the harbouring of mysteries of a chaster kind. It no longer contained bowers or trim lawns, arbours or grottos, but was a place of magnificently ragged greenery that veiled it on all sides. Paphos, the town of Venus, had been turned into Eden, as though purged by some sort of repentance, and the coy retreat, so suspect in its purpose, had become a place of innocence and modesty. Nature had rescued it from the artifices of gallantry, filled it with shade and redesigned it for true love.

And in this solitude a ready heart was waiting. Love had only to show itself, and there to receive it was a temple, composed of verdure and grasses, birdsong, swaying branches, and soft shadow, and a spirit that was all tenderness and trust, candour, hopefulness, yearning, and illusion.

Cosette when she left the convent had been still not much more than a child, a little over fourteen and, as we have seen, at the 'awkward age'. Except for her eyes she was more plain than pretty. Although she had no feature that was ugly, she was uncouth and skinny, at once shy and over-bold—in a word, a big little girl.

Her education was concluded. That is to say, she had been instructed in religion, above all in the arts of devotion; also in history, or what passed for history in the convent, geography, grammar and the parts of speech, the Kings of France, a little music and drawing, and housekeeping. But she was ignorant of all other matters, which is both a charm and a peril. A young girl's mind must not be left too much in darkness or else too startling and too vivid imaginings may arise in it, as in a curtained room. She needs to be gently and cautiously enlightened, more by the reflection of reality than by its direct, harsh glare, a serviceable and gently austere half-light which dispels the terrors of youth and safeguards it against pitfalls. Only a mother's instinct, that intuitive blend of maiden recollection and womanly experience, can understand the composition and the shedding of that half-light; there is no substitute for this. In the forming of a young girl's soul not all the nuns in the world can take the place of a mother.

Cosette had had no mother, only a numerous assortment of mothers. As for Jean Valjean, with all his overflowing love and deep concern he was still no more than an elderly man who knew nothing at all.

But in this work of education, this most serious business of preparing a woman for life, how much wisdom is needed, how much skill in combating that state of profound ignorance that we call innocence! Nothing renders a girl more ripe for passion than a convent. It impels thought towards the unknown. The heart, turned in upon itself, shrinks, being unable to reach outwards, and probes more deeply, being unable to spread elsewhere. Hence the visions and fancies, the speculations, the tales invented and adventures secretly longed for, the castles of fantasy built solely in the mind, vacant and secret dwelling-places where passion may instal itself directly the door is opened. The convent is a prison which, if it is to confine the human heart, must endure for a lifetime.

Nothing could have been more delightful to Cosette when she left the convent, or more dangerous, than that house in the Rue Plumet.

It was at once the continuation of solitude and the beginning of freedom; an enclosed garden filled with a heady riot of nature; the same dream as in the convent, but with young men actually to be seen; a gate like the convent grille but giving on to the street.

Nevertheless, as we have said, when she came there Cosette was still a child. Jean Valjean made her a present of that untended garden. 'Do what you like with it,' he said. Cosette was at first amused by it. She explored the undergrowth and lifted stones in a search for 'little creatures', playing in the garden before she began to dream in it, loving it for the insects she found in the grass before she learned to love it for the stars shining through the branches above her head.

And then she wholeheartedly loved her father—that is to say, Jean Valjean—with an innocent, confiding love which made of him the most charming and desirable of companions. Monsieur Madeleine, we may recall, had read a great deal. Jean Valjean continued to do so, and had in consequence become an excellent talker, displaying the stored riches and eloquence of a humble and honest self-taught mind. His was a tough and gentle spirit, retaining just enough ruggedness to season its natural kindness. During their visits to the Luxembourg he discoursed upon whatever came into his head, drawing upon his wide reading and his past suffering. And Cosette listened while she gazed about her.

She adored him. She constantly sought him out. Where Jean Valjean was, there was contentment; and since he did not frequent the villa or the garden she was happier in the paved back-yard than in the blossoming enclosure, happier in the cottage with its rush-seated chairs than in her own tapestry-hung and richly furnished drawing-room. Jean Valjean would sometimes say, delighted at being thus pursued, 'Now run along and leave me in peace.'

She gently chided him, with that especial charm which graces the scolding of a devoted daughter.

'Father, it's cold in here. Why don't you have a carpet and a stove?'

'Dear child, there are so many people more deserving than I who have not even a roof over their heads.'

'Then why should I have a fire and everything else I want?'

'Because you're a woman and a child.'

'What nonsense! Do you mean that men ought to be cold and uncomfortable?'

'Some men.'

'Very well then. I shall come here so often that you'll *have* to have a fire.'

She also asked:

'Father, why do you eat that horrid bread?'

'For reasons, my dear.'

'Well, if you eat it, so shall I.'

So to prevent Cosette eating black bread Valjean changed to white.

Cosette had only vague recollections of her childhood. She prayed morning and night for the mother she had never known. The Thénardiers haunted her memory like figures in a nightmare. She remembered that one day, 'after dark', she had gone into the wood for water, in some place which she thought must have been far distant from Paris. It seemed to her that she had begun her life in a kind of limbo from which Jean Valjean had rescued her, and that childhood had been a time of beetles, snakes, and spiders. Drowsily meditating at night before she fell asleep, she concluded, since she had no positive reason to believe that she was Valjean's daughter and he her father, that her mother's soul had passed into him and come to live with her. Sometimes when he was seated she would rest her cheek on his white head and shed a silent tear upon it, thinking to herself, 'Perhaps after all this man is my mother!'

It sounds strange, but in her profound ignorance as a convent-bred child, and since in any case maternity is totally incomprehensible to virginity, she had come to believe that her mother had been almost non-existent. She did not even know her name, and when she asked Valjean he would not answer. If she repeated the question he merely smiled, and once, when she persisted, the smile was followed by a tear. Thus did Valjean by his silence hide the figure of Fantine in darkness. Was it from instinctive prudence, from respect for the dead, or from fear of surrendering that name to the hazards of any memory other than his own?

While Cosette had been still a child Valjean had talked to her readily enough about her mother, but now that she was a grown girl he found it impossible to do so. It seemed to him that he dared not. Whether because of Cosette herself, or because of Fantine, he experienced a kind of religious horror at the thought of introducing that shade into her thoughts, and of constituting the dead a third party in their lives. The more he held that shade in reverence, the more awesome did it seem. Thinking of Fantine he was compelled to silence as though amid her darkness he discerned the shape of a finger pressed to the lips. Could it be that all the shame of which Fantine was capable, which had been so savagely driven out of her by the events of her life, had furiously returned to mount fierce guard over her in death? We who have faith in death are not among those who would reject that mystical theory. Hence the impossibility he found in himself of uttering the name of Fantine, even to Cosette.

'Father, last night I saw my mother in a dream. She had two big wings. She must have come near to sainthood in her life.'

'Through martyrdom,' said Jean Valjean.

Otherwise Valjean was content. When he took Cosette out she hung proudly on his arm, happy with a full heart, and at the tokens of affection which she reserved so exclusively for himself and which he alone could inspire, his whole being was suffused with tenderness. In his rapture he told himself, poor man, that this was a state of things that would last as long as he lived; he told himself that he had not suffered enough to warrant such radiant happiness, and he thanked God from the depths of his heart for having caused him, unworthy wretch that he was, to be so loved by a creature so innocent.

V. *The Rose discovers that it is a Weapon of War*

One day Cosette, glancing in her mirror, exclaimed, 'Well!' It struck her that she was almost pretty, and the discovery threw her into a strange state of perturbation. Until that moment she had given no thought to her looks. She had seen herself in the glass but without really looking. She had been told so often that she was plain, and Jean Valjean was the only person who said, 'It's not true.' Despite this she had always considered herself plain, accustoming herself to the thought with the easy acceptance of childhood. And suddenly her mirror had confirmed what Jean Valjean said. She did not sleep that night. 'Suppose I were pretty?' she thought. 'How strange to be pretty!' She thought of girls whose looks had attracted notice in the convent, and she thought, 'Can I really be like them?'

The next day she carefully studied herself and had doubts. 'What can have got into me?' she thought. 'I'm quite ugly.' The fact was simply that she had slept badly; there were shadows under her eyes and her face was pale. It had caused her no great delight on the previous evening to think that she might be a beauty, but now she was sorry that she could not think it. She no longer looked in the glass and for more than two weeks tried to do her hair with her back to the mirror.

She was accustomed in the evenings to do embroidery, or some other kind of convent work, in the salon while Jean Valjean sat reading beside her. Looking up on one occasion, she was dismayed to find her father gazing at her with a troubled expression. And on another occasion when they were out together she thought she heard a man's voice behind her say, 'A pretty girl, but badly dressed.' . . . 'It can't be me,' she thought. 'I'm well dressed and ugly.' She was wearing her plush hat and woollen dress.

Finally, one day when she was in the garden she heard old Toussaint say: 'Has Monsieur noticed how pretty Mademoiselle is growing?' She did not hear her father's reply, but Toussaint's words filled her with amazement. She ran up to her bedroom and, for the first time in three months, looked hard at herself in the glass. She uttered a cry, delighted by what she saw.

She was beautiful as well as pretty; she could no longer doubt the testimony of Toussaint and her mirror. Her figure had filled out, her skin was finer, her hair more lustrous, and there was a new splendour in her blue eyes. The conviction of her beauty came to her in a single instant, like a burst of sunshine; besides, other people had noticed it, Toussaint had said so and the man in the street must, after all, have been talking about her. She ran downstairs and out into the garden feeling like a queen, seeing a golden sun stream through the branches, blossom on the bough, and hearing the song of birds in a state of dizzy rapture.

Jean Valjean, for his part, had a sense of profound, indefinable unease. For some time he had been apprehensively watching this growing radiance of Cosette's beauty, a bright dawn to others but to himself a dawn of ill-omen. She had been beautiful for a long time without realizing it; but he had known it from the first, and the glow which enveloped her represented a threat in his possessive eyes. He saw it as a portent of change in their life together, a life so happy that any change could only be for the worse. He was a man who had endured all the forms of suffering and was still bleeding from the wounds inflicted upon him by life. He had been almost a villain and had become almost a saint; and after being chained with prison irons he was still fettered with a chain that was scarcely less onerous although invisible, that of his prison record. The law had never lost its claim on him. It might at any moment lay hands on him and drag him out of his honourable obscurity into the glare of public infamy. He accepted this, bore no resentment, wished all men well and asked nothing of Providence, of mankind or society or of the law, except one thing—that Cosette should love him.

That Cosette should continue to love him! That God would not prevent her child's heart from being and remaining wholly his! To be loved by Cosette was enough; it was rest and solace, the healing of all wounds, the only recompense and guerdon that he craved. It was all he wanted. Had any man asked him if he wished to be better off he would have answered, 'No.' Had God offered him Heaven itself he would have said, 'I should be the loser.'

Anything that might affect this situation, even ruffle the surface, caused him to tremble as at a portent of something new. He had never known much about the beauty of women, but he knew by instinct that it could be terrible. And across the gulf of his own age and ugliness, his past suffering and ignominy, he watched in dismay the superb and triumphant growth of beauty in the innocent features of this child. 'Such loveliness!' he thought. 'So what will become of me?'

It was in this that the difference lay between his devotion and that of a mother. What caused him anguish would have brought a mother delight.

The first signs of change were not slow to appear.

From the morrow of the day on which she had said to herself, 'After all, I am beautiful!' Cosette began to give thought to her appearance. The words of that unknown man in the street, that unregarded oracle, 'Pretty, but badly dressed,' had implanted in her heart one of the two germs that fill the life of every woman, the germ of coquetry. The other germ is love.

Being now confident of her beauty, her woman's nature flowered within her. Wool and plush were thrust aside. Her father had never refused her anything. Instantly she knew all that there was to know about hats and gowns, cloaks, sleeves and slippers, the material that suits and the colour that matches: all that recondite lore that makes the women of Paris so alluring, so deep and so dangerous. The phrase 'divine charmer' was invented for the Parisienne.

In less than a month little Cosette, in her solitude off the Rue de Babylone, was not merely one of the prettiest women in Paris, which is saying a great deal, but one of the best dressed, which is saying even more. She wished that she could meet that man in the street again, just to 'show him' and hear what he had to say. The truth is that she was ravishing in all respects and wonderfully able to distinguish between a hat by Gérard and one by Herbaut. And Jean Valjean observed this transformation with the utmost misgiving. He who felt that he could never do more than crawl, or at the best walk, watched while Cosette grew wings.

It may be added that any woman glancing at Cosette would have known at once that she had no mother. There were small proprieties and particular conventions which she did not observe. A mother would have told her, for instance, that a young girl does not wear damask.

The first time Cosette went out in her dress and cape of black damask and her white crêpe hat, she clung to Jean Valjean's arm in a pink glow of pride. 'Do you like me like this?' she asked, and he answered in a tone that was almost surly, 'You're charming.'

During their walk he behaved much as usual, but when they were back home he asked:

'Are you never going to wear the other dress and hat again?'

They were in Cosette's bedroom. She turned to the wardrobe where her school clothes were hanging.

'Those old things! Father, what do you expect? Of course I shall never wear them again. With that monstrosity on my head I looked like a scarecrow!'

Jean Valjean sighed deeply.

From then on he found that Cosette, who had hitherto been quite content to stay at home, now constantly wanted to be taken out and about. What is the good, after all, of having a pretty face and delightful clothes if no one ever sees them? He also found that she had lost her fondness for the cottage and the back-yard. She now preferred the garden, and it did not displease her to stroll by the wrought-iron gate. Valjean, always the hunted man, never set foot in the garden. He stayed in the back-yard, like the dog.

Cosette, knowing herself to be beautiful, lost the grace of unawareness: an exquisite grace, for beauty enhanced by innocence is incomparable, and nothing is more enchanting than artless radiance that unwittingly holds the key to a paradise. But what she lost in this respect she gained in meditative charm. Her whole being, suffused with the joy of youth, innocence, and beauty, breathed a touching earnestness.

It was at this point that Marius, after a lapse of six months, again saw her in the Luxembourg.

VI. *The Battle Begins*

Cosette in her solitude, like Marius in his, was ready to be set alight. Fate, with its mysterious and inexorable patience, was slowly bringing together these two beings charged, like thunder-clouds, with electricity, with the latent forces of passion, and destined to meet and mingle in a look as clouds do in a lightning-flash.

So much has been made in love-stories of the power of a glance that we have ended by undervaluing it. We scarcely dare say in these days that two persons fell in love because their eyes met. Yet that is how one falls in love and in no other way. What remains is simply what remains, and it comes later. Nothing is more real than the shock two beings sustain when that spark flies between them.

At the moment when something in Cosette's gaze of which she was unaware so deeply troubled Marius, she herself was no less troubled by something in his eyes of which he was equally unconscious, and each sustained the same hurt and the same good.

She had noticed him long before and had studied him in the way a girl does, without seeming to look. She had thought him handsome when he still thought her plain, but since he took no notice of her she had felt no particular interest in him. Nevertheless she could not prevent herself from noting that he had good hair, fine eyes, white teeth, and a charming voice when he talked to his friends; that although he carried himself badly, if you cared to put it that way, he walked with a grace peculiar to himself; that he seemed to be not at all stupid; that his whole aspect was one of gentle simplicity and pride; and finally that he looked poor but honest.

On the day when their eyes met and at length exchanged those first wordless avowals that a glance haltingly conveys, Cosette did not at once understand. She returned pensively to the house in the Rue de l'Ouest where Jean Valjean, as his custom was, was spending six weeks; and when, next morning, she awoke and remembered the strange young man who after treating her for so long with perfect indifference seemed now disposed to take notice of her, she was by no means sure that she welcomed the change. If anything she was inclined to resent the condescension. With something like defiance astir within her she felt, with a childlike glee, that she was about to take her revenge. Knowing that she was beautiful she perceived, however indistinctly, that she was armed. Women play with their beauty like children with a knife, and sometimes cut themselves.

We may recall Marius's hesitation, his tremors and uncertainties. He stayed on his bench and did not venture to approach. And this provoked Cosette. She said to Valjean, 'Let us walk that way for a change.' Seeing that Marius did not come to her, she went to him. Every woman in these circumstances resembles Mahomet's mountain. And besides, although shyness is the first sign of true love in a youth, boldness is its token in a maid. This may seem strange, but nothing could be more simple. The sexes are drawing close, and in doing so each assumes the qualities of the other.

On that day Cosette's gaze drove Marius wild with delight while his gaze left her trembling. He went away triumphant while she was filled with disquiet. From that day on they adored each other.

Cosette's first feeling was one of confused, profound melancholy. It seemed to her that overnight her soul had turned black, so that she could no longer recognize it. The whiteness of a young girl's soul, compound of chill and gaiety, resembles snow: it melts in the warmth of love, which is its sun.

Cosette did not know what love was. She had never heard the word spoken in an earthly sense. In the volumes of profane music which were admitted into the convent it was always replaced by some scarcely adequate synonym such as 'dove' or 'treasure trove', which had caused the older girls to puzzle over such cryptic lines as 'Ah, the delights of treasure trove' or, 'Pity is akin to the dove'. But Cosette when she left had been still too young to ponder these riddles. She had, in short, no word to express what she was now feeling. Is one the less ill for not knowing the name of the disease?

She loved the more deeply because she did so in ignorance. She did not know if what had happened to her was good or bad, salutary or perilous, permitted or forbidden; she simply loved. She would have been greatly astonished if anyone had said to her: 'You don't sleep at nights? But that is against the rules. You don't eat? But that's very bad! You have palpitations of the heart? How disgraceful! You blush and turn pale at the sight of a figure in a black suit in a green arbour? But that is abominable!' She would have been bewildered and could only have replied: 'How can I be at fault in a matter in which I am powerless and about which I know nothing?'

And it happened that love had come to her in precisely the form that best suited her state of mind, in the form of worship at a distance, silent contemplation, the deification of an unknown. It was youth calling to youth, the night-time dream made manifest while still a dream, the longed-for ghost made flesh but still without a name, without a flaw and making no demands; in a word, the lover of fantasy given a shape but still remote. Any closer contact at that early stage would have frightened Cosette, half-plunged as she still was in the mists of the convent. She had a child's terrors and all the terrors of a nun, and both still assailed her. The spirit of the convent, in which she had been bathed for five years, was only slowly evaporating from her person, and setting all the world outside aquiver. What she needed in this situation was not a lover or even a suitor but a vision. It was in this sense that she loved Marius, as something charming, dazzling and impossible. And since utmost innocence goes hand-in-hand with coquetry she smiled quite openly at him.

She looked forward throughout their walks to the moment when she would see Marius; she had a sense of inexpressible happiness; and she believed she was truly expressing all that was in her mind when she said to Jean Valjean: 'How delightful the Luxembourg Garden is!'

Those two young people were still sundered, each in their own darkness. They did not speak or exchange greetings. They did not know each other. They saw each other, and like stars separated by the measureless spaces of the sky, they lived on the sight of one another.

Thus did Cosette gradually grow into womanhood, beautiful and ardent, conscious of her beauty but ignorant of her love. And, for good measure, a coquette by reason of her innocence.

All situations produce instinctive responses. Eternal Mother Nature obscurely warned Jean Valjean of the approach of Marius, and he trembled in the depths of his mind. He saw and knew nothing precise, but was yet fixedly conscious of an encroaching shadow, seeming to perceive something in process of growth and something in process of decline. Marius, no less on his guard, and warned according to God's immutable law by that same Mother Nature, did his best to hide from the 'father'. Nevertheless it happened now and then that Valjean caught a glimpse of him. Marius's demeanour was anything but natural, he was awkward in his concealments and clumsy in his boldness. He no longer walked casually past as he had once done, but stayed seated at a distance from them with a book which he pretended to read. For whose benefit was he pretending? At one time he had worn his everyday clothes but now he always wore his best. It looked even as though he had had his hair trimmed. His expression was strange and he wore gloves. In short, Jean Valjean took a hearty dislike to the young man.

Cosette, for her part, was giving nothing away. Without knowing precisely what was happening to her, she knew that something had happened and that it must be kept secret. But her sudden interest in clothes, coming at the same time as the young man's suddenly improved appearance, was a coincidence that struck Valjean. It was pure accident, no doubt—indeed, what could it be but accident?— but it was none the less ominous. For a long time he said nothing to her about the stranger, but eventually he could restrain himself no longer, and in a kind of desperation, like the tongue that explores an aching tooth, he remarked: 'That looks a very dull young man.'

A year previously Cosette, still an untroubled child, might have murmured, 'Well, I think he looks rather nice,' and a few years later, with the love of Marius rooted in her heart, she might have said, 'Dull and not worth looking at. I quite agree.' But at that particular moment in her life and in the present state of her feelings, she merely replied, with surpassing calm, 'You mean, that one over there?' as though she had never set eyes on him before. Which caused Jean Valjean to reflect on his own clumsiness. 'She'd never even noticed him,' he thought. 'And now I've pointed him out to her!'

The simplicity of the old and the cunning of the young! . . . And there is another law applying to those youthful years of agitation and turmoil, those frantic struggles of first love against first impediments: it is that the girl never falls into any trap and the young man falls into all of them. Jean Valjean opened a secret campaign against Marius which Marius, in the spell of his youthful passion, quite failed to perceive. Valjean devised countless snares. He changed the time of their visits, changed the bench, came to the garden alone, dropped his handkerchief; and Marius was caught out every time. To every question-mark planted under his nose by Valjean he responded with an ingenuous 'yes'. Meanwhile Cosette remained so solidly fenced in with apparent indifference and unshakeable calm that Valjean ended by concluding, 'The young fool's head over heels in love with her, but she doesn't even know he exists!'

Nevertheless he was acutely apprehensive. Cosette might at any moment fall in love. Do not these things always start with indifference? And on one occasion she let slip a word that frightened him. He rose to leave the bench, where they had been sitting for well over an hour, and she exclaimed: 'So soon?'

Still he did not discontinue their visits to the Luxembourg, not wishing to do anything out-of-the-way and fearing above all things to arouse her suspicions; but during those hours which were so sweet to the lovers, while Cosette covertly smiled at Marius, who in his state of entrancement saw nothing in the world except her smile, he darted fierce and threatening glances at the young man. He who had thought himself no longer capable of any malice now felt the return of an old, wild savagery, a stirring in the depths of a nature that once had harboured much wrath. What the devil did the infernal youth think he was up to, breaking in upon the life of Jean Valjean, prying, peering at his happiness, seeming to calculate his chances of making off with it?

'That's it,' thought Valjean. 'He's looking for an adventure, a love-affair. A love-affair! And I? I who have been the most wretched of men am to be made the most deprived. After living for sixty years on my knees, suffering everything that can be suffered, growing old without having ever been young, living without a family, without wife or children or friends; after leaving my blood on every stone and every thorn, on every milepost and every wall; after returning good for evil and kindness for cruelty; after making myself an honest man in spite of everything, repenting of my sins and forgiving those who have sinned against me—after all this, when at last I have received my reward, when I have got what I want and know that it is good and that I have deserved it—now it is to be snatched from me! I am to lose Cosette and with her my whole life, all the happiness I have ever had, simply because a young oaf chooses to come idling in the Luxembourg!'

At these moments a strange and sinister light shone in his eyes, not that of a man looking at a man, or an enemy facing an enemy, but of a watchdog confronting a thief.

We know what followed. Marius continued to act absurdly. He followed Cosette along the Rue de l'Ouest, and the next day he spoke to the porter, who spoke to Jean Valjean. 'There's a young man been asking about you, Monsieur.' It was on the day after this that Valjean gave Marius the cold glance which even he could not fail to notice, and a week later he moved out of the Rue de l'Ouest, swearing never again to set foot in that street or in the Luxembourg. They returned to the Rue Plumet.

Cosette uttered no complaint. She said nothing, asked no questions, seemed not to wish to know his reasons; she was at the stage when our greatest fear is of discovery and self-betrayal. Jean Valjean had had no experience of those particular troubles, the only attractive ones and the only ones he had never known. That is why he did not grasp the true gravity of Cosette's silence. But he did see that she was unhappy, and this perturbed him. It was a case of inexperience meeting with inexperience.

He tried once to sound her. He asked:

'Would you like to go to the Luxembourg?'

A flush rose on her pale cheek.

'Yes.'

They went there but Marius was not to be seen. Three months had passed, and he had given up going there. When on the following day Valjean again asked if she would like to go there Cosette said sadly and resignedly, 'No.'

He was shocked by her sadness and dismayed by her submissiveness. What was going on in her heart, that was so young but already so inscrutable? What changes were taking place? Sometimes instead of sleeping Valjean would sit for hours by his truckle-bed with his head in his hands; he would spend whole nights wondering what her thoughts might be, what they could possibly be. At these times his own thoughts went back despairingly to the convent, that sheltered Eden with its neglected blossoms and imprisoned virgins, where all scents and all aspirations rose straight to Heaven. How he now longed for it, that Paradise from which he had voluntarily exiled himself; how he now regretted the mood of self-abnegation and folly which had prompted him to bring Cosette out into the world! He was his own sacrificial offering, the victim of his own devotion, and he thought to himself as he sat pondering, 'What have I done?'

But none of this was disclosed to Cosette, never the least ill-humour or unkindness. For her he wore always the same gentle, smiling countenance. If there was any change to be discerned in him it took the form of greater devotion.

And Cosette languished. She missed Marius as she had rejoiced in the sight of him, in her own private fashion, without being fully aware of it. When Valjean changed the order of their daily walk, deep-seated feminine instinct suggested to her that if she displayed no particular interest in the Luxembourg garden he would perhaps take her there again. But he seemed to accept her tacit consent, and as the weeks became months she regretted it. But too late. When at length they returned to the Luxembourg Marius was no longer there. It seemed that he had vanished from her life. That tale was over and there was nothing to be done. Could she hope ever to see him again? There was a weight in her heart that every day grew heavier, so that she no longer knew or cared whether it was winter or summer, rain or shine, whether the birds still sang, whether it was the season of primroses or dahlias, whether the Luxembourg was any different from the Tuileries, whether the laundry brought by the washer-woman was well or badly ironed, whether Toussaint had conscientiously done the day's shopping. She had become indifferent to all everyday matters, her mind occupied with a single thought, as she gazed about her with lack-lustre eyes that saw only the emptiness from which a presence had vanished.

But of this nothing was apparent to Jean Valjean except her pallor. Her manner towards him was unchanged. But the pallor worried him, and now and then he would ask: 'Are you not well?' and she would answer, 'I'm quite well, father.' Then there would come a pause, and feeling his own unhappiness she would ask, 'But you. Are you quite well?' and he would answer, 'There's nothing wrong with me.'

Thus those two beings, so exclusively and touchingly devoted, who had lived so long for each other alone, came to suffer side by side, each through the other, without ever speaking of the matter, without reproaches, each wearing a smile.

VIII. *The Chain-gang*

Jean Valjean was the more unhappy of the two. Youth, whatever its griefs, still has its consolations. There were moments when he suffered to the point of becoming childish, and indeed it is the quality of suffering that it brings out the childish side of a man. He felt overwhelmingly that Cosette was escaping from him, and he sought to combat this, to keep his hold on her, by providing her with dazzling distractions. This notion, childish, as we have said, but at the same time doting, by its very childishness gave him some insight into the effect of gaudy trappings on a girl's imagination. It happened once that he saw a general in full uniform riding along the street, the Comte Coutard, military commander of Paris. He greatly envied that braided, ornate figure, and he thought to himself how splendid it would be to be dressed with a similar magnificence, how it would delight Cosette, so that when they strolled arm-in-arm past the gates of the Tuileries Palace, and the guard presented arms, she would be far too much impressed to take any interest in young men.

An unexpected shock came to dispel these pathetic fancies. They had formed the habit, since coming to live their solitary lives in the Rue Plumet, of going out to watch the sun rise, a quiet pleasure suited to those who are at the beginning of life and those who are approaching its end. To any lover of solitude, a stroll in the early morning is as good as a stroll after dark, with the added attraction of the brightness of nature. The streets are deserted and the birds in full song. Cosette, herself a bird, enjoyed getting up early. They planned these little outings the night before, he proposing and she agreeing. It was a conspiracy between them; they were out before daybreak and this was an especial pleasure to Cosette. Such harmless eccentricities delight the young.

Jean Valjean, as we know, had an especial fondness for unfrequented places, neglected nooks and corners. At this time there were many of these just beyond the Paris barriers, sparse fields that had been almost absorbed into the town, in which crops of stunted corn grew in summer and which, after reaping, looked more shaved than harvested. They were the places Valjean preferred, and Cosette did not dislike them. For him they represented solitude and for her, liberty. She could become a child again, run and frolic, leave her hat on Valjean's knees and fill it with bunches of wild flowers. She could watch the butterflies, although she never tried to catch them; tenderness and compassion are a part of loving, and a girl cherishing something equally fragile in her heart is mindful of the wings of butterflies. She made poppy-wreaths and put them on her head where, red-glowing in the sunshine, they set off her flushed face like a fiery crown.

They kept up this habit of early morning outings even after their lives had become overcast, and so it happened that, on an October morning, in the perfect serenity of the autumn of 1831, they found themselves at daybreak near the Barrière du Maine. It was the first flush of dawn, a still, magical moment, with a few stars yet to be seen in the pale depths of the sky, the earth still dark and a shiver running over the grass. A lark, seeming at one with the stars, was singing high in the heavens, and this voice of littleness, hymning the infinite, seemed to narrow its immensity. To the east the black mass of the Val de Grâce rose against a steel-bright sky, with the planet

Venus shining above it like a soul escaped from darkness. Everywhere was silence and peace. Nothing stirred on the high road, and on the side-lanes only occasional labourers were to be glimpsed in passing on their way to work.

Jean Valjean had seated himself on a pile of logs at the side of a lane, by the gateway of a timber-yard. He was looking towards the high road, seated with his back to the sunrise, which he was ignoring, being absorbed in one of those moments of concentrated thought by which even the eyes are imprisoned, as though in enclosing walls. There are states of meditation which may be termed vertical: when one has plunged into their depths it takes time to return to the surface. Valjean was thinking about Cosette and the happiness which might be theirs if nothing came between them, about the light with which she filled his life, enabling his soul to breathe. He was almost happy in this daydream, while Cosette, standing beside him, watched the clouds turn pink. Suddenly she exclaimed:

'Father, I think something's coming.'

Valjean looked up. The high road leading to the Barrière du Maine is joined at a right angle by the inner boulevard. Sounds were coming from the point of intersection which at that hour were not easy to account for. A strange object appeared, turning the corner into the high road. It seemed to be moving in an orderly fashion, although by fits and starts, and it appeared to be some kind of conveyance, although its load was not distinguishable. There were horses and wheels, shouting voices and the cracking of whips. By degrees, as it emerged from the half-light, it could be seen to be a vehicle of sorts heading for the barrier near which Jean Valjean was sitting. It was followed by a second cart, similar in aspect, and by a third and fourth; altogether seven of these long carts rounded the corner, forming a tight procession with the horses' heads almost touching the back of the vehicle in front. Heads became visible, and here and there a gleam like that of a drawn sabre; there was a sound like the rattle of chains, and as the procession drew nearer, with sounds and outlines growing more distinct, it was like the approach of something in a dream. Bit by bit the details became clear, and the darkly silhouetted heads, bathed in the pallid glow of the rising sun, came to resemble the heads of corpses.

This is what it was. Of the seven vehicles proceeding in line along the high road the first six were of a singular design. They were like coopers' drays, long ladders on wheels with shafts at the forward end. Each of these drays, or ladders, was drawn by four horses in single file and their load consisted of tight clusters of men, twenty-four to each dray, seated in two rows of twelve, back to back with their legs dangling over the side; and the thing rattling at their

71

backs was a chain, and the thing gleaming round their necks was a yoke or collar of iron. Each had his own collar, but the chain was shared by all of them, so that when they descended from the vehicle these parties of twenty-four men had to move in concert like a body with a single backbone, a sort of centipede. Pairs of men armed with muskets stood at the front and rear end of each vehicle, with their feet on the ends of the chain. The iron collars were square. The seventh vehicle, a large four-wheeled wagon with high sides but no roof, was drawn by six horses and carried a clattering load of iron cook-pots, stoves, and chains among which lay a few men with bound wrists and ankles who seemed to be ill. The sides of this wagon were constructed of rusty metal frames which looked as though they might once have served as whipping-blocks.

The procession, moving along the middle of the high road, was escorted on either side by a line of troops of infamous aspect wearing the three-cornered hats of soldiers under the Directory, dirty and bedraggled pensioners' tunics, tattered trousers, something between grey and blue, like those of funeral mutes, red epaulettes and yellow bandoliers; and they were armed with axes, muskets, and clubs. Mercenary soldiers bearing themselves with the abjectness of beggars and the truculence of prison-guards. The man who seemed to be their commander carried a horsewhip. These details, shrouded at first in the half-light, became steadily clearer as the light increased. At the front and rear of the procession rode parties of mounted gendarmes, grim-faced men with drawn sabres.

The procession was so long that by the time its head reached the barrier the last vehicle had only just turned into the high road. A crowd of spectators, sprung up in an instant as so commonly happens in Paris, had gathered on either side of the road to stand and stare. Voices could be heard of men calling to their mates to come and look, followed by the clatter of clogs as they came hurrying in from the fields.

The chained men in the drays, pallid in the chill of the morning, bore the lurching journey in silence. They were all clad in cotton trousers, with clogs on their bare feet. The rest of their attire was a dismally variegated picture of misery, a harlequinade in tatters, with shapeless headgear of felt or tarred cloth, while a few wore women's hats, or even baskets, on their heads and out-at-elbows workers' smocks or black jackets open to uncover hairy chests. Through the rents in their clothing tattoo-marks were visible—temples of love, bleeding hearts, cupids—and also the sores and blotches of disease. One or two had a rope slung from the side of the dray which supported their feet like a stirrup, and one was conveying a hard, black substance to his mouth which looked like rock but was in fact bread. Eyes were expressionless, apathetic or gleaming with an evil light. The men of the escort cursed them but drew not a murmur in reply. Now and then there was the sound of a cudgel thudding on shoulder-blades or on a head. Some of the prisoners yawned while their bodies lurched and swayed, heads knocked together and the chains rattled; others darted venomous looks. Some fists were clenched and others hung limply like the hands of dead men. A party of jeering children followed in the rear of the convoy.

Whatever else it was, this procession of carts was a most melancholy sight. It was certain that sooner or later, within an hour or a day, rain would fall, one shower succeeding another, and that with their miserable garments soaked the poor wretches would have no chance to get dry. Chilled to the bone, they would have no hope of getting warm; the chain would still hold them by the neck, their feet would still dangle in waterlogged clogs; and the thud of cudgels and the crack of whips would do nothing to still the chattering of their teeth. It was impossible to contemplate without a shiver these human creatures exposed like trees or stones to all the fury of the elements.

But suddenly the sun came out, a broad beam of light spread from the east and it was as though it set all those dishevelled heads on fire. Tongues were loosed, and there was an explosion of mocking laughter, oaths, and songs. The horizontal glow cut the picture in two, illuminating heads and torsoes and leaving legs and the wheels of the carts in shadow. This was a terrible moment, for awareness returned to the faces like an unmasking of demons, wild spirits nakedly exposed. But lighted though it was, the picture was still one of darkness. Some of the livelier spirits had quills in their mouths through which they blew spittle at the spectators, for preference at the women. The dawn light threw their haggard faces into relief, not one that was not malformed by misery; and the effect was monstrous, as though the warmth of sunlight had been transformed into the cold brightness of a lightning-flash. The men in the first cart were bellowing the chorus of an old popular song, while the trees shivered and the respectable onlookers in the side-lanes listened with imbecile satisfaction to this rousing clamour of ghosts.

Every aspect of misery was to be seen in that procession, as though it were a depiction of chaos; every animal face was there represented, old men and youths, grey beards and hairless cheeks, cynical monstrosity, embittered resignation, savage leers, half-wit grins, gargoyles wearing caps, faces like those of girls with locks of hair straying over their temples, faces like those of children and the more horrible on that account, fleshless skeleton faces lacking only death.

73

There was a negro in the first cart who perhaps had been a slave and so was familiar with chains. All bore the stamp of ignominy, that dreadful leveller; all had reached that lowest depth of abasement where ignorance changed to witlessness is the equal of intelligence changed to despair. There was no choosing between these men who seemed, from their appearance, to be the scum of the underworld, and it was evident that whoever had organized this procession had made no attempt to distinguish between them. They had been chained together haphazard, probably in alphabetical order, and loaded haphazard on to the carts. But even horror assembled in groups acquires a common denominator, every aggregation of miseries results in a total: each of the separate chain-gangs had a character of its own, each cartload bore its own countenance. Besides the one that sang there was one that merely shouted, one that begged for money, one that ground its teeth, one that uttered threats, one that blasphemed, and the last was silent as the grave. Dante might have seen in them the seven circles of Hell on the move.

It was a march of the condemned on the way to torment, borne not on the flaming chariots of the Apocalypse but on the shabby tumbrils of the damned. One of the guards who had a hook on the end of his club gesticulated with it as though to plunge it into that heap of human garbage. Among the onlookers a woman with a five-year-old boy shook a warning finger at him and said: 'Perhaps that'll teach you to behave!' As the roar of singing and blasphemy increased the man who seemed to be in command of the escort cracked his whip, and at this signal a rain of blows fell on the passengers in the carts, some of whom bellowed while others foamed at the mouth, to the delight of the urchins swarming round the procession like flies round an open wound.

The look in Jean Valjean's eyes was dreadful to behold. They were eyes no longer, but had become those fathomless mirrors which in men who have known the depths of suffering may replace the conscious gaze, so that they no longer see reality but reflect the memory of past events. Valjean was not observing the present scene but was gripped by a vision. He wanted to jump to his feet and run, but could not move. There are times when the thing we see holds us paralysed. He stayed dazedly seated, wondering, in indescribable anguish, what was the meaning of this hideous spectacle and the pandemonium that accompanied it. And presently he clapped a hand to his forehead in a gesture of sudden recollection; he remembered that this was the convoy's usual itinerary, that it was accustomed to make this détour in order to avoid any encounter with royal personages, always possible on the road to Fontainebleau; and

74

he remembered that he himself had passed through that barrier thirty-five years before.

Cosette was no less shaken, although for other reasons. She was staring in breathless bewilderment, scarcely able to believe her eyes. She cried:

'Father, what are those men?'

'Felons condemned to hard labour,' said Valjean.

'Where are they going?'

'To the galleys.'

At this moment the lashing and cudgelling reached its climax, with the flat of swords now being used. The prisoners, yielding to punishment, fell silent, glaring about them like captive wolves. Cosette was trembling. She asked:

'Father, are they still human?'

'Sometimes,' the wretched man replied.

It was in fact the chain-gang from Bicêtre, which was travelling by way of Le Mans to avoid Fontainebleau where the king was in residence. The detour lengthened the unspeakable journey by three or four days, but this was a small matter if thereby the royal susceptibilities could be spared.

Jean Valjean returned home deeply oppressed. The shock of encounters such as this may cause a profound revulsion of the spirit. So absorbed was he in his thoughts that he paid little attention, on their way home, to Cosette's further questions about what they had seen, and perhaps he did not even hear much of what she said. But that evening, when she was about to take leave of him and go to bed, he heard her murmur as though to herself: 'I believe if I were to meet a man like that in the street I should die of fright just from seeing him so close.'

It happened fortunately that on the next day some sort of official celebration was held in Paris, the occasion being marked by a military parade on the Champ de Mars, water-jousting on the Seine, fireworks, festivities and illuminations everywhere. Contrary to his general practice, Valjean took Cosette out to see the sights, hoping thus to efface from her mind the nightmare she had witnessed the previous day, and since the military review was the main event, and the wearing of uniforms was proper to the occasion, he wore his National Guard uniform, partly from an instinctive desire to escape notice. Their outing seemed to be successful. Cosette, who made a point of always seeking to please her father, and for whom in any case every show was a novelty, joined in the fun with the eager, light-hearted acceptance of youth, and gave no sign of despising that hotch-potch of organized rejoicing which is known as a 'public festival'—so much so that Valjean could feel that she had forgotten the previous day's events entirely.

But a few days later they happened to stand together on the steps leading to the garden, warming themselves in the sunshine of a fine morning. This was another departure from Valjean's general rule, and from Cosette's habit, in her unhappy state, of staying indoors. Cosette was wearing a peignoir, one of those gauzy morning garments which adorn a girl like the mist surrounding a star, and, bathed in sunlight, her cheeks still rosy after a sound night's sleep, was playing with a daisy while her father tenderly watched her. Cosette knew nothing of the old children's game, 'He loves me . . . He don't . . . he'll have me . . . he won't . . .'—when had she had the chance to learn it? She was innocently and instinctively picking off the petals, not knowing that the daisy stands for a heart. If to those Graces a fourth could be added bearing the name of Melancholy, but smiling, she might well have played the role. Valjean watched her, fascinated by the contemplation of her slim fingers as she toyed with the little flower, forgetful of all else in the delight of her presence. A redbreast was chirruping on a branch above their heads. White clouds were sailing across the sky, so gaily that one might suppose they had only just been released from confinement. Cosette continued to play with the flower but absently, as though she were thinking of something else—surely it must be something charming. But suddenly, with the slow, graceful movement of a swan, her head turned on her shoulders and she asked:

'Father, that place, the galleys. What does it mean?'

BOOK FOUR

HELP FROM BELOW MAY BE
HELP FROM ABOVE

I. *The Outward Wound and the Inward Healing*

THUS by degrees the shadows deepened over their life. There remained to them only one distraction, one which had once been a source of happiness—the feeding of the hungry and the gift of clothing to those who were cold. During those visits to the poor, on which Cosette often accompanied Jean Valjean, they regained something of the warmth that had formerly existed between them; and sometimes in the evening, after a successful day, when many needy persons had been succoured and many children's lives made brighter, Cosette would be almost gay. It was at this period that they visited the Jondrettes.

On the day following that visit Jean Valjean walked into the villa with his usual air of calm but with a large, inflamed, and suppurating wound resembling a burn on his left forearm, for which he accounted in an off-hand way. It led to his being confined to the house with a fever for more than a month. He refused to see a doctor, and when Cosette begged him to do so he said, 'Call a vet if you like.'

Cosette nursed him so devotedly and with such evident delight in serving him that all his former happiness was restored, the fears and misgivings all dispelled, and he reflected as he gazed at her, 'Oh, most fortunate wound!'

With her father ill Cosette recovered her fondness for the cottage at the back of the villa. She spent nearly all her time at his bedside, reading him the books he most enjoyed, which as a rule were books of travel. And Jean Valjean was a man reborn. The Luxembourg, the strange youth, Cosette's withdrawal—all these shades were banished: to the extent, indeed, that he was inclined to say to himself, 'I'm an old fool. I imagined it all.'

Such was his happiness that his discovery that the so-called Jondrettes were in reality the Thénardiers scarcely troubled him. He had made good his escape and covered his tracks, and what else mattered? If he thought of them at all it was to grieve for their abject state. They were now in prison, and therefore, he assumed, no longer able to harm anyone—but how lamentable a family!

As for the hideous spectacle at the Barrière du Maine, Cosette never referred to it.

Sister Sainte-Mechtilde, at the convent, had given Cosette music lessons. She had the voice of a small wild creature possessed of a soul, and sometimes in the evening, when she sat with the invalid in his cottage, she would sing poignant little songs that rejoiced Jean Valjean's heart.

Spring came, and the garden at that time of year was so delightful that he said to her, 'You never go in it, but I want you to.' . . . 'Why then,' said Cosette, 'I will.'

So to humour her father she resumed her walks in the garden, but generally alone, for Valjean seldom entered it, as we know, probably because he was afraid of being seen through the gate.

Jean Valjean's wound, in short, brought about a great change. When Cosette saw that he was recovering and that he seemed happier, she herself had a sense of contentment of which she was scarcely aware, so gently and naturally did it come to her. This was in March. The winter was ending and the days were growing longer, and winter with its passing always takes with it something of our sorrows. Then came April, the dawn of summer, fresh as all dawns, and merry as childhood, if inclined to be fretful at times, like all young things. Nature in that month sheds rays of enchanted light which, from the sky and the clouds, from trees, meadows, and flowers, pierce to the heart of man.

Cosette was still too young not to be responsive to the magic of April. Insensibly, without her realizing it, the shadows lifted from her heart. Spring brings light to the sorrowing just as the midday sun does to the darkness of a cave. Cosette was no longer really unhappy, although she was scarcely aware of the change in her. When after breakfast she prevailed upon her father to spend a little time in the garden, and strolled up and down with him nursing his injured arm, she was unconscious of her happiness or of how often she laughed.

Jean Valjean watched in rapture as her cheeks regained the glow of health.

'Most fortunate wound!' he thought, and was positively grateful to the Thénardiers.

When he was fully recovered he resumed his habit of solitary night-time walks. It would be a mistake to suppose that one can wander in this fashion through the deserted districts of Paris without ever meeting with an adventure.

It occurred one evening to the boy Gavroche that he had had nothing to eat all day. Nor, for that matter, had he had anything the day before. It was becoming tiresome, so he resolved to go in search of supper. He went on the prowl in the unfrequented regions beyond the Salpêtrière. This was where he thought he might be lucky. In places where there is no one about there are things to be found. He came to a small group of houses which he judged to be the village of Austerlitz.

On one of his previous excursions to those parts he had noticed an old garden, frequented by an old man and woman, in which there was a sizeable apple-tree and a tumbledown storage-shed which might well contain apples. An apple is a meal; it is a source of life. What had been Adam's downfall might be the saving of Gavroche. The garden was flanked by a lane that was otherwise bordered by thickets in default of houses. It had a hedge.

Gavroche located the lane, the garden, the apple-tree, and the shed, and he examined the hedge, which could easily be negotiated. The sun was setting and there was not so much as a cat in the lane; all things seemed propitious. But as Gavroche was starting to get through the hedge he heard the sound of a voice in the garden, and peering through he saw, within a few feet of the spot where he had intended to enter, a fallen stone serving as a garden bench on which was seated the old man belonging to the garden, with the old woman standing in front of him. Gavroche paused and listened.

'Monsieur Mabeuf!' the old woman said.

'Mabeuf! What a crazy name!' reflected Gavroche.

The old man made no response and the woman repeated:

'Monsieur Mabeuf!'

This time, still staring at the ground, the old man deigned to reply.

'Well, Mère Plutarque, what is it?'

'Plutarque—another crazy name,' reflected Gavroche.

'Monsieur Mabeuf,' the woman said in a voice which compelled the old man to listen, 'the landlord's complaining.'

'What about?'

'You owe three quarters rent.'

'So in three months time I shall owe four.'

'He says he's going to turn you out.'

'Then I shall have to go.'

'And the greengrocer says that until she's been paid she won't bring any more faggots. How are we going to heat the place this winter? We shall have no firewood.'

79

'There's always the sun.'

'And the butcher won't let us have any more meat.'

'I'm glad to hear it. Meat disagrees with me. It's too rich.'

'So what are we to live on?'

'On bread.'

'But it's the same with the baker, he won't give us any more credit either.'

'Ah, well.'

'So what are you going to eat?'

'We still have some apples.'

'But, Monsieur, we can't go on like this, without any money at all.'

'I have no money.'

The woman went off, leaving the old man to himself. He sat thinking. Gavroche was also thinking. It was now nearly dark.

The first result of Gavroche's thinking was that instead of scrambling through the hedge he crept into the middle of it at a point where the stems of the bushes were wide enough apart. 'A private bed-chamber,' he reflected. He was now almost directly behind the stone on which Père Mabeuf was seated, so close to him that he could hear the old man's breathing.

Here, for lack of supper, he settled down to sleep; but it was a catlike sleep with one eye open—Gavroche was always on the alert. The faint glow of the night sky cast its pallor on the earth, and the lane was like a white line drawn between two dark rows of undergrowth. And suddenly two figures appeared on the white line, one following at a short distance behind the other.

'Callers,' muttered Gavroche.

The first figure looked like that of a respectable elderly man, clad with the utmost simplicity and walking slowly because of his age, as though he were out for a stroll under the stars. The second figure, also male, was erect and slender. It was matching its pace to that of the first, but in a manner which suggested nimbleness and agility. There was something fierce and disquieting about this second figure, which nevertheless had a look of elegance—a well-shaped hat and a well-cut coat, probably of good cloth, which fitted tightly at the waist. Beneath the hat a youthful face was faintly discernible. There was a rose in the young man's mouth. Gavroche recognized him instantly. It was Montparnasse.

Gavroche crouched and watched, his bed-chamber an admirable post of observation. Clearly the second figure had designs upon the first, and that Montparnasse should be on the hunt at this hour, and in this place, was a fearsome thought. Gavroche's urchin heart went out to the elderly victim.

But what was he to do? For him to attempt to intervene would merely amuse Montparnasse—one weakling going to the rescue of another. There could be no escaping the fact that to that redoubtable eighteen-year-old cut-throat the two of them put together, an ageing man and a child, would be a couple of mouthfuls.

While Gavroche was still deliberating, the attack was launched, swift and ferocious as that of a tiger on a wild ass, or a spider on a fly. Montparnasse, tossing away his rose, flung himself upon his victim, seizing him from behind, and Gavroche could scarcely restrain a cry. A moment later one of the two men was on the ground, writhing and struggling with a knee like marble planted on his chest. But it was not at all what Gavroche had expected. The man on his back was Montparnasse, and the one on top was the elderly man, who had not only withstood the attack but had retaliated so drastically that in the twinkling of an eye the situation of victim and assailant had been reversed.

'What a splendid old boy!' thought Gavroche and could not refrain from clapping his hands; but although he was within a few yards of them the gesture was wasted, since both contestants were too intent upon their struggle.

There was presently a pause. Montparnasse lay motionless and for an instant Gavroche wondered if he were dead. The elderly man had not uttered a sound. He got to his feet and said:

'Get up.'

Montparnasse did so, but the other still had a grip on him. Montparnasse had the abashed and furious look of a wolf savaged by a sheep. Gavroche, delighted by the turn of events, was watching with eyes and ears intent, and he was rewarded for his anxious sympathy by being able to catch most of the ensuing dialogue. The elderly man asked:

'How old are you?'

'I'm nineteen.'

'You're strong and healthy. Why don't you work?'

'It bores me.'

'What is your business in life?'

'Loafer.'

'Talk sense. Can I do anything to help you? What do you want to be?'

'A thief.'

There was another pause. The elderly man seemed plunged in thought; but although he stayed motionless he did not relax his hold on Montparnasse who, lithe and supple, was again kicking and struggling like an animal in a trap. His efforts were disregarded. The other kept him under control with the calm assurance of over-whelming strength. He thought for some time, and when at length he spoke it was to deliver a lecture, rendered the more solemn by the darkness that enshrouded them, which, although it was uttered in low tones, was spoken with such emphasis that Gavroche did not miss a word.

'My poor boy, sheer laziness has started you on the most arduous of careers. You call yourself a loafer, but you will have to work harder than most men. Have you ever seen a treadmill? It is a thing to beware of, a cunning and diabolical device; if it catches you by the coat-tails it will swallow you up. Another name for it is idleness. You should change your ways while there is still time. Otherwise you're done for; in a very little while you will be caught in the machinery, and then there's no more hope. No rest for the idler; nothing but the iron grip of incessant struggle. You don't want to earn your living honestly, do a job, fulfil a duty; the thought of being like other men bores you. But the end is the same. Work is the law of life, and to reject it as boredom is to submit to it as torment. Not wanting to be a workman you will become a slave. If work fails to get you with one hand it will get you with the other; you won't treat it as a friend, and so you will become its negro slave. You flinch from the fatigues of honest men, and for this you will sweat like the damned; where other men sing you will groan, and their work, as you contemplate it from the depths, will look to you like rest. The ploughman and the harvester, the sailor and the blacksmith, they will be bathed for you in radiance like souls in Paradise. The splendid glow of a smith's furnace! The joy of leading a horse, of binding a sheaf of corn! The wonder of a ship sailing in freedom over the seas! But you, the idler, will toil and plod and suffer like an ox in the harness of Hell, when all you wanted to do was—nothing! Not a week will pass, not a day, without its overwhelming pressures; everything you do will cost an effort and every moment will see your muscles strained. What other men find light as a feather for you will have the heaviness of lead. The gentlest slope will seem steep and all life will be a matter of monstrous difficulty. The simplest acts, the very act of breathing, will be a labour to you, your very lungs will seem to have a crushing weight. To go in one direction rather than another will present you with a problem to be solved. The ordinary man when he wants to leave his home has only to open the door, and there he is, outside; but you will have to break through your own wall. What do ordinary people do when they want to go into the street? They simply walk downstairs. But you will have to tear up your sheets and make a rope of them, because you must go out by way of the window; and there you will be, dangling on your rope in darkness, rain or tempest; and if the rope proves too short your only course will be to drop. To drop at random from a doubtful

height, and into what? Into whatever may chance to be below, into the unknown. Or you'll climb by way of a chimney, at the risk of getting burnt, or crawl through a sewer at the risk of drowning. I say nothing about the holes that must be covered up, the stones that must be removed and replaced, the plaster to be disposed of. You are confronted by a lock of which the householder has the key in his pocket, the work of a locksmith. If you want to break it you have to create a masterpiece. First you will take a large sou piece and cut it in two slices. As for the tools you use for this purpose, you will have to invent them. That's your affair. Then you will hollow the inside of the slices, taking care not to damage the outside of the coin, and cut a thread in the rims so that they can be screwed together without any trace being visible. To the world at large it will be nothing but a coin, but to you it will be a box in which you will carry a scrap of steel—a watch-spring in which you have cut teeth, making it into a saw. And with this saw, coiled in a sou piece, you will cut through the bolt of a lock, the shank of a padlock, or the bars of your prison-cell and the fetter on your leg. And what will your reward be for working this miracle of art, skill, and patience if you are found to be its author? It will be prison. That is your future. Indolence and the life of pleasure—what snares they are! Can you not see that to decide to do nothing is the most wretched of all decisions? To live in idleness on the body politic is to be useless, that is to say harmful, and it can only end in misery. Woe to those who choose to be parasites, they become vermin! But you don't want to work. All you want is rich food and drink and a soft bed. You will end by drinking water, eating black bread, and sleeping on a bed of planks with fetters on your limbs, with the night cold piercing to your bones. You will break your chains and escape. All right—but you will crawl on your stomach through the undergrowth and live on grass like the beasts of the field. And you will be caught. After which you will spend years in an underground cell, chained to the wall, groping for the water-jug, gnawing crusts of bread that a dog would not touch, and maggoty beans—like a cockroach in a cellar! Have pity on yourself, my poor lad! You're still young. You were sucking at your mother's breast less than twenty years ago, and doubtless she is still alive. In her name I beseech you to listen to me. You want fine black cloth and glossy pumps, hair smoothly combed and scented; you want to be a gay dog and please the girls! But what you'll get is a shaven head, a red smock, and clogs. You want rings on your fingers, but you'll have one round your neck, and a cut of the whip if you so much as look at a woman. You'll start on that life at twenty and end at fifty. You'll start young and fresh, bright-eyed and white-toothed, and you'll end broken and bent, wrinkled, toothless and repellent, with white hair. My poor boy, you're on the wrong road. Sloth is a bad counsellor. Crime is the hardest of all work. Take my advice, don't be led into the drudgery of idleness. Rascality is a comfortless life; honesty is far less demanding. Now clear out and think about what I have said. Incidentally, what did you want of me? My purse, I suppose. Here it is.'

At length releasing his hold on Montparnasse, the elderly man handed him his purse, and Montparnasse, after weighing it for a moment in his hand, thrust it into the tail-pocket of his coat with as much care as if he had stolen it.

Having said his say, the elderly man turned away and went calmly on with his walk. The reader will have no difficulty in guessing who he was.

'Old babbler!' muttered Montparnasse, and stood staring after him as he vanished in the gloom.

His momentary bemusement was unfortunate for him. While the stranger was disappearing in one direction, Gavroche was approaching from the other.

Gavroche had first glanced through the hedge to make sure that Père Mabeuf, who had presumably fallen asleep, was still in the same place. Then he scrambled out and crept towards where Montparnasse was still standing. Slipping his hand into the pocket of that handsome tail-coat, he deftly removed the purse, after which he slipped away like a lizard into the shadows. Montparnasse, who had no reason to be on his guard and in any case had been moved to thought, perhaps for the first time in his life, was quite unconscious of what had happened. Gavroche got back to the place where Père Mabeuf was sleeping, tossed the purse over the hedge and then made off at top speed.

The purse fell on Père Mabeuf's foot and awakened him. He picked it up and opened it in amazement. It had two compartments, in one of which was some small change while in the other there were six napoleons.

In high excitement Monsieur Mabeuf took it to his housekeeper.

'It must have fallen from Heaven,' said Mère Plutarque.

BOOK FIVE

OF WHICH THE END DOES NOT RESEMBLE
THE BEGINNING

I. *Solitude and the Barracks*

COSETTE'S state of unhappiness, so acute and poignant only a few months earlier, was growing less, even in her own despite. Youth and springtime, her love for her father, the brightness of birds and flowers, were by gradual degrees fostering in that young and virginal spirit something akin to forgetfulness. Did it mean that the fire was quite extinguished, or were the embers still glowing beneath a crust of ashes? The fact is that now she scarcely ever felt any sharp stab of pain. One day, recalling Marius, she thought, 'I don't even think of him!'

It was a few days after this that she observed, passing their garden gate, a handsome young cavalry officer with a wasp waist and a waxed moustache, fair hair and blue eyes, and with a sabre at his side, splendidly elegant in his uniform, a dashing, vainglorious figure, in all respects the opposite of Marius. He was smoking a cigar. Cosette supposed that he belonged to the regiment then quartered in the barracks in the Rue de Babylone.

She saw him again next day, and noted the time. After that— could it have been by accident?—she saw him almost daily as he sauntered past.

The young man's brother officers were not slow to detect that the overgrown garden behind that tiresome rococo gate harboured a good-looking wench who nearly always contrived to be on hand when the lieutenant (whom the reader has already met and whose name was Théodule Gillenormand) went that way.

'There's a girl who's got her eye on you,' they said. 'You ought to give her a glance.' To which he replied: 'Do you really think I've time to stare at all the girls who stare at me?'

This happened at precisely the time when Marius, in the depths of despair, was saying to himself, 'If I could see her just once more before I die!' If he had had his wish and seen Cosette gazing at the young lancer he would have died on the spot.

Which of them was to be blamed? Neither. Marius was one of

those who embrace sorrow and dwell in it; but Cosette was one of those who feel it deeply but recover.

Cosette, in any case, was going through that dangerous stage, fatal to womanhood left to its own devices, when the heart of a lonely girl resembles the tendrils of a vine which may attach itself, as chance dictates, to a marble column or an inn-sign. It is a brief, decisive phase, crucial for any motherless girl whether she be rich or poor, for riches are no defence against error. Misalliance may occur at any level, and the real misalliance is between souls. An unknown young man without birth or fortune may nevertheless be the marble pillar sustaining a temple of lofty sentiments and splendid thought, just as your opulent man of the world, if one looks not at his elegant exterior but at his inner nature, which is the special domain of women, may be no better than a witless wooden post, the resort of violent, drunken passions—an inn-sign, in short.

What was really the state of Cosette's heart? It was a state of passion assuaged or slumbering; of love in flux, limpid and gleaming, tremulous to a certain depth, but sombre below this. The picture of the handsome officer was reflected on the surface, but did a memory still linger in the deepest depths? Perhaps she herself did not know.

And then a singular incident occurred.

II. *Cosette's alarm*

During the first fortnight of April Jean Valjean went on a journey. As we know, it was a thing he occasionally did, at very long intervals. He would be away for a day or two, three at the most. No one knew where he went, not even Cosette; but on one occasion she had accompanied him in a fiacre as far as the corner of a small cul-de-sac bearing the name of the Impasse de la Planchette. Here he had got out and the fiacre had taken Cosette back to the Rue de Babylone. As a rule it was when the household was running short of money that he went on these excursions.

So Valjean was away, having said that he would be back in three days' time. Cosette spent the evening alone in the salon, and to relieve the monotony she sat down at her piano-organ and played and sang the chorus, 'Huntsmen astray in the woods!' from Weber's opera *Euryanthe*, which is perhaps the most beautiful piece of music ever composed. When she had finished she sat musing.

Suddenly she thought she heard the sound of footsteps in the garden.

It was ten o'clock. Her father was away and Toussaint was in bed.

She went to one of the closed shutters and stood listening with her ear to it.

The footsteps sounded like those of a man walking very softly. Cosette ran up to her bedroom, opened the peep-hole in the shutter, and peered out. It was a night of full moon and everything was clearly visible.

There was no one to be seen. She opened the window. The garden was quite empty, and what little could be seen of the street was deserted as usual.

Cosette decided that she was mistaken and that the sound she thought she had heard had been simply an hallucination conjured up by Weber's dark, magnificent chorus, with its terrifying depths, evoking in the minds of its audience the magical forest in which can be heard the snapping of twigs beneath the restless feet of huntsmen half-seen in the dusk.

She thought no more about it; but then, Cosette was not nervous by nature. There was gipsy blood in her veins, that of a barefooted adventuress. We may recall that she was more like a lark than a dove. She had a wild but courageous heart.

At a somewhat earlier hour next day, when it was only beginning to grow dark, she went out into the garden. Intruding upon her random thoughts, she fancied that now and then she heard a sound like that of the previous night, as though someone were walking under the trees quite close to her; but she told herself that nothing more resembled the sound of footsteps in the grass than the sound of two branches rubbing together, and, in any case, she could see nothing.

She emerged from the 'shrubbery' and began to cross the small patch of grass between it and the steps of the villa. The moon, which was at her back, threw her shadow across the grass as she entered its light. And suddenly she stood still, terror-struck.

Beside her own shadow was another and singularly alarming one, a shadow wearing a round hat; it looked like that of a man walking a few paces behind her.

She stayed motionless for a moment, unable to cry out or even to turn her head. Finally, summoning all her courage, she looked round.

There was no one to be seen; and, looking down, she saw that the shadow had vanished. She went bravely back into the shrubbery and searched it, venturing even as far as the gate, but she found nothing.

She was truly alarmed. Could this be another hallucination, the second in two days? She might believe in one hallucination, but to believe in two was not so easy. And, most disturbing, it could not have been a ghost. Ghosts do not wear round hats. Jean Valjean

87

returned home next day and she told him what had happened, expecting to be reassured and to hear him say lightly, 'You're a silly child.' But instead he looked troubled. 'It can't have been anything,' he said.

He made an excuse to leave her and went out into the garden, and she saw him carefully examining the gate.

She awoke during the night, and this time she was certain. She could distinctly near the sound of footsteps beneath her window. She ran to the peep-hole in the shutter and looked out. A man was standing in the garden with a heavy cudgel in his hand. She was about to utter a cry when the moonlight fell upon his face. It was her father. She got back into bed thinking, 'He must be very worried!'

Jean Valjean passed all that night, and the two nights which followed, in the garden. She saw him through her peep-hole.

On the third night, at about one o'clock, when the moon was beginning to wane and rising later, she was awakened by a great burst of laughter and her father's voice calling to her, 'Cosette!' She sprang out of bed, put on her dressing-gown and opened the window. Her father was standing on the lawn.

'I woke you up to tell you everything's all right,' he said. 'Look. Here's your shadow in a round hat!'

He pointed to a shadow on the grass which did indeed look not unlike that of a man wearing a round hat. It was that of a cowled metal chimney belonging to a nearby house.

Cosette, too, began to laugh, with all her fears dispelled, and at breakfast next morning she was very gay on the subject of gardens haunted by the ghosts of chimney-stacks.

Jean Valjean recovered all his calm, and Cosette herself did not give much thought to the question of whether the chimney was really in the line of the shadow she had seen, or thought she had seen, or whether the moon was at the same point in the sky; nor did she question the singular behaviour of a chimney that beats a retreat when it is in danger of being caught—for the shadow had disappeared when she turned back to look for it, she was certain of that. She was quite convinced, and the notion that a stranger had entered their garden vanished from her thoughts.

But a few days later another incident occurred.

There was a stone seat in the garden, close by the railing along the street, sheltered by a hedgerow from the gaze of the passer-by but so near to it that it might have been touched, at a pinch, by anyone reaching an arm through the railing and the hedge. Cosette was sitting on it one evening that April when Valjean was out. She was musing, overtaken by that feeling of sadness that assails us in the dusk and which perhaps arises—who can say?—from the mystery of the grave, of which we have intimations at that hour. Perhaps her mother, Fantine, lurked somewhere in the shadows.

The breeze was freshening. She got up and walked slowly round the garden, through the dew-soaked grass, reflecting idly, in her mood of melancholy abstraction, that she should wear thicker shoes when she went out at that time or she would catch cold.

She returned to the bench, but as she was in the act of sitting down she noticed, in the place where she had been sitting before, a fairly large stone which had not been there a few minutes earlier. She stood looking at it, and it occurred to her, since the stone could not have got there by itself, that it must have been placed there by someone reaching through the hedge. The thought startled her, and this time she was genuinely alarmed. There could be no doubt about the reality of the stone. She did not touch it, but ran back into the house without looking round and hurriedly closed and barred the shutters and bolted the front door. She said to Toussaint:

'Has my father come home?'

'Not yet, Mademoiselle.'

(We have mentioned that Toussaint had a stammer, and we hope to be forgiven for not constantly reproducing it. We dislike the musical notation of an infirmity.)

Valjean, with his fondness for solitary nocturnal walks, often did not return until late at night.

'You're always careful to see that the shutters are properly barred, are you not, Toussaint?' said Cosette. 'Especially on the garden side. And you put those little metal pegs in the rings?'

'Of course, Mademoiselle.'

It was a duty that Toussaint never neglected. Cosette was well aware of the fact, but she could not refrain from adding:

'This is a very lonely spot.'

'Well, that's the truth,' said Toussaint. 'We could be murdered in our beds before you could say knife, especially with Monsieur not sleeping in the villa. But you needn't worry, I lock the place up as though it were a prison. It's not a nice thing, two women alone in a house. Just imagine. You wake suddenly and there's a man in your room, and he tells you to hold your tongue while he cuts your throat! It isn't so much dying one's afraid of, because we've all got to come to that, but it's dreadful to think of being touched by those brutes. Besides which, their knives are probably blunt.'

'That will do,' said Cosette. 'Just make sure of our locks and bars.'

Terrified by this vividly improvised drama, and perhaps recalling her visions of a week or two before, Cosette was afraid to ask Toussaint to go out and look at the stone on the garden bench, from fear that if they opened the front door a party of villains would burst in. After locking and bolting every door and window in the house, and sending Toussaint to inspect the attics and cellars, she locked herself in her bedroom, peered under the bed and that night slept badly, haunted in her dreams by a stone the size of a mountain that was filled with caves.

But the next morning—it being the property of the sunrise to cause us to laugh at our terrors of the night, and our laughter being always proportionate to our fears—Cosette dismissed the whole thing, saying to herself: 'What was I thinking of? It's the same as those footsteps I thought I heard, and the shadow that was nothing but a chimney-stack. Am I turning into a frightened kitten?' And the sunlight, shining through the half-opened shutters and glowing redly through the curtains, so reassured her that she brushed it all away, even the stone. 'It didn't exist, any more than the man in the round hat. I simply imagined it.'

She dressed and ran out into the garden to the bench, and a shiver ran down her spine. The stone was still there.

But her alarm lasted only for a moment. What is terror after dark becomes merely curiosity by daylight. 'Well,' she thought. 'Let me see.'

The stone was quite large. She picked it up and saw that there was something underneath it. It was a white envelope, unaddressed and unsealed. But it was not empty. There was something that looked like a sheaf of folded paper inside. Cosette explored it with her fingers, with a feeling that was no longer one of fear or simple curiosity, but rather the dawning of a new apprehension. Extracting the contents, she found them to be a small paper-covered notebook of which every page was numbered and bore a few lines of very small and, she thought, very elegant handwriting. She looked for a name but found none; the writing was unsigned. For whom was it intended? Presumably for herself, since it had been deposited on her garden bench. Where had it come from? Seized with an overpowering fascination, she sought in vain to look away from the written pages fluttering in her hand, staring at the sky and at the street, at the acacias, bathed in sunshine, and at the pigeons flying over a nearby roof; but her gaze was drawn irresistibly back to the manuscript; she had to know what it had to say.

What follows is what she read.

IV. *The Heart beneath the Stone*

The reduction of the universe to the compass of a single being, and the extension of a single being until it reaches God—that is love.

Love is the salute of the angels to the stars.

How sad the heart is when rendered sad by love!

How great is the void created by the absence of the being who alone fills the world. How true it is that the beloved becomes God. It is understandable that God would grow jealous if the Father of All Things had not so evidently created all things for the soul, and the soul for love.

It needs no more than a smile, glimpsed beneath a hat of white crêpe adorned with lilac, for the soul to be transported into the palace of dreams.

God is behind all things, but all things conceal God. Objects are black and human creatures are opaque. To love a person is to render them transparent.

There are thoughts which are prayers. There are moments when, whatever the posture of the body, the soul is on its knees.

Separated lovers cheat absence by a thousand fancies which have their own reality. They are prevented from seeing one another and they cannot write; nevertheless they find countless mysterious ways of corresponding, by sending each other the song of birds, the scent of flowers, the laughter of children, the light of the sun, the sighing of the wind, and the gleam of the stars—all the beauties of creation. And why should they not? All the works of God are designed to serve love, and love has the power to charge all nature with its messages.

Oh, Spring, you are a letter which I send her!

The future belongs far more to the heart than to the mind. Love is the one thing that can fill and fulfil eternity. The infinite calls for the inexhaustible.

Love partakes of the soul, being of the same nature. Like the soul, it is the divine spark, incorruptible, indivisible, imperishable. It is the fiery particle that dwells in us, immortal and infinite, which nothing can confine and nothing extinguish. We feel its glow in the marrow of our bones and see its brightness reaching to the depths of Heaven.

Oh, love, adoration, the rapture of two spirits which know each other, two hearts which are exchanged, two looks which interpenetrate! You will come to me, will you not, this happiness! To walk together in solitude! Blessed and radiant days! I have sometimes thought that now and then moments may be detached from the lives of angels to enrich the lives of men.

God can add nothing to the happiness of those who love except to make it unending. After a lifetime of love an eternity of love is indeed an increase; but to heighten the intensity, the ineffable happiness that love confers upon the spirit in this world, is an impossibility, even for God. God is the wholeness of Heaven; love is the wholeness of man.

We look up at a star for two reasons, because it shines and because it is impenetrable. But we have at our side a gentler radiance and a greater mystery, that of woman.

Each of us, whoever he may be, has his breathing self. Lacking this, or lacking air, we suffocate. And then we die. To die for lack of love is terrible. It is the stifling of the soul.

When love has melted and merged two persons in a sublime and sacred unity, the secret of life has been revealed to them; they are no longer anything but the two aspects of a single destiny, the wings of a single spirit. To love is to soar!

On the day when a woman in passing sheds light for you as she goes, you are lost, you are in love. There is only one thing to be done, to fix your thoughts upon her so intently that she is compelled to think of you.

That which love begins can be completed only by God.

True love is plunged in despair or rapture by a lost glove or by a found handkerchief; but it needs eternity for all its devotion and its hopes. It is composed of both the infinitely great and the infinitely small.

If you are stone, be magnetic; if a plant, be sensitive; but if you are human, be love.

Nothing satisfies love. We achieve happiness and long for Eden; we gain paradise and long for Heaven.

I say to you who love that all these things are contained in love. You must learn to find them. Love encompasses all heaven, all contemplation, and, more than heaven, physical delight.

'Does she still visit the Luxembourg?' . . . 'No, Monsieur.' . . . 'It is in this church, is it not, that she attends Mass?' . . . 'She does not come here any more.' . . . 'Does she still live in this house?' . . . 'She has moved elsewhere.' . . . 'Where has she gone to live?' . . . 'She did not say.'

How grievous not to know the address of one's soul!

Love has its childishness; other passions have pettiness. Shame on the passions that make us petty; honour to the one that makes us a child!

A strange thing has happened, do you know? I am in darkness. There is a person who, departing, took away the sun.

Oh, to lie side by side in the same tomb and now and then caress with a finger-tip in the shades, that will do for my eternity!

You who suffer because you love, love still more. To die of love is to live by it.

Love! A dark and starry transfiguration is mingled with that torment. There is ecstasy in the agony.

Oh, the happiness of birds! It is because they have a nest that they have a song.

Love is a heavenly breath of the air of paradise.

Deep hearts and wise minds accept life as God made it. It is a long trial, an incomprehensible preparation for an unknown destiny. This destiny, his true one, begins for man on the first stair within the tomb. Something appears to him, and he begins to perceive the finality. Take heed of that word, finality. The living see infinity; the finality may be seen only by the dead. In the meantime, love and suffer, hope and meditate. Woe, alas, to those who have loved only bodies, forms, appearances! Death will rob them of everything. Try to love souls, you will find them again.

I encountered in the street a penniless young man who was in love. His hat was old and his jacket worn, with holes at the elbows; water soaked through his shoes, but starlight flooded through his soul.

How wonderful it is to be loved, but how much greater to love! The heart becomes heroic through passion; it rejects everything that is not pure and arms itself with nothing that is not noble and great. An unworthy thought can no more take root in it than a nettle on a glacier. The lofty and serene spirit, immune from all base passion and emotion, prevailing over the clouds and shadows of this world, the follies, lies, hatreds, vanities and miseries, dwells in the azure of the sky and feels the deep and subterranean shifts of destiny no more than the mountain-peak feels the earthquake.

If there were no one who loved the sun would cease to shine.

V. Cosette after Reading the Letter

As she read this Cosette grew more and more thoughtful. Just as she finished it the young cavalry officer swaggered past the gate, this being his regular time. She thought him odious.

She turned back to the notebook, and now she found the handwriting delightful, always the same hand but in ink that varied in intensity, being sometimes dense black and sometimes pale, as happens when one writes over a period of days and adds water from time to time to the ink. It seemed that these were thoughts that had overflowed on to paper, a string of sighs set down at random, without order or selection or purpose. Cosette had never before read anything like it. The manuscript, in which she saw more clarity than obscurity, affected her like the opening of a closed door. Each of its enigmatic lines, shining with splendour in her eyes, kindled a new awareness in her heart. Her teachers at the convent had talked much of the soul but never of earthly love, rather as one might talk of the poker without mentioning the fire. These fifteen handwritten pages had abruptly but gently opened her eyes to the nature of all love and suffering, destiny, life, eternity, the beginning and the end, as though a hand, suddenly opening, had released a shaft of light. She could discern the author behind them, his passionate, generous, and candid nature, his great unhappiness and great hope, his captive heart and overflowing ecstasy. What was this manuscript if not a letter? A letter unaddressed, without name or date or signature,

urgent, with no demands, a riddle composed of truths, a token of
love to be delivered by a winged messenger and read by virgin eyes,
an appointment to meet in some place not on earth, the love-letter
of a ghost written to a vision. A calm but passionate unknown, who
seemed ready to take refuge in death, had sent to his absent beloved
the secret of human destiny, the key to life and love. He had written
with a foot in the tomb and a finger in the sky. The lines, falling
haphazard on the paper, were like raindrops falling from a soul.

And where did they come from? Who was their author? Cosette
had not a moment's doubt. They could have come from only one
person—from him.

The light of day was revived in her, everything was made good.
She had a sense of inexpressible delight and anguish. It was he!
He had been there, and it was his arm that had been thrust through
the hedge! While she had been forgetful, he had searched and found
her. But had she really forgotten him? Never! She was mad to have
believed so, even for a moment. She had loved him from the first.
The fire had been damped and had died down, but, as she now
knew, it had only burned the more deeply in her, and now it had
burst again into flame and the flame filled her whole being. The
notebook was like a match flung by that other soul into her own,
and she felt the fire break out again. She pored over the written
words, thinking 'How well I know them! I have read it all before
in his eyes.'

As she finished reading it for the third time Lieutenant Théodule
reappeared beyond the gate, clicking his heels on the cobbles.
Cosette was forced to look up. She now thought him fatuous, uncouth, impertinent, and altogether repellent, and she turned her
head away indignantly, wishing she could throw something at him.

She went back into the house and up to her bedroom, to read the
notebook yet again, learn it by heart, ponder on it. At length she
kissed it and hid it in her bosom. The matter was decided. Cosette
was again plunged in the anguished ecstasies of love; the infinity of
Eden had opened for her once again.

She lived through that day in a state of bemusement, scarcely
thinking, a thousand fancies tumbling through her head. She could
guess at nothing, and the hopes amid her tremors were all vague;
she dared be sure of nothing, but she would not reject anything.
Pallors sped over her face, and shivers ran through her body. At
moments she felt that she must be dreaming and asked herself,
'Can it be real?' But then she touched the notebook under her dress
and pressing it to her heart felt its shape against her flesh. If Jean
Valjean had seen her at those moments he would have trembled
at the new look in her eyes. 'Oh, yes,' she thought. 'It can only be

he; it comes to me from him!' And she thought that an intervention of the angels, some celestial chance, had restored him to her.

The wonders conjured up by love! The fantasies! That intervention of the angels, that celestial chance, was like the hunk of bread tossed from one inmate to another, from one courtyard to another, over the walls of the prison of La Force.

VI. *No Place for the Aged*

Jean Valjean went out that evening, and Cosette dressed up.

She did her hair in the way that suited her best and put on a gown that had been cut a little low at the neck so that it allowed the beginning of her bosom to be seen and was, as young ladies say, 'somewhat immodest'. It was not in the least immodest and more pretty than otherwise. She made these preparations without knowing why. Was she going anywhere? Was she expecting a visitor? No.

As evening fell she went into the garden. Toussaint was busy in the kitchen, which looked out on the back-yard. She walked under the trees, thrusting aside the branches now and then since some were very low. She came to the bench and found the stone still there.

She sat down and softly stroked it as though in gratitude. And suddenly she had that feeling that sometimes comes to us, of someone behind her. She looked round and started to her feet.

It was he.

He was bareheaded and he looked pale and thinner. His dark clothing was scarcely visible in the dusk which cast a veil over his forehead and buried his eyes in shadow; beneath his incomparable sweetness of expression there was something of death and something of the night, and his face was faintly illumined with the light of the dying day and the suggestion of a soul in flight, as though he were still not a ghost but no longer a living man. He had dropped his hat, which lay in the bushes.

Cosette, near to fainting, did not utter a sound. She drew slowly away, because she felt herself drawn towards him. He did not move, but something emanated from him, a kind of warmth and sadness which must be in the eyes that she could not see.

In withdrawing Cosette found herself with her back to a tree, and she leaned against it. Without it she would have fallen.

Then he began to speak, in that voice that she had never heard before, speaking so softly that it was scarcely raised above the rustle of the leaves.

'Forgive me for being here. I have been in such distress, I could not go on living the way things were, and so I had to come. Did you read what I left on the bench? Do you perhaps recognize me? You mustn't be afraid. It's a long time ago, but do you remember the day when you first looked at me—in the Luxembourg, near the Gladiator? And the day when you walked past me? Those things happened on the 16th of June and the 2nd of July—nearly a year ago. After that I did not see you for a long time. I asked the woman who collects the chair-rents and she said she hadn't seen you. You were living in a new house in the Rue de l'Ouest, on the third floor. I found out, you see. I followed you. What else could I do? And then you disappeared. I thought I saw you once when I was reading the newspapers under the Odéon arcade and I ran after you, but it wasn't you, only someone wearing a hat like yours. I come here at night, but don't worry, no one sees me. I come and look up at your windows, and I walk very quietly so as not to disturb you. I was behind you the other evening when you looked round, and I hid and ran for it. Once I heard you singing and it made me very happy. Does it matter to you if I listen to you singing through the shutters? It can do you no harm. But you don't mind, do you? To me, you see, you're an angel. You must let me come sometimes. I think I'm going to die. If you knew how I adore you! Forgive me for talking like this, I don't know what I'm saying, perhaps I'm annoying you. Am I annoying you?'

'Mother!' she murmured, and sank down as though she herself were dying.

He caught her as she fell and clasped her tightly in his arms without knowing that he did so. He held her, trembling, feeling as though his head were filled with a mist in which lightnings flashed, feeling, in the tumult of his thoughts, that he was performing a religious rite that was also an act of profanation. For the rest, he felt no spark of physical desire for this enchanting girl whose body was now pressed so closely to his own. He was lost in love.

She took his hand and laid it against her heart, and he felt the shape of the notebook under her dress. He stammered:

'Then—you love me?'

She answered in a voice so low that it was scarcely to be heard: 'Of course! You know I do.' And she hid her russet head against the breast of the triumphant and marvelling young man.

He fell back on to the bench with her at his side. Neither could speak. The stars were beginning to show. How did it happen that their lips came together? How does it happen that birds sing, that snow melts, that the rose unfolds, that the dawn whitens behind the stark shapes of trees on the quivering summit of the hill? A kiss, and all was said.

Both were trembling. They looked at each other with eyes shining in the dusk, unconscious of the cool of the night, the chill of the stone bench, the dampness of the earth, the dew on the grass; they looked at each other, their hearts filled with their thoughts. Without knowing it, they had clasped hands.

She did not ask him, or even wonder, how he had contrived to get into the garden. It seemed to her so right that he should be there. From time to time their knees touched and both quivered. Now and then Cosette stammered a word, her soul trembling on her lips like a dewdrop on the petal of a flower.

And gradually they began to speak. Outpouring followed the silence which is fulfilment. The night was calm and splendid above their heads. Pure as disembodied spirits, they told each other about themselves, their dreams and their follies, their delights, their fantasies, their failings; how they had come to love each other at a distance, to long for each other, and their despair when they no longer saw each other. In an intimacy which nothing could ever make more perfect they told each other of all that was most secret and hidden in themselves, recounting, with an innocent trust in their illusions, everything that love and youth, and the vestiges of childhood that still clung to them, put into their heads. Two hearts were exchanged, so that when an hour had passed they were a youth enriched with the soul of a girl and a girl enriched with a young man's soul. Each pervaded, enchanted, and enraptured the other.

When they had finished, when everything had been said, she laid her head on his shoulder and asked:

'What is your name?'

'My name is Marius. And yours?'

'Cosette.'

BOOK SIX

THE BOY GAVROCHE

I. *Scurvy Trick played by the Wind*

SINCE 1823, while the tavern at Montfermeil was gradually sinking, not in the deeps of bankruptcy but in the sink of petty debt, the Thénardiers had had two more children, both boys, making five altogether, two girls and three boys. It was rather a lot. Mme Thénardier had rid herself of the last two, while they were still very young, in a singularly happy fashion.

'Rid herself' is the right way to put it. She was a woman possessing only a limited store of humanity, a phenomenon of which there are many instances. Like the Maréchale de La Mothe-Houdancourt, who mothered three duchesses, Mme Thénardier was a mother only to her daughters; her maternal instinct extended no further. Her hostility to mankind in general began with her sons, and it was here that her malice reached its peak. She detested the eldest, as we have seen, but she abominated the two others. Why? Because. The most terrible and unanswerable of reasons. 'Because I've no use for a litter of squalling brats,' she said. We must describe how the Thénardiers managed to get rid of their two youngest children and even make a profit out of them.

The woman Magnon, formerly the servant of Monsieur Gillenormand, of whom mention has already been made, had succeeded in getting her employer to support her two sons. She went to live on the Quai des Célestins, at the corner of the ancient Rue du Petit-Musc, of which the name does something to redeem its evil-smelling reputation. Some readers will recall the epidemic of croup which ravaged the riverside quarters of Paris thirty-five years ago and enabled medical science to experiment on a large scale with treatment by insifflations of alum, now superseded by the external application of iodine. Both La Magnon's sons were carried off by the epidemic at a tender age and on the same day—one in the morning and the other in the evening. It was a sad blow to their mother, for the children were valuable, each being worth eighty francs a month. The money was paid with meticulous regularity, on Monsieur Gillenormand's instructions, by his man of affairs, a retired lawyer's clerk living in the Rue du Roi-de-Sicile. The death of the children threatened to bring this happy state of affairs to an end, and La Magnon looked round for a way out of the difficulty. In the dark freemasonry of ill-doing of which she was a member all things are known, all secrets kept and each man helps his fellow. La Magnon needed two children and the Thénardiers had two to dispose of, of the same sex and age, a most fortunate coincidence. So the little Thénardiers became little Magnons, and La Magnon went to live in the Rue Clocheperce. In Paris to change the street in which one lives is to change one's identity.

Officialdom, not having been notified, raised no objection, and the transaction was carried out with the greatest ease. Mme Thénardier demanded a monthly rent of ten francs apiece for the two little boys, which La Magnon agreed to and, in fact, paid. It goes without saying that Monsieur Gillenormand kept up his payments. He visited the children every six months, but noticed no change. 'How like you they're growing, Monsieur!' said La Magnon.

Thénardier, with his usual adaptability, took advantage of the circumstance to turn himself into Jondrette. His two daughters and Gavroche had scarcely had time to notice that they had two small brothers. There is a level of poverty at which we are afflicted with a kind of indifference which causes all things to seem unreal: those closest to us become no more than shadows, scarcely distinguishable against the dark background of our daily life, and easily lost to view.

Nevertheless on the evening of the day on which she handed the boys over to La Magnon, with the firm resolve to be rid of them for ever, the Thénardier woman had, or pretended to have, a fit of conscience. She said to her husband: 'But it's abandoning our children!', to which he replied tersely and magisterially, 'Jean-Jacques Rousseau did even worse.' With her scruples thus disposed of, she became apprehensive: 'But suppose we have the police after us? Is it legal, what we've done, Monsieur Thénardier?' . . . 'Of course it is, and anyway who's going to notice? Who worries about pauper children?'

La Magnon possessed what passed for elegance in her own sphere. She dressed with care. She shared her wretched but showily furnished apartment with a Frenchified Englishwoman who was a skilful thief. This Parisienne by adoption, who had wealthy contacts and a close connexion with the diamonds of Mlle Mars, later became prominent in the police records. She was nicknamed 'Mamselle Miss'.

The two little boys had no reason to complain. Being worth eighty francs a head, they were carefully looked after, like any other valuable property—well-clad, well-fed, treated almost like little gentlemen—far better off under their false mother than under the real one. La Magnon, who aspired to gentility, used no coarse language in their presence.

Thus they lived for some years, and Thénardier began to envisage new possibilities. He said one day to La Magnon, when she brought him the monthly ten francs, 'Their "father" will have to see to their education.'

But suddenly the two unhappy children, hitherto well enough protected, even though it was by their misfortune, were flung neck and crop into real life and forced to start living it.

A mass-arrest of malefactors like that which had taken place in the Jondrettes' garret, which inevitably leads to further police investigation and imprisonments, is a disaster having wide repercussions in the criminal underworld. The downfall of the Thénardiers led to the downfall of La Magnon.

Shortly after La Magnon had passed the letter about the Rue Plumet on to Éponine, the police descended on the Rue Clocheperce. La Magnon and Mamselle Miss were arrested and the whole house, which harboured a number of suspicious characters, was searched. The two little boys were playing in a back-yard when this happened, and knew nothing about it. When they tried to go home they found the doors locked and the house empty. A cobbler, whose shop was across the street, called to them and gave them a written message from their 'mother'. It bore the address of Monsieur Barge, debt-collector, 8 Rue du Roi-de-Sicile—that is to say, Monsieur Gillenormand's man of affairs. 'You don't live here any more,' the cobbler said. 'You must go to this address. It's quite near, first turning on the left. Keep the paper in case you have to ask the way.'

They went off together, the older boy in the lead, clutching the scrap of paper. But he was cold, and his small, stiff fingers did not grip it tightly enough. A gust of wind along the Rue Clocheperce blew it out of his hand, and since it was growing dark he could not find it again.

After this they strayed at random through the streets.

II. *In which the Boy Gavroche profits by the Great Napoleon*

Springtime in Paris is often marred by harsh and bitter winds by which one is chilled if not quite frozen; they may spring up on the finest day, and their effect is like that of an icy draught blowing through a leaky window or ill-closed door into a warm room.

It is as though the grim portals of winter had been left ajar. In the spring of 1832, the year of the first great European epidemic, these winds were more keen and piercing than ever; the door left ajar was not merely the door of winter but of the tomb: those gusts of wind were the breath of cholera. Their peculiarity, from a meteorological point of view, was that they did not exclude a high degree of electrical tension. There were frequent thunderstorms at that time.

On an evening when the wind was particularly vigorous, so much so that it might have been January, and the well-to-do had got out their winter overcoats, the boy Gavroche, shivering in his rags but still cheerful, stood gazing in apparent delight at a hairdresser's window in the neighbourhood of Orme-Saint-Gervais. He had somewhere acquired a woman's shawl, which he was using as a muffler. Ostensibly he was admiring the wax figure of a woman in a bridal gown, with a low-cut decolletée and a headdress of orange-blossom, which smiled at the populace as it slowly revolved on a stand between two lights; but the truth is that he was considering whether he might not 'lift' one or two of the cakes of soap in an open stall in the shop's doorway, thereafter to sell them at a sou apiece to a barber in another part of the town. He had often dined on one of those cakes of soap. It was a form of enterprise for which he had some talent and which he called 'trimming the trimmer'.

While he stood there with one eye on the revolving figure and the other on the array of soap he communed with himself in a low-voiced monologue as follows: 'Tuesday . . . Was it Tuesday? . . . It can't have been . . . Well, but perhaps it was . . . Yes, it was Tuesday.' The subject of the soliloquy is not known, but if it referred to the occasion of his last meal then that must have been three days ago, for the present day was Friday.

The barber, shaving a customer in his well-warmed shop, was keeping a sharp eye on this potential enemy, a frozen, impudent urchin with his hands plunged deep in his pockets but his wits plainly about him.

While Gavroche was studying the situation, glancing from the window to the Brown Windsor soap, two respectably clad small boys, both younger than himself, timidly opened the door and, entering the shop, asked for something in plaintive voices that sounded more like a sob than a plea. Both talked at once, and it was impossible to make out what they were saying because the voice of the younger was choked with misery and the teeth of the elder were chattering with cold. The barber turned furiously upon them and, still with his razor in his hand, thrust them back to the street exclaiming:

'Opening the door and letting the cold in for no reason!'

The children walked dolefully away, and now it was beginning to rain. Gavroche went after them.

'What's up with you two?' he demanded.

'We've nowhere to sleep,' the older boy said.

'Is that all?' said Gavroche. 'Well it's nothing to cry about. You aren't kittens.' And he went on, with a protective note under his air of lofty scorn. 'Come with me, moppets.'

They obeyed him instantly, as though he had been an archbishop, and both stopped crying. Gavroche led them up the Rue Saint-Antoine in the direction of the Bastille, but not without backward glances at the hairdresser's shop.

'That's a cold fish, that one,' he muttered. 'Probably English.'

A woman of the town, seeing them as they walked in single file with Gavroche at the head, gave a loud and disrespectful titter.

'Don't mention it, Miss Open-to-all,' said Gavroche.

But then he returned to the subject of the hairdresser.

'I got the wrong animal. He's not a fish but a snake. I'll get hold of a locksmith and tie a bell to his tail.'

The thought of the hairdresser had made him truculent. Crossing a gutter, they came up with a bearded caretaker, worthy to encounter Faust on the Brocken, with a broom in her hand.

'Madame,' he inquired, 'are you going to fly away on it?'

At the same time he splashed the freshly shined boots of a man who was passing.

'Young devil!' the man exclaimed furiously.

Gavroche stuck his chin out over the shawl.

'Monsieur has a complaint to make?'

'I'm complaining about you!'

'Sorry. No more complaints today. The office is closed.'

But further up the street he noticed, shivering in a doorway, a beggar girl of thirteen or fourteen whose skirts were so short that they left her knees uncovered. She was beginning to be too old to go about like that. These are the tricks that growing up plays. Skirts become too short when nakedness becomes indecent.

'Poor kid,' said Gavroche. 'She hasn't even got drawers on. Here, take this.'

He unwound the thick wool from around his neck and draped it over her skinny shoulders, and the muffler again became a shawl. The girl stared at him in astonishment, accepting the gift in silence. At the level of utmost poverty wits are too dulled to complain at misfortune or give thanks for a benefaction.

'Brrr!' said Gavroche, now shivering more than St. Martin himself, who at least had kept half his cloak. And as though encouraged by the 'brrr' the rain came pouring down. Those black skies punish good deeds. 'And now what?' said Gavroche. 'Raining again. If it goes on like this I shall ask for my money back. All the same,' he went on, looking at the girl as she drew the shawl tightly about her, 'there's one person who can keep warm.' And he glared defiantly at the heavens. 'So that's one up to me!'

He walked on with the two little boys following closely behind him, and when they came to the barred window which was the sign of a baker's shop—for bread must be as rigorously protected as gold —he turned to them and said:

'Talking of which, have you kids had anything to eat?'

'Not since this morning, sir,' the elder boy replied.

'But haven't you any parents?' Gavroche demanded.

'Yes, sir, I beg your pardon, we have a father and mother, but we don't know where they are.'

'We've been walking for hours,' the elder boy went on. 'We've even looked in the gutters for something to eat, but we couldn't find anything.'

'I know,' said Gavroche. 'The dogs get everything.' He paused to consider and then said: 'So—the parents gone astray and no knowing what's become of them. That's bad, my children. It's a mistake to mislay grown-ups. Well, we've got to get a bite somewhere.'

He asked no further questions. To be homeless was no novelty in his life. But the elder of the two little boys, who had now almost entirely recovered the ready heedlessness of childhood, exclaimed:

'It's queer all the same. Mamma said she'd take us to get some box for the decorations of Palm Sunday.'

'My eye!' said Gavroche.

'Mamma's a lady and she lives with Mamselle Miss.'

'Does she now!' said Gavroche.

They were still standing outside the baker's shop, and for some moments he had been exploring the numerous recesses in his ragged attire. Finally he looked up with what he hoped was an air of calm satisfaction but which was really one of triumph.

'Don't worry, lads. This will do for supper for three.' And he brought a single sou out of one of his pockets.

Without giving them time to stare, he pushed them ahead of him into the shop and slapped the sou down on the counter, exclaiming:

'Baker's boy! Five centimes' worth of bread.'

The man behind the counter, who was in fact the baker himself, picked up a loaf and a knife.

'Three slices, boy,' said Gavroche, and added in a dignified manner, 'There are three of us.' Then, seeing that the baker, after a glance at the three diners, had selected a cheap loaf, he put a finger to his nose with a sniff as lordly as if it conveyed a pinch of Frederick the Great's snuff, and cried in outraged indignation:

'Wossat?'

Any reader who may be disposed to mistake this utterance for a word of Russian or Polish, or for one of those cries which the Mohawks or the Ojibasays address to one another across a river in the American far west, is hereby informed that it is an expression which he (the reader) commonly uses in place of the words, 'What is that?' The baker understood perfectly and replied:

'Why, it's bread, of course. Excellent second-class bread.'

'Meaning *larton brutal*, black bread, prison bread,' said Gavroche with cool disdain. 'What I want is white bread. The real, polished stuff. I'm in a spending mood.'

The baker could not restrain a smile, and while he cut the required loaf he surveyed his customers with an expression of sympathy, which outraged Gavroche.

'What do you think you're doing,' he demanded, 'looking us over like that?' The three of them laid end to end would have come to little more than six feet.

When the bread had been cut and the baker had pocketed his sou, Gavroche said to the two children, 'Well, sail in!' They stared in bewilderment and he burst out laughing. 'They're too small to know the language yet. Eat, is what I mean.' He picked up two of the three slices, and thinking that the older boy was more deserving of his notice and should be encouraged to assuage his larger appetite, he handed him the larger of the two. 'Stop your gob with this.'

He kept the smallest slice for himself.

The little boys were ravenous, as was Gavroche. Standing there devouring the bread, they cluttered up the shop, and the owner, having got his money, was beginning to look sourly at them.

'Outside,' said Gavroche, and they continued on their way to the Bastille.

Now and then when they passed a lighted shop-window the smaller boy paused to look at the time by a gunmetal watch hanging on a string round his neck.

'A pampered chick,' reflected Gavroche; but then he muttered between his teeth: 'All the same, if I had brats I'd look after them better than that.'

By the time they had finished the bread they had come to the corner of the dismal Rue des Ballets, at the end of which the low, forbidding doorway of the prison of La Force is to be seen.

'Is that you, Gavroche?' a voice said.

'Is that you, Montparnasse?' said Gavroche.

The man who had spoken was indeed Montparnasse, concealed

behind blue-tinted spectacles but perfectly recognizable to Gavroche.

'My word!' said Gavroche. 'A coat that fits like a poultice and blue goggles like a professor! Classy, that's what we are.'

'Not so bad,' said Montparnasse, and drew him away from the shop lights. The two little boys followed automatically, holding hands. When they were installed under the archway of a house entrance, out of earshot and sheltered from the rain, Montparnasse said:

'Know where I'm going?'

'To the gallows, like as not.'

'Idiot. I'm going to meet Babet.'

'So that's her name,' said Gavroche.

'Not her—him.'

'What—you mean Babet?'

'That's right.'

'But I thought he'd been jugged.'

'Yes, but he's skipped,' said Montparnasse, and he went on to describe how Babet, having been transferred to the Conciergerie, had escaped that same morning by slipping into the wrong file at the inspection parade. Gavroche greatly admired this act of cunning.

'What an artist!' he said.

'But that's not all,' said Montparnasse.

While he was listening to further details Gavroche had taken hold of the case Montparnasse was carrying. He tugged at the handle and the blade of a dagger came to light.

'Hey!' he said, hastily thrusting it back. 'So you're ready for action under the classy get-up!' Montparnasse winked. 'Are you expecting trouble with the cops?'

'You never know,' said Montparnasse airily. 'Just as well to be prepared.'

'Well, what exactly are you up to?'

'Things,' said Montparnasse, resuming his portentous manner. He then changed the subject. 'By the way, a queer thing happened to me the other day.'

'What was that?'

'A few days ago it was. I held up a respectable old gent and he handed me a sermon and his purse. I put it in my pocket, but when I looked for it a few minutes later there was nothing there.'

'Except the sermon,' said Gavroche.

'But what about you? What are you up to?'

'I'm going to put these kids to bed.'

'Put them to bed? Where?'

'In my place.'

'Where's that?'

'My home.'

'You mean you've got a lodging?'

'That's right.'

'Well, where is it?'

'It's in the elephant,' said Gavroche.

Montparnasse was not easily astonished, but this caused him to open his eyes.

'In the elephant?'

'That's right. The Bastille elephant. What's wrong with that?'

Montparnasse's face cleared and he looked approvingly at Gavroche.

'Of course,' he said. 'The elephant. What's it like?'

'Couldn't be better. Real comfort. No draughts like you get under the bridges.'

'But how do you get in?'

'I manage.'

'You mean there's a hole?'

'You bet. But you mustn't let on. It's between the front legs. The cops haven't spotted it.'

'So you climb up. Yes, I see.'

'It takes me about two seconds. But I'll have to find a ladder for these kids.'

Montparnasse glanced at them and laughed.

'How the devil did you come by them?'

'A barber made me a present of them,' said Gavroche simply.

Another thought had now occurred to Montparnasse. 'You recognized me pretty easily,' he muttered.

He got two small objects out of his pocket—two short lengths of quill bound with cotton—and inserted one in each nostril. They gave him a new nose.

'That changes you quite a bit,' said Gavroche. 'A great improvement. You should always wear them.'

Montparnasse was a good-looking youth but he could take a joke.

'Seriously,' he said, 'what's it like?'

His tone of voice had also changed. In the twinkling of an eye he had become a different person.

'Marvellous. How about giving us Punch and Judy?'

At this the two little boys, who had hitherto paid no attention to the conversation, being too busy picking their own noses, turned and looked hopefully up at Montparnasse; but the latter, unfortunately, had grown solemn. He laid a hand on Gavroche's shoulder and said gravely:

'I don't mind telling you, lad, that if I were in the market-place with my *dogue*, my *dague*, and my *digue* and you were so prodigal as to offer me ten sous I wouldn't mind digging for them. But this isn't Mardi Gras.'

This strange utterance had a remarkable effect on the boy. He turned and looked alertly about him, and seeing a policeman standing with his back to them not far away he uttered a grunt of enlightenment, quickly suppressed, and shook Montparnasse by the hand.

'Well, goodnight, I must take these kids along to my place. And by the way, if you need me some night that's where you'll find me. I live on the first floor. There's no hall-porter. Ask for Monsieur Gavroche.'

'Thanks,' said Montparnasse.

They then parted, Montparnasse making for the Grève and Gavroche for the Bastille. The younger of the two little boys, who was being pulled along by his brother, who was being pulled along by Gavroche, looked round several times for a last glimpse of the Punch and Judy man.

The clue to the cryptic utterance which had warned Gavroche of the presence of a policeman was contained in the repetition of the syllable 'dig', either within a word or as a link between two words, meaning, 'Watch out. We can't talk here.' It also contained an elegant literary allusion which escaped Gavroche. The words my '*dogue*,' my '*dague*', and my '*digue*', meaning 'my dog, my dagger, and my woman', were slang of the Temple quarter, commonly used by fairground buskers and camp-followers in the *grand siècle*, when Molière wrote and Callot drew.

Twenty years ago there was still to be seen, in the south-east corner of the Place de la Bastille, near the canal-port dug out of the former moat of the prison-fortress, a weird monument which has vanished from the memory of present-day Parisians but which deserves to have left some trace of itself, for it sprang from the mind of a member of the Institute, none other than the Commander-in-Chief of the Army in Egypt.

We use the word 'monument', although in fact it was no more than a preliminary sketch; but a sketch on the grand scale, the prodigious corpse of a Napoleonic aspiration which successive adverse winds have borne further and further away from us until it has lapsed into history; but the sketch had a look of permanence which was in sharp contrast to its provisional nature. It was an elephant some forty feet high, constructed of wood and plaster, with a tower the size of a house on its back, that once had been roughly painted green but was now blackened by wind and weather. Outlined against the stars at night, in that open space, with its huge body and trunk, its crenellated tower, its four legs like temple columns, it was an astonishing and impressive spectacle. No one knew precisely what it meant. It was in some sort a symbol of the popular will, sombre, enigmatic, and immense; a sort of powerful and visible ghost confronting the invisible spectre of the Bastille.

Few strangers came to view the monster, and the people in the street scarcely glanced at it. It was crumbling to bits, the fallen plaster leaving great wounds in its flanks. The 'aediles', to use the fashionable term, had forgotten about it since 1814. It stood gloomily in its corner, enclosed in a rotting wooden fence soiled by countless drunken cab-drivers, with cracks in its belly, a lath of wood protruding from its tail and tall grass growing between its feet; and since the ground level of the space around it had, by that gradual process common to the soil of all great cities, risen in the past thirty years, it seemed to be standing in a hollow, as though the earth were subsiding beneath it. It was crude, despised, repulsive, and defiant; unsightly to the fastidious, pitiful to the thinker, having about it a contradictory quality of garbage waiting to be swept away and majesty waiting to be beheaded.

As we have said, its aspect changed at night. Night is the true setting for all things that are ghosts. As darkness fell the venerable monster was transformed; amid the serenity of the gathering gloom it acquired a placid and awe-inspiring splendour. Being of the past it belonged to the night; and darkness befitted its nobility.

The ponderous, uncouth, almost misshapen monument, which was certainly majestic and endowed with a sort of savage and magnificent gravity, has since disappeared to make way for the sort of gigantic cooking-stove adorned with a chimney which has replaced the sombre fortress with its nine towers, rather as the era of the bourgeoisie has replaced feudalism. It is very proper that a cooking-stove should be the symbol of an epoch that derives its power from a cook-pot. This epoch will pass—indeed, is already passing. We are beginning to grasp the fact that although power can be contained in a boiler, mastery exists only in the brain: in other words, that it is ideas, not locomotives, that move the world. To harness locomotives to the ideas is good; but do not let us mistake the horse for the rider.

To return to the Place de la Bastille, the architect of the elephant achieved something great in plaster, whereas the architect of the chimney-pot achieved something insignificant in bronze.

In 1832 the chimney-pot, that failed memorial to a failed revolution, grandiloquently baptized the July Column, was—and for our part we regret it—enveloped in a vast array of scaffolding and surrounded by a plank fence, which further isolated the elephant. It was to this deserted corner of the *Place*, dimly lit by a distant street-lamp, that the urchin Gavroche brought the two 'kids'.

May we here break off our narrative to recall that we are dealing with a matter of fact, and that twenty years ago the magistrates tried the case of a child, charged with vagabondage and damaging a public monument, who had been found asleep inside the Elephant of the Bastille.

To proceed. When they reached the monster, Gavroche, conscious of the effect the very large may have on the very small, said reassuringly:

'Don't be afraid, young 'uns.'

He slipped into the enclosure through a gap in the surrounding fence and helped the little boys through. They followed him in silence, both somewhat apprehensive but trusting to this tattered Samaritan who had given them bread and promised them shelter for the night. There was a ladder lying along the fence, used by workmen in a nearby builder's yard. Gavroche hoisted it up with a remarkable display of energy and set it against one of the elephant's front legs. At the top a rough aperture in the creature's belly was visible. Gavroche pointed to this and to the ladder and said:

'Up you go, and inside!'

The little boys exchanged terrified glances.

'What! Mean to say you're scared?' exclaimed Gavroche. 'Well, I'll show you.'

Without deigning to use the ladder he shinned up the rough leg and in no time had reached the aperture, into which he disappeared like a lizard vanishing into a crevice. A moment later the little boys saw the white blur of his face peering down at them out of darkness.

'Well, come on up,' he called, 'and see how nice it is. You go first,' he added to the elder boy. 'I'll lend you a hand.'

The little boys nudged one another, at once scared and heartened; besides which, it was raining heavily. The elder decided to chance it, and at the sight of him on the ladder, while he himself was left alone between the beast's great feet, the younger came near to bursting into tears but did not dare. The elder boy climbed unsteadily while Gavroche encouraged him with a flow of instructions like a fencing-master with a class, or a muleteer with a pack of mules.

'Don't be afraid. That's the way. Now your other foot. Now your hands. That's it. Well done!' Directly he came within reach Gavroche grabbed him by the arm and pulled him towards himself. 'Fine!' he said. The boy was through the entrance.

'Now wait here,' said Gavroche. 'Be so good as to take a seat, Monsieur.'

He slipped out again, slid down the elephant's leg with the nimbleness of a monkey, landed on his feet in the grass, picked up the five-year-old, set him halfway up the ladder, and climbed up behind him, calling to the older boy, 'I'll push, and when he gets to the top you pull!'

The younger boy was pushed, lugged, heaved, and bundled through the aperture almost before he knew where he was, and Gavroche, after kicking away the ladder so that it fell on the grass, clapped his hands and cried:

'We've done it, and long live General Lafayette!' After which outburst he said formally: 'Gentlemen, welcome to my abode.'

It was indeed the only home he had.

The unforeseen usefulness of the superfluous! The charity of great matters, the kindness of giants! That extravagant monument to the fantasy of an Emperor had become the hide-out of an urchin. The pigmy was accepted and sheltered by the colossus. Citizens in their Sunday clothes passing the Elephant of the Bastille might glance at it in dull-eyed indifference saying, 'What use is it?' But it served to protect a homeless, parentless youngster against wind and hail and frost, to preserve him from the slumber in the mud which causes fever and the slumber in the snow which causes death. It housed the innocent rejected by society, and thus in some degree atoned for society's guilt, affording a retreat to one to whom all other doors were closed. It seemed indeed that the crumbling, scabby monster, neglected, despised, and forgotten, a sort of huge beggar crying in vain for the alms of a friendly look, had taken pity on that other beggar, the waif without shoes to his feet or a roof to his head, clad in rags, blowing on numbed fingers, living on such scraps as came his way. That was the use of the Bastille elephant. Napoleon's notion, disdained by men, had been adopted by God, and what could only have been pretentious had been made august. To complete his design the Emperor would have needed copper and marble, porphyry and gold; for God the structure of wood and plaster sufficed. The Emperor had a lordly dream: in that prodigious elephant, bearing its armoured tower and lashing its trunk, he had thought to embody the soul of the people: God had done something greater with it, He had made it a dwelling for a child.

The aperture by which Gavroche had entered was scarcely visible from outside, being, as we have said, hidden under the belly of the elephant and so narrow that only a cat or a small boy could have got through it.

'To start with,' said Gavroche, 'we must tell the doorkeeper that we are not at home.' And diving into the darkness with the ease of one familiar with his surroundings, he produced a plank with which to cover the hole.

He vanished again, and the little boys heard the hiss of a matchstick plunged in a bottle of phosphorus. The chemical match did not then exist: in those days the lighter invented by Fumade represented progress.

A sudden glow caused them to blink. Gavroche had lighted one of the lengths of string soaked in resin which are known as 'rats' tails', and this, although it gave out more smoke than light, made the elephant's interior dimly visible.

Gavroche's two guests gazed about them with something of the feelings of a person inside the great wine-barrel of Heidelberg, or better, the feelings Jonah must have experienced when he found himself inside the whale. They were enclosed in what looked like a huge skeleton. A long beam overhead, to which massive side-members were attached at regular intervals, represented the back-bone and ribs, with plaster stalactites hanging from them like entrails; and everywhere there were great spiders' webs like dusty diaphragms. Here and there in the corners were patches of black that seemed to be alive had changed their position with sudden, startled movements. The litter fallen from the back of the elephant on to its stomach had evened out the concavity of the latter, so that one could walk on it as though on a floor.

The younger of the little boys was clinging to his brother. He whispered:

'It's so dark!'

This drew an outburst from Gavroche. Their state of petrified alarm called for a sharp rebuke.

'What was that?' he demanded. 'Is somebody complaining? Isn't this good enough for you? Perhaps you'd rather have the Tuileries? But I'm no royal lackey, let me tell you, so you might as well stop whimpering.'

A touch of roughness is salutary to weak nerves. The boys drew closer to Gavroche and, touched by the gesture of confidence, his manner changed.

'Lummox,' he said gently to the younger, 'it's outside that it's dark. It's raining outside, but not in here. The wind's blowing but here you don't feel it. There are mobs of people outside, but in here there's no one to bother you. And outside there isn't even a moon, but here we've got a light. What more do you want?'

They began to look less apprehensively about them, but Gavroche did not allow them much time to inspect the premises. 'This way,' he said, and thrust them towards what we have great pleasure in calling his bedchamber.

He had an excellent bed, complete with mattress and coverlet in a curtained sleeping-alcove. The mattress was a piece of straw matting and the coverlet a large blanket of rough wool, warm and almost new. The alcove was devised as follows:

Three thin upright posts, two in front and one at the back, were firmly embedded in the rubble of the floor—that is to say, of the elephant's stomach—and joined with cord at the top so as to form a pyramidal framework. Over this framework wire-netting was draped, carefully stretched and nailed here and there, so as to enclose the whole of it. An array of large stones held it down to the floor and ensured that nothing could get in. The netting, which took the place of curtains, was of the kind used in aviaries, so that Gavroche's bed was in fact in a cage. The general effect was like an Eskimo's tent.

Slightly moving one or two stones, Gavroche drew back two strips of netting and said to the little boys: 'Crawl in on hands and knees.' Having seen them inside, he followed them in, also crawling, and then replaced the stones to secure the entrance. The three of them lay down on the mattress. Small though the two boys were, neither could have stood upright in the cage.

Gavroche was still carrying the rat's tail. 'Silence, everyone,' he said. 'I'm going to dowse the glim.'

But the elder boy pointed to the netting and asked:

'Please, sir, what's that for?'

'To keep the rats out,' said Gavroche gravely. 'And now, silence.'

However, in consideration of their youth and inexperience, he deigned to give his guests a little added information.

'It comes out of the Jardin des Plantes, out of the zoo. They've got all kinds of stuff. You've only got to climb a wall or go in at a window and you can get anything you want.' While he was speaking he was folding the coverlet about the younger boy, who murmured drowsily, 'It's ever so warm.' He looked complacently at the coverlet.

'That comes out of the Jardin des Plantes too, out of the monkey-house.'

He drew the elder boy's attention to the mat on which they were lying, which was very thick and excellently made.

'I got that from the giraffe.'

After a pause he went on: 'The animals had all these things. I pinched them from them, but they didn't mind. I said they were for the elephant.'

Again he was silent and then he summed the matter up:

'You skip over walls and who cares about the government? That's the way it is.'

The little boys were gazing in awed admiration at this intrepid and resourceful adventurer who was a vagabond like themselves, a pauper as lonely and vulnerable as they, but who in their eyes appeared an almost supernatural being, a man of power with the leers and grimaces of a circus clown and the gentlest and most innocent of smiles.

'Please, sir,' said the elder shyly, 'aren't you afraid of the police?'

'We don't call them police,' said Gavroche tersely. 'We call them cops.'

The younger boy's eyes were still open although he was saying nothing. Since he was at the edge of the mat, with his brother in the middle, Gavroche solicitously reached across to make sure that he was properly covered and thrust a few old rags under his head to serve him as pillow. He turned back to the other boy.

'We're pretty well off here, eh?'

'It's wonderful,' the boy said, with a look of overflowing gratitude. As their soaked clothing dried both boys were beginning to feel warm.

'And now,' said Gavroche, 'perhaps you'll tell me what you two were crying about.' He jerked his thumb towards the younger. 'A kid his age, that's excusable; but a big chap like you, blubbering away like a calf, you ought to be ashamed.'

'Well,' protested the older boy, 'but we hadn't any home to go to.'

'You don't call it home,' said Gavroche. 'You call it your shack.'

'And we were scared of being out all night.'

'In the glim,' said Gavroche. 'Now, you listen to me. I don't want any more complaints. From now on I'm looking after you and we're going to have a fine time. You'll see. In the summer we'll go to la Glacière with Mavet, who's a mate of mine, and bathe in the river and run naked along the bank by the Austerlitz bridge, just to annoy the washerwomen. The things they shout at you, it's as good as a pantomime! And we'll go and see the human skeleton. There's one on the Champs Élysées, a real, live man as thin as a skeleton. And I'll take you to the theatre, to the Frédérick-Lemaître. I get tickets, see, because I know the company. In fact, I acted in one of their plays. A gang of boys like me, we crawled about under a canvas to make it look like the sea. Maybe I'll be able to get you both a job. And we'll see the old Indians. Mark you, they aren't real Indians. They wear pink tights that wrinkle and you can see where they've been darned. And we'll go to the Opéra, we'll go into the gallery with the *claque*. It's a very good *claque* at the Opéra. I wouldn't want to go with the boulevard theatre *claques*. But at the Opéra some of them even pay, as much as twenty sous. But that's soft—the dummies, we call them. And we'll go and watch someone being guillotined, and you'll see the Public Executioner, Monsieur Sanson. He lives in the Rue des Marais and he has a letter-box in his door. You'll see! We'll have a high old time!'

At this moment a drop of wax fell on Gavroche's finger, bringing him back to earth.

'*Bigre!* The taper's burning down. We have to watch it. I can't afford more than a sou a month for lighting. When you turn in you go to sleep, you don't sit up reading the novels of Monsieur Paul de Kock. Besides which the light might show through the door and then we'd have the cops after us.'

'And anyway,' ventured the older boy, who alone was brave enough to speak to Gavroche, 'a drop of lighted wax on the straw might set the house on fire.'

'Burn down the shack,' said Gavroche. 'That's right. But not on a night like this.'

The storm had increased, and between the bursts of thunder they could hear the drumming of rain on the monster's back.

'It's coming down in bucketfuls,' said Gavroche. 'I like to hear it pouring down our house's legs. The winter's like another animal. It gives us all it's got, but it's wasting its time and trouble, it can't even wet us, and that makes it roar with fury, the old brute.'

This allusion to the thunder, of which Gavroche, like the nineteenth-century philosopher he was, defied all the consequences, was followed by a particularly brilliant flash of lightning, so vivid that its reflection showed through the crevice in the elephant's belly. At the same time there was another clap of thunder, so loud that the little boys started up in dismay, nearly dislodging the wire netting. Gavroche burst out laughing.

'Easy does it, lads. Don't go breaking up the home. That was a fine old bang, wasn't it? Not one of your damp squibs. Well done, God! It was almost as good as the Théâtre de l'Ambigu.'

This said, he put the netting to rights, thrust the little boys gently back against the straw, pushed down their knees so that they were lying straight and went on:

'Well, as God has lit his candle I can blow out mine. We've got to sleep, my boys, being human. It's bad to go without sleep. It gives you the collywobbles. So snuggle down and I'll blow it out. Are you all right?'

'It's grand,' said the older boy. 'It feels as though I'd got feathers under my head.'

'Not your head,' said Gavroche. 'Your napper. Now let's hear you snore.' And he blew out the taper.

Scarcely was the light extinguished than a strange disturbance shook the netting in which the three children were enclosed, a multitude of small, metallic sounds, as though teeth and claws were worrying the wire, accompanied by small, piercing squeaks. The five-year-old boy, hearing this commotion above his head and petrified with alarm, nudged his brother, but the latter had already obeyed Gavroche's injunction to snore. Finally, when he could bear it no longer, he ventured to address Gavroche, in the lowest of voices and with bated breath.

'Monsieur . . .'

'Well?' said Gavroche with his eyes closed.

'What's that noise?'

'Rats,' said Gavroche, and turned on his side.

The rats, which bred by the thousand in the elephant's carcase and were the living patches of black of which we have spoken, had been kept at bay by the taper while it was alight, but directly that cavernous place, which was their stronghold, was plunged in darkness, and scenting what the excellent storyteller, Perrault, has called 'young flesh', they had swarmed over Gavroche's tent, and were trying to gnaw through the meshes of this new-style mosquito-net.

The little boy was still not happy.

'Monsieur,' he said again.

'Well!' said Gavroche.

'Please, what are rats?'

'A kind of mouse.'

This was fairly reassuring. The little boy had seen white mice and had not been afraid of them. Nonetheless he had another question.

'Monsieur . . .'

'Well?'

'Why don't you keep a cat?'

'I had one,' said Gavroche. 'I brought one in, but they ate it.'

This reply entirely undid the soothing effect of the previous one. The little boy began to tremble again, and the exchanges between him and Gavroche were resumed for the fourth time.

'Monsieur . . .'

'Now what?'

'Who was it who ate the cat?'

'The rats.'

'The mice?'

'Yes, the rats.'

Appalled by this thought of mice that ate cats, the little boy asked:

'But Monsieur, won't they eat us too?'

'Well, blow me!' said Gavroche. But the little boy was now in a state of extreme terror and he turned to him. 'Don't worry, they can't get in. And besides, I'm here. Here, take my hand. Now shut up and go to sleep.'

Reaching across the elder brother, Gavroche gave the younger one his hand, and the little boy clasped it and was comforted. Courage and strength are thus mysteriously transmitted. There was again silence, the sound of voices having frightened the rats away; they were back a few minutes later, but not all their squeakings and gnawings could disturb the three children, who by then were sound asleep.

The night hours passed. Darkness enveloped the immense Place de la Bastille, a winter's wind blew gustily to mingle with the rain, police patrols, peering into doorways, alleyways, and dark corners in search of nocturnal vagabonds, passed indifferently by the elephant. The monster stood motionless, eyes open in the darkness, as though meditating with satisfaction upon its good deed in sheltering three homeless children from the elements and from man.

To understand what follows the reader must recall that at that time the Bastille police-post was situated at the other end of the *Place*, and that the officer on duty there could not see or hear anything that took place in the neighbourhood of the elephant. Towards the end of the last hour before dawn a man came running out of the Rue Saint-Antoine; he crossed the *Place*, rounded the July Column, and, slipping through the palings, came to a stop under the elephant's belly. Had there been any light to see him by, the drenched state of his clothing would have suggested that he had spent the night in the open. Having reached the elephant—he uttered a strange, parrot-cry which is best conveyed by the word *kirikikioo*. He uttered it twice, and the second time it was answered by a clear, youthful voice which simply said:

'Right!'

A moment later the plank masking the hole was removed and Gavroche slid down the elephant's leg and dropped lightly at the man's side. The man was Montparnasse. As for the mysterious call, it was doubtless what had been implied by the words, 'Ask for Monsieur Gavroche.' Upon hearing it Gavroche had crawled out of his sleeping-tent, carefully replaced the netting, and hastened to answer the summons.

They nodded to each other in the darkness, and Montparnasse simply said:

'We need help. Come and lend a hand.'

'I'm ready,' said Gavroche, and asked no further explanation.

They headed for the Rue Saint-Antoine, by which Montparnasse had come, threading their way rapidly through the long file of carts which at that hour were making for the vegetable-market. The market-gardeners, crouched amid their lettuces and cabbages and swathed to the eyes in capes under the beating rain, paid no attention to them.

This is what had happened at the prison of La Force during that night.

A plan of escape had been concerted between Babet, Brujon, Gueulemer, and Thénardier, although Thénardier was in solitary confinement. Babet had managed his own part of the business during the day, as we know from what Montparnasse had said to Gavroche. Montparnasse was to help from outside.

Brujon, having spent a month in a punishment-cell, had had time, first, to plait a rope, and secondly to evolve the plan. At one time a solitary confinement cell consisted of stone walls, a stone ceiling, a tiled floor, a camp bed, a small, barred window, and a door reinforced with iron bands, the whole being known as a *cachot*. But the *cachot* was considered too severe. The cell now consists of an iron door, a barred window, a camp bed, a tiled floor, stone walls, and a stone ceiling, and is called a 'punishment-cell'. A faint light penetrates at mid-day. The drawback to these cells which, as we see, are not *cachots*, is that they leave men to their thoughts when they should be made to work.

Brujon had taken thought and got out of the punishment-cell with his rope. Since he was reputed to be highly dangerous he was transferred from the Cour Charlemagne to the New Building. Here he found, first Gueulemer and second a nail. The first meant crime and the second meant liberty.

Brujon, at whom we must now take a closer look, was, beneath his carefully calculated appearance of fragility and languor, a well-mannered, intelligent, thieving rogue with a disarming gaze and an abominable grin. The gaze was rehearsed, but the grin was natural. He had first concentrated on roof-tops, and had made strides in the business of robbing roofs and gutters of their lead by the process known as *gras-double*, or tripe-stripping.

What made that moment particularly favourable for a break-out was the fact that a part of the prison roof was being re-timbered and re-tiled. The Cour Saint-Bernard was no longer entirely cut off from the Cour Charlemagne and the Cour Saint-Louis. There were scaffolding and ladders; in other words, bridges and stairways for the use of the escaper.

The so-called New Building, which was in a state of lamentable decrepitude, was the prison's weakest point. Its walls had so crumbled under the effects of saltpetre that the dormitories had had to be lined with wooden panelling, because otherwise rubble was liable to fall on the sleepers in their beds. Despite its inadequacy, this New Building was where the most dangerous prisoners were housed, the 'hard cases', to use the prison term. The building contained four superimposed dormitories, with an attic above them known as the Bel-Air. A large chimney, probably a survival from the former kitchen of the Dukes of La Force, rose up from the ground floor, passing through the four dormitories like a flattened central column and emerging through the roof.

Gueulemer and Brujon were in the same dormitory, having been put as a precaution on the lowest floor. The heads of their beds, as it happened, were both against this chimney. Thénardier was exactly above them in the Bel-Air attic.

The stroller who pauses in the Rue Culture-Sainte-Catherine, at the gateway of the bath-house beyond the fire-station, will see a courtyard filled with flowers and bushes in tubs, at the far end of which is a small rotunda with two wings, painted white with green blinds—the pastoral dream of Jean-Jacques Rousseau. Not more than ten years ago it had at its back a tall, black wall, which was the outer wall of the prison of La Force. High though it was, this wall was over-topped by an even blacker roof rising behind it, that of the New Building, in which four barred dormer windows were to be seen. They were the windows of the Bel-Air attic dormitory, and the chimney rising above the roof was the one which passed through the lower dormitories.

The Bel-Air attic was a kind of sloping-roofed gallery partitioned by triple-grilles and metal-lined doors studded with huge nail-heads. Entering it at the northern end one had the four windows on one's left, and on one's right, facing the windows, four fairly large square cages separated by narrow passage-ways and built of brick-work up to shoulder level and iron grilles reaching to the ceiling.

Thénardier had been confined in one of these cages since the night of 3rd February. No one ever discovered how, and with what assistance, he managed to obtain and hide a bottle of the wine invented, it is said, by the prisoner Desrues, which contains a narcotic and was made famous by the gang known as the *Endormeurs*, the 'dopers'. There are in many prisons treacherous employees, thieves as well as gaolers, who sell a fraudulent loyalty to their masters and make their pickings on the side.

And so it happened that on the night when the boy Gavroche gave shelter to two forlorn children, Brujon and Gueulemer, knowing that Babet, who had escaped that morning, was waiting for them with Montparnasse in the street outside, rose softly from their beds and began to burrow into the chimney, using the nail that Brujon had acquired. The débris fell on Brujon's bed and made no sound. The noises of hail and thunder shook the doors on their hinges, filling the prison with an alarming but convenient din. Those of their fellow-inmates who were awakened pretended to be still asleep and did not interfere. Brujon was skilful and Gueulemer was powerful. Without any sound reaching the warder in the cell with a window looking into the dormitory, the chimney-flue was pierced, the chimney climbed, the grille at the top forced and the two redoubtable ruffians were out on the roof. The wind and rain were at their height and the roof was slippery. 'A fine night for a getaway,' said Brujon.

A gap six feet wide and eighty feet deep separated them from the outer wall, and below them they could discern the faint gleam of a guard's musket. They attached one end of the rope which Brujon had plaited to the bars of the metal grille, which they had twisted back, and flung the other end over the outer wall. Then, jumping the gap on to the top of the wall, they slid down the rope to the roof of a small building adjoining the bath-house, pulled the rope down after them, jumped over into the bath-house courtyard, crossed it and pushed open the porter's window, beside which hung the *cordon*. They pulled the *cordon*, opened the gate, and walked out into the street.

It was less than three-quarters of an hour since they had stood on their beds in the darkness, nail in hand and their plans all laid. Within a minute or so they had joined Babet and Montparnasse, who were lurking nearby.

They had broken their rope in retrieving it, so that a part remained still attached to the grille at the top of the chimney; otherwise no harm was done except that they had very little skin left on their hands.

Thénardier had been warned of what was to happen, although it is not known how, and had stayed awake. At about one o'clock in the morning, the night being very dark, he had seen, through the window opposite his cage, two figures moving along the roof in the wind and rain. One of them stopped for an instant to look in at the window, and Thénardier recognized Brujon. It was all he needed to know.

Being registered as a dangerous criminal sentenced for attempted armed robbery, Thénardier was kept under close surveillance. A warder with a loaded musket, who was relieved every two hours, did sentry-duty outside his cage. The attic was lighted by a wall-lantern. The prisoner had fifty-pound irons on his legs. At four o'clock every afternoon a prison guard accompanied by two police dogs— this was still customary in those days—entered the cage, deposited a loaf of black bread on the floor by the bed, together with a jug of water and a bowl of thin broth with a few beans swimming in it, examined the prisoner's fetters and tapped on the bars of the cage. He and his dogs paid two further visits during the night.

Thénardier had obtained permission to keep a small iron spike with which he used to skewer his bread to a crack in the wall— 'to keep it out of reach of the rats,' he said. Since he was under constant supervision this was not thought dangerous; but it was later recalled that one of the warders had remarked, 'It would be better if he had a wooden spike.'

At two in the morning the warder, a regular army veteran, was relieved by a younger man, a conscript. Shortly afterwards the guard with the dogs paid his visit and noted nothing out of the way except the extreme youth and 'doltish air' of the new man. But two hours after this, at four o'clock, when it was the new man's turn to be relieved he was found prostrate and sleeping like a log outside Thénardier's cage. Thénardier was gone, and his broken leg-irons lay on the floor. There was a hole in the ceiling of the cage and another hole above it, in the roof of the building. A plank had been wrenched off the bed and presumably taken away, since it was not to be found. But a half-empty bottle was found containing the remains of the drugged wine that had put the soldier to sleep. His bayonet had disappeared.

At the time when the discovery was made Thénardier was thought to be well out of reach; but the truth is that although he was no longer in the New Building he was still in considerable danger. He had not yet made good his escape. After climbing out on to the roof he had found the length of rope attached to the grille protecting the chimney, but this broken remnant was far too short for him to be able to negotiate the outside wall as Brujon and Gueulemer had done.

Turning out of the Rue des Ballets into the Rue Roi-de-Sicile, one comes almost immediately to a sort of squalid recess. A house occupied it in the last century of which only the back wall is still standing, a dingy pile of masonry rising to a height of three storeys, with buildings on either side. It contains two square windows, one of which is partly blocked by a worm-eaten beam of wood that props up the wall. At one time one could see through these windows a further expanse of forbidding masonry, the outer wall of the prison.

The empty space left by the demolished house is half-filled by a fence of rotting planks reinforced by stone posts, and within this enclosure there is a small lean-to shed built against the remaining wall. There is a gate in the fence which, until a few years ago, was fastened only with a latch.

Thénardier reached the top of this wall at about three o'clock in the morning.

How had he got there? This is something that no one has ever been able to explain or understand. The lightning must have both hindered and helped him. Had he made use of the roof-menders' scaffolding and ladders to convey himself from roof-top to roof-top over the ill-assorted cluster of buildings, from the Cour Charlemagne to the Cour Saint-Louis, thence to the outer wall of the prison, and so, eventually, to the ruined wall? But there were so many gaps in this route as to make it seem impossible. Had he made the plank from his bed serve as a bridge from the attic to the outer wall, and then crawled on his stomach along that wall until he came to the ruin? But the top of the outer wall of the prison presented a very jagged outline, with steep ups and downs; it went down at the firemen's quarters and rose sharply at the bath-house; it was broken by intersections and was lower at the Hotel Lamoignon than over the Rue Pavée; there were sudden drops and right-angles. Taking all this into account, the exact manner of Thénardier's escape becomes inexplicable. Escape by either of these two routes was virtually impossible. Had Thénardier, actuated by that overwhelming passion for liberty that turns precipices into ditches, iron bars into wooden slats, an office clerk into an athlete, stupidity into instinct, instinct into intelligence and intelligence into genius, devised some quite other method? This has never been known.

There is in a prison escape an element of the miraculous that is not always realized. The man on the run, let us repeat, is a man inspired. There is starlight and lightning in the mysterious glow of flight, and the straining for liberty is no less remarkable than the soaring of the spirit to the sublime. To ask, of the escaped prisoner, how did he manage to achieve the impossible, is to ask, as we do of Corneille, 'When did he know *that he was dying*?'

However it may be, Thénardier, dripping with sweat and soaked with rain, clothes in shreds, hands skinned and knees and elbows bleeding, reached the top of the ruined wall and lay stretched at full length along it, his strength exhausted. There was a drop of three storeys to the ground, and the rope he had with him was too short.

He lay there pale and helpless, all hope abandoned, still sheltered by the darkness but knowing that it would soon be light, expecting at any moment to hear the clock of the Church of Saint-Paul strike four, at which hour they would come to relieve the guard outside his cage and find him in a drugged slumber. He lay there contemplating in a kind of stupor the wet, dark surface gleaming faintly in the street lights at a terrible depth below him, the solid earth of liberty that could be his death. He was wondering if his three confederates had made good their escape, if they were awaiting him, if they would come to his aid. Excepting a police-patrol no one had gone along the street while he was there. Nearly all the market-gardeners from Montreuil, Charonne, Vincennes, and Bercy went to the market by way of the Rue Saint-Antoine.

Four o'clock struck, and he started. Very shortly afterwards the confused hubbub which accompanies the discovery of an escape broke out in the prison, the opening and slamming of doors, the screech of hinges, the thud of running feet, the voices hoarsely shouting; until finally the clatter of musket-butts on the paving of the courtyard sounded almost below him. Lights shone behind the barred windows of the dormitory and a torch moved along the attic roof of the New Building. The firemen from the nearby station had been summoned to assist, and their helmets, gleaming in torch-light under the rain, could be seen on the rooftops. At the same time he saw the first pallid glow of sunrise in the sky beyond the Bastille.

He was lying, incapable of movement, along a wall some ten inches wide, with a sheer drop on either side of him, dizzy at the possibility of falling and in horror at the certainty of capture, his thoughts swinging between these two alternatives like the pendulum of a clock—'I'm dead if I fall and caught if I don't.' But suddenly he perceived amid the darkness of the street the figure of a man creep cautiously past the housefronts from the Rue Pavée and come to a stop in the recess, above which Thénardier was as it were suspended. He was joined by a second man moving with the same caution, then by a third and a fourth. When they were all together one of them opened the gate in the fence and they moved into the enclosure where the shed was—that is to say, almost directly below Thénardier. They had evidently chosen the recess as a place where they might confer without being seen by anyone in the street or by the sentry at the prison-gate, which was only a few yards away. In any case, the sentry was being kept in his box by the rain. Thénardier, unable to distinguish their faces, listened to what they said with the desperate attentiveness of a man at his last gasp. And suddenly he had a ray of hope. The men were talking *argot*, that is to say, thieves' slang.

One of them said, speaking in a low voice but quite clearly:

'*Décarrons. Qu'est-ce que nous maquillons icigo?*—We've got to clear out. What's the good of hanging about here?'

Another said:

'*Il lansquine à éteindre le riffe du rabouin. Et puis les coqueurs vont passer, il y a là un grivier qui porte gaffe, nous allons nous faire emballer icicaille.*—It's raining fit to dowse the fires of hell. Besides, the law will be along. There's a soldier on guard back there. We'll be copped if we stay here.'*

The two words, *icigo* and *icicaille*, both meaning *ici* (here), and

* Hugo himself added footnotes with translations in conventional French of these passages of *argot*, which are here reproduced as a sample of the cant. In the subsequent dialogue only his translations have been rendered into English.   Trs.

of which the first belongs to barrier-slang and the second to the slang of the Temple, were highly enlightening to Thénardier. The first pointed to Brujon, who was a barrier-prowler, and the second to Babet, who among his many callings had once been a huckster in the Temple market. It was only in the Temple that the ancient slang of the Grand Siècle was still spoken, and Babet was the only one who spoke it perfectly. Without that *icicaille* Thénardier would not have recognized him, for he had entirely disguised his voice.

Another of the men said:

'There's no hurry, we might as well wait a little. We can't be sure he won't need us.'

From this, which was in plain French, Thénardier recognized Montparnasse, who made it a point of pride to understand all the slangs and speak none of them.

The fourth man said nothing, but his huge shoulders were enough. Thénardier had no doubt that it was Gueulemer.

Brujon answered almost excitedly, but still keeping his voice low.

'What are you getting at? The innkeeper hasn't made it because he doesn't know how. He's an amateur. To weave a sound rope out of a blanket, bore holes in a door, cook up false papers, make skeleton keys, cut through leg-irons, hide everything and get away using the rope, it takes skill to do all that. You've got to know your business. The old fellow wasn't up to it.'

Babet added, speaking still in the recondite, classical *argot* used by Poulailler and Cartouche, which, compared with the coarse, lurid slang of Brujon, is like the language of Racine compared with that of André Chenier:

'He's probably been caught. He's nothing but a novice. He may have talked and given himself away. You can hear that shindy in the prison, can't you, Montparnasse? You can see the lights. He's been caught for certain. He'll be inside for another twenty years. I'm no coward, no one's ever said that of me; but there's nothing to be done and no sense in hanging about here until we're all in the bag. It's no use worrying, come along and we'll split a bottle or two of wine.'

'You can't leave a friend in the lurch,' muttered Montparnasse.

'I tell you he's caught,' repeated Brujon. 'He's sunk and there's nothing we can do. Let's clear out. I'm expecting to feel a hand on my shoulder any minute.'

Montparnasse continued to protest, but only weakly; the fact is that the four men, true to the code of loyalty among thieves, had spent the night hanging round the prison, regardless of the risk to themselves, hoping to see the form of Thénardier appear on top of some part of the wall. But it had been too much for them. The streets emptied by the pouring rain, themselves numbed with cold in their drenched clothes, the disturbing sounds issuing from within the prison, the time wasted, the police patrols, the waning of hope and growth of anxiety—all this prompted them to retreat. Even Montparnasse, who may have been especially beholden to Thénardier, being perhaps his unofficial son-in-law, was disposed to give way. In another moment they would have gone, and Thénardier on his wall groaned like the Men of the Medusa on their raft when the ship they had sighted vanished over the horizon.

He dared not call out, since by doing so he might give himself away, but one resource was left to him. He fished out of his pocket the short length of rope he had detached from the grille over the chimney, and tossed it into the enclosure. It fell at the men's feet.

'That's my rope,' said Brujon.

'The innkeeper's up there,' said Montparnasse.

They looked up and Thénardier thrust his head into view.

'Quick,' said Montparnasse to Brujon. 'Have you got the rest of the rope?'

'Yes.'

'Tie the two bits together and chuck one end up to him. He'll have to fix it to the wall. There'll be enough for him to slide down.'

Thénardier ventured to speak.

'I'm numb with cold.'

'We'll soon get you warm.'

'I can't move.'

'You've only got to slide down. We'll catch you.'

'My hands are frozen.'

'Just tie the rope to the wall.'

'I couldn't do it.'

'One of us will have to go up,' said Montparnasse.

'Three storeys!' said Brujon.

An old plaster flue, part of a stove which at some time had burned in the shed, ran up the wall very near where Thénardier was lying. It has broken off since then, being very much the worse for wear, but traces of it are still to be seen. It was very thin.

'Someone could climb up by that,' said Montparnasse.

'That bit of piping?' said Babet. 'A grown man? You're crazy. Only a kid could do it.'

'That's right,' said Brujon. 'We need a boy. But where are we to find one?'

'I know where. I'll fetch him,' said Montparnasse.

Softly opening the gate and peering up and down the street to make sure that there was no one about, he closed it carefully behind him and set off at a run in the direction of the Bastille.

Some seven or eight minutes elapsed during which Babet, Brujon, and Gueulemer did not speak. Then the gate was opened again and Montparnasse reappeared, panting, with Gavroche at his side. The street was still deserted.

Gavroche stood calmly surveying the men with rainwater dripping from his hair.

'Well, lad,' said Gueulemer, 'can you do a man's job?'

Gavroche shrugged his shoulders and replied in the broadest *argot*:

'Kids like me are grown up and coves like you are kids.'

'He's got the gab all right!' said Brujon.

'So what do you want me to do?' asked Gavroche.

'Climb up that chimney-pipe,' said Montparnasse.

'Taking this rope with you,' said Babet.

'And tie it near the top of the wall,' said Brujon. 'To the crossbar of the window.'

'And then?' said Gavroche.

'That's all,' said Gueulemer.

Gavroche considered the rope, the flue, the wall, and the window and clicked his tongue in an expression of scorn at the simplicity of the task.

'There's a man up there,' said Montparnasse. 'You'll be saving him.'

'Will you do it?' asked Brujon.

'Don't be daft,' said Gavroche, as though the question were insulting, and he slipped off his shoes.

Gueulemer picked him up and set him on the roof of the shed, the planks of which sagged under his weight, then passed him the rope, which Brujon had re-tied during Montparnasse's absence. Gavroche went up to the flue, which ran through a hole in the lean-to roof; but as he was about to start his climb, Thénardier, seeing the approach of rescue and safety, peered down from the wall. The pallid light of dawn fell upon his sweat-dewed face, the white cheekbones, flat, barbarous nose and tangled grey beard, and Gavroche recognized him.

'Blow me,' he exclaimed, 'if it isn't my father! Well, no matter.'

Taking the rope between his teeth, he began to climb. He reached the top of the ruined wall and, sitting astride it, tied the rope securely to the upper crossbar of the window. Within a minute Thénardier was down in the street.

The moment his feet touched the ground, feeling himself out of danger, he lost all sense of fatigue, chill, and terror; the sufferings of the past hours vanished from his recollection like a puff of smoke, and that strange, ferocious intelligence was instantly alert and free, ready for further action. These are the first words he spoke.

'Well, so now who are we going to eat?'

No need to dwell upon the significance of that horridly lucid word, which meant to murder, to beat to death, to plunder—'eat' in the literal sense of 'devour'.

'Let's get away fast,' said Brujon. 'Just a word and then we separate. There was a job that looked hopeful in the Rue Plumet, two women living alone in an isolated house in an empty street, with a rusty iron gate to the garden.'

'Well, what's wrong with it?' asked Thénardier.

'Your wench, Éponine, had a look round and she gave Magnon the "biscuit". There's nothing to be done there.'

'She's no fool,' said Thénardier. 'All the same, we ought to make sure.'

'Yes,' said Brujon. 'We might look it over.'

The men had paid no further heed to Gavroche, who during this conversation had seated himself on one of the stones supporting the fence. He waited a little longer, perhaps expecting his father to say something to him, then he pulled on his shoes and said:

'Is that all? You don't want me any more? Well, I've done the job, so I'll be going. I've got to see to those kids of mine.'

He then left them.

The five men left separately. When Gavroche had disappeared round the corner of the Rue des Ballets Babet drew Thénardier aside and said:

'Did you look at that youngster?'

'What youngster?'

'The one who climbed the wall and brought you the rope.'

'Can't say I did much.'

'Well, I'm not sure, but I have an idea he's your son.'

'What!' said Thénardier. 'You don't say!'

And he departed.

[Book Seven: Argot, will be found in Appendix B at page 455]

BOOK EIGHT

ENCHANTMENT AND DESPAIR

I. *Broad Daylight*

THE READER will have gathered that Éponine, having recognized the girl behind the wrought-iron gate in the Rue Plumet, whither she had been sent by Magnon, had begun by putting the ruffians off that particular house, and then had led Marius to it; and that Marius, after spending several days of ecstatic contemplation outside the gate, gripped by the force that draws iron to a magnet and the lover to the stones of his beloved's dwelling, had finally entered Cosette's garden much as Romeo had entered that of Juliet. It had indeed been less troublesome to him than to Romeo. Romeo had had to climb a wall, whereas Marius had needed only to force one of the rusty bars of the gate, which were already as loose in their sockets as an old man's teeth. He was slender and had had no difficulty in wriggling through; nor, since there was never anyone in the street and he went only after dark, did he run any risk of being seen.

Following that blessed and hallowed hour when a kiss had sealed the lovers' vows, he went there every evening. If at this moment in her life Cosette had had to do with an unscrupulous libertine, she would have been lost; for there are warm hearts whose instinct is to give, and she was one of those. Among the most great-hearted qualities of women is that of yielding. Love, when it holds absolute sway, afflicts modesty with a kind of blindness. The risks they run, those generous spirits! Often they give their hearts where we take only their bodies. That heart remains their own, for them to contemplate in shivering darkness. For with love there is no middle course: it destroys, or else it saves. All human destiny is contained in that dilemma, the choice between destruction and salvation, which is nowhere more implacably posed than in love. Love is life, or it is death. It is the cradle, but also the coffin. One and the same impulse moves the human heart to say yes or no. Of all things God has created it is the human heart that sheds the brightest light, and, alas, the blackest despair.

God decreed that the love which came to Cosette was a love that saves. During that month of May in the year 1832, in that wild garden with its dense tangle of undergrowth that grew daily more impenetrable and richly scented, two beings composed wholly of chastity and innocence, bathed in all the felicities under Heaven, nearer to the angels than to men, pure, truthful, intoxicated and enraptured, shone for each other in the gloom. To Cosette it seemed that Marius wore a crown, and to Marius Cosette bore a halo. They touched and gazed, held hands and clung together; but there was a gulf that they did not seek to cross, not because they feared it but because they ignored it. To Marius the purity of Cosette was a barrier, and to Cosette his steadfast self-restraint was a safeguard. The first kiss they had exchanged was also the last. Since then Marius had gone no further than to touch her hand with his lips, or her shawl, or a lock of her hair. To him she was an essence, rather than a woman. He breathed her in. She denied him nothing and he demanded nothing. She was happy and he was content. They existed in that state of ravishment which may be termed the enchantment of one soul by another, the ineffable first encounter of two virgin spirits in an idyllic world, two swans meeting on the Jungfrau.

In that first stage of their love, the stage when physical desire is wholly subdued beneath the omnipotence of spiritual ecstasy, Marius would have been more capable of going with a street-girl than of lifting the hem of Cosette's skirt, even to above her ankle. When on one occasion she bent down to pick something up and her corsage gaped to disclose the top of her bosom, he turned his head away.

What did take place, then, between those two? Nothing. They adored each other. The garden, when they met there after dark, seemed to them a living and consecrated place. Its blossoms opened to enrich them with their scent, and they poured out their hearts to the blossoms. A vigorous, carnal world of flowing sap surrounded those two innocents, and the words of love they spoke set up a quiver in the trees.

As to the words they spoke, they were breaths and nothing more, but breaths that set all Nature stirring. They were a magic which would have little meaning were they to be set down on paper, those murmurs destined to be borne away like puffs of smoke under the leaves. If we rob the words of lovers of the melody from the heart that accompanies them like a lyre, what remains is but the shadow. Is that really all?—mere childishness, things said and said again, triteness, foolishness and reasonless laughter? Yes that is all, but there is nothing on earth more exquisite or more profound. Those are the only things that are really worth saying and worth hearing, and the man who has never heard or uttered them is a bad man and a fool.

'You know . . .' said Cosette. (They addressed each other instinctively as 'tu', neither knowing how this had come to pass.) 'You know, my real name is Euphrasia.'

'Euphrasia? But you're called Cosette.'

'Oh, that's just a silly name they gave me when I was a child. I'm really Euphrasia. Do you like Euphrasia?'

'Yes . . . But I don't think Cosette is silly.'

'Do you like it better than Euphrasia?'

'Well—yes.'

'Then so do I. You're quite right. It's a nice name. So you must always call me Cosette.'

And the smile accompanying the words made of that scrap of conversation an idyll worthy of a woodland in Heaven.

Another time, after looking hard at him she exclaimed:

'Allow me to tell you, Monsieur, that you're good-looking, you're very handsome, and you're clever, not a bit stupid, much more learned than I am. But I can match you in one thing—I love you!'

Marius in his rapture might have been hearing the melody of the spheres.

Then again, when he happened to cough, she gave him a little reproving pat and said: 'You're not to cough. No one is allowed to cough in my house without permission. It's naughty of you to cough and worry me. I want you to be well always, because if you aren't I shall be very unhappy.'

He said to her once: 'Do you know, at one time I thought your name was Ursula?' This thought kept them amused for the rest of the evening.

And during another conversation he suddenly exclaimed:

'Well, there was one time in the Luxembourg when I would have liked to break an army veteran's neck.'

But he did not go on with that story. He could not have done so without mentioning her garter, and this was out of the question. There was a whole world, that of the flesh, from which their innocent love recoiled with a kind of religious awe.

It was thus, and with nothing added, that Marius envisaged his life with Cosette—his coming every evening to the Rue Plumet, wriggling through that convenient gate, sitting beside her on the bench, the fold of his trouser mingling with the spread of her skirts while they watched the growing glitter of starlight through the trees, softly stroking her thumb-nail, addressing her as 'tu', breathing with her the scent of the same flowers—all this was to continue indefinitely, to last for ever. Meanwhile the clouds drifted above their heads. When the wind blows it blows away more human dreams than clouds in the sky.

But that is not to say that this almost fiercely chaste love was wholly lacking in gallantry. No. To 'pay compliments' to the loved person is the first step on the way to caresses, tentative audacity trying out its wings. A compliment is something like a kiss through a veil. Physical fulfilment makes its presence known, while still remaining hidden. The heart draws back from this fulfilment in order to love the more. Marius's wooing, pervaded as it was with fantasy, was, so to speak, ethereal. The birds when they fly aloft in company with the angels must understand words such as he spoke. Yet there was life in them, manliness, all that was positive in Marius. They were words spoken in the grotto, the foreshadowing of those to be spoken in the alcove, lyrical effusions of mingled prose and poetry, soft flatteries, all love's most delicate refinements arranged in a scented and subtle bouquet, the ineffable murmur of heart to heart.

'How lovely you are!' sighed Marius. 'I scarcely dare look at you, and so I have to contemplate you at a distance. You are grace itself and my senses reel even at the sight of your slipper beneath the hem of your skirt. And the light that dawns when I catch a glimpse of what you are thinking! Such good sense. There are moments when you seem to me a figure in a dream. Go on talking and let me listen. Oh, Cosette, how strange and wonderful it is! I think I am a little mad. I so worship you. I study your feet with a magnifying glass and your soul with a telescope.'

To which she replied:

'I love you more with every minute that passes.'

Random conversations in which question and answer must take their chance, always returning to the subject of love, like those weighted dolls which always come upright.

Cosette's whole being expressed artlessness and ingenuousness, a white transparency, candour and light. One might say of her that she was light itself. She conveyed to the beholder a sense of April and daybreak; there was dew in her eyes. She was the condensation of dawn light in a woman's form.

It was natural that Marius should admire as well as adore her; but the truth is that that little schoolgirl, so newly shaped by the convent, talked with great sagacity and said many things that were both true and perceptive. Her very babblings had meaning. She saw clearly and was not easily deceived, being guided by the soft, infallible instinct of the feminine heart. Only women have this gift for saying things that are at once tender and profound. Tenderness and depth: all womanhood resides in these, and all Heaven.

In this state of utter felicity tears rose constantly to their eyes. A crushed insect, a feather fallen from a nest, a broken sprig of hawthorn, these things moved them to pity, and their rapture, always near to melancholy, found relief in tears. The sovereign manifestation of love is a sense of compassion that at times is well-nigh intolerable.

And with all this—for these contradictions form the lightning-play of love—they laughed constantly and unrestrainedly, so familiarly that they might have been a pair of boys at play. Yet even in hearts intoxicated with chastity Nature is always present, always in pursuit of her sublime, remorseless aims; and, however great the purity of souls, even in the most innocent of relationships the wonderful and mysterious difference is still to be felt which separates a pair of lovers from a pair of friends.

They adored each other; but still the permanent and the immutable subsist. We may love and laugh, pout, clasp hands, smile and exchange endearments, but that does not affect eternity. Two lovers hide in the dusk of evening, amid flowers and the twittering of birds, and enchant each other with their hearts shining in their eyes; but the stars in their courses still circle through infinite space.

II. *The Bemusement of Perfect Happiness*

Thus, bathed in happiness, they lived untroubled by the world. They paid no heed to the epidemic of cholera which during that month ravaged Paris. They had told each other as much about themselves as they could, but it did not go very far beyond their names. Marius had told Cosette that he was an orphan, that his name was Marius Pontmercy, that he was a lawyer and that he got his living by working for publishers; that his father had been a colonel and a hero, and that he, Marius, had quarrelled with his grandfather, who was rich. He had also mentioned in passing that he was a baron, but this had made no impression on Cosette. Marius a baron? She had not understood, not knowing what the word meant. Marius was Marius. And on her side she had told him that she had been brought up in the Petit-Picpus convent, that her mother was dead, like his own, that her father was Monsieur Fauchelevent, that he was a good man who gave generously to the poor although he was poor himself, and that he denied himself everything while denying her nothing.

Strangely, to Marius in his present state of entrancement, all past events, even the most recent, seemed so misty and remote that he was quite satisfied with what Cosette told him. It did not occur to him even to mention the drama in the tenement, the Thénardiers, the burnt arm and the strange behaviour and remarkable disappearance of her father. All this had for the time being completely escaped his mind. He forgot in the evening what he had done in the morning, whether he had breakfasted, whether he had spoken to anyone. The trilling of birds deafened his ears to all other sounds; he was only really alive when he was with Cosette. And so, being in Heaven, it was easy for him to lose sight of earth. Both of them languorously bore the impalpable burden of unfleshly delights. It is thus that the sleep-walkers who are called lovers live.

Alas, who has not known that enchanted state? Why must the moment come when we emerge from that bliss, and why must life go on afterwards?

Loving is almost a substitute for thinking. Love is a burning forgetfulness of all other things. How shall we ask passion to be logical? Absolute logic is no more to be found in the human heart than you may find a perfect geometrical figure in the structure of the heavens. Nothing else existed for Cosette and Marius except Marius and Cosette. The world around them had vanished in a cloud. They lived in a golden moment, seeing nothing ahead of them and nothing behind. Marius was scarcely conscious of the fact that Cosette had a father; his wits were drugged with happiness. So what did they talk about, those lovers? They talked about flowers and swallows, sunset and moonrise, everything that to them was important; about everything and about nothing. The everything of lovers is a nothing. But as for her father, real life, the gang of ruffians, and the adventure in the attic—why bother to talk about all that? Was it even certain that that nightmare had really happened? They were together and they adored each other and that was all that concerned them. Other things did not exist. It is probable that the vanishing of Hell at our backs is inherent in the coming of Paradise. Have we really seen devils?—are there such things?—have we trembled and suffered? We no longer remember. They are lost in a rosy haze.

The two of them lived in that exalted state, in all the make-believe that is a part of nature, neither at the nadir nor at the zenith; somewhere between mankind and the angels; above the mire but below the upper air—in the clouds; scarcely flesh and blood, but spirit and ecstasy from head to foot; too exalted to walk on earth but still too human to disappear into the blue, suspended in life like molecules in solution that await precipitation; seemingly beyond the reach of fate; escaped from the rut of yesterday, today, tomorrow; marvelling, breathless and swaying, at moments light enough to fly off into infinite space, almost ready to vanish into eternity.

They drowsed wide-eyed in that cradled state, in the splendid lethargy of the real overwhelmed by the ideal. Such was Cosette's beauty that at moments Marius closed his eyes; and that is the best way to see the soul, with the eyes closed.

They did not ask where this was taking them; they felt that they had arrived. It is one of the strange demands of mankind that love must take them somewhere.

III. *The First Shadows*

Jean Valjean suspected nothing.

Cosette, less given to dreaming than Marius, was gay, and that was enough to make him happy. The thoughts in Cosette's mind, her tender preoccupations, the picture of Marius that dwelt in her heart, all this in no way diminished the purity of her chaste and smiling countenance. She was at the age when a virgin girl bears her love like an angel carrying a lily. So Valjean was easy in his mind. And then when two lovers are in perfect harmony everything is easy to them; any third party who might disturb their love is kept in ignorance by those small concealments which are practised by all lovers. Thus, Cosette never opposed any wish of Valjean's. Did he want to go out? Yes, dear father. He would rather stay at home? Very well. He wanted to spend the evening with her? She was delighted. Since he always went to bed at ten, Marius on these occasions never entered the garden until after that hour, and after hearing Cosette open the door on to the terrace. It goes without saying that Marius never showed himself by daytime, and indeed Valjean had forgotten his existence. But it happened one morning that he remarked to Cosette: 'Your back's all white.' The evening before Marius, in a moment of rapture, had pressed her against the wall.

Old Toussaint, who went to bed early and only wanted to sleep once her work was done, was as ignorant as Valjean of what was going on.

Marius never set foot in the house. He and Cosette were accustomed to hide in a recess near the steps, where they could not be seen or heard from the street, and being seated were often content merely to clasp hands in silence while they gazed up at the branches of the trees. A thunderbolt might have fallen a few yards away without their noticing, so absorbed was each in the other. A state of limpid purity. Hours that were all white and nearly all the same. Love-affairs such as this are like a collection of lily-petals and doves' feathers.

The whole stretch of garden lay between them and the street. Every time Marius entered or left he carefully re-arranged the bars of the gate, so that the fact that they had been moved would not be noticed.

He left as a rule at midnight and walked back to Courfeyrac's lodging. Courfeyrac said to Bahorel:

'Would you believe it! Marius has taken to coming home at one in the morning!'

'Well, what of it?' said Bahorel. 'Still waters run deep.'

And sometimes Courfeyrac would fold his arms and say sternly to Marius:

'You're going off the rails, young fellow-me-lad.'

Courfeyrac, being of a practical turn of mind, did not take kindly to this glow of a secret paradise that surrounded Marius. He was not accustomed to undisclosed raptures. They bored him, and from time to time he would try to bring Marius down to earth. He said to him on one occasion:

'My dear fellow, you seem to me these days to be living on the moon, in the kingdom of dreams of which the capital is the City of Soap-Bubble. Be a good chap and tell me her name.'

But nothing would make Marius talk. Not even torture could have extracted from him the sacred syllables of the name, Cosette. True love is as radiant as the dawn and as silent as the tomb. But Courfeyrac perceived this change in Marius, seeing that his very secretiveness was radiant.

Throughout that mild month of May Marius and Cosette discovered these tremendous sources of happiness: The happiness of quarrelling simply for the fun of making up; of discussing at length and in exhaustive detail persons in whom they took no interest whatever, which is one more proof that in the ravishing opera that is called love the libretto is of almost no importance. The happiness, for Marius, of listening to Cosette talk about frills and furbelows, and, for Cosette, of listening to Marius talk about politics. The happiness for both of them, while they sat with knee touching knee, of hearing the distant sound of traffic on the Rue de Babylone; of looking upwards to speculate on the same star in the sky, or downwards to study the same glow-worm in the grass; of being silent together, which is even more delightful than to talk . . . And so on.

But meanwhile complications were looming.

One evening when Marius was on his way along the Boulevard des Invalides to keep their nightly rendezvous, walking as usual with his eyes on the ground, just as he was about to turn into the Rue Plumet a voice spoke to him.

'Good evening, Monsieur Marius.'

He looked up and saw Éponine.

The encounter gave him a shock. He had not given the girl a

thought since the day she had led him to the Rue Plumet; he had not seen her again, and the memory of her had completely slipped his mind. He had every reason to be grateful to her; he owed his present happiness to her, and yet it embarrassed him to meet her.

It is a mistake to suppose that the state of being in love, be it never so happy and innocent, makes a man perfect. As we have seen, it simply makes him forgetful. If he forgets to be evil, he also forgets to be good. The sense of gratitude and obligation, the recollection of everyday essentials, all this tends to disappear. At any other time Marius would have treated Éponine quite differently; but absorbed as he was in the thought of Cosette he scarcely remembered that her full name was Éponine Thénardier, that she bore a name bequeathed to him by his father and one which, a few months earlier, he had longed to serve. We have to depict Marius as he was. Even the memory of his father had faded a little in the splendour of his love-affair.

He said awkwardly:

'Oh, it's you, Éponine.'

'Why do you speak to me in that cold way? Have I done something wrong?'

'No,' he said.

Certainly he had nothing against her—far from it. It was simply that, with all his warmth bestowed on Cosette he had none for Éponine.

He stayed silent and she burst out, 'But why——?' But then she stopped. It seemed that words had failed the once so brazen and heedless creature. She tried to smile but could not. She said, 'Well . . .' and then again was wordless, standing with lowered eyes.

'Goodnight, Monsieur Marius,' she said abruptly, and left him.

IV. *The Watch-dog*

The next day was 3 June 1832, a date which must be set down because of the grave events now impending, that loomed like thunder-clouds over Paris. Marius that evening was going the same way as on the previous evening, his head filled with the same thoughts and his heart charged with the same happiness, when he saw Éponine coming towards him past the trees on the boulevard. Two days in succession was too much. He turned sharply off the boulevard and made for the Rue Plumet by way of the Rue Monsieur.

This caused Éponine to follow him as far as the Rue Plumet, a thing which she had not previously done. Hitherto she had been content to watch him on his way along the boulevard without seeking to attract his notice. The previous evening was the first time she had ventured to speak to him.

So, without his knowing it, she followed him, and saw him slip through the wrought-iron gate into the garden. 'Well! He's going into the house!' she concluded, and, testing the bars of the gate, rapidly discovered his means of entry. 'Not for you, dearie,' she murmured sadly.

As though taking up guard duty, she sat down on the step at the point where the stone gatepost adjoined the neighbouring wall. It was a dark corner which hid her entirely. She stayed there for more than an hour without moving, her mind busy with its thoughts. At about ten o'clock one of the two or three persons accustomed to use the Rue Plumet, an elderly gentleman hastening to get away from that lonely and ill-famed street, heard a low resentful voice say, 'I shouldn't be surprised if he came here every night!' He looked round but could see no one, and, not daring to peer into the dark corner, hurried on in great alarm.

He did well to hurry, for a very short time afterwards six men entered the Rue Plumet. They came in single file, walking at some distance from one another and skirting the edge of the street like a scouting patrol. The first of them stopped at the wrought-iron gate, where he waited for the rest to catch up, until all six of them were gathered together.

They conferred in low voices.

'Sure this is the place?'

'Is there a dog?'

'I don't know. Anyway, I've brought something for it to eat.'

'Have you brought the gummed paper to do the window-pane?'

'Yes.'

'It's an old gate,' said a fifth man, speaking in a voice like that of a ventriloquist.

'So much the better. We can cut through the bars all the easier.'

The sixth man, who had not yet spoken, proceeded to examine the gate as Éponine had done an hour before and was not slow to discover the bar loosened by Marius. But as he was about to wrench it aside a hand emerging from the darkness seized him by the arm. He felt himself thrust backward and a husky voice said in a warning undertone, 'There's a dog!' The lanky figure of a girl rose up before him.

The man recoiled with the shock of the unexpected. He seemed to bristle, and nothing is more dismaying than the sight of a startled wild animal; their very fright is frightening. He drew back, exclaiming:

'Who the devil are you?'

'Your daughter.'

The man was Thénardier.

At this the five other men, Claquesous, Gueulemer, Babet, Montparnasse, and Brujon, gathered round them, moving silently, without haste and without speech, in the slow, deliberate manner that is proper to creatures of the night. They were equipped with a variety of sinister implements. Gueulemer had one of those curved crowbars that are known as jemmies.

'What are you doing here? What do you want? Have you gone crazy?' cried Thénardier, so far as anyone can be said to cry who is keeping his voice low. 'Have you come to try and put me off?'

Éponine laughed and flung her arms round his neck.

'I'm here because I'm here, dearest father. Aren't I even allowed to sit down in the street? You're the one who shouldn't be here. What's the use of coming here when it's no good? I told Magnon it was a biscuit. There's nothing to be got here. But you might at least kiss me. It's a long time since we saw each other. So you're out again?'

Thénardier grunted, trying to release himself from her arms:

'That's enough. You've kissed me. Yes, I'm not inside any more. And now, clear out.'

But Éponine still clung to him.

'But how did you do it? It was very clever of you to get out. You must tell me how you did it. And mother—where is she? You must tell me about mother.'

'She's all right,' said Thénardier. 'I don't know where she is. And now, clear out, can't you?'

'But I don't want to go,' said Éponine, pouting like a spoilt child. 'I haven't seen you for four months, and you want to send me away.' And she tightened her grip on him.

'This is getting silly,' said Babet.

'Hurry it up,' said Gueulemer. 'The cops'll be along.'

Éponine turned to the other men.

'Why, it's Monsieur Brujon! And Monsieur Babet. Good evening, Monsieur Claquesous. Don't you recognize me, Monsieur Gueulemer? And how are you, Montparnasse?'

'That's all right, they all know you,' said Thénardier. 'Well, you've said hallo, and now for God's sake go away and leave us in peace.'

'This is a time for foxes, not for hens,' said Montparnasse.

'You can see we've got a job to do,' said Babet.

Éponine took Montparnasse's hand.

'Careful,' he said. 'You'll cut yourself. My knife's open.'

'Montparnasse, my love,' said Éponine very sweetly, 'you must learn to trust people. Aren't I my father's daughter? Don't you remember, Monsieur Babet and Monsieur Gueulemer, that I was sent to look this place over?'

It is worthy of note that Éponine did not speak a word of argot. Since she had known Marius thieves' slang had become impossible for her. She pressed her thin, bony fingers into Gueulemer's rugged palm and went on:

'You know I'm not stupid. People generally believe me. I've been useful to you more than once. Well, I've found things out, and I swear there's nothing for you here. You'd be running risks for no reason.'

'Two women alone,' said Gueulemer.

'No. The people have left.'

'The candles haven't,' said Babet.

And he pointed through the tree-tops to a flickering light in the attic, where Toussaint, staying up later than usual, was hanging out washing to dry.

Éponine made a last effort.

'Anyway, they're very poor, nothing there of any value.'

'Go to the devil!' exclaimed Thénardier. 'When we've ransacked the house from top to bottom we'll know if there's anything worth having.'

He thrust her aside.

'Montparnasse, you're my friend,' said Éponine. 'You're a good lad. Don't go in!'

'Watch out you don't cut yourself,' said Montparnasse.

Thénardier spoke with the authority he knew how to assume.

'Off you go, girl, and leave the men to get on with their business.'

Éponine let go of Montparnasse's hand and said:

'So you're determined to break in!'

'That's right,' said the ventriloquist and chuckled.

'Well, I won't let you,' said Éponine.

She stood with her back to the gate, facing the six men, all armed to the teeth and looking like demons in the dark. She went on in a low, resolute voice:

'Listen to me. I mean this. If you try to get into the garden, if you so much as touch this gate, I'll scream the place down. I'll rouse the whole neighbourhood and have the lot of you pinched.'

'She will, too,' muttered Thénardier to Brujon and the ventriloquist.

Éponine nodded vigorously, adding, 'And my father for a start!'

Thénardier moved towards her.

'You keep your distance,' she said.

He drew back, furiously muttering, 'What's got into her?' And he spat the word at her: 'Bitch!'

She laughed derisively.

'Say what you like, you aren't going in. I'm not a dog's daughter but a wolf's. There are six of you, six men and I'm one woman, but I'm not afraid of you. You aren't going to break into this house, because I don't choose to let you. I'm the watch-dog, and if you try it I'll bark. So you might as well be on your way. Go anywhere you like, but don't come here. I won't have it.'

She took a step towards them, and she was awe-inspiring. She laughed again.

'My God, do you think I'm scared? I'm used to starving in summer and freezing in winter. You poor fools, you think you can frighten any woman because you've got soft little sluts of mistresses who cower under the bedclothes when you talk rough. But I'm not scared.' She looked at her father. 'Not even of you.' With fiery eyes she glared round at the other men. 'What do I care if my body's picked up in the street tomorrow morning, beaten to death by my own father—or found in a year's time in the ditches round Saint-Cloud or the Île des Cygnes, along with the garbage and the dead dogs?'

She was interrupted by a fit of coughing, a hollow sound that came from the depths of her narrow, sickly chest.

'I've only got to yell, you know, and people will come running. There are six of you, but I'm the public.'

Thénardier again made a move towards her. 'Keep away!' she cried. He stopped and said mildly: 'All right, I won't come any nearer, but don't talk so loud. My girl, are you trying to prevent me working? After all, we have to earn our living. Have you no more feeling for your father?'

'You sicken me,' said Éponine.

'But we've got to eat.'

'I don't care if you starve.'

Having said which she sat down again on the step, humming the refrain of '*Ma grand'mère*' by Béranger, the most renowned songwriter of the day:

> *Combien je regrette*
> *Mon bras si dodu,*
> *Ma jambe bien faite*
> *Et le temps perdu.**

> * *How sadly I miss*
> *My smooth, round arm,*
> *My well-turned leg*
> *And the time that is gone.*

She sat with her legs crossed, her elbow on her knee and her chin on her hand, swinging her foot with an air of indifference, the glow of a nearby street-lamp illuminating her posture and her profile. Through the rents in her tattered garment her thin shoulder-blades were to be seen. It would be hard to conceive a picture more determined or more surprising.

The six ruffians, disconcerted at being kept at bay by a girl, withdrew into the shadows and conferred together with furious shruggings of their shoulders, while she calmly but resolutely surveyed them.

'There must be some reason,' said Babet. 'D'you think she's fallen in love with the dog? But it would be a shame to pass it up. Two women and an old man who lives in the back-yard. There are good curtains in the windows. If you ask me, the man's a Jew. I reckon it's worth trying.'

'Well, you lot go in,' said Montparnasse. 'I'll stick with the girl, and if she gives so much as a squeak . . .' He flourished the knife which he kept up his sleeve.

Thénardier said nothing, seeming content to leave the decision to the others.

Brujon, who was something of an oracle, and who, as we know, was the original promoter of the enterprise, had not so far spoken. He seemed to be thinking. It was said of him that he would stop at nothing, and he was known to have looted a police post out of sheer bravado. Moreover, he made up poems and songs, and this caused him to be highly esteemed.

Babet now looked at him:

'Why aren't you saying anything?'

Brujon remained silent for some moments, and then, portentously wagging his head, spoke as follows:

'Well, listen. This morning I saw two sparrows fighting, and this afternoon I bumped into a woman who abused me. Those are bad signs. Let's go.'

So they went away. Montparnasse muttered:

'All the same, if wanted, I was ready to give the girl a clout.'

'I wouldn't have,' said Babet. 'I don't hit women.'

At the bend of the street they paused to exchange a few cryptic words.

'Where are we going to sleep tonight?'

'Under the town.'

'Have you the key to the grating, Thénardier?'

'Maybe.'

Éponine, intently watching, saw them move off the way they had come. She got up and stole along behind them, keeping close to walls and house-fronts until they reached the boulevard. Here they separated, and melted like shadows into the night.

V. *Things of the Night*

With the departure of the robber band the Rue Plumet resumed its night-time aspect.

What had happened in that street would not have been unusual in a jungle. Trees and thickets, tangled branches, creepers and under-growth live their own dark lives, witnessing amid their savage growth sudden manifestations of the life they cannot grasp. What lives on a higher plane than man peers down through the mist at what is lower, and things unknown by daylight encounter each other in the dark. Wild, bristling Nature takes fright at what it feels to be supernatural. The powers of darkness know each other and preserve a mysterious balance between them. Tooth and claw respect the intangible. Animals that drink blood, voracious appetites in search of prey, instinct equipped with jaws and talons, with no source or aim other than the belly, apprehensively sniff the shrouded, spectral figure, stalking in filmy, fluttering garments, that seems to them imbued with a terrible dead life. Those brutish creatures, wholly material, instinctively fight shy of the measureless obscurity contained in any unknown being. A dark figure barring the way stops a wild animal in its tracks. What emerges from the burial-ground alarms and dismays that which emerges from the lair; the bloodthirsty fears the sinister; the wolf recoils from the ghoul.

VI. *Marius gives Cosette his Address*

While that human watchdog was guarding the gate, and the six ruffians were giving in to a girl, Marius was with Cosette.

Never had the night been more starry and enchanting, the trees more tremulous, the scent of grass more pungent; never had the birds twittered more sweetly as they fell asleep amid the leaves, or the harmonies of a serene universe been more in tune with the un-sung music of love; and never had Marius been more enraptured and entranced. But he had found Cosette unhappy. She had been weeping and her eyes were red. It was the first cloud in their clear sky.

His first words to her were, 'What's the matter?', and seated beside him on their bench by the steps into the villa she told him of her troubles.

'My father said this morning that I must be ready. He has business to attend to and we may have to leave this place.'

Marius trembled. At the end of life death is a departure; but at life's beginning a departure is a death.

In the past six weeks Marius, by gradual degrees, had been taking possession of Cosette: possession in ideal terms but deeply rooted. As we have said, in a first love it is the soul that is first captured, then the body; later the body comes before the soul, which may be forgotten altogether. Cynics may maintain that this is because the soul does not exist, but fortunately that sarcasm is a blasphemy. Marius possessed Cosette only in spirit; but his whole soul bound her jealously to him, and with overwhelming assurance. He possessed her smiles, the light of her blue eyes and the fragrance of her breath, the softness of her skin when he touched her hand, the magical grace of her neck, her every thought. They had vowed never to sleep without each dreaming of the other, and so he possessed all Cosette's dreams. His gaze dwelt endlessly on the small hairs on the nape of her neck, which sometimes he stirred with his breathing, and he told himself that there was not one of them that did not belong to him. He studied and adored the things she wore— ribbons, gloves, cuffs, slippers—seeing them as hallowed objects of which he was the proprietor. He thought of himself as the owner of the tortoiseshell comb in her hair, and went so far—such are the first stirrings of a growing sensuality—as to consider that there was not a tape in her garments, a stitch in her stockings, a fold in her corset, that did not belong to him. Seated beside Cosette he felt himself to be lord of his domain, master of his estate, near his ruler and his slave. It seemed to him, so deeply merged were their souls, that if they had tried to separate them they would not have been able to tell which part belonged to which . . . 'That bit's mine.' . . . 'No, it's mine.' . . . 'I'm sure you're wrong. That bit is me.' . . . 'No. What you think is you is really me.' . . . Marius was a part of Cosette, and Cosette was a part of Marius; he felt her life within him. To have Cosette, to possess her, this to him was no different from breathing. It was into this entranced state of absolute, virginal possession, this state of sovereignty, that the words, 'We may be going away' suddenly fell: and it was the peremptory voice of reality warning him, 'Cosette is not yours!'

Marius suddenly woke up. For six weeks he had been living outside life. Now he was brought harshly back to earth.

He could not speak, but Cosette felt his hand grow cold. She asked, as he had done, 'What's the matter?' and he replied, so low that she could scarcely hear:

'I don't understand what you mean.'

'Father told me this morning that I must get ready,' she said. 'He said that he had to go on a journey and we would go together. He would give me his clothes to pack, and I must see to everything— a big trunk for me and a little one for him. It must all be ready within a week, and perhaps we should be going to England.'

'But that's monstrous!' cried Marius.

It is unquestionable that, to Marius at that moment, no act of despotic tyranny in the whole course of history, from Tiberius to Henry VIII, could rank with this in infamy—that Monsieur Fauchelevent should take his daughter to England because he had business there! He asked in a stifled voice:

'And when, precisely, will you be leaving?'

'He didn't say.'

'And when will you be coming back?'

'He didn't tell me that, either.'

Marius rose to his feet and said coldly:

'Cosette, are you going?'

She looked distractedly up at him.

'But——'

'Are you going to England?'

'Why are you being so cruel to me?'

'I'm simply asking if you're going.'

'But what else can I do?' she cried, wringing her hands.

'So you are going?'

'But if my father goes . . .'

Cosette reached for Marius's hand. 'Very well,' he said. 'Then I shall go away.'

Cosette felt the words, rather than understood them, and turned so pale that her face gleamed whitely in the darkness. She murmured:

'What do you mean?'

Marius looked away from her without answering; but then, looking back at her, he found that she was smiling. The smile of a woman one loves is discernible even in the dark.

'Marius, how silly we're being! I've got an idea.'

'What is it?'

'If we go you must come too. I'll tell you where, and you must meet me there, wherever it is.'

Marius was now fully awake. He had come down to earth with a bump.

'How can I possibly do that?' he cried. 'Are you crazy? It takes money to go to England, and I haven't any. I already owe Courfeyrac more than ten louis—he's a friend of mine. And I wear a hat that isn't worth three francs, and I've lost half the buttons off my jacket, and my cuffs are frayed and my boots leak. I haven't thought about things like that for six weeks. I haven't told you, Cosette, but I'm a pauper. You only see me at night and you give me your hand; if you saw me by daylight you'd give me alms. England! I can't even afford a passport.'

He got up and stood with his face pressed to the trunk of a tree with his arms above his head, unconscious of the roughness of the bark against his cheek and almost ready to collapse—a statue of despair. He stayed in this posture for a long time; depths such as these are timeless. Finally he turned, having heard a small, stifled sound behind him. Cosette was in tears.

He fell on his knees in front of her, and bending down, kissed the foot that showed beneath the hem of her skirt. She made no response. There are moments when, like a saddened and resigned goddess, a woman silently accepts the gestures of love.

'Don't cry,' he said.

'But if I've got to go away and you can't come too . . .'

'Do you love me?'

She answered him with the divine word that is never more moving than when spoken amid tears:

'I adore you.'

His voice as he spoke again was the gentlest of caresses.

'Then don't cry. Do that much for me—stop crying.'

'Do you love me?' she asked.

He took her hand.

'Cosette, I have never given anyone my word of honour because it frightens me to do so. I feel my father watching me. But I give you my most sacred word of honour that if you leave me I shall die.'

These words were uttered with so much quiet solemnity that she trembled, feeling chilled as though at a ghostly touch, terrifying but true. She stopped crying.

'Now listen,' he said. 'Don't expect me here tomorrow.'

'Why not?'

'Not until the day after.'

'But why?'

'You'll see.'

'A whole day without seeing you! But that's dreadful!'

'We must sacrifice a day for the sake of our whole lives.' And Marius murmured, half to himself: 'He won't change his habits. He never sees anyone except in the evening.'

'Who are you talking about?' asked Cosette.

'Never mind.'

145

'But what are you going to do?'

'Wait until the day after tomorrow.'

'Must I really?'

'Yes, Cosette.'

She took his head in her hands and, rising on tip-toe, sought to read his secret in his eyes.

'While I think of it,' said Marius, 'you must have my address in case you need it. I'm living with this friend of mine, Courfeyrac, at 16, Rue de la Verrerie.'

He got a penknife out of his pocket and scratched it on the plaster of the wall—16, Rue de la Verrerie.

Cosette was intently watching him.

'Tell me what you're thinking. Marius, you're thinking of something. Tell me what it is, or how shall I sleep tonight?'

'I'm thinking this—that God can't possibly mean us to be separated. I shall be here the evening after tomorrow.'

'But what am I to do until then? It's all very well for you, you'll be out and about. You'll be doing things. Men are so lucky! But I shall be all alone. I shall be so wretched. Where are you going tomorrow evening?'

'I'm going to try something.'

'Well, I'll pray for you to succeed and I'll never stop thinking about you. I'll ask no more questions because you don't want me to. You're the master. I'll spend tomorrow evening singing the music from *Euryanthe* that you like so much—you listened to it once outside the window. But you must be here in good time the day after tomorrow. I shall expect you at nine o'clock exactly. Oh, two whole days is such a long time! Do you hear me? At exactly nine o'clock I shall be waiting in the garden!'

'I shall be there.'

And without further speech, prompted by the same impulse, the electric current that unites lovers in their every thought, passionate even in their sorrow, they fell into each other's arms, unconscious that their lips were joined while their tear-filled eyes looked upward at the stars.

By the time Marius left the street was deserted. Éponine had just departed to follow the robber band as far as the boulevard.

While he had stood reflecting with his face against the tree-trunk, Marius had had an idea—one that alas he himself thought hopeless and impossible. He had taken a drastic decision.

Monsieur Gillenormand had now passed his ninety-first year. He was still living with his daughter in the old house which he owned in the Rue des Filles-du-Calvaire. He was, we may recall, one of those veterans cast in the antique mould who await death upright, burdened but not softened by age, and whom even bitter disappointment cannot bend.

Nevertheless for some time Mlle Gillenormand had been saying, 'My father is failing'. He no longer cuffed his servants or so vigorously rapped the banister on the landing with his cane when Basque was slow in opening the door. His fury at the July Revolution had lasted barely six months, and his calm had been scarcely ruffled when in the *Moniteur* he had come upon that monstrous conjunction of words, 'Monsieur Humblot-Conte, Peer of France'. The truth is that the old man was filled with despair. He did not give way to it, he did not surrender, since it was not in his physical or moral nature to do so; but he was conscious of an inner weakening. For four years he had sturdily—that is the right word—awaited Marius's return, convinced that sooner or later the young scamp would knock at his door; but now there were melancholy moments when he reflected that if the boy did not come soon . . . It was not the approach of death that he found unbearable, but the thought that he might never see Marius again. Until quite recently this thought had never entered his head, but now it haunted and terrified him. Absence, as happens always in the case of true and natural feeling, had served only to increase his affection for the graceless boy who had deserted him. It is in the dark and cold December nights that we most ardently desire the sun. Monsieur Gillenormand, the grandfather, was wholly incapable—or thought he was—of making any move towards reconciliation with his grandson—'I would rather die,' he thought. Although aware of no fault in himself, he thought of Marius with the profound tenderness and silent desolation of an old man on the threshold of the grave.

He was beginning to lose his teeth, which added to his unhappiness.

Without confessing it to himself, for the avowal would have made him furious and ashamed, Monsieur Gillenormand had never loved any of his mistresses as well as he loved Marius. He had had hung in his bedroom, facing the end of his bed so that it was the first thing he saw when he awoke, an old portrait of his other daughter, the one now dead who had become Madame Pontmercy, which had been painted when she was eighteen. He gazed at it constantly, and on one occasion remarked:

'I think he's like her.'

'Like my sister?' said Mlle Gillenormand. 'Yes, he is.'

'Like him, too,' the old man said.

Once, when he was sitting huddled with his knees together and his eyes half-closed in a posture of dejection, his daughter ventured to say:

'Father, are you still so angry with——' She broke off, afraid to say more.

'With whom?'

'With poor Marius.'

He looked up sharply, thumped with his old, wrinkled fist on the table, and cried in a voice ringing with fury:

'Poor Marius, indeed! That gentleman is a worthless scoundrel without heart or feeling or gratitude, a monster of conceit, a villainous rogue.' And he turned away his head so that she should not see the tears in his eyes.

Three days after this he broke a silence that had lasted four hours to say without preliminaries to his daughter:

'I have already requested Mademoiselle Gillenormand never to mention that subject again.'

After this Aunt Gillenormand gave up the attempt, having arrived at the following conclusion—'Father never greatly cared for my sister after she made a fool of herself. Clearly, he detests Marius'. By 'made a fool of herself' she meant marrying the colonel.

Apart from this, as the reader will have surmised, Mlle Gillenormand had failed in her attempt to find a substitute for Marius. Lieutenant Théodule had not brought it off. Monsieur Gillenormand had disdained him. The ravaged heart does not so readily accept palliatives. And for his part, Théodule, while interested in the possible inheritance, had disliked the business of ingratiating himself. The old man had bored the cavalry officer, and the cavalry officer had exasperated the old man. Théodule was cheerful but over-talkative, frivolous but commonplace, a high-liver but in shabby company; it was true that he had mistresses and that he talked about them, but he talked badly. All his virtues were flawed. Monsieur Gillenormand was outraged by his tales of casual encounters near the barracks in the Rue de Babylone. And then again, he sometimes turned up in uniform, his cap adorned with a tricolour cockade. This alone ruled him out. It had ended with the old gentleman saying to his daughter: 'I've had enough of Théodule. You can see him if you like, but I don't much care for peacetime warriors. I'm not sure that I don't prefer adventurers to men who simply wear a sword. The clash of blades in battle is a less depressing sound than the rattle of a scabbard on the pavement. And then, to parade oneself as a fighting man and be titivated like a woman, with a corset under one's *cuirasse*, is to be fatuous twice over. A real man avoids display as much as he does effeminacy. You can have your Théodule, he's neither one thing or the other."

His daughter's argument that Théodule was his great-nephew was unavailing. Monsieur Gillenormand, it seemed, was a grandfather to his finger-tips, but not in the least a great-uncle. Indeed, the comparison being forced on him, Théodule had served only to make him miss Marius the more.

An evening came—it was the 4th of June, but that did not prevent him from having a fire blazing in the hearth—when Monsieur Gillenormand, having dismissed his daughter, was alone in his room with its pastoral tapestries, seated in his armchair with his feet on the hob, half-enclosed in his nine-leafed screen, with two green-shaded candles on the table at his elbow and with a book in his hand which, however, he was not reading. According to his habit he was dressed in the fashion of the *incroyables* and looked like an old-style portrait of Garat, the Minister of Justice at the time of the execution of Louis XVI. This would have caused him to be stared at in the streets, but whenever he went out his daughter saw to it that he was enveloped in a sort of bishop's cloak which hid his costume. At home he never wore any sort of house-gown except in his bedroom. 'They make you look old,' he said.

He was thinking of Marius with both affection and bitterness, and, as usual, bitterness came uppermost. His exacerbated tenderness always ended by boiling up into anger. He was at the point where we seek to come to terms with a situation and to accept the worst. There was no reason, after all, why Marius should ever come back to him; if he had been going to do so he would have done so already. There was no more hope, and Monsieur Gillenormand was trying to resign himself to the idea that all was over, and that he must go to his grave without ever seeing 'that gentleman' again. But he could not do so; his whole being recoiled from the thought, his every instinct rejected it. 'What—never! He'll *never* come back? Never again?' His bald head had sunk on to his chest, and he was gazing with grievous, exasperated eyes into the fire.

And while this mood was on him his old man-servant Basque entered the room and asked:

'Will Monsieur receive Monsieur Marius?'

Monsieur Gillenormand started upright, ashen-faced and looking like a corpse revived by a galvanic shock. All the blood seemed to have been drained out of his body. He stammered:

'Monsieur—who?'

'I don't know,' said Basque, alarmed by his master's appearance.

'I haven't seen him. Nicolette says that a young man has called and I'm to tell you that it's Monsieur Marius.'

Monsieur Gillenormand said in a very low voice:

'Show him in.'

He waited, quivering, with his eyes fixed on the door until at length it opened and the young man entered. It was Marius.

He stood uncertainly in the doorway, as though waiting to be invited in. The shabbiness of his clothes was not apparent in the half-darkness of the room. Nothing of him was clearly visible but his face, which was calm and grave but strangely sad.

Monsieur Gillenormand, in the turmoil of his stupefaction and delight, was incapable for some moments of seeing anything but a sort of glimmer, as though he had been visited by an apparition. He was near to swooning. He saw Marius through a haze. But it was really he; it was Marius!

At last! After four years! When at length he was able to look him over he found him handsome, noble, distinguished, grown into a whole man, correct in bearing and agreeable in manner. He wanted to open his arms and summon him to his embrace; his whole being cried out to him . . . until finally this surge of feeling found expression in words springing from the harsh underside of his nature, and he asked abruptly:

'What have you come for?'

Marius murmured in embarrassment:

'Monsieur . . .'

Monsieur Gillenormand had wanted him to rush into his arms. He was vexed both with Marius and with himself. He felt that he had been too brusque and that Marius's response was too cold. It was an intolerable exasperation to him that he should be so tenderly moved inside and outwardly so hard. His bitterness revived. He cut Marius short, saying:

'Well, why are you here?'

The significance of that 'Well——' was, 'if you have not come to embrace me'. Marius stared at the old man's face, whose pallor gave it a look of marble.

'Have you come to apologize? Do you now see that you were wrong?'

Hard though the words sounded, they were intended to be helpful, to pave the way for the 'boy's' surrender. But Marius shivered. He was being asked to disavow his father. He lowered his eyes, and said:

'No, Monsieur.'

'Well then,' the old man burst out in an access of pain and anger, 'what do you want of me?'

Marius clasped his hands, and moving a step towards him said in a low and trembling voice:

'Monsieur, I ask you to have pity on me.'

The words touched Monsieur Gillenormand. Had they been spoken sooner they would have melted him, but they came too late. The old man rose to his feet and stood white-lipped, leaning on his stick with his head swaying on his shoulders, but by his taller stature dominating Marius, whose eyes were still cast down.

'Pity indeed! A youth your age asking pity of a man aged ninety-one! You're beginning life and I'm leaving it. You go to the theatre, the dance, the café, the billiard-hall; you've got wits and looks to attract the women—while I huddle in midsummer spitting into the fire. You have all the riches that matter while I have all the poverty of age, infirmity, and loneliness. You have all your teeth and a sound digestion, a clear eye, health, strength, and gaiety and a good crop of dark hair, while I haven't even any white hairs left. I've lost my teeth, I'm losing the use of my legs and I'm losing my memory. I can't even remember the name of the streets round this house. Rue Charlot, Rue du Chaume, Rue Saint-Claude, I'm always muddling them up. That's the state I'm in. You have the whole world at your feet, bathed in sunshine, but for me there's nothing but darkness. You're in love, it goes without saying, but nobody on earth loves me. And then you come here asking for pity. That's something even Molière didn't think of. If it's the kind of joke you lawyers crack in the courts, I congratulate you! You're a waggish lot.' Then he said impatiently but more seriously, 'Well, and what is it you really want?'

'Monsieur,' said Marius, 'I know that I am not welcome here. I have come to ask for only one thing, and then I will go away at once.'

'You're a young fool,' the old man said. 'Who said you were to go away?'

It was the nearest he could get to the words that were in his heart—'Ask my forgiveness! Fling yourself into my arms!' He realized that Marius was on the verge of leaving, driven away by the coldness of his reception; he knew all this and his unhappiness was sharpened by the knowledge; and since, with him, unhappiness was transformed instantly into rage, so did his harshness increase. He wanted Marius to understand, but Marius did not understand, and this made him more angry still.

'You deserted me, your grandfather! You left my house to go God knows where. You almost broke your aunt's heart. I've no doubt you found a bachelor life very much more pleasant—aping the young man-about-town, playing the fool, coming home at all hours, having a high old time. And not a word to us. You've run up debts, I suppose, without even asking me to pay them. You've joined in demonstrations, no doubt, behaved like a street hooligan. And now, after four years, you come back to me, and this is all you have to say!'

This rough attempt to evoke in Marius a display of affection simply had the effect of reducing him to silence. Monsieur Gillenormand folded his arms, a particularly lordly gesture as he used it, and concluded bitterly:

'Well, let's get to the point. You say you've come to ask for something. What is it?'

'Monsieur,' said Marius, with the expression of a man about to jump off a precipice, 'I have come to ask your consent to my marriage.'

Monsieur Gillenormand rang the bell and Basque appeared.

'Will you please ask my daughter to come here.'

The door was again opened a few moments later. Mlle Gillenormand showed herself in the doorway but did not enter the room. Marius was standing dumbly with his arms hanging, looking like a criminal. Monsieur Gillenormand was pacing up and down. He glanced at his daughter and said:

'A trifling matter. Here, as you see, is Monsieur Marius. Bid him good-day. He wants to get married. That's all. Now go away.'

The terse, harsh tone of the old man's utterance conveyed a strange fullness of emotion. Aunt Gillenormand darted a startled glance at Marius, seeming scarcely to recognize him, and then, without speaking or making any gesture, scuttled away from her father's fury like a dead leaf in a gale of wind. Monsieur Gillenormand resumed his place in front of the hearth.

'And so you want to get married—at the age of twenty-one. You've arranged it all except for one trifling formality—my consent. Please be seated, Monsieur. There has been a revolution since I last had the privilege of seeing you, and the Jacobins came off best. You must have been highly gratified. No doubt you've become a republican since you became a baron. The two things go together. The republic adds savour to the barony, does it not? Were you awarded any July decorations? Did you help to take the Louvre, Monsieur? Quite near here, in the Rue Saint-Antoine, opposite the Rue des Nonnains-d'Hyères, there's a cannon ball lodged in the third storey of a house wall, bearing the inscription, 28 July 1830. You should go and look at it, it is most impressive. They do such charming things, these friends of yours. They're putting up a fountain, I believe, in place of the statue of the Duc de Berry. And so you want to get married? Would it be indiscreet to ask to whom?'

The old man paused, but before Marius could reply he burst out:

'So I suppose you've got some sort of position. Perhaps you've made a fortune. What do you earn as a lawyer?'

'Nothing,' said Marius in a voice of almost savage firmness and defiance.

'Nothing? So all you have to live on are the twelve hundred *livres* I allow you?'

Marius made no reply, and Monsieur Gillenormand went on.

'Well then, I take it the girl is rich.'

'No richer than I am.'

'You mean, she won't have a dowry?'

'No.'

'Expectations?'

'I think not.'

'Not a rag to her back! And what does her father do?'

'I don't know.'

'Well, what's her name?'

'Mademoiselle Fauchelevent.'

'Fauche—— what?'

'Fauchelevent.'

'Pshaw!' said the old man.

'Monsieur!' cried Marius.

Monsieur Gillenormand cut him short, speaking in an aside to himself.

'So that's it. Twenty-one years old and no position, nothing but twelve hundred *livres* a year. Madame la Baronne Pontmercy will have to count her sous when she goes to market.'

'Monsieur,' cried Marius, in the distraction of seeing his last hope vanish, 'I beg of you, I beseech you in Heaven's name on my bended knees, to allow me to marry her!'

The old man uttered a shrill, anguished laugh which turned into a fit of coughing, then burst again into speech.

'So you said to yourself, "I'll have to go and see him, that old fossil, that old mountebank. It's too bad I'm not yet twenty-five. I wouldn't have to worry about him and his consent. As it is, I'll go there and crawl to him, and the old fool will be so happy to see me that he won't care who I marry. I haven't a sound pair of shoes and she hasn't a chemise to her back, but no matter. I'm proposing to throw away my career, my prospects, my youth, my whole life and plunge into poverty with a woman round my neck. That's what I intend to do, I'll tell him, and I'll ask his consent. And the old fossil will oblige . . ." That's what you think, isn't it? Well, my lad, you can do what you please. Hamstring yourself, if you must. Marry your Pousselevent or Coupelevent or whatever her name is. But as for my consent, the answer is, Never!'

'Grandfather——'

'Never!'

The tone in which the word was uttered robbed Marius of all hope. He rose and crossed the room slowly, swaying a little, with his head bowed, more like someone in the act of dying than someone merely taking his leave. Monsieur Gillenormand stood watching him, but then, when he was about to open the door, moving with the jerky liveliness of a spoilt, imperious old man, he darted after him, seized him by the coat collar, dragged him vigorously back into the room, thrust him into an armchair and said:

'Tell me about it.'

It was the word 'grandfather' that had brought about the change in him. Marius stared in amazement. Monsieur Gillenormand's expression had become one of coarse, implicit bonhomie. The stern guardian had given way to the grandfather.

'Come on. Tell me all about your love affairs. Don't be afraid to talk. Lord, what fools you young fellows are.'

'Grandfather . . .' Marius said again, and the old man's face lighted up.

'That's it. Don't forget I'm your grandfather.'

There was so much bluff, fatherly indulgence in his manner that Marius, now suddenly transported from despair to hope, was quite bewildered. He was seated near the table and the light of the two candles, disclosing the dilapidated state of his attire, caused Monsieur Gillenormand to survey him with astonishment.

'You really are penniless, aren't you!' he said. 'You look like a tramp'. He pulled open a drawer and got out a purse which he put on the table. 'Here's a hundred louis. Buy yourself some clothes.'

'Oh, grandfather,' said Marius, 'if you knew how much I love her. The first time I saw her was in the Luxembourg, she was there every day. I didn't take much notice of her at first, but then—I don't know how it was—I fell in love with her. I was terribly unhappy, but in the end—well, now I see her every day at her home—her father doesn't know—we meet in the garden in the evening—and they're going away, he's going to take her to England. So when I heard this I thought to myself, I'll go and see my grandfather and tell him about it. Because otherwise I'll get ill, or go mad and throw myself in the river. I've got to marry her, I *must* marry her, or I shall go mad. Well, that's the whole truth. I don't think I've left anything out. She lives in a house in the Rue Plumet, with a garden and a wrought-iron gate. It's near the Invalides.'

Monsieur Gillenormand was seated radiantly beside him, adding

zest to his delight in his presence and the sound of his voice with an occasional long pinch of snuff. But at the mention of the Rue Plumet he started, with his fingers to his nose, and let the snuff fall on his knees.

'The Rue Plumet? Wait a minute. Isn't there a barracks near there? That's it, your cousin Théodule—you know, the cavalry officer—he told me about her. In the Rue Plumet. It used to be the Rue Blomet. I remember perfectly—a girl in a garden with a wrought-iron gate in the Rue Plumet. Another Pamela. You have good taste, my boy. A pretty wench, from what I hear. I fancy that fool Théodule had his eye on her, but I don't know how far it went. Anyway, it doesn't matter, you can't believe a word he says, he's always boasting. My dear Marius, I think it entirely right that a young fellow like you should be in love. It's natural at your age. I'd far sooner have you in love with a wench than with revolution. I'd sooner have you crazy about a dancing partner, or twenty dancing partners, than about Monsieur de Robespierre. I'm bound to say that the only kind of *sans-culottes* I've ever cared for are the ones in skirts. A pretty wench is a pretty wench, and what's wrong with that? So she lets you in without her father knowing, does she? That's quite in order. I've had that kind of adventure myself, and more than once. But listen, you don't want to take it too seriously, you mustn't go asking for trouble—no drama, no talk of marriage or anything of that sort. You're a gay young blade, but you've got a head on your shoulders. You have your fun, but you don't marry. You come to see your grandfather, who's not a bad old boy at heart and always has a few louis stuffed away in a drawer, and you ask him to help you out. And grandfather says, "Why, that's easy!" Youth profits and age provides. I've been young, and one day you'll be old. Here you are, lad, and you'll pay it back to your own grandson. Two hundred pistoles. Have your fun, and what could be better? That's how it should be. You don't marry, but that needn't stop you—you understand?'

Marius, too shocked to be capable of speech, shook his head. The old man burst out laughing, winked an aged eyelid, tapped him on the knee and gazing conspiratorially at him said with an indulgent shrug of his shoulders:

'Why, you young nincompoop—make her your steady mistress!'

Marius turned pale. He had understood nothing of what his grandfather had said. The talk of the Rue Blomet, Pamela, the barracks, and the cavalry officer had been to him a meaningless rigmarole. None of it had anything to do with his lily-white Cosette. The old man had been babbling; but his babbling had ended in an admonition which Marius had understood. 'Make her your mistress!'

The mere suggestion was an insult to Cosette, and it wounded her high-minded young lover like a swordthrust to his heart.

He rose, picked up his hat off the floor and walked firmly and resolutely towards the door. Here he turned, bowed deeply to his grandfather, straightened himself and said:

'Five years ago you insulted my father; today you have insulted my future wife. I shall ask nothing more of you, Monsieur. Farewell.'

Monsieur Gillenormand opened his mouth in stupefaction, reached out an arm and sought to get up from his chair; but before he could say anything the door had closed and Marius was gone.

The old man stayed motionless for some moments, unable to speak or breathe, as though a hand had clutched him by the throat. Finally he struggled to his feet. He ran to the door, so far as his ninety-one years permitted him to run, opened it and cried:

'Help! Help!'

His daughter appeared, followed by the servants. He croaked pitifully:

'After him! Catch him! What have I done to him? He must be mad. He's going away again. Oh, my God, my God, this time he'll never come back!'

He ran to the window looking on to the street, opened it with aged, trembling hands and leaned out while Basque and Nicolette held him from behind.

'Marius!' he called. 'Marius! Marius!'

But Marius, turning the corner of the Rue Saint-Louis, was already out of earshot.

Monsieur Gillenormand clasped his hands to his head and with an anguished expression withdrew from the window. He sank into an armchair, breathless, speechless, and tearless, wagging his head and soundlessly moving his lips, with nothing more in his eyes or his heart than a blankness like the coming of night.

BOOK NINE

WHERE ARE THEY GOING?

I. *Jean Valjean*

AT ABOUT four o'clock on the afternoon of that same day, Jean Valjean had been seated alone on the shady side of one of the more isolated slopes of the Champ de Mars. From caution, from the desire for solitude, or simply because of one of those unconscious changes of habit which occur in all our lives, he now seldom went out with Cosette. He was wearing his workman's smock, grey linen trousers, and the long-peaked cap which hid his face. He was again on easy and happy terms with Cosette, his earlier anxieties having been put to rest; but during the past week or so other things had occurred to trouble him. One day as he walked along the boulevard he had seen Thénardier. Thanks to his disguise the latter had not recognized him, but since then he had seen him several times, often enough to convince him that Thénardier was now frequenting that part of the town. This had prompted him to take a major decision. Thénardier was the embodiment of all the dangers that threatened him.

Besides which, Paris was in an unsettled state, and for anyone with something to hide the present political unrest had the disadvantage that the police had become more than usually obtrusive, and might, in their search for agitators, light upon someone like Jean Valjean.

All these considerations troubled him. And something else had occurred to add to his unease, an unaccountable circumstance of which he had become aware only that morning. Rising early, before Cosette's shutters were opened, he had gone out into the garden and had suddenly noticed an address scratched on the wall, apparently with a nail—*16, Rue de la Verrerie.*

It was evidently recent. The letters stood out white against the dingy plaster, and there was fresh dust on the weeds at the foot of the wall. It might well have been done the previous night. Was it intended as a message for some third party, or was it a warning to himself? In any case it was certain that the garden had been broken into. Valjean was reminded of the other curious incidents that had disturbed the household. He pondered these matters, but said nothing to Cosette about this latest development, not wishing to alarm her.

The upshot was that, after due consideration, Jean Valjean had decided to leave Paris, and even France, and go to England. He had warned Cosette that he wanted to leave within a week. And now he sat on the grass in the Champ de Mars turning it all over in his mind —Thénardier, the police, the letters scratched on the wall, their prospective journey, and the difficulty of procuring a passport.

While he was thus engaged he saw, by the shadow cast by the sun, that someone was standing on the ridge of the slope at his back. He was about to turn when a scrap of folded paper fell on his knee, seeming to have been tossed over his head. Unfolding it, he read two words, pencilled in capital letters:

'CLEAR OUT.'

He got up quickly, but now there was no one on the slope. Looking about him he saw a queer figure, too tall for a child but too slight for a man, clad in a grey smock and drab-coloured corduroy trousers, scramble over the parapet and drop into the ditch encircling the Champ de Mars.

Valjean went home at once, his mind much exercised.

II. *Marius*

Marius dejectedly left his grandfather's house. He had gone there with only a gleam of hope; he left in utter despair.

The mention of a cavalry officer, his strutting cousin, Théodule, had made no impression on him, none whatever, as any student of the youthful human heart will readily understand. A playwright might have evolved complications arising out of this blunt disclosure from grandfather to grandson, but what the drama would have gained the truth would have lost. Marius was at the age when, in the matter of evil, we believe nothing; there comes a later age when we believe everything. Suspicions are nothing but wrinkles. Youth does not possess them. What overwhelms Othello leaves Candide untouched. As for suspecting Cosette, there were countless crimes which Marius could more easily have committed.

Taking refuge in the resource of the sore in heart, he wandered aimlessly through the streets, thinking of nothing that he could afterwards remember. At two in the morning he returned to Courfeyrac's lodging and flung himself fully dressed on his mattress. It was daylight before he fell into that state of troubled slumber in which the mind goes on working, and when he awoke he found that Courfeyrac, Enjolras, Feuilly, and Combeferre were all in the room, dressed for the street and seeming very agitated.

Courfeyrac asked him:

'Are you coming to the funeral of General Lamarque?'

For all they meant to him, the words might have been Chinese.

He went out some time after them, having put in his pocket the pistols Javert had loaned him on the occasion of the affair in February, which he had never returned. They were still loaded. It would be difficult to say what thought at the back of his mind prompted him to do this.

He roamed about all that day without knowing where he went. There were one or two showers of rain, but he did not notice them. He bought a roll at a baker's shop, thrust it in his pocket and forgot to eat it. It seems, even, that he bathed in the Seine without knowing that he did so. There are times when the head is on fire, and Marius was in that condition. He neither hoped for anything nor feared anything; this was what he had come to since the previous evening. He was waiting feverishly for the present evening, having only one clear thought in his mind, that at nine o'clock he would see Cosette. This last brief happiness was all that the future held for him; beyond it lay darkness. At moments, as he strayed along the frequented boulevards, it struck him that there was a strange hubbub in the town, and he emerged from his preoccupations to wonder, 'Are people fighting?'

At nightfall, at nine o'clock precisely in accordance with his promise, he was in the Rue Plumet, and as he drew near the wrought-iron gate he forgot all else. It was forty-eight hours since he had seen Cosette and now he was to see her again; all other thoughts were dispelled by this present rapture. Those minutes in which we live through centuries have the sovereign and admirable quality that at the time of their passing they wholly fill our hearts.

Marius slipped through the gate and hurried into the garden. Cosette was not in the place where ordinarily she awaited him. He crossed through the shrubbery and made for the recess by the steps. 'She'll be there,' he thought—but she was not there. Looking up he saw that all the shutters were closed. He explored the garden and found it empty. Returning to the house, half-crazed with love and grief and terror, like a householder returning home at an un-propitious moment, he banged with his fists on the shutters. He banged and banged again, regardless of the risk that a window might open to reveal the scowling face of her father demanding to know what he was about. This meant nothing to him compared with what he feared. He gave up banging and began to shout. 'Cosette! Cosette, where are you?' There was no reply. There was no one in the house or garden, no one anywhere.

Marius stared up with despairing eyes at the mournful dwelling, as dark and silent but more empty than a tomb. He looked at the stone bench where with Cosette he had passed so many enchanted hours. Finally he sat down on the steps, his heart swelling with tenderness and resolve. He blessed his love from the depths of his being, and said to himself that, now she was gone, there was nothing for him to do but die.

Suddenly he heard a voice calling through the trees, apparently from the street.

'Monsieur Marius!'

He looked up.

'Who's that?'

'Is that you, Monsieur Marius?'

'Yes.'

'Monsieur Marius, your friends are waiting for you at the barricade in the Rue de la Chanvrerie.'

The voice was not quite unfamiliar; it resembled the coarse, husky croak of Éponine. Marius ran to the gate, shifted the loose bar and, thrusting his head through, saw someone who looked like a youth vanish at a run into the darkness.

III. *Monsieur Mabeuf*

Jean Valjean's purse was of no service to Monsieur Mabeuf. His aged, childlike austerity had never encouraged gifts from heaven; nor was he disposed to admit that the stars could be transformed into *louis d'or*. Not knowing where the purse came from he took it to the local police post and left it there as an item of lost property to await a claimant. Needless to say, it was never claimed and did Monsieur Mabeuf no good.

For the rest, Monsieur Mabeuf continued on his downward course. His experiments with indigo were no more successful in the Jardin des Plantes than they had been in the Austerlitz garden. Last year he had owed his housekeeper her wages, this year he owed the rent. The pawnbroker had sold the plates of his *Flora* after thirteen months, and a tinker had made them into saucepans. Deprived of his plates, and unable even to finish off the incomplete sets of the *Flora* that he still possessed, he had sold the sheets of text and illustrations to a secondhand dealer at a knock-down price as 'remainders'. Nothing was now left to him of his life's work. He lived for a time on the proceeds of the sheets, and when he found that even this meagre nest-egg was nearly exhausted he gave up gardening and let his plot lie fallow. He had long ago given up the two eggs and occasional piece of beef on which he had once lived; his meals now consisted of bread and potatoes. He had sold the last of his furniture and everything he could spare in the way of clothes and bedding, also the majority of his books and engravings. But he still kept the most precious of his books, some of which, such as *La Concordance des Bibles*, by Pierre de Besse, and *Les Marguerites de la Marguerite* by Jean de la Haye, dedicated to the Queen of Navarre, were extremely rare. Monsieur Mabeuf never had a fire in his bedroom and went to bed when it grew dark to save candles. He seemed no longer to have neighbours; people avoided him when he went out, and he was aware of this. The plight of a child concerns its mother and the plight of a young man may concern a girl; but the plight of an old man concerns no one, it is the most lonely of all despairs. Nevertheless Monsieur Mabeuf had not wholly lost his childlike serenity. His eyes still lighted up when they fell upon a book, and he could still smile while he pored over his edition of Diogenes Laertius, printed in 1644, which was the only copy extant. His glass-fronted bookcase was the only article of furniture he had retained, apart from bare essentials.

Mère Plutarque said to him one morning:

'I've no money to buy dinner.'

By 'dinner' she meant a small loaf and four or five potatoes.

'Can't you owe for it?' asked Monsieur Mabeuf.

'You know very well they won't let me.'

Monsieur Mabeuf opened the bookcase and spent a long time contemplating his books, each one in turn, like a parent compelled to sacrifice one of his children. Finally he snatched one off the shelf and went out with it under his arm. He returned two hours later with nothing under his arm and laid thirty sous on the table.

'That will do for dinner.'

But the same thing happened next day and the day after and every day. Monsieur Mabeuf went out with a book and came back with a trifling sum of money. Seeing that he was forced to sell, the second-hand bookseller paid him twenty sous for a volume he had bought for twenty francs, sometimes at the same establishment. Thus his library dwindled. He remarked now and then, 'After all, I'm eighty' —perhaps with a lingering thought that he would come to the end of his days before he came to the end of his books. His melancholy increased. But one day he had a triumph. He went off with a Robert Estienne which he sold for thirty-five sous on the Quai Malaquais and came back with a volume of Alde which he had bought for forty sous in the Rue des Grès. 'I owe five sous,' he said happily to Mère Plutarque. That day he had no dinner.

He was a member of the Société d'Horticulture. When his state of impoverishment became known the president of the society undertook to speak on his behalf to the Minister of Agriculture and Commerce. 'Why certainly!' said the minister. 'A worthy, harmless old man, a scholar, and a botanist—certainly we must do something for him.' Next day Monsieur Mabeuf received an invitation to dine at the minister's home, which, trembling with delight, he displayed to Mère Plutarque. 'We're saved!' he said. Arriving on the appointed evening, he noted that his ragged cravat, his rusty, old-fashioned jacket and his shoes, which had been polished with white of egg, greatly astonished the footmen. Nobody spoke to him, not even the minister. At about ten o'clock, still hoping for a word from someone, he heard the minister's wife, a handsome lady in a low-cut evening dress whom he had not ventured to approach, ask, 'Who is that old person?' He went home on foot, at midnight and in pouring rain, having sold a volume of Elzevir to pay for a fiacre to take him there.

He had fallen into the habit, before going to bed, of reading a few pages of his Diogenes Laertius, having sufficient knowledge of Greek to be able to savour the particularities of the version he possessed. This was now his only pleasure. A few weeks after the dinner-party Mère Plutarque fell suddenly ill. There is something even more distressing than the lack of means to buy a loaf of bread, from the baker, and that is to lack the means to buy drugs from the apothecary. The ailment grew worse, and the doctor prescribed a very expensive medicine. Monsieur Mabeuf went to his bookcase but it was now empty. The last volume had gone. All he had left was his Diogenes Laertius.

Monsieur Mabeuf put the unique volume under his arm and went out. This was on 4 June 1832. He went to Royol's successor in the Rue Saint-Jacques and came back with a hundred francs. He put the pile of five-franc pieces on his old servant's bedside table and retired to his bedroom without saying a word.

At dawn the next day he sat down on the overturned milestone which served him as a bench, and contemplated the still morning and his neglected garden. It rained now and then, but he did not seem to notice. During the afternoon he heard a strange commotion coming from the direction of the town, sounds that resembled rifle fire and the clamour of a vast crowd.

Monsieur Mabeuf looked up, and seeing a gardener passing on the other side of his hedge asked him what was happening. The gardener, with a spade over his shoulder, answered in the most unconcerned of voices:

'It's a riot.'

'What do you mean, a riot?'

'The people are fighting.'

'What about?'

'Blessed if I know,' said the gardener.

'Where is this happening?' asked Monsieur Mabeuf.

'Round by the Arsenal.'

Monsieur Mabeuf went into the house for his hat, looked round automatically for a book to tuck under his arm, found none, muttered, 'Oh, of course', and set off for the town with a wild light in his eyes.

BOOK TEN

5 JUNE 1832

I. *The Outward Aspect*

OF WHAT does a revolt consist? Of everything and nothing, a spring slowly released, a fire suddenly breaking out, force operating at random, a passing breeze. The breeze stirs heads that think and minds that dream, spirits that suffer, passions that smoulder, wrongs crying out to be righted, and carries them away.

Whither?

Where chance may dictate. In defiance of the State and the laws, of the prosperity and insolence of other men.

Outraged convictions, embittered enthusiasms, hot indignation, suppressed instincts of aggression; gallant exaltation, blind warmth of heart, curiosity, a taste for change, a hankering after the unexpected, the impulse which makes us look with interest at the announcement of a new play, and the delight we take in those three knocks on the stage; vague dislikes, rancours, frustrations—the vanity that believes Fate is against us; discomforts, idle dreams, ambition hedged with obstacles; the hope that upheaval will provide an outlet; and finally, at the bottom of it all, the peat, the soil that catches fire—such are the elements of a revolt.

The greatest and the smallest; the beings on the fringe of life who wait upon chance, the footloose, men without convictions, hangers-on at the crossroads; those who sleep at nights in the desert of houses with no roof of their own other than the clouds in the sky; those who look to luck, not labour, for their daily bread; the unknown denizens of misery and squalor, bare-footed and bare-armed—all these belong to the revolt.

All those who cherish in their souls a secret grudge against some action of the State, or of life or destiny, are attracted to the revolt; and when it manifests itself they shiver and feel themselves uplifted by the tempest.

A revolt is a sort of whirlwind in the social atmosphere which swiftly forms in certain temperatures and, rising and travelling as it spins, uproots, crushes, and demolishes, bearing with it great and sickly spirits alike, strong men and weaklings, the tree-trunk and the wisp of straw. Woe to those it carries away no less than to those it seeks to destroy; it smashes one against the other.

It inspires those it lays hold of with extraordinary and mysterious powers, raising everyman to the level of events and making all men weapons of destruction; it makes a pebble into a cannon-ball, a labourer into a general.

If we accept the doctrine of certain exponents of political strategy, a weak revolt, from the point of view of those in power, is not undesirable: in principle any revolt strengthens the government it fails to overthrow. It tests the reliability of the army, unites the bourgeoisie, flexes the muscles of the police, and demonstrates the strength of the social framework. It is an exercise, almost a course of treatment. Power feels revived after a revolt, like a man after a massage.

But thirty years ago revolts were viewed differently.

There is in all matters a theoretical approach which calls itself 'common sense'. It is Molière's Philinte as opposed to his Alceste : the offer of compromise between what is true and what is false; discourse, admonition, rather patronizing extenuation which, because it is a mingling of blame and excess, supposes itself to be wisdom and is often no more than sophistry. A whole school of political thought, called 'moderate', springs from this approach. It is something between hot and cold—the tepid water. This school of thought, superficial but with simulated depth, analyses effects without looking to their cause, and with the loftiness of a pseudo-science rebukes the fever of the market-place.

This is what they say:

The riots which succeeded the achievement of 1830 robbed that great event of something of its purity. The July Revolution was a salutary blowing of the popular wind which instantly cleared the air. The subsequent rioting brought back the clouds, debasing a revolution that had been remarkable for its unanimity to the level of a brawl. In the July Revolution, as always when progress proceeds by jerks, there were hidden lesions; the rioting brought these to light. One could see that this or that thing had been broken. The July Revolution itself brought nothing but a feeling of deliverance; but after the riots one had a sense of catastrophe.

Any uprising causes the shops to shut and the funds to fall; it creates consternation on the Bourse, interferes with trade, causes bankruptcies; money runs short, the rich are apprehensive, public credit is shattered and industry thrown out of gear; capital is withheld and employment dwindles; there is insecurity everywhere, and countermeasures are adopted in every town. Hence the great fissures that arise. It has been estimated that the first day of the revolt cost

France twenty million francs, the second forty, and the third sixty. Simply in financial terms, the three days' revolt cost a hundred and twenty million—that is to say, the equivalent of a lost naval battle ending in the destruction of sixty ships-of-the-line.

In the historical perspective, no doubt, the rioting was not without beauty: the war of the street barricades is no less grandiose and dramatic than war in the undergrowth, the one being inspired by the spirit of the town, the other by the spirit of the countryside. The riots threw a garish but splendid light on what is most particular to the character of Paris—hot-blooded devotion and tempestuous gaiety, students who proved that courage is a part of intelligence, the unshakeable Garde Nationale, the encampments of shopkeepers and fortifications of street-urchins, and the defiance of death displayed by the ordinary man in the street. The schools did battle with the soldiery. When all is said, between the combatants there was only a difference of age; they were of the same race; the young men who at twenty were ready to die for their ideas would at forty be ready to die for their families. The army, always unhappy in times of civil disturbance, opposed prudence to audacity. The riots, while they made manifest the reckless daring of the masses, stiffened the courage of the bourgeoisie.

All this is true, but did it justify the blood that was shed? And to the shedding of blood must be added the darkened future, the setback to progress, the disquiet of decent people, the despair of honest liberals, wounds inflicted by foreign absolutism on the revolution it had itself provoked, and the triumph of those defeated in 1830, who could now proclaim, 'We told you so!' It may be that Paris was aggrandized, but certainly France was diminished. Nor may we ignore—for everything must be taken into account—the massacres which too often dishonoured the forces of order grown ferocious in their repression of the spirit of liberty run mad. All in all, this revolt was a disaster.

Such is the summing up of that approximation of wisdom which the bourgeoisie, that approximation of the people, is all too ready to accept.

For our part we reject that over-flexible and, in consequence, over-convenient term 'revolt'. We seek to distinguish between popular movements. We do not ask if a revolt costs as much as a battle. In any case, why have a battle? This brings us to the question of war. Is external war less of a disaster than internal revolt? And is every insurrection a disaster? And what if the insurrection of 14 July did cost a hundred and twenty million? The installation of Philip V upon the throne of Spain cost France two milliards. Even had the cost been the same, we should prefer 14 July. Moreover, we do not accept those figures, which sound like argument but are simply words. Accepting the fact of a revolt, we seek to examine the thing itself. The doctrinaire attitude depicted above deals only with effects: we must look for the cause.

II. *The Root of the Question*

There is the street riot and the national insurrection: two expressions of anger, the one wrong and the other right. In democratic states, the only ones based on justice, it may happen that a minority usurps power; the nation as a whole rises, and in the necessary assertion of its rights it may have recourse to violence. In any matter affecting the collective sovereignty, the war of the whole against the part is the insurrection, and the war of the part against the whole is a form of mutiny: the Tuileries may be justly or unjustly assailed according to whether they harbour the King or the Assembly. The guns turned on the mob were wrong on 10 August and right on 14 Vendémiaire. It looks the same, but the basis is different: the Swiss guards were defending an unrighteous cause, Bonaparte a righteous one. What has been done in the free exercise of its sovereign powers by universal suffrage cannot be undone by an uprising in the street. The same is true of matters of pure civilization: the instinct of the crowd, which yesterday was clear-sighted, may tomorrow be befogged. The fury which was justified against Terray was absurd when directed against Turgot, since the one stood for privilege and the other for the reform of abuses.* The wrecking of machines, looting of warehouses, tearing up of railway lines, destruction of docks; mobs led astray, the denial of progress by the people's justice, Ramus murdered by his own students, the stoning of Rousseau—all this is mob violence; it is Israel in revolt against Moses, Athens against Phocion, Rome against Scipio. But Paris rising against the Bastille— that is insurrection. His soldiers rising against Alexander, his sailors against Christopher Columbus, these are mere acts of mutiny. Alexander with the sword did for Asia what Columbus did for America with the compass—he opened up a world; and the gift of a new world to civilization is so great a spreading of light that resistance to it is culpable. Sometimes the mass counterfeits fidelity to itself. The mob betrays the people. Can anything be more strange, for example, than the action of the salt-makers who, after a long and bloody and wholly justified revolt, at the very moment of victory,

* Both were Finance Ministers—Terray from 1769 to 1774, Turgot from 1774 to 1776.

167

when their cause was won, went over to the King in a counter-revolution against the popular uprising on their behalf. A sad triumph of ignorance! The salt-makers escaped the royal gallows, and, with the rope still round their necks, donned the white cockade. 'Down with the salt-tax!' became 'Long live the King!' The massacre of St Bartholomew's Eve, the September massacre, the massacre at Avignon (Coligny murdered in the first, Madame de Lamballe in the second, Marshal Brune in the third)—these were all acts of riot. The Vendée was a huge Catholic revolt.

The sound of righteousness in movement is clearly recognizable, and it does not always come from the tumult of an over-excited mob. There are insane outbursts of rage just as there are flawed bells: not all tocsins sound the true note. The clash of passion and ignorance is different from the shock of progress. Rise up by all means, but do so in order to grow. Show me which way you are going; true insurrection can only go forward. All other uprisings are evil. Every violent step backwards is mutiny, and to retreat is to do injury to the human cause. Insurrection is the furious assertion of truth, and the sparks struck by its flung paving-stones are righteous sparks. But the stones flung in mutiny stir up nothing but mud. Danton versus Louis XVI was insurrection, but Hébert versus Danton was mutiny.

Thus it is that if, as Lafayette said, insurrection is the most sacred of duties, sporadic revolt may be the most disastrous of blunders.

There is also the difference of temperature. Insurrection is often a volcano, revolt often a hedgerow fire.

Sometimes insurrection is resurrection.

Since the solution of all problems by universal suffrage is a wholly modern concept, and since history prior to it has for four thousand years been a tale of violated rights and the suffering of the masses, every period of history discloses such acts of protest as are within its means. There was no insurrection under the Caesars, but there was Juvenal, who wrote: '*Si natura negat, facit indignatio versum.*'* There was also Tacitus.

We need not speak of the exile in Patmos who mightily assailed the world as it was with a protest in the name of an ideal world, a huge, visionary satire which cast upon Rome-that-was-Nineveh, Rome-that-was-Babylon, and Rome-that-was-Sodom the thunderous light of his *Revelation*. John on his rock is the Sphinx on its pedestal; he is beyond our understanding; he was a Jew and a Hebrew. But Tacitus, who wrote the *Annals*, was a Latin, and, better still, a Roman.

Since the rule of a Nero is black, it must be blackly depicted. The
* 'Where talent is lacking, anger writes poetry.'

work of the graving-tool alone would be too weak; the lines must be drawn with the acid of a prose that bites deep.

Despots play their part in the works of thinkers. Fettered words are terrible words. The writer doubles and trebles the power of his writing when a ruler imposes silence on the people. Something emerges from that enforced silence, a mysterious fullness which filters through and becomes steely in the thought. Repression in history leads to conciseness in the historian, and the rocklike hardness of much celebrated prose is due to the tempering of the tyrant. The tyrant enforces upon the writer a condensation which is a gain in strength. The Ciceronian periods, scarcely adequate on the subject of Verres, would sound flowery applied to Caligula. Less roundness in the phrase produces more hitting power. Tacitus thinks with clenched fists. The honesty of a great spirit, fined down to justice and truth, is devastating.

It may be remarked in passing that Tacitus was not the historical contemporary of Caesar. His field was the Tiberii. Caesar and Tacitus are successive phenomena whose clash seems to have been mysteriously prevented by the Dramatist who down the centuries decrees entrances and exits. Both were great, and God spared their greatness by not bringing them into collision.* The passer of judgement assailing Caesar might have hit too hard and dealt unjustly with him. God did not desire this. The great African and Spanish campaigns, the rooting out of the Silician pirates, the spread of civilization to Gaul, Britain, and Germany—those are the glories that crossed the Rubicon. There is a kind of delicacy in the divine justice, in its reluctance to let loose the redoubtable historian upon the illustrious usurper, preserving Caesar from Tacitus and allowing genius the benefit of extenuating circumstances.

Certainly despotism is always despotism, even under a despot of genius. There is corruption under the most illustrious of tyrants, but moral depravity is even more abominable under an ignoble tyrant. In those reigns nothing masks the shame, and the pointers of morals, a Tacitus or a Juvenal, can more usefully castigate the vileness that is indefensible in the eyes of men.

Rome had a fouler stench under Vitellius than under Sulla; under Claudius and Domitian there was a manner of baseness corresponding to the baseness of the tyrant. The institution of slavery is a direct product of despotism. A miasma arises from blunted consciences reflecting the mind of the master; public authorities are infamous, hearts shrunken, scruples dulled, souls like crawling

* Prof. Guyard remarks that Hugo was here thinking of the first Napoleon (Caesar) and himself. He was the Tacitus of Napoleon III, that modern Tiberius.

slugs. So it was under Caracalla, under Commodus and Heliogabalus; but the Roman Senator under Caesar exhales only the rank odour proper to an eagle's eyrie. Hence the seemingly late appearance of a Tacitus or a Juvenal: it is when the evil is manifest that its denouncer shows himself.

But Juvenal and Tacitus, like Isaiah in the Old Testament and Dante in the Middle Ages, were individual men, whereas revolt and insurrection are the multitude, which is sometimes right and sometimes wrong.

Most commonly revolt is born of material circumstances; but insurrection is always a moral phenomenon. Revolt is Masaniello, who led the Neapolitan insurgents in 1647; but insurrection is Spartacus. Insurrection is a thing of the spirit, revolt is a thing of the stomach. John Citizen grows angry, and not always without cause. Where it is a question of famine the street uprising—that of Buzançais, for example, in 1847—has a real and moving validity. Nevertheless, it remains no more than an uprising. Why? Because although it has good reason it is wrong in method. It is ill-directed although right, violent although morally powerful; it hits out at random, thunders on like a blinded elephant, crushing everything in its path and leaving behind it the bodies of old men, women, and children. It sheds the blood of innocents, without knowing why. The feeding of the people is a rightful objective, but their massacre is a wrongful means.

All armed acts of protest, however warranted, even those of 10 August and 14 July, take the same course. First come the sound and fury, before the rightful cause emerges. Insurrection itself is no more than a street riot at the beginning, a stream that swells into a torrent. Ordinarily the stream flows into the ocean, which is revolution. But sometimes, pouring down from those mountain heights which dominate our moral horizon, justice, wisdom, reason, law, born of the pure source of idealism, after the long descent from rock to rock, after reflecting the heavens in the limpidity of its waters and being swollen by a hundred tributaries in its splendid show of triumph, the insurrection wastes itself eventually in some bourgeois quagmire, as if the river Rhine were to end in a marsh.

All that belongs to the past; the future is another matter. It is the particular virtue of universal suffrage that it cuts the ground from under the feet of violent revolt and, by giving insurrection the vote, disarms it. The elimination of war—warfare in the streets or warfare across frontiers—is the fruit of progress. Whatever may be happening today, peace is the meaning of tomorrow.

For the rest, whatever the difference may be between insurrection and revolt, the bourgeoisie are little aware of the distinction. For

the bourgeois, both are sedition, rebellion pure and simple, a rebellion of the dog against its master which has to be restrained with chain and collar—until such time as the dog's head, vaguely discernible in the shadows, is found to have grown into the head of a lion. Whereupon the bourgeois cries, 'Long live the people!'

Having thus defined our terms we must ask, how will history assess the events of June 1832? Were they a revolt or an insurrection? They were an insurrection.

It may happen, in the course of our account of that formidable convulsion, that we shall use words such as 'riot' and 'revolt', but this is to describe the facts on the surface, without losing sight of the distinction between revolt in appearance and insurrection in principle.

In its rapid explosion and melancholy suppression, the outburst of 1832 was possessed of such nobility that even those who regard it as no more than a riot cannot talk of it without respect. To them it is like a last echo of 1830. Over-heated imaginations, they maintain, do not cool in a day. Revolution does not come abruptly to an end. There must be a gradual aftermath, further rises and falls, before it settles down into a state of stability, like the lower slopes of a mountain merging into the plain. There are no Alps without their Jura, no Pyrenees without their Asturias.

That pathetic crisis in contemporary history which is known to latter-day Paris as 'the time of riots' was undoubtedly characteristic of the tempestuous occasions in the tale of the present century. We must add a last word before beginning our account of it.

The events to be related belong to that order of vivid and dramatic happenings which historians sometimes pass over for lack of time and space. But it is here, we must insist, that the reality of life is to be found, the stir and tremor of human beings. Small details are as it were the separate foliage of great events, lost to sight in the distant perspective of history. The so-called time of riots abounds in details such as these. And for reasons differing from those of history, the subsequent judicial investigations do not disclose everything, nor, perhaps, have they got to the bottom of everything. We propose to bring to light, amid the known and published details, things hitherto unknown, facts scattered by the forgetfulness of some men and the death of others. Most of the actors in that great drama have vanished; they fell silent upon the morrow; but we can truly say of what we have to relate, 'These are things which we saw'. We shall change certain names, for it is the function of history to chronicle, not to denounce; but we shall depict the truth. Confined within the bounds of the book we are writing, we shall deal with only one aspect and one incident, certainly the least known, of the events of 5 and 6 June 1832; but we shall do it in such a manner as to enable the reader to catch a glimpse, behind the dark curtain that we shall raise, of the true face of that terrible occurrence.

III. *A Burial and a Rebirth*

By the spring of 1832, although for three months cholera had chilled men's spirits and in some sort damped their state of unrest, Paris was more than ripe for an upheaval. The town was like a loaded gun, needing only a spark to set it off. The spark, in June 1832, was the death of General Lamarque.

Lamarque was a man of action and of high repute. Under the Empire and the Restoration he had possessed the two forms of courage required by those two epochs—courage on the battlefield and courage in the debating chamber. He was as eloquent as he had been brave: one sensed the swordthrust in his words. Like Foy, his predecessor, having staunchly borne the command he staunchly upheld the cause of liberty. He took his stand midway between the extremes of left and right, was esteemed by the people as a whole because he faced the hazards of the future and by the crowd because he had loyally served the Emperor. With Counts Gérard and Brouet, he had been one of Napoleon's marshals *in petto*—that is to say, his possible successor in the military command. The treaties of 1815 had outraged him like a personal affront. He detested Wellington with a forthright hatred that pleased the masses; and for seventeen years, taking little note of subsequent events, Lamarque had mourned the tragedy of Waterloo. On his deathbed he had pressed to his heart the sword bestowed on him by his fellow officers of the Hundred Days, and he had died with the word *patrie* on his lips, as Napoleon had died with the word *armée*.

His death, which was not unexpected, had been feared by the people as a loss, and by the Government as a pretext. It was a day of national mourning, and, like all other bitterness, mourning may be transformed into revolt. That is what happened.

On the eve of 5 June, the day fixed for Lamarque's funeral, and on the morning of that day, the Faubourg Saint-Antoine, through which the funeral procession was to pass, assumed a formidable aspect. The crowded network of streets became a hive of activity. Men were arming themselves with whatever they could lay hands on. There were joiners who snatched up the tools of their trade to 'break down doors', or converted them into daggers. One man in a state of bellicose fever had slept in his clothes for three nights. A carpenter named Lombier was accosted by a friend in the street who asked him where he was going. 'I haven't got a weapon,' said Lombier . . . 'So?' . . . 'I'm going to fetch a pair of dividers from my workshop' . . . 'What will you do with them?' . . . 'Blessed if I know.' . . . A man named Jacqueline, a carrier, accosted passing workmen with offers of a drink. Having stood them a glass of wine he asked, 'Have you got a job?' . . . 'No.' . . . 'Well, go to Filspierre, between the Montreuil and the Charronne barriers. There's a job for you there.' There were weapons and ammunition at Filspierre's establishment. Certain recognized leaders 'did the round-up'—went from door to door collecting their followers. In cafés such as Barthélemy, near the Barrière du Trône, Capel, and the Petit-Chapeau, the drinkers enquired of one another, 'Where are you hiding your pistol?' . . . 'Under my jacket.' . . . 'And you?' . . . 'Under my shirt.' . . . There were whispering groups outside workshops in the Rue Traversière and in the courtyard of the Maison-Brûlée. Among the most ardent of the agitators was a certain Mavot, who never stayed more than a week in any one job, being dismissed because the masters found 'one had to be constantly arguing with him'. He was killed the day after the funeral at the barricade in the Rue Ménilmontant. Pretot, who also died in the fighting, was his second-in-command: when asked what his aim was, he answered, 'Insurrection'. A group of workers gathered at the corner of the Rue de Bercy to await a man named Lemarin, the revolutionary agent for the Faubourg Saint-Marceau. Orders were issued almost publicly.

So on 5 June, on a day of alternating rain and sunshine, General Lamarque's funeral procession crossed Paris with full military ceremonial, somewhat swollen by special safety precautions. The escort consisted of two battalions of infantry with draped drums and reversed arms; ten thousand National Guards armed with sabres, and the National Guard batteries of artillery. The hearse was drawn by a team of young men. Invalided officers followed immediately behind it carrying branches of laurel. Then came a motley, excited, numerous crowd, representatives of the *Amis du Peuple*, the Schools of Law and Medicine, refugees from all nations bearing Spanish, Italian, German and Polish flags and banners of all kinds, children waving bunches of greenery, stonemasons and carpenters who were at that moment on strike, printers, recognizable by their paper caps—marching in pairs and in threes, shouting, nearly all carrying cudgels and a few armed with sabres, disorderly yet infused with a single spirit, both a mob and an organized body. The different groups had their own leaders. A man armed with a pair of pistols which he made no effort to conceal seemed to be inspecting them, and the files parted to make room for him. The streets leading to the boulevards, trees, balconies, and windows, all were packed with men, women and children anxiously watching. An armed crowd was on the march while an apprehensive crowd looked on.

Authority was also on the alert, with a hand on its sword-hilt. In the Place Louis XV were four mounted squadrons of carabineers, with muskets and musketoons loaded and full ammunition pouches, ready to go into action with trumpeters at their head; detachments of the Garde Municipale were drawn up in the streets of the Latin Quarter and in the Jardin des Plantes; there was a squadron of Dragoons in the Halle-aux-Vins; the 12th Light Infantry was divided between the Grève and the Bastille; the 6th Dragoons were on the Quai des Célestins and the courtyard of the Louvre was packed with artillery. The rest of the troops were held in reserve in barracks, to say nothing of the regiments on the outskirts of Paris. A disquieted government confronted the threatening multitude with 24,000 soldiers in the town itself and another 30,000 in the environs.

Rumours ran up and down the procession. There was talk of a legitimist conspiracy and of the Duc de Reichstadt, whom God had marked for death at the moment when the crowd was electing him to Empire (he died a few weeks later). Some person who has never been identified announced that when the time came two suborned works foremen would open the doors of an arms factory to admit the mob. The prevailing expression among the majority of the bare-headed spectators was one of mingled ardour and bewilderment, but here and there, amid that multitude so seized with violent but not ignoble emotion, the faces were to be seen of authentic evil-doers, base mouths that talked of loot. There are certain kinds of civil disturbances that stir up the mud at the bottom of the pond, and any experienced police force is aware of the fact.

The procession moved slowly but feverishly along the boulevard from the mortuary chapel to the Bastille. The occasional showers of rain did nothing to deter the crowd. There were a number of incidents. While the coffin was borne round the Vendôme column stones were thrown at the Duc de Fitz-James, who was seen on a balcony with his hat on his head: the Gallic cock, emblem of the July Monarchy, was torn off a standard and trampled in the mud; a police sergeant was wounded with a swordthrust at the Porte Saint-Martin; a party from the École Polytechnique, the students of which had been confined to the school premises, broke out and joined the procession, to be greeted with cries of, 'Long live the École Polytechnique, long live the Republic!' At the Place de la Bastille long and impressive columns of interested spectators from the Faubourg Saint-Antoine added themselves to the procession, and signs of commotion became apparent. A man was heard to say to

174

his neighbour, 'You see that fellow with the red beard? He's the one who'll give the order to shoot'. It seems that this red-bearded man, whose name was Quénisset, was some years later to be involved in another affair, the attempted assassination of the Dukes of Orleans and Aumale.

The hearse passed the Bastille, and, following the canal, crossed the small bridge and came to the esplanade of the Pont d'Austerlitz. Here it paused. A bird's-eye view of the procession at this moment would have displayed a comet with its head at the esplanade and its tail extending over the Quai Bourdon and along the boulevard, across the Place de la Bastille and on to the Porte Saint-Martin. A circle formed round the hearse, and the vast crowd fell silent. Lafayette delivered a farewell address to Lamarque. It was a moving and uplifting moment, with all heads bared and all hearts beating in sympathy. But suddenly a rider on horseback clad in black and carrying a red flag (some say that it was a pike surmounted by a red bonnet) appeared within the circle. Lafayette looked away, and General Exelmans left the procession.

The red flag unloosed a tempest and vanished in it. From the Boulevard Bourdon to the Pont d'Austerlitz a clamour arose from the multitude that was like the rising of a tide. Two tremendous cries were raised—'Lamarque to the Panthéon!' and 'Lafayette to the Hôtel de Ville!' Two parties of young men, amid the applause of the crowd, harnessed themselves and began to drag Lamarque in his hearse across the Pont d'Austerlitz and Lafayette in a fiacre along the Quai Morland.

Meanwhile a detachment of the Cavalerie Municipale had appeared on the left bank and were barring the exit from the bridge, while on the right bank a detachment of dragoons moved along the Quai Morland. The young men dragging Lafayette's fiacre saw these as they debouched on to the *quai* and cried, 'Watch out! Dragoons!' The dragoons advanced grimly and purposefully at a walking pace and in silence, sabres sheathed, pistols in their holsters, musketoons in their rests.

Two hundred paces from the little bridge they halted. Lafayette's fiacre was moving towards them. They parted their ranks to let him through and then closed up behind him. At that moment the dragoons and the crowd were in direct contact. The women ran away in terror.

What happened in that fateful minute? No one will ever know. It was the dark moment when two clouds converge. Some people say that a bugle-call sounding the charge was heard from the direction of the Arsenal, others that a youth attacked one of the dragoons with a dagger. What is certain is that suddenly three shots were fired. The first killed the squadron commander, Cholet; the second killed a deaf old woman in the act of shutting her window in the Rue Coutrescarpe and the third singed an officer's epaulette. A woman cried, 'They're starting too soon!', and suddenly there appeared at the other end of the Quai Morland another squadron of dragoons which had been held in reserve. They galloped with bared sabres down the Rue Bassompierre and the Boulevard Bourdon, clearing a path in front of them.

And that is the whole story. The tempest was unleashed, stones fell like hail, volleys were fired and a mass of people rushed to the river and crossed that narrow arm of the Seine that has since been filled in. The builders' yards on the Île Louviers, that vast, ready-made fortress, bristled with combatants. Stakes were pulled up, pistols fired, a makeshift barricade erected. The young men who had been held up on the Pont d'Austerlitz now crossed the bridge at the double, dragging the hearse, and charged the Garde Municipale. The carabineers came up, the dragoons used their sabres, the crowd scattered in all directions while sounds of war echoed to the four corners of Paris. The cry, 'To arms' rang out and there were clashes everywhere. Fury fanned the uprising as the wind fans a forest fire.

IV. *Earlier Occasions*

Nothing is more remarkable than the first stir of a popular uprising. Everything, everywhere happens at once. It was foreseen but is unprepared for; it springs up from the pavements, falls from the clouds, looks in one place like an ordered campaign and in another like a spontaneous outburst. A chance-comer may place himself at the head of a section of the crowd and lead it where he chooses. This first phase is filled with terror mingled with a sort of terrible gaiety. There is rowdiness and the shops put up their shutters; people take to their heels; blows thunder on barred doors, and servants within enclosed courtyards can be heard gleefully exclaiming, 'There's going to be a bust-up!'

These are the things that happened in different parts of Paris within the first quarter of an hour.

In the Rue-Sainte-Croix-de-la-Bretonnerie a band of some twenty young men, bearded and long-haired, entered a café to re-emerge a minute later carrying a tri-colour flag still wrapped in crêpe, and having three armed men at their head, one carrying a sabre, the second a musket, and the third a pike.

In the Rue des Nonnains-d'Hyères a well-dressed citizen, bald and round-bellied, with a black beard, a bristling moustache and a loud voice, was openly offering cartridges to the passers-by.

Bare-armed men were parading the Rue Saint-Pierre-Montmartre with a black banner on which was inscribed in white letters the legend, 'Republic or Death', and in the Rue des Jeûneurs, the Rue de Cadran, the Rue Montorgueil, and the Rue Mendar there were groups waving flags bearing the word '*section*' and a number in letters of gold. One of these flags was red and blue, separated by a faint white stripe.

An arms factory on the Boulevard Saint-Martin was looted, as were three arms shops in the Rue Beaubourg, the Rue Michel-le-Comte, and the Rue du Temple. Within a few minutes the crowd had secured possession of 230 muskets, nearly all double-loaders, 64 sabres, and 63 pistols. Muskets and bayonets were distributed separately, that more men might be armed.

Young men armed with muskets took possession of apartments overlooking the Quai de la Grève for use as firing-posts. They rang the bell, walked in and set about making cartridges. A woman said afterwards: 'I didn't know they were cartridges until my husband told me.'

A party burst into a curio-shop in the Rue des Vieilles-Haudriettes and helped themselves to scimitars and other Turkish weapons.

The body of a builder's labourer, killed by a musket-ball, lay in the Rue de la Perle.

And on both banks of the river, on the boulevards, in the Latin Quarter and the quarter round Les Halles, breathless men—workmen, students, section-leaders—were reading out proclamations and shouting, 'To arms!' Street-lamps were being smashed, carriages unharnessed, cobblestones torn up, trees uprooted, house-doors battered down, and piles of timber, paving-stones, barrels, and furniture built up into barricades.

The citizenry were forcibly enlisted. Houses were broken into and women forced to surrender any weapons belonging to their absent husbands, and a note of the proceeding was chalked on the door—'Weapons handed over.' Some men even signed a formal receipt for a musket or sabre, saying, 'You can get it back tomorrow at the Mairie'. Isolated sentries and national guards on their way to their local headquarters were disarmed in the streets. Officers had their epaulettes ripped off. An officer of the Garde Nationale, being pursued by a band armed with cudgels and swords, was forced to take refuge in a house in the Rue du Cimetière-Saint-Nicolas from which he was not able to escape until after dark and in disguise.

In the Saint-Jacques quarter students poured out of their lodging-houses up the Rue Saint-Hyacinthe to the Café du Progrès or down to the Café des Sept-Billards in the Rue des Mathurins. Here the young men distributed arms, standing on curbstones outside the doors. The timber-yard in the Rue Transnonain was looted to build barricades. Only in one place did the inhabitants resist, at the corner of the Rues Sainte-Avoye and Simon-le-Franc, where they pulled down a barricade. And in one place the insurgents gave ground. After firing on a detachment of the Garde Nationale they abandoned a half-constructed barricade in the Rue du Temple and fled along the Rue de la Corderie. The detachment found a red flag on the barricade, a bag of cartridges and 300 pistol bullets. They tore up the flag and bore off the fragments on the points of their bayonets.

All these incidents, here slowly related in succession, occurred almost simultaneously in separate parts of the town amid a vast tumult, like a string of lightning flashes in a single clap of thunder.

Within less than an hour twenty-seven barricades had sprung up in the quarter of Les Halles alone. At the centre was the famous House No. 50, which became the fortress of the workers' leader, Jeanne, and his 106 followers, and which, with the Saint-Merry barricade on one side and the Rue Maubuée barricade on the other, commanded three streets, the Rue des Arcis, the Rue Saint-Martin, and the Rue Aubry-le-Boucher, which faced it. Two barricades set at right angles ran from the Rue Montorgueil to the Grande-Truanderie, and from the Rue Geoffroy-Langevin to the Rue Sainte-Avoye. No need to specify the countless barricades in twenty other quarters. There was one in the Rue Ménilmontant with a *porte cochère* lifted off its hinges and another within a hundred yards of the Préfecture de Police on which was an overturned coach.

A well-dressed man distributed money to the workers manning the barricade in the Rue des Ménétriers, and a mounted man rode up to the Rue Grenéta barricade and handed the leader something that looked like a roll of coins, saying, 'This is to cover expenses, wine, and so forth'. A fair-haired young man without a cravat went from one barricade to another passing on orders. Another, wearing a blue police cap and carrying a drawn sabre, was posting sentries. Within the barricades, cafés and porters' lodges were converted for use as guard-posts. In general the uprising conformed to accepted military procedure. The streets it made use of, narrow and with many twists and turns, were admirably chosen, particularly in the neighbourhood of Les Halles, where the network was more tangled than footpaths in a forest. It was said that the *Société des Amis du Peuple* had taken charge of operations in the Sainte-Avoye quarter. A man killed in the Rue du Ponceau was found to have on him a street-map of Paris.

But what had really taken charge of the uprising was a kind of wild exhilaration in the air. While rapidly building barricades, the insurgents had also seized nearly all the garrison-posts. In less than three hours, like a lighted powder-train, they had assailed and occupied, on the Right Bank, the Arsenal, the Mairie in the Place Royale, all the Marais, the Popincourt arms factory and all the streets round Les Halles; and on the Left Bank the Veterans' Barracks, the Place Maubert, the Deux-Moulins powder-factory and all the city barriers. By five o'clock in the evening they were masters of the Place de la Bastille, the Place de la Lingerie, and the Place des Blancs-Manteaux; their patrols were moving into the Place des Victoires and threatening the Banque de France, the Petits-Pères barracks, and the central Post Office. In a word, they held one third of Paris.

Everywhere battle had been joined on the largest scale, and through the disarming of soldiers, house-to-house requisitions and the looting of arms-shops, what had started as a brawl with brick-bats had become an engagement with musketry.

At about six o'clock that evening the Passage du Saumon had become a battlefield, with the insurgents at one end and the military at the other. An observer, the marvelling author of these lines, who had gone to witness the upheaval at first hand, found himself caught between two fires, with nothing but the half-pillars separating the shops to protect him from the bullets. He was pinned in this unhappy position for nearly half an hour.

Meanwhile, the drums were beating and the men of the Garde Nationale were putting on their uniforms, snatching up their arms, and pouring out of houses while the regiments of soldiers marched out of barracks. Opposite the Passage de l'Ancre a drummer-boy received a dagger-thrust, and another, in the Rue du Cygne, was assailed by some thirty youths who destroyed his drum and took away his sabre. Yet another was killed in the Rue Grenier-Saint-Lazare. Three officers died in the Rue Michel-le-Comte, and a number of wounded members of the Garde Municipale beat a retreat along the Rue des Lombards.

A detachment of the Garde Nationale found, outside the Cour Batave, a red flag bearing the inscription, 'Révolution républicaine No. 127'. Was it in fact a revolution?

The uprising had turned the centre of Paris into a vast, labyrinthine citadel. This was its focal point, and it was here that the matter had to be decided. The rest was mere skirmishing: and the proof that this was the real centre lay in the fact that thus far no fighting had gone on there.

The soldiers in certain regiments were of doubtful reliability, and this added to the terrifying uncertainty of the situation. They remembered the popular ovation with which, in July 1830, the neutrality of the 53rd regiment of the line had been rewarded. Two tried veterans of the great wars, Maréchal de Lobau and Général Bugeaud, were in command of the government forces, Bugeaud being subordinate to Lobau. Very large patrols consisting of detachments of regular soldiers flanked by entire companies of the Garde Nationale, and preceded by a Police Commissioner in ceremonial attire, set out to reconnoitre the streets held by the insurgents, while on their side the insurgents stationed outposts at the crossroads and audaciously sent out patrols beyond their barricades. Each side was probing the other. The Government, with an army at its disposal, was hesitant. It would soon be dark, and the Saint-Merry tocsin was beginning to sound.

The then Minister for War, Marshal Soult, who had fought at Austerlitz, was sombrely following the course of events. Oldstagers such as he, warriors accustomed to text-book manoeuvres and having no other guide than orthodox military tactics, are dismayed by the huge and formless blast of public anger. The wind of revolution is not easily controlled.

The suburban units of the Garde Nationale rallied hastily and in disorder. A battalion of the 12th Light Infantry arrived at the double from Saint-Denis; the 14th line regiment came in from Courbevoie; the École Militaire batteries had taken up their station in the Place du Carrousel and the guns were brought in from Vincennes.

The Tuileries were a solitude. Louis-Philippe was entirely calm.

V. *The Uniqueness of Paris*

In the past two years, as we have said, Paris had witnessed more than one upheaval. Outside its rebellious districts nothing as a rule is more strangely untroubled than the face of Paris during an uprising. She very quickly adapts herself—'After all, it's only a riot'—and Paris has too much else to do to let herself be disturbed by trifles. Only the largest of cities can offer this strange contrast between a state of civil war and a kind of unnatural tranquillity. Ordinarily, when the uprising begins, when the drums and the summons to arms are heard, the shopkeeper in another part of the town remarks to his neighbour, 'Seems there's trouble in the Rue Saint-Martin' . . . or 'in the Faubourg Saint-Antoine' . . . and he will very likely add unconcernedly, '—or somewhere that way'. And when later he hears the heartrending sound of musket-fire he comments, 'Seems to be hotting up'.

But then, if the trouble seems to be coming his way, he will hastily shut up shop and don his uniform—that is to say, safeguard his merchandise and risk his life.

There is shooting at a crossroads or in a street or alleyway, barricades are besieged, captured and recaptured, houses are pock-marked with bullets, blood flows, corpses litter the pavements—and two streets away one may hear the click of billiard-balls in a café. Curious onlookers laugh and gossip within a stone's throw of streets echoing with the sounds of war, theatres open their doors and present vaudeville, fiacres proceed along the street with parties on their way to dine, sometimes in the very quarter where the battle is in progress. In 1831 the firing stopped to allow a wedding to pass.

In the uprising of 12 May 1839, an old man in the Rue Saint-Martin, pulling a handcart adorned with a tricolour flag and con-taining bottles of some nondescript beverage, shuttled between the Government forces and the forces of anarchy, offering his wares impartially to either side.

Nothing could be more strange: and this is the peculiar character-istic of Paris uprisings, to be found in no other capital. For such things to happen, two qualities are requisite—the greatness of Paris and her gaiety. It calls for the city of Voltaire and of Napoleon.

But on this occasion, in the battle of 5 June 1832, the great city encountered something that was perhaps even greater than herself. She was stricken with fear. Everywhere, even in the remotest and most 'uninvolved' districts, closed windows and shutters were to be seen in broad daylight. Brave men reached for their weapons, and cowards hid. The heedless and preoccupied pedestrian vanished from the streets, many of which were as deserted as in the small hours of the night. Strange tales were told and terrifying rumours circulated—that *they* had captured the Banque de France—that there were six hundred of them in the Saint-Merry monastery alone, barricaded in the chapel—that the army was not to be trusted—that Armand Carrel had been to see Marshal Clauzel, one of La-marque's pall-bearers, who had said, 'Find me one reliable regiment' —that Lafayette was ill but had nevertheless said to them, 'I'm on your side. I'll go wherever there's room for a chair'—that one had to be on one's guard against bands of pillagers who were looting isolated houses in the less frequented parts of the town (in this last one may discern the vivid imagination of the police, that Ann Radcliffe* of the government)—that a battery of artillery had been installed in the Rue Aubry-le-Boucher—that Lobau and Bugeaud had concocted a plan whereby four columns were to march upon the centre of the insurrection, coming respectively from the Bastille, the Porte Saint-Martin, the Place de la Grève and Les Halles—but

* Author of *The Mysteries of Udolpho*. Trs.

on the other hand that the troops might evacuate Paris altogether and withdraw to the Champ de Mars—that no one knew what was going to happen, but the position was undoubtedly serious—that Marshal Soult's hesitation was disturbing—why did he not attack at once? The old lion was certainly very much perplexed, seeming to discern amid the confusion a monster hitherto unknown.

That evening the theatres did not open. The police patrols were evidently on edge, searching pedestrians and arresting suspects. By nine o'clock more than eight hundred persons had been arrested and the prisons were full to bursting point, the Conciergerie in particular, where the long underground passage known as the 'Rue de Paris' was floored with bales of straw for the accommodation of the dense mass of prisoners whom Lagrange, the revolutionary from Lyon, was boldly haranguing. The rustling of so much straw, under so many bodies, was like the sound of a downpour. Elsewhere the prisoners were in the open air, huddled together in prison yards. There was apprehension everywhere, a tremulousness unusual to Paris.

People were barricading their houses, while wives and mothers waited anxiously for men who did not come home. Occasionally there was a distant rumble of cartwheels, and doorways echoed with a subdued tumult of voices reporting the latest developments— 'That was the cavalry . . . there go the ammunition tenders . . .' The sound of drums and bugle-calls, of sporadic firing; above all the dismal tolling of the Saint-Merry tocsin. The first thunder of cannon-fire was awaited. Armed men appeared at street corners and swiftly vanished, shouting, 'Go home!' Doors were hastily bolted while householders asked each other, 'Where will it end?' With every minute that passed Paris in the gathering dusk seemed more and more ominously tinged with the red glow of revolution.

BOOK ELEVEN

THE STRAW IN THE WIND

I. *The Poetry of Gavroche*

THE MOMENT when rebellion, arising out of the clash between civilians and the military in front of the Arsenal, enforced a backward movement of the crowd following the hearse, which, winding through the boulevards, brought its weight to bear, so to speak, on the head of the procession, was a moment of terrible recoil. The crowd broke ranks and scattered, some uttering bellicose cries, others in the pale terror of flight. The river of humanity filling the boulevards overflowed to left and right, breaking up into lesser streams along a hundred side streets with a sound like the bursting of a dam. At this moment a ragged small boy, coming down the Rue Ménilmontant with a sprig of flowering laburnum which he had picked on the heights of Belleville, noticed in a stall outside an antique shop an old cavalry pistol. Throwing away his flowers, he snatched it up, shouted to the proprietress, 'Missus, I'm borrowing your thingamajig!' and made off with it.

A few minutes later the terrified citizenry making their escape along the Rue Amelot and the Rue Basse found him flourishing his weapon and singing:

> *Nothing to be seen at night,*
> *But in daytime all is bright*
> *And the gentlefolk turn pale*
> *At the writing on the wall.*
> *Do your duty, my fine lads,*
> *Blow away their silly hats!*

Gavroche was going to war. Not until he reached the boulevard did he notice that the pistol had no hammer.

Where did they come from, that marching-song and the many other songs he sang? Who can say? Perhaps he made them up himself. Certainly he knew all the popular ditties of the day, to which he brought his own improvements. Ragamuffin that he was, he sang with the voice of Nature and the voice of Paris, mingling the song of the birds with the songs of the studio. He was well acquainted with art students, a tribe related to his own. He had, it seems, been for three months apprenticed to a printer. He had once run an errand for Monsieur Baour-Lormian, a Member of the Academy. In short, Gavroche was a lettered urchin.

But Gavroche still did not know that when on that stormy night he had offered the hospitality of his elephant to two homeless little boys he had been playing providence to his own brothers. Brothers rescued in the evening, father in the morning, that was how his night had been spent. After leaving the Rue des Ballets in the early hours he had hurried back to the elephant, from which he had skilfully extracted the two children; and after sharing with them the breakfast that he had somehow conjured up he had gone off on his own affairs, entrusting them to the mercy of the streets, his own foster-mother. His parting words had been: 'I'm leaving you now, in other words, buzzing off, or, as they say in polite circles, hooking it. You kids, if you can't find your mum and dad, come back here this evening and I'll fix you up with supper and a bed'. But the two children, whether because they had been picked up by a *sergeant de ville* and taken to the nearest police post, or kidnapped by some street performer, or had simply lost their way in the vast labyrinth of Paris, had not come back. Such disappearances are common enough at the lowest level of our society. Gavroche had not seen them again. In the ten or twelve weeks that had passed he had more than once scratched his head and wondered, 'Where the devil have my two kids got to?'

And now, still flourishing his pistol, he had arrived at the Pont-aux-Choux. He saw that only one shop in the street was open, and, which made the circumstance worthy of note, that this was a pastry-cook's. It was a heaven-sent opportunity to eat one last apple-puff before embarking upon new adventures. Gavroche tapped his clothing and turned out his trouser-pockets, and found nothing, not so much as a sou. He was tempted to cry out in vexation. It is a bitter thing to miss the most delicious of all confections.

He continued on his way, and two minutes later he was in the Rue Saint-Louis. Passing through the Rue du Parc-Royal, and feeling the need to console himself for the loss of the apple-puff, he allowed himself the huge satisfaction of pulling down theatre-posters in broad daylight. A little further on, coming upon a group of well-dressed citizens who looked to him like house-owners, he gesticulated and delivered himself of the following objurgation:

'A fine, plump lot they are, the well-to-do! They do themselves proud. They wallow in rich dinners. Ask them where their money goes and they can't tell you. They've eaten it, that's all—gone with the wind!'

II. *Gavroche goes to War*

To flourish a hammerless pistol in the public street is so splendid a gesture of defiance that Gavroche felt his spirits rising with every step he took. In the intervals of singing bursts of the *Marseillaise* he discoursed as follows:

'All's well. My left foot's sore and I've got the rheumatics, but I'm feeling fine. The gentry have only to listen and I'll sing them revolutionary songs. Who cares for the coppers' narks, they're a lot of dirty dogs. Not that I've anything against dogs. But I wish my pistol had a hammer. I've come from the boulevard, mates, it's getting hot there, things are boiling up nicely. It's time to skim the pot. Forward, lads, and may the furrows run red with traitors' blood! I give my life to *la patrie*, and I shan't be seeing my best girl any more. No more Nini, but who cares? Let's make a fight of it— I've had enough of despotism.'

At this moment the horse of a trooper of the Garde Nationale fell in the street. Gavroche put down his pistol, helped the man up and helped him to get the horse on its feet. He then picked up the pistol and strode on.

All was peace and quiet in the Rue de Thorigny, and its indifferent calm, so proper to the Marais, was in marked contrast to the surrounding tumult. Four housewives were gossiping in a doorway. Scotland has its trios of weird sisters, but Paris has its foursomes of old biddies; and the 'thou shalt be King hereafter' flung at Macbeth on the blasted heath can have been no more ominous than the same words flung at Napoleon in the Rue Baudoyer. The hoarse croaking would have sounded much the same.

The ladies in the Rue de Thorigny were wholly intent upon their own affairs. Three were concierges and one was a *chiffonnière* (garbage-collector, rag-picker, and street-cleaner) with her hook and basket. Between them they seemed to represent the four extremities of age, which are decay, decrepitude, ruin and misery. The chiffonnière was humble. In that doorstep world it was she who made obeisance and the concierge who patronized, and this has to do with the accommodation arrived at between the exactions of the concierge and the compliance of the street-cleaner. There can be good will even in a broom. This chiffonnière was a grateful body, and fulsome in her smiles for the three concierges. Their talk was on the following lines:

'So your cat's still being a nuisance?'

'Well, you know what cats are, the natural enemies of dogs. It's the dogs that make the fuss.'

'Besides people.'

'And yet cat fleas don't get on to people.'

'Besides which, dogs are dangerous. I remember one year there were so many dogs that they had to write about it in the newspapers. It was the time when there were big sheep in the Tuileries, pulling the Roi de Rome in his little carriage. Do you remember the Roi de Rome?'

'The one I liked was the Duc de Bordeaux.'

'Well, I once saw Louis XVIII. I like Louis XVIII best.'

'The way the price of meat has gone up, Mme Patagon!'

'Don't talk of it! Butcher's shops are the limit, a perfect horror. All one can afford are the worst cuts.'

The chiffonnière remarked:

'My business is going from bad to worse. The rubbish heaps are worthless. Nobody gets rid of anything these days, they eat everything.'

'There are some who are worse off than you, Mme Vargoulème.'

'Well that's true,' said the chiffonnière deferentially. 'At least I have a regular position.' And yielding to the love of showing off that exists in all of us, she went on: 'When I got home this morning I cleared out my basket and did the sorting. I've got separate places for everything. Rags in a box, applecores in a bucket, linens in my cupboard, woollens in the chest of drawers, old papers on the window-sill, eatables in the cookpot, bits of glass in the fireplace, slippers behind the door, and bones under the bed.'

Gavroche, who had paused to listen, now inquired:

'Why are you old girls bothering with politics?'

He was met with a four-barrelled volley of abuse.

'Another of those ruffians!'

'What's that he's got in his paw? A pistol!'

'I ask you, a boy that age!'

'They're never happy except when they're going against the law.'

By way of reply Gavroche thumbed his nose with his fingers spread, and the chiffonnière exclaimed:

'Nasty little ragamuffin!'

The lady who answered to the name of Patagon clapped her hands together in outrage.

'There's going to be trouble, that's for sure. The errand boy next door, the one that's growing a beard, I've watched him go past every morning with his arm round a hussy in a pink cap, but this morning it was a musket he had under his arm. Mme Bacheux says there was a revolution last week in—in—well, where was it?— in Pontoise. And look at that little demon, carrying a pistol! It seems that the Rue des Célestins is full of cannons. Well, what do you expect, when the Government has to deal with rascals like him,

always inventing new ways of upsetting everything, and just when things were quietening down after all the trouble we've had. Lord have mercy on us, when I think of that poor Queen that I saw go by in the tumbril! And what's more, it'll send up the price of tobacco. It's monstrous, that's what it is. Well anyway, I'll live to see you guillotined, my fine cocksparrow!'

'Your nose is running, old lady,' said Gavroche. 'Better wipe it.'

And he passed on. At the Rue Pavée the thought of the chiffonnière crossed his mind and he addressed her thus in fancy:

'You shouldn't abuse the revolutionaries, Mother Streetcorner. My pistol is on your side. It's to help you find more things worth eating in your basket.'

There was a sound of footsteps behind him, and he turned to see that Mme Patagon had followed and was shaking her fist at him.

'You're nothing but somebody's bastard!'

'As to that,' said Gavroche, 'I am profoundly indifferent.'

Shortly after this he passed the Hôtel Lamoignon, to which he addressed a ringing appeal: 'On the way, lads—on to battle!'

Then he was seized with melancholy, and looking reproachfully at his pistol he said: 'I'm ready for action, but you won't act.'

He came upon a very thin dog and was moved to sympathy.

'Poor old fellow, you look like a barrel with all the hoops showing.'

He headed for the Orme-Saint-Gervais.

III. *Righteous Wrath of a Barber*

The worthy barber who had driven away the two little boys whom Gavroche had entertained in his elephant was at that moment engaged in shaving a veteran legionary who had served under Napoleon. After discussing the present disorders and the late General Lamarque, they had eventually arrived at the subject of the Emperor. From this had ensued a conversation which a sober citizen with a literary turn might have entitled, 'Dialogue between a Razor and a Sabre.'

'Monsieur,' said the barber, 'how was the Emperor as a horseman?'

'He didn't know how to fall. That's why he never did fall.'

'I'm sure he had very fine horses.'

'I studied the one he was riding the day he pinned the cross on me. It was a racy mare, all white, with ears set wide apart, deep withers, a narrow head with a black star, very long neck, good

187

strong ribs and fetlocks, sloping shoulders and powerful hind-quarters. A little over fifteen hands.'

'A pretty horse,' said the barber.

'Well, it belonged to His Majesty.'

The barber paused, feeling that after this dictum a momentary silence was called for. He then said:

'It's true, is it not, that the Emperor was only once wounded.'

'In the heel. At Ratisbon. I've never seen him so well turned out as he was that day—neat as a new pin.'

'But you, Monsieur, you must have been wounded many times.'

'Oh, nothing to speak of, a couple of sabre-cuts at Marengo, a ball in the right arm at Austerlitz and one in the left thigh at Iéna, a bayonet wound at Friedland, just there, and seven or eight lance wounds at Moskowa, all over the place they were. And at Lützen I had a finger smashed by a shell-burst. Oh, and at Waterloo I got a bit of grape in the thigh. But that's all.'

'How splendid,' rhapsodized the barber, 'to die on the field of battle! I give you my word I'd sooner be killed by a cannon-ball in the belly than die slowly of illness in my bed, with doctors and medicines and all the rest of it.'

'You've got the right idea,' said the soldier.

He had scarcely spoken the words when there was a crash and one of the windowpanes lay shattered on the floor of the shop. The barber turned pale.

'Oh, my God!' he cried. 'There's one now.'

'One what?'

'A cannon-ball.

'Think so?' said the soldier. 'Here it is.' And he stooped and picked up a large stone.

The barber got to the window just in time to see Gavroche making off at top speed towards the Marché Saint-Jean. With the thought of the two forlorn little boys in his mind, he had not been able to resist paying his respects to the barber.

'There, you see!' bellowed the barber, turning from white to crimson. 'They do damage just for the fun of it. What harm have I ever done that young devil?'

IV. *The Boy marvels at an Old Man*

Gavroche, having arrived at the Marché Saint-Jean, where the police post had already been put out of action, proceeded to join forces with a party led by Enjolras, Courfeyrac, Combeferre and

Feuilly. Nearly all were armed, Enjolras with a double-barrelled fowling-piece, Combeferre with two pistols in his belt and a National Guard musket bearing an old regimental number, Jean Prouvaire with an old cavalry musketoon, and Bahorel with a carbine, while Courfeyrac was brandishing an unsheathed swordstick. Feuilly, with a naked sabre in his fist, was striding ahead shouting, 'Long live Poland!'

They had reached the Quai Morland hatless, collarless, breathless and soaked by the downpour, but starry-eyed, when Gavroche went calmly up to them.

'Where are you off to?'

'Join us,' said Courfeyrac.

Behind Feuilly was Bahorel, skipping rather than walking, a fish in the waters of insurrection. He had a crimson waistcoat and, as always, a ready tongue. The waistcoat startled an onlooker, who cried in alarm:

'Here come the Reds!'

'Red—reds!' repeated Bahorel. 'That's a fine thing to be frightened of, Mister. Speaking for myself, I'm not afraid of poppies, and little Red Ridinghood doesn't scare me out of my wits. Take my word for it, leave the fear of red to horned cattle.' He pointed to the most pacific of notices on a nearby wall, a dispensation on the part of the Archbishop of Paris to his flock, informing them that they might eat eggs in Lent. 'Flock!' he exclaimed. 'A polite way of saying geese.'

He tore down the placard and in doing so won the heart of Gavroche, who from that moment never took his eyes off him.

'You were wrong to do that,' Enjolras said to Bahorel. 'You should have left it alone. We've no quarrel with the Church. Don't waste your anger, save it for where it's needed.'

'It's all according to how you look at things,' said Bahorel. 'The clerical tone of voice annoys me. I want to be able to eat eggs without any by-your-leave. You're the cold zealot type, Enjolras, but I'm enjoying myself. And I'm not wasting anything, simply getting up steam. I tore down the placard because, by Hercules, I felt like it.'

The word 'Hercules' struck Gavroche, who was always anxious to learn.

'What does it mean?' he asked.

'It's the Latin for "thunder and lightning",' said Bahorel.

A tumultuous crowd was following them, composed of students, artists, youthful members of the Cougourde d'Aix, navvies and dock-labourers, armed with cudgels and bayonets, and a few, like Combeferre, with pistols in their belts. Among them was an old man who looked very old. He had no weapon and was trotting to keep up, although his expression was vague.

'Who's that?' asked Gavroche.

'Just an old man,' said Courfeyrac.

It was Monsieur Mabeuf.

V. *The Old Man*

We must relate what had happened.

Enjolras and his friends had been on the Boulevard Bourdon near the reserve warehouses, when the dragoons had charged, and Enjolras, Courfeyrac, and Combeferre had been among those who had gone off down the Rue Bassompierre, shouting, 'To the barricades!' On the Rue Lesdiguières they had encountered an old man wandering along the street.

What had attracted their notice was the fact that he was staggering as he walked, as though he were drunk. Moreover, although it had been raining all the morning and was now coming down harder than ever, he was carrying his hat in his hand. Courfeyrac recognized Monsieur Mabeuf, whom he had seen on several occasions when he had accompanied Marius to his door. Knowing the peaceable and more than timid nature of the old bibliophile he was horrified to find him there, hatless in the downpour and amid the tumult of charging cavalry and musket-shots. He had gone up to him and the following dialogue had ensued between them, the twenty-five-year-old rebel and the octogenarian:

'Monsieur Mabeuf, you must go home.'

'Why?'

'There's going to be fighting.'

'I don't mind.'

'Sabre-thrusts and bullets, Monsieur Mabeuf.'

'I don't mind.'

'Possibly cannon-fire.'

'Very well. And where are you going?'

'We're going to overthrow the Government.'

'Good.'

And the old man had joined their column. From then on he had not spoken a word, but his tread had grown firmer and when a workman had offered an arm for his support he had refused it with a shake of his head. He had advanced nearly to the front of the column, his movements those of a man on the march, his eyes those of a man in a dream.

'The old fire-eater!' one of the students exclaimed, and the word went round that he was a former member of the Convention, a regicide.

The column turned into the Rue de la Verrerie. Gavroche, now in the forefront, was singing some doggerel with the full strength of his lungs, so that his voice rang out like a trumpet-call.

> '*Now that the moon is risen high*
> *Into the forest let us fly,*'
> *Said Charlot to Charlotte.*

VI. *Reinforcements*

Their numbers were steadily increasing. They were joined in the Rue des Billettes by a tall, grey-haired man whose bold, vigorous appearance impressed Enjolras and his friends, although none of them knew him. Gavroche, still striding along at the head of the column, whistling, humming, and banging on shop-shutters with his hammerless pistol, had not noticed him.

They went past Courfeyrac's door in the Rue de la Verrerie. 'Good,' said Courfeyrac. 'I came out without my purse and I've lost my hat'. Leaving the party, he ran upstairs to his room, picked up his purse and an old hat, and also seized a large, square box about the size of a suitcase which was hidden under his dirty linen. As he hurried down again the concierge called to him:

'Monsieur de Courfeyrac!'

'Concierge, what is your name?' demanded Courfeyrac.

She was astonished.

'Why, you know it perfectly well. I'm the concierge, Mère Veuvain.'

'Well, if you insist on calling me Monsieur *de* Courfeyrac I shall have to call you Mère *de* Veuvain. And now, what is it you want?'

'There's someone waiting to see you.'

'Who is it?'

'I don't know.'

'Well, where is he?'

'In my lodge.'

'Damn!' said Courfeyrac.

'He's been waiting over an hour,' said the concierge.

At this moment a youth who seemed to be some sort of workman, slight of figure, pale-faced and freckled, wearing a torn smock and patched velveteen trousers, looking rather like a girl dressed in man's garments, came out of the lodge and said in a voice that was not in the least like that of a woman:

'I'm looking for Monsieur Marius.'

'He's not here.'

'Will he be back this evening?'

'I couldn't tell you. I certainly shan't be here myself,' said Courfeyrac.

The youth looked hard at him and asked:

'Why not?'

'Because I shan't.'

'Where are you going?'

'What's that got to do with you?'

'Would you like me to carry your box?'

'I'm going to the barricades.'

'Shall I come with you?'

'If you want to,' said Courfeyrac. 'The streets are open to everyone.'

He ran off to rejoin his friends, and when he had caught up with them gave two of them his box to carry. It was some time before he noticed that the youth had followed him.

A makeshift crowd does not always go where it first intended; it is borne on the wind, as we have said. They passed by Saint-Merry and presently, without quite knowing why, found themselves in the Rue Saint-Denis.

BOOK TWELVE

CORINTH

I. *History of Corinth from its Foundation*

THE PARISIAN of today who enters the Rue Rambuteau from the direction of Les Halles and sees on his right, facing the Rue Mondé-tour, a basket-maker's shop bearing as its sign a basket shaped like the great Napoleon with the inscription, 'Napoleon all made of osier', can scarcely imagine the terrible events witnessed by that place a bare thirty years ago.

This was the site of the Rue de la Chanvrerie, spelt Chanverrerie in old documents, and of the celebrated tavern known as Corinthe.

The reader will recall what has been said about the barricade set up at this point, which was, however, overshadowed by the one at Saint-Merry. It is upon this Rue de la Chanvrerie barricade, the tale of which has now vanished from memory, that we hope to shed some light.

For the purpose of clarity we may revert to the method used in our account of the battle of Waterloo. Any person wishing to visualize with some degree of accuracy the situation of the buildings at that time standing round the Pointe Sainte-Eustache, to the north-east of Les Halles, at what is the entrance to the Rue Rambuteau, has only to imagine a letter N, with the Rue Saint-Denis at one end and Les Halles at the other, its two uprights being the Rue de la Grande-Truanderie and the Rue de la Chanvrerie, and the Rue de la Petite-Truanderie its diagonal line. The old Rue Mondétour cut sharply through all three lines, so that the relatively small rectangle between Les Halles and the Rue Saint-Denis on the one side and the Rue du Cygne and the Rue des Prêcheurs on the other, was divided into seven blocks of houses of different styles and sizes, seemingly set up at random and at all angles, and separated, like the blocks of stone in a builder's yard, by narrow passageways.

'Narrow passageways' is the best idea we can give of those dark, twisting alleys, running between tenements eight storeys high. The buildings themselves were so decrepit that in the Rue de la Chan-vrerie and the Rue de la Petite-Truanderie they were buttressed by wooden beams running from one house-front to the one opposite.

The streets were extremely narrow and the central gutters wide, so that the pedestrian, walking along pavements that were always wet, passed shops like cellars, big, ironbound curbstones, over-large garbage heaps and doorways fortified with wrought-iron grilles. All this has now vanished to make way for the Rue Rambuteau.

The name 'Mondétour' or 'my detour' admirably depicts that labyrinth; and a little further on it was even better represented by the Rue Pirouette, which ran into the Rue Mondétour. The pedestrian going from the Rue Saint-Denis into the Rue de la Chanvrerie found the latter narrowing ahead of him as though he had entered a funnel. At the end of the short street he found his passage barred on the side of Les Halles by a block of tall houses, and might have thought himself in a blind alley if he had not discovered dark alleyways like trenches on either side affording him a way out. This was the Rue Mondétour, running from the Rue des Prêcheurs to the Rue du Cygne and the Rue de la Petite-Truanderie. At the end of this seeming blind-alley, on the corner of the righthand trench, there was a house much lower than the rest that formed a kind of break in the street.

It is in this house, only two storeys high, that three centuries ago a renowned tavern was light-heartedly installed, sounding a note of festivity on a site of which the poet, Théophile, has recorded:

Here swings the awesome skeleton
Of a sad lover who hanged himself.

Being well located, the tavern flourished and was handed down from father to son. In the days of Mathurin Régnier it was known as the Pot-aux-Roses, and, wordplay being fashionable at the time, its sign was a wooden post, or *poteau*, painted pink. In the last century the estimable Charles-Joseph Natoire, one of those masters of fantasy whose works are despised by our present-day realists, adorned the pink post with a bunch of Corinth grapes in celebration of the fact that he had on numerous occasions got mellow at the table where Régnier had got drunk. The delighted tavern-keeper had accordingly changed the name of his establishment and caused the words *Au Raisin de Corinthe* to be painted in gold across the top of the sign. Hence the name 'Corinth'. Nothing pleases the drinking man more than transitions of this kind, mental zig-zags appropriate to the lurching of his homeward-bound feet. The latest tavern-keeper of the dynasty, Père Hucheloup, had so far lost touch with ancient tradition as to have the post painted blue.

A ground-floor room with a bar and an upstairs room with a billiard-table, a spiral staircase through the ceiling, wine on the tables, smoke on the walls, candles in broad daylight—such was the tavern. A trapdoor in the lower room led to the cellar, and the Hucheloup apartment was on the upper storey, being reached by a flight of stairs that was more like a ladder than a stairway, its only entrance a curtained doorway in the ground-floor room. There were also two attics under the roof where the serving women were housed. The kitchen shared the ground floor with the main room.

Père Hucheloup may have been born to be a chemist; he was certainly a cook. People came to his establishment to eat as well as drink. He had invented one particular dish which was to be had nowhere else, consisting of stuffed carp, which he called *carpes au gras*. This was eaten by the light of a tallow candle or a lamp of the Louis XVI period on tables with nailed coverings of waxed muslin in lieu of tablecloths. People came from far and wide. Hucheloup had the notion one day of drawing the attention of the passer-by to his speciality. He dipped his brush in a pot of black paint, and, since his spelling was as original as his cooking, adorned his façade with the following striking announcement: 'CARPES HO GRAS. A freak of heavy rainfall and hail one winter washed out the first S and the G, so that it read CARPE HO RAS. With the aid of wind and weather a plain gastronomic advertisement was thus transformed into the injunction of the poet Horace, '*Carpe horas*'—profit by the hours. From which it appeared that Père Hucheloup, although ignorant of French, had been a master of Latin, and that in seeking to abolish Lent he had become a philosopher. But it was also a plain invitation to step inside.

All that has since vanished. The Mondétour labyrinth was largely done away with in 1847, and probably none of it now remains. The Rue de la Chanvrerie and Corinth have vanished under the cobbles of the Rue Rambuteau.

Corinth, as we have said, was a meeting-place, if not a rallying-point, of Courfeyrac and his circle. Grantaire had discovered it. Having been beguiled first by the '*Carpe horas*' he had gone back for the '*Carpes au gras*', and to eat and drink and argue with his friends. The price was modest. They paid little and sometimes not at all, but were always welcome. Père Hucheloup was a kindly man.

He was also a tavern-keeper with a moustache and a quirky nature. He had a surly look, as though to overawe his regular customers, and he scowled at all comers, seeming more ready to quarrel than to serve them with soup. And yet, we must repeat, all were made welcome. His oddities had brought renown to his establishment, so that young men said to one another, 'Let's go and watch the old man huff and puff.' He had been a master-at-arms. But then suddenly he would explode with laughter: a thunderous voice and a good fellow. He was a comic spirit in gloomy guise; and his fondness for intimidating his guests was like those snuff-boxes that are shaped like pistols—the only detonation was a sneeze.

His wife, Mère Hucheloup, was bearded and extremely ugly.

Père Hucheloup died in 1830, taking with him the secret of the *carpes au gras*. His widow, scarcely to be consoled, continued to preside over the tavern. But the cooking degenerated and became lamentable, and the wine, which had always been poor, became even worse. Nevertheless, Courfeyrac and his friends still went there—'From piety', as Bossuet said.

The widow Hucheloup was short-winded and ill-shaped but she had country memories and country speech. Her manner of telling a tale added a spice to her village and springtime recollections. Her greatest delight, she declared, had been to hear 'the redbreasts twittering in the bushes'.

The room on the upper floor housing the 'restaurant' was a long place cluttered with tables, benches, chairs, stools, and the ancient, ricketty billiard-table. One reached it by way of the spiral staircase, which ended in a square hole in the corner, like a ship's hatchway. Lighted by a single narrow window and a lamp that was always kept burning, it had the look of a lumber-room. Every article of furniture with four legs behaved as though it had only three. The whitewashed walls were unadorned except for the following verse, dedicated to Mère Hucheloup:

> '*She startles at ten yards, at two you feel weak.*
> *There's a wart at the side of her pendulous beak:*
> *One is always afraid that if ever she blows it,*
> *It will come off and fall in her mouth ere she knows it.*'

This was inscribed in charcoal on the wall.

Mère Hucheloup, of whom this was a not unfaithful portrait, spent her days passing unconcernedly in front of this legend. Two waitresses called Matelote and Gibelotte, who had never been known by any other name, helped with laying the tables, fetching the carafes of blue-tinted wine, and dishing up the various messes served to the customers in earthenware pots. Matelote, who was fat, flabby, red-haired and strident of voice, had been the favoured handmaiden of the late Père Hucheloup. Ugly she certainly was, as repulsive as any mythological monster; but, since the servant must always give way to the lady of the house, she was less ugly than Mère Hucheloup. Gibelotte, who was long and thin, pale with a lymphatic pallor, with dark-circled eyes and drooping lids, and was afflicted with what may be termed chronic exhaustion, was always first up in the morning and last to bed at night, gently and silently waiting upon everyone, even her fellow-waitress, and smiling drowsily in her fatigue.

There was a mirror over the bar-counter.

On the door of the restaurant were the words, written in chalk by Courfeyrac: 'Revel if you can and eat if you dare.'

II. *Preliminary Frolics*

Laigle de Meaux, as we know, lodged more often with Joly than elsewhere. He perched there like a bird on a branch. The two friends lived, ate, and slept together, sharing everything, even the girl Musichetta from time to time. On the morning of 5 June they breakfasted at Corinth, Joly with a cold in the head that Laigle was also beginning to share. Laigle's clothes were the worse for wear, but Joly was neatly dressed. They entered the dining room on the first floor at about nine o'clock in the morning, to be welcomed by Matelote and Gibelotte.

'Oysters, cheese, and ham,' Laigle ordered as they sat down. The place was empty except for themselves, but as they were starting on their oysters a head appeared through the stairway hatch and Grantaire said:

'I was passing outside when I caught a delicious whiff of Brie, so here I am.'

Seeing that it was Grantaire, Gibelotte brought two more bottles of wine, making three in all.

'Are you going to drink both bottles?' Laigle asked.

'We're all ingenious, but you alone are ingenuous,' said Grantaire. 'Two bottles never hurt anyone.'

The others had begun by eating, but Grantaire began by drinking and one bottle was soon half empty.

'You must have a hole in your stomach,' said Laigle.

'You've certainly got one in your elbow,' said Grantaire, and having drained his glass he went on, 'My dear Laigle of the funeral oration, that's a very shabby jacket you're wearing.'

'I hope it is,' said Laigle. 'That's why we get on so well together, my jacket and I. It matches its creases with mine, moulds itself to my deformities, adapts itself to my every movement so that I only know it's there because it keeps me warm. Old clothes are like old friends. Have you just come from the boulevard?'

'No, I didn't come that way.'

'Joly and I saw the head of the procession go past.'

'It was a wonderful sight,' said Joly, speaking for the first time.

'And think how quiet this street is,' said Laigle. 'You'd never guess that Paris was being turned upside down. At one time, you know, it was all monasteries round here, monks of all descriptions, bearded and shaven, sandalled and barefooted, black and white, Franciscans, Capuchins, Carmelites, great, small and ancient Augustines . . . The place swarmed with them.'

'Don't talk to me about monks,' said Grantaire. 'The thought of those hair-shirts makes me itch.'

A moment later he uttered an exclamation of disgust.

'I've just swallowed a bad oyster! My hypochondria's starting again. Bad oysters and ugly waitresses, how I hate the human race! I came by way of the Rue Richelieu, past the big public library. The place is like a pile of oyster-shells. All those books, all that paper and ink, all those scribbled words. Somebody had to write them. Who was the idiot who said that man was a biped without a quill? And then I ran into a girl I know, a girl as lovely as a spring morning, worthy to be called April, and the little wretch was in a transport of delight because some poxed-up old banker has taken a fancy to her. The smell of money attracts women like the scent of lilac; they're like all the other cats, they don't care whether they're killing mice or birds. Two months ago that wench was living virtuously in an attic, sewing metal eye-holes into corsets, sleeping on a truckle-bed and living happily with a flower-pot for company. Now she's a banker's doxy. It seems it happened last night, and when I met her this morning she was jubilant. And what's so disgusting is that she's just as pretty as ever. Not a sign of high finance on her face. Roses are better or worse than women in this respect, that you can see when the grubs have been at them. There's no morality in this world. Look at our symbols—myrtle, the symbol of love, laurel, the symbol of war, the fatuous olive-branch, symbol of peace, the apple-tree, which nearly did for Adam with its pips, and the fig-leaf, the first forebear of the petticoat. As for right and justice, shall I tell you what they are? The Gauls wanted Clusium. Rome defended Clusium, asking what harm it had done them. Brennus replied, "The same harm that Alba did you, to say nothing of the Volscians and the Sabines. They were your neighbours; just as the Clusians are ours. Proximity means the same to us as it does to you. You seized Alba and we're taking Clusium." Rome would not allow it and so Brennus seized Rome, after which he cried, "Vae victis!—Woe to the conquered." That's right and justice for you. A world full of beasts of prey, a world full of eagles! It makes my flesh creep.'

Grantaire held out his glass to be refilled and then resumed his discourse, all three of them unconscious of the interruption.

'Brennus, who captured Rome, was an eagle. The banker who

captures a grisette is an eagle of another kind, but one is as shameless as the other. So there is nothing for us to believe in. Drink is the only reality. It makes no odds what your opinions are—whether you're on the side of the skinny fowl, like the Canton d'Uri, or the plump fowl, like the Canton de Glaris—drink. You were talking about the boulevard and the procession and all that. So what of it? There's going to be another revolution. What astounds me is the clumsy means that God employs. He's always having to grease the wheels of events. There's a hitch, the machine isn't working, so quick, let's have a revolution! God's hands are always blackened with that particular grease. If I were he I'd do things more straight-forwardly. I wouldn't be for ever tinkering with the works; I'd keep the human race in order and string the facts together so that they made sense—no ifs and buts, and no miracles. The thing you call "progress" is driven by two motors, men and events. But unfortunately it happens now and then that something exceptional is called for. Whether it's men or events, the run-of-the-mill is not enough; you need geniuses in terms of men, and revolutions in terms of events. Huge accidents are the law, and the natural order of things can't do without them—and when you think of comets you can't help feeling that Heaven itself needs its star performers. God puts up a meteor when you least expect it, like a poster on a wall, or a weird star with an enormous tail attached to it for emphasis. And so Caesar dies. Brutus gives him a dagger-thrust and God sends a comet. Bingo!—And you have the aurora borealis or a revolution or a great man. You have the year '93 in capital letters, Napoleon the star and 1811 at the top of the bill. And a very fine poster it is, midnight blue and studded with tongues of fire. "This remarkable spectacle!" But watch out, you groundlings, because suddenly the whole thing's in ruins, the star and the drama as well. Good God, that's too much—and still it's not enough! These devices, snatched haphazard, they look magnificent but they're really feeble. The fact is Providence is simply playing tricks. What does a revolution prove?—simply that God's at his wits' end. He brings about a coup d'état because there's a break in continuity between the present and the future that He hasn't known how to mend. Which only confirms my theory about the unhappy state of Jehovah's fortunes. When I think of the unease up aloft and here below, the baseness and rascality and misery in Heaven and on earth, extending from the bird that can't find a grain of corn to me that can't find an income of a hundred thousand livres; when I think of human destiny, which is wearing very thin, even the destiny of kings, haunted by the rope like the hanged Prince de Condé; when I think of winter, which is nothing but a rift in the firmament through which the winds

199

break loose, the shreds of cloud over the hilltops in the new blue of the morning—and dew-drops, those false pearls, and frost, that beauty powder, and mankind in disarray and events out of joint, and so many spots on the sun and so many craters in the moon and so much wretchedness everywhere—when I think of all this I can't help feeling that God is not rich. He has the appearance of riches, certainly, but I can feel his embarrassment. He gives us a revolution the way a bankrupt merchant gives a ball. We must not judge any god by appearances. I see a shoddy universe beyond the splendour of the sky. Creation itself is bankrupt, and that's why I'm a malcontent. Today is the fifth of June and it's almost dark; I've been waiting since early morning for the sun to shine. But it hasn't shone yet, and I'll bet you it won't shine all day—an oversight, no doubt, on the part of some under-paid subordinate. Yes, everything is badly managed, nothing fits with anything else, this old world is in a mess and I've joined the opposition. Everything's at odds, and the whole world is exasperating. It's like with children, those that ask don't get, and those that don't need, do. So I'm opting out. Besides, the sight of Laigle de Meaux's bald head afflicts me; it's humiliating to think that I'm the same age as that shiny pate. Well, I may criticize but I don't abuse. The world's what it is. I'm talking without malice, simply to relieve my mind. Be assured, Eternal Father, of my distinguished sentiments. Alas, by all the saints of Olympus and all the gods in Paradise, I was not born to be a Parisian—that is to say, to hover indefinitely, like a shuttlecock bouncing between two rackets, between the lookers-on and the activists. I was born to be a Turk and spend my days watching exquisite girls perform those lubricious oriental dances that are like the dreams of virtuous men; or a well-to-do countryman; or a gentleman of Venice attended by fair ladies; or a German princeling contributing half an infantry soldier to the German Confederation and occupying his spare time with drying his socks on his hedge, that is to say, his frontier. That's what I was really born for. I said a Turk, and I'm not gainsaying it. I don't know why people should be so against the Turks. There was good in Mahomet. The invention of the seraglio with houris and a paradise with odalisques is deserving of our respect. Let us not abuse Mahomedanism, the only creed that includes a hen-roost. I insist on drinking to it. This earth is a great imbecility. And now it seems the fools are going to fight one another, bash one another's heads in, in this month of high summer, when they might be out with a wench in the fields, breathing the scent of new-mown hay. Really people are too stupid. An old broken lantern that I saw the other day in an antique shop put a thought in my mind—it's time to bring light to the human race. And that thought has made me unhappy again. What good does it do to gulp down an oyster or a revolution? Again I'm growing dismal. This hideous old world. We struggle and fall destitute, we prostitute ourselves, we kill each other—and in the end we swallow it all!'

After this prolonged fit of eloquence Grantaire subsided in a fit of coughing, not undeserved.

'Talking about revolution,' said Joly, struggling with his stuffed-up nose, 'it seems that Barius—Marius—is head over heels in love.'

'Does anyone know who with?' asked Laigle.

'No.'

'Marius in love!' cried Grantaire. 'I can imagine Marius in a fog, and he has found himself a mist. He belongs to the tribe of poets, which is as good as saying that he's crazy. Marius and his Marie or Maria or Mariette, whatever she's called, they must be a rum pair of lovers. I can guess what it's like—rarefied ecstasies with kisses all forgotten, chastity on earth and couplings in the infinite. Two sensitive spirits sleeping together amid the stars.'

Grantaire was embarking on his second bottle, and perhaps his second harangue, when a newcomer appeared in the hatchway, a boy less than ten years old, ragged, very small, sallow and pug-faced but bright-eyed, thoroughly unkempt and soaked to the skin, but looking pleased with himself. Without hesitating, although plainly he knew none of them, he addressed Laigle de Meaux.

'Are you Monsieur Bossuet?'

'That's my nickname,' said Laigle. 'What do you want?'

'Well, listen, a tall, fair-haired cove on the boulevard asked me if I knew Mère Hucheloup. "You mean the one in the Rue Chanvrerie, the old man's widow?" I said. "That's right," he said. "I want you to go there and ask for Monsieur Bossuet. You're to give him this message, 'A—B—C.'" I reckon it's a joke someone's playing on you. He gave me ten sous.'

'Joly, lend me ten sous,' said Laigle. 'And you, too, Grantaire.'

So the boy got another twenty sous.

'What's your name?' asked Laigle.

'Navet. I'm a pal of Gavroche.'

'You'd better stay with us,' said Laigle.

'And have some breakfast,' said Grantaire.

'I can't. I'm in the procession. I'm the one that shouts, "Down with Polignac!"'

And dragging one foot behind him, which is the most respectful of all salutations, the lad departed.

'That's a specimen of urchin pure and simple,' said Grantaire. 'There are a lot of varieties. There's the lawyer's *gamin*, known as a *saute-ruisseau*, the cook's *gamin*, or *marmiton*, the baker's *gamin*, or *mitron*—' he reeled off a long list, ending with '—royal *gamin*, or *dauphin*, and holy *gamin*, or *bambino*.'

Meanwhile Laigle was considering.

'A—B—C . . . Meaning, Lamarque's burial.'

'And I suppose the tall fair-haired cove was Enjolras sending for you,' said Grantaire.

'Are we going?' asked Bossuet.

'It's raining,' said Joly. 'I swore to go through fire, but not water. I don't want to make my cold worse.'

'I'm staying here,' said Grantaire. 'Better a breakfast table than a hearse.'

'Very well, we stay where we are,' said Laigle. 'We might as well have some more to drink. Anyway, we can skip the funeral without skipping the insurrection.'

'I'm all in favour of that,' cried Joly.

'We're going on where 1830 left off,' said Laigle, rubbing his hands. 'The people are thoroughly worked up.'

'I care precious little about your revolution,' said Grantaire. 'I don't abominate this government—the Crown made homely with a cotton cap, the Sceptre ending in an umbrella. Come to think of him, in this weather Louis-Philippe can manifest his royalty in two ways, by waving his sceptre over the people and flourishing his umbrella at the gods.'

The room was dark, with dense clouds smothering the daylight. There was no one in the tavern or in the street, everyone having gone off to witness the happenings.

'It might be midnight,' said Bossuet. 'One can't see a thing. Gibelotte, fetch a light.'

Grantaire was sadly drinking.

'Enjolras despises me,' he murmured. 'He said to himself, "Joly's not well and Grantaire's sure to be drunk. I'll send the boy to Bossuet." If he'd come after me himself I'd have gone with him. To the devil with Enjolras, he can have his funeral.'

The matter being thus decided, the three of them stayed in the tavern. By two o'clock that afternoon their table was covered with empty bottles. Two candles were burning, one in a copper candlestick that was green all over and the other in the neck of a cracked carafe. Grantaire had tempted Joly and Bossuet to drink, and they had done something to restore his spirits.

But by midday Grantaire had gone beyond wine, that moderate source of dreaming. To the serious drinker wine is only an appetizer. In this matter of insobriety there is black as well as white magic, and wine is of the latter kind. Grantaire was an adventurous drinker. The black approach of real drunkenness, far from appalling, allured him. He had deserted the wine-bottle and gone on to the *chope*, the bottomless pit. Having neither opium nor hashish to hand, and wanting to befog his mind, he had had recourse to that terrible mixture of eau-de-vie, stout, and absinthe, which so utterly drugs the spirit. Those three ingredients are a dead weight on the soul, three darknesses in which the butterfly life of the mind is drowned; they create a vapour, tenuous yet with the membranous substance of a bat's wing, in which three furies lurk—Nightmare, Night, and Death, hovering over the slumbering Psyche.

Grantaire was still far from having reached that last stage; he was uproariously gay, and Bossuet and Joly were keeping up with him. They raised their glasses in a series of toasts, and to high-flown speech Grantaire added extravagance of gesture. Seated with dignity astride a chair, with his left hand on his knee, the arm akimbo, and his right hand holding his glass, he solemnly addressed the plump waitress, Matelote:

'Let the doors of the palace be flung wide! Let all men become members of the Académie Française and all have the right to embrace Madame Hucheloup. And let me drink!' Then he added, addressing Madame Hucheloup, 'Antique lady, hallowed by custom, draw near that I may gaze upon you.'

'Matelote and Gibelotte,' cried Joly, 'don't for Heaven's sake give Grantaire anything more to drink. He spends money like water. He has squandered two francs ninety-five centimes in reckless dissipation this morning alone.'

'Who is the person,' Grantaire intoned, 'who without my leave has plucked stars from the sky and set them on this table in the guise of candles?'

Bossuet, although very drunk, had remained calm. Seated on the ledge of the open window, with the rain beating on his back, he was gravely contemplating his friends.

But suddenly tumult broke out behind him, the sound of running feet and the cry of 'To arms!' Looking round he saw a party consisting of Enjolras, with a musket, Gavroche with his pistol, Feuilly with a sabre, Courfeyrac with a sword, Jean Prouvaire with a musketoon, Combeferre with a musket, and Bahorel with a carbine. They were proceeding along the Rue Saint-Denis, past the end of the Rue de la Chanvrerie, followed by an excited crowd.

The Rue de la Chanvrerie was short. Making a trumpet of his hands, Bossuet bellowed, 'Courfeyrac! Courfeyrac! Hoy!'

Courfeyrac heard the call and, seeing who it was, turned and advanced a few paces into the Rue de la Chanvrerie. His 'What do you want?' clashed with Bossuet's 'Where are you going?'

'To build a barricade,' shouted Courfeyrac.

'Why not here? This is a good place.'

'You're right, Laigle,' said Courfeyrac.

Beckoning to the others, he led them into the Rue de la Chanvrerie.

III. *Darkness gathers about Grantaire*

The place was indeed particularly suitable, with the wide entrance from the street rapidly narrowing to the bottleneck constituted by Corinth, the Rue de Mondétour easily blocked on either side and direct, frontal attack impossible from the Rue Saint-Denis. Bossuet drunk had had the clear vision of a Hannibal sober.

Dismay gripped the whole street when the newcomers poured in. Casual loiterers took to their heels. In the twinkling of an eye doors were bolted and windows shuttered from one end to the other and from ground-floor to attic, and an old dame had rigged a mattress across her window as a protection against musket-fire. Only the tavern remained open, for the good reason that the party made straight for it. 'May the saints preserve us!' moaned Mère Hucheloup.

Bossuet had run down to greet Courfeyrac while Joly shouted to him from the window:

'Why haven't you got your umbrella? You'll catch cold like me.'

Within a few minutes twenty iron bars had been wrenched out of the tavern's window-grilles and street cobbles and paving-stones had been torn up over a distance of perhaps a dozen yards. A cart containing three barrels of lime, the property of a lime-merchant named Anceau, had been overturned by Gavroche and Bahorel, and the barrels had been surrounded by piles of paving-stones and flanked by empty wine-casks which Enjolras had brought up from Mère Hucheloup's cellar. Feuilly, with hands more accustomed to decorating the fragile blades of fans, had buttressed the whole with solid heaps of stone, procured no one knew where, and the large timbers used to prop up a nearby housefront had been laid across the casks. By the time Bossuet and Courfeyrac desisted from their labour half the street was blocked with a rampart higher than a man. Nothing can exceed the zeal of the populace when it is a matter of building up by pulling down.

The two waitresses had joined in the work, Gibelotte going to and fro with loads of rubble. Her weariness was equal to any task. She served paving-stones as she might have served bottles of wine, still looking half asleep.

An omnibus drawn by two white horses appeared at the end of the street. Climbing on the barricade, Bossuet ran after it, ordered the driver to pull up and the passengers to get out. After assisting the ladies to descend he dismissed the driver and brought the omnibus back with him, leading the horses. 'No omnibus,' he said, 'is allowed to pass Corinth. *Non licet omnibus adire Corinthum.*'

The horses were unharnessed and turned loose along the Rue Mondétour, and the omnibus, pushed over on its side, made a useful addition to the barricade.

The distraught Mère Hucheloup had taken refuge on the upper floor, where she sat gazing wild-eyed at these proceedings and muttering about the end of the world. Joly deposited a kiss on her thick red neck and remarked to Grantaire: 'You know, I have always considered a woman's neck a thing of infinite delicacy.'

But Grantaire had now achieved the highest flights of dithyramb. When Matelote came upstairs he grabbed her round the waist and then bellowed with laughter out of the window.

'Matelote is ugly!' he shouted. 'Matelote is a dream of ugliness, a chimera! I will tell you the secret of her birth. A gothic Pygmalion carving cathedral gargoyles fell in love with one of them. He besought the God of Love to bring the stone to life, and that was Matelote. Look at her, everyone! She has hair the colour of lead-oxide, like Titian's mistress, and she's a good wench. I guarantee she'll fight well; there's a hero in every good wench. As for Mère Hucheloup, she's a sturdy old soul. Look at that moustache, inherited from her husband; a real hussar, she is, and she'll fight too. These two alone will terrify the neighbourhood. Comrades, we're going to throw out the Government and that's the truth, as true as the fact that between margaric acid and formic acid there are fifteen intermediate acids. Not that I care a straw about that. My father always abominated me because I couldn't understand mathematics. The only things I understand are love and liberty. I'm good old Grantaire. Never having had any money I've never got into the way of having it and so I've never missed it; but if I'd been rich, no one else would have been poor. You'd have seen! This would be a far better world if the generous hearts had the fat purses. Think of Jesus Christ with Rothschild's fortune, the good he'd have done! Matelote, come and kiss me. You are sensual and shy. You have cheeks which call for a sister's kiss and lips which call for a lover.'

'Stow it, you wine-cask!' said Courfeyrac.

'I am High Magistrate and Master of Ceremonies!' proclaimed Grantaire.

Enjolras, who was standing on the barricade, musket in hand, looked sternly round at him. Enjolras, as we know, was a Spartan and a puritan. He would have died with Leonidas at Thermopylae or massacred the garrison of Drogheda with Cromwell.

'Grantaire,' he called, 'go and sleep your wine off somewhere else. This is a place for intoxication but not for drunkenness. Don't dishonour the barricade.'

The sharp rebuke had a remarkable effect on Grantaire, as though he had received a douche of cold water. Suddenly he was sober. He sat down with his elbows on a table by the window, and looking with great sweetness at Enjolras called back:

'You know I believe in you.'

'Go away.'

'Let me sleep it off here.'

'Go and sleep somewhere else,' said Enjolras.

But Grantaire, still regarding him with troubled, gentle eyes, persisted:

'Let me sleep here, and if need be, die here.'

Enjolras looked scornfully at him.

'Grantaire, you're incapable of believing or thinking or willing or living or dying.'

'You'll see,' said Grantaire gravely. 'You'll see.'

He muttered a few more unintelligible words; then his head fell heavily on the table and—a not uncommon effect of the second stage of inebriety, into which Enjolras had so harshly thrust him— fell instantly asleep.

IV. *Efforts to console Mère Hucheloup*

Bahorel, delighted with the barricade, exclaimed:

'Now the street's stripped for action. Doesn't it look fine!'

Courfeyrac, while partly demolishing the tavern, was doing his best to comfort the proprietress.

'Mère Hucheloup, weren't you complaining the other day that someone brought a charge against you because Gibelotte shook a rug out of the window?'

'That's true, Monsieur Courfeyrac . . . Saints preserve us, are you going to put that table on your horrible pile as well? . . . It was for the rug and a flower-pot that fell out of the attic window into the street. The Government fined me a hundred francs. Don't you think that is disgraceful?'

'Mère Hucheloup, we will avenge you.'

Mère Hucheloup seemed doubtful of the practical value of this vengeance, in which she resembled the Arab woman who complained to her father that her husband had smacked her face. 'You must pay him back, father—an affront for an affront.' . . . 'Which cheek did he smack?' . . . 'The left.' . . . The father thereupon smacked her right cheek. 'There you are. You can tell your husband that he chastised my daughter and I have chastised his wife.'

The rain had stopped and new recruits were arriving. Workmen brought in kegs of gunpowder under their overalls, a basket containing bottles of vitriol, some carnival torches and a hamper filled with fairy-lights 'left over from the king's birthday', a festival of fairly recent date, having taken place on 1 May.

These munitions were said to have come from a grocer named Pépin in the Faubourg Saint-Antoine. The single street-lamp in the Rue de la Chanvrerie was smashed, as were the lamps in surrounding streets.

Enjolras, Combeferre, and Courfeyrac were directing all operations. A second barricade was going up at the same time, both barricades flanked by the Corinth tavern and set at right angles. The larger of the two blocked the Rue de la Chanvrerie, while the other blocked the Rue Mondétour on the Rue de la Cygne side. This second barricade was very narrow, being constructed only of barrels and paving-stones. They were manned by about fifty workers, some thirty of whom were equipped with muskets, having raided an armourer's shop on the way.

The rebels were an ill-assorted and motley crowd. One man, wearing a short, formal jacket, was armed with a cavalry sabre and two saddle-pistols; another, in his shirtsleeves, wore a billycock hat and had a powder-bag slung round his neck, and a third had made himself a breastplate of nine sheets of packing paper and carried a saddler's bradawl. One man was shouting, 'Let us die to the last man, bayonet in hand!'—as it happened, he had no bayonet. Another, clad in a frock-coat, was equipped with the belt and ammunition-pouch of the Garde Nationale, the latter stamped with the words, 'Public Order'. There were a good many muskets bearing regimental numbers, very few hats, no neckties, a great many bare arms and a few pikes—and their bearers were men of all ages and varieties, from pallid youths to burly, weather-beaten dock-labourers. All were working feverishly while at the same time they discussed their prospects—that help would arrive between two and three in the morning, that they could count on such-and-such a regiment, that the whole of Paris would rise—dire prediction mingled with a kind of bluff joviality. They might have been brothers, although they did not know one another's names. It is the ennobling quality of danger that it brings to light the fraternity of strangers.

A fire had been lighted in the kitchen, and pitchers, spoons, and forks, in short all the metal-ware in the establishment, were being melted down for casting into bullets. Drink was circulating everywhere. Percussion caps and small-shot were scattered amid wine glasses over the tables. In the upstairs room Mère Hucheloup, Matelote, and Gibelotte, variously affected by their state of alarm, the first dazed, the second breathless and the third, at last, wide awake, were tearing up old rags for dressings assisted by three of the rebels, three hairy and bearded stalwarts who worked with uncommon deftness and quite over-awed them.

The tall man whom Courfeyrac, Combeferre, and Enjolras had noticed when, uninvited, he joined their party at the corner of the Rue des Billettes, was doing useful work on the larger barricade. Gavroche was working on the smaller. As for the youth who had called at Courfeyrac's lodging asking for Marius, he had disappeared at about the time when the omnibus was overturned.

Gavroche, radiantly in his element, seemed to have constituted himself overseer. He bustled to and fro, pushing, pulling, laughing, and chattering as though it was his function to keep up everyone's spirits. What spurred him on, no doubt, was his state of homeless poverty; but what lent him wings was sheer delight. He was like a whirlwind, constantly to be seen and always to be heard, filling the air with the sound of his excited voice. His seeming ubiquity acted as a kind of goad; there was no pausing when he was by. The whole working-party felt him on its back. He disconcerted the dawdlers, roused the idlers, stimulated the weary, and exasperated the more thoughtful, amusing some and enraging others, exchanging banter with the students and epithets with the working-men; he was here, there, and everywhere, a gadfly buzzing about the lumbering revolutionary coach.

'Come on now, we want more paving-stones, more barrels, more of everything. Let's have a basket of rubble to stuff up that hole. This barricade's still not big enough, it's got to be higher. Shove everything on it, break up the house if necessary. Hullo, there's a glass-paned door!'

'So what are we going to do with a glass-paned door, my young lummox?' a workman demanded.

'Lummox yourself. A glass-paned door is a very good thing to have on a barricade—easy to attack, but not so easy to get past. Haven't you ever tried stealing apples over a wall with broken glass on top? Nothing like a bit of glass for cutting the soldiers' arms. The trouble is, you've no imagination, you lot.'

But what really worried Gavroche was his hammerless pistol. He went about exclaiming: 'A musket! I must have a musket! Why will no one give me a musket?'

'A musket at your age?' said Combeferre.

'And why not? I had one in 1830, when we kicked out Charles X.'

'When there are enough for all the men we'll start handing them out to the children,' said Enjolras, shrugging his shoulders.

Gavroche turned upon him and said with dignity:

'If you're killed before me I shall take yours.'

'Urchin!' said Enjolras.

'Greenhorn!' said Gavroche.

The sight of a dandified young man straying in bewilderment past the end of the street created a diversion. Gavroche shouted:

'Come and join us, mate! Aren't you ready to do a turn for your poor old country?'

The young man fled.

V. *The Preparations*

The newspapers of the day, which reported that the 'almost unassailable' barricade in the Rue de la Chanvrerie reached the level of the second storey, were in error. The fact is that it was nowhere more than six or seven feet high, and so constructed that the defenders could shelter behind it or peer over it or climb on top of it by means of four piles of superimposed paving stones arranged to form a broad flight of steps. The outer side of the barricade, consisting of paving-stones and barrels reinforced by wooden beams and planks interlaced in the wheels of the cart and the overturned omnibus, had a bristling, unassailable appearance. A gap wide enough for a man to pass through had been left at the end furthest from the tavern to afford a means of exit. The shaft of the omnibus had been set upright and was held in position with ropes. It had a red flag affixed to it which fluttered over the barricade.

The small Mondétour barricade was not visible from that side, being concealed behind the tavern. Between them the two barricades constituted a formidable stronghold. Enjolras and Courfeyrac had not seen fit to barricade the other section of the Rue Mondétour, affording an outlet to Les Halles by way of the Rue des Prêcheurs, no doubt because they wished to preserve a means of communication with the outside world and considered that an attack by way of that tortuous alleyway was unlikely.

With the exception of this outlet, which might be technically termed a *boyau*, or communicating trench, and the narrow gap in the Rue de la Chanvrerie, the area enclosed by the two barricades, with the tavern forming a salient between them, was in the shape of an irregular quadrilateral, sealed on all sides. The distance between the main barricade and the tall houses behind it, facing the street, was about twenty yards, so that it could be said that the barricade was backed on to those houses, all of which were occupied but bolted and shuttered from top to bottom.

All this work was completed without interruption in less than an hour, and without the handful of intrepid defenders catching sight of a bearskin or bayonet. The few citizens who at that stage of the uprising ventured into the Rue Saint-Denis after glancing along the Rue de la Chanvrerie and seeing the barricade, went hurriedly on their way.

When both barricades were completed and the flag had been hoisted, a table was brought out of the tavern and Courfeyrac climbed on to it. Enjolras brought out the square box and Courfeyrac opened it. It was filled with cartridges, and at the sight of these even the stoutest hearts quivered and there was a momentary silence. Courfeyrac, smiling, proceeded to pass them out.

Every man was issued with thirty cartridges. Those who had brought powder with them set about making more, using the bullets that were being cast in the tavern. As for the barrel of powder, this was placed handy to the door and kept in reserve.

The roll of drums calling the forces of law and order to arms was sounding throughout Paris, but by now it had become a monotonous background noise to which no one paid any attention. It rose and fell, drawing nearer and receding, with a dismal regularity.

Together and without haste, with a solemn gravity, they charged muskets and carbines. Enjolras posted three sentinels outside the stronghold, in the Rue de la Chanvrerie, the Rue des Prêcheurs, and the Rue de la Petite-Truanderie. Then, with the work done, the weapons loaded and the orders given, alone in those gloomy, narrow streets where now there were no strollers, surrounded by silent houses in which there was no stir of human life, plunged in the gathering shadows of the dusk, amid a silence in which the approach of tragic and terrible events could be felt, isolated, armed, resolute and calm, they waited.

VI. *Waiting*

What did they do during those hours of waiting? We must tell of this, since this, too, is history.

While the men were busy making cartridges and the women busy with their bandages, while the lead for musket-balls was bubbling in a large cooking-pot on the stove, while armed look-outs kept guard on the barricades and Enjolras, whom nothing could distract,

inspected his dispositions, Combeferre, Courfeyrac, Jean Prouvaire, Feuilly, Bossuet, Joly, Bahorel, and a few others gathered together as though this were the most peaceful of student occasions, and, seated within a few feet of the defences they had built, with their loaded weapons leaning against their chairs, in a corner of the tavern which they had transformed into a fortress, these gallant young men, brothers in this supreme moment of their lives, recited love-poems.

> *Do you recall how life was kind*
> *When youth and hope still filled our breast,*
> *And we'd no other thought in our mind*
> *Than to be lovers and well-dressed?*
>
> *When your age added in with mine*
> *Made forty by our reckoning;*
> *And, paupers, we did not repine,*
> *For every winter's day was spring.*
>
> *Brave days of modesty and pride,*
> *When Paris was a lover's feast!*
> *I brought you flowers at Eastertide,*
> *And pricked my finger on your breast.*
>
> *And men's eyes watched you with desire*
> *When in the crowded streets we strolled.*
> *Your beauty was a living fire*
> *That had no thought of growing old;*
>
> *No thought of strife and angry men,*
> *Heads bowed beneath the tyrant's rod . . .*
> *When first I kissed you, it was then,*
> *Ah, then I believed in God . . .*

The time and place, the youthful recollections, the first stars showing in the sky, the funereal quiet of those deserted streets and the inexorable approach of desperate adventure, all this lent a touching pathos to the verses, and there were many of them, recited low-voiced in the dusk by Jean Prouvaire, who, as we know, was a poet.

Meanwhile, a fairy-light had been set on the small barricade, and on the larger one a wax torch of the kind that one sees on Mardi-Gras preceding carriages bearing masked revellers on their way to the ball. These torches, we may recall, had come from the Faubourg Saint-Antoine. The torch had been placed in a kind of enclosure made of paving-stones, which sheltered it on three sides from the wind, but left the fourth side open so that its light fell on the red flag. The street and the barricade remained in darkness, with nothing visible except that flag, lighted as though by a dark lantern, the rays of which lent to the crimson of the flag an ominous purple tinge.

VII. *The Recruit from the Rue des Billettes*

Night fell, but nothing happened. Only a confused, distant murmur was to be heard, broken occasionally by bursts of musket-fire, but these were rare, meagre, and remote. The prolonged pause was a sign that the Government was taking its time and assembling its forces. Those fifty men were awaiting the onslaught of sixty thousand.

Enjolras was seized with the impatience that afflicts strong characters on the threshold of great events. He went to look for Gavroche, who was now making cartridges in the downstairs room by the uncertain light of two candles set from precaution on the bar-counter because of the powder scattered over the tables. Their light was not visible from outside, and the rebels had also been at pains to ensure that there was no light on the upper floors.

Gavroche was very much preoccupied at that moment, but not precisely with cartridges. The man who had joined them in the Rue des Billettes had come into the downstairs room and seated him-self at a table in the darkest corner. He had been issued with a large-bore musket, which was now propped between his knees. Until that moment Gavroche, his attention distracted by a thousand fascin-ating matters, had not so much as looked at him. He did so auto-matically when he entered the room, admiring the musket; but then, as the man sat down, he got to his feet. Anyone who had been watching the man until that moment might have noticed that he was observing everything around him, everything to do with the barricades and the rebel band, with a singular intentness; but from the moment when he entered the room he seemed to withdraw into himself and to take no further interest in what was going on. Gavroche, drawing nearer, walked round the detached and brooding figure with extreme caution, going on tiptoe like someone anxious not to awaken a sleeper. At the same time a series of expressions passed over his youthful countenance that was at once so impudent and so eager, so volatile and so profound, so gay and so heart-rending, a series of grimaces like those of an aged man communing with himself—'Rubbish! . . . It's not possible . . . I'm seeing things. I'm dreaming . . . Could it possibly be . . .? No, it can't be!' And Gavroche, rocking on his feet with his fists clenched in his pockets, head and neck wagging like the neck of a bird, expressed in an exaggerated pout all the sagacity of his lower lip. He was at once astounded, sceptical, convinced, and amazed; he had the look of a Chief Eunuch at the slave-market discovering a Venus among the offerings, or an art-lover coming upon a Raphael in a pile of discarded canvases. Every faculty was at work, the instinct that scents and the wits that contrive. Clearly something tremendous had happened to Gavroche.

And it was at this moment that Enjolras came up to him.

'You're small enough,' Enjolras said. 'You won't be noticed. I want you to slip out along the housefronts, out into the streets, and come back and tell me what's going on.'

Gavroche flung back his head.

'So we're good for something after all, us little 'uns. Well, that's fine. I'll do it. You trust the little 'uns, guv'nor, but keep an eye on the big 'uns. For instance, that one there.' He had lowered his voice as he nodded towards the man from the Rue des Billettes.

'What about him?'

'He's a police spy, a copper's nark.'

'You're sure?'

'He picked me up less than a fortnight ago by the Pont Royal, where I was having a stroll.'

Enjolras hurriedly left him and said a word in the ear of a dock-labourer who happened to be near. The man left the room and returned almost instantly with three others. The four men, four burly stevedores, grouped themselves unobtrusively round the table at which the man from the Rue des Billettes was seated, evidently ready to fling themselves upon him. Enjolras then went up to him and asked:

'Who are you?'

The abrupt question caused the man to start. Looking hard into Enjolras's eyes, he seemed to discern exactly what was in his mind, and smiling the most disdainful, unabashed, and resolute of smiles he answered:

'I see how it is . . . Yes, I am.'

'You're a police informer?'

'I'm a representative of the law.'

'And your name?'

'Javert.'

Enjolras nodded to the four men. Before Javert had time to move he was seized, overpowered, bound, and searched. A small round card was found on him, enclosed between two pieces of glass and bearing on one side the words 'Surveillance et Vigilance', and on the other the following particulars: 'Javert, Inspector of Police, aged

52' signed by the Prefect of Police of the time, M. Henri-Joseph Gisquet.

He also had a watch on him and a purse containing a few gold pieces. These were restored to him. But at the bottom of his watch-pocket was a scrap of paper in an envelope on which were his orders, written in the Prefect's own hand.

'Having fulfilled his political mission Inspector Javert will endeavour to confirm the truth of the report that the miscreants have places of resort on the right bank of the Seine, near the Pont d'Iéna.'

After being searched Javert was stood upright with his hands tied behind his back and bound to the wooden pillar in the centre of the room that had given the tavern its original name.

Gavroche, who had intently followed the proceedings, nodding his head in approval, now addressed Javert:

'So the mouse has caught the cat!'

Everything had happened so swiftly that it was all over before the news became known. Javert had not uttered a sound. Hearing what had happened, Courfeyrac, Bossuet, Joly, Combeferre, and some of the men on the barricades came trooping in. Javert, so securely lashed to the post that he could not move, confronted them with the cool serenity of a man who has never in his life told a lie.

'He's a police spy,' said Enjolras. And to Javert he said: 'You will be shot two minutes before the barricade falls.'

'Why not now?' Javert inquired with the utmost composure.

'We don't want to waste ammunition.'

'You could use a knife.'

'Policeman,' said the high-minded Enjolras, 'we are judges, not murderers.' He gestured to Gavroche. 'You! Get started. Do what I told you.'

'I'm off,' said Gavroche.

But at the door he paused.

'Anyway, let me have his musket. I'm leaving you the musician, but I'd like to have his trumpet.'

He made them a military salute and slipped happily through the gap in the large barricade.

VIII. *Questions regarding a Man called Le Cabuc*

The tragic picture we are printing would be incomplete, the reader would not see in their true proportions those momentous hours of civic travail and revolutionary birth wherein confusion was mingled with noble striving, were we to omit from this summary account the incident of epic and savage horror which took place almost immediately after the departure of Gavroche.

Crowds gather and then, as we know, grow like rolling snowballs, attracting violent men who do not ask each other where they come from. Among those who joined the contingent led by Enjolras and the others, there was a man in worn labourer's clothes whose wild shouts and gestures were those of an uncontrolled drunkard. This man, who went by the name of Le Cabuc, but who was in reality quite unknown to the people who pretended to recognize him and who was either very drunk or pretending to be, had seated himself with several others at a table which they had dragged out of the tavern. While encouraging his companions to drink he seemed to be surveying the house at the back of the barricade, a five-storey house, looking along the street to the Rue Saint-Denis. Suddenly he cried:

'You know what, comrades? That house is the place to shoot from. With marksmen at all the windows, devil a soul could come along the street!'

'But the house is shut.'

'We can knock, can't we?'

'They won't open.'

'Then we'll break down the door.'

The door had a massive knocker. Le Cabuc went and hammered on it, without result. He knocked a second and a third time, but there was still no response.

'Is anyone in?' shouted Le Cabuc.

Silence.

So then he picked up a musket and hammered on the door with the butt. It was an old-fashioned arched doorway, low and narrow, the door made solidly of oak, lined with sheet metal and reinforced with iron bands, a real fortress door. The blows of the musket-butt shook the house but left the door unshattered. However, they had evidently alarmed the inmates, because eventually a light showed and a small window on the third floor opened to disclose the grey head of a man who was presumably the doorkeeper.

'Messieurs,' he asked, 'What do you want?'

'Open the door!' shouted Le Cabuc.

'I'm not allowed to, Monsieur.'

'Do it all the same.'

'Out of the question.'

Le Cabuc levelled his musket, aiming at the man's head; but since he was standing in the street, and it was very dark, the doorkeeper did not see him.

'Are you going to open, or aren't you?'

'No, Monsieur.'

'You refuse?'

'I do, my good——'

The sentence was cut short by the report of the musket. The ball took the old man under the chin and travelled through his neck, severing the jugular vein. He sank forward without a sound, and the candle he had been holding fell from his hand and went out. Nothing was now to be seen but a motionless head resting on the window-ledge and a rising wisp of smoke.

'There you are!' said Le Cabuc, grounding his musket on the cobbles.

Scarcely had he uttered the words than a hand fell on his shoulder, gripping it as tightly as an eagle's talon, and a voice said:

'On your knees!'

He turned to confront the white, cold face of Enjolras, who had a pistol in his other hand. He had been brought out at the sound of the shot.

'On your knees,' he repeated; and with an imperious gesture the slender youth of twenty, compelling the muscular broad-shouldered dock-worker to bend like a reed before him, forced him to kneel in the mud. Le Cabuc tried to resist, but seemed to be in the grip of a superhuman power. Enjolras, with his girlish face, his bare neck and untidy hair, had at that moment something of the look of an antique god. The dilated nostrils and glaring eyes conferred upon his implacable Greek countenance that expression of chaste and righteous anger which in the ancient world was the face of justice.

The men on the barricades had come hurrying to the scene and now stood silently a short distance away, finding it impossible to utter any word of protest at what was about to take place.

Le Cabuc, wholly subdued, made no further attempt to struggle. He was now trembling in every limb. Enjolras released his hold on him and got out his watch.

'Pull yourself together,' he said. 'Pray or ponder. You have one minute.'

'Mercy!' the murderer gasped, and then, with his head bowed, fell to muttering inarticulate profanities.

Enjolras did not take his eyes off his watch, and when the minute had passed he returned it to his pocket. He gripped Le Cabuc by the hair, and as the man knelt screaming pressed the muzzle of the pistol to his ear. Many of those hot-blooded men, who had so lightly engaged upon a desperate enterprise, turned away their heads.

The shot rang out, the murderer fell face down on the cobbles, and Enjolras, straightening, gazed sternly and assuredly about him. He thrust aside the body with his foot and said:

'Get rid of that.'

Three men picked it up, still twitching in its last death-throes, and flung it over the smaller barricade into the Rue Mondétour.

Enjolras stayed deep in thought, and who shall say what fearful shadows were massing behind his outward calm. Suddenly he raised his voice, and there was silence.

'Citizens,' said Enjolras, 'what that man did was abominable and what I have done is horrible. He killed, and that is why I killed. I was obliged to do it, for this rebellion must be disciplined. Murder is an even greater crime here than elsewhere. We are under the eyes of the revolution, priests of the republic, the tokens of a cause, and our actions must not be subject to calumny. Therefore I judged this man and condemned him to death. But at the same time, compelled to do what I did but also abhorring it, I have passed judgement on myself, and you will learn in due course what my sentence is.'

A quiver ran through his audience.

'We will share your fate,' cried Combeferre.

'It may be,' said Enjolras. 'I have more to say. In executing that man I bowed to necessity. But the necessity was a monster conceived in the old world, and its name is fatality. By the law of progress, this fatality must give way to fraternity. This is a bad moment for speaking the word "love"; nevertheless I do speak it, and glory in it. Love is the future. I have had resort to death, but I hate it. In the future, citizens, there will be no darkness or lightnings, no savage ignorance or blood-feuds. Since there will be no Satan there will be no Michael. No man will kill his fellow, the earth will be radiant, mankind will be moved by love. That time will come, citizens, the time of peace, light, and harmony, of joy and life. It will come. And the purpose of our death is to hasten its coming.'

Enjolras fell silent. His virgin lips closed, and he remained for some moments standing like a statue on the spot where he had shed blood, while his steadfast gaze subdued the murmur of voices about him. Jean Prouvaire and Combeferre silently clasped hands and, standing together at the corner of the barricade, gazed in admiration mingled with compassion at the stern-faced young man who was at once priest and executioner, shining like a crystal but unshakeable as a rock.

We may say here that when, after the business was over, the bodies were taken to the morgue and searched, a police-card was found on Le Cabuc. In 1848 the author of this work saw the special report on this episode delivered to the Prefect of Police in 1832.

It may be added that, according to a police surmise which seems to have been not without substance, Le Cabuc was Claquesous. The fact is that after the death of Le Cabuc nothing more was heard of Claquesous. He vanished without trace, seeming to have faded into invisibility. His life had been lived in shadow, his end was total darkness.

The band of rebels was still oppressed by that tragic trial, so rapidly conducted and so summarily concluded, when Courfeyrac caught sight of the slim young man who that morning had come to his lodging in search of Marius. This youth, who had a bold and heedless air, had come to rejoin them.

BOOK THIRTEEN

MARIUS ENTERS THE DARKNESS

I. *From the Rue Plumet to the Quartier Saint-Denis*

THE VOICE summoning Marius in the dusk to join the barricade on the Rue de la Chanvrerie, had sounded to him like the voice of Fate. He wished to die and here was the means; his knock on the door of the tomb was answered by a hand tendering him the key. There is a fascination in the melancholy inducements that darkness offers to the despairing. Marius parted the bars of the gate, as he had done so many times before, and leaving the garden behind him said, 'So be it!' Half-crazed with grief, with nothing clear or settled in his mind, unable to face the realities of life after those two intoxicated months of youthfulness and love, overwhelmed by the bewilderment of despair, his only thought was to put a rapid end to his misery. He set out at a brisk walk. As it happened, he was already armed, having Javert's pistols on him. The youth he thought he had discerned in the shadows had vanished.

He went from the Rue Plumet to the boulevard, crossed the Esplanade, the Pont des Invalides, the Champs-Élysées, and the Place Louis XV (both before and after this the Place de la Concorde) and so came to the Rue de Rivoli. The shops were open and women were shopping under the lights of the arcade or eating ices at the Café Laiter or cakes at the English pastry-cook's. But now and then a post-chaise set off at a gallop from the Hôtel des Princes or the Hôtel Meurice.

Marius went by way of the Passage Delorme into the Rue Saint-Honoré. Here the shops were shut. Shopkeepers were talking in their half-closed doorways, people were passing along the pavements, the street lamps were lit and the houses were lighted as usual above the first floor. There was a detachment of cavalry in the Place du Palais-Royal.

But as he left the Palais-Royal behind him, following the Rue Saint-Honoré, Marius noted that there were fewer lighted windows. Doors were locked and there were no gossipers in the doorways. The street grew darker and the crowd more dense: for the number of people in the street had become a crowd—a crowd in which no one spoke, but from which a deep, heavy murmur arose. Around the Fontaine de l'Arbre-Sec there were 'rallying points', motionless groups of men detached from the ebb and flow of passers-by like rocks in a stream.

By the time it reached the end of the Rue des Prouvaires the crowd could move no more. It had become a solid, almost impenetrable mass of people talking in undertones. Scarcely any black coats and round hats were to be seen here. There were smocks and tradesmen's jackets, caps, sallow faces and bare heads of unkempt hair. This multitude swayed confusedly in the night mist, and its low-voiced muttering resembled a shudder. Although no man was walking there was nevertheless a sound of feet stamping in the mud. Beyond this concentration, in the Rue du Roule, the Rue des Prouvaires, and the further length of the Rue Saint-Honoré, not a lighted window was to be seen. The single lines of street lamps were seen to dwindle along the street. The lamps in those days were like red stars slung on ropes which cast a pool of light like a great spider on the pavement. But these streets were not empty. Stacked muskets were to be seen in them, bayonets moving on sentry-go and bivouacking troops. No sightseer penetrated as far as this. All traffic had stopped. Here the crowd ended and the army began.

Marius was imbued with the pertinacity of a man who has ceased to hope. He had been summoned and he must go. He contrived to pass through the crowd and the army bivouacs, dodging sentries and patrols. By means of a détour he reached the Rue de Bethisy and made for Les Halles. At the end of the Rue des Bourdonnais the street-lamps ceased. After passing first through the zone of the crowd and then through the military zone he found himself in a zone that to him seemed terrible—not a civilian or a soldier, not a light; a place of solitary silence and darkness. A chill assailed him. To turn into any street was like entering a cellar. But he continued on his way.

There was a sound of running footsteps passing close by him, whether those of a man or woman, of one person or more than one, he could not tell. They echoed and died away.

By twists and turns he arrived at an alley which he thought must be the Rue de la Poterie. Half way along it he bumped into something which he found to be an overturned cask. His feet discovered puddles. There were potholes in the street and piles of loose paving stones. A barricade had been started and then abandoned. Climbing over this obstacle, he moved further down the street, feeling his way along the housefronts. A little further on he saw a blur of white which, when he drew nearer to it, turned out to be the two white horses unharnessed from the omnibus that morning by Bossuet.

After straying all day about the streets they had come to rest in this place with the tired patience of animals that no more understand the ways of men than men understand the ways of Providence.

Marius went past them. As he entered a street which he thought must be the Rue du Contrat-Social there was the report of a musket, and the ball, fired at random from Heaven knew where, pierced a copper shaving bowl just above his head, hanging outside a barber's shop. That punctured shaving bowl was still to be seen in the Rue du Contrat-Social, near the pillars of Les Halles, in 1846.

It was at least a sign of life, but nothing else happened. Marius's journey was like a descent down a pitch-dark stairway. Nevertheless, he went on.

II. *Paris—A Bird's-eye View*

Anyone capable at that moment of soaring over Paris on the wings of a bat or an owl would have had a dismal spectacle beneath his eyes.

The ancient quarter of Les Halles, intersected by the Rues Saint-Denis, Saint-Martin, and countless alleyways, which is like a town within a town, and which the insurgents had made their base and arms depot, would have looked to him like a huge patch of darkness in the centre of Paris, a black gulf. Owing to the breaking of street-lamps and the shuttering of windows, no light was to be seen there, nor was any sound of life or movement to be heard. The invisible guardian of the uprising, that is to say, darkness, was everywhere on duty and everywhere kept order. This is the necessary tactic of insurrection, to veil smallness of numbers in a vast obscurity and enhance the stature of every combatant by the possibilities which obscurity affords. At nightfall every window where a light showed had been visited by a musket-ball; the light had gone out, and sometimes the occupant had been killed. Now nothing stirred; nothing dwelt in the houses but fear, mourning, and amazement; nothing in the streets but a kind of awestruck horror. Not even the long rows of storeyed windows were visible, nor the jagged outline of housetops and chimneys, the dim sheen of lights reflected on wet, muddy pavements. The eye looking from a height into that mass of shadow might have discerned here and there at remote intervals faint gleams of light throwing into relief the irregular shapes of singular constructions, like lanterns moving amid ruins; these were the barricades. The rest was a pool of utter darkness, misty and oppressive, above which rose the still, brooding outlines of the Tour Saint-Jacques, the Église Saint-Merry, and two or three others of those great edifices which man makes into giants and night turns into ghosts.

All round that silent, ominous labyrinth, in those quarters where the Paris traffic had not been brought to a standstill and where a few street-lamps still shone, the aerial observer might have perceived the metallic glitter of drawn swords and bayonets, the rumbling wheels of artillery and the silent gathering of battalions growing in numbers from one minute to the next—a formidable girdle slowly tightening around the uprising.

The besieged quarter was nothing but a sort of monstrous cavern, everything within it seeming motionless or slumbering, and the roads to it were all plunged in darkness, as we have seen.

A menacing darkness filled with traps and pitfalls, sinister to approach and more sinister still to penetrate, where those who entered trembled at the thought of those waiting to receive them, and those who waited dreaded those who must come. Invisible warriors crouched at every street corner; deadly ambushes hidden in the depths of night. All uncertainty was ended. No other greeting was to be expected than the flash of a musket, no other encounter than the sudden, swift emergence of death; and no one to say whence or when it would come, only that it was certain. In that place designated for combat, the two sides were soon to come cautiously to grips—Government and insurrection, the Garde Nationale and the groups of workers, the bourgeoisie and the rebels. Each was under the same necessity, to end up dead or victorious. There was no other way. So far had things gone, so heavy was the darkness, that the most timid was filled with resolution and the boldest with fear. And for the rest, fury and fervour were equal on either side. On the one hand, to go forward was to die, but no man thought of going back; on the other, to stand fast was to die, but no man thought of flight.

It was necessary that on the next day the matter should be settled, that one side or the other should triumph, that the insurrection should become revolution or else a damp squib. The Government understood this as did the rebels; the humblest citizen knew it. Hence the feeling of anguish that pervaded the impenetrable darkness of that place where all was to be decided; the heightened tension pervading the silence from which so soon a disastrous clamour was to arise. Only one sound was to be heard, awesome as a death-rattle, sinister as a malediction, the tocsin of Saint-Merry. Nothing could have chilled the blood so surely as did the tolling of that desperate bell crying its lament into the night.

As often happens, Nature seemed to have matched herself to the undertakings of men. Nothing conflicted with the fateful harmonies of that set stage. No stars showed, and the scene was overhung with heavy cloud. A black sky brooded over the dead streets like a vast pall draping a vast tomb.

And while a battle that was still political was preparing in that place that had witnessed so many revolutionary acts; while the young people, the secret societies, and the schools, inspired by principle, and the middle-class inspired by self-interest, were advancing upon each other to clash and grapple; while each side hastened and sought the moment of crisis and decision—remote from all this and from the battlefield itself, in the deepest recesses of that ancient Paris of the poor and destitute which lay hidden beneath the brilliance of the rich and fortunate Paris, there was to be heard the sombre growling of the masses: a fearful and awe-inspiring voice in which were mingled the snarl of animals and the words of God, a terror to the faint-hearted and a warning to the wise, coming at once from the depths, like the roaring of a lion, and from the heights, like the voice of thunder.

III. *The Extreme Edge*

Marius had reached Les Halles. Here everything was even quieter, darker and more immobile than in the surrounding streets, as though the icy peace of the tomb had risen up from the earth to spread beneath the sky. Nevertheless a glare was visible in the darkness, lighting the roofs of the houses separating the Rue de la Chanvrerie from Saint-Eustache. It was the torch that stood burning on the Corinth barricade. Marius, making his way towards it, was guided to the Marché-aux-Poirées, whence he could see the dark mouth of the Rue des Prêcheurs. He entered it, without being seen by the rebel sentry, who was at the far end. Feeling himself to be near his destination, he walked on with extreme caution and thus came to the turning into the short stretch of the Mondétour alleyway which, as we know, Enjolras had kept open as a channel of communication with the outside world. Reaching the corner, he peered into the alleyway past the house on his left.

Himself hidden in the shadow of the house he saw, reflected on the cobbles, a faint glow coming from a small flickering light on top of what looked like a crudely constructed wall adjoining the tavern building, of which he could see a part; and, crouched in front of it, a number of men with muskets on their knees. This, within twenty yards of him, was the interior of the stronghold. The houses on his right hid the rest of the tavern, the larger barricade and the flag.

Marius had now only a step to go; whereupon the unhappy young man seated himself on a curb-stone, folded his arms and fell to thinking about his father.

He was brooding on the heroic Colonel Pontmercy, that proud soldier who under the Republic had defended the frontiers of France and under Napoleon had reached the borders of Asia; who had seen Genoa, Alexandria, Milan, Turin, Madrid, Vienna, Dresden, Berlin, and Moscow, leaving on all the victorious battlefields of Europe drops of the same blood that flowed in Marius's veins; whose hair had turned prematurely white in a life of discipline and command; who had lived with his sword-belt buckled, epaulettes falling over his breast, cockade blackened by powder, forehead creased by the weight of his helmet, in barrack-rooms, in encampments, under canvas, and in ambulances, and who after twenty years had returned from the wars with a scarred cheek and a smiling countenance, simple, tranquil, admirable, pure-hearted as a child, having done all that he could for France and nothing against her.

Marius said to himself that now it was his turn, his hour had sounded; that following his father he too must be bold and resolute, braving the musket-balls, baring his breast to the bayonets, shedding his blood seeking out the enemy and finding death if need be; that he too was going to war—but that his battlefield would be the streets, and it was a civil war that he would be fighting. It was civil war that opened like an abyss before him; it was into that abyss that he must fall.

And thinking of this he shivered.

He thought of his father's sword, which his grandfather had sold to a secondhand dealer and which he himself so sorely regretted. He told himself that it had done well, that chaste and gallant sword, to escape from him and take indignant refuge in oblivion; that it had taken flight because it had good sense and knew what the future held; that it had had a presentiment of this uprising, this war of gutters and paving-stones—volleys fired from loopholes in cellars, stabs in the back. Having known Marengo and Friedland it had no wish to visit the Rue de la Chanvrerie, and having served honourably with the father it was not minded to degrade itself with the son. Marius said to himself that if he had it with him now, if he had retrieved it from his dying parent's bedside to bear it with him into this dark brawl between Frenchmen and Frenchmen, the sword would have burnt his hand, flaming like a weapon of supernatural wrath. He said to himself that he was glad it was not there, that it was just and right that it had vanished, that the true guardian of his father's fame had been his grandfather, that it was better that the sword should have been auctioned, sold to a huckster, tossed on the scrap-heap rather than be buried in their country's flank . . . And Marius wept bitterly.

His plight was terrible, but what else could he do? To live without Cosette was impossible. Since she had left him, he could only die. Had he not sworn to her that he would die? She had left him knowing this; therefore his death must be agreeable to her. In any case, it was clear that she no longer loved him, since she had gone off in this fashion without a word of warning, without a letter, although she knew his address. Why go on living, what was there left for him to live for? And then, how could he now draw back, having come so far? To sniff at danger and then run away, peep into the barricade and go off trembling—'I've had a look and that's enough. That's all I want. It's civil war, and I'm clearing out . . .!' To desert the friends who were awaiting him, who perhaps had need of him—a handful against an army! To fail in all things, love, friendship, and his pledged word, making patriotic sentiment the excuse for cowardice! This was unthinkable. If his father's ghost had seen him retreat he would have thrashed him with the flat of his sword crying, 'Coward, go forward!'

Marius had been sitting with his head bowed, while the argument surged this way and that. But suddenly he straightened as a splendid thought occurred to stiffen his resolve. There is a lucidity inspired by the nearness of the grave: to be close to death is to see clearly. The course on which he was perhaps on the verge of embarking seemed to him no longer shameful but splendid. The thought of street warfare was by some process of spiritual alchemy suddenly transformed in his mind. The questions he had been asking came crowding back, but they no longer troubled him. He had an answer to each one.

Why should his father be angry? Were there no circumstances in which rebellion acquired the dignity of a duty? How could it be degrading for the son of Colonel Pontmercy to play a part in the conflict that had now begun? This was not Montmirail or Champaubert but another matter entirely. It was a question, not of sacred soil but of a noble idea. The country might lament, but humanity would applaud. And indeed, would the country lament? France might bleed, but the cause of liberty would prosper, and in the triumph of liberty France would forget her wounds. And furthermore, looking at the matter still more broadly, why should there be any talk of civil war?

Civil war . . . What did the words mean? Was there any such thing as 'foreign war'? Was not all warfare between men warfare between brothers? Wars could only be defined by their aims. There were no 'foreign' or 'civil' wars, only wars that were just or unjust. Until the great universal concord could be arrived at, warfare, at least when it was the battle between the urgent future and the dragging past, might be unavoidable. How could such a war be condemned? War is not shameful, nor the sword-thrust a stab in the back, except when it serves to kill right and progress, reason, civilization, and truth. When this is war's purpose it makes no difference whether it is civil or foreign war—it is a crime. Outside the sacred cause of justice, what grounds has one kind of war for denigrating another? By what right does the sword of Washington despise the pike of Camille Desmoulins? Which is the greater—Leonidas fighting the foreign enemy or Timoleon slaying the tyrant who was his brother? One was a defender, the other a liberator. Are we to condemn every resort to arms that takes place within the citadel, without concerning ourselves with its aim? Then we must condemn Brutus and Coligny. Fighting in the undergrowth or in the streets—why not? That was the warfare of Ambiorix, of Arta-velde, of Marnix, of Pelage. But Ambiorix fought against Rome, Artavelde fought against France, Marnix against Spain, and Pelage against the Moors—all fought against foreigners. But monarchy is also a foreigner; oppression and divine right, both are foreigners. Despotism violates the moral frontier just as foreign invasion violates the geographical frontier. To drive out the tyrant or to drive out the English is in either case the reconquest of one's own territory. The moment comes when protest is not enough; reason must give way to action, and force ensure what thought has conceived. The Encyclopaedia enlightens minds, but 10 August sets them in motion. After Aeschylus came Thrasybulus, and after Diderot came Danton. Multitudes are inclined to accept the existing master; their very mass creates apathy. Crowds lapse readily into compliance. They have to be stirred and driven, shaken by the very benefits conferred on them by deliverance, their eyes dazzled by truth, enlightenment forced on them with blows. They need to be a little shocked by their own salvation, and this it is that arouses them. Hence the necessity of fanfares and of wars. Great fighters have to arise, to stir nations with their audacity and shake loose the pitiful humanity buried in the shadow of Divine Right and Caesarian glory, of force and fanaticism, irresponsible power and absolute monarchy—the foolish mass that gazes open-mouthed at those dark and tawdry splendours. Down with the tyrant? But to whom are you referring? To Louis-Philippe? He was no more a tyrant than Louis XVI. Both were what history is accustomed to term 'good kings'. But principles cannot be fragmented: truth is the whole, and it does not admit of compromises. There can be no concessions, no indulgence for the man who must be removed. Louis XVI

was a king by divine right. Louis-Philippe became king because he was a Bourbon: both in some degree represent the seizure of rights, and this world-wide usurpation must be contested. It is necessary, since France is for ever that which is beginning. When the ruler falls in France, he falls everywhere. In brief, what cause can be more just, what war more righteous, than that which restores social truth, restores liberty to its throne, restores their proper sovereignty to all men, displaces the purple from the head of France, reasserts the fullness of reason and equity, eliminates the seeds of antagonism by allowing each man to be himself, abolishes the hindrance to universal concord represented by monarchy and makes all mankind equal before the law? It is wars such as these that build peace. A vast citadel of prejudice, privilege, superstition, lies, exactions, abuses, violence and iniquity still looms over the world, enclosed within towers of hatred. It must be overthrown, its monstrous bulk reduced to rubble. To win Austerlitz is glorious; but to seize the Bastille is immense.

Every man has discovered in himself that the human spirit—and this is the miracle of its complex, ubiquitous unity—has the strange gift of being able to reason almost coldly in the most desperate extremity, and that in desolation and utmost despair, in the travail of our darkest meditation, we may still view our situation with detachment and weigh arguments. Logic enters our state of turmoil, and the thread of syllogism runs unbroken through the tempest of our thought. This was Marius's state of mind.

Thinking these things, utterly downcast but resolute, still hesitant, and indeed trembling at the thought of what he was about to do, his gaze travelled over the interior of the barricade. The rebels were talking in low voices, not moving, and one could feel the unreal silence which denotes the last stage of expectancy. Above their heads, at a third-floor window, Marius could make out the form of what seemed to be a spectator or witness, who was listening with a singular attention. It was the door-keeper killed by Le Cabuc. From below, by the light of the torch on the barricade, the figure was only dimly visible. Nothing could have been more eerie, in that flickering, uncertain light, than that head of tangled hair, the livid, motionless, astonished face, wide-eyed and open-mouthed, leaning over the street in a posture of intent curiosity. It was as though the man who was dead was contemplating those about to die. A long trail of blood from the head flowed in streaks down the wall as far as the first floor, where it stopped.

BOOK FOURTEEN

THE GREATNESS OF DESPAIR

I. *The Flag—Act One*

STILL nothing had happened. The clock of Saint-Merry had struck ten, and Enjolras and Combeferre had seated themselves with their carbines near the narrow breach in the main barricade. They were not talking; both were listening with ears strained to catch the least, most distant sound of marching feet.

Suddenly the brooding silence was broken by the sound of a gay young voice, seeming to come from the Rue Saint-Denis, raised in an improvised ditty to the tune of *Au clair de la lune,* and ending with a cockcrow.

> *Save me if I swoon, mates,*
> *That old man, Bugeaud,*
> *He's not on the moon, mates,*
> *Though he's pretty slow.*
> *Cock-tails* on their caps, mates,*
> *Uniforms of blue,*
> *The troops are in our laps, mates,—*
> *Cock-a-doodle-doo!*

'It's Gavroche,' said Enjolras, and he and Combeferre shook hands.

Running footsteps echoed down the empty street, a figure nimble as a circus clown scrambled over the omnibus and Gavroche, very much out of breath, leapt down from the barricade.

'They're coming! Where's my musket?'

An electric stir ran through the defenders and there was a sound of hands snatching up weapons.

'Would you like my carbine?' Enjolras asked.

'No, I want the big musket,' said Gavroche. He meant Javert's musket.

Two of the sentries had fallen back and re-entered the barricade almost at the same moment as Gavroche. They were the ones who had been posted at the end of the street and in the Petite-Truanderie.

---

* The Gallic cock was the emblem of the July Monarchy.

The sentry in the Rue des Prêcheurs was still at his post, which indicated that so far nothing was approaching from the direction of the bridges and the markets. The Rue de la Chanvrerie, of which only a short stretch was dimly visible in the light falling on the flag, looked to the defenders like a cavernous doorway opening into the mist.

Every man took up his action station. Forty-three defenders, among them Enjolras, Combeferre, Courfeyrac, Bossuet, Joly, Bahorel, and Gavroche, knelt behind the main barricade with muskets and carbines thrust through the gaps between the paving-stones, alert and ready to fire. Six others, commanded by Feuilly, waited with loaded muskets at the windows on the two upper floors of the tavern.

A short time passed and then the tramp of marching feet, heavy, measured, and numerous, was clearly to be heard from the direction of Saint-Leu. The sound, faint at first but growing in volume, drew steadily nearer, approaching without a pause, with a calm, inexorable rhythm. Nothing else was to be heard; the mingled silence and sound recalled the entrance of the statue of the Commendatore in *Don Giovanni*; but that stony tread conveyed an impression of vastness, a suggestion not only of an army on the move but also of something spectral, the march of an unseen Legion. It drew nearer and nearer still, and then stopped. It was as though one could hear the breathing of many men at the end of the street. But still nothing was to be seen, except, in the depths of the murky darkness, a multitude of metallic gleams, needle-thin, scarcely perceptible and constantly in motion, like the phosphorescent threads that quiver beneath our eyelids in the first mists of sleep. They were bayonets and musket-barrels faintly illumined by the distant light of the torch.

There was a pause, as though both sides were waiting. Suddenly a voice called out of the darkness, the more awesome because no speaker was to be seen, so that it sounded like the voice of the darkness itself:

'Who's there?'

At the same time they heard the clicking of muskets being cocked.

Enjolras responded in lofty and resonant tones:

'The French Revolution!'

'Fire!' ordered the voice, and an instant glare of light shone upon the front of the houses as though a furnace-door had been swiftly opened and closed.

A hideous blow shook the barricade. The red flag fell. So heavy and concentrated was that volley that it carried away the flagstaff— that is to say, the tip of the shaft of the omnibus. Bullets ricocheting back off the houses behind them wounded several of the defenders.

The effect of that first discharge was stupefying, its sheer weight enough to make the boldest man think twice. They were evidently confronted by, at the least, a whole regiment.

'Comrades,' shouted Courfeyrac, 'don't waste your powder. Wait till they show themselves before shooting back.'

'And first of all,' cried Enjolras, 'we must hoist the flag again.'

He picked it up from where it had fallen, right at his feet. At the same time they heard the rattle of ramrods in the muskets as the soldiers re-loaded.

'Who is brave enough?' demanded Enjolras. 'Who's going to put back the flag on the barricade?'

There was no reply. To climb on to the barricade at that moment, when the muskets were again being levelled, was simply to invite death. Enjolras himself trembled at the thought. He repeated:

'Does no one volunteer?'

II. *The Flag—Act Two*

Since they had installed themselves in Corinth and set about building the barricade no one had paid any attention to Père Mabeuf. But he had not deserted the troop. He had found a seat behind the counter on the ground floor of the tavern, and here he had so to speak withdrawn into himself, seeming unaware of what was going on around him. Courfeyrac and others had spoken to him once or twice, warning him of the danger and advising him to get away, but he had seemed not to hear them. His lips moved when no one had spoken to him as though in reply to a question, but when anyone addressed him his lips were still and his eyes vacant. For some hours before the attack on the barricade he had remained seated in the same posture, with his fists clenched on his knees and his head bowed forward as though he were staring over a precipice. Nothing had caused him to change this attitude; it was as though his conscious self were not present within the barricades. After the rest had run out to take up their position only three persons were left in that ground-floor room—Javert, lashed to his pillar, the rebel with a drawn sabre who was mounting guard over him, and Monsieur Mabeuf. But the thunder of that first volley, the physical shock, seemed to bring him to life. He jumped up and crossed the room, and at the moment when Enjolras repeated the words, 'Does no one volunteer?' he showed himself in the doorway of the tavern.

His appearance created a stir among the defenders. Someone shouted:

'That's the Man of the Convention who voted for the King's death—the Representative of the People!'

Probably he did not hear.

Walking up to Enjolras, while the rebels made way for him with a sort of awe, he snatched the flag from the young man's startled hands, and, no one venturing to stop him, began slowly to mount the makeshift flight of paving-stones leading to the top of the barricade—an eighty-year-old man, his head swaying on his shoulders but his feet firm. So tragic and noble was the spectacle that the men around cried, 'Hats off!' Each step he took was terrifying to watch, the white hair, the shrunken face with its high, wrinkled forehead, the deep-set eyes, the open, astonished mouth, the old arms lifting the red flag on high, these things rose up out of the darkness, seeming to grow larger in the ruddy glare of the torch. It might have been the ghost of '93 arising from the tomb and bearing aloft the flag of the Terror. When he reached the topmost step, a quivering, terrible ghost, and stood on the pile of rubble facing twelve hundred invisible muskets, facing death as though he were stronger than death, the whole dark barricade acquired a new and awe-inspiring supernatural dimension.

A silence fell, of the kind that only accompanies some prodigious event; and in the silence the old man flourished the red flag and cried:

'Long live the Revolution! Long live the Republic! Fraternity, Equality—and Death!'

Those behind the barricade heard a distant, rapid murmur like that of a hurried priest gabbling a prayer. It was probably the Commissioner of Police delivering the statutory warning from the other end of the street. The stentorian voice which had called to them before now shouted:

'Go away!'

Monsieur Mabeuf, white and haggard, eyes glowing with the wild light of madness, waved the flag and repeated:

'Long live the Republic!'

'Fire!' ordered the voice.

A second volley, like a charge of grapeshot, crashed into the barricade.

The old man tottered on his legs, attempted to recover, then let go the flag and fell backwards like a log, to lie full length on the ground with arms outstretched. Blood was pouring from him, and his sad, pale face seemed to be looking up to Heaven.

The rebels pressed forward, forgetful of their own safety, stirred by feelings loftier than man, and gazed with respectful awe at the dead body.

231

'They were gallant men, those regicides,' said Enjolras.

Courfeyrac drew close and whispered in his ear.

'This is between ourselves—I don't want to damp the enthusiasm —but no one was ever less of a regicide. I knew him. His name was Mabeuf. I don't know what got into him today. He was a brave old simpleton. Look at his expression.'

'A simpleton with the heart of a Brutus,' said Enjolras.

Then he raised his voice:

'Citizens, this is the example which our elders set the young. While we hesitated he volunteered. We drew back, but he went forward. This is the lesson which those who tremble with age teach those who tremble with fear. This old man is noble in the eyes of his country. He had a long life and a splendid death. Now we must safeguard his body, each of us must defend this dead old man as he would defend his living father, so that his presence among us makes our fortress unconquerable.'

A murmur of grim approval greeted these words.

Bending down, Enjolras lifted the old man's head and kissed him gently on the forehead. Then, handling him with the utmost tenderness, as though he feared to hurt him, he removed his coat and held it up so that all might see its bloodstained holes.

'This is our new flag,' he said.

III. *Gavroche's Musket*

A long black shawl belonging to the Widow Hucheloup was draped over Père Mabeuf's body. Six men made a stretcher of their muskets and, with bared heads, bore him slowly and reverently into the tavern, where they laid him on the big table in the ground-floor room. Wholly intent upon the solemn nature of their task, they gave no thought to their own perilous situation.

When the body passed by Javert, who remained expressionless as ever, Enjolras said to him:

'You—it won't be long!'

Meanwhile Gavroche, who alone had stayed at his post keeping watch, thought he saw men moving stealthily towards the barricade. He shouted:

'Watch out!'

Courfeyrac, Enjolras, and the others came rushing out of the tavern. They were barely in time. A dense glitter of bayonets was now visible on the other side of the barricade. The tall forms of Municipal Guardsmen surged in, some climbing over the omnibus and others coming by way of the breach. Gavroche was forced to give ground, but he did not run away.

It was a critical instant, like the moment when floodwaters rise to the topmost level of an embankment and begin to seep over. In another minute the stronghold might have been taken.

Bahorel sprang towards the first man to enter and shot him at point-blank range; a second man killed him with a bayonet-thrust. Courfeyrac was felled by another man and called for help. The biggest of all the attackers, a giant of a man, bore down with his bayonet on Gavroche. Raising Javert's heavy musket, the boy took aim and pulled the trigger. Nothing happened. Javert had not loaded the musket. The Municipal Guardsman laughed and thrust at the youngster with his bayonet.

But before the bayonet could reach Gavroche the musket fell from the man's hands and he himself fell backwards with a bullet in his forehead. A second bullet took the man assailing Courfeyrac in the chest and laid him low.

Marius had entered the stronghold.

IV. *The Powder-keg*

Crouched at the turning of the Rue Mondétour, Marius had witnessed the beginning of the battle, still irresolute and trembling. But he had not long been able to withstand that mysterious and overwhelming impulse that may be termed the call of the abyss. The imminence of the peril—the death of Monsieur Mabeuf, that tragic enigma, the killing of Bahorel, Courfeyrac's call for help, the threat to Gavroche; friends to be rescued or avenged—all this had thrown hesitation to the winds. He had rushed into the mêlée with a pistol in either hand, and one had saved Gavroche, the other Courfeyrac.

Amid the din of musket-fire and the cries of the wounded the attackers had climbed on to the barricade, the top of which was now occupied by Municipal and Regional Guards and foot-soldiers of the line. They covered two thirds of its length but had not yet jumped down into the enclosure, seeming uncertain, as though they feared a trap. They hesitated, peering into the dark stronghold as they might have peered into a lion's den. The glare of the torch fell upon bayonets, bearskin caps and the upper part of menacing but apprehensive faces.

Marius was now weaponless, having flung away his discharged pistols; but he had seen the keg of powder near the door in the lower room of the tavern. While he was looking at it, a soldier levelled his musket at him, but as he was in the act of firing a hand was thrust over the muzzle, diverting it. The person who had flung himself forward was the young workman in corduroy trousers. The ball shattered his hand and perhaps entered his body, for he fell; but it did not touch Marius. It was an episode in misted darkness, half-seen rather than seen. Marius, on his way into the tavern, was scarcely aware of it. He had vaguely seen the musket levelled at him and the hand thrust out to block it, and he had heard the discharge. But at moments such as these, when events follow at breathless speed, we are not to be distracted from whatever purpose we have in mind. We plunge on blindly amid the fog around us.

The rebels, shaken but not panic-stricken, had rallied. Enjolras shouted, 'Steady! Don't fire at random!' In that first confusion they might indeed have hit each other. The greater number had retreated into the tavern, from the upper windows of which they dominated their assailants; but the most resolute, with Enjolras, Courfeyrac, Jean Prouvaire, and Combeferre, had taken up their stand with their backs to the house at the end of the street, where they stood confronting the soldiers and National Guardsmen on the barricade. All this had been accomplished without undue haste, with the strange and threatening gravity that precedes a set battle. Muskets were levelled on both sides at point-blank range; they were so close that they could talk without shouting. At this point, when the spark was about to be struck, an officer in a stiff collar and large epaulettes raised his sword and said:

'Lay down your arms!'

'Fire!' ordered Enjolras.

The two volleys rang out simultaneously, and the scene was enveloped in thick, acrid smoke filled with the groans of the wounded and the dying. When it had cleared both sides could be seen, diminished but still in the same place, re-charging their weapons in silence. But suddenly a ringing voice cried:

'Clear out or I'll blow up the barricade!'

All heads were turned to stare in the direction of the voice.

Marius, seizing the powder-keg in the tavern, had taken advantage of the smoke-filled lull to slip along the barricade until he reached the structure of paving-stones in which the torch was fixed. To detach the torch and set the powder-keg in its place, thrusting aside the paving-stones, had taken him, urged on by a sort of terrible compulsion, only the time he needed to bend down and then stand upright; and now the men grouped at the other end of the barricade, officers, soldiers, men of the National and Municipal Guard, stared

in stupefaction at the figure holding the flaming torch over the opened keg while he repeated his challenge:

'Clear out or I'll blow up the whole place!'

First the octogenarian and then the youthful Marius: it was the revolution of the young following the ghost of the old!

'If you blow up the barricade,' a sergeant called, 'you'll blow up yourself as well!'

'And myself as well,' said Marius, and lowered the torch towards the keg.

But there was no longer anyone on the barricade. The attackers had made off in a disorderly stampede, leaving their dead and wounded behind, and were now vanishing into the darkness at the far end of the street. It was a rout, and the fortress had been relieved.

V. *The Last Poem of Jean Prouvaire*

His friends flocked round Marius, and Courfeyrac flung his arms about his neck.

'So you've come!' he cried.

'And welcome!' said Combeferre.

'At the right moment!' said Bossuet.

'I'd be dead otherwise,' said Courfeyrac.

'I'd have copped it too,' said Gavroche.

'Where is the leader?' Marius asked.

'You're now the leader,' Enjolras said.

Throughout that day Marius had had a furnace in his brain, but now it was a whirlwind, a tempest from outside himself that carried him away. He seemed to have been borne a huge distance outside life. The two radiant months of happiness ending abruptly in this inferno, the sight of Monsieur Mabeuf dying for the Republic, himself a rebel leader—all this was like an outrageous nightmare, so that it cost him an effort to realize that what was happening was real. He had not yet lived long enough to have discovered that nothing is more close at hand than the impossible, and that what must be looked for is always the unforeseen. He was observing his own drama as though it were a play he did not understand.

In his confused state of mind he did not recognize Javert, who, lashed to his pillar, had not turned a hair during the attack on the barricade and was observing the commotion around him with the resignation of a martyr and the detachment of a judge. Marius had not even noticed him.

The attackers made no further move. Although the sound of them could be heard at the far end of the street, they seemed disinclined to take the initiative, either because they were awaiting fresh orders, or because they were hoping for reinforcements before again assailing that formidable stronghold. The rebels had posted sentries, and the medical students among them were attending to the wounded.

All the tables had been taken out of the tavern except the two in use for the making of bandages and cartridges and the one on which Monsieur Mabeuf's body lay; they had been piled on to the barricade, being replaced in the downstairs room by mattresses from the beds of the Widow Hucheloup and her two waitresses. The wounded were laid on these mattresses. As for the three luckless women whose home was Corinth, no one knew what had become of them. They were eventually found huddled in the cellar.

A sad blow had damped the students' rejoicing at their temporary triumph. When the roll was called, one of them was found to be missing, one of the bravest and best, Jean Prouvaire. He was not to be found among the wounded or the dead. It seemed, then, that he must have been taken prisoner. Combeferre said to Enjolras:

'They've got our friend and we've got their agent. Are you really so set on the death of this spy?'

'Yes,' said Enjolras, 'but less than on the life of Jean Prouvaire.'

They were talking in the downstair room near Javert's pillar.

'Well then,' said Combeferre, 'I'll tie a handkerchief to my stick and go and bargain with them—their man in exchange for ours.'

'Wait,' said Enjolras, laying a hand on his. 'Listen!'

An ominous rattle of muskets had come from the other end of the street. A brave voice shouted:

'Long live France! Long live the future!'

It was the voice of Jean Prouvaire.

'They've shot him!' cried Combeferre.

Enjolras turned to Javert and said:

'Your friends have killed you as well.'

VI. *The Throes of Death after the Throes of Life*

It is a peculiarity of this type of warfare that the attack on a barricade is nearly always delivered from the front and that as a rule the attacker makes no attempt to outflank the defence, either because he fears an ambush or because he is reluctant to engage his forces in narrow, tortuous streets. The rebels' attention was therefore concentrated on the main barricade which was constantly threatened and where the battle would undoubtedly be resumed. However, Marius thought of the smaller barricade and went to inspect it. It was unguarded except by the lamp flickering on the paving-stones. The Mondétour alleyway, and the small streets running into it, the Petite-Truanderie and the Rue du Cygne, were entirely quiet.

As he was leaving, having concluded his inspection, he heard his own name faintly spoken in the darkness.

'Monsieur Marius!'

He started, recognizing the husky voice that two hours previously had called to him through the gate in the Rue Plumet. But now it was scarcely more than a whisper.

He looked about him, but, seeing no one, thought that he had imagined it, that it was no more than an hallucination to be added to the many extraordinary vicissitudes of that day. He started to move away from the barricade and the voice repeated:

'Monsieur Marius!'

This time he knew that he had heard it, but although he peered hard into the darkness he could see nothing.

'I'm at your feet,' the voice said.

Looking down, Marius saw a dark shape crawling over the cobbles towards him. The gleam of the lamp was enough to enable him to make out a smock, a pair of torn corduroy trousers, two bare feet and something that looked like a trail of blood. A white face was turned towards him and the voice asked:

'Don't you recognize me?'

'No.'

'Éponine.'

Marius bent hastily down and saw that it was indeed that unhappy girl, clad in a man's clothes.

'How do you come to be here? What are you doing?'

'I'm dying,' she said.

There are words and happenings which arouse even souls in the depths of despair. Marius cried, as though starting out of sleep:

'You're wounded! I'll carry you into the tavern. They'll dress your wound. Is it very bad? How am I to lift you without hurting you? Help, someone! But what are you doing here?'

He tried to get an arm underneath her to raise her up, and in doing so touched her hand. She uttered a weak cry.

'Did I hurt you?'

'A little.'

'But I only touched your hand.'

She lifted her hand for him to see, and he saw a hole in the centre of the palm.

237

'What happened?' he asked.

'A bullet went through it.'

'A bullet? But how?'

'Don't you remember a musket being aimed at you?'

'Yes, and a hand was clapped over it.'

'That was mine.'

Marius shuddered.

'What madness! You poor child! Still, if that's all, it might be worse. I'll get you to a bed and they'll bind you up. One doesn't die of a wounded hand.'

She murmured:

'The ball passed through my hand, but it came out through my back. It's no use trying to move me. I'll tell you how you can treat my wound better than any surgeon. Sit down on that stone, close beside me.'

Marius did so. She rested her head on his knee and said without looking at him:

'Oh, what happiness! What bliss! Now I don't feel any pain.'

For a moment she was silent, then with an effort she turned to look at Marius.

'You know, Monsieur Marius, it vexed me when you went into that garden. That was silly, because after all I'd shown you the way there, and anyway I should have known that a young gentleman like you—' She broke off and, passing from one unhappy thought to another, said with a touching smile: 'You think I'm ugly, don't you?' She went on: 'But now you're done for! No one will get out of this place alive. And I'm the one who brought you here! You're going to die. I was expecting it, and yet I put my hand over that musket barrel. How queer. But I wanted to die before you did. I dragged myself here when I got hurt, and nobody noticed. I've been waiting for you. I thought, "Won't he ever come?" I had to bite my smock, the pain was so bad. But now it's all right. Do you remember the time when I came into your room and looked at myself in your glass, and the day when I found you by the Champ de l'Alouette? So many birds were singing! It's not so very long ago. You offered me a hundred sous, and I said, "I don't want your money." Did you pick the coin up? I know you weren't rich. I didn't think of telling you to pick it up. It was a fine, sunny day, not a bit cold. Do you remember, Monsieur Marius? Oh, I'm so happy! We're all going to die.'

She was talking distractedly, in a manner that was grave and heartrending. The torn smock disclosed her naked bosom. While she spoke she pressed her injured hand to her breast, where there was another hole from which at that moment the blood spurted

238

like wine from a newly tapped cask. Marius looked down at her in deep compassion, desolate creature that she was.

'Oh!' she cried suddenly. 'It's starting again. I can't breathe!'

At this moment the voice of Gavroche rang out in another burst of song like a cock-crow. He was sitting on a table loading his musket, and the song was a highly popular song of the moment:

When Lafayette comes in sight,
All the gendarmes take to flight—
Sauvons-nous! Sauvons-nous! Sauvons-nous! . . .

Éponine had raised herself on one arm and was listening.

'That's him,' she said. She looked up at Marius. 'That's my brother. He mustn't see me. He'd scold.'

'Your brother?' Marius repeated, while in the bitterest and most painful depths of his heart he recalled the obligation to the Thénardier family laid upon him by his father. 'Whom do you mean?'

'The boy.'

'The one who's singing?'

'Yes.'

Marius made a movement.

'Oh, don't go!' she said. 'It won't be long.'

She was sitting almost upright, but her voice was very low and broken by hiccoughs. At moments she struggled for breath. Raising her face as near as she could to Marius's, she said, with a strange expression:

'Look, I can't cheat you. I have a letter for you in my pocket. I've had it since yesterday. I was asked to post it, but I didn't. I didn't want you to get it. But you might be angry with me when we meet again. Because we shall all meet again, shan't we? Take your letter.'

With a convulsive movement she seized Marius's hand with her own injured one, but without seeming to feel the pain, and guided it to her pocket.

'Take it,' she said.

Marius took out the letter, and she made a little gesture of satisfaction and acceptance.

'Now you must promise me something for my trouble . . .' She paused.

'What?' asked Marius.

'Do you promise?'

'Yes, I promise.'

'You must kiss me on the forehead after I'm dead . . . I shall know.'

She let her head fall back on his knees; her lids fluttered, and then

239

she was motionless. He thought that the sad soul had left her. But then, when he thought it was all over, she slowly opened her eyes that were now deep with the shadow of death, and said in a voice so sweet that it seemed already to come from another world:

'You know, Monsieur Marius, I think I was a little bit in love with you.'

She tried to smile, and died.

VII. *Gavroche reckons Distances*

Marius kept his promise. He kissed the pale forehead, bedewed with an icy sweat. It was no act of infidelity to Cosette, but a deliberate, tender farewell to an unhappy spirit.

He had trembled as he took the letter Éponine had brought him. Instantly sensing its importance, he longed to read it. Such is the nature of man—scarcely had the poor girl closed her eyes than he wanted to open it. But first he laid her gently on the ground, feeling instinctively that he could not read it beside her dead body.

Going into the tavern, he unfolded it by the light of a candle. It was a short note, folded and wafered with feminine elegance, and addressed in a feminine hand to 'Monsieur Marius Pontmercy, chez M. Courfeyrac, No. 16, Rue de la Verrerie.' Breaking the seal he read:

My dearest,

Alas, father insists that we must leave here at once. We go tonight to No.7, Rue de l'Homme-Armé, and in a week we shall be in England.

Cosette 4th June.

Such was the innocence of their love that Marius had not even known her handwriting.

What had happened may be briefly told: Éponine was responsible for everything. After the evening of 3 June she had had two things in mind, to frustrate the plan of her father and his friends for robbing the house in the Rue Plumet, and to separate Marius and Cosette. She had exchanged clothes with a youth who thought it amusing to go about dressed as a woman, while she dressed up as a man. It was she who, in the Champ de Mars, had given Jean Valjean the note warning him to change his address. Valjean had gone home and said to Cosette, 'We're moving this evening, with Toussaint, to the Rue de L'Homme-Armé, and next week we're going to London.' Cosette, shattered by this unexpected blow, had hurriedly written her letter to Marius. But how was it to be posted? She never went out alone and Toussaint, surprised by an errand of this nature, would certainly show the letter to her master. While she was debating the matter Cosette had caught sight of Éponine through the garden gate, wandering in her male attire up and down the street. Thinking she had to do with a young workman, she had called to the girl and given her five francs and the letter, asking her to take it at once to the address given. Éponine had put the letter in her pocket and the next day, the 5th, had gone to Courfeyrac's lodging, not to give him the letter but simply, as any jealous lover will understand, 'to have a look'. She had waited there for Marius, or anyway for Courfeyrac, still only 'having a look'; but when Courfeyrac told her that he and his friends were going to the barricade a sudden impulse had seized her—to plunge into that death, as she would have plunged into any other, and take Marius with her. She had followed Courfeyrac to find out where the barricade was situated, and then, since she was certain, having intercepted Cosette's letter, that Marius would go as usual to the Rue Plumet, she had gone there herself and passed on the summons, supposedly from his friend, which she had no doubt would lead him to join them. She had counted on Marius's despair at not finding Cosette, and in this had judged rightly. She had returned separately to the Rue de la Chanvrerie, and we know what had happened there. She had died in the tragic rapture of jealous hearts, who take the beloved with them into death, saying, 'No one else shall have him!'

Marius covered Cosette's letter with kisses. So she still loved him! He thought for a moment that now he must not die, but then he thought, 'She's going away!' She was going with her father to England, and his grandfather had refused to consent to their marriage. Nothing was changed in the fate that pursued them. Dreamers such as Marius have their moments of overwhelming despair, from which desperate courses ensue: the burden of life seems insupportable, and dying is soon over.

But he reflected that he had two duties to perform. He must tell Cosette of his death and send her a last message of farewell; and he must save that poor little boy, Éponine's brother and Thénardier's son, from the disaster that so nearly threatened them all.

He had his wallet on him, the same one which had contained the notebook in which he had written so many loving thoughts for Cosette. He got out a sheet of paper, and with a pencil wrote the following lines:

'Our marriage was impossible. I went to my grandfather, and he refused his consent. I have no fortune; neither have you. I hurried to see you but you were no longer there. You remember the pledge

I gave you. I shall keep it. I shall die. I love you. When you read this my soul will be very near at hand and smiling at you.'

Having nothing with which to seal the letter he simply folded the paper in four and addressed it as follows: 'To Mademoiselle Cosette Fauchelevent, chez M. Fauchelevent, 7 Rue de l'Homme-Armé.'

Then after a moment's reflection he wrote on another sheet of paper:

'My name is Marius Pontmercy. My body is to be taken to the house of my grandfather, M. Gillenormand, 6 Rue des Filles-du-Calvaire, in the Marais.'

He returned the wallet to his jacket pocket and called to Gavroche.

'Will you do something for me?'

'Anything you like,' said Gavroche. 'Lord love us, if it weren't for you I'd have copped it.'

'You see this letter?'

'Yes.'

'I want you to deliver it. You must leave here at once'—at this Gavroche began to scratch his head—'and take it to Mademoiselle Cosette at the address written on the outside—care of Monsieur Fauchelevent, number seven, Rue de l'Homme-Armé.'

'Yes, but look here,' said the valiant Gavroche, 'the barricade may be taken while I'm away.'

'The chances are that they won't attack again until daybreak, and the barricade won't fall until noon.'

The respite granted to the defenders did indeed give every sign of continuing. It was one of those lulls which commonly occur in night fighting, and which are always followed by an assault of redoubled fury.

'Well, then,' said Gavroche, 'why shouldn't I deliver the letter tomorrow morning?'

'It would be too late. By then all the streets round us will be guarded and you'd never get out. You must go at once.'

Gavroche had no reply to this. He continued to hesitate, unhappily scratching his head. But then, with one of those swift, birdlike movements that characterized him, he took the letter.

'Very well,' he said. And he went off at a run down the narrow Rue Mondétour.

The thought that had decided Gavroche was one that he did not disclose to Marius, for fear that he might raise objections. He had reflected that it was only just midnight, that the Rue de L'Homme-Armé was not far off, and that he could deliver the letter and be back in plenty of time.

BOOK FIFTEEN

IN THE RUE DE L'HOMME-ARMÉ

I. *The Treacherous Blotter*

WHAT is the turmoil in a city compared with that of the human heart? Man the individual is a deeper being than man in the mass. Jean Valjean, at that moment, was in a state of appalling shock, with all his worst terrors realized. Like Paris itself he was trembling on the verge of a revolution that was both formidable and deep-seated. A few hours had sufficed to bring it about. His destiny and his conscience were both suddenly plunged in shadow. It might be said of him, as of Paris, that within him two principles were at war. The angel of light was about to grapple with the angel of darkness on the bridge over the abyss. Which would overthrow the other? Which would gain the day?

On the evening of that 5 June, Valjean, with Cosette and Toussaint, had removed to the Rue de l'Homme-Armé, and it was here that the unforeseen awaited him.

Cosette had not left the Rue Plumet without protest. For the first time in their life together her wishes and those of Jean Valjean had shown themselves to be separate matters which, if not wholly opposed, were at least contradictory. Objections on the one side had been met by inflexibility on the other. The abrupt warning to Valjean to change his abode, flung at him by a stranger, had so alarmed him as to make him overbearing. He had thought that his secret was discovered and that the police were after him. Cosette had been forced to give way.

They had arrived in tight-lipped silence at the Rue de l'Homme-Armé, each concerned with a personal problem, Valjean so perturbed that he did not perceive Cosette's distress, and Cosette so unhappy that she failed to discern his state of alarm.

Valjean had brought Toussaint with them, a thing he had never done on their previous removals. He foresaw that he might never go back to the Rue Plumet, and he could neither leave Toussaint behind nor tell her his secret. In any event, he could trust her to be faithful. The start of betrayal, as between servant and master, is curiosity. But Toussaint, as though she had been born to be Valjean's servant, was quite incurious. She said in her stumbling peasant dialect, 'It's all one to me. I do my work, and the rest is no affair of mine.'

In their departure from the Rue Plumet, so hasty as to be almost flight, Jean Valjean had taken nothing with him except the cherished box of child's clothing which Cosette had nicknamed his 'inseparable'. A pile of luggage would have necessitated the services of a carrier, and a carrier is a witness. A fiacre had been summoned to the door in the Rue de Babylone, and they had driven off. It was only with difficulty that Toussaint had obtained permission to make up a few packages of clothes and toilet articles. Cosette had taken nothing but her letter-case and blotter. Valjean, as a further precaution, had arranged for them to leave at nightfall, which had allowed her time to write her letter to Marius. It was dark when they reached the Rue de l'Homme-Armé.

They went to bed in silence. The apartment in the Rue de l'Homme-Armé was on the second floor overlooking the courtyard at the back of the house, and consisted of two bedrooms, a living-room with a kitchen adjoining, and an attic room furnished with a truckle-bed, which fell to Toussaint. The living-room was also the entrance-lobby and it separated the two bedrooms. The apartment was equipped with all the necessary domestic paraphernalia.

Panic, such is human nature, may die down as irrationally as it arises. Scarcely had they reached their new dwelling than Valjean's alarm subsided until finally it had vanished altogether. There are places of which the calm communicates itself almost mechanically to the human spirit. The Rue de l'Homme-Armé is a small, unimportant street inhabited by peaceful citizens, so narrow that it is barred to vehicles at either end, silent amid the tumult of Paris, dark even in broad daylight, seemingly incapable of any emotion between its two rows of tall, century-old houses which keep themselves to themselves like the ancients they are. It is a street of placid forgetfulness, and Jean Valjean, breathing its odour of tranquillity, was caught by the contagion. How could anyone find him here?

His first act was to put the 'inseparable' beside his bed. He slept well. The night brings counsel, and, one may add, it soothes. He was almost light-hearted when he got up next morning. He found the living-room delightful, hideous though it was with its old round dining-table, the low sideboard with a mirror hanging on the wall above it, a worm-eaten armchair, and a few other chairs loaded with Toussaint's packages. A tear in one of these showed that it contained Valjean's National Guard uniform.

As for Cosette, she had asked Toussaint to bring her a cup of soup in her bedroom and she did not appear until the evening. At about five o'clock Toussaint, who had been busy all day putting things to rights, set a dish of cold chicken on the table and Cosette deigned to attend the meal, out of deference to her father.

This done, and saying that she had a headache, Cosette bade her father goodnight and went back to her bedroom. Valjean, having eaten a wing of chicken with a good appetite, sat with his elbows on the table, basking in his present security. He had been vaguely aware, while he was eating, of Toussaint's stammer as she tried to tell him the news—'Monsieur, there's something happening. There's fighting in the town'. Absorbed in his own thoughts, he had paid no attention to this. In fact, he had not really listened. He got up presently and began to walk up and down the room, from the door to the window and back, feeling more and more at ease.

And with his growing serenity the thought of Cosette, his constant preoccupation, returned to him. Not that he was troubled by her headache, which he regarded as nothing but a trifling *crise de nerfs*, a girlish sulk that would wear off in a day or two; but he was thinking of her future, and, as always, with affectionate concern. After all, there seemed to be no reason why their happy life should not continue. There are times when all things look impossible, and times when all things look easy. For Valjean this was one of the latter occasions. As a rule they follow bad times as day follows night, by that law of succession and contrast which is at the heart of Nature, and which superficial minds call antithesis. In the placid street where he had taken refuge, Valjean shrugged off all the anxieties which for some time had been troubling him. From the very fact of having seen so many dark clouds, he now had glimpses of a clearer sky. To have left the Rue Plumet without difficulty or any untoward incident was in itself a gain.

It might well be prudent to leave France, if only for a few months, and go to London. Well then, that was what they would do. What did it matter where they were provided they were together? Cosette was his only country, all that he needed for his happiness. The thought that perhaps he might not be all that Cosette needed for happiness, which at one time had caused him sleepless nights, did not now enter his mind. He was rid of all past troubles, in a state of brimming optimism. Cosette, being near him, seemed part of him— an optical illusion which everyone has experienced. He mentally planned their journey to England, endowing it with every imaginable comfort, and, in his day-dream, saw his happiness reborn no matter where they were.

But as he paced slowly up and down the room something suddenly caught his eye. He came face to face with the mirror hanging at an inclined angle over the sideboard, and, reflected in it, he read the following lines:

My dearest,

Alas, father insists that we must leave here at once. We go tonight to No. 7, Rue de l'Homme-Armé, and in a week we shall be in England.

Cosette 4th June.

Jean Valjean stood aghast.

Cosette when they arrived had put her blotting-book on the dresser, and in her distress had forgotten to remove it, leaving it open at the page on which she had blotted her letter to Marius; and the mirror, reflecting the reversed handwriting, had made it clearly legible. It was simple and it was devastating.

Valjean moved closer to the mirror. He re-read the lines without believing in their existence. They were like something seen in a lightning-flash, a hallucination. The thing was impossible; it could not be true.

Slowly his wits returned to him. He examined the blotter with a renewed sense of reality, studying the blotted lines which, in their reversed state, were a meaningless scrawl. He thought, 'But there's no sense in this, it's not handwriting,' and drew a deep breath of irrational relief. Which of us has not known these aberrations in moments of intense shock? The spirit does not give way to despair until it has exhausted every possibility of self-deception.

He stood staring stupidly at the blotter in his hand, almost ready to laugh at the hallucination which had so nearly deceived him. But then he looked again in the mirror and saw the words reflected in remorseless clarity. This was no illusion. The reflection of a fact is in itself a fact. This was Cosette's handwriting. He saw it all.

He trembled and, putting down the blotter, sank into the arm-chair by the sideboard, to sit there with his head lolling, his eyes dulled in utter dismay. He said to himself that there was no escape, the light of his world had gone out, since Cosette had written this to someone other than himself. But then he heard his own spirit, become again terrible, roar sullenly in the darkness. Try to rob a lion of its cub!

What is strange and sad is that at that time Marius had not received the letter. Fate had treacherously delivered it into Valjean's hands before Marius had seen it.

Until that moment no trial had been too much for Jean Valjean. He had endured hideous ordeals; no extremity of ill-fortune had been spared him; every utmost hardship, every vindictiveness and all the spite of which society was capable had been visited upon him. He had stood his ground unflinching, accepting, when he had to, the bitterest blows. He had sacrificed the inviolability he had gained as a man restored to life, surrendered his freedom, risked his neck, lost everything and suffered everything, and had remained tolerant and stoical to the point that at moments he seemed to have achieved the self-abnegation of a martyr. His conscience, fortified by so many battles with a malignant fate, had seemed unassailable. But anyone able to see into his heart would have been forced to admit that now he weakened.

Of all the torments he had suffered in his long trial by adversity, this was the worst. Never had the rack and thumbscrew been more shrewdly applied. He felt the stirring of forgotten sensibilities, the quiver of deep-buried nerves. Alas, the supreme ordeal—indeed, the one true ordeal—is the loss of the beloved.

It is true that the poor, ageing man loved Cosette only as a father; but, as we have already said, the emptiness of his life had caused this paternal love to embrace all others. He loved Cosette as his daughter, his mother, his sister; and since he had had neither mistress nor wife, since human nature is a creditor who accepts no compromise, that kind of love, too, was mingled with the others, confused and unrealized, pure with the purity of blindness, innocent, unconscious and sublime, less an emotion than an instinct, and less an instinct than a bond, impalpable, indefinable, but real. The true essence of love was threaded through his immense tenderness for Cosette like the seam of gold hidden unsullied beneath the mountainside.

We must recall the relationship between them that we have already described. No marriage between them was possible, not even a marriage of souls, and yet their destinies were assuredly joined. Except Cosette—that is to say, except a child—Jean Valjean had known nothing of the things that men love. No succession of loves and passions had coloured his life with those changing shades of green, fresh green followed by dark green, which we see in trees that have lived through a winter and men who have lived for more than fifty years. In short, as we have more than once emphasized, that inner fusion, that whole of which the sum was a lofty virtue, had resulted in making Jean Valjean a father to Cosette. A strange father compounded of the parent, son, brother and husband who all existed within him; a father in whom there was even something of the mother; a father who loved and worshipped Cosette, for whom she was light and dwelling-place, family, country, paradise.

So that now, when he realized that this was positively ended, that she was escaping from him, slipping through his fingers like water, like a mist; when he was confronted by the crushing evidence that another possessed her heart and was the end and purpose of her life, and that he was no more than the father, someone who no longer existed; when he could no longer doubt this, but was forced to say, 'She is going to leave me', the intensity of his pain was past enduring. To have done so much for it to end like this; to be no one, of no account! He was shaken throughout his being by a tempest of revolt, and he felt to the very roots of his hair an overweening rebirth of egotism—self bellowed from the depths of his emptiness.

There is such a thing as spiritual collapse. The thrust of a desperate certainty into a man cannot occur without the disruption of certain profound elements which are sometimes the man himself. Anguish, when it has reached this stage, becomes a panic-flight of all the powers of conscience. There are mortal crises from which few of us emerge in our right mind, with our sense of duty still intact. When the limit of suffering is overpassed the most impregnable virtue is plunged in disarray. Jean Valjean picked up the blotter again, and again convinced himself. As though turned to stone, he stood with eyes intent on those irrefutable lines, and such a darkness filled his mind as to make it seem that all his soul had crumbled.

He studied the revelation, and the exaggerations which his own imagination supplied, with an appearance of calm that in itself was frightening, for it is a dreadful thing when the calm of a man becomes the coldness of a statue. He measured this change effected by a remorseless destiny of which he had been quite unaware, recalling his fears of the summer, so lightly dismissed. It was the same precipice, it had not changed; but now he was not standing at the edge, he was at the bottom. And, which was of all things most bitter and outrageous, he had fallen without knowing. The light of his life had vanished while he thought that the sun still shone.

His instinct spared him nothing. He recalled incidents, dates, certain flushes and pallors on Cosette's cheek, and he thought, 'That was he!' The lucid percipience of despair is like an arrow that never fails to find its target. His thoughts flew instantly to Marius. He did not know the name, but he promptly placed the man. He clearly saw, in the implacable revival of memory, the youthful stranger in the Luxembourg, the contemptible chaser of girls, the love-lorn idler, the fool, the cheat—for it is treachery to make eyes at a girl with a loving parent at her side.

Having decided in his mind that this young man was at the bottom of it all, Jean Valjean, the man who had redeemed himself, who had mastered his soul and with such painful effort resolved all life, hardship and suffering in love, turned his inward vision upon himself: and a ghost rose before his eyes—hatred.

Great suffering brings great weakness; it undermines the will to live. In youth it is perilous, but later it may be disastrous. For if despair is terrible when the blood is hot, the hair dark, the head still held high like the flame of a torch; when the thread of destiny has still to be unreeled and the heart may still beat faster with a worthy love; when there are still women and laughter and the whole wide world; when the force of life is undiminished—if despair even then is terrible, what must it be in age, when the years rush past with a growing pallor and through the dusk we begin to see the stars of eternity?

While he sat brooding Toussaint entered the room. Valjean turned to her and asked:

'Where is it happening? Do you know?'

She stared at him in bewilderment.

'I don't understand.'

'Didn't you say there was fighting going on somewhere?'

'Oh, I see,' said Toussaint. 'It's near Saint-Merry.'

There are actions which arise, without our knowing it, from the depths of our thought. No doubt it was owing to an impulse of this kind, of which he was scarcely conscious, that a few minutes later Valjean was out in the street. He was seated, bareheaded, on the curbstone outside the house. He seemed to be listening.

Darkness had fallen.

II. *A Boy at War with Street-lamps*

How long did he stay there? What was the ebb and flow of his tragic meditation? Did he seek to recover himself? Was he so bowed down as to be broken, or could he still stand upright, finding within himself something still solid on which to set his feet? Probably he himself did not know.

The street was empty. The occasional apprehensive inhabitant, hurriedly returning home, scarcely noticed him. In times of peril it is every man for himself. The lamplighter, on his accustomed round, lit the lamp, which was just opposite the door of No. 7, and went his way. To anyone pausing to examine him in the half-light, Jean Valjean would not have seemed a living man. Seated on the curbstone outside his door he was like a figure carved in ice. There is a frozen aspect of despair. Vague sounds of distant tumult, tocsins and fanfares, were to be heard, and mingled with these the clock of the Église de Saint-Paul, gravely and without haste striking the hour of eleven: for the tocsin is man, but the hour is God. The passing of time made no impression on Valjean; he did not move. But at about that time a sudden burst of firing sounded from the direction of the market, followed by a second, even more violent. Probably this was the attack on the Rue de Chanvrerie barricade which, as we know, Marius repulsed. The two volleys, their savagery seeming heightened by the outraged stillness of the night, caused Valjean to get to his feet and stand facing the direction from which the din had come; but then he sat down again, and, crossing his arms, let his chin sink slowly on to his chest while he resumed his inward debate.

The sound of footsteps caused him to raise his head. By the light of the street lamp he saw a youthful figure approaching, pale-faced but glowing with life. Gavroche had arrived in the Rue de l'Homme-Armé.

He was gazing at the house fronts, apparently in search of a number. Although he could see Valjean he paid no attention to him. He stared up and then down, and, rising on tip-toe, rapped on doors and ground floor windows. All were locked and barred. After trying five or six houses in vain he shrugged his shoulders and commented on the situation as follows:

'Well, blow me!'

Jean Valjean, who in his present state of mind would not have addressed or answered any other person, was irresistibly moved to question this lively small boy.

'Well, youngster, what are you up to?'

'What I'm after is that I'm hungry,' said Gavroche crisply; and he added, 'Youngster yourself.'

Valjean felt in his pocket and produced a five-franc piece. But Gavroche, skipping from one subject to another like the sparrow he was, had become aware of the street-lamp. He picked up a stone.

'You've still got lights burning in these parts,' he said. 'That's not right, mate. No discipline. I'll have to smash it.'

He flung the stone, and the lamp-glass fell with a clatter which caused the occupants of the nearby houses, huddled behind their curtains, to exclaim, 'It's '93 all over again!'

'There you are, you old street,' said Gavroche. 'Now you've got your nightcap on.' He turned to Valjean. 'What's that monstrous great building at the end of the street? The Archives, isn't it? You ought to pull down some of those pillars and make them into a barricade.'

Jean Valjean went towards him.

'Poor little chap,' he muttered. 'He's half-starved.' And he pressed the five-franc piece into his hand.

Startled by the size of the offering, Gavroche stared at the coin, charmed by its whiteness as it glimmered faintly in his hand. He had heard of five-franc pieces, he knew them by reputation, and he was

delighted to see one at close quarters. Something worth looking at, he thought, and did so for some moments with pleasure. But then he held out the coin to Valjean, saying in a lordly fashion:

'Thank you, guv'nor, but I'd sooner smash street lamps. Take back your bribe. It doesn't work with me.'

'Have you a mother?' Valjean asked.

'More than you have perhaps.'

'Then keep it and give it to her.'

Gavroche was melted by this. Besides, the man was hatless, and this predisposed him in his favour.

'You mean I can have it?' he said. 'It's not just to stop me smashing lamps?'

'Smash as many as you like.'

'You're all right,' said Gavroche. He put the coin in one of his pockets, and with a growing assurance, asked: 'Do you live in this street?'

'Yes. Why?'

'Would you mind telling me which is Number Seven?'

'Why do you want to know?'

Gavroche was brought up short, feeling that he had already said too much. He ran a hand through his hair and said cryptically:

'Because.'

A thought occurred to Jean Valjean. Acute distress has these moments of lucidity. He asked:

'Have you brought me the letter I've been waiting for?'

'You?' said Gavroche. 'But you're not a woman.'

'A letter addressed to Mademoiselle Cosette.'

'Cosette,' muttered Gavroche. 'I think that's a rummy name.'

'Well then, I'm to give it to her. May I have it?'

'I take it you know that I've come from the barricades.'

'Of course . . .' said Valjean.

Gavroche fished in another pocket and got out the folded sheet of paper. He then gave a military salute.

'Confidential despatch,' he said, 'from the Provisional Government.'

'Let me have it,' said Valjean.

Gavroche held the missive above his head.

'Don't go getting the idea that this is just a *billet doux*. It's addressed to a woman, but it's for the people. Our lot, we may be rebels, but we respect the weaker sex. We aren't like the fine world where it's all wolves chasing after geese.'

'Give it to me.'

'I'm bound to say,' said Gavroche, 'you look to me like a decent cove.'

'Quickly, please.'

'Well, here you are.' Gavroche handed over the letter. 'And hurry it up, Monsieur Chose. You mustn't keep Mamselle Chosette waiting.' He was pleased with this happy play on words.

'One thing,' said Jean Valjean. 'Should I take the reply to Saint-Merry?'

'If you did you'd be making what's called a floater,' said Gavroche. 'That letter comes from the barricade in the Rue de la Chanvrerie, to which I am now returning. Good night, citizen.'

Whereupon Gavroche departed—or, better, returned like a homing pigeon to its nest. He sped away into the night with the swift certainty of a bullet, and the narrow Rue de l'Homme-Armé was again plunged in empty silence. In the twinkling of an eye the strange little boy, that creature of darkness and fantasy, had disappeared into the gloom amid the tall rows of houses, vanishing like a puff of smoke; and one might have thought that he had vanished for ever if, a minute after his departure, the indignant dwellers in the Rue du Chaume had not been startled by the crash of another street-lamp.

III. *While Cosette and Toussaint Sleep*

Jean Valjean went back into the house with Marius's letter. As grateful for the darkness as an owl clutching its prey, he groped his way upstairs, gently opened his door and closed it behind him, stood listening until he was assured that Cosette and Toussaint were asleep. Then, so greatly was his hand shaking, he made several vain attempts before extracting a spark from the Fumade tinder-box. His every action was like that of a thief in the night. Finally, with his candle lighted, he sat down at the table and unfolded the letter.

We cannot be said to read when in a state of violent emotion. Rather, we twist the paper in our hands, mutilating it as though it were an enemy, scoring it with the finger-nails of our anger or delight. Our eyes skip the beginning, hurrying on to the end. With a feverish acuteness we grasp the general sense, seize upon the main point and ignore the rest. In the letter written by Marius, Jean Valjean was conscious only of the following: 'I shall die . . . When you read this my soul will be very near . . .'

The effect of these words was to kindle in him a horrid exaltation, so that for a moment he was as it were dumbfounded by the sudden change of feeling in himself. He stared in a kind of drunken bemusement at the letter. There, beneath his eyes, was a marvel—the death of the hated person.

His triumph cried out hideously within him. So it was done with! His problem was solved, more rapidly than he had dared to hope. The individual who threatened his happiness was to vanish from the scene; and of his own free will. Without any action on the part of Jean Valjean, through no fault of his, this 'other man' was about to die, perhaps was already dead. Valjean's fevered mind made calculations. No, he was not yet dead. The letter was evidently intended to be read by Cosette tomorrow morning. Nothing had happened after those two bursts of musket fire between eleven and midnight. The real attack on the barricade would not begin until daylight. But it made no difference. Having joined in the battle the 'other man' was doomed to die, swept away in the stream of events . . . Valjean felt that he was saved. Once again he would have Cosette to himself, without any rival, and their life together would continue as before. He had only to keep this letter in his pocket. Cosette would never know what had happened to that other man. 'I have only to let things take their course. There is no escape for the youth. If he is not yet dead he will certainly die. What happiness!'

But having assured himself of this, Valjean's gloom returned; and presently he went downstairs and roused the porter.

About an hour later he left the house again, clad in the full uniform of the National Guard and fully armed. The porter had had no difficulty in finding in the neighbourhood the means to complete his equipment. With a loaded musket and a pouch filled with cartridges he set off for Les Halles.

IV. *Excess of Zeal on the Part of Gavroche*

Gavroche, meanwhile, had been having an adventure. Having conscientiously shattered the street-lamp in the Rue du Chaume, he had passed on into the Rue des Vieilles-Haudriettes where, finding nothing worthy of his attention, he had seen fit to unburden himself of a lusty repertoire of song. The sleeping or terrified houses had been favoured with subversive ditties of which the following is a sample:

The birds sit brooding in the trees
Where distantly the river swirls
Their chirping lingers on the breeze—
But where are all the golden girls?

Pierrot, my friend, you're on your knees,
While through your head fair fortune whirls,
And prayer perhaps may bring you ease—
But where are all the golden girls?

Toiling and buzzing like the bees
You dream of houses decked with pearls,
But I love Agnes and Louise—
And where are all the golden girls? . . .

And so on . . . While he walked Gavroche was acting his song, for the weight of the refrain is in the gesture that accompanies it. His face, with its endless variety of expressions, writhed in a series of grimaces more fantastic and extraordinary than those of a torn cloth flying in the wind. Unhappily, since he was alone and in darkness, no one saw or could have seen him: and this wealth was scattered in vain.

But suddenly he stopped short—'Away with sentiment,' he said.

His cat's eyes had discerned in the recess of a doorway what is known to painters as an ensemble—a composition, that is to say, of man and object. The object was a handcart, the man was an Auvergnat, a peasant from the Auvergne, lying asleep in it. The handles of the cart were resting on the pavement and the man's head was resting against the tail-board, so that he lay sloping downwards with his feet touching the ground. Gavroche, rich in worldly experience, at once knew what he had to deal with—a street carrier who had drunk rather too much and was now sleeping it off.

'So here's the use of a summer night,' reflected Gavroche. 'The Auvergnat is asleep in his cart. We requisition the cart for the service of the Republic and leave the Auvergnat to the Monarchy.' For it had instantly occurred to him that the cart would come in very handy on the barricade.

The man was snoring. Gavroche gently pulled the cart one way and the man the other by his feet, so that in a very short time the Auvergnat, undisturbed, was lying on the pavement. The cart was now free.

Gavroche, being always prepared for emergencies, was as always well equipped. He got out of his pocket a scrap of paper and a stub of red pencil pinched from a carpenter's shop, and wrote as follows:

French Republic
Received—one handcart.
(signed) GAVROCHE

He then put the receipt in the pocket of the snoring Auvergnat's waistcoat, grasped the handcart by the handles, and set off for the market at a run, pushing it with a glorious clatter in front of him.

This was dangerous, for there was a military post in the Imprimerie Royale, the royal printing-works. Gavroche did not think of this. The post was occupied by a section of the Garde Nationale from outside Paris. For some time there had been a certain restiveness in the section and heads had been raised from camp beds. The smashing of two street-lamps, followed by a song delivered at full lung-power, all this was rather surprising in unadventurous streets which were accustomed to put out their candles and go to bed at nightfall. For the past hour the urchin Gavroche had been setting up a stir in that peaceful neighbourhood that was like the buzzing of a fly in a bottle. The out-of-town sergeant was listening. But he was also waiting, being a prudent man.

The clatter of the handcart over the cobbles robbed him of all further excuse for delay, and he decided to go out and reconnoitre. '—there must be a whole gang of them,' he reflected. 'Gently does it.' Who could doubt that the Hydra of Anarchy had raised its head and was rampaging through the quarter? He ventured cautiously out of the post.

And Gavroche, pushing the handcart into the Rue des Vieilles-Haudriettes, found himself suddenly confronted by a uniform, a plumed helmet, and a musket. For the second time he was brought up short.

'So here we are,' he said. 'Authority in person. Good day to you.' Gavroche was never long put out of countenance.

'Where are you going, rascal?' barked the sergeant.

'Citizen,' said Gavroche, 'I haven't called you a bourgeois. Why should you insult me?'

'Where are you going, clown?'

'Monsieur,' said Gavroche, 'yesterday you were perhaps a man of wit, but today your wits have failed you.'

'I'm asking where you're going.'

'How politely you talk! You know, you don't look your age. You should sell your hair at a hundred francs apiece. That would net you five hundred francs.

'Where are you going? Where are you off to? What are you doing, you young scoundrel?'

'That's a very ugly word. Before you have another drink you should wash your mouth out.'

The sergeant levelled his musket.

'Will you or will you not tell me where you're going?'

'My lord General,' said Gavroche, 'I'm on my way to fetch the doctor for my wife, who's in labour.'

'To arms!' shouted the sergeant.

It is the hall-mark of great men that they can turn weakness into triumph. Gavroche summed up the situation at a glance. The handcart had got him into trouble and the handcart must get him out of it. As the sergeant bore down upon him the cart, driven forward like a battering ram, took him in the stomach and he fell backwards into the gutter while his musket was discharged into the air. The sound of his shout brought his men rushing out of the post, and that first shot was followed by a ragged burst of firing, after which they reloaded and began again. This blind-man's-buff engagement lasted a quarter of an hour. The casualties were a number of window-panes.

Meanwhile, Gavroche, who had taken to his heels, pulled up half-a-dozen streets away and sat down on a curbstone to get his breath. He sat listening, and presently turned in the direction of the shooting. He raised his left hand to the level of his nose and jerked it forward three times, at the same time slapping the back of his head with his right hand—the sovereign gesture with which the Paris street-urchin sums up all French irony, and which is evidently efficacious, since it has endured for half a century.

But his triumph was damped by a sobering thought.

'It's all very fine,' he reflected. 'I'm laughing fit to split and having a high old time, but now I'm on the wrong road and I've got a long way to go. It won't do for me to get back too late.'

Running on he resumed his song, and the following stanza echoed through the sombre streets:

We drain the wine-cup to the lees,
And cheer the flag when it unfurls;
And life and death are as you please—
But where are all the golden girls?

The armed sortie from the post was not without a sequel. The handcart was captured and its drunken owner taken prisoner. The one was impounded and the other half-heartedly tried by court martial as an accomplice of the rebels. Thus did authority display its zeal in the protection of society.

Gavroche's adventure, now a part of the folk-lore of the Temple quarter, is among the most terrifying memories of aged citizens of the Marais, its title being *Night attack on the post at the Imprimerie Royale.*

PART FIVE

Jean Valjean

BOOK ONE

WAR WITHIN FOUR WALLS

I. *Scylla and Charybdis*

THE TWO barricades most likely to be recalled by the student of social disorder do not come within the period of this story. Both of them, each symbolic of a particular aspect of a redoubtable situation, were flung up during the insurrection of June 1848, the biggest street-war in history.

It sometimes happens in defiance of principle, regardless of liberty, equality and fraternity, universal suffrage, and the government of the whole by the whole, that an outcast sector of the populace, the riff-raff, rises up in its anguish and frustration, its miseries and privation, its fever, ignorance, darkness, and despair, to challenge the rest of society. The down-and-outs do battle with the common law: mobocracy rebels against demos.

Those are melancholy occasions, for their dementia always contains an element of justice, and the conflict an element of suicide. The very words accepted as terms of abuse—down-and-outs, riff-raff, mobocracy—point, alas, rather to the faults of those who rule than to the sins of those who suffer, to the misdeeds of privilege rather than to those of the disinherited. For our own part, we can never utter those words without a feeling of grief and respect, for where history scrutinizes the facts to which they correspond it often finds greatness hand-in-hand with misery. Athens was a mobocracy: down-and-outs made Holland: the common people more than once saved Rome, and the rabble followed Jesus Christ.

There is no thinker who has not at times contemplated the splendour rising from below. It was of the rabble that St. Jerome must surely have been thinking—the vagabond poor, the outcasts from which the apostles and martyrs sprang—when he uttered the words, *Fex urbis, lex orbis*, 'Dregs of the city, law of the world'.

The fury of the mob which suffers and bleeds, its violence running counter to the principles which bring it life, its assault upon the rule of law, these are popular upheavals which must be suppressed. The man of probity stands firm, and from very love of the people opposes them. But he deeply understands their reason, and does so with respect. It is one of those rare occasions when doing what we are in duty bound to do, we have a sense of misgiving which almost calls on us to stay our hand. We go on because we must but with uneasy conscience: duty is burdened with a heavy heart.

June 1848, let me hasten to say, was exceptional, an event which history finds it almost impossible to classify. All the words we have used must be discarded in respect of that extraordinary uprising, which embodied all the warranted apprehensions of labour demanding its rights. It had to be combated; this was necessary: for it was an attack on the Republic. But what, finally, was June 1848? It was a revolt of the populace against itself.

Where the theme is not lost sight of there can be no digression. We may therefore permit ourselves to direct the reader's attention to those two wholly unique strongholds which characterized that insurrection.

One barred the entrance to the Faubourg Saint-Antoine, and the other blocked the approach to the Faubourg du Temple. No one who beheld under that brilliant June sky those two formidable creations of civil war will ever forget them.

The Saint-Antoine barricade was enormous—some three storeys high and seven hundred feet in length. It ran from one end to the other of the vast mouth of the Faubourg—that is to say, across three streets. It was jagged, makeshift, and irregular, castellated like an immense mediaeval survival, buttressed with piles of rubble that were bastions in themselves, with bays and headlands and, in solid support, the two larger promontories formed by the houses at the end of the streets—a giant's causeway along one side of the famous Place de la Bastille that had witnessed 14 July. Nineteen lesser barricades were arrayed in depth along the street behind it. The sight of this barricade alone conveyed a sense of intolerable distress which had reached the point where suffering becomes disaster. Of what was it built? Of the material of three six-storey houses demolished for the purpose, some people said. Of the phenomenon of overwhelming anger, said others. It bore the lamentable aspect of all things built by hatred—a look of destruction. One might ask, 'Who built all that?'; but one might equally ask, 'Who destroyed all that?' Everything had gone on to it, doors, grilles, screens, bedroom furniture, wrecked cooking stoves and pots and pans, piled up haphazard, the whole a composite of paving stones and rubble, timbers, iron bars, broken window panes, seatless chairs, rags, odds and ends of every kind—and curses. It was great and it was trivial, a chaotic parody of emptiness, a mingling of debris. Sisyphus had cast his rock upon it and Job his potsherd. In short it was terrible, an Acropolis of the destitute. Overturned carts protruded from its outer slope, axles pointing to the sky like scars on a rugged hillside: an omnibus, blithely hoisted by vigorous arms to its summit, as though the architects had sought to add impudence to terror, offered empty shafts to imaginary horses. The huge mass, jetsam of rebellion, was Pelion piled on the Ossa of all previous revolutions— 1793 on 1789, 9 Thermidor on 10 August, 18 Brumaire on 21 January, 1848 on 1830. The site was highly appropriate: it was a barricade worthy to appear on the place from which the grim prison had vanished. If the ocean built dykes, it was thus that it would build them: the fury of the tide itself was imprinted on that shapeless mound. And the tide was the mob. One seemed to behold riot turned to rubble. One seemed to hear, buzzing over that barricade as though it were their hive, the gigantic dark-bodied bees of violent progress. Was it a cluster of thickets, a bacchanalian orgy, or a fortress? Delirium seemed to have built it with the beating of its wings. There was something of the cloaca about it, and something of Olympus. One might see, in that hugger-mugger of desperation, roofing-ridges, fragments from garrets with their coloured wallpaper, window frames with panes intact set upright and defying cannon fire amid the rubble, uprooted fireplaces, wardrobes, tables, benches, piled in clamouring disorder, a thousand beggarly objects disdained even by beggars, the expression of fury and nothingness. One might have said that it was the tattered clothing of the people— a clothing of wood, stone and iron—which the Faubourg Saint-Antoine had swept out of doors with a huge stroke of the broom, making of its poverty its protective barrier. Hunks of wood like chopping-blocks, brackets attached to wooden frames that looked like gibbets, wheels lying flat upon the rubble—all these lent to the anarchic edifice a recollection of tortures once suffered by the people. The Saint-Antoine barricade used everything as a weapon, everything that civil war can hurl at the head of society. It was not a battle but a paroxysm. The fire-arms defending the stronghold, among which were a number of blunderbusses, poured out fragments of pottery, knuckle-bones, coat buttons, and even castors, dangerous missiles because of their metalwork. That barricade was a mad thing, flinging an inexpressible clamour into the sky. At moments when it defied the army, it was covered with bodies and with tempest, surmounted by a dense array of flaming heads. It was a thing of swarming activity, with a bristling fringe of muskets, sabres, cudgels, axes, pikes and bayonets. A huge red flag flapped in the wind. The shouting of orders was to be heard, warlike song, the roll of drums, the sobbing of women, and the dark raucous laughter of the half-starved. It was beyond reason and it was alive; and, as though from the back of some electric-coated animal, lightning crackled over it.

The spirit of revolution cast its shadow over that mound, resonant with the voice of the people, which resembles the voice of God: a strange nobility emanated from it. It was a pile of garbage, and it was Sinai.

As we have said, it was raised in the name of the Revolution. But what was it fighting? It was fighting the Revolution. That barricade, which was chance, disorder, terror, misunderstanding and the unknown, was at war with the Constituent Assembly, the sovereignty of the people, universal suffrage, the nation and the Republic. It was the *Carmagnole* defying the *Marseillaise*. An insane but heroic defiance, for that ancient faubourg is a hero.

The faubourg and its stronghold sustained one another, the faubourg lending a shoulder to the stronghold and the stronghold bracing itself against the faubourg. The huge barricade was like a cliff against which the strategy of the generals from Africa was shattered. Its recesses and excrescences, its warts and swellings grinned, so to speak, and jeered through the smoke. Grapeshot vanished in its depths: shells were swallowed up in it; musket balls did no more than make small holes. What good does it do to bombard chaos? The soldiers, accustomed to the most fearful manifestations of war, were dismayed by this fortress that was like a wild beast, by its boar-like bristling and its mountainous size.

Some half a mile away, near the Château d'Eau where the Rue du Temple runs into the boulevard, the onlooker, if he was not afraid to risk his head by peering round the promontory formed by the Magasin Dallemagne, might see, far off, looking across the canal and along the street rising up to the heights of Belleville, at the summit of the rise a strange-looking wall about two storeys high, a sort of hyphen between the houses on either side—as though the street had folded in upon itself to shut itself off. This wall, built of paving-stones, was straight and perpendicular, as though it had been constructed with the aid of a T-square. It was, no doubt, lacking in cement, but, as with some Roman walls, this in no way impaired the rigidity of its structure. A view from above enabled one to ascertain its thickness: it was mathematically even from top to bottom. Its grey surface was pierced at regular intervals with almost invisible loopholes, like dark threads. The street bore every sign of being deserted: all doors and windows were closed. The wall erected across it, a motionless, silent barrier, had made of it a cul-de-sac in which no person was to be seen, no sound heard. Bathed in the dazzling June sunshine, it had the look of a sepulchre. This was the Faubourg du Temple barricade.

Coming to that place, and seeing that remarkable structure, even the boldest spirit was moved to ponder. It was immaculate in design, flawless in alignment, symmetrical, rectilinear and funereal, a thing of craftsmanship and darkness. One felt that its presiding spirit must be either a mathematician or a ghost: and, contemplating it, one spoke in a lowered voice.

When, as happened from time to time, someone ventured to enter that deserted stretch of road—a soldier or a representative of the people—there was a faint, shrill whistle, and he fell, either wounded or dead; or, if he escaped, a bullet buried itself in a shutter or housefront. Sometimes it was a burst of grapeshot, for the defenders had contrived to make two small cannon out of gas-piping blocked at one end with oakum and fire-clay. Nearly every bullet found its mark. There were corpses here and there and pools of blood. I remember seeing a butterfly flutter up and down that street. Summer does not abdicate.

The entrances to the houses in the neighbouring street were filled with wounded. One felt in that place the gaze of an unseen observer, as though the street itself were taking aim. Massed behind the hump of the narrow bridge across the canal, at the approach to the Faubourg du Temple, the attacking troops, grim-faced and wary, kept watch on that silent and impassive stronghold which spat death. Some crawled on their stomachs on to the hump, taking care that their tall helmets should not show.

The gallant Colonel Monteynard observed the barricade with a shuddering admiration. 'The way it's built!' he exclaimed. 'Not a stone out of line. It might be made of earthenware!'—and as he spoke the words, a bullet smashed the cross on his breast and he fell.

'The cowards!' men said. 'Why don't they show themselves? Why do they skulk in hiding?' . . . That barricade at the Faubourg du Temple, defended by eighty men against ten thousand, held out for three days. On the fourth day, it was captured by the device of breaking through the adjoining houses and clambering over the roofs. Not one of the eighty 'cowards' attempted to escape. All were killed except their leader, Barthélemy, of whom we shall have more to say.

The Saint-Antoine barricade was a place of thunderous defiance, the one at the Temple a place of silence. The difference between these two strongholds was the difference between the savage and the sinister, the one a roaring open mouth, the other a mask. The huge, mysterious insurrection of June '48 was at once an outburst of fury and an enigma: in the first of these barricades the dragon was discernible; in the second, the sphinx.

The two strongholds were the work of two men, Cournet and Barthélemy, and each bore the image of the man responsible.

Cournet of Saint-Antoine was a burly broad-shouldered man, red-faced, heavy-fisted, daring, and loyal, his gaze candid but awe-inspiring. He was intrepid, energetic, irascible and temperamental, the warmest of friends and the most formidable of enemies. War and conflict, the *mêlée*, were the air he breathed, they put him in high spirits. He had been a naval officer, and his voice and bearing had the flavour of sea and tempest—he brought the gale with him into battle. Except for genius there was in Cournet something of Danton, just as, except for divinity, there was in Danton something of Hercules.

Barthélemy, of the Temple, was thin and puny, sallow-faced and taciturn, a sort of tragic outcast who, having been beaten by a police officer, waited for the chance and killed him. He was sent to the galleys at the age of seventeen, and when he came out he built this barricade.

Later a terrible thing happened in London, where both men were in hiding. Barthélemy killed Cournet. It was a duel to the death, one of those mysterious affairs of passion in which French justice sees extenuating circumstances and English justice sees only the death penalty. Barthélemy was hanged. Thanks to the sombre ordering of society, that luckless man, who possessed a mind that was certainly resolute and perhaps great, by reason of material privation and moral darkness, began his life in a French prison, and ended it on an English scaffold. Barthélemy at all times flew one flag only, and it was black.

II. *What to do in a Bottomless Pit except Talk?*

Sixteen years are a useful period in the underground instruction of rebellion, and they were wiser in June 1848 than in June 1832. The barricade in the Rue de la Chanvrerie was nothing but a first outline, an embryo, compared with those we have been describing. Nevertheless, it was impressive for its time.

Under the eye of Enjolras, for Marius no longer took count of anything, the rebels made good use of the hours of darkness. The barricade was not merely repaired but strengthened, its height raised by two feet. Iron bars projected from between the paving-stones like couched lances. Fresh material had been brought in to add to the complexity of its outer face and it had been cunningly rebuilt so that on the one side it resembled a thicket and on the other side a wall. The stairway of paving-stones which made it possible to climb to the top, as on to the battlements of a fortress, had been restored. The whole area within the barricades had been tidied up, the ground-floor room of the tavern cleared and the kitchen converted into a first-aid post where all wounds had been dressed. More bullets had been cast and cartridges made. The weapons of the fallen had been redistributed, and the bodies of the dead removed. They were heaped in the Mondétour alleyway, still commanded by the rebels, of which the pavement had long been red with blood. Among the dead were four suburban National Guards. Enjolras had their uniforms laid aside.

Enjolras had advised everyone to get two hours sleep, and a hint from him amounted to a command. Nevertheless, only three or four obeyed it. Feuilly spent the two hours carving the words 'Long Live the People!' on the house facing the tavern. They were still there, carved with a nail on a beam, in 1848.

The three women had taken advantage of the darkness to vanish finally from the scene, which was a relief to the rebels. They were now hiding in a nearby house.

The majority of the casualties were still able and willing to fight; but five badly wounded men lay on a bed of straw and mattresses in the kitchen, two of them National Guards. These latter were the first to be attended to.

No one remained in the downstairs room except Monsieur Mabeuf under his black shroud and Javert, lashed to his pillar.

'The house of the dead,' said Enjolras.

The table on which Monsieur Mabeuf lay was at the far end of the room, lighted by a single candle, its horizontal outline visible behind the pillar, so that the two figures, Javert upright and Mabeuf prone, vaguely suggested the form of a cross.

The shaft of the omnibus, damaged though it was by musket fire, was still sufficiently upright to fly a flag; and Enjolras, who possessed the especial virtue of a leader, in that he always did what he said he would do, had attached the old man's bloodstained jacket to it.

No meal was possible, since there was neither bread nor meat. In the sixteen hours they had been there the fifty defenders of the barricade had devoured all the tavern's scanty store. There comes a point when every fortress that holds out becomes a raft of Medusa. They had to put up with being hungry. It was on that Spartan day of 6 June that Jeanne, the commander of the Saint-Merry barricade, surrounded by supporters clamouring to be fed, retorted: 'What for? It is now three—by four o'clock we shall be dead.'

Since there was nothing to eat, Enjolras placed a ban on drinking, withholding wine altogether and rationing eau-de-vie. Fifteen hermetically sealed bottles were found in the cellar. Enjolras and Combeferre went down to inspect them, and Combeferre said when they came back:

'They must be some of Père Hucheloup's original stock. He started life as a grocer.'

'Probably good wine,' said Bossuet. 'It's lucky Grantaire's still asleep. Otherwise we should have had a job protecting them.'

Despite murmurs of protest, Enjolras vetoed the fifteen bottles, and, to prevent anyone touching them, to make them as it were sacrosanct, he had them placed under Monsieur Mabeuf's table.

At two o'clock in the morning roll was called. There were thirty-seven of them.

Dawn was beginning to show, and the torch, replaced in its screen of paving-stones, had been extinguished. The interior of the strong-hold, the small area of street which it enclosed, was still in shadow, and in that vaguely ominous first light it resembled the deck of a ship in distress. The dark forms of the defenders passed to and fro, while, overhanging the sombre redoubt, the house-fronts and chimney-tops grew gradually distinct. The sky was in that state of fragile uncertainty which hovers between white and blue. Birds flew happily. The roof of the tall house at the back of the strong-hold, which faced east, had a pinkish glow, and a morning breeze was stirring in the grey locks of the dead man in the third-storey window.

'I'm glad we've put out the torch,' Courfeyrac said to Feuilly. 'I didn't like the way it flared in the wind, as though it was afraid. A torch-flame resembles the wisdom of cowards: it gives a poor light because it trembles.'

Dawn rouses the spirits as it does the birds. Everyone was talking. Joly, seeing a cat exploring the gutter, was moved to philosophize.

'After all, what is a cat?' he demanded. 'It's a correction. Having created the mouse God said to himself, "That was silly of me!" and so he created the cat. The cat is the *erratum* of the mouse. Mouse and cat together represent the revised proofs of Creation.'

Combeferre was discoursing to a circle of students and workmen on the subject of the dead—Jean Prouvaire, Bahorel, Mabeuf, even Cabuc—and Enjolras's stern sadness.

'All those who have killed have suffered,' he said. 'Harmodius and Aristogeiton, Brutus, St. Stephen, Cromwell, Charlotte Corday —all have had their moments of anguish. Our hearts are so sensitive, and human life is so great a mystery, that even after a civic murder, a liberating murder, if such exists, our feeling of remorse at having killed a man exceeds the joy of having served mankind.'

A minute later, such are the twists and turns of conversation, they had arrived, by way of the verse of Jean Prouvaire and a comparison of different translations of the Georgics, particularly of the passage describing the prodigies which heralded the death of

Caesar, at the subject of Caesar himself, whence their discussion returned to Brutus.

'Caesar,' said Combeferre, 'was justly killed. Cicero was hard on him, but with reason. When Zoilus attacked Homer, Maevius attacked Virgil, Vise attacked Molière, Pope attacked Shakespeare, and Fréron attacked Voltaire, these insults were merely in accord with the age-old law of envy and hatred: genius invites hostility. Great men are always more or less assailed. But Zoilus and Cicero are two birds of a different kind. Cicero did justice with the mind just as Brutus did justice with the sword. For my part, I condemn that latter kind of justice, but the ancient world accepted it. Caesar, in crossing the Rubicon, conferring, as though they came from himself, dignities which came from the people, and not rising to greet the Senate, performed, as Eutropius said, the acts of a king and almost of a tyrant—*regia ac paene tyrannica*. He was a great man, and so much the worse or so much the better—the lesson was the greater. His twenty-three wounds afflict me less than the spittle on the forehead of Christ. Caesar was stabbed to death by senators; Christ was mauled by underlings. In the greater outrage we perceive the God.'

Bossuet, dominating the talkers from the top of a heap of paving-stones and flourishing his carbine, cried:

'Oh Cydathenaeum! Oh Myrrhinus! Oh Probalinthus! Oh Graces of the Aeantides! Who will teach me to speak the lines of Homer like a Greek from Laurium or Edapteon?'

III. *Light and Shadow*

Enjolras made a tour of reconnaissance. He went out by the Mondétour alleyway, moving cautiously along the housefronts.

The rebels, be it said, were filled with hope. Their success in repelling the night attack had made them almost disdainful of the attack that must come with the dawn. They awaited it with confident smiles, no more doubtful of success than they were of their cause. Besides which, help must assuredly be on the way. They counted on this. With the gift of sanguine prophecy which is one of the strengths of the embattled French, they divided the coming day into three parts: at six o'clock in the morning a regiment which had been 'worked on' could come over to their side; at midday all Paris would rise in revolt, and by sundown the revolution would be accomplished. The tolling of the Saint-Merry tocsin, which had not ceased for a minute since the previous evening, was still to be heard, and this was evidence that the other stronghold, the big one commanded by Jeanne, was still holding out.

Heady prognostications of this ran from group to group in a kind of grim and gay murmur resembling the buzz of war in a hive of bees.

Enjolras returned from his cautious patrol of the surrounding darkness. He stood for a moment listening to this exuberance with arms folded and a hand pressed to his mouth. Then, cool and flushed with the growing light of the morning, he said:

'The whole Paris army is involved. A third of it is concentrated on us, besides a contingent of the Garde Nationale. I made out the shakos of the fifth infantry of the line and the colours of the sixth. We shall be attacked within the hour. As for the populace, they were excited enough yesterday but now they aren't stirring. We've nothing to hope for—not a single faubourg or a single regiment. They have failed us.'

The effect of these words on the gossiping groups was like that of rainfall on a swarm of bees. All were silent. There was a moment of inexpressible terror, overshadowed by the wings of death.

But it swiftly passed. A voice from one of the groups cried:

'All right, then we'll build the barricade up to twenty feet high, citizens, and defend it with our dead bodies. We'll show the world that if the people have deserted the republicans, the republicans have not deserted the people!'

The speech, releasing men from their private terror, was greeted with cheers.

No one can say who delivered it—some ordinary working man, one of the unnamed, random heroes who crop up in moments of human crisis and social evolution to speak decisive words, and then, having in a lightning flash given utterance to the spirit of the people and of God, relapse into anonymity. So much was it in tune with the mood of that 6 June 1832, that, at almost the same moment, defenders of the Saint-Merry stronghold raised their voices in a bellow that has gone down to history—'No matter whether they come to our aid or not, we'll die to the last man!'

As we see, the two strongholds, separated though they were, were together in spirit.

IV. *Five Fewer; One More*

After that unknown man, demanding that they should 'protest with their dead bodies', had voiced the resolution of them all there arose a roar of strange satisfaction, deadly in its impact but triumphant in tone.

'To the death! We'll all stay here.'

'Why all?' asked Enjolras.

'All of us—all!'

Enjolras said:

'It's a strong position. The barricade is sound. Thirty men can hold it. Why sacrifice forty?'

'Because no one wants to leave,' was the reply.

'Citizens,' cried Enjolras, with a hint of exasperation in his voice. 'The Republic is not so rich in men that it can afford to waste them. Heroics are wasteful. If it is the duty of some of us to leave, that duty should be carried out like any other.'

Enjolras, their acknowledged leader, possessed over his followers the kind of authority that is born of absolute conviction. Nevertheless, there were rebellious murmurs. A leader to his finger-tips, Enjolras stood his ground and demanded coolly:

'Will those who are afraid of our being no more than thirty kindly say so?'

The murmurs grew louder.

'Besides,' a voice said, 'it's all very well to talk about leaving, but we're surrounded.'

'Not on the side of Les Halles,' said Enjolras. 'The Rue Mondétour is clear. You can get to the Marché des Innocents by way of the Rue des Prêcheurs.'

'And there we'll be taken,' said another voice. 'They'll see a man in a smock and cap and they'll want to know where he comes from. They'll look at his hands, they'll smell powder, and he'll be shot.'

Without replying Enjolras touched Combeferre's shoulder and the two of them went into the tavern. They re-emerged a minute later, Enjolras carrying the four uniforms stripped off the bodies of the dead soldiers and Combeferre with their belts and helmets.

'Anyone can pass through the soldiers' ranks wearing these,' Enjolras said. 'They'll do for four of you.' He dropped the uniforms on the ground.

Their stoical audience still showed no sign of obeying, and Combeferre now addressed them:

'We must show a little pity,' he said. 'Don't you see what this means? It concerns the women. Have none of you any womenfolk, or any children? Have you or haven't you? What of the mothers rocking the cradles with their young around them? If there is one among you who has never seen a nursing breast let him raise his hand. You want to get yourselves killed, and so do I, but I don't like the thought of women wringing their phantom hands over me. Die by all means, but do not cause others to die. The act of suicide we have resolved upon is sublime; but suicide is a private matter that admits of no extension, and when it is passed on to those nearest us it becomes murder. Think of small heads of fair hair, and old, white heads. Enjolras has just told me that on the fifth floor of a house at the corner of the Rue du Cygne he saw a candle burning and, silhouetted against the window-pane, the nodding head of an old woman who looked as though she had sat up waiting all night. If she is the mother of any one of you then he should hurry back to her and say, "Mother, here I am". He need not worry, the rest of us will do the job here. Those supporting a family by their labour have no right to sacrifice their lives—it is an act of desertion. Those of you who have daughters or sisters—have you thought of them? Who will feed them when you are dead? It is a terrible thing for a girl to go hungry. A man may beg, but a woman has to sell. Those charming creatures who are the delight of your life, the Jeannes or Lises or Mimis who fill your home with innocent gaiety and fragrance— are you to leave them to starve? What am I to say to you? There is a market in human flesh, and it is not your disembodied hands, fluttering over them, that will protect them from being drawn into it. Think of the streets, the shops outside which women go to and fro in low-cut gowns with their feet in the mud. Those women, too, were once chaste. Think of your sisters, those of you who have any. Prostitution, the police, the Saint-Lazare prison—that is what they will come to, those delicate, modest creatures, those marvels of gentleness and beauty. And you will no longer be there to protect them. You wanted to rescue the people from Royalty, and so you have handed your daughter over to the police. Take care, my friends; show compassion. Women, poor souls, are not much given to thinking. We pride ourselves in the fact that they are less educated than men. We prevent them from reading, from thinking, from concerning themselves with politics. Will you not also prevent them from going to the morgue tonight to identify your bodies? Those of you who have families must be sensible fellows and shake us by the hand and clear out leaving the rest of us to see this business through. I know it is not easy to run away. It's difficult. But the greater the difficulty the greater the merit. You say to yourself: "I've got a musket and here I am, and here I stay". It is easily said. But there is tomorrow, friends. You won't be living, but your families will. Think of their sufferings. Have you thought of what will happen to the rosy-cheeked, laughing, chattering infant that feels so warm in your embrace? I remember one such, no higher than my knee. The father died and some poor people took it in out of charity, but they had not enough to eat themselves. The child was always hungry.

It never cried. It huddled near the cooking-stove, which was never lighted. The chimney had been patched with clay. The child with its small hands scratched out fragments of the clay and ate them. It breathed with difficulty; it was white-faced, with weak limbs and a swollen stomach. It said nothing and did not answer when it was spoken to. It was taken to the Necker hospital, which is where I saw it. I was a junior physician at that hospital. The child died. If there are parents among you, fathers who know the happiness of going for a walk on Sunday with a child clinging to his strong, protective hand, they should think of that dead child as though it were their own. I can see him now, that poor little boy, lying naked on the dissecting-table, with the ribs standing out under his skin like the furrows of a ploughed field. We found mud in his stomach and ashes in his teeth. Let us search our conscience and take counsel with our hearts. Statistics show that fifty-five per cent of abandoned children die. I repeat, we have the women to consider—mothers, girls and babies. Have I said anything about yourselves? I know very well what you are. I know that you are brave, and that your hearts are uplifted at the thought of shedding your lives in our great cause. I know that each of you feels that he has been chosen to die usefully and magnificently and that each wants his share in the triumph. That is splendid, but you are not alone in the world. You have to think of others. You must not be egoists.'

His audience gloomily bowed their heads.

Strange are the contradictions of the human heart, even in its noblest moments! Combeferre, who said these things, was not an orphan. He remembered other men's mothers, but not his own. He was himself one of the 'egoists'.

Marius, fasting and feverish, plunged from the heights of hope to the depths of despair and, seeing his personal shipwreck approach its end, was becoming ever more deeply sunk in that state of visionary stupor which precedes the fateful moment deliberately invited. A psychologist might have studied in him the increasing symptoms of that classic condition well known to science, which bears the same relation to suffering as sensuality does to physical delight. Despair has its own ecstasies and Marius had reached them. He was witnessing events as though from outside, and the things going on around him seemed to him remote, a pattern to be conscious of, but of which the details were disregarded. He saw the figures of men coming and going in a haze, and heard the sound of voices speaking in a void.

But one thing troubled him. There was in his situation one thought that touched and aroused him. Although his only desire was to die, and nothing must be allowed to distract him from his purpose, the thought reoccurred to him in his desolate, befogged state, that this resolve must not prevent him from saving the life of some other person.

He suddenly spoke.

'Enjolras and Combeferre are right,' he said. 'I agree with them that there must be no unnecessary sacrifice. And there is no time to be lost. As Combeferre has said, some of you have families—mothers, wives, and children. Those men must leave at once.'

No man stirred.

'Married men and the supporters of families are to break ranks!' Marius repeated.

His authority was great. Enjolras was captain of the fortress, but Marius was its saviour.

'That is an order!' shouted Enjolras.

'I beseech you,' said Marius.

And then, stirred by Combeferre's address, shaken by Enjolras's order, and touched by Marius's plea, the heroic defenders began to denounce one another. 'That's right,' a youth said to another man. 'You're the father of a family. You must go.' . . . 'You're keeping your two sisters,' the older man replied. And the strangest of altercations broke out, as to who should not stay to be killed.

'Be quick,' said Courfeyrac. 'In another quarter of an hour it will be too late.'

'Citizens,' said Enjolras, 'this is the Republic, where universal suffrage prevails. You must decide by vote who is to go.'

He was obeyed. Within a few minutes five men had been selected and they stepped out of the ranks.

'Five!' exclaimed Marius. 'But there are only four uniforms.'

'Then,' said the five men, 'one of us must stay.'

And the noble-hearted dispute was resumed, as to which had the best reason for going.

'You have a wife who loves you . . . you have an old mother . . . you have neither father nor mother, but what about your three younger brothers? . . . You're the father of five children . . . You have a right to go on living; at seventeen you're too young to die . . .'

Those great revolutionary barricades were gathering places of heroism. The improbable became natural, and no man surprised his fellow.

'Hurry up!' repeated Courfeyrac.

Someone shouted to Marius:

'You decide which one's to stay.'

'Yes,' said the five men. 'You choose and we'll obey.'

Marius had thought that he was no longer capable of any profound emotion, but at the idea that he should select a man for death he felt his blood run cold. He could have turned pale, had he not been pale already.

He moved forward and the five men, their eyes blazing with the fire that is the message of Thermopylae, greeted him with cries of 'Me! . . . Me! . . . Me! . . .'

Marius, in his stupor, counted them. There were still five. Then he looked down at the four uniforms.

As he did so a fifth uniform was added to the heap, as though it had fallen from the clouds. The fifth man was saved!

Looking round, Marius recognized Monsieur Fauchelevent.

Jean Valjean had entered the stronghold.

Whether acting on information, or by instinct or chance, he had come by way of the Rue Mondétour, and, in his National Guard uniform, had had no difficulty in getting through. The rebel sentry posted in the alley had seen no reason to raise the alarm on account of a single man but had let him pass, reflecting that either he had come to join them or, at the worst, would be taken prisoner. In any event, the situation was too acute for the sentry to leave his post.

No one had noticed Valjean when he appeared, all eyes being intent on the five men and the four uniforms. Valjean had stood listening, and, grasping the situation, had silently stripped off his uniform and dropped it on the pile.

The sensation was enormous.

'Who is this man?' demanded Bossuet.

'At least,' said Combeferre, 'he's ready to save another man's life.'

Marius said authoritatively:

'I know him.'

This was enough for them. Enjolras turned to Jean Valjean.

'Citizen, you are welcome.' And he added. 'You know that we are about to die.'

Valjean, without replying, helped the man he had saved to put on his uniform.

V. *The World as seen from the Top of the Barricade*

Their situation, in that fateful hour and that inexorable place, found its ultimate and utmost expression in the supreme melancholy of Enjolras.

Enjolras embodied in himself the fullness of revolution. Yet he was incomplete, in so far as the absolute may be incomplete. There

was in him too much of Saint-Just, too little of Anacharsis Clootz.*
Nevertheless his thinking, in the ABC society, had been to some
extent influenced by the outlook of Combeferre. Gradually ridding
himself of the narrow restrictions of dogma, he had begun to consider the wider aspect of progress, and had come to accept, as the
final, magnificent goal of social evolution, the expansion of the
great French Republic into the republic of all mankind. As for the
immediate steps to be taken, since they were in a situation of
violence he desired them to be violent; in this he was unshakeable,
a follower of that epic, redoubtable school of thought which may
be summed up in a date, the year 1793.

Enjolras was standing on the steps of the barricade with one arm
resting on the muzzle of his carbine. He was thinking, quivering as
though swayed in a breeze under the gallows—influenced by that
place of death. A kind of dark fire smouldered in his absent, meditative eye. Suddenly he raised his head, and with his fair hair flowing
back like that of the angel on his dark chariot of stars, or like a
lion's mane, he cried:

'Citizens, can you conceive of the future? Streets in cities bathed
in light, green branches on the thresholds of the houses and all
nations sisters, all men upright; old men blessing the young, and the
past loving the present; thinkers wholly free to pursue their thought,
and religious believers all equal before the law; Heaven itself the
one religion, God its immediate priest and the conscience of mankind its altar. An end to hatred: the brotherhood of the workshop
and the school; notoriety both punishment and reward; work for
all men, justice for all men, and peace, an end to bloodshed and to
war. To tame the natural world is the first step, and the second step
is to achieve the ideal. Consider what progress has already been
accomplished. The primitive races of mankind were terrified by the
hydra that flew upon the water, by the dragon that belched fire, by
the griffin, that aerial monster with the wings of an eagle and a tiger's
claws—fearful creatures beyond the control of men. But man set
his traps, the miraculous traps conceived by human intelligence, and
in the end he captured them.

'We have tamed the hydra, and its new name is the steamship;
we have tamed the dragon, and it is the locomotive; we have not
yet tamed the griffin, but we have captured it and its name is the
balloon. On the day when this Promethean task is completed and
man has finally harnessed to his will the ancient triple chimera of
the hydra, the dragon, and the griffin he will be the master of fire,
air, and water, and he will have become to the rest of living Creation

* A German visionary and follower of Hébert who went to the guillotine in 1794.

what the Gods of antiquity were to him. Have courage, citizens! We must go forward. But what are we aiming at? At government by knowledge, with the nature of things the only social force, natural law containing its penalties and sanctions within itself, and based on its evident truth: a dawn of truth corresponding to the laws of daylight. We are moving towards the union of nations and the unity of mankind. No more make-believers and no more parasites. Reality governed by truth, that is our aim. Civilization will hold its court in Europe and later will preside over all the continents in a Grand Parliament of Intelligence. History has already known something of the kind. The Amphictyonic League held two sessions a year, one at Delphi, the place of the Gods, and the other at Thermopylae, the place of heroes. Europe will have its Amphictyon, and presently the whole world. France carries this sublime future in her loins. It is here that the nineteenth century is being conceived. What Greece first essayed is worthy to be achieved by France. Listen to me, my friend Feuilly, sturdy workman that you are, man of the people and of all peoples. I honour you. You see clearly into the future, and see rightly. You knew neither father nor mother, Feuilly; you have made humanity your mother and justice your father. You are to die in this place, which is to say that you are to triumph. Citizens, no matter what happens today, in defeat no less than victory, we shall be making a revolution. Just as a great fire lights up all the town, so a revolution lights up all mankind. And what is the revolution that we shall make? I have already told you: it is the revolution of Truth. In terms of policy there is only one principle, the sovereignty of man over himself, and this sovereignty of me over me is called Liberty. Where two or more of these sovereignties are gathered together, that is where the State begins. But there can be no withdrawal from this association. Each sovereignty must concede some portion of itself to establish the common law, and the portion is the same for all. The common law is nothing but the protection of all men based on the rights of each, and the equivalent sacrifice that all men make is called Equality. The protection of all men by every man is Fraternity, and the point at which all these sovereignties intersect is called Society. Since this intersection is a meeting point, the point is a knot—hence what is called the "social bond". It is sometimes called the social contract, which comes to the same thing, since the word "contract" is etymologically based on the idea of drawing together. But equality, citizens, does not mean that all plants must grow to the same height—a society of tall grass and dwarf trees, a jostle of conflicting jealousies. It means, in civic terms, an equal outlet for all talents; in political terms, that all votes will carry the same weight; and in religious terms that all

beliefs will enjoy equal rights. Equality has a means at its disposal—
compulsory free education. The right to learn the alphabet, that is
where we must start. Primary school made obligatory for everyone
and secondary school available to everyone, that must be the law.
And from those identical schools the egalitarian society will emerge.
Yes, education! Light!—light—all things are born of light and all
things return to it! Citizens, our nineteenth century is great, but
the twentieth century will be *happy*. Nothing in it will resemble
ancient history. Today's fears will all have been abolished—war
and conquest, the clash of armed nations, the course of civilization
dependent on royal marriages, the birth of hereditary tyrannies,
nations partitioned by a congress or the collapse of a dynasty,
religions beating their heads together like rams in the wilderness of
the infinite. Men will no longer fear famine or exploitation, prostitution from want, destitution born of unemployment—or the
scaffold, or the sword, or any other malice of chance in the tangle
of events. One might almost say, indeed, that there will be no more
events. Men will be happy. Mankind will fulfil its own laws as does
the terrestrial globe, and harmony will be restored between the
human souls and the heavens. The souls will circle about the Truth
as the planets circle round the sun. I am speaking to you, friends,
in a dark hour; but this is the hard price that must be paid for the
future. A revolution is a toll-gate. But mankind will be liberated,
uplifted and consoled. We here affirm it, on this barricade. Whence
should the cry of love proceed, if not from the sacrificial altar?
Brothers, this is the meeting place of those who reflect and those
who suffer. This barricade is not a matter of rubble and paving-
stone; it is built of two components, of ideas and of suffering. Here
wretchedness and idealism come together. Day embraces night and
says to her, "I shall die with you, and you will be reborn with me."
It is of the embraces of despair that faith is born. Suffering brings
death, but the idea brings immortality. That agony and immortality
will be mingled and merged in one death. Brothers, we who die
here will die in the radiance of the future. We go to a tomb flooded
with the light of dawn.'

Enjolras fell silent rather than ceased to speak; his lips continued
to move as though he were still speaking to himself, with the result
that his audience continued to regard him, waiting to hear more.
There was no applause, but much whispering. Words being but a
breath, the stir of awakened minds is like the rustling of leaves.

VI. *Marius and Javert*

We must describe what was going on in Marius's mind.

His general situation we know. We have said already that the world for him had ceased to be real. He no longer grasped things clearly. He was moving, we must repeat, in the shadow of the great dark wings that spread over the dying. He felt that he was already in the grave, that he had crossed over to the other side, whence he could see the faces of the living only with the eyes of the dead.

How did Monsieur Fauchelevent come to be here? Why was he here? What had he come for? Marius did not ask himself these several questions. In any event, the quality of the state of despair being that we extend it to others besides ourselves, it seemed to him natural that everyone should have come there to die. But the thought of Cosette clutched at his heart.

Monsieur Fauchelevent did not speak to Marius or even look at him, and seemed not to have heard when Marius said, 'I know him'. This was a relief to Marius, and indeed, if the word can be used in such a context, it may be said to have pleased him. He had been always conscious of the impossibility of his addressing a word to this enigmatic figure who was to him both suspect and impressive. Besides, it was a very long time since he had seen him, and to anyone as shy and reserved as Marius this increased the impossibility.

The five selected men left the stronghold by way of the Rue Mondétour, looking precisely like members of the National Guard. One of them was weeping. Before leaving they embraced all those who were staying behind.

When the men restored to life had departed, the thoughts of Enjolras turned to the man condemned to death. He went into the tavern and asked:

'Do you want anything?'

Javert replied:

'When are you going to kill me?'

'You must wait. At the moment we need all our ammunition.'

'Then give me something to drink,' said Javert.

Enjolras brought him a glass of water, and, since his arms were bound, held it for him to drink.

'Is that all?' he asked.

'I'm not at all comfortable,' said Javert. 'It was scarcely kind to keep me lashed to this pillar all night. You can tie me up as much as you like, but you might at least let me lie on a table like that other fellow.' And he nodded in the direction of Monsieur Mabeuf.

It will be remembered that at the back of the ground-floor room there was a large table that had been used for the making of bullets and cartridges. Now that this was done, and the supply of powder used up, the table was no longer required. At Enjolras's order, four of the rebels released Javert from the pillar, a fifth holding a bayonet to his breast while they were untying him. Keeping his hands tied behind his back and holding him with a length of stout cord which permitted him to take a pace fifteen inches long, like a man mounting the scaffold, they walked him to the table and, stretching him out on it, tied him to it securely with a rope passed round his body. As a further precaution, to render any attempt at escape impossible, they passed a rope round his neck, ran the two ends between his legs and tied them to his wrists—the device known in prisons as the 'martingale'.

While they were doing this a man appeared in the doorway and stood staring with a singular fixity at Javert. The shadow he cast caused Javert to turn his head. He looked round and recognized Jean Valjean. He gave no sign of emotion. Coolly averting his gaze, he simply said, 'So here we are!'

VII. *The Situation Deteriorates*

The sky was growing rapidly lighter: but not a door or a window opened in the street. It was daybreak but not yet the hour of awakening. As we have said, the troops had been withdrawn from the far end of the Rue de la Chanvrerie, opposite the barricade; the street seemed clear, open to the public with a sinister tranquillity. The Rue Saint-Denis was as silent as the Avenue of the Sphinx at Thebes, with not a soul to be seen at the intersections now brightening in the reflected light of the dawn. Nothing is more dreary than this gathering of light in an empty street.

There was nothing to be seen but something to be heard. Mysterious movements were taking place some distance away. Clearly the crisis was imminent, and the sentries withdrew as they had done on the previous evening; but this time they all went.

The barricade was stronger than it had been at the first assault. After the departure of the five men it had been still further reinforced. Acting on the advice of the scout who was keeping an eye on the Halles area, Enjolras had taken a serious step. He had blocked the narrowest part of the Rue Mondétour, which until then had remained open, uprooting the paving-stones over a length of several more houses for the purpose. The stronghold, being now protected in front by the barricade across the Rue de la Chanvrerie, and on either flank by the barricades across the Rue du Cygne and the Rue Mondétour, had been rendered almost impregnable; but, on the other hand, it was totally enclosed. It had three fighting fronts but no outlet. 'A fortress, but also a mousetrap,' said Combeferre, chuckling. Enjolras had had some thirty paving-stones torn up for no reason, as Bossuet said, and piled up by the door of the tavern.

The silence in the direction from which the main attack was to be expected was now so ominous that Enjolras sent all his men to their action stations and a ration of eau-de-vie was distributed.

Nothing is more singular than a barricade preparing for an assault. Men take their places as though at the play, jostling and elbowing each other. Some make seats for themselves. The awkward corner is avoided, and the niche which may afford protection is occupied. Left-handed men are invaluable: they can fill places unsuited to the rest. Many men prefer to fight sitting down, to be able to kill and die in comfort. In the savage fighting of June 1848 a renowned marksman operating from a roof-terrace had an armchair of the Voltaire pattern brought up to him: he was caught by a discharge of grapeshot.

Directly the commander orders the men to action-stations all disorder ceases—the exchange of ribaldries, the gossiping groups, the groups of personal friends. Each man, seized with the common purpose, concentrates his thoughts on the enemy. A barricade not in immediate danger is chaos; but in the face of danger it is disciplined. Peril brings order.

When Enjolras, with his double-barrelled carbine, took up his position in the sort of redoubt he had reserved for himself, complete silence fell, broken only by a series of clicks along the wall as the men cocked their muskets.

For the rest, their state of mind was more proud and confident than ever. Extravagance of sacrifice is a stiffener of the spirit. They had nothing to hope for, but they had despair, that last resort which, as Virgil said, sometimes brings victory. Supreme resources may be born of supreme resolution. To plunge into the sea is sometimes to escape shipwreck; a coffin-lid may be a safety plank.

As on the previous evening, all eyes were intent on the end of the street, which was now bathed in daylight. They did not have long to wait. Sounds of movement were now clearly to be heard from the direction of Saint-Leu; but they were unlike the sounds that had preceded the first attack. There was a rattling of chains and a clatter of massive wheels over the cobbles—a sort of solemn commotion heralding the approach of more sinister ironmongery. And the old streets trembled, built as they were for the fruitful passage of commerce and ideas, not for the monstrous rumbling of engines of war. All eyes widened as the defenders stared through the barricade.

A piece of artillery came in sight.

It was being pushed by its gun-crew and was all ready stripped for action, with the front bogey-wheels removed. Two men supported the barrel, four were at the wheels, and the others followed, pulling the ammunition tender. A lighted fusee was visible.

'Fire,' shouted Enjolras.

The whole barricade flashed fire, and following the thunderous detonations a wave of smoke engulfed the gun and its crew. But when after some moments this cleared the men were seen to be hauling the gun into its position facing the barricade, working without haste, in correct, military fashion. Not one had been hit. The chief gunner, lowering the breech to get the range, was aiming the gun with the gravity of an astronomer adjusting a telescope.

'Well done the gunners!' cried Bossuet, and all the defenders clapped their hands.

In a matter of instants the gun was ready for action, its wheels straddling the gutter in the middle of the street, its formidable mouthpiece pointing at the barricade.

'Cheer up!' said Courfeyrac. 'This is where it gets rough. First the sparring and now the punch. The army is showing its fist. We are about to be seriously shaken. Musketry paves the way, but artillery does the job.'

'It's one of the new model bronze eight-pounders,' said Combeferre. 'If the proportion of tin to copper exceeds one tenth, the barrel's liable to get distorted. Too much tin weakens it, and the whole thing goes out of shape. Perhaps the best way of avoiding this would be to revert to the fourteenth-century practice of hooping —a series of steel rings, not welded to the barrel but encircling it at intervals from end to end. Meanwhile the fault has to be rectified as best it can. One can use a gauge to discover where the inside of the barrel bulges or narrows. But there's a better method, Gribeaural's "Moving Star".'

'They grooved cannon in the sixteenth century,' said Bossuet.

'Yes. It increased ballistic force but diminished accuracy. Besides, at short range the trajectory isn't level enough. There's too much of a curve for the projectile to be able to hit an intermediate object, which is necessary in battle, and the more so according to the proximity of the enemy and the rate of fire. The trouble with those grooved or rifled sixteenth-century cannon was due to the weakness of the charge, which itself was due to practical considerations such as the need to preserve the gun-mounting. In other words, the cannon, that lord of battle, can't do all it would like to do: its very strength is a weakness. A cannon-ball travels only at the speed of six hundred leagues an hour, whereas light travels at seventy thousand leagues a second—and that is the superiority of God over Napoleon.'

Enjolras meanwhile had ordered his men to reload, and the artillery men were loading their gun. The question was, however, would the barricade stand up to cannon-fire? Would it be breached? The discharge was awaited with tense anxiety.

The blow fell, accompanied by a roaring explosion; and a cheerful voice cried:

'I'm back!'

Gavroche had reappeared at the precise moment that the ball ploughed into the barricade, having come by way of the Rue du Cygne and scrambled over the small barrier confronting the maze of the Petite-Truanderie. His arrival made more impression than did the cannon-ball, which simply buried itself in the rubble, having done nothing worse than shatter a wheel of the omnibus and demolish the old Ancean handcart. Seeing which, the defenders burst out laughing.

'Carry on!' shouted Bossuet to the gunners.

VIII. *The Gunners show their Worth*

The defenders crowded round Gavroche, but he had no time to tell them anything. Marius, trembling, dragged him aside.

'Why have you come back here?'

'If it comes to that,' said Gavroche, 'why are you here at all?' And he surveyed Marius with his customary effrontery, his eyes widening with the glow of his own achievement.

'Who told you to come back?' Marius demanded sternly. 'Did you at least deliver my letter?'

Gavroche was feeling somewhat remorseful about that letter. In his haste to get back to the barricade he had got rid of it rather than delivered it. He was bound to admit to himself that he had behaved casually in bestowing it on an unknown man whose features he had not been able to distinguish. Certainly the man had been hatless, but that in itself was not enough. In short, he was not too pleased with himself in this matter, and he feared Marius's rebuke. So he took the easiest way out: he lied outrageously.

'Citizen, I gave the letter to the doorkeeper. The lady was asleep. She'll get it when she wakes up.'

Marius had sent the letter with two objects in mind, to bid farewell to Cosette and to save Gavroche. He had to content himself with having accomplished only one of them.

But the thought of the letter reminded him of the presence of Monsieur Fauchelevent in the stronghold, and it occurred to him that the two things might be connected. Pointing to Monsieur Fauchelevent, he asked:

'Do you know that man?'

'No,' said Gavroche.

It will be remembered that he had encountered Jean Valjean after dark. Marius's uneasy suspicions were dispelled. What did he know, after all, of Monsieur Fauchelevent's political opinions? He might be a convinced republican, which would account for his having come to join them.

Gavroche, meanwhile, at the other end of the barricade, was demanding, 'Where's my musket?' Courfeyrac had it given back to him. Gavroche went on to tell the 'comrades', as he called them, that they were now entirely surrounded. He had had great difficulty in getting back. A battalion of the line, based on the Petite-Truanderie, was keeping a watch round the Rue du Cygne, and the Rue des Prêcheurs, on the other side, was occupied by the Garde Municipale. The main strength of the army was facing them.

'And I authorize you to give them a boot up the backside,' said Gavroche, having concluded his report.

All this time Enjolras in his redoubt was watching and intently listening.

The enemy, evidently disappointed by the failure of their cannonball, had not fired the gun again. A company of infantry of the line had now moved into position at the end of the street, behind the gun. They were digging up the paving-stones and using them to build a low wall, a sort of breastwork not more than eighteen inches high, facing the barricade. At the left-hand end of this breastwork the head of another column of troops, massed along the Rue Saint-Denis, could be seen.

Enjolras caught a sound that he thought he recognized, the rattle of grape-cannisters when they are taken out of the ammunition-tender. He saw the leader of the gun-crew readjust his aim, pointing the gun-muzzle slightly to the left. The crew reloaded the gun, and the leading gunner himself took the linstock and held it over the touch-hole.

'Heads down and get back to the wall', shouted Enjolras. 'All of you down on your knees.'

The rebels, who had left their posts to listen to Gavroche, dashed frantically back, but the gun was fired before the order could be carried out, and they heard the hideous whistle of grapeshot.

The gun was aimed at the narrow breach between the end of the barricade and the house wall. The bullets ricocheted off the wall, killing two men and wounding three. If it went on like that the barricade would cease to be tenable. It was not proof against grape-shot.

There was a murmur of dismay.

'We must not let that happen again,' said Enjolras.

He levelled his carbine at the leading gunner, who, bent over the breach of the gun, was finally adjusting its aim. He was a gunnery sergeant, a fair-haired, handsome young man with a gentle face and the look of intelligence appropriate to that formidable, predestined weapon which, by its very perfection of horror, must finally put an end to war.

Combeferre, at Enjolras's side, was staring at him.

'What a shame!' said Combeferre. 'How hideous this butchery is! Well, when there are no more kings there will be no more war-fare. You're aiming at that sergeant, Enjolras, but you're not looking at him. He looks a charming young man, and he is certainly brave. One can see that he thinks—these young artillery-men are highly educated. No doubt he has a family, a father and mother, and probably he's in love. He can't be more than twenty-five. He could be your brother.'

'He is,' said Enjolras.

'Yes,' said Combeferre, 'and mine too. We mustn't kill him.'

'We must. It has got to be done.' A tear rolled slowly down Enjolras's pallid cheek.

At the same moment he pressed the trigger. The young gunner spun round twice with arms extended and head flung back as though gasping for air, then fell sideways on to the gun and stayed motion-less. Blood poured from the middle of his back, which was turned towards them.

His body had to be removed and a relief appointed in his place. It meant that a few minutes had been gained.

IX. *Use of an Old Poacher's Talent*

Urgent views were exchanged along the barricade. The gun would soon fire again. They could not survive more than a quarter of an hour against grapeshot. Something had to be done to lessen its effect.

'Stuff that gap with a mattress,' ordered Enjolras.

'There isn't one to spare,' said Combeferre. 'The wounded are using them all.'

Jean Valjean, seated on a curbstone at the corner of the tavern with his musket between his knees, had thus far kept aloof from the rest of the company and taken no part in the proceedings, seeming not to hear the remarks that were being made around him. Now, however, he got to his feet.

It will be recalled that when the party had entered the Rue de la Chanvrerie an old woman in one of the houses had rigged a mattress outside her window as a precaution against bullets. It was an attic window six storeys above ground, and the house was situated just outside the barricade. The mattress was suspended from two clothes-poles held by two cords running from nails driven into the woodwork of the window. The cords, at that distance, looked no thicker than a hair.

'Will someone lend me a double-barrelled carbine?' said Valjean.

Enjolras passed him his own, which he had just reloaded.

Jean Valjean took aim and fired, and one of the cords parted, leaving the mattress hanging by the other. He fired again, and the second cord whipped against the window. The mattress slid between the two poles and fell into the street.

There was a burst of applause from the defenders and someone cried:

'There's your mattress.'

'Yes,' said Combeferre, 'but who's going to fetch it?'

The mattress had fallen outside the barricade, into the no-man's land between attackers and defenders. But the soldiers, infuriated by the death of their sergeant, were now lying on their stomachs behind the breastwork of paving-stones and keeping up a steady fire on the barricade while they waited for the gun to come into action again. The defenders had not been returning their fire because of the need to save ammunition. The bullets buried themselves harmlessly in the barricade; but the street in front of it was a place of hideous danger.

Jean Valjean went out through the breach, dashed through the hail of bullets, picked up the mattress and, carrying it on his back, brought it into the stronghold. He then used it to block the breach, fixing it against the house wall in a position where the gunners could not see it.

Then the defenders awaited the next salvo of grape, which was not slow in coming. The gun thundered out its charge of smallshot, but this time there was no ricochet. The mattress had had the desired effect; it had damped the spread of the bullets. The stronghold was spared this peril.

'Citizen,' said Enjolras to Jean Valjean, 'the Republic thanks you.'

Bossuet was laughing as he marvelled.

'How immoral that a mattress should prove so effective! A triumph of submissiveness over aggression! Glory be to the mattress, which neutralizes cannon!'

X. *Dawn*

It was at this moment that Cosette awakened.

Her bedroom was small, clean and modest, with a tall window giving on to the back courtyard of the house.

Cosette knew nothing of what was happening in Paris. She had retired to bed when Toussaint said, 'There seems to be trouble'. She had not slept for very long but she had slept soundly. She had had sweet dreams, which perhaps was due in part to the fact that the narrow bed was very white. A vision of Marius had appeared to her in a glow of light, and when she awoke with the sun in her eyes it was like the continuation of her dream.

Her first thoughts as she woke up were happy ones. She felt quite reassured. Like Jean Valjean a few hours before, she was experiencing that reaction of the spirit which rejects absolutely the thought of misfortune. She was filled with hope, without knowing why. Then she felt a clutching at her throat. It was three days since she had seen Marius. But she told herself that by now he must have got her letter, so that he knew where she was; and he was so clever that he was sure to find some means of reaching her. What was more, he would certainly come today, perhaps even this morning. Although it was now daylight, the sun was still low. It must be very early in the morning. But still she must get up, to be ready for Marius.

She knew now that she could not live without Marius, and this in itself was a sufficient reason for his coming. So much was certain. It was bad enough that she should have suffered for three days. Three days without Marius, which was horribly unkind of God. But at least she had survived it, that cruel joke played on her by Heaven, and today Marius would come, bringing good news. Such is youth! It quickly dries its tears and having no use for sorrow refuses to accept it. Youth is the future smiling at a stranger, which is itself. It is natural for youth to be happy. It seems that its very breath is made of happiness.

Moreover, Cosette could not exactly remember what Marius had told her about his enforced absence, which was to last only one day, or what explanation he had given her. We all know the artfulness with which a dropped coin hides itself, and the job we have to find it again. There are thoughts which play the same trick on us, rolling into a buried corner of our minds; and there it is, they've gone for ever, we can't put our finger on them. Cosette was decidedly vexed by the insufficiency of her memory. It was very wrong of her, and she felt guilty at having forgotten any words spoken by Marius.

She got out of bed and performed those two ablutions of the spirit and the body—her prayers and her toilet.

The reader may at a pinch be introduced into a marital bedchamber, but not into a young girl's bedroom. This is something that verse scarcely dares; to prose it is utterly forbidden. It is the interior of a bud not yet opened, whiteness in shadow, the secret resort of a closed lily not to be seen by man until it has been looked upon by the sun. A budding woman is sacred. The innocent bed with its coverlet tossed back, the enchanting semi-nudity that is afraid of itself, the white foot taking refuge in a slipper, the bosom that veils itself before a mirror as though the mirror were a watching eye, the chemise hastily pulled up to hide a shoulder from a piece of furniture that creaks as a carriage passes in the street, the ribbons, hooks and laces, the tremors, small shivers of cold and modesty, the exquisite shyness of every movement, the small, mothlike flutterings where there is nothing to be afraid of, the successive donning of garments as charming as the mists of dawn—such matters may not be dwelt upon; even to have hinted at them is too much.

The masculine gaze must display even more reverence at the rising of a girl from her bed than at the rising of a star; the very possibility that she can be touched should increase our respect. The down on a peach, the dust on a plum, the crystal gleam of snow, the powdered butterfly's wing, these are gross matters compared with the chastity that does not know that it is chaste. A virgin girl is a vision in a dream, not yet become a thing to be looked at. Her alcove is buried in the depths of the ideal. An indiscreet caress of the eyes is a ravishment of this intangible veil. Even a glance is a profanation. Therefore we shall depict nothing whatever of the soft commotion of Cosette's uprising. According to an eastern fable, the rose was white when God created it, but when, as it unfolded, it felt Adam's eyes upon it, it blushed in modesty and turned pink. We are among those who are moved to silence by young girls and flowers, finding them objects of veneration.

Cosette quickly dressed and did her hair—a simple matter in those days, when women did not pad out their tresses and ringlets, or insert any kind of framework. Then she opened her window and leaned out, hoping to be able to see a small length of street beyond the corner of the house, so that she could keep watch for Marius. But she could not do so. The back courtyard of the house was enclosed in high walls, beyond which were only gardens. She decided that they were hideous; for the first time in her life she found flowers ugly. The least glimpse of the street gutter would have suited her better. So she looked up at the sky, as though hoping that Marius might come that way.

And suddenly she burst into tears, not from any oversensibility but from disappointed hope and the misery of her present situation. She had an obscure sense of disaster. It was in the air about her. She told herself that she could be sure of nothing, that to be lost to sight was to be wholly lost; and the thought that Marius might drop down from the heavens no longer seemed to her charming but most miserable. Then, such are these fantasies, calm returned to her and hopefulness, a sort of unwitting smile of trust in God.

Everyone was still in bed and a provincial silence reigned in the house. Not a shutter had been thrust open and the porter's lodge was still closed. Toussaint was not yet up, and Cosette naturally supposed that her father was asleep. She must have suffered greatly, and must still be unhappy, because she told herself that her father had been unkind; but she still relied on Marius. The extinction of that light was quite simply inconceivable. She began to pray. Now and then she heard the sound of thudding some distance away, and she thought it strange that people should be opening and slamming house-doors so early in the morning. In fact, this was the sound of cannon-fire from the barricades.

A few feet below Cosette's window, in the blackened cornice of the wall, there was a nest of house-martins. It stuck out a little beyond the cornice, so that she could see inside it. The mother-bird was there, with her wings spread over her brood, while the father flew back and forth bringing them food. The morning sun gilded that happy sight, that smiling instance of the glory of the morning. Cosette, with her hair in the sunshine and her mind filled with dreams, glowing inwardly with love and outwardly in the dawn, leaned mechanically further forward and, scarcely venturing to admit that she was also thinking of Marius, contemplated that family of birds, male and female, mother and children, with the sense of profound disturbance that a bird's nest imparts to a virgin girl.

XI. *A Musket-shot that does not Miss but does not Kill*

The attackers kept up their fire, alternating musketry with grapeshot, but, it must be said, without doing any great damage. Only the upper part of the tavern suffered, the first-floor window and those in the attics gradually crumbling as they were riddled with grape and musket-balls. The men posted there had had to withdraw. In general, this is a tactic commonly used in attacking a street barricade: a steady fire is kept up to draw the fire of the insurgents, if they are so foolish as to return it. When they are seen to be running out of powder and shot the assault goes in. But Enjolras had not fallen into this trap. The fire was not returned.

At every volley Gavroche thrust his tongue into his cheek in a grimace of lofty disdain and Courfeyrac mocked the gunners—'You might be scattering confetti, my good fellows.'

Inquisitiveness is as much present in battle as at a ball. Probably the muteness of the stronghold was beginning to perturb the attackers, causing them to fear some unforeseen development, so that they were consumed with the desire to know what was going on behind that impressive wall. The rebels suddenly perceived the gleam of a helmet on a nearby roof. A sapper had appeared, standing with his back to a tall chimney, having evidently been posted as a look-out. He could see straight down into the stronghold.

'That's tiresome,' said Enjolras.

Jean Valjean had returned Enjolras's carbine, but he had his musket. Without speaking he took aim at the sapper, and a moment later the helmet, struck by a bullet, clattered down into the street. The soldier hurriedly retreated.

Another look-out took his place, this time an officer. Valjean, having reloaded, fired again, and the officer's helmet went to join that of the first man. The officer was not stubborn; he, too, hastily withdrew. This time the point had been taken. No other observer appeared to spy on the fortress.

'Why did you fire at the helmet instead of killing the man?' Bossuet asked Valjean.

He did not reply.

XII. *Disorder the Upholder of Order*

Bossuet murmured to Combeferre:

'He didn't answer my question.'

'He's a man who does kindness with bullets,' said Combeferre.

Those readers with any recollection of that already distant epoch will know that the volunteer Garde Nationale from the districts surrounding Paris, always sturdily opposed to insurrection, were particularly ruthless and intrepid during those days of June 1832. Your honest cabaret proprietor in Pantin or Les Vertus or La Cunette, seeing a threat to the prosperity of his establishment, was lionhearted in the defence of his dance-floor, ready to risk his life to preserve the state of order in which he flourished. In those days which were both bourgeois and heroic, faced by concepts which had their knightly champions, private profit also had its paladins. Prosaic motives in no way detracted from the gallantry of their conduct. The shrinkage in the value of money caused bankers to sing the *Marseillaise*. Blood was lyrically shed to safeguard the cash box, and the shop, that microcosm of the nation, was defended with a Spartan tenacity. It must be said that all this was extremely serious. Two sections of the populace were at war, pending the establishment of a balance between them.

Another sign of the times was the mingling of anarchy and governmentalism (the barbarous word then used by the orthodox). A mixture of order and indiscipline. The drums beat capriciously at the order of some hot-blooded colonel of the Garde Nationale; the order to fire was given by excited captains, and the men under them fought according to their own ideas and for their own purpose. In moments of crisis, the 'big days', instinct was more often consulted than the official leaders. There were freelance warriors in the ranks of order, fighters with the sword, like Fannicot, and fighters with the pen, like the journalist, Henri Fonfrède.

Civilization, of which the unhappy embodiment at that time was an aggregation of interests rather than a collection of principles, believing itself to be threatened raised a cry of alarm; and the individual, seeing himself as its centre, sought to defend it after his own fashion. Everyman took it upon himself to save society.

Zeal was sometimes carried to excess. A platoon of the Garde Nationale might constitute itself a court-martial and try and execute a captured rebel in five minutes. It was this kind of improvisation that had caused the death of Jean Prouvaire—a ferocious lynch-law with which neither side is entitled to reproach the other, for it was used by the republicans in America no less than by the monarchists in Europe. It was the source of many blunders. In one uprising, for example, a young poet named Paul-Aimé Garnier was chased across the Place Royale with bayonets at his back and had difficulty in escaping through the doorway of No. 6. He had been mistaken for a 'Saint-Simonien', a follower of the radical philosopher, Saint-Simon. The fact is that the book he was carrying under his arm was a volume of the memoirs of the Duc de Saint-Simon. A member of the Garde Nationale, seeing only the name, had clamoured for his death.*

On 6 June 1832, a suburban company of the Garde Nationale,

* This episode, described in *Choses vues* as having happened to Hugo himself in 1834, is here attributed to another person. The poet, Paul-Aimé Garnier, died in 1846.

commanded by the Captain Fannicot already referred to, allowed itself from pure self-indulgence to be decimated in the Rue de la Chanvrerie. The fact, singular as it is, was established by the judicial inquiry held after the 1832 insurrection. The zealous and hot-blooded captain, a condottiere of troops of the kind we have been describing, and a fanatical and insubordinate supporter of the Government, could not resist the temptation to open fire before the appointed time so as to overthrow the barricade single-handed— that is to say, with his own company. Exasperated by the hoisting of the red flag followed by an old coat which he took to be a black flag, he loudly criticized the authorities and army leaders, then in council, who had decided that the time for the final assault was not yet ripe, and, in the phrase made famous by one of them, were letting the insurrection 'stew in its own juice'. His own view was that the barricade itself was ripe, and since ripe fruit is ready to fall he put his theory to the test.

The men under his command were as hot-blooded as himself— 'wild men', as a witness described them. His company, which had been responsible for the shooting of Jean Prouvaire, was at the head of the battalion drawn up beyond the corner of the street. At the moment when it was least expected, the captain flung his men against the barricade. The attack, executed with more zeal than military skill, cost the Fannicot company dear. Before it had covered two-thirds of the Rue de la Chanvrerie it was met with a volley from all the defenders. The four boldest men, who were in the forefront, were shot at point-blank range and fell at the foot of the barricade, and the courageous mob of National Guards, men of the utmost bravery but lacking the steadiness of regular soldiers, fell back after some hesitation, leaving fifteen dead bodies in the street. That moment of hesitation gave the rebels time to reload, and a second, murderous volley caught them before they had got round the corner into safety. Indeed they were caught between two fires, because they also received a charge of grapeshot from the cannon, which went on firing, not having been ordered to stop. The bold but rash Fannicot was one of the casualties—killed, that is to say, by the forces of order.

The attack, which was more hot-headed than serious, annoyed Enjolras.

'The idiots!' he exclaimed. 'They're getting themselves killed and wasting our ammunition for no reason.'

Enjolras had spoken like the born rebel leader he was. Insurrection and repression fight with different weapons. Insurrection, with limited resources, can fire only so many shots and lose only so many men. An ammunition-pouch emptied, or a man killed, cannot be replaced. Repression, with the army at its disposal, has no need to spare men or, with its arsenals, to spare bullets; it has as many regiments as there are defenders on the barricades, and as many factories as the barricades have cartridge-cases. So these battles of one against a hundred must always end in the crushing of the rebels unless the spirit of revolution, spontaneously arising, casts its flaming sword into the balance. This can happen. And then it becomes a universal uprising, the very stones rise up, the strongholds of the populace teem with men, all Paris trembles; something more than human is unloosed and it is another 10 August or 29 July. A prodigious light shines, and the gaping jaws of force recoil; the lion which is the army comes face to face with the erect and tranquil figure of the prophet, which is France.

XIII. *Passing Gleams*

All things are to be found in the chaos of sentiment and passions defending a barricade: there is gallantry, youth, honour, enthusiasm, idealism, conviction, the frenzy of the gambler and, above all, the fluctuations of hope.

One of these fluctuations, one of the vague surges of hope, suddenly, and at the most unforeseeable moment, ran through the defenders of the barricade in the Rue de la Chanvrerie.

'Listen!' shouted Enjolras, always on the alert. 'It sounds to me as though Paris were on the move.'

It is certain that for an hour or two on that morning of 6 June the insurrection gained a degree of impetus. The persistent summons of the Saint-Merry tocsin stirred latent impulses. Barricades went up in the Rue du Poirier and the Rue des Gravilliers. A young man with a carbine launched a single-handed attack on a cavalry squadron at the Porte Saint-Martin. Kneeling without cover on the boulevard, he aimed at, and killed, the squadron commander, saying when he had done so, 'Well, that's another who won't do us any more harm!' He was cut down with sabres. In the Rue Saint-Denis a woman fired at the National Guard from behind a Venetian blind, of which the slats were seen to tremble with every shot. A boy of fourteen was caught in the Rue de la Cossonerie with his pockets filled with cartridges. A regiment of cuirassiers, with General Cavaignac de Baragne at its head, was greeted as it entered the Rue Bertin-Poirée with a very lively and quite unexpected volley. In the Rue Planche-Mibray pots and pans and other domestic articles were flung at the troops from the roof-tops. A bad sign, this; and when it was reported to Marshal Soult, that Napoleonic veteran looked thoughtful, recalling an observation made by Suchet at Saragossa—'When we get the old women emptying chamber-pots on our heads we're done for.'

These widespread portents, coming at a time when the uprising was thought to have been localized—manifestations of a growing anger, spurts of flame rising here and there out of the great mass of combustible material which is Paris—disquieted the army commander, and great haste was made to put out the fire before it spread. Accordingly the assault on the strongholds of Maubuée, de la Chanvrerie, and Saint-Merry was delayed until these lesser affairs had been dealt with, so that then only the three major outbreaks would remain and they could be crushed in a single operation. Preventive columns were sent through the fermenting streets, clearing the larger and probing the smaller ones to left and right, sometimes slowly and cautiously, sometimes at the double. The doors of houses from which shots had been fired were battered down while at the same time a cavalry operation cleared the gathering groups off the boulevards. The process was not soundless or free from the uproar that accompanies any clash between the army and the people. This was what Enjolras heard in the pauses between gun and musket-fire. Moreover, he saw wounded men on stretchers being carried past the end of the street, and he said to Courfeyrac, 'Those wounded don't come from here'.

But the hope did not last for long; the gleam was soon extinguished. Within half an hour the stir had died down as though it were a lightning-flash not followed by thunder, and the rebels again felt the weight of that pall of indifference that the people bestow on zealots whom they have abandoned. The general upheaval which had given signs of taking shape had been frustrated, and the attention of the Minister for War and the strategy of the generals could again be concentrated on the three or four strongholds remaining.

The sun had risen in the sky. A man called to Enjolras:

'We're hungry down here. Have we really got to die without getting a bite to eat?'

Crouched in his redoubt, with his eyes intent on the end of the street, Enjolras merely nodded.

Seated on a paving-stone near Enjolras, Courfeyrac continued to jeer at the cannon, and every passage of that sinister cloud of projectiles that is called grapeshot, accompanied by its monstrous din, drew from him an ironical comment.

'You're wearing yourself out, you poor old brute. You're getting hoarse. You're not thundering, only spluttering. It's breaking my heart.'

His remarks were greeted with laughter. He and Bossuet, whose valiant high spirits increased with danger, like Madame Scarron were substituting pleasantry for nourishment and, since wine was not to be had, spreading gaiety around them.

'I admire Enjolras,' said Bossuet. 'I marvel at his cool steadfastness. He lives alone, and this perhaps makes him unhappy; he resents the greatness which compels him to celibacy. We others have mistresses to rob us of our wits—make us brave, in other words. A man in love is like a tiger, and the least he can do is to fight like a lion. It's a way of getting our own back for the tricks the wenches play on us. Roland got himself killed to score off Angélique. All our heroism stems from our womenfolk. A man without a woman is like a pistol without a hammer; the woman sparks the charge. But Enjolras has no woman. He contrives to be brave without being in love. It's a very remarkable thing to be cold as ice and still as hot as fire.'

Enjolras seemed not to be listening, but anyone near enough might have heard him murmur the word *Patria*.

Bossuet was still laughing when Courfeyrac exclaimed: 'Here's another!' And in the voice of a ceremonial usher he announced: 'My lord Eight-Pounder!'

And indeed a second cannon had been brought into action. The gunners rapidly manoeuvred it into position alongside the first.

It was the beginning of the end.

A minute later both pieces fired together, accompanied by a volley of musketry from the supporting troops. Gunfire was also to be heard not far off. While the two guns were bombarding the stronghold in the Rue de la Chanvrerie, others, in the Rue Saint-Denis and the Rue Aubry-le-Boucher, were in action against the Saint-Merry redoubt, this simultaneous fire setting up an ominous echo.

Of the two pieces now battering the Rue de la Chanvrerie barricade, one was charged with grape, the other with ball. The one loaded with ball was aimed a little high so as to hit the upper edge of the barricade and fill the air with the splinters of paving-stones, the intention being to drive the defenders off the barricade itself and under cover. It was a preliminary to the main assault. Once the barricade had been cleared by cannon-fire, and musketry had driven the defenders away from the windows of the tavern, it would be possible for the attacking troops to advance along the street without being shot at, possibly without being seen, and over-run the barricade as they had done on the evening before, perhaps even taking it by surprise.

'We really must abate this nuisance,' said Enjolras, and he shouted: 'Open fire on the gunners.'

Everything was in readiness. The barricade, so long silent, burst furiously into flame, six or seven volleys following one another in a mingling of rage and joy. The street was filled with blinding smoke, but after a few minutes the bodies of two-thirds of the gunners could be dimly discerned, prostrate round the gun. Those still on their feet continued with rigid composure to serve the guns, but the rate of fire slackened.

'Good!' said Bossuet to Enjolras. 'A success.'

Enjolras shrugged his shoulders.

'Another quarter of an hour of that kind of success and we shan't have ten cartridges left.'

It seemed that Gavroche must have heard those words.

XV. *Gavroche*

Courfeyrac suddenly perceived someone crouched in the street just beyond the barricade. Gavroche, having fetched a basket from the tavern, had slipped out through the break and was calmly engaged in filling it with ammunition from the pouches of the men killed in the previous assault.

'What are you doing?' demanded Courfeyrac.

Gavroche looked up perkily.

'I'm filling my basket.'

'Haven't you ever heard of grapeshot?'

'So it's raining,' said Gavroche. 'So what?'

'Come back at once!'

'All in good time,' said Gavroche, and moved further along the street.

It will be remembered that Fannicot's retreating company had left a trail of dead behind them. Some twenty corpses were scattered over the length of the street, twenty ammunition pouches to be looted.

Smoke filled the street like a fog. Anyone who has seen low cloud at the bottom of a sheer mountain gorge will be able to picture it, that dense mist eddying and swirling between the two dark lines of tall houses. It slowly rose but was constantly renewed, a dark veil drawn over the face of the sun, so that the combatants at either end of the street, short though it was, could scarcely see each other.

This state of affairs, probably reckoned with and desired by the leaders of the assault, was very helpful to Gavroche. Under cover of the smoke, and thanks to his small size, he could move some distance into the street without being seen. He looted the first seven or eight pouches without being in much danger, creeping along on hands and knees, wriggling from one body to the next and emptying pouches and cartridge-belts like a monkey cracking nuts.

He was still not far from the barricade, but no-one dared shout to him to come back for fear of drawing attention to him.

On one body, that of a corporal, he found a powder-flask.

'Handy in case of thirst,' he said and put it in his pocket.

As he moved further along the street the veil of smoke grew thinner, so that presently the soldiers of the line behind their breast-work and the men of the Garde Nationale clustered at the corner of the street were able to discern something moving in the haze. He was ransacking the pouch of a sergeant lying near a curbstone when the body was hit by a bullet.

'Blazes!' said Gavroche. 'Now they're killing dead men.'

A second bullet struck a spark from the nearby cobbles and a third overturned his basket. Looking up, Gavroche saw that it had come from the street-corner. He got to his feet, and standing erect with his hands on his hips, his eyes fixed on the men of the Garde Nationale, he sang:

> They're ugly at Nanterre,
> It's the fault of Voltaire;
> And stupid at Palaiseau,
> All because of Rousseau.

Then he picked up his basket, retrieved the cartridges that had fallen out of it without losing one, and moved still nearer to the attackers to loot another pouch. A fourth bullet narrowly missed him. He sang:

> I'm no lawyer, I declare,
> It's the fault of Voltaire.
> I'm nothing but a sparrow
> All because of Rousseau.

295

A fifth bullet succeeded only in drawing another verse from him:

There's joy in the air,
Thanks to Voltaire;
But misery below,
So says Rousseau.

This went on for some time, a touching and heartrending scene. Gavroche, being shot at, mocked the shooters. He seemed to be thoroughly enjoying himself, a sparrow pecking at the bird-catchers. Every shot inspired him to another verse. They fired again and again at him and missed, and the soldiers and the men of the Garde Nationale laughed as they took aim. He leapt and dodged, ducked into doorways, vanished and reappeared, cocking a snook at the foe, and all the time continued to empty pouches and fill his basket. The rebels watched in breathless anxiety. The barricade trembled, and he sang. He was neither child nor man but a puckish sprite, a dwarf, it seemed, invulnerable in battle. The bullets pursued him, but he was more agile than they. The urchin played his game of hide-and-seek with death, and whenever the dread spectre appeared he tweaked its nose.

But at length a bullet caught him, better aimed or more treacherous than the rest. Gavroche was seen to stagger, and then he collapsed. A cry went up from the barricade. But there was an Antaeus concealed in that pygmy. A Paris urchin touching the pavement is a giant drawing strength from his mother earth. Gavroche had fallen only to rise again. He sat upright with blood streaming down his face, and raising his arms above his head and gazing in the direction of the shot, he again began to sing.

I have fallen I swear
It's the fault of Voltaire
Or else this hard blow
Has been dealt by——

He did not finish the verse. A second ball from the same musket cut him short. This time he fell face down and moved no more. His gallant soul had fled.

XVI. *How a Brother becomes a Father*

At that same moment two little boys in the Luxembourg Gardens —for the eyes of the dramatist must be everywhere at once—were walking hand in hand. One was perhaps seven years old, the other about five. After being soaked by the downpour they were keeping to the sunnier paths, the elder leading the way. They were ragged and pale, with the look of lost birds. The younger said, 'I'm very hungry.'

The elder, who was developing a protective attitude, was holding his brother with his left hand while he clutched a stick in his right. The gardens were deserted, the gates having been closed as a precautionary measure in view of the uprising. The troops who had been encamped there during the night had left to go about their duties.

How, then, had those two children got there? They might have slipped through the half-open door of a police-post, or possibly have run away from a party of strolling players who had set up their booth nearby, at the Barrière de l'Enfer or on the Esplanade de l'Observatoire; or perhaps they had escaped the notice of the park-keepers at closing time the evening before, and spent the night in one of those sheltered corners where people sit and read their newspapers. In any event they were wandering at large and seemed unattached. To be astray and free is to be lost, which is what these children were.

They were the two little boys whom Gavroche had once sheltered, as the reader will remember—the Thénardier children, disposed of to La Magnon and attributed by that lady to Monsieur Gillenormand, and now become leaves fallen from those rootless branches, blown helter-skelter by the wind. Their clothes, which had been clean and neat in La Magnon's day, and had served to justify her in the eye of Monsieur Gillenormand, were now in tatters. In short, they had become a statistic, recorded by the police under the heading *Enfants Abandonnés* and picked up by them in the streets of Paris.

Only at a time of disorder could outcasts such as these have been found in a place like the Luxembourg, at any other time they would have been turned out. The children of the poor are not allowed in public gardens, although it might be thought that, like any other children, they have a right to flowers.

But there they were, thanks to the closed gates. They had slipped in, regardless of regulations, and had stayed there. The closing of the gates does not relieve the park attendants of their duties. Their supervision is supposed to be maintained, but it tends to grow lax. Besides which the attendants, infected by the disturbance, were more interested in events outside the gardens than in what was going on inside, and failed to notice the delinquents.

It had rained during the night and even a little in the morning; but June showers are no great matter. One scarcely remembers, on a day of radiant sunshine, that an hour ago there was a downpour.

The earth in summer dries as quickly as an infant's cheek. At the summer solstice the noonday sun is, so to speak, grasping. It envelops everything, applying a kind of suction to the earth, as though the sun itself were thirsty. A shower is a mere glass of water; any rainfall is instantly swallowed. The streaming morning becomes the delightful afternoon.

Nothing is more pleasant than greenery washed by the rain and dried by the sun into cleanliness and warmth. Gardens and meadows, with moisture at their roots and sunshine on their blossoms, become jars of incense, each giving out its scent. The world smiles and sings and bestows itself, and we feel a gentle intoxication. Springtime is a foretaste of paradise. The sun teaches men to endure.

At eleven o'clock on that morning of 6 June the Luxembourg, empty of people, was particularly charming. Lawns and flowerbeds mingled their colour and their fragrance, and the branches of trees seemed locked in an extravagant embrace in the warmth of the midday sun. Linnets were chirruping in the sycamores, sparrows flew rejoicing, woodpeckers assiduously tapped the trunks of the chestnut trees. The beds did dutiful obeisance to the legitimate royalty of the lily, the noblest of scents being that which comes from whiteness. Marie de Medici's old rooks were cawing in the tall trees, and the sun was gilding and crimsoning the tulips, which are simply every hue of flame made into flowers; and over the tulip beds darted the bees, like sparks from flames. All was grace and gaiety and there was no real threat in the shower that was approaching, which would be welcomed by honeysuckle and lily-of-the-valley and was causing the swallows to fly low. Any person there must have breathed happiness, security, innocence and benevolence. The thoughts falling from the sky were as soft as a child's hand that one bends down to kiss.

The statues under the trees, white and naked, were clad in garments of shadow dappled with light, goddesses in the tattered vesture of sunshine, its rags enclosing them on all sides. The earth around the big pond was already dried and almost burnt, and there was wind enough to cause little scurries of dust to arise. A few yellowed leaves, survivals from the autumn, fluttered gaily in pursuit of one another as though they were at play.

There was an inexpressible reassurance in this lavishness of light, this overflowing of life and sap, perfume and warmth. In the puffs of wind laden with love, the mingling of harmonies and reflections; in the lavish expense of the sun's gaze, that prodigious outpouring of liquid gold, one had a sense of inexhaustible abundance. And beyond it all, as though beyond a curtain of flames, one sensed the presence of God, that millionaire of the stars.

All had been washed clean, all the magnificence was immaculate, so that an army veteran from the nearby barracks, looking through the railing, could proclaim, 'nature's presenting arms in full-dress uniform'. And in the vast silence of contented Nature all Nature breakfasted. This was the hour. Creation took its seat at table, with a blue cloth in the heavens and a green cloth on earth, sunshine to light the feast. God served a universal repast, in which each creature found its rightful food—hempseed for the dove, millet for the chaffinch, worms for the robin, flowers for the bee, infusoria for the flies—and flies for the linnet. If to some extent one creature preyed upon another, that is a token of the mysterious mingling of bad with good; but no creature went hungry.

The two forlorn little boys had found their way to the pond, and, half-scared by the brilliant light, with the instinct of the poor and weak confronted by magnificence, even when it is impersonal, were crouched behind the swanhouse. Now and then a puff of wind brought distant sounds of tumult to their ears, shouting voices, the rattle of musketry and the heavy thud of cannon-fire. Smoke was rising above the house-tops in the direction of Les Halles; and a bell that sounded like a summons was tolling somewhere far away. The children paid little heed to this. From time to time the younger repeated in a mournful voice, 'I'm hungry.'

But at about the same time two other persons were approaching the pond. They were a gentleman nearing fifty and a six-year-old boy, evidently father and son. The boy was clutching a large bun.

In those days, certain nearby houses in the Rue Madame and the Rue d'Enfer had keys to the Luxembourg which their occupants could use when the gates were closed—a privilege that has since been abolished. No doubt this accounted for the presence of the new arrivals.

The two strays, seeing the 'quality' approach, tried to hide more securely.

The gentleman was of the middle-class, possibly the same one whom Marius, in the fever of love, had overheard in this very place counselling his child to avoid all excesses. He had a complacent, affable manner and a mouth which, since it never closed, was always smiling; a mechanical smile, the result of too much jaw and too little flesh, which displayed his teeth rather than his nature. The child, who had bitten into his bun but not finished it, looked over-fed. He was dressed in the uniform of the Garde Nationale, whereas his father was prudently wearing civilian attire.

Father and son stopped by the pond to look at its two swans, for which the gentleman seemed to have an especial admiration. He even resembled them, in the sense that he walked like them. At that moment, however, the swans were swimming, this being their principal talent, and they looked, and were, superb.

If the two ragamuffins had been near enough, and old enough to understand, they might have profited by the words of a citizen of solid worth.

'A wise man contents himself with little,' said the father. 'Look at me, my boy. I have no love of display. You'll never see me in robes of gold and precious stones. I leave such false adornments to persons of less regulated minds.'

Here there was a louder burst of sound from the direction of Les Halles, an uproar of voices and the tolling of a bell.

'What is that?' the boy asked.

'Saturnalia,' the sage replied. He had suddenly noticed the ragamuffins, huddled and motionless behind the green-painted shanty that housed the swans. 'And this is the beginning,' he said, adding after an impressive pause. 'Anarchy has entered the garden.'

His son, meanwhile, had taken a mouthful of his bun. He spat it out and suddenly burst into tears.

'What are you crying about?' the father asked.

'I'm not hungry,' the boy replied.

The father's smile expanded.

'One doesn't need to be hungry to eat a cake.'

'I don't like it. It's stale.'

'You don't want any more?'

'No.'

'Then throw it to our web-footed friends.'

The son hesitated. The fact that one does not want one's cake is not a reason for giving it away.

'Be generous,' said the father. 'We must always be kind to animals.'

Taking the bun, he tossed it into the pond. It fell not far from the edge, and the swans, who were plunging their heads in the middle of the pond, did not see it. The sage, fearing that it might be wasted, flapped his arms like a semaphore to attract their attention. Upon which, seeing something floating on the water, they proceeded slowly towards it, with the solemn stateliness that befits white creatures.

'You see?' said the sage, and delivered himself of a happy play on words. '*Les cygnes comprennent les signes.*'

There was another and still louder burst of tumult from that distant part of the town, and this time it sounded ominous. It can happen that one puff of wind may speak more authoritatively than another. This one clearly conveyed to the Luxembourg the roll of drums, the rat-a-tat of musketry, the bellow of voices, the thud of cannon, and the mournful tolling of the bell. Moreover at that moment a cloud obscured the sun.

The swans were still on their way.

'We must go home,' the father said. 'They're attacking the Tuileries.' He took his son's hand. 'It is no great distance from the Tuileries to the Luxembourg, no greater than the distance separating Royalty from the peerage.* There will be shooting.' He glanced up at the cloud. 'And perhaps it is going to rain as well. Even the heavens are taking a hand. We must hurry.'

'I want to see the swans eat my bun,' the little boy said.

'That would be imprudent,' the father said. And he led away his bourgeois offspring, who kept looking back until a clump of trees got in the way.

The bun was still floating on the surface of the pond, and now the two ragamuffins, as well as the swans, were approaching it, the younger with his eyes intent upon it and the elder with an eye on the retreating gentleman.

When father and son were out of sight the older boy flung himself down at the water's edge and, leaning over the stone rim of the pond as far as he dared, tried to fish out the bun with the stick he was holding in his right hand. The swans, seeing a rival, increased their speed and in doing so set up a ripple which helped the small fisherman. The bun was driven gently towards him, and by the time the swans arrived it was within reach of his stick. He swiftly drew it in, flourished his stick to frighten off the swans, then fished it out and got to his feet. The bun was soaked, but the boys were both hungry and thirsty. The elder boy divided it into two parts, one large and one small, and handing his brother the larger of the two said, 'There you are. Stop your gob with that.'

XVII. *Interlude*

Marius had dashed out beyond the barricade with Combeferre behind him. But it was too late. Gavroche was dead. Combeferre brought back the basket of ammunition while Marius brought back the boy, reflecting sadly as he did so that he was repaying the service Thénardier had done his father, with the difference that his father had been still alive. When he returned to the stronghold with the body in his arms his face, like that of Gavroche, was covered with blood. A bullet had grazed his scalp without his noticing it.

* The Palais du Luxembourg, at that time, was the hall of assembly of the French Senate or House of Peers.

Courfeyrac loosened his cravat and bandaged his forehead. Gavroche was laid on the table beside Monsieur Mabeuf, and the same black shawl sufficed to cover the bodies of the old man and the boy.

Combeferre doled out the captured cartridges—fifteen rounds to each man. But when he offered his share to Jean Valjean, who had not moved but was still seated motionless on his curbstone, the latter shook his head.

'An eccentric fellow,' Combeferre muttered to Enjolras. 'He comes to join us but doesn't want to fight.'

'Which doesn't prevent him lending a hand,' said Enjolras.

'Heroes come in all shapes,' said Combeferre; and Courfeyrac, overhearing, remarked: 'He's a different kind from Père Mabeuf.'

It is worthy of note that the fire hammering the barricade scarcely troubled the defenders within the stronghold. Persons who have never experienced this kind of warfare can have no idea of the strange lulls which punctuate its more violent moments. Men move about, talking, jesting, even loitering. An acquaintance of the writer heard a combatant remark in the middle of an attack with grapeshot, 'We might be at a school picnic'. The interior of this stronghold in the Rue de la Chanvrerie appeared, we must repeat, extremely calm. Every possible contingency and development had been, or was soon to be, experienced. From being critical the situation had become menacing, and before long, no doubt, it would become desperate. And as it worsened so did the heroism of the defenders glow more brightly, presided over by a dour-faced Enjolras, like a young Spartan devoting his drawn sword to the genius of Epidotas.

Combeferre, with an apron tied round him, was bandaging the wounded. Bossuet and Feuilly were making more cartridges with the powder taken by Gavroche from the dead corporal, and Bossuet remarked to his companion, 'We shall soon be taking a trip to another world.' Courfeyrac was spreading out his entire arsenal on the small heap of paving-stones he had constructed for himself near Enjolras—his swordstick, his musket, two cavalry-pistols, and a pocket pistol—arranging them with the meticulous care of a girl tidying her workbox. Jean Valjean was silently contemplating the wall opposite him. A workman was tying a large straw hat belonging to Mère Hucheloup on his head—'To guard against sunstroke,' he said. The young men of the Cougourde d'Aix were gaily chatting together, as though not to waste the chance of talking their native patois for the last time. Joly had got Mère Hucheloup's mirror down from the wall. Several men, having found some rather mouldy crusts of bread in a drawer, were avidly devouring them. Marius was worrying about what his father would have to say to him.

We must lay stress on a psychological fact peculiar to the barricades. Nothing characteristic of this astonishing street warfare should be omitted.

Despite their strange aspect of interior calm, these strongholds have for those within them a kind of unreality. Civil war, wherein the fog of the unknown mingles with the flame of furious outburst, has always an apocalyptic quality; revolution is a sphinx, and he who has undergone the experience of fighting on the barricades may feel that he has lived through a dream.

What one experiences, as we have indicated in the case of Marius (and we shall see the consequences of this), is something at once greater and less than life. Emerging from the barricade, we are no longer fully conscious of what we have seen. We have done terrible things and do not know it. We have been caught up in a conflict of ideas endorsed with human faces, our heads bathed in the light of the future. There were corpses prostrate and ghosts walking erect. The hours were immeasurable, like the hours of eternity. We lived in death. Shadows passed before our eyes, and what were they? We saw bloodstained hands. It was a state of appalling deafness, but also of dreadful silence. There were open mouths that cried aloud, and open mouths that uttered no sound. We were enveloped in smoke, perhaps in darkness, seeming to touch the sinister exhalations of unknown depths. We see something red in a finger-nail, but we do not remember.

To return to the Rue de la Chanvrerie: suddenly, in between two volleys, they heard the striking of a clock.

'Midday,' said Combeferre.

Before it had finished striking Enjolras sprang to his feet and gave the following order in a ringing voice:

'Paving-stones are to be brought into the house to reinforce the first floor and attic window-sills. Half the men to stand by with muskets, the rest to bring in the paving-stones. There's not a minute to be lost.'

A squad of sappers with axes over their shoulders had appeared in battle-order at the end of the street. They could only be the head of a column, surely an attacking column, since the sappers, whose business was to break down the barricade, always preceded the soldiers who had to climb over it.

Enjolras's order was carried out with the precise haste that is proper to fighting ships and barricades, these being the two places whence escape is impossible. In less than a minute two-thirds of the paving-stones which Enjolras had caused to be piled in the

Corinth doorway had been carried up to the first floor and the attic, and before another minute had passed they had been neatly disposed so as to block half the first floor window and the attic windows. A few loopholes, carefully arranged by Feuilly, the chief architect, permitted the passage of the musket barrels. This precaution was the more easily carried out since there had been a lull in the firing of grapeshot. The two cannons were now trained on the middle of the barricade for the purpose of making a hole in it and, if possible, creating a breach through which the assault might pass.

When the paving-stones, that ultimate rampart, were in position, Enjolras had the bottles which he had placed under the table on which Mabeuf was lying taken up to the first floor.

'Who's to drink them?' Bossuet asked.

'The defenders,' said Enjolras.

The ground-floor window was then barricaded and the iron bars used to fasten the tavern door at night were placed in readiness.

The fortress was now completely prepared. The barricade was its outer rampart, and the tavern was its keep. Such paving-stones as remained were used to fill the gap in the barricade.

Since the defenders of a street barricade are always obliged to husband their ammunition, and the attackers are aware of this, the attackers go about their business with an irritating deliberation, taking their time and exposing themselves before the fighting starts, although more in appearance than in reality. The preparations for the attack are always carried out with a certain methodical slowness, after which comes the holocaust.

This delay enabled Enjolras to oversee and perfect everything. He felt that since men such as these were about to die, their death must be a masterpiece. He said to Marius: 'We are the two leaders. I shall give the last orders inside while you keep watch on the outside.'

Marius took up his post of observation on top of the barricade.

Enjolras had the door of the kitchen, which as we know was the casualty ward, nailed up.

'To keep the wounded from being hit by splinters,' he said.

He gave his last orders in the downstairs room, speaking tersely but in a profoundly calm voice. Feuilly took note of them and spoke for everyone.

'Axes to cut down the stairs should be ready on the first floor. Are they there?'

'Yes,' said Fleury.

'How many?'

'Two, and a pole-axe.'

'Good. We are twenty-six able-bodied defenders. How many muskets are there?'

'Thirty-four.'

'Eight more than we need. They should be loaded like the rest and kept handy. Sabres and pistols in men's belts. Twenty men on the barricade and six in the attic and on the first floor to fire through the loopholes. Not a man must be wasted. When the drum beats for the assault the twenty men down below must make a rush for the barricade. Those who get there first will have the best positions.'

Having thus made his plans, Enjolras turned to Javert.

'I haven't forgotten you,' he said. Putting a pistol on the table, he went on, 'The last man to leave this place will blow out this spy's brains.'

'Here?' someone asked.

'No. We don't want his body to be mixed up with our own. Anyone can get over the small barricade in the Rue Mondétour. It's only four feet high. The man's securely bound. He's to be taken there and executed.'

Only one man at that moment was more impassive than Enjolras; it was Javert himself.

At this point Jean Valjean intervened. He had been in the main group of defenders. He now left them and said to Enjolras:

'You're the leader, are you not?'

'Yes.'

'A short time ago you thanked me.'

'I thanked you in the name of the Republic. Two men saved the barricade—Marius Pontmercy and yourself.'

'Do you think I deserve a reward?'

'Certainly.'

'Then I will ask for one.'

'What is it?'

'That I may be allowed to blow that man's brains out.'

Javert looked up and, seeing Valjean, made a slight movement of his head.

'That's fair.'

Enjolras was reloading his carbine. He looked about him and asked:

'Does anyone object?'

There was silence and he turned to Valjean.

'All right. You can have the spy.'

Valjean took possession of Javert by seating himself on the end of the table. He picked up the pistol, and the sound of a click indicated that he had cocked it. But at almost the same instant there was a sound of trumpets.

'On guard!' cried Marius from the top of the barricade.

Javert laughed in the silent manner that was peculiar to himself. He looked coolly at the defenders.

'You're scarcely in any better case than I am.'

'Everybody out!' cried Enjolras.

The men rushed out, receiving in their backs, if we may be allowed the expression, Javert's parting words.

'It won't be long!'

XIX. *The Vengeance of Jean Valjean*

When Jean Valjean was alone with Javert he undid the rope tied round the prisoner's body, of which the knot was under the table. He then signed to him to stand up. Javert obeyed with the indefinable smile which is the expression of captive supremacy. Valjean took him by the belt of his greatcoat, much as one takes an animal by its halter, and tugging him behind him led him out of the tavern, but slowly, because Javert, his legs stiff, could walk only with difficulty. Valjean had a pistol in his other hand.

Thus they crossed the interior of the stronghold, while its defenders, intent upon the coming attack, had their backs to them. Only Marius, at the end of the barricade, saw them pass, and that sinister pair, victim and executioner, reflected the sense of doom in his own spirit.

Jean Valjean with some difficulty helped Javert, bound as he was, to climb over the barricade leading to the Rue Mondétour, without, however, letting go of him for an instant. Having done so they were in the narrow alleyway, where the corner of the house hid them from the insurgents. The dead bodies dragged off the barricade formed a dreadful heap a few paces away, and among them was an ashen face, a pierced heart and the breast of a half-naked woman—Éponine.

Javert glanced sidelong at the dead body and murmured in a voice of profound calm:

'I think I know that girl.'

Then he turned to Valjean who, with the pistol under his arm, was regarding him in a manner which rendered the words, 'You know me, too,' unnecessary.

'Take your revenge,' said Javert.

Valjean got a clasp-knife out of his pocket and opened it.

'A knife-thrust!' exclaimed Javert. 'You're quite right. That suits you better.'

Jean Valjean cut the halter round Javert's neck, then the ropes binding his wrists and ankles; then, standing upright, he said:

'You're free to go.'

Javert was not easily taken aback but, with all his self-discipline, he could not conceal his amazement. He stared open-mouthed.

'I don't suppose I shall leave here alive,' Valjean went on. 'But if I do, I am lodging at No. 7, Rue de l'Homme-Armé, under the name of Fauchelevent.'

A swift tigerish grimace curled the corner of Javert's lip.

'Take care!' he said.

'Now go,' said Jean Valjean.

'Fauchelevent, you said? In the Rue de l'Homme-Armé?'

'Number seven.'

'Number seven,' repeated Javert.

He re-buttoned his greatcoat, straightened his shoulders, turned, and with folded arms, supporting his chin in one hand, he marched off in the direction of the market. Valjean stood watching him. After he had gone a few paces Javert turned and said:

'I find this embarrassing. I'd rather you killed me.'

He did not notice that he had ceased to address Valjean disrespectfully as 'tu'.

'Clear out,' said Valjean.

Javert walked on slowly and a moment later had turned into the Rue des Prêcheurs. When he had vanished from sight Valjean fired the pistol into the air.

Then he went back into the stronghold and said, 'It's done.'

In the meantime the following had occurred.

Marius, more concerned with what was happening outside the stronghold, had paid little attention to the spy tied up in the obscure downstairs room of the tavern; but when he saw him in full daylight climbing over the barricade to his death, he recognized him. He suddenly recalled the police inspector in the Rue de Pontoise who had given him the two pistols which he had only recently used. Not only did he recall his face but he remembered his name.

The recollection was, however, hazy and uncertain, as were all his thoughts at that time. He did not put it to himself in the form of a positive statement but rather as a question. 'Is not that the police inspector who told me his name was Javert?' Perhaps there was still time to intercede in his favour, but first he must make sure that he was right. He turned to Enjolras, who had come from the other end of the barricade.

'What is the name of that man?'

'Which man?'

'The policeman. Do you know his name?'

'Of course. He told us.'

'Well, what is it?'

'Javert.'

Marius started forward, but at this moment there was the sound of a pistol-shot and Jean Valjean returned saying, 'It's done.'

A chill pierced Marius to the heart.

XX. *The Dead are Right, but the Living are not Wrong*

The death-throes of the stronghold were about to begin.

All things combined to create the tragic majesty of that supreme moment, a thousand mysterious shudders in the air, the breath of armed bodies of men moving along streets where they were not yet visible, the occasional galloping of cavalry, the heavy rumble of artillery on the move, musketry and cannon fire clashing in the labyrinth of Paris, the smoke of battle rising golden above the roofs, occasional distant cries that were vaguely terrible, the lightnings of danger everywhere, the Saint-Merry tocsin that now had the sound of a sob, the mildness of the season, the splendour of a sky filled with sun and cloud, the beauty of the day and the dreadful silence of the houses.

For since the previous evening the two rows of houses in the Rue de la Chanvrerie had become fiercely defiant ramparts, with bolted doors, windows, and shutters.

In those days, so different from our present time, when the hour had struck when the people wanted to have done with a situation that had gone on too long, a charter offered to them, or a body of law; when universal anger was suspended in the air, when the town acquiesced in the uprooting of its pavements, when insurrection won a smile from the bourgeois by whispering orders in their ear; in such times the citizen, penetrated with rebellion, as one might say, was the ally of the combatant, the private house fraternized with the improvised fortress into which it had been turned. But when the time was not ripe, when the insurrection was decidedly not agreed to, when the majority repudiated the movement, then there was no hope for the combatant; the town became a desert surrounding the revolt, hearts were frozen, all ways of escape were closed and the streets lay open to the army in its assault upon the barricades.

One cannot goad people into moving faster than they are prepared to go. Woe to him who tries to force their hands. A whole people does not let itself be driven. It leaves the insurrection to its own devices. The insurgent becomes a pestilence. The house is an escarpment, its door a refusal, its façade a closed wall. A wall that sees and hears and will have none of it. It might open its doors and save you, but it does not do so. The wall is a judge. It looks at you and passes sentence. How sombre are those barred houses! They seem dead, but are alive. Life in them, though it seems suspended, still persists. No one has emerged from them in twenty-four hours, but no one is missing. Within that rock people come and go, retire to bed and rise; they are a family, they eat and drink, and they are frightened, a terrible thing. Fear excuses that formidable inhospitableness, and it brings with it the extenuating circumstances of panic. Sometimes indeed, and this has been known, fear becomes passion, panic can turn into fury as prudence can turn into rage. Hence that profound expression, 'The fury of the moderates'. There can be a flare-up of terror from which, like a sinister smoke, anger arises . . . 'What do those people want? They're never satisfied. They compromise peaceful men. As if we had not had enough of this sort of disorder! Why did they choose to come here? Well, they must get out of it as best they can, and so much the worse for them. It's their own doing, they'll only get what they deserve. It's no affair of ours. Look at our poor street, pocked with bullet-holes. They're a gang of ruffians. Mind you keep that door shut!' . . . And the house acquires the semblance of a tomb. The insurgent crouches in deadly peril outside that door, seeing the guns and naked sabres. If he calls for help he knows that he is heard but that no one will answer; there are walls that might protect him, men who might save him— the walls have living ears, but the men have bowels of stone.

Whom shall we blame?

Nobody, and everybody.

The incomplete times in which we live.

It is always at its risk and peril that Utopia takes the form of Insurrection, substituting armed for reasoned protest, transforming Minerva into Pallas. The Utopia which grows impatient and becomes an uprising knows what awaits it; it nearly always happens too soon. So then it resigns itself, stoically accepting disaster in place of triumph. Without complaint it serves those who have disavowed it, even acquitting them, and its magnanimity lies in acceptance of desertion. It is indomitable in the face of obstacles and mild in the face of ingratitude.

In any case, is it ingratitude? Yes, in terms of the human species. No, in terms of the individual.

Progress is the life-style of man. The general life of the human race is called Progress, and so is its collective march. Progress advances, it makes the great human and earthly journey towards what is heavenly and divine; it has its pauses, when it rallies the stragglers, its stopping places when it meditates, contemplating some new and splendid promised land that has suddenly appeared on its horizon. It has its nights of slumber; and it is one of the poignant anxieties of the thinker to see the human spirit lost in shadow, and to grope in the darkness without being able to awake sleeping progress.

'Perhaps God is dead,' Gérard de Nerval once said to the writer of these lines, confusing progress with God and mistaking the pause in its movement for the death of the Supreme Being.

It is wrong to despair. Progress invariably reawakens, and indeed it may be said that she walks in her sleep, for she has grown. Seeing her again on her feet, we find that she is taller. To be always peaceful is no more a part of progress than it is of a river, which piles up rocks and creates barriers as it flows; these obstacles cause the water to froth and humanity to seethe. This leads to disturbance; but when the disturbance is over we realize that something has been gained. Until order, which is nothing less than universal peace, has been established, until harmony and unity prevail, the stages of progress will be marked by revolutions.

What, then, is Progress? We have just said it. It is the permanent life of all people. But it sometimes happens that the momentary life of individuals is opposed to the eternal life of the human race.

Let us admit the fact without bitterness: the individual has his separate interests and may legitimately seek to further and defend them; the present has its excusable quantity of egotisms; the life of the moment has its own rights and is not obliged to sacrifice itself incessantly for the future. The generation which now has its time upon earth is not obliged to shorten this time for the sake of generations—its equals, after all—which will later have their turn. 'I exist,' murmurs someone whose name is Everyone. 'I'm young and in love; I am old and want rest; I work, I prosper, I do good business, I have houses to rent, money in State Securities; I am happy, I have a wife and children; I like all these things and I want to go on living, so leave me alone.' . . . There are moments when all this casts a deep chill on the large-minded pioneers of the human race.

Moreover Utopia, let us agree, emerges from its starry-eyed state when it goes to war. Being tomorrow's truth she borrows her method, which is war, from yesterday's lies. She is the future, but she acts like the past; she is the ideal, but she becomes the actuality, sullying her heroism with a violence for which it is right that she should be held responsible—tactical and expedient violence, against all principle, and for which she is inevitably punished. Utopia in rebellion defies the established military code: she shoots spies, executes traitors, destroys living beings and casts them into unknown shadow. She makes use of death, which is a grave matter. It seems that

Utopia no longer believes in its own ideal, that irresistible and incorruptible force. She wields the sword. But no sword is simple; all are two-edged, and he who inflicts wounds with the one edge wounds himself with the other.

But subject to that reservation, made in all severity, it is impossible for us not to admire the glorious warriors of the future, the prophets of Utopia, whether they are successful or not. Even when they fail they are deserving of reverence, and perhaps it is in failure that they appear most noble. Victory, if it is in accord with progress, deserves the applause of mankind; but an heroic defeat deserves one's heartfelt sympathy. The one is magnificent, the other sublime. For ourselves, since we prefer martyrdom to success, John Brown is greater than Washington, Pisacane greater than Garibaldi.

It is necessary that someone should be on the side of the defeated. We are unjust to those great fighters for the future when they fail. We accuse revolutionaries of spreading terror. Every barricade seems to be an act of aggression. We stigmatize their theories, suspect their aims, mistrust their afterthoughts, and denounce their scruples. We reproach them with piling up a structure of misery and suffering, iniquities, grievances and despairs against the existing social order, and with dredging up shadows from the lowest depths as a pretext for conflict. We say to them: 'You are robbing Hell of its pavements!' To which they might reply: 'That is why our barricade is built of good intentions'.

Certainly the best solution is the one peacefully arrived at. We may agree, in short, that at the sight of paving-stones we think of the monster, and his good intentions are disquieting to society. But it is for society to save itself, and it is to its own good intentions that we appeal. No violent remedy is called for. To examine the evil with good-will, define it and then cure it—that is what we urge society to do.

However this may be, those men in all parts of the world who, with their eyes fixed upon France, struggle in the great cause with the inflexible logic of idealism, are deserving of honour. They offer their lives as a gift to progress, they fulfil the will of Providence, they perform a religious rite. When the time comes, with as much indifference as an actor taking his cue in accordance with the divine scenario, they pass on into the tomb. They accept the hopeless battle and their own stoical disappearance, for the sake of the splendid and supreme universal outcome of the magnificent human movement which began with irresistible force on 14 July 1789. Those soldiers are priests. The French Revolution is a gesture of God.

For the rest, there are—and we must add this distinction to those already made in an earlier chapter—there are accepted insurrections which we call revolutions, and there are rejected revolutions which we call uprisings. An insurrection when it breaks out is an idea which submits itself to trial by the people. If the people turn down their thumbs then the idea is dead fruit, the insurrection has failed.

To go into battle on every pretext, and whenever Utopia desires it, is not the will of the people. Nations are not always and at every moment endowed with the temperament of heroes and martyrs. They are positive. In principle they find insurrection repugnant, first because it often leads to disaster, and secondly because its starting-point is always an abstract idea.

It is always for the ideal, the ideal alone—and this is splendid—that its devotees are prepared to sacrifice themselves. An insurrection is an outburst of enthusiasm. This enthusiasm may turn to rage, hence the recourse to arms. But every insurrection levelled at a government or a regime is aiming higher than this. We must insist, for example, that the leader of this insurrection of 1832, and most especially the youthful enthusiasts in the Rue de la Chanvrerie, were not precisely doing battle with Louis-Philippe. Most of them, in their conversation, did justice to the qualities of that king who was midway between monarchy and revolution; none hated him. But they were attacking in Louis-Philippe the younger branch of the divine right, precisely as they had attacked the older branch in Charles X; and, as we have said, what they were seeking to overthrow, in overthrowing monarchy in France, was the usurpation of man over man and of privilege over law throughout the world. Paris without a king signified a world without despots. That was how they reasoned. Their objective was a remote one, no doubt, perhaps vague, and one which receded as they strove to draw near it; but it was great.

That is how it is. And men sacrifice themselves for visions which for the sacrificed are nearly always illusions, but illusions, after all, in which all human certainties are mingled. The insurgent poeticizes and gilds the insurrection. He flings himself into the tragedy intoxicated with the thought of what he will achieve. And who can be sure that he will not succeed? We are small in numbers, with a whole army arrayed against us; but we are defenders of the right, of the natural law, the sovereignty of each man over himself which cannot possibly be renounced, of justice and truth, and if need be we will die like the Spartan three hundred. We do not think of Don Quixote but of Leonidas. We go forward and, being engaged in battle, do not retreat; we charge with our heads down, impelled by the hope of unimaginable victory, the revolution successful, progress set free, the human race made great, universal deliverance; or, at the worst, another Thermopylae.

These resorts to arms in the name of progress frequently fail, and we have said why. The crowd mistrusts the allurement of paladins. The masses, ponderous bodies that they are, and fragile on account of their very heaviness, fear adventure; and there is adventure in the ideal.

Moreover we must not forget that there are interests which have little sympathy with the ideal and the sentimental. Sometimes the stomach paralyses the heart.

It is the grandeur and the beauty of France that she is less concerned with the belly than other peoples; she slips readily into harness. She is the first to awaken, the last to fall asleep. She presses forward. She is a searcher.

All this depends on the fact that she is an artist. The ideal is nothing but the culmination of logic, just as beauty is the apex of truth. Artistic peoples are logical peoples. To love beauty is to seek for light. That is why the torch of Europe, which is civilization, was carried first by Greece, which passed it to Italy, which has passed it to France. Divine pioneering peoples—*Vitai lampada tradunt.*

What is admirable is that the poetry of a people is at the head of its progress. The quantity of civilization is measured by the quality of imagination. But a civilizing race must be a masculine race; it must be Corinth, not Sybaris. Those who become effeminate bastardize themselves. It is necessary to be neither a dilettante nor a virtuoso; but it is necessary to be an artist. In the matter of civilization one must not refine but sublimate. Subject to this condition, we endow mankind with the mastery of the ideal.

The modern ideal finds its prototype in art and its method in science. It is through science that we shall realize that sublime vision of poets: social beauty. We shall rebuild Eden in terms of A + B. At the stage which civilization has reached, the exact is a necessary element in what is splendid, and artistic feeling is not only served but completed by the scientific approach; the dream must know how to calculate. Art, which is the conqueror, must have as its point of stress science, which is the prime mover. The solidity of the mount is important. The modern spirit is composed of the genius of Greece mounted on the genius of India—Alexander on the elephant.

Races petrified in dogma or demoralized by wealth are unfitted for the conduct of civilization. Genuflexion before the idol or the golden crown weakens the muscles which march and the will-power which impels. Hieratic or mercantile preoccupations decrease the luminous quality of a people, narrow its horizon by lowering its level, and withhold from it that instinct, at once human and divine, which makes missionary nations. Babylon had no ideal, nor did

Carthage. Athens and Rome had, and still, through all the darkness of centuries, they retain the glow of civilization.

France is a people of the same quality as Greece and Italy. She is Athenian in beauty and Roman in grandeur. Moreover, she is generous. She gives herself. More often than other peoples, she knows the mood of devotion and sacrifice. But it is a mood that comes and goes; and this is the great danger for those who seek to run when she is content to walk, and to walk when she wishes to stay still. France has her relapses into materialism, and at certain moments the ideas which obstruct the working of her splendid mind contain nothing that recalls her greatness but are rather of the dimensions of Missouri or some other southern state. What can be done about it? The giantess plays the dwarf; great France has her fantasies of smallness. That is all.

There is nothing to be said about that. Nations, like stars, are entitled to eclipse. All is well, provided the light returns and the eclipse does not become endless night. Dawn and resurrection are synonymous. The reappearance of the light is the same as the survival of the soul.

We may note the facts with calm. Death on the barricades or an exile's grave are, to those devoted to a cause, acceptable alternatives. The true name for devotion is disinterest. Let the deserted accept desertion and the exiled resign themselves to exile: we can only beseech the great people, when they withdraw, not to withdraw too far. They must not, on the pretext of returning to reason, advance too far on the downward path.

Matter exists, and the moment exists, as do the self-interest and the belly; but the belly must not be the sole source of wisdom. The life of the moment has its rights, and we admit them; but enduring life also has rights. Alas, to have climbed high does not preclude a fall. We see this in history more often than we would like. A nation is illustrious, it knows the taste of the ideal; then it lapses into squalor and finds this good. And if you ask why it has abandoned Socrates for Falstaff it replies: 'The truth is, I like statesmen'.

One last word before we return to battle.

A conflict like the one we are describing is nothing but a convulsive movement towards the ideal. Frustrated progress is sickly, and it is from this that these tragic epilepsies arise. We were bound to meet it on our journey, that affliction of progress, civil war. It is one of the fateful stages, both act and interval, in this play which centres upon a social outcast, and of which the real title is, *Progress*.

Progress!

That cry which we so often utter encompasses all our thought;

and, at the point in the drama which we have now reached, the idea
it contains having yet more than one trial to undergo, we may
perhaps be allowed, if not to lift the veil, at least to let a clear light
shine through it.

The book which the reader now holds in his hands, from one
end to the other, as a whole and in its details, whatever gaps,
exceptions, or weaknesses it may contain, treats of the advance from
evil to good, from injustice to justice, from falsity to truth, from
darkness to daylight, from blind appetite to conscience, from decay
to life, from bestiality to duty, from Hell to Heaven, from limbo to
God. Matter itself is the starting-point, and the point of arrival is the
soul. Hydra at the beginning, an angel at the end.

XXI. *The Heroes*

Suddenly a drum beat the charge.

The attack was a hurricane. During the night, under cover of
darkness, the barricade had been stealthily approached. In the present
broad daylight, and in that open street, there was no possibility of
surprise: it was a matter of naked force, cannon-fire paving the
way while the infantry rushed the barricade. Ferocity was now allied
to skill. A powerful column of infantry of the line, broken at equal
intervals by contingents of foot-soldiers from the national and
municipal guards, and reinforced in depth by additional bodies of
soldiery which could be heard but not seen, advanced at the double
down the street, drums playing and trumpets sounding, bayonets
fixed, sappers in the lead and, unshaken by the counter-fire, flung
itself upon the barricade with the weight of a metal battering ram
against a wall.

The wall held.

The insurgents fired impetuously. The barricade under the assault
had a crest of flashes like a lion's mane. The counter-attack was so
violent that although at one moment it was submerged beneath the
attackers, it shrugged off the soldiers as the lion shrugs off the dogs
and was covered only as a cliff is covered with sea-foam, to re-emerge
an instant later, sheer, black, and formidable.

The attacking column, forced to retreat, stayed massed in the
street, exposed but terrible, and replied with a terrifying burst of
musket-fire. Anyone who has witnessed a firework display will
recall the pattern made by the cluster of rockets that is called a
'bouquet'. We must think of this bouquet as being not vertical but
horizontal, with musket bullets or grapeshot at each of its points

of fire, and carrying death in its patterned thunders. The barricade was subjected to this.

Determination was equal on either side. Bravery became almost barbarous and to it was added a sort of heroic ferocity beginning with the sacrifice of self. It was the time when members of the Garde Nationale fought like zouaves. The troops wanted to be done with it; the rebels wanted to fight. The acceptance of death in the fullness of youth and health turns daring into frenzy. Everyone in that mêlée was filled with the inspiration of a supreme moment. The street was littered with bodies.

Enjolras was at one end of the barricade, Marius at the other: Enjolras, who carried the whole affair in his head, was keeping under cover and reserving himself; three soldiers fell under his redoubt without even seeing him. Marius had no cover. He set himself up as a target. Half his body was exposed above the top of the barricade. There is no greater spendthrift than the miser who throws over the traces, and no man more terrible in action than a dreamer. Marius was formidable and reflective, engaged in the battle as though it was a dream, as it were a ghost firing a musket.

The defenders' ammunition was running low, but not their sarcasm. They still laughed, even amid that deadly whirlwind.

Courfeyrac was bare-headed.

'What have you done with your hat?' Bossuet asked.

'It was taken off by a cannon-ball,' Courfeyrac replied.

Or they said more serious things. Feuilly cried bitterly:

'What are we to make of the men'—and he cited well-known and even celebrated names, some belonging to the old army—'who promised to join us and swore to assist us, who gave us their word of honour, who were to have been our leaders and who have deserted us?'

To which Combeferre replied with a melancholy smile:

'There are people who observe the rules of honour as we do the stars, from a very long way off.'

The ground within the barricade was so covered with used cartridge-cases that it might have been a snowstorm.

The attackers had the advantage of numbers; the rebels had the advantage of position. They were defending a wall whence they shot down at point-blank range the soldiers staggering amid their dead and wounded or enmeshed in the barricade itself. The barricade, constructed as it was and admirably buttressed, did indeed present one of those positions where a handful of men could defy a legion. Nevertheless, being constantly reinforced and expanding under the hail of bullets, the attacking column inexorably moved forward and now, little by little and step by step, but with certainty, the army was compressing the barricade like the screw of a wine-press.

The assaults continued one after another. The horror was steadily growing.

There ensued, on that heap of paving-stones in the Rue de la Chanvrerie, a struggle worthy of the ruins of Troy. That handful of haggard, ragged, and exhausted men, who had not eaten for twenty-four hours, who had not slept, who had only a few shots left to fire, so that they searched their empty pockets for cartridges, nearly all wounded, with head or arm swathed in rough, blackening bandages, having holes in their clothing through which the blood flowed, ill-armed with insufficient muskets and old, worn sabres, became Titans. The barricade was ten times assailed and climbed, but still it did not fall.

To form an idea of that conflict one must imagine a terrible pyre of courage set on fire and oneself watching the blaze. It was not a battle but the inside of a furnace; mouths breathed out fumes; faces were extraordinary, seeming no longer human but living flames; and it was awe-inspiring to watch those salamanders of battle move to and fro in the red haze. We shall not seek to depict the successive stages of the slaughter. Only an epic is entitled to fill twelve thousand lines with an account of battle. It might have been that Hell of Brahminism, the most awful of the seventeen abysses, which the Veda calls 'the forest of swords'.

They fought body to body, hand to hand, with pistol shots, sabre-thrusts, bare fists, from above and below, from all quarters, the roof of the house, the windows of the tavern, the vent-holes of the cellars into which some had slipped. They were one against sixty. The façade of Corinth, half pounded to rubble, was made hideous. The window, peppered with grape-shot, had lost both glass and framework and was nothing but a shapeless hole hastily blocked with paving-stones. Bossuet, Feuilly, Courfeyrac, Joly all were killed; Combeferre, pierced by three bayonet thrusts while he was picking up a wounded soldier, had only time to look up to the sky before he died.

Marius, still fighting, was so covered with wounds, particularly on the head, that his face was smothered with blood as though he had a red scarf tied round it.

Enjolras alone was unscathed. When he was weaponless he reached to right or left and a blade of sorts was placed by a fellow rebel in his hand. Of four swords, one more than François I had had at Marignano, he had only the stump of one left.

Homer wrote: 'Diomed slays Axylus, the son of Teuthranis, who lived in happy Arisbe; Euryalus, the son of Mecisteus, destroys Dresos, Opheltios, Esepes, and that Pedasus whom the Naiad

Abarbarea bore to the irreproachable Bucolion; Ulysses overthrows Pidutes of Percote, Antilochus, Ablerus; Polypaetes, Astyalus, Polydamas, Otus of Cyllend, Teucer and Aretaon. Meganthis dies beneath the pike-thrusts of Euripylus. Agamemnon, the king of heroes, fells Elatos, who was born in the fortified town washed by the rippling River Satnois.' In our old poems of battle Esplandian attacks with a two-forked flame the giant Marquis Swantibore, who defends himself by pelting the knight with the stones of towers he uproots. Ancient mural frescoes depict for us the dukes of Brittany and of Bourbon, armed and accoutred for battle, mounted and encountering each other, battle-axe in hand, visored with iron, shod with iron, gauntletted with iron, the one caprisoned with ermine, the other draped in blue; Brittany with a lion's head between the two horns of his crown, Bourbon adorned with a huge fleur-de-lys at his visor. But to be superb it is not necessary to flaunt, like Yvon, the ducal morion, or to carry in the hand a living flame, like Esplandian, or, like Phyles, the father of Polydamas, to have brought back a suit of armour from Ephyrae, the present of the king of Corinth; it is only necessary to give one's life for a conviction or for a loyalty. The simple-minded soldier, yesterday a peasant in la Beauce or Le Limousin, who strays, pigsticker at his side, round the children's nurses in the Luxembourg; the pale young student bent over a piece of anatomy or a book; a blond adolescent who trims his beard with scissors—infuse these with a sense of duty and plant them face to face in the Carrefour Boucherat or the blind alley Blanche Mibray, the one fighting for his flag, the other for his ideals, and both believing that they are fighting for their country, and you will find that the shadow cast by the country bumpkin and the aspirant doctor, in the epic field where mankind struggles, will be no less great than the shadow cast by Megaryon, the king of tiger-filled Lycia, in his struggle with the giant Ajax, the equal of the Gods.

XXII. *Close Quarters*

When only two of the leaders were left alive, Marius and Enjolras at either end of the barricade, the centre, which for so long had been sustained by Courfeyrac, Joly, Bossuet, Feuilly, and Combeferre, gave way. The cannon-fire, without making an effective breach in the wall, had sufficiently damaged it. The top had been shot away, falling on either side, so that the débris formed two inclines, one within the stronghold and the other outside it, the one outside providing a ramp for the attackers.

A supreme assault was launched, and this time it succeeded. The mass of soldiery, bristling with bayonets and advancing at the double, was irresistible, and the dense front line of the attacking force appeared amid the smoke on the top of the barricade. This time all was over. The group of rebels defending the centre beat a hasty retreat.

And then in some of them the deeply implanted love of life was revived. Faced by that forest of muskets, several no longer wanted to die. It is a moment when the instinct of self-preservation cries out loud and the animal reappears in man. They were pressed against the six-storey house which formed the back of the stronghold. This house might be the saving of them. It was barricaded and, so to speak, walled in from top to bottom. Before the troops had penetrated into the stronghold, there was time for a door to open and close, only a moment was needed, and that door might be life itself to the handful of desperate men. Beyond the house lay streets, space, the possibility of flight. They began to hammer on the door with musket-butts, and to kick it, calling out and begging with clasped hands. But no one opened the door. From the window in the third floor the dead head looked down on them.

But Enjolras and Marius, and the seven or eight who rallied round them, gave the rest some protection. Enjolras had cried to the soldiers, 'Stand back!' and when an officer had refused to obey he had killed him. He stood now in the little interior courtyard of the stronghold, his back to the tavern, a sword in one hand, a carbine in the other, defending the door against the attackers and cried to his men, 'This is the only open door.' Covering them with his body, defying a battalion single-handed, he let them pass behind him. They hastened to do so; and Enjolras, using his carbine as a cudgel to batter down the bayonets that threatened him, was the last to enter. There was a terrible moment, with the soldiers striving to force open the door and the rebels striving to close it. Finally it was closed with such violence that, as it was slammed to, it still bore, adhering to the woodwork, the severed finger of a soldier who had clutched it.

Marius had stayed outside. A ball had shattered his shoulder-blade. He felt himself grow dizzy and he fell. At this moment, when his eyes were already closed, he felt himself grasped by a vigorous hand, and in the moment before he sank into unconsciousness he had just time to think, mingled with the memory of Cosette, 'I'm taken prisoner. I shall be shot'.

Enjolras, not seeing Marius among those who had taken refuge in the tavern, thought the same. But it was a moment when there was no time to think of any death except one's own. Enjolras barred and double-bolted the door while a thunder of blows from musket-butts and the axes of the sappers descended on it from outside. Their attackers were now concentrating upon the door. The siege of the tavern had begun.

The soldiers were furiously angry. The death of the artillery sergeant had enraged them and, worse still, the rumour had gone round during the hours preceding the attack that the rebels were mutilating their prisoners, and that the headless body of a soldier lay in the tavern. Hideous rumours of this kind are a normal accompaniment of civil war, and it was a similar rumour which was later to lead to the disaster in the Rue Transnonain.

When the door was secured, Enjolras said to his fellows:

'We must sell our lives dearly.'

Then he went to the table on which the bodies of Mabeuf and Gavroche were lying. Two rigid, motionless forms, one large, one small, lay covered by a black cloth, and the two faces could be faintly discerned beneath the stiff folds of the shroud. A hand had escaped its covering and hung down towards the floor. It was that of the old man.

Enjolras bent down and kissed the venerable hand as on the previous evening he had kissed the forehead. They were the only two kisses he had ever bestowed in his life.

In brief, the barricade had fought like a doorway of Thebes, and the tavern fought like a house in Saragossa. Those were obstinate defences. No quarter was given, no discussion was possible. Men are ready to die provided they also kill. When Suchet cried, 'Surrender!' Palafox replied, 'After the battle with firearms comes the battle with knives'. Nothing was lacking in the capture by assault of the Hucheloup tavern, neither the paving-stones rained down upon the besiegers from the upper window and roof, causing hideous injuries, nor shots fired from the cellars and attics, neither fury in the attack nor rage in the defence—nor finally, when the door gave way, the frantic dementia of slaughter. The attackers, rushing into the tavern, their feet entangled in the panels of the broken door, found not a single defender. The circular staircase, cut in halves with an axe, lay in the middle of the lower room, where a few wounded men were in process of dying. All those remaining alive were on the upper floor, and from here, by way of the hole in the ceiling which had been the entrance to the staircase, there came a terrible burst of fire. Those were the last cartridges. When they had been fired, and when the heroic defenders were left with neither powder nor shot, each seized two of the bottles set aside by Enjolras, of which we have spoken, and held back the attack with these most fragile cudgels. They were bottles of brandy. We are depicting these sombre aspects of the carnage as they happened. The besieged, alas, makes a weapon of everything. Greek fire did no dishonour to Archimedes, nor boiling pitch to Bayard. All forms of warfare are terror, and there is nothing to choose between them. The musketry of the attackers, although harassed and aiming upwards, was murderous. The edge of that hole in the ceiling was soon surrounded by dead heads from which hung long, streaming red threads. The din was indescribable; and a reeking cloud of smoke plunged the battle in darkness. Words are lacking to depict a horror that has reached this point. There were no longer men engaged in a struggle that was now infernal, no longer giants against Titans; it was nearer to Milton and Dante than to Homer. Demons attacked and spectres resisted. It was heroism become monstrous.

XXIII. *Orestes fasting and Pylades Drunk*

Eventually, lending each other a back and making use of the remains of the staircase, climbing up the walls and clinging to the ceiling, and hacking down the last resistance at the edge of the hatchway, some twenty of the attackers, soldiers and national and municipal guards, most of them suffering from wounds sustained in that final advance, blinded with their own blood, enraged and now savage, succeeded in reaching the upper room. Only one man in it was still on his feet—Enjolras. Without cartridges or a sword, his only weapon was the barrel of his carbine, the butt of which he had broken on the heads of the attackers. He had put the billiard-table between his assailants and himself, and had retreated to the corner of the room; but here, proud-eyed and erect, armed with nothing but that last fragment of a weapon, he was still sufficiently impressive for a space to be left around him. A voice cried:

'He's the leader. He's the one who killed the artilleryman. Well, he's set himself up for us. He's only got to stay there and we can shoot him on the spot.'

'Shoot me,' said Enjolras.

Flinging away the remains of the carbine and folding his arms, he offered them his breast.

The bold defiance of death is always moving. On the instant when Enjolras folded his arms, accepting his fate, the din of battle ceased in the room and chaos was succeeded by a sort of sepulchral solemnity. It seemed that the dignity of Enjolras, weaponless and motionless, weighed upon the tumult, and that this young man, the only one unwounded, proud, blood-spattered, charming, and disdainful as though he were invulnerable, impelled the sinister group to kill him with respect. His beauty, now enhanced by pride, was radiant, and as though he could be neither fatigued nor wounded, even after the appalling twenty-four hours which had passed, his cheeks were flushed with health. Perhaps it was to him that a witness was referring when later he said to the tribunal, 'There was one of the insurgents whom I heard called Apollo'. A national guard who aimed his musket at Enjolras, lowered it and said: 'I feel as though I'd be shooting a flower.'

Twelve men formed up in the opposite corner of the room and silently charged their muskets.

A sergeant cried, 'Take aim!', but an officer intervened.

'Wait', he said.

He spoke to Enjolras:

'Would you like your eyes to be bandaged?'

'No.'

'It really was you who killed the artillery sergeant?'

'Yes.'

Grantaire had woken up a few moments previously.

As we may recall, he had been asleep since the previous day in the upper room of the tavern, seated on a chair and sprawled over a table.

He had been the perfect embodiment, in all its forcefulness, of the old expression, 'dead drunk'. The awesome mixture of absinthe, stout, and raw spirit had plunged him into a coma. Since his table was small and of no use to the defence, he had been left there. He was in his original posture, with his head resting on his arms, surrounded by glasses, tankards, and empty bottles, deep in the annihilating slumber of a hibernating bear or a bloated leech. Nothing had penetrated it, not the firing or the bullets and grape-shot that came in through the window, nor even the tremendous uproar of the final assault. Only the cannon had drawn an occasional snore from him; he seemed to be waiting for a ball to save him the trouble of waking up. Several dead bodies lay around him; and at first glance there was nothing to distinguish him from the truly dead.

It is not noise that awakens a drunken man, but silence. This is a singular fact that has often been observed. The collapse of everything around him had merely served to increase Grantaire's unconsciousness, as though it were a rocking cradle. But the pause induced by Enjolras came as a shock to his slumbers, the effect being that of a carriage drawn at a gallop which comes suddenly to a stop. The sleeper awoke. Grantaire sat up with a start, stretched his arms, rubbed his eyes, stared, yawned, and understood.

The ending of drunkenness is like the tearing down of a curtain. One sees, as a whole and at a single glance, everything that it concealed. Memory suddenly returns, and the drunkard who knows nothing of what has happened in the past twenty-four hours, has scarcely opened his eyes before he is aware of the situation. His thoughts return to him with a brisk lucidity; the non-being of drunkenness, a sort of fog that blinds the brain, vanishes to be replaced by an instant, clear grasp of things as they are.

The soldiers, intent upon Enjolras, had not even noticed Grantaire, who had been slumbering in a corner, partly concealed from them by the billiard-table. The sergeant was about to repeat the order, 'Take aim!' when suddenly a loud voice cried:

'Long live the Republic! I'm one of them.'

Grantaire had risen to his feet.

The blazing light of the battle of which he had seen nothing, and in which he had taken no part, shone in the eyes of the transfigured sot. He repeated, 'Long live the Republic!' and walking steadily across the room took his stand beside Enjolras, confronting the muskets.

'Might as well kill two birds with one stone,' he said; and then, turning to Enjolras, he added gently: 'If you don't mind.'

Enjolras clasped his hand and smiled.

The smile had not ended when the volley rang out. Enjolras, pierced by eight shots, stayed leaning against the wall as though the bullets had nailed him there; only his head hung down. Grantaire collapsed at his feet.

Within a few minutes the soldiers had driven out the last of the rebels sheltering at the top of the house. They fired through a wooden lattice into the attic. There was fighting under the roof and bodies were flung out of windows, some of them still living. Two sappers who were trying to set the overturned omnibus upright were killed by carbine-shots from the attic. A man in a smock was flung out of it with a bayonet-thrust in his belly and lay groaning on the ground. A soldier and a rebel slid together down the sloping roof-tiles and, refusing to let go of each other, fell together in a fierce embrace. There was a similar struggle in the cellar—cries, shots, desperate exertion. Then silence. The stronghold was taken.

The soldiers began to search the surrounding houses and pursue the fugitives.

XXIV. *Prisoner*

Marius was indeed a prisoner, and of Jean Valjean. It was Valjean's hand that had grasped him as he fell, and whose grip he had felt before losing consciousness.

Valjean had taken no part in the battle other than in exposing himself to it. Had it not been for him, no one in those last desperate moments would have thought of the wounded. Thanks to him, present everywhere in the carnage like a providence, those who fell were picked up, carried into the tavern, and their wounds dressed. In the intervals he mended the barricade. But he did not strike a blow, even in self-defence. He silently assisted. And, as it happened, he had scarcely a scratch. The bullets would have none of him. If he had had any thought of suicide when he entered that deadly place, he had failed in this. But we question whether he had thought of suicide, an irreligious act.

In the dense reek of battle Valjean had not seemed to see Marius; but the truth is that he had never taken his eyes off him. When a bullet laid Marius low, Valjean leapt forward with the agility of a tiger, seized him as though he were his prey, and carried him off.

The attack at that moment was so intensely concentrated upon Enjolras and the door of the tavern that no one saw Valjean carry Marius's unconscious form across the stronghold and vanish round the corner of the house. This, it will be remembered, made a sort of promontory in the street, affording shelter for a few square feet from bullets and also out of sight. In the same way there is sometimes one room in a blazing house that does not burn, or a quiet stretch of water behind an outcrop of land in a storm-lashed sea. It was in this retreat within the barricades that Éponine had died.

Here Jean Valjean stopped, lowered Marius to the ground, and with his back to the wall stood looking about him.

The situation was appalling. For perhaps two or three minutes this corner of wall might afford them shelter; but how to escape from the inferno? He remembered his torments eight years earlier in the Rue Polonceau, and how he had eventually got away; that had been difficult, but this time it seemed impossible. Facing him was that silent, implacable house that seemed to be inhabited only by a dead man leaning out of a window; to his right was the low barricade closing the Rue de la Petite-Truanderie, an obstacle easily surmounted; but beyond the barricade a row of bayonets was visible, those of the soldiers posted to block this way of escape. To climb the barricade would be to encounter a volley of musket-fire. And on Valjean's left was the field of battle. Death lurked round the corner.

It was a situation such as only a bird could have escaped from. But the matter had to be instantly decided, a device contrived, a plan made. The fight was going on within a few yards of him, and, by good fortune, it was concentrated on a single point, the door of the tavern; but if a single soldier had the idea of going round the house to attack it from the side all would be over.

Valjean looked at the house opposite, at the barricade and then at the ground, with the intentness of utmost extremity, as though he were seeking to dig a hole in it with his eyes.

As he looked something like a possibility emerged, as though the very intensity of his gaze had brought it to light. He saw, a few feet away, at the foot of that rigorously guarded lower barricade, half-hidden by tumbled paving-stones, an iron grille let into the street. Made of stout iron transverse bars, it was about two feet square. The stones surrounding it had been uprooted, so that it was, as it were, unsealed. Beneath the bars was a dark aperture, something like a chimney flue or a boiler cylinder. Valjean leapt forward, all his old experience of escape springing like inspiration into his mind. To shift the paving-stones, raise the grille, lift Marius's inert body on to his shoulder, and, charged with this burden, using elbows and knees, to climb down into this fortunately shallow well; to let the heavy grille fall shut behind him, over which the stones again tumbled, and find footing on a tile surface some ten feet underground—all this was done as though in delirium, with immense strength and hawklike speed. It took only a few minutes.

Valjean, with the still unconscious Marius, found himself in a long subterranean passage, a place of absolute peace, silence, and darkness. He was reminded of the time when he had fallen out of the street into the garden of the convent; but then it had been with Cosette.

Like a subdued echo above his head he could still hear the formidable uproar which accompanied the capture of the tavern.

BOOK TWO

THE ENTRAILS OF THE MONSTER

I. *Land Impoverished by the Sea*

PARIS pours twenty-four million francs a year into the water. That is no metaphor. She does so by day and by night, thoughtlessly and to no purpose. She does so through her entrails, that is to say, her sewers. Twenty-five millions is the most modest of the approximate figures arrived at by statistical science.

After many experiments science today knows that the most fruitful and efficacious of all manures is human excrement. The Chinese, be it said to our shame, knew it before us. No Chinese peasant, according to Eckeberg, goes to the town without bringing back, at either end of his bamboo pole, two buckets filled with unmentionable matter; and it is thanks to this human manure that the Chinese earth is as fruitful as in the days of Abraham. The Chinese corn harvest amounts to 120 times the amount of seed. No guano is to be compared in fertility with the droppings of a town. A big city is the most powerful of dunging animals. To use the town to manure the country is to ensure prosperity. If our gold is so much waste, then, on the other hand, our waste is so much gold.

And what do we do with this golden dung? We throw it away. At great expense we send ships to the South Pole to collect the droppings of petrels and penguins, and the incalculable wealth we ourselves produce we throw back into the sea. The human and animal manure which is lost to the world because it is returned to the sea instead of to the land would suffice to feed all mankind. Do you know what all this is—the heaps of muck piled up on the streets during the night, the scavengers' carts and the foetid flow of sludge that the pavement hides from you? It is the flowering meadow, green grass, marjoram and thyme and sage, the lowing of contented cattle in the evening, the scented hay and the golden wheat, the bread on your table and the warm blood in your veins—health and joy and life. Such is the purpose of that mystery of creation which is transformation on earth and transfiguration in Heaven.

Return all that to the great crucible and you will reap abundance. The feeding of the fields becomes the feeding of men. You are free to lose that richness and to find me absurd into the bargain; that will be the high point of your ignorance.

It has been calculated that France alone through her rivers every year pours into the Atlantic half a milliard francs. You must note that those five hundred millions represent a quarter of our budget expenditure. Such is man's astuteness that he prefers to rid himself of this sum in the streams. It is the people's substance that is being carried away, in drops or in floods, the wretched vomit of our sewers into the rivers, and the huge vomit of the rivers into the sea. Each belch of our cloaca costs us a thousand francs, and the result is that the land is impoverished and the water made foul. Hunger lurks in the furrow and disease in the stream.

It is notorious, for example, that in recent years the Thames has been poisoning London. As for Paris, the outlet of most of the sewers has had to be brought below the last of the bridges.

A two-channel arrangement of locks and sluices, sucking in and pouring out, an elementary drainage system as simple as the human lung, such as is already functioning in some parts of England, would suffice to bring to our towns the pure water of the fields and to return to the fields the enriched water of the towns; and this very simple exchange would save us the five hundred millions which we fling away.

The present process does harm in seeking to do good. The intention is good, the result lamentable. We think to cleanse the town but weaken the population. A sewer is a mistake. When drainage, with its double function of restoring what it takes away, shall have replaced the sewer, which is mere impoverishment, then this, combined with a new social economy, will increase by a hundredfold the produce of the earth and the problem of poverty will be immeasurably lessened. Add to this the elimination of parasites, and the problem is solved.

Meanwhile wastage continues and public wealth flows into the river. Wastage is the word. Europe is exhausting itself to the point of ruin. As for France, we have named the figures. But since Paris amounts to one twenty-fifth of the total French population, and the Paris manure is the richest of all, to assess at twenty-five millions Paris's share in the annual loss of half a milliard is an underestimate. Those twenty-five millions, used for relief-work and for amenities, would double the splendour of Paris. The city wastes them in its sewers; so that one may say that the abundance of Paris, her festivities, her noble buildings, her elegance, luxury and magnificence, and the money that she squanders with both hands—all this is sewage.

It is in this fashion, in the blindness of a false political economy, that the well-being of the whole community is allowed to pour away. There should be nets at Saint-Cloud to trap the public wealth. Economically one may sum it up as follows: Paris is a leaky basket. This model capital city, of which every nation seeks to have a copy, this ideal metropolis, this noble stronghold of initiative, drive, and experiment, this centre and dwelling-place of minds, this nation-town and hive of the future, a composite of Babylon and Corinth, would, seen in this aspect, cause a peasant of Fo-Kian to shrug his shoulders.

To copy Paris is to invite ruin. And Paris, in this matter of immemorial and senseless waste, copies herself. There is nothing new in her ineptitude; it is not a youthful folly. The ancients behaved like the moderns. 'The cloaca of Rome,' wrote Liebig, 'absorbed all the well-being of the Roman peasant.' When the Roman countryside was ruined by the Roman sewer, Rome exhausted Italy, and when she had poured Italy through her drains she disposed of Sicily, then Sardinia, then Africa. The Roman sewer engulfed the world, sapping town and country alike. *Urbi et orbi* or the Eternal City, the bottomless drain.

In this, as in other matters, Rome set the example; and Paris follows it with the stupidity proper to intelligent towns. For the purpose of the operation she has beneath her another Paris, with its roads and intersections, its arteries and alleyways—the Paris of the sewers, a city of slime only lacking human kind.

We must avoid flattery, even of a great people. Where there is everything there is ignominy as well as sublimity: and if Paris contains Athens, the city of light, Tyre, the city of power, Sparta, the city of stern virtue, Nineveh, the city of prodigy, she also contains Lutetia, the city of mud. Moreover, the mark of her greatness is there also. The huge bilge of Paris achieves the strange feat that among men only a few, such as Machiavelli, Bacon, and Mirabeau, have achieved—an abjectness of grandeur.

The underside of Paris, if the eye could perceive it, would have the appearance of a vast sea-plant. A sponge has no more apertures and passageways than the patch of earth, six leagues around, on which the ancient city stands. Apart from the catacombs, the intricate network of gas-pipes and of piping that distributes fresh water to the street pumps, each a separate system, the sewers alone form a huge, dark labyrinth on either side of the river—a maze to which the only key is itself.

And here, in the foetid darkness, the rat is to be found, apparently the sole product of Paris's labour.

If one thinks of Paris lifted up like a lid, the view of the sewers from above would resemble a great tree-trunk grafted onto the river. On the right bank the main sewer would be the trunk of the tree, its lesser channels being the branches and its dead ends the twigs.

This is a condensed and inexact simile, for the right-angle, which is characteristic of this form of underground ramification, is very rare in vegetable growths. One may form a more appropriate image by supposing that one is looking down on a grotesque jumble of eastern letters attached to each other haphazard, by their sides or their extremities.

Bilges and sewers played a great part in the Middle Ages, in the Lower Empire and the far East. Plague was born in them, despots died in them. The masses contemplated with an almost religious awe those hotbeds of putrescence, vast cradles of death. The Pit of Vermin at Benares was no less deep than the Pit of Lions at Babylon. Tiglath-Pilezar, according to the rabbinical books, swore by the vents of Nineveh. It is from the sewer of Münster that John of Leyden raised his false moon, and from the pit of Kekhscheb that Mokanna, the veiled prophet of Khorassan, raised his false sun.

The history of mankind is reflected in the history of cloaca. The Gemoniae depicted Rome. The sewer of Paris was a formidable ancient thing, both sepulchre and refuge. Crime, intelligence, social protest, liberty of conscience, thought and theft, everything that human laws pursue or have pursued has been hidden in it—the Maillotins in the fourteenth century, the Tire-laines in the fifteenth, the Huguenots in the sixteenth, the Illuminati in the seventeenth, the Chauffeurs in the eighteenth. A century ago the night-time dagger thrust came out of it, the footpad in danger vanished into it. The forest had its caves, and Paris had its sewer. The *truanderie*, that Gallic gipsy band, accepted the sewer as a part of the Court of Miracles, and at night, cunning and ferocious, crouched under the Maubuée vomitoria as in a bedchamber.

It was natural that those whose daily work was in the alley Vide-Gousset or the Rue Coupe-Gorge should have this night-time dwelling in the culvert of the Chemin-vert bridge or the Hurepoix kennel. From these come a host of memories. All sorts of ghosts haunt those long, lonely corridors; foulness and miasma are everywhere, with here and there a vent-hole through which Villon from within converses with Rabelais without.

The sewer, in ancient Paris, is the resting-place of all failure and all effort. To political economy it is a detritus, and to social philosophy a residue. It is the conscience of the town where all things converge and clash. There is darkness here, but no secrets. Everything has its true or at least its definitive form. There is this to be said for the muck-heap, that it does not lie. Innocence dwells in it. The mask of Basil is there, the cardboard and the strings, accented with honest filth; and beside it, the false nose of Scapin. Every foulness of civilization, fallen into disuse, sinks into that ditch of truth wherein ends the huge social down-slide, to be swallowed, but to spread. It is a vast confusion. No false appearance, no white-washing, is possible; filth strips off its shirt in utter starkness, all illusions and mirages scattered, nothing left except what is, showing the ugly face of what ends. Reality and disappearance: here, a bottle neck proclaims drunkenness, a basket-handle tells of home life; and there the apple-core that had literary opinions again becomes an apple-core. The face on the coin turns frankly green, the spittle of Caiaphas encounters the vomit of Falstaff, the gold piece from the gaming house rattles against the nail from which the suicide hung, a livid foetus is wrapped in the spangles which last Shrove Tuesday danced at the Opera, a wig which passed judgement on men wallows near the decay which was the skirt of Margoton. It is more than fraternity, it is close intimacy. That which was painted is besmeared. The last veil is stripped away. A sewer is a cynic. It says everything.

This sincerity of filth pleases us and soothes the spirit. When one has spent one's time on earth suffering the windy outpourings which call themselves statesmanship, political wisdom, human justice, professional probity, the robes of incorruptibility, it is soothing to go into the sewer and see the mire which is appropriate to all this. And at the same time it teaches us. As we have said, history flows through the sewer. Saint Bartholomew seeps drop by drop through the paving-stones. The great assassinations, the political and religious butcheries, pass through that underworld of civilization with their bodies. To the thoughtful eye, all the murderers of history are there on their knees in that hideous penumbra, with a fragment of shroud for their apron, sadly washing out their offence. Louis XI is there with Tristan, François I with Duprat, Charles IX with his mother, Richelieu with Louis XIII; Louvois, Letellier, Hébert, and Maillard seek to efface the traces of their lives. One may hear the swish of spectral brooms and breathe the huge miasma of social catastrophe and see red reflections in the corners. A terrible water flows that has washed blood-stained hands.

The social observer should enter that darkness; it is a part of his laboratory. Philosophy is the microscope of thought, from which everything seeks to fly but nothing escapes. To compromise is useless: what side of oneself does one show by compromise; except what is shameful? Philosophy pursues evil with its unflinching

gaze and does not allow it to escape into nothingness. Amid the vanishing and the shrinking it detects all things, reconstructing the purple from the shred of rag and the woman from the wisp. Through the cloaca it reconstructs the town, from the mire it recreates its customs; from the shard it deduces the amphora or the jug. From the impress of a fingernail on parchment it distinguishes between the Jewry of the Judengasse and that of the Ghetto. From what remains it rediscovers what has been, good, bad, false, true—the spot of blood in the palace, the inkspot in the cavern, the drop of grease in the brothel, the torments suffered, temptations encountered, orgies vomited up, the wrinkles of self-abasement, the traces of prostitution in souls rendered capable of it by their vileness, and on the smock of the Roman porter the elbow-mark of Messalina.

III. *Bruneseau*

The Paris sewer in the Middle Ages was a legend. In the sixteenth century Henri II attempted a sounding which failed. Less than a hundred years ago, as Mercier attests, the cloaca was left to itself, to make of itself what it could.

Such was ancient Paris, the victim of quarrels, indecisiveness, and false starts. For a long time it was stupid. Then the year '89 showed how sense comes to cities. But in the good old days the capital had little discernment; she did not know how to order her affairs either morally or materially, and could no more dispose of ordure than of abuses. Everything was difficult, everything raised questions. The sewerage itself was opposed to any discipline. A course could no more be laid down for it than could agreement be reached in the town; above was the unintelligible, below the inextricable; beneath the confusions of tongues lay the confusion of cellars, the labyrinth below Babel.

Sometimes the Paris sewer chose to overflow, as though that hidden Nile were suddenly angry. There were infamous sewer floods. That stomach of civilization digested badly; the cloaca at times flowed back into the town, giving Paris a taste of bile. These parallels of sewage and remorse had their virtue. They were warnings, very badly received it must be said. The town was angered by the audacity of its filth, and could not accept that its ordure should return; it must be better disposed of.

The flood of 1802 is within the memory of eighty-year-old Parisians. The mire formed a cross in the Place des Victoires, with its statue of Louis XIV. It entered the Rue Saint-Honoré by the two sewer mouths of the Champs-Élysées, the Rue Popincourt by the Chemin-Vert mouth, the Rue de la Roquette by the Rue de Sappe sewer. It covered the Rue des Champs-Élysées to a depth of thirty-five centimetres; and at midday, when the vomitorium of the Seine performed its function in reverse, it reached the Rue des Marais among other streets, covering a distance of a hundred and nine metres, only a few paces from the house where Racine had lived, respecting the poet more than it had the king. It attained its greatest depth in the Rue Saint-Pierre, where it rose three feet above the roof-gutters, and its greatest extent in the Rue Saint-Sabin, when it stretched over a distance of two hundred and thirty-eight metres.

At the beginning of this century the Paris sewer was still a place of mystery. Muck has never had a good name, but here it was a subject for alarm. Paris was confusedly aware that beneath her lay a dreadful hollow, resembling the monstrous bog of Thebes inhabited by worms fifteen feet long, and which might have served as a bath-tub for Behemoth. The great boots of the sewage workers never ventured beyond certain known points. It was still very near the time when the carts of the street-scavengers, from one of which Sainte-Foix had fraternized with the Marquis de Créqui, were simply emptied into the sewer. As for cleansing, this was left to the rain-storms, which obstructed more than they carried away. Rome invested her cloaca with a touch of poetry, calling it Gemoniae; Paris insulted hers, calling it the stench-hole. Science and superstition were agreed as to the horror. The stench-hole was as repellent to hygiene as to legend. Spectral figures emerged from the Mouffetard sewer, corpses had been flung into that of the Barillerie. Fagon attributed the terrible malignant fever of 1685 to the break in the Marais sewer, which until 1833 lay open in the Rue Saint-Louis, almost opposite the inn-sign of the Messager-Galant. The sewer-mouth in the Rue de la Mortellerie was famous for the plagues which spread from it: with the pointed bars of its grille resembling a row of teeth, it was like a dragon's mouth breathing hell upon men. Popular imagination credited that dark Parisian sink with a hideous endlessness. The idea of exploring it did not occur to the police. Who would have dared to sound those depths, to venture into that unknown? It was terrible. Nevertheless someone did venture. The cloaca found its Christopher Columbus.

On a day in 1805, during one of the Emperor's rare visits to Paris, the Minister of the Interior attended his *petit lever*. The rattle of sabres of those extraordinary soldiers of the Republic and the Empire could be heard in the Carrousel. There was an over-abundance of heroes at Napoleon's door—men from the Rhine, the

Adige, and the Nile, comrades of Joubert, Desaix, Marceau, Hoche, and Kléber, men who had followed Bonaparte on the bridge at Lodi, who had accompanied Murat in the trenches of Mantua, who had preceded Lannes in the sunken road of Montebello. All the army, represented by a squad or a platoon, was there in that courtyard of the Tuileries, guarding Napoleon's rest. It was the splendid time when the Grande Armée had Marengo behind it and Austerlitz ahead of it. . . . 'Sire,' said the Minister to Napoleon, 'yesterday I saw the bravest man in your empire.' . . . 'Who is he?' the Emperor asked. 'And what has he done?' . . . 'It is what he wants to do, Sire.' . . . 'What is that?' . . . 'To explore the sewers of Paris'.

The man's name was Bruneseau.

IV. *Unknown Details*

The inspection took place. It was a formidable undertaking, a battle in darkness against pestilence and asphyxia. And also a voyage of discovery. One of the survivors, an intelligent workman who was then very young, later recalled certain details which Bruneseau had seen fit to omit from his report to the Prefect of Police as being unworthy of an official document. Methods of disinfection were at that time very rudimentary. Bruneseau had hardly entered the underground network when eight of his twenty workers refused to go further. The operation was complicated; it entailed cleaning and also measuring, noting the entry-points, counting the grilles and mouths, recording the branches with some indication of the current at various points, examining the different basins, determining the width and height of each corridor both from the floor of the sewer and in relation to the street surface. Progress was slow. It happened not infrequently that the ladders sank into three feet of slime. Lanterns flickered and died in the poisonous air, and from time to time a fainting man had to be carried out. There were pitfalls at certain places where the floor had collapsed and the sewer became a bottomless well; one man suddenly disappeared and they had great difficulty in rescuing him. On the advice of Fourcroy, the noted chemist, they lighted reasonably clear places with cages filled with oakum steeped in resin. The walls were here and there covered with shapeless fungi resembling tumours; the very stonework seemed diseased.

Bruneseau proceeded downstream in his survey. At the junction of two channels at the Grand Hurleur he detected on a jutting stone the date 1550, which indicated the limit reached by Philibert Delorne, charged by Henri II with inspecting the underground labyrinth of Paris. This stone was the token of the sixteenth century. Bruneseau found the handicraft of the seventeenth century in the Ponceau conduit and that of the Rue Vieille-du-Temple, vaulted over between 1600 and 1650, and of the eighteenth in the western section of the main canal, lined and vaulted over in 1740. The two vaults, especially the more recent, that of 1740, were more cracked and decrepit than the masonry of the ring sewer, dating from 1412, when the open stream of Ménilmontant was invested with the dignity of the main sewer of Paris—a promotion resembling that of a peasant who becomes the King's valet.

Here and there, notably under the Palais de Justice, dungeon cells were found built into the sewer itself. An iron collar hung in one of them. All were walled up. There were strange discoveries, among others the skeleton of an orang-utan that had vanished from the Jardin des Plantes in 1800, a disappearance probably connected with the famous appearance of the Devil in the Rue des Bernardins. The poor devil had been drowned in the sewer.

Under the long, vaulted corridor that ends at the Arche-Marion a rag-picker's hod was found in a state of perfect preservation. The slime everywhere, being bravely ransacked by the sewage workers, abounded in precious objects of jewellery and gold and silver, and coins. A giant filtering the cloaca might have scraped up the wealth of centuries. At the junction of the Rue du Temple and the Rue Sainte-Avoye a strange copper medal was found, of Huguenot origin, having on one side a pig wearing a cardinal's hat and on the other a wolf in a tiara.

But the most surprising discovery was made at the entrance to the main sewer. This entrance had formerly been closed by a barred gate of which only the hinges remained. A dingy shred of material was attached to one of the hinges, having no doubt been caught on it as it floated by. Bruneseau examined it by the light of his lantern. It was of very fine cambric, and on its least worn part he discovered a heraldic coronet embroidered above the seven letters LAVBESP. The coronet was that of a marquis, and the seven letters signified Laubespine. He realized that he was looking at a fragment of Marat's shroud. Marat in his youth, at the time when he was veterinary surgeon to the household of the Comte d'Artois, had had a love-affair, historically attested, with a great lady, of which a sheet was his only souvenir. On his death, since it was the only scrap of decent linen he possessed, he had been wrapped in it. Old women had dressed him for the grave, the tragic Ami du Peuple, in that relic of sensual delight.

Bruneseau left the rag there without destroying it, whether from contempt or respect who can say? Marat merited both. It was so imprinted with destiny that one might hesitate to touch it. Besides, the things of the tomb should be left where they choose to be. In short, it was a strange relic: a marquise had slept in it, Marat had rotted in it and it had crossed the Panthéon to end up with the sewer rats. The bed-chamber rag, of which Watteau might have exquisitely drawn the folds, had in the end been worthy of the dark gaze of Dante.

The total inspection of that unspeakable underside of Paris took seven years, from 1805 to 1812. While exploring, Bruneseau originated, planned, and carried out considerable construction work. In 1808 he lowered the Ponceau level, and, creating new channels everywhere, he drove the sewer in 1809 under the Rue Saint-Denis to the Fontaine des Innocents; in 1810 under the Rue Froidmanteau and the Salpêtrière; in 1811 under the Rue Neuve-des-Petits-Pères, the Rue du Mail, the Rue de l'Écharpe, and the Place Royale; in 1812 under the Rue de la Paix and the Chaussée d'Antin. At the same time he had the whole network disinfected. He was assisted from the second year by his son-in-law Nargaud.

Thus at the beginning of this century society cleansed its underside and performed the toilet of its sewer. So much at least was made clean.

Tortuous, fissured and unpaved, interspersed with quagmires, rising and falling, twisting and turning without reason, foetid and bathed in obscurity, with scars on its floor and gashes in its walls, altogether horrible—such, in retrospect, was the ancient sewer of Paris. Ramifications all ways, intersections, branches, crow's feet, blind alleys, salt-rimed vaults, reeking cesspits, poisonous ooze on the walls, drops falling from the roof, darkness: nothing could equal in horror that excremental crypt, Babylon's digestive system, a cavern pierced with roads, a vast molehill in which the mind seems to perceive, straying through the darkness amid the rot of what was once magnificence, that huge blind mole, the Past.

This, we repeat, was the sewer of former days.

V. *Present Progress*

Today the sewer is clean, cold, straight, and correct, almost achieving that ideal which the English convey by the word 'respectable'. It is orthodox and sober, sedately in line, one might almost say, neat as a new pin—like a tradesman become Counsellor of State. One can see almost clearly in it. The filth is well-behaved. At first sight one might mistake it for one of those subterranean passages that aided the flight of princes in those good old days when 'the people loved their kings'. The present sewer is a good sewer, pure in style. The classic rectilinear alexandrine, having been driven out of poetry, seems to have taken refuge in architecture and to be part of the stone-work of the long, shady, whitish vault. Every outlet is an arcade; the Rue de Rivoli has its counterpart in the cloaca. Moreover, if a geometrical line is to have a place anywhere, it is surely in the stercorary trench of a great city. The sewer today has a certain official aspect. Even the police reports of which it is sometimes the object treat it with some respect. Words referring to it in adminis-trative language are lofty and dignified. What was once called a sluice is now a gallery, and a hole has become a clearing. Villon would no longer recognize his emergency lodgings. But the network still has its immemorial rodent population, more numerous than ever. Now and then a veteran rat will risk his neck at a sewer-window to survey the Parisians; but even these vermin are tame, being well-content with their subterranean palace. Nothing is left of the cloaca's primitive ferocity. The rain, which once sullied it, now washes it. But we should not trust it too much on this account. Miasmas still infest it. It is more hypocritical than irreproachable. Despite the efforts of the police and the Health Commission, despite all attempts to purify it, it still exhales a vaguely suspect odour, like Tartuffe after confession.

We may agree then, when all is said, that cleaning is a tribute which the sewer pays to civilization; and since, in this respect, the conscience of Tartuffe is an advance on the Augean stable, so the Paris sewer is a step forward.

It is more than an advance, it is a transformation. Between the old and the present sewer a revolution has taken place. And who was responsible? The man whom everyone forgets, and whom we have named—Bruneseau.

VI. *Future Progress*

The digging of the Paris sewer was no small matter. Ten centuries had worked at it without completing it, any more than they had completed Paris. It was a sort of dark, multi-armed polyp which grew with the city above it. When the city put out a street, the sewer stretched an arm. The old monarchy had constructed only twenty-three thousand metres of sewer: that was the point reached in Paris on 1 January 1806. From that time, to which we shall refer later, the work was effectively and energetically carried forward. Napoleon —the figures are curious—built 4,804 metres, Louis XVIII built 5,709, Charles X 10,836, Louis-Philippe 89,020, the Republic of 1848 23,381 and the present regime has built 70,500; in all, at this date, 226,610 metres, or 60 leagues of sewers, constitute the vast entrails of Paris. A dark network always in growth, unknown and enormous.

As we see, the underground labyrinth of Paris is today ten times what it was at the start of the century. It is hard to conceive of the perseverance and effort needed to bring it to its present state of relative perfection. It was with great difficulty that the monarchical authority, and the revolutionary in the last decade of the eighteenth century, succeeded in digging the five leagues of sewer which existed before 1806. Every kind of obstacle hindered the operation, some due to the nature of the ground, others to the prejudice of the working population of Paris. Paris is built on a site strangely opposed to pick and shovel, to all human management. Nothing is more difficult to penetrate than the geological formation on which is set the marvellous historical formation which is Paris; underground resistance is manifest whenever, and by whatever means, the attempt is made. There are liquid clays, live springs, rocks, and the deep sludgy pits known to science as *moutardes*. The pick advances laboriously through chalky strata alternating with seams of very fine clay, and layers of schist encrusted with oyster-shells, relics of the prehistoric ocean. Sometimes a stream destroys the beginning of a tunnel, drenching the workers; or a fall of rubble sweeps down like a cataract, shattering the stoutest roof-props. Only recently, when it became necessary to run a sewer under the Saint-Martin canal without emptying the canal or interfering with its use, a fissure developed in the canal bottom so that more water poured into the lower gallery than the pumps could handle; a diver had to find the fissure, which was in the neck of the great basin, and it was blocked only with difficulty. Elsewhere, near the Seine and even at some distance from the river, there are shifting sands in which a man may sink. There is also the danger of asphyxiation in the foul air and burial beneath falls of earth. There is a typhus, with which the workers become slowly infected. In our time, after four months of day and night labour principally designed to rid Paris of the pouring waters of Montmartre, and after constructing the Rue Barre-du-Bec sewer some six metres underground, the foreman, Monnot, died. The engineer, Duleau, died after constructing 3,000 metres of sewer which included the formidable task of lowering the floor of the Notre-Dame-de-Nazareth cutting. No bulletins signalled these acts of bravery, more useful than any battlefield slaughter.

The Paris sewers in 1832 were very different from what they are today. Bruneseau had made a start, but it needed cholera to supply the impetus for the huge reconstruction which took place later. It is surprising to know, for example, that in 1821 a part of the ring sewer, known, as in Venice, as the Grand Canal, still lay open to the sky in the Rue des Gourdes. Not until 1823 did Paris find the 266,080 francs 6 centimes necessary to cover this disgrace. The three absorbent wells of the Combat, the Cunette, and Saint-Mande, with their ancillary outlets, date from only 1836. The intestinal canal of Paris has been rebuilt and, as we have said, increased more than tenfold in the last twenty-five years.

Thirty years ago, at the time of the insurrection of 5 and 6 June, it was still in many places almost the ancient sewer. A great many streets, now cambered, were then sunken. One often saw, at a point where the gutters of two streets met, large square grilles whose thick iron bars, burnished by the feet of pedestrians, were slippery for carts and dangerous for horses. And in 1832, in countless streets, the old gothic cloaca was still shamelessly manifest in great gaping blocks of stone.

In Paris in 1806 the figure was not much more than that for May 1663—5,328 fathoms. After Bruneseau, on 1 January 1832, it amounted to 40,300 metres. From 1806 to 1831 an annual average of 750 metres had been built; after which the figure rose to eight and even ten thousand a year, galleries built of cemented rubble on a foundation of concrete.

Apart from economic progress, the Paris sewer is part of an immense problem of public hygiene. Paris exists between two layers, of water and of air. The water layer, some distance underground but fed by two sources, is borne on the stratum of sandstone situated between chalk and jurassic limestone, and may be represented by a disc of some twenty-five leagues radius into which a host of rivers and streams seep. One may drink the mingled waters of Seine, Marne, Yonne, Oise, Aisne, Cher, Vienne, and Loire in a glass of water drawn from a well in Grenelle. The layer of water is healthy, coming first from the sky and then from the earth; the layer of air is unhealthy, for it comes from the sewer. All the miasmas of the cloaca are mingled with the breath of the town, hence its poor quality. It has been scientifically demonstrated that air taken from immediately above a dung-heap is purer than the air of Paris. In time, with the aid of progress, perfected mechanisms and fuller knowledge, the layer of water will be used to purify the layer of air—that is to say, to cleanse the sewer. By cleansing the sewer we mean the return of mire to the earth, of manure to the soil, and fertilizer to the fields. This simple fact will bring about a decrease in misery and increase in health for the whole community. As things are, the maladies of Paris spread some fifty leagues from the Louvre, taking this as the hub of the pestilential wheel.

It may be said that for ten centuries the sewer has been the disease of Paris, the evil in the city's blood. Popular instinct has never doubted it. The trade of sewage worker was more perilous and nearly as repugnant to the people as the trade of executioner, and held in abhorrence. High wages were needed to induce a mason to vanish into that foetid ooze. 'To go into the sewer is to go into the grave,' men said. All sorts of legends covered that colossal sink with horror, that dreadful place which bears the impress of the revolution of the earth and of men, in which the remains of every cataclysm is to be found, from the flood to the death of Marat.

BOOK THREE

MIRE, BUT THE SOUL

I. *The Cloaca and its Surprises*

JEAN VALJEAN was in the Paris sewer. And here is another resemblance between Paris and the sea; as with the sea, the diver can
vanish into it.

The change was unbelievable. In the very heart of the town,
Valjean had left the town; in a matter of moments, the time to
lift a lid and let it fall, he had passed from daylight into total darkness,
from midday to midnight, from tumult to silence and the stillness
of the tomb; and, by a chance even more prodigious than that in
the Rue Polonceau, from utmost peril to absolute safety. He stayed
for some moments listening, as though in a stupor. The trap-door
salvation had suddenly opened beneath him. Celestial benevolence
had in some sort caught him by betrayal; the wonderful ambushes
of Providence!

Meanwhile the injured man did not move, and Valjean did not
know whether his burden was living or dead.

His first sensation was one of utter blindness; he could see nothing.
It seemed to him also that he had suddenly become deaf. He could
hear nothing. The tempest of slaughter going on only a few feet
above his head reached him only as a distant murmur. He could feel
solid ground beneath his feet and that was all, but it was enough.
He reached out one arm and then the other, touching the wall on
either side, and perceived the narrowness of the passage; he slipped,
and knew that the floor was wet. He cautiously advanced a foot,
fearing a pitfall, and noted that the floor continued. A gust of foetid
air told him where he was.

After some moments, as his eyes became adjusted, he began to see
by the dim light of the hatchway by which he had entered. He could
make out that the passage in which he had landed was walled up
behind him. It was a dead-end. In front of him was another wall,
a wall of darkness. The light from the hatchway died a few paces
from where he stood, throwing a pallid gleam on a few feet of
damp wall. Beyond was massive blackness, to enter which was to be
swallowed up. Nevertheless it could and must be done, and with

speed. Valjean reflected that the grille he had perceived might also be seen by the soldiers, who might come in search of him. There was no time to be lost. He had laid Marius on the ground; he picked him up and taking him on his shoulders marched resolutely into the darkness.

The truth is that they were less safe than Valjean supposed. Other dangers, no less fearful, might await them. After the turbulence of battle came the cave of evil mists and pitfalls; after chaos, the cloaca. Valjean had moved from one circle of Hell into another. After walking fifty paces he had to stop. A question had arisen. The passage ran into another, so that now there were two ways he might go. Which to choose—left or right? How was he to steer in that black labyrinth? But the labyrinth, as we have said, provides a clue— its slope. Follow the downward slope and you must come to the river.

Jean Valjean instantly realized this. He thought that he was probably in the sewer of Les Halles, and that if he went left, following the slope, he would arrive within a quarter of an hour at some outlet to the Seine between the Pont-au-Change and the Pont-Neuf— appear, that is to say, in broad daylight in the most frequented part of Paris, perhaps even at a crossroads, to the stupefaction of the passers-by. Arrest would then be certain. It was better to press deeper into the labyrinthine darkness, trusting to chance to provide a way out. He moved upwards, turning to the right.

When he had turned the corner into the new passageway the distant light from the hatch vanished completely and he was again blind. He pressed on nonetheless, as rapidly as he could. Marius's arms were round his neck while his feet hung down behind. He held both arms with one hand, following the wall with the other. Marius's cheek was pressed against his own and stuck to it, since it was bleeding; he felt the warm stream trickling beneath his clothes. But the faint breathing in his ear was a sign of life. The passage he was now following was less narrow than the first, but he struggled painfully along it. Yesterday's rain had not yet drained away; it made a stream in the middle of the floor, and he had to keep close to the wall if he was not to have his feet in water. Thus he went darkly on, like some creature of the night.

But little by little, either because widely-spaced openings let through a glimmer of light, or because his eyes had grown accustomed to the darkness, he recovered some degree of sight, so that he had a dim perception of the wall he was touching or the vaulted roof. The pupil dilates in darkness and in the end finds light, just as the soul dilates in misfortune and in the end finds God. It was difficult to choose his path. The direction of the sewers in general follows that of the streets above them. At that time there were 2,200 streets in Paris; and one may picture a similar tangle below. The system of sewers existing at that time laid end to end would have had a length of eleven leagues. As we have said, the present network, thanks to the work of the past thirty years, has a length of not less than sixty leagues.

Valjean started by making a mistake. He thought he was under the Rue Saint-Denis and it was unfortunate that he was not. There is an old stone sewer dating from Louis XIII under the Rue Saint-Denis, having only a single turn, under the former Cour des Miracles, and a single branch, the Saint-Martin sewer, of which the four arms intersect. But the Petite-Truanderie passage, of which the entrance is near the Corinth tavern, has never communicated with that under the Rue Saint-Denis; it runs into the Montmartre sewer, and this was the way Valjean had followed. Here there are endless chances of going astray, the Montmartre sewer being one of the most labyrinthine of all. Fortunately he had left behind him the Les Halles sewer, the plan of which is like a forest of ship's masts; but more than one perplexity lay ahead of him, more than one street corner (for streets are what they really are) offered itself in the darkness like a question mark. First, on his left, the huge Plâtrière sewer, a sort of Chinese puzzle, running with countless twists and turns under the Hotel des Postes and the cornmarket to the Seine; secondly, on his right, the Rue du Cadran with its three blind alleys; thirdly, again on the left, a sort of fork zig-zagging into the basin of the Louvre; and finally, on the right, the blind alley of the Rue des Jeûneurs, without counting small offshoots here and there—all this before he reached the ring sewer, which alone could take him to some place sufficiently far off to be safe.

Had Valjean known all this he would have realized, simply by feeling the wall, that he could not be under the Rue Saint-Denis. Instead of the old cut stone, the costly old-time architecture which had dignity even in its sewers, he would have felt cheap modern materials under his hand, bourgeois masonry; but he knew nothing of this. He went anxiously but calmly ahead, seeing and knowing nothing, trusting to chance, or to providence.

And by degrees the horror grew upon him, the darkness pierced his soul. He was walking through a riddle. He had to pick his way, almost to invent it, without seeing it. Every step he took might be his last. Would he find a way out, and in time? Would this huge underground sponge with interstices of stone allow itself to be conquered? Would he come to some impenetrable place where Marius would bleed to death and he himself would die of hunger, leaving two skeletons in the darkness? He asked himself these questions and had no answer; he was Jonah in the body of the whale.

Suddenly he was startled. He perceived that he was no longer going uphill. The stream washed round the heels of his boots, instead of round the toes. The sewer was going downwards. Would he arrive suddenly at the Seine? The danger was great, but the danger of turning back was greater still. He pressed on.

He was not going towards the Seine. The ridge of land on the right bank caused one of the streams to flow into the Seine, the other into the main sewer. The crest of the ridge follows a capricious line, its culminating point, where the streams separate, being beneath the Rue Sainte-Avoye and the Rue Montmartre. This was the point which Valjean had reached. He was on the right road, moving towards the ring-sewer; but this he did not know.

Whenever he came to a branch he measured its dimensions with his hand, and if he found the opening less wide than the passage he was following he passed it, rightly considering that every smaller passageway must be a dead end. Thus he avoided the four-fold trap we have described.

A moment came when he realized that he had left behind the Paris petrified by the uprising and was under the Paris living its everyday life. There was a sound like distant steady thunder above his head, the sound of cartwheels. He had been walking for half an hour, according to his reckoning, without any thought of rest, only changing the hand with which he held Marius. The darkness was greater than ever, but this reassured him.

Suddenly he saw his own shadow, faintly visible on the floor of the passage in front of him. He was conscious of a dim light on the viscous walls. He looked back in stupefaction.

Behind him, at what seemed a great distance, there shone a dim, flickering light, as it were a star that was observing him. It was a police lantern, and within its glow some eight or ten moving figures were to be seen.

II. *Explanation*

On that morning a search of the sewers had been ordered, since it was considered that these might be used by the defeated rebels. Hidden Paris was to be ransacked while General Bugeaud cleared the open streets: a combined operation involving both the army and the police. Three squads of police agents and sewage men were exploring the underside of Paris, one the right bank, the second the left bank and the third the Cité. The police were armed with carbines, batons, swords and daggers. What Jean Valjean now saw was the lantern of the right-bank squad.

The squad had visited the curved passage and the three dead-ends under the Rue du Cadran. Valjean had passed them while they were in one of the dead-ends, which he found to be narrower than the main passageway. The police, emerging from the Cadran passageway, had thought they heard footsteps in the direction of the ring sewer. They were those of Valjean. The sergeant raised his lantern and they stared in his direction.

It was a bad moment for Valjean. Fortunately, although he could see the lantern, the lantern saw very little. It was light and he was in shadow, far from it and buried in darkness. He stopped, pressed against the wall. He did not know what was behind him. Sleeplessness, lack of food, and strong emotion had brought him to a state of hallucination. He saw a glow and moving forms, but did not know what they were.

When he ceased to move the sound ceased. The men listened and heard nothing, stared and saw nothing. They consulted together.

There was at this time an open space in the Montmartre sewer which has since been abolished because of the pool that formed in it when the heavy rains came down. The squad were able to assemble here. Valjean saw them form a sort of circle, heads close together. The outcome of their discussion was that they had heard nothing and there was no one there. To move towards the ring sewer would be a waste of time, and it would be better to make haste towards Saint-Merry where, if any rebel had escaped, he was more likely to be found.

The sergeant gave the order to go left towards the Seine. If they had divided into two parties and followed both directions Valjean would have been captured. It was as near as that. Probably, to guard against the possibility of an encounter with a number of rebels, they had been ordered not to separate. They turned away, leaving Valjean behind, but all he knew of it was the sudden vanishing of the lantern. For a long time he stayed motionless with his back to the wall, hearing the receding echo of that spectral patrol.

III. *The Man Pursued*

It must be said for the police of that time that even in the gravest circumstances they continued imperturbably to perform their duties. An uprising was not, in their view, a reason for giving villains a free hand, nor could society be neglected because the government was in danger. Ordinary duties were correctly carried out together with extraordinary ones. In the midst of an incalculable political event, and under the threat of revolution, without letting himself be distracted by all this, the policeman pursued the criminal.

This is precisely what happened on the right bank of the Seine on that afternoon of 6 June, a short way beyond the Pont des Invalides.

There is no bank there now. The aspect of the place has changed. But on that bank, some distance apart, two men seemed to be observing one another, one seeking to avoid the other. It was like a game of chess played remotely and in silence. Neither seemed in a hurry; both moved slowly as though each feared that by hastening he might speed up the other. As it were, an appetite in pursuit of a prey, without seeming to be acting with intent. The prey was wary and constantly alert. Due distance between tracker and tracked was preserved. The would-be escaper was a puny creature; the hunter a tall robust man, hard of aspect and probably of person.

The first, the weaker, sought to avoid the second, but he did so in a furious manner, and anyone looking closely at him would have seen in his eyes all the dark hostility of flight, the menace that resides in fear.

The river-bank was deserted. There were no strollers, nor even a boatman on any of the barges moored here and there. The men could best be seen from the opposite bank, and to anyone viewing them at that distance the first would have appeared a ragged, furtive creature, shivering under a thin smock, while the other had an aspect of officialdom, with the coat of authority buttoned close under his chin.

The reader would perhaps recognize the men, could he see them more closely. What was the second man seeking to do? Probably to clothe the first more warmly. When a man clothed by the State pursues a man clad in rags, it is to make him, too, a man clothed by the State. But the matter of colour is important. To be clad in blue is splendid; to be clad in red is disagreeable. There is a purple of the depths. It was probably this disagreeable purple that the first man was anxious to avoid.

If the other let him go on without attempting to lay hands on him, it was probably because he hoped to see him reach some significant spot—the delicate operation known as 'shadowing'. What makes this appear likely is that the uniformed man, seeing an empty fiacre pass along the quay, signalled to the driver, and the latter, evidently knowing with whom he had to deal, turned and kept pace with the two men. This was not noticed by the ragged fugitive.

The fiacre rolled past the trees of the Champs-Élysées, its driver being visible above the parapet, whip in hand. Among the secret instructions issued to the police is the following: 'Always have a vehicle handy, in case of need.'

Each manoeuvring with admirable strategy, the two men drew near a ramp running from the quay down to the bank, which enabled cab-drivers reaching Passy to water their horses. This has since been abolished in the name of symmetry. The horses go thirsty, but the eye is flattered.

It seemed likely that the man in the smock intended to climb this ramp and attempt to escape by the Champs-Élysées, a place abounding in trees but also in policemen. That part of the quay is very little distant from the house brought from Moret to Paris in 1824 by Colonel Brack, known as the house of François I. There is a guard-post very near it.

Surprisingly, the pursued man did not go up the ramp to the quay, but continued to move along the bank. His position was plainly becoming desperate. Apart from plunging into the Seine, what was he to do? He had no access to the quay other than the ramp or stairway, and he was near the spot, at the bend of the Seine towards the Pont d'Iéna, where the bank growing ever more narrow, finally vanished underwater. There he would find himself trapped between the sheer wall on his right and the river on his left, with authority close behind him. It is true that the ending of the bank was concealed from him by a heap of rubble some seven or eight feet high, the remains of some demolition. But did he really hope to hide behind it? Surely not. The ingenuousness of thieves is not so great.

The heap of rubble formed a sort of hillock running from the water's edge to the quay wall. The fugitive reached this hillock and hurried round it, so that his pursuer could not see him. The latter, not seeing, was himself unseen; accordingly he abandoned all pretence and quickened his pace. He reached the heap and went round it, and then stood still in amazement. The man he was pursuing was not there! He had completely disappeared. Only some thirty feet of bank lay beyond the heap before it vanished into the river. The fugitive could not have plunged into the Seine or climbed on to the quay without being seen by his pursuer. What had become of him?

The man in the buttoned coat went to the extreme end of the bank and stood there reflecting, fists clenched and eyes gleaming. Suddenly he clapped a hand to his forehead. He had seen, at the point where the bank ended, a wide, low iron grille with a heavy lock and three massive hinges. It opened as much on to the river as on to the bank, and a dark stream flowed from it, running into the Seine.

Beyond the thick, rusty bars a dark vaulted corridor was to be seen. The man folded his arms and looked angrily at the grille. Since this served no purpose, he attempted to force it open, but it resisted all his shaking. It must certainly have been opened, although he had heard nothing, which was strange considering its rusty state. And it had been closed. This meant that whoever had opened it had done so not with a hook but with a key. The idea dawned suddenly on the pursuer and drew from him a roar of indignation:

'Upon my soul, a government key!'

Calming down immediately, he gave vent to his thoughts in a series of ironic monosyllables:

'Well! Well! Well! Well!'

Having said this, and hoping for he knew not what—to see the man emerge or other men arrive—he settled down by the heap of rubble to keep watch with the patience of a game-dog.

The driver of the fiacre, following all his movements, had come to a stop near the parapet above him. Foreseeing a long wait, he put nosebags on his horses. Occasional strollers from the Pont d'Iéna paused to observe those two motionless features of the landscape— the man on the bank and the fiacre on the quay.

IV. *He too Bears his Cross*

Jean Valjean had resumed his journey without again stopping. It became more and more laborious. The height of the passageway varies, being of an average five feet six inches; Valjean had to bend down to prevent Marius rubbing against the roof, and he had to feel his way constantly along the wall. The dampness of the stone and the slipperiness of the floor offered insecure hand- and foot-holds. He staggered in the horrid excrement of the town. The lights of vent-holes appeared only at long intervals, so pallid that what was sunlight might have been moonlight; all else was mist, miasma, and darkness. Valjean was both hungry and thirsty, especially thirsty, in that place of water where there was none to drink. Even his great strength, so little diminished with age, was beginning to flag, and the weight of his burden increased with his fatigue. He was carrying Marius so as best to allow him freedom to breathe. He felt the scuttle of rats between his feet, and one was so startled as to bite him. From time to time he was revived by a gust of fresh air from the vent-holes.

It was perhaps three o'clock in the afternoon when he reached the ring sewer. He was at first astonished by the suddenly increased width, finding himself in a passageway where his outstretched hands could not touch both walls nor his head the roof. This main sewer is in fact eight feet wide and seven feet high.

At the point where the Montmartre sewer joins the main sewer two other passageways form an intersection. Faced by four alternatives, a less sagacious man might have been undecided. Valjean took the widest way, the ring sewer. But here again the question arose—to go up or down? He felt that time was running out and that he must at all costs try to reach the Seine. That is to say, downward; and he turned to the left.

It was well that he did so, for the main sewer, being nothing but the former stream of Ménilmontant, ends, if one goes upwards, in a cul-de-sac, at the spring which was its original source. Had Valjean gone upwards he would finally have arrived, exhausted, at a blank wall. At a pinch, by turning back he might eventually have reached the Amelot sewer and thence, if he did not go astray in the maze beneath the Bastille, have come to the outlet to the Seine near the Arsenal. But for this he would have needed a detailed knowledge of the system, and, we must repeat, he knew nothing of it. Had he been asked where he was he could only have answered, 'In darkness'.

Instinct served him well. Descent was the way of safety. A little way beyond an effluent which probably came from the Madeleine, he stopped. A large hatchway, probably in the Rue d'Anjou, gave a light that was almost bright. With the gentleness of a man handling a wounded brother, Valjean laid Marius down at the edge of the sewer. Marius's bloodstained face in the pallid light of the hatchway was like a face of death. His eyes were closed, the hair plastered to his temples, his hands limp and dangling, and there was blood at the corners of his mouth. Gently thrusting inside his shirt, Valjean laid a hand on his chest and found that his heart was still beating. Tearing strips off his own shirt, he bandaged Marius's wounds as best he could.

Then, bending over the unconscious form in that dim light, he stared at him with inexpressible hatred.

He found two objects in Marius's clothing, the piece of bread left from the day before and his wallet. He ate the bread and, opening the wallet, found on the first page the lines Marius had written. 'My name is Marius Pontmercy. My body is to be taken to the house of my grandfather, M. Gillenormand, 6 Rue des Filles-du-Calvaire, in the Marais.'

Valjean pored over the message, memorizing the address; then he replaced the wallet in Marius's pocket. He had eaten and regained his strength. Taking Marius on his back with his head on his right shoulder, he resumed his downward path.

The main sewer, following the slope of the Ménilmontant valley, is nearly two leagues in length, and paved to a large extent; but the list of names with which we have enlightened the reader was not known to Valjean. He did not know what part of the town he was passing under or how far he had come. Only the increasing dimness of the occasional hatchways told him that the sun was setting, and the rumble of vehicles above his head had now almost ceased. He concluded that he was no longer under the centre of Paris but was nearing some outlying district where there were fewer streets and houses and, in consequence, fewer hatchways. He pressed on, feeling his way in the darkness, which suddenly became terrible.

V. *The Treachery of Sand*

He found that he was moving in water, and that what he had under his feet was not stone but sludge.

It happens sometimes on the sea coast that a man walking at low tide far out along the beach suddenly finds that he is moving with difficulty. The going is heavy beneath his feet, no longer sand but glue. The surface is dry, but every footprint fills with water. Yet all the beach wears the same aspect, so that the eye cannot distinguish between what is firm and what is not. The walker continues on his way, tending to move inland and feeling no disquiet. Why should he? But it is as though the heaviness of his feet increases with every step he takes. Suddenly he sinks several inches. He pauses, and looking down at his feet sees that they have disappeared. He picks up his feet and tries to turn back, but only sinks in deeper. The sand is over his ankles. He struggles and finds it reaching his calves. With indescribable terror he realizes that he is in a patch of shifting sand, where a man cannot walk any more than a fish can swim. He flings away whatever he is carrying, shedding his cargo like a vessel in distress. It is too late, the sand has reached his knees.

He shouts, waving hat or handkerchief, while the sand gains upon him. If the beach is deserted and there is no heroic rescuer at hand, then he is done for, destined to be swallowed up, condemned to that appalling burial which can be neither hastened nor delayed, which may take hours, dragging down a strong and healthy man the more remorselessly the more he struggles. He sees the world vanish from his gaze; sky, land, and sea. There is nothing he can do. The sand creeps up to his stomach, his chest. He waves his arms, shouts and groans in torment; the sand reaches his shoulders and neck, until nothing is left but staring eyes and a crying mouth that is suddenly silenced. Only an extended arm remains. The man is gone.

This fateful occurrence, still possible on some seashores, was also possible thirty years ago in the Paris sewer. During the work begun in 1833 the underground network was subject to sudden collapses, when in particularly friable stretches of soil the bottom, whether of paving stones as in the old sewers, or concrete, as in the new, gave way. There were crevasses composed of shifting sand from the seashore, neither earth nor water. Sometimes the depth was very great.

Terrible to die in such a fashion. Death may mitigate its horror with dignity; at the stake or in a shipwreck nobility is possible. But this suffocation in the sewer is unclean. It is humiliating. Filth is synonymous with shame; it is squalid and infamous. To die in a butt of Malmsey, like the Duke of Clarence, may pass; but to die in a pit of slime . . . There is the darkness of Hell, the filth of evil; the dying man does not know whether he is to become a ghost or a toad.

Everywhere else the grave is sinister; here it is shapeless. The depth of these pits varied as did their length and density, according to the nature of the subsoil. Some were three or four feet in depth, others eight or ten; some had no bottom. The slime was almost solid in some places, almost liquid in others. A man might have taken a day to be swallowed up in the Lunière pit, a few minutes only in that of Phélippeaux, depending on the thickness of the slime. A child might be safe where a man would be lost. The first resource was to rid oneself of every burden, fling away one's bag of tools or whatever it might be; and this was what every sewage-man did when he felt the ground unsafe beneath his feet.

The pits were due to various causes; the friability of the earth, collapses at some lower level, heavy showers in summer, incessant rain in winter, long steady drizzle. Sometimes the weight of the houses broke the roof of a gallery or caused a floor to give way. The settling of the Panthéon, a quarter of a century ago, destroyed a part of the caves under the Mont Sainte-Geneviève. When such things happened the evil in some cases was manifest in cracks in the street, and could be quickly remedied. But it also happened that nothing was visible from above, in which case, woe to the sewage-men. Entering the collapsed place unawares, they might be lost. Such cases are entered in the records. There are a number of names, including that of one Blaise Poutrain, buried in a pit under the Rue Carème-Prenant.

There was also the youthful and charming Vicomte d'Escoubleau, one of the heroes of the siege of Lerida, which they assailed in silk stockings, violins leading the way. D'Escoubleau, surprised one night in the bed of his cousin the Duchesse de Sourdis, was drowned in a pit in the Beautrellis sewer, when he sought to escape from the duke. Madame de Sourdis, learning the manner of his death, called for her smelling salts and was too busy inhaling them to weep. No love can survive such an event. Hero refuses to wash the corpse of Leander; Thisbe holds her nose before Pyramus, saying, 'Pooh!'.

VI. *The Pit*

Jean Valjean had come to a pit. These were numerous under the Champs-Élysées, which because of its excessive fluidity did not lend itself to the work of construction and conservation. When in 1836 the old stone sewer beneath the Faubourg Saint-Honoré, where we find Valjean at this moment, was rebuilt, the shifting sand which runs from the Champs-Élysées to the Seine delayed the operation for six months, to the indignation of the surface dwellers, particularly those with private houses and carriages. The work was not only difficult but dangerous. It is true that there were four and a half months of rain, and the Seine was three times flooded.

The pit Valjean reached had been caused by the rain of the previous day. A depression in the flooring, insufficiently supported by the sand beneath, had led to a flood of rainwater, and the collapse of the floor had followed. The broken floor had subsided into the swamp, it was impossible to say over what distance. The darkness was greater here than anywhere else. It was a hole of mud in a cavern of night.

Valjean felt the surface slip away from under him, water on top, sludge beneath. He had to go on. Marius was at death's door and he himself exhausted. So he struggled on, and at first the bog did not seem unduly deep. But then it grew deeper—slime halfway up his legs and water above his knees. He had to keep Marius as best he could above the water, which had now reached his waist. The mire, thick enough to support a single man, evidently could not sustain two. Either of them might have passed through separately. Valjean went on, carrying what might already be a corpse.

The water reached his armpits and he felt himself sinking; it was all he could do to move. His own sturdiness that kept him upright was also an obstacle. Still carrying Marius, and by the use of unbelievable strength, he pressed on, sinking ever deeper. Only his head was now above water, and his two arms carrying Marius. In old paintings of the flood there is one of a mother carrying her child in this fashion.

He went on, tilting his face upwards so that he could continue to breathe. Anyone seeing him at that moment might have thought him a mask floating in the darkness. Dimly above him he could see the livid face of Marius. He made a last desperate effort, thrusting a foot forward, and it rested upon something solid—only just in time. He straightened and thrust with a kind of fury on this support, feeling that he had found the first step of a stairway back to life.

In fact this foothold, reached at the supreme moment, was the other end of the floor, which had sagged under the weight of water but without breaking. Well-built floors have this solidity; the floor still existed, and, climbing its further slope, Valjean was saved.

Emerging from the water, he stumbled on a stone and fell on his knees. This he thought proper, and he stayed in this posture for some time, his spirit absorbed in the thought of God. Then he stood upright, shivering and foul, bowed beneath his burden, dripping with mire; but with his soul filled with a strange lightness.

VII. *Sometimes We fail with Success in Sight*

He went on again. If he had not left his life in that pit, he seemed certainly to have left his strength there. The final effort had exhausted him. His weariness was now such that at every few paces he had to pause for breath. Once he had to sit down while he altered Marius's position, and he thought that he would never get up again. But if his strength was flagging his will was not, and he rose.

He went on despairingly, but almost quickly, and covered a hundred paces without looking up, almost without breathing, until suddenly he bumped into the wall. He had reached a turning without seeing it. Looking up, he saw in the far distance a light, and this was no cavern light, but the clear white light of day.

He saw the way of escape, and his feelings were those of a damned soul seeing the way out of Hell. He was no longer conscious of fatigue or of the weight of Marius; his muscles were revived, and he ran rather than walked. As he drew near to it he saw the outlet more plainly. It was a pointed arch, less high than the ceiling, which was growing gradually lower, and less wide than the passageway, which was narrowing. The tunnel ended in a bottleneck, logical enough in a prison but not in a sewer, and something which has now been corrected.

But when he reached it, Valjean stopped short. It was an outlet, but it offered no way out. The arch was closed with a stout grille, fastened with a huge, rusty lock. He could see the keyhole and the bolt securely in place—clearly it was double-locked. It was one of those prison locks that were common in Paris at that time. And beyond the grille was open air, daylight, the river and a strip of bank, very narrow but sufficient to escape by. All Paris, all liberty, lay beyond it; to the right, downstream, the Pont d'Iéna, to the left the Pont des Invalides. One of the most deserted spots in Paris, a good place to escape from after dark. Flies came and went through the grille.

The time was perhaps half past eight in the evening, and dusk was falling. Valjean set Marius down by the wall, where the floor was dry; then, going to the grille, he seized it with both hands. But his frantic shaking had no effect. He tried one bar after another hoping to find one less solid that might be used as a lever, or to break the lock. But no bar shifted. He had no lever, no possible purchase, no way of opening the gate.

Was this to be the end of it? He had not the strength to turn back, and could not, in any case, have struggled again through the pit from which he had so miraculously emerged. And could he hope to escape the police patrol for a second time? In any event, where was he to go? Another outlet might be similarly obstructed. Probably all outlets were closed in this way. By chance he had entered by one that was not, and in so doing had escaped into a prison. It was the end. All his efforts had been futile. God had rejected him.

Both men were caught in the great, grim cobweb of death, and Valjean felt the running feet of the deadly spider. He turned his back to the grille and sank on to the floor beside the motionless form of Marius, crouched rather than seated, his head sunk between his knees. There was no way out. It was the last extreme of anguish. Of whom did he think in that moment? Not of himself or of Marius. He thought of Cosette.

VIII. *A Fragment of Torn Clothing*

While he was in this state of despair a hand was laid on his shoulder and a low voice said:

'We'll go halves.'

Valjean thought he was dreaming. He had not heard a sound. He looked up and saw a man standing beside him.

The man was clad in a smock. His feet were bare and he carried his shoes in his hand, having removed them so that he might approach Valjean in silence. Valjean did not hesitate. Unexpected though this meeting was, he knew the man instantly. It was Thénardier.

Despite his astonishment, Valjean was too accustomed to sudden emergencies, too weary and alert, to lose his self-possession. In any event his situation could not be made worse by the presence of Thénardier. There was a brief pause. Thénardier raised a hand to his forehead, knitting his brow and pursing his lips in the manner of a man seeking to recognize another. He failed to do so. Jean Valjean had his back to the light, and was anyway so begrimed and blood-stained that even in the brightest light he would have been un-recognizable. Thénardier, on the other hand, his face illumined by the light from the grille, faint though it was, was immediately known to Valjean, and this gave the latter a certain advantage in the dialogue that was to take place between them.

Valjean saw at once that Thénardier did not know him. The two men contemplated one another in the dim light, each taking the measure of the other. It was Thénardier who broke the silence.

'How are you going to get out?'

Valjean made no reply. Thénardier went on:

'No way of unlocking the door. But you've got to get away from here.'

'That's true.'

'So we'll go halves.'

'How do you mean?'

'You've killed a man. All right. I have a key.' Thénardier pointed at Marius and went on: 'I don't know you but I'm ready to help you. You must be a friend.'

Valjean began to understand. Thénardier supposed him to be a murderer.

'Listen, comrade,' Thénardier went on. 'You won't have killed that man without looking to see what he has in his pocket. Give me half and I'll unlock the door.' He produced a large key from under his smock. 'Want to see what a master key looks like? Here it is.'

Valjean 'stayed stupid', in Corneille's phrase, to the point of scarcely believing his ears. Providence had come to his rescue in a horrid guise, sending a good angel in the shape of Thénardier.

Thénardier fished in a large pocket concealed under his smock and brought out a length of rope which he offered to Valjean.

'I'll give you this as well.'

'What for?'

'And you'll need a stone. But you'll find plenty of those outside.'

'What am I to do with it?'

'Fool. You'll have to chuck the body in the river, and if it isn't tied to a stone it'll float.'

Valjean took the rope. We are all subject to such mechanical gestures. Thénardier snapped his fingers as a thought occurred to him.

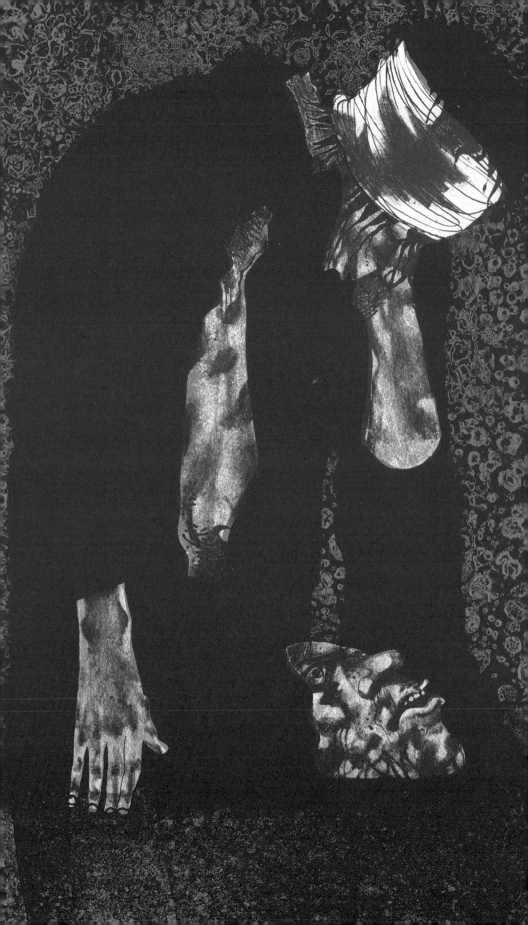

'Come to that, how did you manage to get through the pit down there? I wouldn't have risked it. You smell foul.'

After a pause he went on:

'I keep asking questions and you're right not to answer. It's a preparation for the nasty quarter of an hour in court. And by not talking you don't risk talking too loud. Anyway, just because I can't see your face and don't know your name, that isn't to say I don't know what you are and what you want. I know, all right. You've done that cove in, and now you've got to get rid of him. Well, I'll help you. Helping a good man in trouble, that's my line.'

While professing to approve of Valjean's silence, he was evidently trying to get him to talk. He nudged his shoulder, seeking to see his profile, and exclaimed without raising his voice;

'Talking of that pit, you're a fine fool, aren't you? Why didn't you leave him there?'

Valjean remained silent. Thénardier tightened the rag that served him as a neck-tie, putting a finishing touch to his appearance of a capable, reliable man. He went on:

'Well, perhaps you were right. The workmen will be along to-morrow to fill in the pit. They'd find him, and bit by bit, one way or another, it would have been traced to you. Somebody must have come through the sewer. Who was it, and how did he get out? The police have their wits about them. The sewer would give you away. A discovery like that's uncommon, it attracts notice; not many people use the sewer for their business, while the river belongs to everyone. The river's the real drain. In a month's time your man is fished out at Saint-Cloud. So what does that prove? Nothing. A lump of carcass. And who killed him? Paris. No need for any inquiry. You were right.'

The more loquacious Thénardier became, the more silent was Valjean. Thénardier again shook his shoulder.

'Well now, let's settle up. I've shown you my key, let's see your money.'

Thénardier was haggard, wild, shabby, slightly threatening but friendly. And his manner was strangely equivocal. He did not seem quite at his ease, talking furtively in a low voice, and now and then putting a finger to his lips. It was hard to guess why. There were only the two of them. Valjean reflected that there might be other footpads hidden somewhere near, and that Thénardier did not want to share with them.

'Let's have it,' he said. 'How much did the chap have on him?'

Valjean searched his pockets. We may recall that he always carried money on him from the necessity of the hazardous life he lived. But this time he was caught short. In his preoccupation when he had donned his National Guard uniform the previous evening he had forgotten to take his wallet. He had only a little change in his waistcoat pocket, a mere thirty francs. He turned the muddy garment inside out and spread them on the floor—a louis d'or, two five-franc pieces and five or six sous.

'You didn't kill for much,' said Thénardier.

He began familiarly to pat Valjean's pockets and those of Marius, and Valjean, anxious to keep his back to the light, did not stop him. While searching Marius, Thénardier, with a pickpocket's adroitness, managed to tear off a fragment of material which he hid in his smock without Valjean's noticing; probably he thought that this would later help him to identify the murdered man and his murderer. But he found no more money.

'It's true,' he said. 'That's all there is.'

Forgetting what he had said about sharing, he took the lot. He hesitated over the sous, but on consideration took those as well.

'It's helping a cove on the cheap,' he said.

He again produced the key.

'Well, pal, you'd better go out. It's like a fair, you pay when you leave. You've paid.' And he laughed. In helping an unknown man to escape, was he disinterestedly concerned to save a murderer? We may doubt it.

After helping Valjean to lift Marius on to his shoulders he crept to the grille on his bare feet and peered out with a finger to his lips. Then he put the key in the lock. The bolt slid back and the gate opened without a sound; evidently the hinges were carefully oiled and it was used more often than one might think, presumably by some criminal gang, for which the sewer was a place of refuge.

Thénardier opened the gate just enough to allow Valjean to pass through, closed it after him, turned the key in the lock and then vanished into the darkness, as silently as if he walked on tiger's paws. An instant later the sinister agent of providence was invisible.

And Valjean was outside.

IX. *Marius appears to be Dead*

He laid Marius on the bank. He was outside!

The darkness, stench, and horror were all behind him. He was bathed in pure, fresh air and surrounded by silence, the delicious silence of sunset in a clear sky. It was dusk; night was falling, the great liberator, the friend of all those needing darkness to escape from distress. The sky offered a prospect of immense calm; the river lapped at his feet with the sound of a kiss. There was a goodnight murmur from the nests in the trees on the Champs-Élysées and a few stars faintly showed in the deepening blue of the sky. The evening bestowed on Jean Valjean all the tenderness of infinity, in that enchanting hour which says neither no nor yes, dark enough for distance to be lost, but light enough for nearness to be seen.

For some moments he was overwhelmed by this serenity, and forgetful of what had passed, all suffering lost in this drowsy glow of dark and light, where his spirit soared. He could not refrain from contemplating the huge chiaroscuro above him, and the majestic silence of the eternal sky moved him to ecstasy and prayer. Then, recalled to a sense of duty, he bent over Marius and sprinkled a few drops of water on his face from the hollow of his hand. Marius's eyelids did not move, but his open mouth still breathed.

Valjean was again about to dip his hand in the water when he had that familiar sense of someone behind him. He looked sharply round and found this to be the case. A tall man in a long coat, with folded arms and a cudgel in his right hand, was standing a few paces away. In the half-darkness it seemed a spectral figure; but Valjean recognized Javert.

The reader has doubtless guessed that the pursuer of Thénardier was Javert. After his unhoped-for escape from the rebel stronghold the inspector had gone to the Préfecture de Police, where he had reported to the prefect in person. He had then immediately returned to his duties, which entailed keeping watch on the right bank near the Champs-Élysées, a spot which for some time had been attracting the notice of the police. Seeing Thénardier, he had followed him. The rest we know.

We may also gather that the gate so obligingly opened for Valjean was a stratagem on the part of Thénardier. With the instinct of a hunted man, Thénardier had sensed that Javert was still there and he wanted to distract him. What could be better than to supply him with a murderer? Producing Valjean in his place, Thénardier would send the police off on another trail: Javert would be rewarded for his patience, and he himself, besides gaining thirty francs, would have a better chance of getting away.

Valjean had fallen out of the frying-pan into the fire. The two encounters, first with Thénardier and then Javert, caused him a severe shock.

Javert did not recognize Valjean, who, as we have said, looked quite unlike himself. Without unfolding his arms, but securely gripping his cudgel, he asked calmly:

'Who are you?'

'Myself.'

'Who is that?'

'Jean Valjean.'

Javert put the cudgel between his teeth and leaning forward clapped his hands on Valjean's shoulders, seizing them in a vice-like grip. Staring hard, he recognized him. Their faces were nearly touching. Javert's gaze was terrible. Jean Valjean stayed unresisting, like a lion consenting to the clutch of a lynx.

'Inspector Javert,' he said, 'you have got me. In any case, since this morning I have considered myself your prisoner. I did not give you my address in order to escape from you. But grant me one thing.'

Javert did not seem to hear. He was gazing intently at Valjean with an expression of wild surmise. Finally, releasing him, he took his cudgel again in his hand, and, as though in a dream, murmured:

'What are you doing here? Who is this man?'

'It is about him I wished to speak,' said Valjean. 'You may do what you like with me, but help me first to take him home. That is all I ask.'

Javert's face twitched, as always happened when someone thought him capable of making a concession. But he did not refuse. Bending down, he took a handkerchief from his pocket, soaked it in water, and bathed Marius's blood-stained forehead.

'He was at the barricade,' he muttered; 'the one called Marius.' First-class agent that he was, he had taken note of everything, even when he thought himself on the verge of death. He took Marius's wrist, feeling for his pulse.

'He's wounded,' said Valjean.

'He's dead,' said Javert.

'No. Not yet.'

'You brought him here from the barricade?' asked Javert. His state of preoccupation must have been great indeed for him not to have dwelt on that disquieting rescue, or even to have noted Valjean's failure to reply.

Jean Valjean, for his part, seemed to have only one thought in mind.

'He lives in the Marais, Rue des Filles-du-Calvaire,' he said, 'with a relative whose name I forget.' He felt in Marius's jacket, found the wallet, opened it at the written page and handed it to Javert.

There was still just light enough to read by, and Javert, in any case, had the eyes of a cat. He studied the words and grunted. 'Gillenormand, 6 Rue des Filles-du-Calvaire.' Then he shouted: 'Coachman!'

We may recall the fiacre which was waiting 'just in case'. In a very short time it had come down the ramp and Marius had been placed on the back seat, while Javert and Valjean sat in front. The fiacre drove off rapidly along the quay in the direction of the Bastille.

Leaving the quay it entered the streets, the coachman whipping up his horses. There was stony silence in the fiacre. Marius was prostrate in a corner, head drooping, arms and legs limp, as though he had only a coffin to look forward to. Valjean was a figure of shadow and Javert like a figure carved in stone. The dark interior of the fiacre, when it passed under a street lamp, was momentarily lighted and the three tragic figures were thrown into relief—the seeming corpse, the spectre, and the statue.

X. *The Prodigal Returns to Life*

At every lurch a drop of blood fell from Marius's hair. It was quite dark when they reached 6 Rue des Filles-du-Calvaire. Javert got out first, and raising the heavy iron knocker, moulded in the ancient design of goat and satyr, knocked loudly. The door opened to disclose a yawning porter with a candle. Everyone was asleep. They retire early in the Marais, particularly in times of upheaval. That respectable old quarter, terrified of revolution, takes refuge in slumber like a child hiding its head under the sheets.

Jean Valjean and the coachman brought Marius from the fiacre, Valjean carrying him under the armpits and the coachman carrying him by the legs. As they did so Valjean thrust a hand under his torn clothes to feel his chest and make sure that his heart was still beating. It was in fact beating a little less feebly, as though the jolting of the fiacre had restored to it some degree of life.

Javert questioned the porter in a brisk, official tone.

'Anyone live here called Gillenormand?'

'Yes. What do you want of him?'

'We're bringing back his son.'

'His son?' exclaimed the porter in amazement.

'He's dead.'

Valjean, at whom the porter had been staring with horror as he stood, ragged and covered in mud in the background, shook his head. The porter seemed to understand neither of them.

'He was at the barricade,' said Javert, 'and here he is.'

'At the barricade!'

'He got himself killed. Go and wake his father.' The porter did not stir. 'Go on,' said Javert, and added: 'He'll be buried tomorrow.'

For Javert, the common incidents of the town were strictly classified, this being the basis of foresight and alertness, and every contingency had its place. Possible facts were, so to speak, in drawers from which they could be brought out as the case required, in varying quantities. Happenings in the street came under the headings of commotion, upheaval, carnival, funeral.

The porter awakened Basque. Basque awakened Nicolette, who awakened Aunt Gillenormand. They let the old man sleep on, thinking that he would know soon enough.

Marius was taken up to the first floor, without anyone in other parts of the house knowing what went on, and laid on an old settee in Monsieur Gillenormand's sitting-room. While Basque went in search of a doctor and Nicolette ransacked the linen cupboard, Valjean felt Javert's hand on his arm. He understood and went downstairs, with Javert close behind him. The porter watched them go as he had watched them arrive, with startled drowsiness. They got back into the fiacre, and the driver climbed on to his seat.

'Inspector,' said Valjean, 'grant me one last favour.'

'What is it?' Javert asked harshly.

'Let me go home for a minute. After that you can do what you like with me.'

Javert was silent for some moments, his chin sunk in the collar of his greatcoat. Then he pulled down the window in front of him.

'Drive to No. 7 Rue de l'Homme-Armé,' he said.

XI. *Collapse of the Absolute*

Neither spoke a word during the journey.

What did Jean Valjean wish to do? He wished to finish what he had begun; to tell Cosette the news of Marius, give her perhaps some other useful information and, if possible, make certain final arrangements. Where he personally was concerned, all was over. He had been taken by Javert and had made no resistance. Another man in his place might have thought of the rope Thénardier had given him and the bars of the first prison cell he would enter; but since his encounter with the bishop there was in Valjean a profound religious abhorrence of any act of violence, even against himself. Suicide, that mysterious plunge into the unknown, which might entail some degree of death of the soul, was impossible for Jean Valjean.

At the entrance to the Rue de l'Homme-Armé, the fiacre stopped, since the street was too narrow to admit vehicles. Javert and Valjean got out. The coachman respectfully pointed out to Monsieur l'Inspecteur that the velvet upholstery of his cab was stained by the blood of the murdered man and the mud of his murderer, which is what he understood them to be. Bringing a notebook out of his pocket he requested the inspector to write a few words to this effect. Javert thrust the book aside.

'How much does it come to, including the time of waiting and the distance travelled?'

'I waited seven hours and a quarter,' the coachman replied, 'and my upholstery is new. It comes to eighty francs, Monsieur.'

Javert got four napoleons out of his pocket and dismissed him.

Valjean thought that Javert intended to escort him on foot to either the Blancs-Manteaux or the Archives police post, both of which were near at hand. They walked along the street which, as usual, was deserted. Valjean knocked on the door of No. 7 and it was opened.

'Go up,' said Javert. He had a strange expression, as though it cost him an effort to speak. 'I'll wait for you here.'

Valjean looked at him. This was little in accordance with his usual habits. But Javert now had an air of lofty confidence, that of a cat that allows a mouse a moment's respite; and since Valjean had resolved to give himself up and be done with it, this did not greatly surprise him. He entered the house, called 'It's me' to the porter, who had pulled the cord from his bed, and went upstairs.

On the first floor he paused. All Calvaries have their stations. The sash window was open. As in many old houses the staircase looked on to the street and was lighted at night by the street lamp immediately outside. Perhaps automatically, or simply to draw breath, Valjean thrust out his head. He looked down into the street, which was short and lighted from end to end by its single lamp. He gave a start of amazement. There was no one there.

Javert had gone.

XII. *The Grandfather*

Basque and the porter had carried Marius, lying motionless on the settee, into the salon. The doctor had arrived and Aunt Gillenormand had got up. Aunt Gillenormand paced to and fro wringing her hands, incapable of doing more than say, 'Heavens, is it possible!' After the first shock she took a more philosophical view, to the point of saying, 'It was bound to end like this'. But she did not go so far as to say, 'I told you so', as is customary on these occasions.

At the doctor's orders a camp-bed was set up beside the settee. The doctor found that Marius's pulse was still beating, that he had no deep wound in his chest and that the blood at the corner of his lips came from the nasal cavity. He had him laid flat on the bed, without a pillow, his torso bare and his head on the same level as his body, to facilitate breathing. Seeing that he was to be undressed,

Mlle Gillenormand withdrew and went to tell her beads in her own room.

There was no sign of internal injury. A bullet, diverted by his wallet, had inflicted an ugly gash along the ribs but had not gone deep, so that this was not dangerous. The long underground journey had completed the dislocation of the shattered shoulderblade, and this was more serious. The arms had been slashed, but there was no injury to the face. The head, on the other hand, was covered with cuts, and it remained to be seen how deep they went, and whether they had penetrated the skull. What was serious was that they had caused unconsciousness of a kind from which one does not always recover. The haemorrhage had exhausted the patient; but there was no injury to the lower part of the body, which had been protected by the barricade.

Basque and Nicolette tore up rags for bandages. Lacking lint, the doctor temporarily staunched the wounds with wadding. Three candles burned on the bedside table, on which his instruments were spread. He washed Marius's face and hair with cold water, which rapidly turned red in the bowl.

The doctor looked despondent, now and then shaking his head as though in answer to himself. A doctor's voiceless dialogue is a bad omen for the patient. Suddenly, as he was gently touching the closed lids, the door of the room opened and a long, pale face appeared. It was the grandfather.

The fighting had greatly agitated and angered Monsieur Gillenormand. He had not been able to sleep the previous night, and had been in a fever all day. That night he had gone to bed early, ordering every door in the house to be locked, and had quickly fallen asleep. But old men sleep lightly. His bedroom was next to the salon, and despite all precautions the noise had awakened him. Seeing light under his door, he had got out of bed.

He stood in the doorway with a hand on the door-handle, his head thrust forward, his body covered by a white bedgown that hung straight down without folds like a shroud, so that he looked like a ghost peering into a tomb. He saw the bed and the wax-white young man, eyes closed and mouth open, lips colourless, bared to the waist and covered with bright red scars.

He shook from head to foot with the tremor that afflicts old bones; his eyes, yellowed with age, had a glassy look, while his whole face took on the sharp contours of a skull. His arms sank to his sides as though a spring had been broken, and his stupefaction was manifest in the way he spread out his old, shaking fingers. His knees thrust forward, disclosing through the opening of his garment his skinny legs. He muttered:

'Marius!'

'He has just been brought here, Monsieur,' said Basque. 'He was on the barricade, and . . .'

'He's dead!' cried the old man in a terrible voice. 'The brigand!'

A sort of sepulchral transformation caused him to straighten up like a young man. 'You're the doctor?' he went on. 'Tell me one thing. Is he truly dead?'

The doctor, filled with anxiety, said nothing. Monsieur Gillenormand wrung his hands and burst into dreadful laughter.

'Dead! Dead on the barricade, in hatred of me! He did this against me, the bloodthirsty ruffian, and this is how he comes back to me. Misery of my life, he's dead!'

He went to the window, flung it wide as though he were stifling, and talked into the night:

'Gashed, slashed and done for, that's what he is now! He knew I was waiting for him, that his room was kept in readiness and his boyhood picture at my bedside. He knew he had only to return and I would be waiting at the fireside half mad with longing. You knew it. You had only to say, "Here I am", and you would be master of the house and I would obey you in all things, your old fool of a grandfather. You knew it and you said, "No, he's a royalist, I won't go". You went to the barricade instead and got yourself killed from sheer perversity. That is what is infamous! Well, sleep in peace. That is my word to you.'

The doctor, feeling that he had two patients to worry about, went to Monsieur Gillenormand and took his arm. The old man turned, and gazing at him with eyes that seemed to have grown larger, said quietly:

'Thank you, but I am calm, I am a man. I saw the death of Louis XVI, I can confront events. What is terrible is the thought that it is your newspapers that make all the trouble. Scribbles, orators, tribunes, debates, the rights of man, the freedom of the press—that's what your children are brought up on. Oh, Marius, it's abominable! Dead before me! The barricades! Doctor, you live in this quarter, I believe. Yes, I know you. I see you pass by in your cabriolet. I tell you, you are wrong to think that I am angry. To rage against death is folly. This was a child I brought up. I was old already, and he was small. He played in the Tuileries, and to save him from the keeper's wrath I filled in the holes that he dug with his spade. One day he cried, "Down with Louis XVIII!" and off he went. It is not my fault. He was pink and fair-haired. His mother is dead. Have you noticed that all small children are fair? Why is that? He was the son of one of the brigands of the Loire, but children are not responsible for their father's crimes. I remember when he was so high.

He could not pronounce the letter "d". He talked like a little bird. I remember people turning to look at him, he was so beautiful, pretty as a picture. I talked sternly to him and flourished my stick, but he knew that it was only a joke. When he came to my room in the morning I might be grumpy, but it was as though the sun had come in. There is no defence against those little creatures. They take you and hold you and never let you go. The truth is that there was no one more lovely than that child. You talk of your Lafayettes, your revolutionaries—they kill me. It can't go on like this.'

He moved towards the still motionless Marius, to whom the doctor had returned, and again wrung his hands. His old lips moved mechanically, emitting disjointed words—'Heartless! The rebel! The scoundrel!'—words loaded with reproach. By degrees coherence returned to him, but it seemed that he had scarcely strength to utter the words he spoke, so low and distant was his voice.

'It makes no difference, I too shall die. To think that in all Paris there was no wench to make that wretched boy happy! A young fool who went and fought instead of enjoying life. And for what? For a republic, instead of dancing, as a young man should do. What use is it to be twenty years old? A republic, what imbecility! Woe to the mothers who make pretty boys. So he's dead. Two funerals to go through the door of this house. So he did it for the glory of General Lamarque, that ranting swashbuckler—he got himself killed for the sake of a dead man. At twenty. It's enough to drive one mad. And never looking round to see what he was leaving behind. So now the old men have to die alone. Well, so much the better, it's what I hoped for, it will finish me off. I'm too old—a hundred, a thousand years old—I should have been dead long ago. This settles it. What good does it do to make him breathe ammonia and those other things you're trying on him? You're wasting your time, you fool of a doctor. He's well and truly dead. I should know, being dead myself. He hasn't done it by halves. Oh, this is a disgusting time, and that's what I think of you all, your ideas, your systems, your masters, your oracles, your learned doctors, your rascally writers and threadbare philosophers—and all the revolutions which for sixty years have startled the crows in the Tuileries! And since without pity you got yourself killed I shall not grieve for your death—do you hear me, murderer?'

At this moment Marius's eyes slowly opened and his gaze, in drowsy astonishment, rested upon Monsieur Gillenormand.

'Marius!' the old man cried. 'Marius, my child, my beloved son! You're living after all!'

And he fell fainting to the floor.

BOOK FOUR

JAVERT IN DISARRAY

JAVERT had walked slowly away from the Rue de l'Homme-Armé, walking for the first time in his life with his head bowed and, also for the first time, with his hands behind his back. Until then Javert had adopted of Napoleon's two attitudes only the one expressive of determination, arms folded over the chest; the attitude of indecision, hands behind the back, was unknown to him. Now a change had come over him; his whole person bore the imprint of uncertainty.

Walking through the silent streets, he took the shortest way to the Seine, finally arriving near the police-post in the Place du Châtelet, by the Pont Notre-Dame. Between the Pont Notre-Dame and the Pont au Change, on the one hand, and the Quai de la Mégisserie and the Quai aux Fleurs, the Seine forms a sort of pool traversed by a swift current. It is a place feared by boatmen. Nothing is more dangerous than that current, aggravated in those days by the piles of the bridges, which have since been done away with. The current speeds up formidably, swelling in waves which seem to be trying to sweep the bridges away. A man falling into the river at this point, even a strong swimmer, does not emerge.

Javert leaned with his elbows on the parapet, his chin resting on his hands. Something new, a revolution, a disaster, had occurred to him, and he had to think it over. He was suffering deeply. For some hours past he had ceased to be the simple creature he had been; his blinkered, one-track mind had been disturbed. There was a flaw in the crystal. He felt that his sense of duty was impaired, and he could not hide this from himself. When he had so unexpectedly encountered Jean Valjean on the edge of the river his feelings had been partly those of a wolf catching its prey and partly those of a dog finding its master.

He could see two ways ahead of him, and this appalled him, because hitherto he had never seen more than one straight line. And the paths led in opposite directions. One ruled out the other. Which was the true one?

To owe his life to a man wanted by the law and to pay the debt in equal terms; to have accepted the words, 'You may go', and now to say, 'Go free', this was to sacrifice duty to personal motive, while at the same time feeling that the personal motive had a wider and perhaps higher application; it was to betray society while keeping faith with his own conscience. That this dilemma should have come upon him was what so overwhelmed him. He was amazed that Valjean should have shown him mercy, and that he should have shown Valjean mercy in return.

And now what was he to do? It would be bad to arrest Valjean, bad also to let him go. In the first case an officer of the law would be sinking to the level of a criminal, and in the second the criminal would be rising above the law. There are occasions when we find ourselves with an abyss on either side, and this was one of them.

His trouble was that he was forced to reflect—the very strength of his feelings made this unavoidable. Reflection was something to which he was unused, and he found it singularly painful. There is in it always an element of conflict, and this irritated him. Reflection, on any subject outside the narrow circle of his duties, had always been to him a useless and wearisome procedure; but now, after today's happenings, it was torture. Yet he was obliged to study his shaken conscience and account for himself to himself.

What he had done made him shudder. Against all regulations, all social and legal organization, against the whole code he, Javert, had taken it upon himself to let a prisoner go. He had substituted private considerations for those of the community: was it not inexcusable? He trembled when he thought of this. What to do? Only one proper course lay open to him—to hurry back to the Rue de l'Homme-Armé and seize Valjean. He knew it well, but he could not do it.

Something prevented him. What was it? Could there be other things in life besides trials and sentences, authority and the police? Javert was in utter dismay. A condemned man to escape justice through his act! That these two men, the one meant to enforce, the other to submit to the law, should thus place themselves outside the law—was not this a dreadful thing? Jean Valjean, in defiance of society, would be free, and he, Javert, would continue to live at the government's expense. His thoughts grew blacker and blacker.

The thought of the rebel taken to the Rue des Filles-du-Calvaire might have occurred to him, but it did not. The lesser fault was lost in the greater. In any case, he was probably dead. It was the thought of Jean Valjean that oppressed and dismayed him. All the principles on which his estimate of man had been based were over-thrown. Valjean's generosity towards himself amazed him. Behind Valjean loomed the figure of Monsieur Madeleine, and they merged into one, into a figure deserving of veneration. Something dreadful was forcing its way into Javert's consciousness—admiration for a convicted felon. He shivered, but could not evade it. Try as he might, he had in his heart to admit the scoundrel's greatness. It was abhorrent. A benevolent evildoer, a man who returned good for evil, a man near to the angels—Javert was forced to admit that this monstrosity could exist. He did not accept the fact without a struggle. He did not for a moment deny that the law was the law. What more simple than to enforce it? But when he sought to raise his hand to lay it on Valjean's shoulder an inner voice restrained him: 'You will deliver up your deliverer? Then go and find Pontius Pilate's bowl and wash your hands!' He felt himself diminished beside Jean Valjean.

But his greatest anguish was the loss of certainty. He had been torn up by the roots. The code he lived by was in fragments in his hand. He was confronted by scruples that were utterly strange to him. He could no longer live by his lifelong principles; he had entered a new strange world of humanity, mercy, gratitude and justice other than that of the law. He contemplated with horror the rising of a new sun—an owl required to see with eagle's eyes. He was forced to admit that kindness existed. The felon had been kind, and, a thing unheard of, so had he. Therefore he had failed himself. He felt himself to be a coward. Javert's ideal was to be more than human; to be above reproach. And he had failed.

All kinds of new questions arose in his mind, and the answers appalled him. Had the man performed a duty in showing him mercy? No, he had done something more. And he, in returning mercy, had denied his duty. So it seemed that there was something other than duty? Here all balance left him, the whole structure of his life collapsed; what was high was no more deserving of honour than what was low. Although instinctively he held the Church in respect, he regarded it as no more than an august part of the social order; and order was his dogma, and had hitherto sufficed him. The police force had been his true religion. He had a superior officer, Monsieur Gisquet; he had given no thought to that higher superior, which is God.

Now he became conscious of God and was troubled in spirit, thrown into disarray by that unexpected presence. He did not know how to treat this superior, knowing that the subordinate must always give way, never disobey or dispute orders, and that, faced by a superior with whom he does not agree, he can only resign. But how resign from God?

What it all came down to was that he was guilty of an unpardonable infraction of the rules. He had let a felon go. He felt that his life

367

was in ruins. Authority was dead within him, and he had no reason to go on living.

To feel emotion was terrible. To be carved in stone, the very figure of chastisement, and to discover suddenly under the granite of our face something contradictory that is almost a heart. To return good for a good that hitherto one had held to be evil; to be of ice, and melt; to see a pincer become a hand with fingers that parted. To let go! The man of action had lost his way. He was forced to admit that infallibility is not always infallible, that there may be error in dogma, that society is not perfect, that a flaw in the unalterable is possible, that judges are men and even the law may do wrong. What was happening to Javert resembled the de-railing of a train—the straight line of the soul broken by the presence of God. God, the inwardness of man, the true conscience as opposed to the false; the eternal, splendid presence. Did he understand or fully realize this? No; and faced by the incomprehensibility he felt that his head must explode.

He was not so much transformed as a victim of this miracle. He submitted in exasperation, feeling that henceforth his very breath must fail. He was not used to confronting the unknown. Until now what had been above him had been plain and simple, clearly defined and exact. Authority . . . Javert had been conscious of nothing unknowable. The unexpected, the glimpse of chaos, these belonged to some unknown, recalcitrant, miserable world. But now, recoiling, he was appalled by a new manifestation—an abyss above him. It meant that he was wholly at a loss. In what was he to believe?

The chink in society's armour might be found by a wretched act of mercy. An honest servant of the law might find himself caught between two crimes, the crime of mercy and the crime of duty. Nothing any longer was certain in the duties laid upon him. It seemed that a one-time felon might rise again and in the end prove right. Was it conceivable? Were there then cases when the law, mumbling excuses, must bow to transfigured crime? Yes, there were! Javert saw, and not only could not deny it but himself shared in it. This was reality. It was abominable that true fact should wear so distorted a face. If facts did their duty they would simply reinforce the law. Facts were God-given. Did anarchy itself descend from Heaven?

So then—and in the extremity of his anguish everything that might have corrected this impression was lost, and society and human kind assumed a hideous aspect—then the settled verdict, the force of law, official wisdom, legal infallibility, all dogma on which social stability reposed, all was chaos; and he, Javert, the guardian of these things was in utter disarray. Was this state of things to be borne? It was not. There were only two ways out. To go determinedly to Jean Valjean and return him to prison; or else . . .

Javert left the parapet and, now with his head held high, walked firmly to the police-post lighted by a lantern in the corner of the Place du Châtelet. He thrust open the door, showed the duty sergeant his card and sat down at a table on which were pens, inkstand and paper. It was something to be found in every police-post, fully equipped for the writing of reports. Javert settled down to write.

SOME NOTES FOR THE GOOD OF THE SERVICE

First: I beg Monsieur le Préfet to consider this.

Second: Prisoners returning from interrogation are made to take off their shoes and wait with their bare feet on the tiles. Many are coughing when they go back to prison. This leads to hospital expenses.

Third: Surveillance is well performed, with relief agents at regular distances; but in all important cases there should be at least two agents within sight of one another, able to come to each other's support.

Four: The special regulation at the Madelonnettes prison, whereby prisoners are not allowed a chair even if they pay for it, is hard to justify.

Five: There are only two bars over the canteen counter at the Madelonnettes, which enables the canteen-woman to touch the prisoners' hands.

Six: The prisoners called 'barkers' who summon prisoners to the parlour charge two sous for calling a man's name distinctly. This is robbery.

Seven: The prisoner who drops a thread in the weaving-room loses ten sous. This is an abuse on the part of the contractor, since the cloth is none the worse for it.

Eight: It is unsatisfactory that visitors to La Force should have to cross the Cour des Mômes to reach the Sainte-Marie-l'Egyptienne parlour.

Nine: Gendarmes in the courtyard of the Préfecture are often heard discussing Court proceedings. A gendarme should never repeat what he has heard in the course of his official duties.

Ten: Mme Henry is an excellent woman who keeps her canteen in good order. But it is wrong that a woman should be at the entrance to the secret cells. This is unworthy of the Conciergerie.

Having methodically written these lines without omitting a comma, Javert signed as follows:

369

'Javert, inspector of the First Class, writing at the Place du Châtelet post.

'7 June 1832, at about one o'clock in the morning.'

He blotted and folded the sheet of paper, and addressing it to the Administration, left it on the table. He went out, and the barred, glass-paned door closed behind him.

Crossing the Place du Châtelet, he returned automatically to the spot he had left a quarter of an hour before and stood leaning with his elbows on the parapet as though he had never left it. It was the sepulchral moment that succeeds midnight, with the stars hidden by cloud and not a light to be seen in the houses of the Cité, not a passer-by, only the faint, distant gleam of a street-lamp and the shadowy outlines of Notre Dame and the Palais de Justice.

The place where Javert stood, we may recall, was where the river flows in a dangerous rapid. He looked down. There was a sound of running water, but the river itself was not to be seen. What lay below him was a void, so that he might have been standing at the edge of infinity. He stayed motionless for some minutes, staring into nothingness. Abruptly he took off his hat and laid it on the parapet. A moment later a tall, dark figure, which a passer-by might have taken for a ghost, stood upright on the parapet. It leaned forward and dropped into the darkness.

There was a splash, and that was all.

BOOK FIVE

GRANDSON AND GRANDFATHER

I. *We again see the Tree with a Zinc Plate*

SOME time after the events we have described Boulatruelle had a severe shock.

Boulatruelle was the Montfermeil road-mender whom we met in an earlier part of this tale. He was a man of many troubles, whose stone-breaking caused vexation to travellers on the road. But he cherished a dream. He believed in the treasure buried in the woods of Montfermeil and hoped to find it. In the meantime he picked the pockets of passers-by when he could.

But for the present he was being prudent. He had had a narrow escape, having been rounded up in the Jondrette garret with the other gangsters. Drunkenness had saved him, since it could not be proved that he had been there with criminal intent, and so he had been granted an acquittal, based on his undeniably drunken state. He had then returned to the woods and the road from Gagny to Lagny where under administrative supervision and in a subdued manner, warmed only by his fondness for wine, he had continued to break stones.

The shock was as follows. One morning just before daybreak, going as usual to work but perhaps a little more awake than on most days, he had seen among the trees the back view of a stranger who did not appear wholly unfamiliar. Drinker though he was, Boulatruelle had an excellent memory, a necessary weapon for anyone somewhat at odds with the law.

'Where the devil have I seen him?' he wondered, but could find no answer to the question. He considered the matter. The man was not local. He must have come on foot, since no public conveyance passed at that hour. He could not have come from any great distance, since he had no bundle or haversack. Perhaps he had come from Paris. But what was he doing there? Boulatruelle thought of the hidden treasure. Ransacking his memory, he recalled a similar encounter some years before. He had bowed his head while thinking, which was natural but unwise. When he looked up the man was no longer to be seen.

'By God I'll find him,' said Boulatruelle. 'I'll find out who he is and what he's up to. Can't have secrets in my woods.' He took up his pick, which was very sharp. 'Good for digging into the earth, or into a man.'

He set off in the general direction taken by the man. Before long he was helped by the growing daylight. Footprints here and there, crushed bushes and other indications, afforded him a rough trail, which, however, he lost. Pushing further into the wood, he climbed a small hillock and then had the idea of climbing a tree. Despite his age he was agile. There was a tall beech, and he climbed it as high as he could. From this eminence he saw the man, only to lose him again. The man had vanished into a clearing surrounded by tall trees. But Boulatruelle knew the clearing well because one of the trees was a chestnut that had been mended with a sheet of zinc nailed to the bark. Doubtless the heap of stones in the clearing is still there. There is nothing to equal the longevity of a heap of stones.

Boulatruelle almost fell out of the tree in his delight. He had run his man to earth, and doubtless the treasure as well. But to reach the clearing was not easy. Following the twisted paths, it took a quarter of an hour; but to go direct, forcing one's way through the toughest undergrowth, took twice as long. Boulatruelle made a mistake. For once in his life he took the straight line.

It was a laborious business. When, breathless, he reached the clearing some half an hour later, he found no one there. Only the heap of stones was there; no one had taken that away. But the man himself had vanished, no one could say in what direction. Worse still, behind the heap of stones and near the tree with its zinc plate, was a pile of earth, an abandoned pick-axe, and a hole.

The hole was empty.

'Scoundrel!' cried Boulatruelle, flinging up his arms.

II. *From Street Warfare to Domestic Conflict*

Marius lay for a long time between life and death, in a state of fever and delirious, endlessly repeating the name of Cosette. The extent of some of his wounds was serious because of the risk of gangrene, and every change in the weather caused the doctor anxiety.

'Above all,' he said, 'he must not be excited.' Dressings were difficult, sticking-plaster being unknown at that time. Nicolette tore up countless sheets, 'enough to cover the ceiling'. While the peril remained Monsieur Gillenormand, hovering distractedly at the bedside, was like Marius himself—neither dead nor alive.

Every day, and sometimes twice a day, a white-haired, well-dressed gentleman, according to the porter, came to ask for news of the sick man and brought with him a bundle of rags for bandages.

Finally, on 7 September, three months to the day after Marius had been brought to his grandfather's house, the doctor announced that he was out of danger. But because of the damage to his shoulder-blade he had to spend a further two months resting in a chaise-longue. There are always injuries which refuse to heal and cause great vexation to the sufferers, but on the other hand his long illness and convalescence saved Marius from the authorities. In France there is no anger, not even official, that six months do not extinguish; and uprisings, in the present state of society, are so much the fault of everyone, that it is better for eyes to be closed. We may add that Gisquet's inexcusable order, instructing doctors to denounce the wounded, outraged not only public opinion but that of the King himself, and this protected them. Apart from one or two who were captured in the fighting, they were not troubled; and so Marius was left in peace.

Monsieur Gillenormand at first went through every kind of torment, and then through every kind of rapture. It was with great difficulty that he was restrained from spending all his nights at the bedside. He insisted that his daughter should use the best linen in the house for the patient's bandages; but Mlle Gillenormand, prudent woman, contrived to save the best without his knowing. He personally supervised all the dressings, from which Mlle Gillenormand modestly withdrew, and when rotted flesh had to be scraped away he exclaimed in pain. Nothing was more touching than to see him tender the patient a cup of tisane with his old, shaking hand. He overwhelmed the doctor with questions, which he endlessly repeated. And on the day when the doctor announced that the danger was past, such was his happiness that he tipped the porter three louis. That night in his bedroom he danced a gavotte, snapping his fingers and singing a little song. Then he knelt down at a chair, and Basque, peeping through the partly open door, was sure that he was praying. Until then he had never believed in God.

His state of rapture grew as the patient's condition improved. He did absurd, extravagant things, such as running up and down stairs without knowing why. His neighbour, a pretty woman be it said, was astonished to receive a large bouquet from him, greatly to her husband's annoyance. He even tried to take Nicolette on his knee. He addressed Marius as 'Monsieur le Baron' and cried, 'Long live the Republic!' He watched over the prodigal like a mother, no longer thinking of himself. Marius had become the master of the house, and he, surrendering, was his grandson's grandson, the most venerable of children, such was his state of happiness. He was radiant and young, his white hair lending dignity to the warmth shining in his face.

As for Marius, during all his convalescence he had but one thought in mind, that of Cosette. When he ceased to be delirious he ceased to speak her name, but this was precisely because she meant so much to him. He did not know what had happened to her or to himself. Vague pictures lingered in his mind—Éponine, Gavroche, Mabeuf, the Thénardiers, and the friends who had been with him at the barricade. The appearance of Monsieur Fauchelevent in that sanguinary affair was a riddle to him. He did not know how he had come to be saved, and no one could tell him. All they could say was that he had been brought there in a fiacre. Past, present, and future, all were befogged in his mind. There was but one clear, fixed point: his resolve to find Cosette. In this he was unshakeable, regardless of what it might cost, or the demands he might have to make of his grandfather or of life.

He did not conceal the difficulties from himself. And we must stress one point: he was not won over or much moved by his grandfather's kindness, for one thing because he did not know of it all, and also because, in the wandering thoughts of a sick man, he saw in this new phenomenon an attempt to bring him to heel. He remained cool, and his grandfather's aged tenderness was wasted. He thought that all would be well while things remained as they were, but that any mention of Cosette would lead to a changed situation—the old quarrel revived. So he hardened his heart in advance. And with returning life his old grievances returned, so that the figure of Colonel Pontmercy came between him and his grandfather. He felt that he could not hope for kindness from one whose attitude to his father had been so harsh. With growing health he felt a kind of acrimony towards the old man, from which the latter suffered. Without giving any sign, Monsieur Gillenormand noted that Marius now never addressed him as 'father'. He did not, it is true, say 'Monsieur', but found ways of avoiding either.

Clearly a crisis was approaching. As nearly always happens, Marius skirmished before joining battle. It happened one morning that Monsieur Gillenormand, glancing at the newspaper, let fall a frivolously royalist remark on the Convention and Danton, Saint-Just and Robespierre.

'Those men of '93 were giants,' Marius said angrily.

The old man did not say another word, and Marius, never forgetting the inflexible grandparent of former years, saw in his silence a manifestation of deeply buried anger, and prepared himself for the struggle that must come. He was resolved that if Cosette were denied him he would strip the bandages off his wounds and refuse all food. His wounds were his armoury. He would have Cosette or die.

With the crafty patience of the invalid he awaited the moment. And the moment came.

III. *Marius attacks*

One day while his daughter was tidying the room Monsieur Gillenormand bent over Marius's bed and said to him most tenderly:

'If I were you, dear Marius, I would begin to eat more meat than fish. A fried sole is excellent at the beginning of convalescence; but a good chop is what a man needs to put him on his feet.'

Marius, whose strength was now almost quite restored, sat up with clenched fists and glared at his grandfather.

'There is something I have to say to you.'

'What is it?'

'I want to get married.'

'But of course,' said the old man, laughing.

'How do you mean—of course?'

'That's understood. You shall have your little girl.'

Marius trembled with sheer amazement.

'You shall have her,' Monsieur Gillenormand repeated. 'She comes here every day in the shape of an elderly gentleman who asks for news of you. Since your injury she has spent her time weeping and making bandages. I know all about her. She lives at No. 7, Rue de l'Homme-Armé. You didn't think of that, did you? You thought to yourself, "I'll put it to him squarely, that old relic of the *ancien régime*. He was a beau once; he had his flutter and his wenches. He had his fun, and now we'll see". A battle, you thought, and you'd take the bull by the horns. So I suggest that you should eat a chop and you say you want to get married! What a jump! You thought there was bound to be an argument, not knowing what an old coward I am. You didn't expect to find your grandfather even sillier than yourself, too busy thinking of all the things you were going to say to me. But I'm not so foolish. I've made inquiries. I know that she's charming and good and that she adores you. If you had died there would have been three of us—her coffin and mine alongside your own. I had thought, when you were better, of simply bringing her to your bedside; but that's the sort of romantic situation that only happens in novels. What would your aunt have said? And the doctor? A pretty girl is no cure for fever. So there you are, and no need to say any more. I knew you did not care for me, and I thought, what can I do to make him love me? I thought, I can give him Cosette. You expected me to play the tyrant and ruin everything. Not a bit of it—Cosette is yours. Nothing could be better. Be so good as to get married, my dear sir. And be happy, my dear, dear boy.'

Having said which the old man burst into tears. He clasped Marius's head to his chest and they wept together.

'Father!' cried Marius.

'At last you love me!' the old man said.

There was a moment of supreme happiness during which neither could speak. Then the old man stammered:

'So at last you've said it—father.'

Marius gently disengaged his head.

'Father, now that I'm so much better I think I should be allowed to see her.'

'You shall. You shall see her tomorrow.'

'But father—'

'Well?'

'Why not today?'

'Well then, today. You have called me "father" three times and that has earned it. It is like the end of a poem by André Chénier, whose throat was cut by those vill—— those giants of '93.'

Monsieur Gillenormand thought he had caught the trace of a frown on Marius's face, although the truth is that, his mind filled with thoughts of Cosette, Marius had not even heard him. Trembling at the thought that he might have blundered in that reference to the murderers of André Chénier, the old man hurriedly went out.

'Well, that was not the way to put it. There was nothing evil about those great men of the Revolution. They were heroes, not a doubt of it. But they found André Chénier troublesome, and so they had him guillo—— I mean, they asked him in the public interest if he wouldn't mind . . .'

But he could find no way of ending the sentence. While his daughter smoothed Marius's pillows he ran out of the room as hurriedly as his age allowed, shut the door behind him, and, foaming with rage, found himself face to face with Basque. He seized him by the collar and cried:

'By all the gods, those villains murdered him!'

'Murdered who?'

'André Chénier.'

'Certainly, monsieur,' said the startled Basque.

Cosette and Marius saw one another again. What it meant to them we shall not attempt to say. There are things beyond description, of which the sun is one.

All the household, including Basque and Nicolette, were assembled in Marius's room when she entered. She stood in the doorway, seeming enveloped in a glow of light. The old man, at that moment, had been about to blow his nose. He stopped short, gazing at Cosette over his handkerchief.

'Exquisite,' he cried and loudly blew.

Cosette was in Heaven, as dazed as a person can be by sheer happiness. She stood stammering, pale and pink, waiting to fling herself into Marius's arms, but not venturing to do so, afraid of thus showing her love to the world. We are pitiless to happy lovers, hampering them with our presence when they only want to be alone.

Standing behind Cosette was a white-haired man, grave but nevertheless smiling—a vaguely touching smile. It was 'Monsieur Fauchelevent'—that is to say, Jean Valjean. As the porter had said, he was very well dressed, entirely in new black garments, with a white cravat.

The porter was not within miles of discerning, in that respectable figure, the ragged, mud-smeared person who on 7 June had brought the unconscious Marius to the door. Nevertheless his porter's instinct was aroused, and he had not been able to refrain from saying to his wife, 'I don't know why it is, but I can't help feeling I've seen him somewhere before.'

Monsieur Fauchelevent was standing somewhat apart from the others. He had under his arm a package that looked like a volume wrapped in paper, the paper being greenish in colour and seeming damp.

'Does the gentleman always have a book under his arm?' Nicolette murmured to Mlle Gillenormand, who did not care for books.

'Why,' said Monsieur Gillenormand in the same low tone, 'he's a man of learning. So what is wrong with that? Monsieur Boulard, whom I used to know, never went anywhere without a book under his arm.'

Raising his voice and bowing, he said:

'Monsieur Tranchelevent . . .' He did not do it on purpose; but inattention to proper names was one of his aristocratic habits. 'Monsieur Tranchelevent, I have the honour, on behalf of my grandson, Baron Marius Pontmercy, to ask for your daughter's hand in marriage.'

Monsieur Tranchelevent bowed.

'Then that is settled,' said the old man, and turning to Marius and Cosette with arms upraised he said: 'My children, you are free to love one another.'

They did not need telling twice. The billing and cooing began. 'To see you again,' Cosette murmured, standing by the chaise-longue. 'To know that it is really you! Why did you go and fight? How dreadful! For four months I have felt that I was dead. How cruel of you, when I had done you no harm. You are forgiven, but you must never do it again. When I had the message asking me to come here I thought that I should die of joy. I have not even troubled to dress up. I must look terrible . . . But you don't say anything. Why do you let me do all the talking? We're still in the Rue de l'Homme-Armé. And your dreadful wound—I cried my eyes out. That anyone should suffer so much. Your grandfather looks very nice. No, don't try to stand up, it might be bad for you. Oh, I'm so happy, wild with happiness! Do you still love me? We live in the Rue de l'Homme-Armé. There's no garden. I've done nothing but make bandages, look at the blister on my finger, you bad man!' . . .'Angel!' Marius said: the word that never wears out, the one most often used by lovers . . . And then, since there were others present, they fell silent, only touching each other's hand. Monsieur Gillenormand turned to the rest of the company and cried:

'Well talk, can't you! Make a little noise so that they can chatter in comfort!' He bent over them. 'And call each other *tu*. Don't be afraid.'

Aunt Gillenormand with a kind of amazement was observing the bright scene in her faded home. There was nothing shocked or envious in her gaze: it was that of an innocent creature of fifty-seven, a wasted life witnessing the triumph of love. Her father said to her:

'I told you this would happen to you . . .' He paused and went on after a moment's silence, '. . . to see the happiness of others.' Then he turned to Cosette. 'So sweetly pretty, like a painting by Greuze. And to think that she's to be all yours, you rascal! If I weren't fifteen years too old we'd fight a duel for her. Young lady, I am in love with you, and no wonder. What a charming wedding it will be! Saint-Denis du Saint-Sacrement is our parish, but I'll get a dispensation for you to be married in Saint-Paul, which is a nicer church, built by the Jesuits. The masterpiece of Jesuit architecture is at Namur, the church of Saint-Loup. You must go there when you're married. I am wholly on your side, Mademoiselle; all young ladies should get married, it's what they're for. Be fruitful and multiply. What can be better than that?' The old man skipped on his ninety-

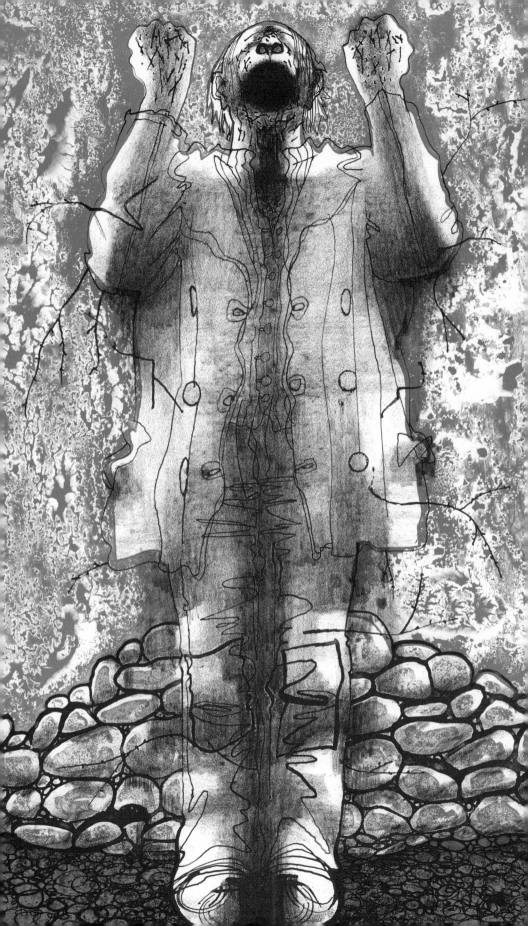

year-old heels and said to Marius: 'By the way—did you not have a close friend?'

'There was Courfeyrac.'

'What's become of him?'

'He's dead.'

'Ah, well.'

He made Cosette sit down, sat beside them and took their four hands in his own.

'So enchanting, this Cosette, a true masterpiece. A young girl and a great lady. It's a pity she'll only be a baroness, she should be a marquise. Get it well into your heads, my children, that you are on the right road. Love is the folly of men and the wisdom of God. Love one another. But now I come to think of it, more than half of all I possess is tied up in an annuity. My poor children, what will you do after my death in twenty years' time?'

A quiet voice said: 'Mademoiselle Euphrasie Fauchelevent has six hundred thousand francs.'

It was Jean Valjean who had spoken. Hitherto he had not uttered a word, but had stood silently contemplating the happy group.

'And who is this Mademoiselle Euphrasie?' the old man asked.

'It's me,' said Cosette.

'Six hundred thousand!' exclaimed the old man.

'Less a few thousand francs,' said Valjean, and he put the parcel which Aunt Gillenormand had supposed to be a book on the table. Opening it he disclosed a bundle of banknotes, which, being counted, amounted to five hundred thousand-franc notes and one hundred and sixty-eight five-hundred-franc notes—in all, five hundred and eighty-four thousand francs.

'Well that's a very handsome book,' said Monsieur Gillenormand.

'Five hundred and eight-four thousand francs,' murmured the aunt.

'That settles matters very nicely, does it not, Mlle Gillenormand?' the old man said. 'This young rogue of a Marius, he finds a million-airess in his dreamland. Trust the young people of nowadays. Students find girl-students worth six hundred thousand francs. Cherubino is a better man that Rothschild.'

'Five hundred and eighty-four thousand francs!' Mlle Gillenormand murmured again. 'As good as six hundred thousand!'

And as to Marius and Cosette, they were gazing into each other's eyes, scarcely aware of this trifle.

V. *How to Safeguard your Money*

No lengthy explanation is needed for the reader to understand that after the Champmathieu affair Jean Valjean had been able, during his brief escape, to come to Paris and withdraw from the Laffitte bank the money he had accumulated as Monsieur Madeleine. Fearing recapture, he had buried it in the clearing in the Montfermeil wood. The sum of 630,000 francs in banknotes was not bulky and could be put in a box; but to safeguard the box from damp he had put it in an oak chest filled with chestnut shavings. In this he had also put the bishop's candlesticks which he had taken from Montreuil-sur-mer. It was Valjean whom the road-mender, Boulatruelle, had seen. When he needed money Valjean had returned to the clearing, which accounts for the absences we have referred to; and when he knew Marius to be convalescent, foreseeing that the entire sum would come in useful, he had gone to retrieve it. This was the last time Boulatruelle had seen him. He had inherited his pickaxe.

The sum then remaining had amounted to 584,500 francs. Valjean had kept the five hundred for himself. 'We shall see how it works out,' he reflected.

The difference between this sum and the 630,000 francs withdrawn from Laffitte represented the expenditure of ten years—from 1823 to 1833. The time in the convent had cost only 5,000 francs. Valjean had put the silver candlesticks on the mantelpiece, where they glittered to the great admiration of Toussaint.

For the rest, Valjean knew that he had nothing more to fear from Javert. It had been reported in the *Moniteur* that his drowned body had been found under a washerwoman's boat between the Pont au Change and the Pont Neuf. He had been a policeman with an irreproachable record, highly-esteemed by his superiors, who concluded that he must have committed suicide while of unsound mind. 'Well,' reflected Jean Valjean, 'since he had me and let me go, that may well be true.'

VI. *Two Old Gentlemen prepare for the Happiness of Cosette*

Preparations for the wedding were put in hand. The month was December and the doctor, being consulted, declared that it might take place in February. Several weeks of perfect bliss ensued, and Monsieur Gillenormand was far from being the least happy. He spent hours in the contemplation of Cosette.

'The sweet, pretty girl,' he said. 'So gentle and so good. Never have I seen so delightful a girl. Who could live anything but nobly with such a creature? Marius, my boy, you are a baron and you are rich. Don't, I beseech you, waste your time lawyering.'

Cosette and Marius had been transported so rapidly from the depths to the heights that they would have been dazed had they not been dazzled.

'Do you understand it all?' he asked Cosette.

'No,' she replied. 'But I feel that God is watching over us.'

Jean Valjean arranged everything and made everything easy, speeding Cosette's happiness with as much pleasure, or so it appeared, as she felt herself. Having been a mayor, he knew how to solve an awkward problem, that of Cosette's civic status. To reveal the truth about her origin might, who knows, have prevented the marriage. He endowed her with a dead family, which meant that no one could make demands on her. She was not his daughter but the daughter of another Fauchelevent. Two Fauchelevent brothers had worked as gardeners in the Petit-Picpus convent; and the fact was confirmed by the nuns, who, little interested in the matter of paternity, had never troubled to inquire which of them was her father. They willingly said what was wanted, a document was prepared and Cosette acquired the legal state of Mademoiselle Euphrasie Fauchelevent, an orphan. Jean Valjean, under the name of Fauchelevent, became her guardian and Monsieur Gillenormand her deputy guardian.

As for the money, it had been bequeathed to Cosette by a person who had preferred to remain anonymous. The original sum had been 594,000 francs; but of this 10,000 francs had been spent on little Euphrasie's education, 500 going to the convent. The legacy, held by a trustee, was to go to Cosette when she attained her majority or when she married. All of which, it will be seen, was highly acceptable, particularly since the sum involved exceeded half a million. There were one or two trifling oddities, but these passed unnoticed.

Cosette had to learn that she was not the daughter of the old man whom for so long she had addressed as father, and that another Fauchelevent was her real parent. At any other time she would have been greatly distressed, but in her present state of happiness this scarcely troubled her. She had Marius; and the coming of the young man made the older less important. And all her life she had been surrounded by mystery, so that this last change was not hard to accept. In any case she continued to call Jean Valjean 'father'.

She had taken a great liking to Monsieur Gillenormand, who showered presents on her. While Jean Valjean arranged her civic status, he attended to her trousseau, delighting in its magnificence.

He gave her a dress of Binche lace which had come to him from his grandmother, saying that it was again becoming fashionable. 'Old styles are all the rage,' he said. 'The young women nowadays dress just as they did when I was young'. He rifled wardrobes filled with the belongings of his wives and mistresses; damask and moire and painted Indian cloths, lacework from Genoa and Alençon, all kinds of elegant frivolity were lavished on the rapturous Cosette, whose soul soared skyward on Mechlin lace wings. It was a time of endless festivity in the Rue des Filles-du-Calvaire.

One day Marius, who with all his happiness enjoyed serious conversation, remarked for some reason that I do not recall:

'The men of the Revolution were so great that their deathless fame is already assured. Like Cato and Phocion they have become figures of antiquity.'

'Antiquity—antique moire!' the old man cried. 'Marius, I thank you—just the idea I was looking for!' And the next day a magnificent dress of antique moire the colour of tea was added to Cosette's wardrobe.

The old man drew morals from this finery.

'Love is all very well, but something more is needed. There must be extravagance in happiness, rapture must be spiced with super-fluity. Let me have a milkmaid, but make her a duchess. Let me view an endless countryside from a colonnade of marble. Happiness unadorned is like unbuttered bread: one may eat it but one does not dine. I want the superfluous, the embellishment, the thing that serves no purpose. In Strasbourg Cathedral there is a clock the size of a three-storey house which condescends to tell you the time but does not seem to exist for that alone. Whatever hour it strikes, midday, the hour of the sun, or midnight, the hour of love, it seems to be giving you the sun and the stars, earth and ocean, kings, emperors and the twelve apostles, and a troop of little gilded men playing the trumpet—all this thrown in! How does a mere bare dial pointing the hours compare with that? The great clock of Strasbourg, and not just a Black Forest cuckoo-clock, is what suits me.'

Monsieur Gillenormand dwelt especially on the subject of festivity, invoking all the gaieties of the eighteenth century.

'You have lost the art in these days,' he cried. 'This nineteenth century is flat, lacking in excess, ignorant of what is rich and noble, insipid, colourless, and without form. Your bourgeois ideal is a chintz upholstered boudoir! But I can look back. On the day in 1787 when I saw the Duc du Rohan, who was Prince de Léon, and other peers of France drive to Longchamps, not in stately coaches but in chaises, I knew it was the beginning of the end. Look what follows. In these days people do business, play the market, make money and are rotten—smooth, neat, polished, irreproachable on the surface; but go deeper and you will raise a stench that would make a cow-hand hold his nose! You must not mind, Marius, if I talk like this. I say nothing against the people, but I have a bone to pick with the bourgeoisie. I am one myself, and that is how I know. There is so much that I regret—the elegance, the chivalry, the courtly manners, and the songs . . . The bride's garter, which was akin to the girdle of Venus. What else caused the Trojan war, if not Helen's garter? Why else did Hector and Achilles deal each other mortal blows? Homer might have made the *Iliad* out of Cosette's garter, and put in an old babbler like me whom he would call Nestor. In the good old days, my friends, people married wisely —a good marriage contract followed by a good blow-out. One did oneself proud, sitting beside a pretty woman who did not unduly hide her bosom. Those laughing mouths, how gay they were! People set out to look pretty with make-up and embroidery. Your bourgeois looked like a flower, your marquis like a statue. It was a great time, fastidious on the one hand and splendid on the other— and how we enjoyed ourselves! People nowadays are serious. The bourgeois is miserly and a prude. A wretched century—the Graces would be considered too lightly clad. Beauty is hidden as though it were ugliness. Everyone wears pantaloons since the Revolution, even the dancers. Songs are solemn, they have to have a message. People have to look important, and the result is that they all look insignificant. Listen, my children—joy is not simply joyous, it is great! Be gaily in love, and when you marry do so in all the fever and excitement of happiness. Decorum in church is proper, but when that's over—bang! A wedding should be royal and magical, I detest solemn weddings. That moment in life should be a flight to Heaven with the birds, even if next day you have to fall back to earth among the bourgeoisie and the frogs. There should be nothing meagre about that day. If I had my way it would be a day of enchantment, with violins in the trees, a sky of silver and blue, and the singing of nymphs and nereids, a chorus of naked girls. That is the programme I would like to see.'

Aunt Gillenormand viewed these matters with her customary placidity. She had had much to unsettle her in recent months— Marius fighting on the barricades, brought home more dead than alive, reconciled to his grandfather, engaged to be married to a pauper who turned out to be an heiress. The 600,000 francs were the culminating astonishment, after which she had reverted to her customary state of religious torpor, regularly attending Mass, telling her beads, murmuring *Aves* in one corner of the house while the words 'I love you' were being exchanged in another. There is a state of asceticism in which the benumbed spirit, remote from everything that we call living, is scarcely aware of any happening less catastrophic than an earthquake, nothing human, whether pleasant or unpleasant. 'It's like a bad cold in the head,' Monsieur Gillenormand said. 'You can't smell a thing, good or bad.'

It was the money that had decided the matter for her. Her father was so in the habit of ignoring her that he had not asked her whether he should give his consent to Marius's marriage, and this had ruffled her, although she had given no sign of it. She had thought to herself: 'Well, my father may decide about the marriage but I can decide about the means'. She was in fact rich, which her father was not. She had kept an open mind, but the probability is that if they had been poor she would have let them go on being poor—if her nephew chose to marry a pauper that was his affair. But a fortune of six hundred thousand francs is deserving of esteem, and since they no longer needed it she would undoubtedly leave them her own fortune.

It was arranged that the couple should live with Marius's grandfather. The old man insisted on giving up his bedroom, the best room in the house. 'It will make me young again,' he said. 'I have always wanted to have a honeymoon in that room'. He filled it with old, gay furniture and hung it with a remarkable material, golden flowers on a satin background, which he believed had come from Utrecht. 'The same as draped the bed of the Duchesse d'Anville à la Roche Guyon,' he said. And on the mantelpiece he put a little Saxon figurine holding a muff over her naked tummy. His library became Marius's advocate's office, this, as we know, being a legal requirement.

VII. *Happiness and Dreams*

The lovers saw each other every day, Cosette coming with Monsieur Fauchelevent. 'It's not at all right,' said Mlle Gillenormand, 'for the lady to come to the gentleman'. But they had got into the habit during Marius's convalescence, and the greater comfort of the armchairs in the Rue des Filles-du-Calvaire, more suited to the tête-à-tête, had been an added inducement. Marius and Monsieur Fauchelevent saw one another but scarcely spoke, as though by tacit agreement. Every girl needs a chaperon, and so Cosette could not have come without him. Marius accepted him for this reason. They exchanged an occasional word on the political situation and once, when Marius asserted his conviction that education should be free and available to everyone, they found themselves in agreement and had a brief discussion. Marius found that although Monsieur Fauchelevent talked well, with an excellent command of language, there was something lacking in him. He was something less than a man of the world, and something more.

All sorts of questions concerning Monsieur Fauchelevent, who treated him with a cool civility, were at the back of Marius's mind. His illness had left a gap in his memory in which much had been lost. He found himself wondering whether he could really have seen that calm, sober man at the barricade. But no amount of happiness can prevent us from looking back into the past. There were moments when Marius, taking his head in his hands, recalled the death of Mabeuf, heard Gavroche singing amid the musket-fire and felt his lips pressed to Éponine's cold forehead. Enjolras, Courfeyrac, Jean Prouvaire—the figures of all his friends appeared to him and then vanished. Had they really existed, and where were they now? Was it true that they were all dead—all gone, except himself? All that had vanished like the fall of the curtain at the ending of a play. And was he himself the same man? He had been poor and now was rich, solitary and now he had a family, desolate and now he was to marry Cosette. He felt that he had passed through a tomb, black when he entered it but white when he emerged—and the others had remained in it. There were moments when those figures from the past crowded in upon him and filled his mind with darkness; then the thought of Cosette restored him to serenity. Nothing less than his present happiness could have washed out that disaster.

And Monsieur Fauchelevent had become almost one of those vanished figures. Seeing him quietly seated beside Cosette, Marius found it hard to believe that this was the man who had been with him at the barricade. That earlier Fauchelevent seemed rather a figment of his delirium. And there was a gap between them which Marius did not think of bridging. It is less rare than one may think for two men sharing a common experience to agree by tacit consent never to refer to it. Only once did Marius make the attempt. Bringing the Rue de la Chanvrerie into the conversation, he turned to Monsieur Fauchelevent and said:

'You know the street, do you not?'

'What street was that?'

'The Rue de la Chanvrerie.'

'I don't know the name of any such street,' replied Monsieur Fauchelevent with the greatest calm.

This reply, bearing simply on the name of the street, appeared to Marius more conclusive than it really was.

'I must have dreamed it,' he reflected. 'It was someone like him, but certainly not Monsieur Fauchelevent.'

VIII. *Two Men Impossible to Find*

His state of rapture, great though it was, did not relieve Marius's mind of other preoccupations; and while the wedding preparations were going forward he subjected himself to scrupulous self-examination. He owed debts of gratitude both on his father's account and on his own. There was Thénardier, and there was the stranger who had brought him to Monsieur Gillenormand's house. He was resolved to find these two men, since otherwise they might cast a shadow on his life. Before moving joyously into the future he wanted to feel that he had paid due quittance to the past.

That Thénardier was a villain did not alter the fact that he had saved the life of Colonel Pontmercy. He was a rogue in the eyes of all the world except Marius. And Marius, not knowing what had really happened at Waterloo, was ignorant of the fact that although his father owed Thénardier his life, he owed him no gratitude. But the agents employed by Marius could find no trace of Thénardier. The woman had died in prison during the trial, and the man and his daughter Azelma, the sole survivors of that lamentable group, had vanished into obscurity.

The woman being dead, Boulatruelle acquitted, Claquesous vanished and the leading members of the gang having escaped from prison, the matter of the Gorbeau tenement conspiracy had been more or less abandoned. Two minor figures, Panchaud, known as Bigrenaille, and Demi-Liard, known as Deux Milliards, had been sentenced to ten years in the galleys, while their accomplices had been condemned in their absence to hard labour for life. Thénardier, as the instigator and leader, had been condemned to death, also in his absence. And that was all that was known of Thénardier.

As for that other man, the one who had saved Marius, the inquiries had at first produced some result but then had come to a dead end. The fiacre was found which had brought Marius to the Rue des Filles-du-Calvaire. The coachman declared that on the afternoon of 6 June, acting on the orders of a police agent, he had remained stationed on the Quai des Champs-Élysées from three o'clock until nightfall, and that about nine o'clock that evening the sewer-gate giving on to the river had opened and a man had come out carrying another man who seemed to be dead. The police agent had arrested the living man, and on his orders the cab-driver had 'taken the whole lot' to the Rue des Filles-du-Calvaire. He recognized Marius as the supposedly dead man. He had then driven the two other men to a spot near the Porte des Archives. And that was all he knew. Marius himself remembered nothing except that a strong hand had gripped him just as he was sinking unconscious to the ground at the barricade.

He was lost in conjecture. How had it happened that, having fallen in the Rue de la Chanvrerie, he had been picked up by a policeman on the bank of the Seine near the Pont des Invalides? Someone must have carried him there from the quarter of Les Halles, and how could he have done so except by way of the sewer? It was a wonderful act of devotion. This man, his saviour, was the man whom Marius sought, without discovering any trace of him. Although it had to be done with great discretion, he pursued his inquiries even as far as the Préfecture de Police, only to discover that they knew even less than the driver of the fiacre. They knew nothing of any arrest at the gate of the main sewer, and were inclined to think that the coachman had invented the story. A cabby looking for a tip is capable of anything, even of imagination. But Marius could no more doubt the truth of the story than he could doubt his own identity.

The whole thing was wrapped in mystery. What had become of this man who had rescued him and then been arrested, presumably as a rebel? And what had become of the agent who had arrested him? Why had he kept silent? And how had the man escaped? Had he bribed the agent? Why had he not got in touch with Marius, who owed him so much? No one could tell him anything. Basque and Nicolette had had no eyes for anyone except their young master. Only the porter with his candle had noticed the man, and all he could say was, 'He was a terrible sight'. In the hope that they might provide him with some clue, Marius had kept the blood-stained garments in which he had been rescued. He made a queer discovery when he examined the jacket. A small piece was missing.

One evening when Marius was talking to Cosette and Jean Valjean about the mystery and his fruitless efforts to solve it, he became irritated by 'Monsieur Fauchelevent's' air of apparent indifference. He exclaimed almost angrily.

'Whoever he was, that man was sublime. Do you realize, Monsieur, what he did? He came to my rescue like an angel from Heaven. He plunged into the battle, picked me up, opened the sewer and then carried me for a league and a half through those appalling underground passages, bent double with a man on his back! And why did he do it? Simply to save a dying man. He said to himself, "There may be a chance for him, and so I must risk my life". He risked it twenty times over, with every step he took! And the proof is that no sooner had we left the sewer than he was arrested. And he did all this without any thought of reward. What was I to him? Simply a rebel. Oh, if all Cosette's money were mine.'

'It is yours,' Jean Valjean interrupted.

'I would give it all,' said Marius, 'to find that man!'

Jean Valjean was silent.

BOOK SIX

THE SLEEPLESS NIGHT

I. *16 February 1833*

THE NIGHT of 16 February was a blessed one, with a clear sky shading into darkness. It was the night of Marius and Cosette's wedding day.

The day itself had been delightful, not perhaps Monsieur Gillenormand's vision of cherubs and cupids fluttering above the heads of the bridal pair, but gentle and gay.

Wedding customs in 1833 were not what they are today. France had not yet borrowed from England the supreme refinement of abducting the bride, carrying her off from the church as though ashamed of her happiness like an escaping bankrupt or like rape in the manner of the Song of Songs. The chastity and propriety of whisking one's paradise into a post-chaise to consummate it in a tavern-bed at so much a night, mingling the most sacred of life's memories with a hired driver and tavern serving maids, was not yet understood in France.

In this second half of the nineteenth century in which we live the mayor in his robes and the priest in his chasuble are not enough. We must have the Longjumeau postilion in his blue waistcoat with brass buttons, his green leather breeches, waxed hat, whip and top boots. France has not yet carried elegance, like the English nobility, to the point of showering the bridal pair with worn-out slippers, in memory of Marlborough, who was assailed by an angry aunt at his wedding by way of wishing him luck. These are not yet a part of our wedding celebrations—but patience, they will doubtless come.

There was a strange belief in those days that a wedding was a quiet family affair, that a patriarchal banquet in no way marred its solemnity, that even an excess of gaiety, provided it was honest, did no harm to happiness, and finally that it was right and proper that the linking of two lives from which a family was to ensue should take place in the domestic nuptial chamber. In short, people were so shameless as to get married at home.

So the wedding reception took place, in this now outmoded fashion, at the house of Monsieur Gillenormand. But there are formalities in these matters, banns to be read and so forth, and they could not be ready before the 16th. This, as it happened, was *Mardi gras*, to the perturbation of Aunt Gillenormand.

'*Mardi gras!*' exclaimed the old man. 'Well, why not? There's a proverb which says that no graceless child is ever born of a *Mardi gras* marriage. Do you want to put it off, Marius?'

'Certainly not,' said the young man.

'Very well then, the sixteenth it is.'

And so it was, regardless of public festivity. The day was a rainy one, as it happened, but there is always a patch of blue sky visible to lovers, although the rest of the world may see nothing but their umbrellas.

On the previous day Jean Valjean, in the presence of Monsieur Gillenormand, had handed Marius the 584,000 francs. The marriage deeds were very simple.

Since Valjean no longer needed Toussaint he had passed her on to Cosette, who had promoted her to the rank of lady's maid. As for Valjean himself, a handsome room in Monsieur Gillenormand's house had been expressly furnished for him, and Cosette had said so bewitchingly, 'Father, I beseech you!', that he had almost promised to live in it. But a few days before the wedding he had an accident, injuring his right thumb. It was a trifling matter, but it obliged him to wrap up his hand and keep his arm in a sling, which meant that he could not sign any documents. Monsieur Gillenormand, as deputy-guardian, had done so in his place.

We shall not take the reader to the mairie or the church ceremony, but will confine ourselves to recounting an incident, unperceived by the wedding-party, which occurred on the way from the Rue des Filles-du-Calvaire to the church of Saint Paul.

At that time the northern end of the Rue Saint-Louis was being re-paved and there was a barrier across the Rue du Parc-Royal. This made it impossible for the wedding-party to go the shortest way to the church; they had to go round by the boulevard. One of the wedding-guests remarked that, being *Mardi gras*, there would be a great deal of traffic . . . 'Why?' asked Monsieur Gillenormand . . . 'Because of the masks.' . . . 'Splendid,' said the old man. 'We'll go that way. These young folk are entering upon the serious business of life. It will do them good to start with a masquerade.'

So they went by way of the boulevard. The first carriage contained Cosette and Aunt Gillenormand, Monsieur Gillenormand and Jean Valjean; Marius, still kept separate from his bride as custom required, came in the second. Upon leaving the Rue des Filles-du-Calvaire they found themselves in a procession of vehicles stretching from the Madeleine to the Bastille and back. There were masks in abundance. Although it rained occasionally, Paillasse, Pantalon, and Gilles were not to be put off. Paris, in the happy humour of that winter of 1833, had put on the guise of Venice. We do not see a *Mardi gras* like that any more. Since everything is now an overblown carnival, carnivals no longer exist.

The side-streets, like the house windows, were thronged with spectators. Besides the masks there was the *Mardi gras* procession of vehicles, fiacres, hackney cabs, gigs, cabriolets, and others, kept so strictly in order by the police that they might have been running on rails. A person in one of those vehicles was both spectator and participant. The endless, parallel files of conveyances, going in opposite directions towards the Chaussée d'Antin and the Faubourg Saint-Antoine, were like rivers flowing up- and downstream. Important vehicles bearing the quarterings of peers of France, or belonging to ambassadors, were allowed free passage in the middle of the road. England, too, cracked her whip in that scene of Parisian gaiety. My Lord Seymour, who had been endowed with a vulgar nickname, made a great show in his postchaise. And also in the double file, escorted by gendarmes as conscientious as sheepdogs, were family barouches with grandmothers and aunts and charming clusters of children in fancy dress, six- and seven-year-old pierrots and pierrettes, very conscious of the dignity of taking part in this public ceremony.

Now and then there was a hold-up in one or other of the lines of vehicles, and they had to stop until the blockage was cleared. Then they went on again. The wedding party, heading in the direction of the Bastille, was on the right-hand side of the road. It was brought to a stop at the entrance to the Rue du Pont-aux-Choux, and the line going in the opposite direction stopped at almost the same moment. There was a carriage of masks in that line.

These carriages or, better, these cart-loads of masks are well known to the Parisians—so much so that if a *Mardi gras* or *mi-carême* were to go by without them people would say, 'There must be some reason. Probably the government's going to fall'. They are filled with clusters of Cassandras, Harlequins, and Columbines, figures of fantasy and mythology of every conceivable kind, and their tradition goes back to the early days of the monarchy. The household accounts of Louis XI include an item of 'twenty sous for three carts of masqueraders'. In these days they travel noisily in hired vans, inside and on top, twenty where there is room for six, girls seated on the men's knees, all laughing and screaming—hillocks of raucous merriment amid the crowds. But it is a gaiety too cynical to be honest. It exists simply to prove to the Parisians that this is a day of carnival.

There is a moral in those blowzy conveyances, a sort of protocol. One senses a mysterious affinity between public men and public women. How many infamous plots have been hatched beneath the semblance of gaiety, how often has prostitution served the purposes of espionage? It is sad that the crowds should be amused by what should outrage them, these manifestations of riotous vulgarity; but what is to be done? The insult to the public is exonerated by the public's laughter. The laughter of everyman is the accomplice of universal degradation. The populace, like all tyrants, must have its buffoons. Paris is the great, mad town whenever she is not the sublime city, and carnival is a part of politics. Paris, let us admit it, is very ready to be amused by what is ignoble. All she asks of her masters is—make squalor pleasant to look at. Rome was the same. She loved Nero, that monstrous exhibitionist.

As it happened, one of these bevies of masked men and women, in a big wagon, stopped on the left-hand side of the street at the moment when the wedding party stopped on the right.

'Hallo,' said one of the masks. 'A wedding.'

'A sham one,' said another. 'We're the real celebration.'

Too far off to converse with the wedding party, and in any case afraid of getting into trouble with the police, the two masks looked elsewhere. A moment later they and their companions had plenty to occupy them. The crowd began to howl and shower insults on them, and not all the extensive vocabulary they had picked up in the market-place could drown that lusty voice. There was a lurid exchange of abuse. Meanwhile two other members of the same company, one a Spaniard with an exaggerated nose and enormous black moustache, and the other a skinny young girl in a wolf-mask, had noticed the wedding party and were talking together amid the hubbub. It was a cold day, and the open cart was soaked with rain. The girl in her low-necked dress coughed and shivered as she spoke. Their dialogue was as follows, the man speaking first:

'Hey!'

'Well?'

'See that old man?'

'Which?'

'The one in the first wedding coach, on our side.'

'The one with his arm in a sling?'

'That's him.'

'Well?'

'I'm sure I know him.'

'You do?'

'I'll take my oath on it. Can you see the bride if you stretch?'

'No.'

'Or the groom?'

'There isn't one, not in that carriage, unless it's the old man.'

'Try to see the bride. Crane your neck a bit more.'

'I still can't.'

'Well, never mind. There's something about that chap—I'll swear I've seen him somewhere.'

'And so what?'

'I dunno. Sometimes it comes in handy.'

'A fat lot I care.'

'I'll swear I know him.'

'Anything you say.'

'What the devil's he doing at a wedding?'

'Search me.'

'And where do that lot come from?'

'How do I know?'

'Well, look—there's something you can do.'

'What's that?'

'Get off the cart and follow them.'

'What for?'

'To find out who they are and where they're going. Hurry up, my girl. You're young.'

'I don't want to.'

'Why not?'

'I'm watched. I owe my day off to the cops. If I get off the cart they'll pick me up next instant. You know they will.'

'That's true. It's a nuisance. I'm interested in that fellow.'

'Anyone 'ud think you were a girl.'

'He's in the first carriage, the bride's carriage.'

'So?'

'That means he's the father.'

'There's other fathers.'

'Now listen—I can scarcely go anywhere unless I'm masked. That's all right for today, but there won't be any masks tomorrow. I'll have to keep under cover or I'm liable to be picked up. But you're free.'

'Not all that much.'

'More than I am, anyway. So you've got to try and find out where that wedding party was going, and who the people are and where they live.'

'Sounds easy, doesn't it? A wedding party going somewhere or other on *Mardi gras*. Like looking for a needle in a haystack!'

'All the same, you've got to try, Azelma, do you hear?'

Then the two lines resumed their progress in opposite directions, and the wagon of masks lost sight of the wedding party.

II. *Jean Valjean still has his Arm in a Sling*

To how many of us is it given to realize our dream? Perhaps the matter is decided by elections in Heaven, with the angels voting and all of us candidates. Cosette and Marius had been elected. Cosette at the church and the mairie was glowingly and dazzlingly pretty. She had been dressed by Toussaint, with the help of Nicolette, in a dress of Binche lace with a white taffeta under-skirt, a veil of English stitching, a necklace of small pearls, and a crown of orange blossom, and she was dazzling in this whiteness, she might have been a virgin in process of being transformed into a goddess.

Marius's beautiful hair was lustrous and scented, but here and there beneath its thick locks the scars left by the wounds he had received on the barricade were still to be discerned.

Monsieur Gillenormand, proudly erect, his costume and his manners more than ever depicting the elegance of the days of Barras, escorted Cosette, replacing Jean Valjean, who could not give her his arm since he still wore it in a sling. Clad in black, he followed them smiling.

'Monsieur Fauchelevent,' the old man said to him, 'this is a great day. I decree happiness, the end of all grief and affliction. Nothing bad may be allowed to show itself. That in fact there are unhappy people is a disgrace to the blue of the sky. Evil does not come to the man who is good at heart. All human miseries have their capital and seat of government in Hell itself—in other words, those infernal Tuileries. But I'm not going to make a speech. I no longer have political opinions. All I want is for everyone to be rich and happy.'

When at length all the ceremonies were completed, at the mairie and at the church, when all the documents were signed, rings exchanged, and, hand in hand, he in black and she in white, the wedded couple emerged through the church doors between rows of admiring spectators to return to the carriage, Cosette could scarcely believe that it was all true. She looked at Marius, at the people, and at the sky, half afraid of waking out of a dream, and this look of doubtful amazement lent her an added charm. They returned home with Marius and Cosette seated side by side, while Monsieur Gillenormand and Jean Valjean sat facing them, Aunt Gillenormand being relegated to the second carriage. 'My children,' said the old gentleman, 'you are now a baron and baroness with thirty thousand francs a year'. And Cosette, leaning towards Marius, whispered angelically: 'It's true. My name is now the same as yours. I'm Madame You.'

Both were radiant in that supreme and unrepeatable moment, the union of youth and happiness. Between them they were less than forty years of age. It was the sublimation of marriage, and the two

young creatures were like lilies. Cosette saw Marius in a haze of glory, and Marius saw Cosette as though on an altar; and somehow, behind these two visions, a mist for Cosette, a flame for Marius, there was the ideal and the real, the place of kisses and dreams, the marriage-bed.

All the tribulations they had gone through, the griefs, despairs and sleepless nights, all these added to the enchantment of the hour that was approaching, past sorrow was an embellishment of rapture, unhappiness an added glow to present delight. They were two hearts caught in the same spell, tinged with carnality in the case of Marius, of modest apprehension in the case of Cosette. 'We shall see our garden in the Rue Plumet again,' she whispered, while the fold of her dress flowed over his knee.

They returned to their house in the Rue des Filles-du-Calvaire, and triumphantly mounted the stairs up which Marius's unconscious form has been carried, months before. The poor, gathered at the doorway, received alms and blessed them. There were flowers everywhere, as many as there had been in the church; after the incense came the roses. They seemed to hear voices singing and felt Heaven in their hearts. And suddenly the clock struck. Marius gazed at Cosette's sweet bare arms and at the pink objects vaguely to be perceived beneath the lace of her corsage, and Cosette, seeing his eyes upon her, blushed a deep red.

Many old friends of the Gillenormand family had been invited, and they made much of Cosette, addressing her as Madame la Baronne. Théodule Gillenormand, now promoted captain, had come from Chartres, where he was stationed, to attend his cousin Pont-mercy's wedding. Cosette did not recognize him; nor did he, the man of many light loves, recognize her. 'How right I was to take no notice of that tale of a cavalry officer,' old Monsieur Gillenormand murmured to himself. He pointed the joy of the occasion with a flow of maxims and aphorisms, in which Cosette supported him, spreading love and kindness as though it were a perfume around her. She talked with a particular tenderness to Jean Valjean, using inflections that recalled the innocent chatter of her childhood.

A banquet had been spread in the dining-room. Bright light is essential to great occasions. Dimness is unthinkable. It may be night outside, but there must be no shadows within. The dining-room was a scene of utmost gaiety. Hanging over the centre of the richly adorned table was a great Venetian chandelier with little birds of every colour perched among its candles. There were triple mirrors on the walls, and glass and crystal, porcelain, gold and silver shone and glittered. Gaps between the candelabra were filled with bouquets, so that wherever there was a candle there was a flower. In the antechamber three violins and a flute were softly playing Haydn quartets.

Jean Valjean was seated in a corner of the room by the open door, which almost hid him from sight. Just before they took their places at the table Cosette came over to him, and making a slow curtsey asked with a half-teasing tenderness:

'Dear Father, are you happy?'

'Yes,' he said. 'I'm happy.'

'Then why aren't you smiling?'

Valjean obediently smiled, and a moment later Basque announced that dinner was served.

The company proceeded into the dining-room led by Monsieur Gillenormand with Cosette on his arm and seated themselves in their pre-arranged places. There were armchairs on either side of the bride, one for the old gentleman and the other for Jean Valjean. But when they looked round for 'Monsieur Fauchelevent' they found that he was not there. Monsieur Gillenormand asked Basque if he knew what had become of him.

'Monsieur Fauchelevent requested me to say, monsieur, that his hand was paining him,' said Basque. 'He has therefore asked to be excused. He has gone out, but will be back tomorrow morning.'

This cast something of a chill upon the gathering, but fortunately Monsieur Gillenormand had high spirits enough for two. He said that Monsieur Fauchelevent had been quite right to go to bed early if he was in pain, slight though the injury was. This put everyone at their ease. Besides, what difference could a small patch of shadow make in such a wealth of light? Cosette and Marius were in one of those moments of bliss when they could be aware of nothing but happiness. And Monsieur Gillenormand had an idea.

'Since Monsieur Fauchelevent will not be with us,' he said, 'Marius shall occupy his chair. It should by rights go to his aunt, but I know she will not begrudge it him. Come and sit beside Cosette, Marius.'

Marius did as he was bidden, to the general applause; and so it fell out that Cosette, who had been momentarily distressed by Jean Valjean's absence, was made happy. She would not have regretted the absence of God himself, had Marius been there to take his place; and she laid her small, satin-clad foot upon his.

With the dessert Monsieur rose to his feet holding a glass of champagne (half-filled to allow for the shakiness of his ninety-two-year-old hand) and proposed the health of the young couple.

'You are obliged to listen to two sermons,' he said. 'The curé this morning and this evening the old grandfather. I will give you a piece of advice—adore one another. Be happy. There are no wiser creatures in all creation than the turtle-doves. The philosophers say, "Be moderate in your pleasures," but I say, enjoy them to the full. Go mad with pleasure and let the philosophers stuff their dull counsels down their throats. Can there be too much perfume in the world, too many rosebuds or green leaves or singing nightingales or breathless dawns? Can two people charm and delight one another too much, be too happy, too much alive? Moderate your pleasures—what nonsense it is! Down with the philosophers! Rapture is the true wisdom. Are we happy because we are good, or good because we are happy? I don't know. Life is made up of such riddles. What matters is to be happy without pretence; to be a blind worshipper of the sun. For what is the sun if not love, and what is love if not a woman! It is woman who is all-powerful. Is not Marius, that young demagogue, enslaved by the tyranny of that little Cosette? And gladly so! Woman! You may talk of Robespierre, but it is the woman who rules. That is the only kind of royalty I recognize. What was Adam except Eve's kingdom? What revolution did she need? Think of all the sceptres there have been—the royal sceptre surmounted by a *fleur de lys*, the imperial sceptre surmounted by a globe, Charlemagne's sceptre which was of iron, and that of Louis le Grand which was gold—and the Revolution took them between thumb and forefingers and squashed them flat! So much for sceptres; but show me a revolution against a little scented handkerchief—I should like to see that! What makes it so powerful when it is nothing but a scrap of material? Ah, well, we who belonged to the eighteenth century were just as foolish as you are. You needn't think you have changed the world just because you have discovered a cure for cholera and invented a dance called the cachucha. We still have to love women and there's no getting away from it. Love, women and kisses are a magic circle from which I defy you to escape, and for my part I wish I could get back into it. How many of you have seen the rising of the planet Venus, that great courtesan of the skies? A man can be in a fury, but when she appears he has to smile. We are all the same, we have our rages, but when a woman appears on the scene we're on our knees. Six months ago Marius was fighting, and today he has got married. It is well done, and he and Cosette are both right. You must live boldly each for the other, cling and caress, frantic only because you cannot do more. To love and be loved, that is the miracle of youth. Don't think I'm just inventing it. I too have had my dreams and sighs; I too have moonlight in my soul. Love is a child six thousand years old who should be wearing a long white beard. Compared with Cupid, Methuselah is the merest urchin. For sixty centuries men and women have settled their affairs by loving one another. The devil, who is cunning, elected to hate man; but man, more cunning still, chose to love woman, and in this way did more good than all the harm done by the devil. My children, love is an old invention but it is one that is always new. Make the most of it. You must be so close that when you are together you lack nothing, Cosette the sun for Marius and Marius the whole world for Cosette. Fine weather, for Cosette, must be her husband's smiles, and for Marius the rain should be his wife's tears. You have drawn the winning number in the lottery and you must treasure it. Each must be a religion to the other. We all have our own way of worshipping God, but the best of all, Heaven knows, is to love one's wife. Every lover is orthodox. The oath sworn by Henri IV puts sanctity somewhere between riot and drunkenness. I've no use for that oath, which makes no mention of women. They tell me I'm old, but it's wonderful how young I feel. I should like to hear the piping in the woods. Young folk who continue to be both beautiful and happy, these delight me. I would gladly marry again if anyone would have me. It is impossible to suppose that God made us for any other purpose than to enact all the fantasies and delights of love. That is what we believed when I was young, and how enchanting, how tender and gracious, the women were! I made my conquests! And so I say to you, love one another. If it weren't for love-making I don't know what use the spring would be, and for my part I would ask God to take away all the lovely things he has made for us—flowers and birds and pretty girls. My dear children, accept an old man's blessing!'

It was a gay, delightful evening, the tone being set by their host, who was so nearly a hundred years old. There was a little dancing and a great deal of laughter and happy commotion. But suddenly a silence fell. The newly married pair had disappeared. Shortly after midnight Monsieur Gillenormand's house became a temple.

And here we must pause. At the door of every bridal bedchamber an angel stands, smiling, with a finger to his lips.

There should be a radiance about houses such as this, the rapture they contain should somehow escape through their stones. Love is the sublime melting-pot in which man and woman are fused together, and this melting of two souls into one must stir the outer darkness. The lover is a priest, the ravished virgin a consenting, trembling sacrifice. If it were given to us to peer into a higher world, should we not see beneficent forms clustered over that glowing house; and would not the lovers, thinking themselves alone in their ecstasies, hear the flutter of wings? That small and secret bedchamber is wide open to Heaven. When two mouths, consecrated by love, draw close together in the act of creation it is impossible that this ineffable kiss does not cause a tremor among the stars.

This is the true felicity and there is no joy outside the ecstasy of love. The rest is tears. To love or to have loved is all-sufficing. We must not ask for more. No other pearl is to be found in the shadowed folds of life. To love is an accomplishment.

III. *Inseparable*

What had become of Jean Valjean?

After he had smiled at Cosette's gentle request, he had risen unnoticed and gone into the room next door, the same room into which, ragged and caked with mud, he had eight months earlier carried Monsieur Gillenormand's grandson. Its ancient woodwork was now decked with flowers, and the musicians were seated on the settee on which Marius had been laid. Basque was there, clad in black knee-breeches, white stockings, and white gloves, placing small bouquets on the dinner-plates. Valjean told him the reason for his departure and left.

The dining-room windows looked out on to the street, and Jean Valjean stood beneath them for a few moments listening to the sounds of the party behind him, the predominating voice of Monsieur Gillenormand, the violins, the laughter, the rattle of crockery and, distinguishable amid it all, the gentle happy voice of Cosette. Then he left the Rue des Filles-du-Calvaire and returned to the Rue de l'Homme-Armé.

He went by way of the Rue Saint-Louis and the Blancs-Manteaux, which was rather longer but the route he was accustomed to follow, when walking between the two houses, to avoid the crowds and muddiness of the Rue Vieille-du-Temple. It was the way he had always come with Cosette, so he could take no other.

He arrived home, lit his candle, and went upstairs. The apartment was empty. Toussaint was not there and the sound of his footsteps was louder than usual. All the cupboards were empty and Cosette's bed was unmade, the pillow, without its lacy pillowslip, lying on a pile of folded blankets. All the feminine knick-knacks that had been Cosette's had been taken away, nothing remained in the room but its heavy furniture and bare walls. Toussaint's bed was also stripped. The only one that could be slept in was his own. He wandered from one room to another, shutting the cupboard doors. Then he went back to his own bedroom and put his candle on the table. He had taken his arm out of its sling and was using it as though it caused him no discomfort.

He went towards his bed, and as he did so his eye rested—was it by chance or was it intentional?—on the little black box that

Cosette had called his 'inseparable'. When they had moved into the Rue de l'Homme-Armé he had placed it on a foot-stool beside his bed. He now got a key out of his pocket and opened it.

Slowly he took out the clothes in which Cosette had left Montfermeil, ten years before. First the little black dress, then the black scarf, then the stout child's shoes which Cosette could still have worn, so small were her feet, then the thick fustian camisole, the woollen petticoat, and, still bearing the impress of a small leg, two stockings scarcely longer than his hand. Everything was black, and it was he who had brought them when he took her from Montfermeil. He laid the garments on the bed, recalling that occasion. It had been a very cold December, and she had been shivering in rags, her small feet red from the clogs she wore. Her mother in her grave must have been happy to know that her daughter was in mourning, and that she was decently and warmly clad. He thought of those Montfermeil woods, through which they had walked together, the leafless trees, the absence of birds, the sunless sky; but still it had been delightful. He spread the garments on the bed and stood looking at them. She had been so little, carrying that big doll and with her golden louis in her apron pocket. She had laughed as they walked hand-in-hand, and he had become all the world to her.

Then the ageing white head sank forward, the stoical heart gave way and his face was buried in Cosette's garments. Anyone passing on the stairs at that moment would have heard the sound of dreadful sobbing.

IV. *Undying Faith*

The fearful struggle, of which we have recorded more than one phase, had begun again. Jacob's battle with the angel lasted only one night; but how often had Jean Valjean been darkly joined in mortal conflict with his own conscience! A desperate struggle: his foot slipping at moments and, at others, the ground seeming to give way beneath his feet. How stubbornly his conscience had fought against him! How often had inexorable truth borne down like a great weight on his breast. How often, in that implacable light, had he begged for mercy—the light that the bishop had lit for him. How often had his rebellious spirit groaned beneath the knowledge of his plain duty. Opposition to God himself: self-inflicted wounds of whose bleeding he alone was conscious. Until finally, shaken, he had risen from despair above himself to say, 'Now it is settled. I may go in peace'. A melancholy peace!

But this night Valjean knew that the struggle had reached its climax. An agonizing question presented itself. Predestination does not always offer a straight road to the predestined; there are many twists and turns, forks and crossroads. Valjean had come to the most perilous of these. He had reached the ultimate intersection between good and evil and he saw it clearly. As had happened before, at critical moments of his life, two roads lay open to him, one seductive and the other terrifying. Which was he to take?

The road that appalled him was the one indicated by that mysterious finger that we always see when we try to peer into the darkness. Once more he was faced by the choice between the terrible haven and the alluring trap.

Is it true then, that though the soul may be cured, destiny may not? Incurable destiny—how terrible a thing!

The question was this: how was he, Jean Valjean, to ensure the continued happiness of Cosette and Marius? It was he who had brought about that happiness, he who had forged it, and he could contemplate it with something of the satisfaction of the armourer who has worked well. They had each other, Marius and Cosette, and they were wealthy into the bargain; and all this was his doing.

But what was he now to do with it, this happiness that he had brought about? Should he take advantage of it, treat it as though it belonged to him? Cosette was another man's, but he still retained as much of her as he could ever possess. Could he not continue to be almost her father, respected as he had always been, able when he chose to enter her house? And could he, without saying a word, bring his past into that future, seat himself by that fireside as though it were his right? Could he greet them smiling with his tragic hands, and cross that innocent threshold casting behind him the infamous shadow of the law? Could he still keep silent?

One must have grown accustomed to the harsher face of destiny to be able to confront facts in all their hideous nakedness. Good and evil are behind the vigorous question-mark: 'Well,' demands the sphinx, 'what are you going to do?' Valjean, from long habit, looked it steadily in the eye. Pitilessly he considered the facts in all their aspects. Cosette, that exquisite creature, was his lifeline. Was he to cling to it or let it go? If he clung to it, then he was safe; he could go on living. But if he let it go . . . Then, the abyss.

Thus did he wrestle with himself, torn between conviction and desire. It was a relief to him that he had been able to weep. This may have calmed him, although the beginning had been fearful, a tempest fiercer than the one that had once driven him to Arras. But now he was brought to a stop. It is terrible, in the battle *à outrance* between self-will and duty, when we seek in vain for a way out, to find ourselves caught with our back to the wall. But there is no end to conscience, for this is God himself. It is a bottomless well into which one may fling the labour of a lifetime, liberty and country, peace of mind and happiness; but in the end one has to fling in one's heart. In the shades of the ancient hells there are pits like that.

Is it not permissible in the end to refuse? Cannot an endless bond be too much for human strength? Who would blame Sisyphus or Jean Valjean if at the last they said, 'That is enough.' The movement of matter is delimited by the forces to which it is subjected; may there not be a similar limitation on the movement of the soul? If perpetual motion is impossible, must we then insist upon perpetual devotion? The first step is nothing; it is the last which is difficult. Compared with Cosette's marriage and all that would ensue from it, what was the Champmathieu affair? What was the return to prison compared with entry into limbo? The first step downward may be obscured, but the second is pitch black. Why not this time look the other way?

Martyrdom is a sublimation, but a sublimation that corrodes. It is a torment that sanctifies. One may endure it at first, the pincers, the red-hot iron, but must not the tortured flesh give way in the end?

In the calm of exhaustion, Jean Valjean considered the two alternatives, the balance between light and dark. Was he to inflict his prison record on those two happy children, or accept the loss of his own soul? Was Cosette to be sacrificed, or himself?

His meditation lasted through the night. He remained until day-light in the same posture, seated and bent double on the bed, with fists clenched and arms out-flung like those of a man cut down from the cross. He was motionless as a corpse, while the thoughts flew and tumbled in his mind. Until suddenly he shuddered convulsively and pressed Cosette's garments to his lips. Only then did one see that he was alive.

One. Who was that one, when there was no one else there?

The One who is present in the shadows.

BOOK SEVEN

THE BITTER CUP

I. *The Seventh Circle and the Eighth Heaven*

THE DAY after a wedding is one of solitude. We respect the privacy of the newly-weds and perhaps their late arising. The hubbub of visits and congratulations does not begin until later. It was a little after midday when Basque, busily 'doing the antechamber', heard a tap on the door. There had been no ring, which showed discretion on that particular day. Basque opened and found Monsieur Fauchelevent. He showed him into the salon, which was still in a state of disorder.

'We're up late this morning, Monsieur,' said Basque.

'Is your master up?' asked Jean Valjean.

'How's monsieur's arm?' asked Basque.

'It's better. Is your master up?'

'Which master, the old or the new?'

'Monsieur Pontmercy.'

'Ah, Monsieur le Baron,' said Basque.

Titles are important to servants, upon whom something of their lustre is shed. Marius, as we know, was a militant republican and had fought to prove it; but despite himself he was a baron. The matter had caused something of a revolution in the family. It was now Monsieur Gillenormand who insisted upon the title and Marius who was disposed to ignore it; but since his father had written, 'My son will bear my title,' he obeyed. And then Cosette, in whom the woman was beginning to show, was delighted to be Madame la Baronne.

'I'll go and see,' said Basque. 'I'll tell him you're here.'

'No. Don't tell him that it's me. Tell him it is someone who wishes to speak to him in private, but don't mention my name.'

'Ah,' said Basque.

'I want to surprise him.'

'Ah,' said Basque again, as though this second 'ah' explained the first.

He went out, leaving Valjean alone.

The salon, as we have said, was in great disorder, almost as though anyone who happened to be listening could still have heard the echoes of last night's party. Flowers had fallen on the parquet floor, and burnt-out candles had draped the crystal lustre with stalactites of wax. Nothing was in its proper place. Three or four armchairs, grouped together in a corner, seemed to be still carrying on a conversation. But it was a gay disorder, for this had been a happy party. The sun had replaced the candles and shone bravely into the room.

Some minutes elapsed during which Jean Valjean remained motionless where Basque had left him. He was very pale. His eyes were so sunken with sleeplessness that they had almost disappeared, and his black coat had the tired creases of a garment that has been worn all night. He stood looking down at the glow of light cast by the sunshine on the floor.

The sound of the door opening caused him to look up. Marius entered, head up and face aglow with triumphant happiness. He, too, had not slept all night.

'Why, it's you, father!' he exclaimed. 'That silly fellow Basque chose to make a mystery of it. But you're early. It's only half-past twelve and Cosette is still asleep.'

His use of the word 'father' was most felicitous. As we know, there had always been a certain constraint between them, ice to be broken or melted. Such was Marius's state of rapture that this no longer existed: 'Monsieur Fauchelevent' was father to him as he was to Cosette. He went on, the words pouring out of him:

'I'm so delighted to see you. We missed you so much last night. Is your hand better?' He did not wait for a reply. 'We've talked so much about you, Cosette and I. She's so fond of you. You haven't forgotten, I hope, that you have a room here. We don't want any more of the Rue de l'Homme-Armé. That ugly, squalid little street— how in the world did you ever come to live in it? But now you're coming here, and today, what's more, or you'll be in trouble with Cosette. I warn you, she means to have you here if she has to pull you by the nose! You've seen your room, it's very near our own, and it looks out over the garden. It's all in perfect order. Cosette put a big old velvet-upholstered armchair by the bedside, to open its arms to you, as she said. Every spring a nightingale nests in the acacias, you'll be hearing it in a couple of months. You'll have its nest on one side of you and ours on the other. It will sing in the nighttime and Cosette will chatter in the daytime. She'll arrange your books for you and all your belongings. I understand there's a little valise that you particularly value, and I've thought of a special place for it. My grandfather has taken a great liking to you, and if you play whist that will make it perfect. And of course you'll take

Cosette for walks when I'm working, just as you used to do, in the Luxembourg. We're absolutely determined to be very happy, and you're part of it, father, do you understand? Talking of which, you'll be lunching with us today?'

'Monsieur,' said Jean Valjean, 'I have something to tell you. I am an ex-convict.'

There are sounds that the mind cannot absorb although they are registered by the ear. Those words 'I am an ex-convict', emerging from the lips of Monsieur Fauchelevent and entering the ear of Marius, went beyond the limit. He knew that something had been said, but he could not grasp what it was. He stood open-mouthed.

And now he perceived what in his blissful state he had not noticed, that the man addressing him was in very bad shape. He was terribly pale.

Valjean took his arm out of the sling which still supported it, removed the bandage, and held his hand out to Marius.

'There's nothing wrong with my thumb,' he said. 'There never has been.' He went on: 'It was right that I should not attend your wedding-party. I have kept in the background as much as possible, I invented this injury in order to avoid signing the marriage deeds, which might have nullified them.'

Marius stammered: 'But what does it mean?'

'It means,' said Valjean, 'that I have been in the galleys. I was imprisoned for nineteen years, first for theft and later as a recidivist. I am at present breaking parole.'

Marius might recoil in horror, might refuse to believe, but in the end he was forced to accept it. Indeed, as commonly happens, he went further. He shuddered as an appalling thought occurred to him.

'You must tell me everything—everything!' he cried. 'You are really Cosette's father!' And in horror he took a step backwards.

Jean Valjean raised his head with a gesture of such dignity that he seemed to grow in stature.

'In this you must believe me,' he said, 'although the sworn oaths of such as I are not accepted in any court of law. I swear to you before God, Monsieur Pontmercy, that I am not Cosette's father or in any way related to her. My name is not Fauchelevent but Jean Valjean. I am a peasant from Faverolles, where once I earned my living as a tree-pruner. You may be sure of that.'

'But what proof—?' stammered Marius.

'My word is the proof.'

Marius looked at him. He was melancholy but calm, with a kind of stony sincerity from which no lie could emerge. The truth was apparent in his very coldness.

'I believe you,' said Marius.

Jean Valjean bowed his head in acknowledgement.

'So what am I to Cosette?' he went on. 'Someone who came upon her quite by chance. Ten years ago I did not know that she existed. I love her certainly, as who would not? When one is growing old one has a fatherly feeling for all small children. You may perhaps be prepared to believe that I have something that can be called a heart. She was an orphan and she needed me. That is how I came to love her. Children are so defenceless that any man, even a man like me, may want to protect them. That is what I did for Cosette. Whether an act so trifling can be termed a good deed I do not know; but if it is, then let it be said that I did it. Let it be set down in extenuation. Now she has gone out of my life; our roads run in different directions. Besides, there is nothing more that I can do for her. She is Madame Pontmercy. Her life has changed, and she has gained by the change. As for the six hundred thousand francs, I will anticipate your question. It was a sum held for her in trust. As to how it came into my hands, that is quite unimportant. I have fulfilled my trust, and nothing more can be required of me. And I have concluded the matter by telling you my name. I have done so for my own sake, because I wanted you to know who I am.'

Jean Valjean looked steadily at Marius.

As for Marius, his thoughts were tumultuous and incoherent. We all have moments of bewilderment in which our wits seem to desert us; we say the first thing that comes into our head, although it is not the right thing. There are sudden revelations that cannot be endured, inducing a state of intoxication like that caused by a draught of some insidious wine. Marius was so stupefied that he talked almost as though Valjean had done him a deliberate injury.

'Why have you told me all this? Nobody forced you to. You could have kept it to yourself. You aren't being pursued, are you? No one has denounced you. You must have some reason of your own for blurting it out like this. Why have you done so? There must be more—something that you haven't told me. I want to know what it is.'

'My reason . . .' said Jean Valjean, in a voice so low that he might have been talking to himself. 'Why should an ex-convict proclaim himself to be an ex-convict? Well, it's a strange reason— a matter of honesty. There is a bond in my heart that cannot be broken, and such bonds become stronger as one grows older. Whatever may happen in one's life, they still hold. If I could have broken that bond, dishonoured it, all would have been well. I could simply have gone away. Coaches leave from the Rue Bouloi and you are happy, there was nothing to keep me. I tried to tear out that bond, but I could not do it without tearing out my heart as well.

I thought to myself, since I cannot live anywhere else, I must stay here. You will think me a fool, and rightly. Why not just stay and say nothing? You have offered me a home. Cosette—but I should now call her Madame Pontmercy—loves me. Your grandfather would welcome me. We could live together as a happy, united family.'

But as he spoke that last word Jean Valjean's expression changed. He stood scowling at the floor as though he would like to kick a hole in it, and there was a new ring in his voice.

'A family! But I belong to no family, least of all yours. I am sundered from all mankind. There are moments when I wonder whether I ever had a father and mother. Everything ended for me with that child's marriage. She is happy with the man she loves, a worthy old man to watch over her, a comfortable home, servants, everything that makes for happiness; but I said to myself, "That is not for me." I might have lied and deceived you all by continuing to be "Monsieur Fauchelevent". I did it where she was concerned; but now it is a matter of my own conscience and I can do it no longer. That is my answer to you when you ask me why I have felt compelled to speak. Conscience is a strange thing. It would have been so easy to say nothing. I spent the whole night trying to persuade myself to do so. I did my utmost. I gave myself excellent reasons. But it was no use. I could not break that bond in my heart or silence the voice that speaks to me when I am alone. That is why I have come here to confess everything to you, or nearly everything. There is no point in telling you things that only concern myself. I have told you what matters, disclosed my secret to you, and, believe me, it was not easy to do. I had to wrestle with myself all night. You may believe me when I say that in concealing my real name I was harming no one. It was Fauchelevent himself who gave it me, in return for a service I had done him. I could have been very happy in the home you have offered me, keeping to my own corner, disturbing no one, content to be under the same roof as Cosette. To continue to be Monsieur Fauchelevent would have settled everything—except my conscience. No matter how great the happiness around me, my soul would have been in darkness. The circumstances of happiness are not enough, there must also be peace of mind. I should have been a figure of deceit, a shadow in your sunshine, sitting at your table with the thought that if you knew who and what I really was you would turn me out—the very servants would have exclaimed in horror! When we were alone together, your grandfather, you two children and myself, talking unconstrainedly, all seeming at our ease, one of us would have been a stranger, a dead man battening on the living; and condemned to this for the rest of his life! Does it not make you shudder? I should have been not only the most desolate of men but the most infamous, living the same lie day after day. Cheating you day after day, my beloved, trusting children! It is not so easy to keep silent when the silence is a lie. I should never have ceased to be sickened by my own treachery and cowardice. My "good-morning" would have been a lie, and my "good-night". I should have slept with the lie, eaten with it, returned Cosette's angelic smile with a grimace of the damned. And all for what? To be happy! But what right have I to happiness? I tell you, monsieur, I am an outcast from life.'

Jean Valjean paused. Marius had been listening without attempting to interrupt, for there are times when interruption is impossible. Valjean again lowered his voice, but now it contained a harsh note.

'You may ask why I should tell you this, if I have not been exposed and am not in any danger of pursuit. But I *have* been exposed, I *am* pursued—by myself! That is a pursuer that does not readily let go.' He gripped his coat collar and thrust it out towards Marius. 'Look at that fist,' he said. 'Don't you think it has a firm grip on that collar? That is what conscience is like. If you want to be happy you must have no sense of duty, because a sense of duty is implacable. To have it is to be punished, but it is also to be rewarded, for it thrusts you into a hell in which you feel the presence of God at your side. Your heart may be broken, but you are at peace with yourself.'

Then again his voice changed, containing a note of poignancy.

'This is not a matter of commonsense, Monsieur Pontmercy. I am an honourable man. In debasing myself in your eyes I am raising myself in my own. Yes, an honourable man; but I should not be one if, through my fault, you continued to esteem me. That is the cross I bear, that any esteem I may win is falsely won; it is a thought that humiliates and shames me, that I can only win the respect of others at the cost of despising myself. So I have to take a stand. I am a felon acting according to his conscience. It may be a contradiction in terms, but what else can I do? I made a pact with myself and I am holding to it. There are chances that create duties. So many things, Monsieur Pontmercy, have happened to me in my life.'

Once again Jean Valjean paused. Then he resumed talking with an effort, as though the words left a bitter taste in his mouth.

'When a man is under a shadow of this kind he has no more right to inflict it upon others without their knowledge than he has to infect them with the plague. To draw near to the healthy, to touch them with hands that are secretly contagious, that is a shameful thing. Fauchelevent may have lent me his name, but I have no right to use it. A name is an identity. Although I was born a peasant, monsieur, I have done a little reading and thinking in my time; I have learnt the value of things. As you see, I can express myself fluently. I have oned something to educate myself. To make use of a borrowed name is an act of dishonesty, as much a theft as to steal a purse or a watch. I cannot cheat decent people in that way— never, never, never! Better to suffer the tortures of the damned! And that is why I have told you all this'. He sighed and added a last word: 'Once I stole a loaf of bread to stay alive; but now I cannot steal a name in order to go on living.'

'Go on living!' cried Marius. 'Surely you don't need the name simply for that.'

'I know what it means to me,' said Valjean and nodded his head several times.

For a time there was silence. Both men were occupied with their own thoughts. Marius was seated by a table with his chin resting on his hand. Valjean had been pacing up and down. He stopped in front of a mirror and stood motionless, staring into it but seeing nothing. Then, as though replying to some observation of his own, he said:

'For the present, at least, I have a sense of relief.'

He began once more to pace the room. Then, seeing Marius's eyes upon him, he said:

'I drag my leg a little as I walk. Now you know why . . . I ask you to consider this, monsieur. Let us suppose that I had said nothing but had come to live with you as Monsieur Fauchelevent, to share your daily lives, to walk with Madame Pontmercy in the Tuileries and the Place Royale, to be accepted as one of yourselves and then one day, when we are talking and laughing together, a voice cries "Jean Valjean!" and the terrible hand of the police descends on my shoulder and strips the mask away! . . . What do you think of that?'

Marius had nothing to say.

'Now you know why I could not keep silent. But no matter. Be happy, be Cosette's guardian angel, live in the sun and do not worry about how an outcast goes about his duty. You are facing a wretched man, monsieur.'

Marius walked slowly across the room, holding out his hand. But he had to reach for Valjean's hand, which made no response, and it was like grasping a hand of marble.

'My grandfather has friends,' he said. 'I will get you a reprieve.'

'There is no need,' said Valjean. 'The fact that I am presumed dead is enough.' Releasing his hand from Marius's clasp he added, with an implacable dignity: 'All that matters is that I should do my duty. The only reprieve I need is that of my own conscience.'

At this moment the door at the other end of the salon was half-opened and Cosette's head peeped round it. Her hair was charmingly disordered and her eyes still heavy with sleep. With a movement like that of a bird peeping out of its nest she looked first at her husband and then at Jean Valjean, and exclaimed laughingly,

'I'm sure you've been talking politics. How absurd of you, when you might have been talking to me!'

Valjean started. Marius stammered, 'Cosette . . .' and then was silent. They might have been two guilty men.

Cosette continued to gaze at them, her eyes shining.

'I've caught you out,' she said. 'I heard a few words that father Fauchelevent spoke just as I opened the door. Something about conscience and duty. Well, that's politics and I won't have it. Nobody's allowed to talk politics the day after a wedding.'

'You're mistaken,' said Marius. 'We were talking business. We were discussing how to invest your six hundred thousand francs.'

'Is that all?' said Cosette. 'Then I'm going to join you.' And she walked determinedly into the room.

She was wearing a voluminous white peignoir with wide sleeves which covered her from neck to toes. She looked herself over in a long mirror and then exclaimed in sheer delight.

'Once upon a time there was a king and queen . . . Oh, I'm so happy!' After which she curtseyed to Marius and Valjean. 'And now I'm going to sit down with you. Luncheon is in half an hour. You can talk about anything you like and I won't interrupt. I'm a very good girl. I know men have to talk.'

Marius took her by the arm and said affectionately:

'We were talking business.'

'By the way,' said Cosette, 'when I opened my window I saw a flock of starlings in the garden—real ones, not masks. This is Ash Wednesday, but the birds can't be expected to know that.'

'I said we were talking business, dearest. Figures and that sort of thing. It would only bore you.'

'What a nice necktie you're wearing, Marius. You're looking very smart. No, it wouldn't bore me.'

'I'm sure it would.'

'No. I shan't understand, but I shall enjoy listening. When it's two people you love the words don't matter, the sound of their voices is enough. I just want to be with you, and so I'm going to stay.'

'My beloved Cosette, it's really impossible.'

'Impossible!'

'Yes.'

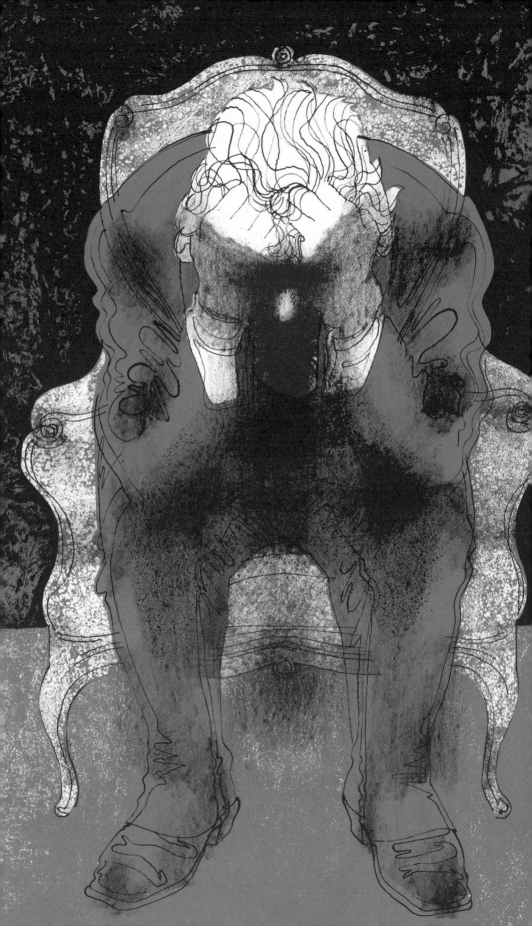

'Well,' said Cosette. 'And I was going to tell you such interesting things. For instance, that grandfather is still asleep and Aunt Gillenormand has gone to Mass, and father Fauchelevent's chimney is smoking and Nicolette has sent for the sweep, and she and Toussaint have quarrelled already because she teased Toussaint about her stammer. You see, you don't know a thing about what's going on. Impossible, is it? Well, you be careful, or I'll say "impossible" to you, and then where would you be! Darling Marius, please, please let me stay with you.'

'My sweet Cosette, I do promise you that we have to be alone.'

'But surely I don't count as just anyone.'

Jean Valjean had not spoken a word. She turned to him.

'In the first place, father, I must ask you to come and kiss me. Why haven't you been standing up for me? What sort of a father are you? Can't you see how unhappy I am? My husband beats me. So come and kiss me at once.'

Valjean moved towards her and she turned back to Marius.

'As for you, I'm frowning at you.'

Valjean had drawn close, and she offered him her forehead to kiss. But then she took a step back.

'Father, how pale you are! Is your hand still hurting you?'

'No, it's better,' said Valjean.

'Well, did you sleep badly?'

'No.'

'Are you feeling unhappy?'

'No.'

'Then kiss me. If you're well and happy I shan't scold you.'

Again she offered him her forehead, and he touched it with his lips.

'But you must smile.'

He did so, a spectral smile.

'And now you must take my side against my husband.'

'Cosette . . .' said Marius.

'Be cross with him. Tell him I can stay here. You can talk in front of me. You must think I'm very silly. Business indeed, investing money and all that nonsense—as if it were so difficult to understand! Men make mysteries out of nothing. I want to stay. I'm looking particularly pretty this morning, aren't I, Marius?'

She turned to him with a look of enchanting archness and it was as though a spark passed between them. The presence of a third party was unimportant.

'I love you,' said Marius.

'I adore you.'

And they fell into each other's arms.

'And now,' said Cosette smoothing her peignoir with a little smile of triumph, 'I'm staying.'

'My dear, no,' said Marius beseechingly. 'There's something we have got to settle.'

'It's still no?'

'I assure you, it's impossible.'

'Well, of course, when you talk to me in that solemn voice . . . Very well then, I'll go. Father, you didn't support me. You and my husband are both tyrants. I shall complain to grandfather. And if you think I'm going to come back and talk sweet nothings to you, you're very much mistaken. I shall wait for you to come to me, and you'll find that you'll very soon get bored without me. So now I'm going.'

She went out; but a moment later the door opened again and her glowing face reappeared peeping round it. 'I'm very cross with you both!' she said.

The door closed once more and the darkness returned. It was as though a ray of light had lost its way and flashed through a world of shadow.

Marius made sure that the door was firmly closed.

'Poor Cosette!' he murmured. 'When she hears . . .'

At these words Jean Valjean trembled in every limb and gazed frantically at Marius.

'Of course that's true. You'll tell Cosette. I hadn't thought of that. One has the strength to bear some things but not others. Monsieur, I beseech you to promise me not to tell her. Surely if you yourself know, that is enough. I might have told her of my own accord; I might have told everyone. But Cosette—she doesn't even know what it means. A felon, a man condemned for life to forced labour, a man who has been in the galleys. She would be appalled! Once she saw a convict chain-gang pass . . . Oh, my God!'

He sank into an armchair and buried his face in his hands. He made no sound, but the heaving of his shoulders showed that he was weeping. He was overtaken by a sort of convulsion and lay back in the chair as though he were unable to breathe, with his arms hanging limply at his sides. Marius saw his tear-stained face and heard his murmur, 'I wish I were dead.'

'Don't worry,' said Marius. 'I'll keep your secret.'

He went on in a voice that was perhaps less sympathetic than it should have been, conscious as he was of the new situation that had arisen and the huge gulf that lay between them:

'I am bound to speak of the trust money that you have so honourably and faithfully handed over. It was an act of probity for which you deserve to be rewarded. You yourself shall name the sum, and you need not hesitate to make it a large one.'

'I thank you, monsieur,' Valjean said gently. He sat thinking, mechanically rubbing thumb and forefinger together. 'Nearly everything is now settled, except for one last thing.'

'What is that?'

Making a supreme effort, Valjean said in a scarcely audible voice:

'You are the master. Do you think, now you know everything, that I should not see Cosette again?'

'I think it would be better,' Marius said coldly.

'Then I will not do so,' said Valjean, and getting up, he went to the door.

But with the door half-opened he stood for a moment motionless, then closed it again and came back to Marius. He was now no longer pale but deathly white, and instead of tears in his eyes there was a sort of tragic flame. His voice had become strangely calm.

'Monsieur,' he said, 'if you will permit me I would like to come and see her. Believe me, I greatly desire to do so. If I had not wanted to go on seeing Cosette I should not have told you what I have; I should simply have gone away. But because I so wanted to go on seeing her, I was bound in honour to tell you everything. You understand, I am sure. She has been my constant companion for nine years. We lived first in that tenement, then at the convent and then not far from the Luxembourg, where you saw her for the first time. Later we moved to the Invalides quarter, to a house in the Rue Plumet with a garden and a wrought-iron gate. My own dwelling was in the backyard, where I could hear her play the piano. That has been my life. We were never separated during those nine years and a few months. She was like my own child. To go away and never see or speak to her again—to have nothing left to live for—that would be very hard. I wouldn't come often or stay for long. We could meet in that little room on the ground floor. I would be quite willing to come by the servants' entrance, but that would give rise to talk, and so it might be better for me to come by the ordinary way. Monsieur, if I cannot see her from time to time there will be nothing left for me in life, but it will be for you to decide how often. And there is another thing. We have to be careful. If I never came at all, that too would give rise to talk. It occurs to me that I might come in the evening, when it's beginning to grow dark.'

'You shall come every evening,' said Marius.

'Monsieur, you are very kind,' said Jean Valjean.

They shook hands. Happiness escorted despair to the door, and so they parted.

413

II. *Questions that may be Contained in a Revelation*

Marius was distracted. The lack of contact he had always felt for the man he had supposed to be Cosette's father was now explained . . . He had felt instinctively that Monsieur Fauchelevent was concealing something, and now he knew what it was. To have learned this secret in the midst of his happiness was like discovering a scorpion in a dove's nest. Was his happiness and that of Cosette henceforth to depend upon that man, was he to be accepted as a part of their marriage bond? Was there nothing more to be done? Was he linked to an ex-convict? It was a thought to make even angels shudder.

But then, as always happens, he began to wonder whether he himself were not also at fault. Had he been lacking in perspicacity and prudence, had he deliberately closed his eyes? Perhaps there was some truth in this; perhaps he had plunged impulsively into the love-affair with Cosette without paying sufficient attention to the circumstances of her life. He could even admit (and it is by admissions of this kind that life teaches us self-knowledge) that there was a visionary side of his nature, a kind of imaginative haziness that pervaded his whole being. We have more than once drawn attention to this. He remembered how during those six or seven rapturous weeks in the Rue Plumet he had not once referred to the drama in the Gorbeau tenement in which the victim had behaved so strangely. Why had he never asked her about it, or mentioned the Thénardiers, particularly on the day when he had met Éponine? He could not account for this, but he took note of it. Looking back coolly, he recalled the ecstasy of their falling in love, the absolute fusion of their souls, and the vague instinct which had impelled him to put that episode—in which, after all, he had played no part— out of his mind. In any event those few weeks had sped by like a dream; there had been no time to do anything except love one another. And what would have happened if he had told Cosette that story, naming Thénardier? If he had learned the truth about Jean Valjean? Would it have changed his feeling for Cosette, caused him to love her less? Assuredly not. So he had nothing to regret, no reason to reproach himself, and all was well. He had blindly followed the path he would have followed with eyes wide open. Love, in blinding him, had led him to Paradise.

But that paradise now had its infernal aspect. The slight coolness that had existed between himself and the man whom he now knew as Jean Valjean contained an element of horror; pity as well, it must be said, and also amazement. That thief, that recidivist convict, had handed over the sum of six hundred thousand francs, all of which he might have kept for himself. Also, although nothing had

414

obliged him to do so, he had revealed his secret, accepting both the humiliation and the risk. A false name is a safeguard to a condemned man. He might have lived out his life with a respectable family, but he had not yielded to that temptation, simply, it seemed, from motives of conscience. Whatever else Jean Valjean might be, he was assuredly a man of principle. It seemed that at some time or other a mysterious transformation must have taken place in him, since when his life had been changed. Such rectitude was not to be found in base motives; it was an indication of greatness of soul. And his sincerity could not be doubted; the very suffering his avowal had caused him, the painful meticulousness with which he had omitted no detail, was sufficient evidence. And here a contradiction occurred to Marius. About Monsieur Fauchelevent there had always been a hint of defiance; but in Jean Valjean it was trustfulness.

In his consideration of Jean Valjean, weighing one thing with another, Marius sought to achieve a balance. But it was like peering through a tempest. The more he strove to see him as a whole, as it were to penetrate to his heart, the more he lost him only to find again a figure in a mist. On the one hand there was his honourable handing over of the trust money, on the other hand the extraordinary affair in the Jondrette attic. Why had he slipped away when the police arrived, instead of staying to testify against his persecutors? Here at least the answer was not far to seek. He was a man wanted by the police. But then again, how had he come to be on the barricade and what was he doing there? As Marius now recalled, he had taken no active part in the fighting. At this question a ghost arose to supply an answer, Javert. Marius perfectly remembered Javert's bound form being taken outside by Valjean, and soon afterwards the sound of a pistol shot. So presumably there had been a personal vendetta between the two men and Valjean had gone there from motives of revenge. The fact that he had been late in arriving suggested that he had only just discovered that Javert had been taken prisoner. The Corsican vendetta had penetrated to certain sectors of the underworld where it was accepted as law; and there were men, more or less reformed, who, although they would be scrupulous in the matter of theft, would not be deterred from an act of vengeance. There seemed to be no doubt that Valjean had killed Javert.

A final question remained to which there was no reply, one that tortured Marius's mind. How had this long association with Cosette been formed? What strange fatality had brought them together? Were there links forged in Heaven with which it pleased God to join angels and demons, and could crime and innocence be united in some mysterious prison of the underworld? How was it to be explained? By what extraordinary conjunction of circumstances had it come about, the lamb attached to the wolf—or, still more inexplicable, the wolf attached to the lamb? For the wolf truly loved the lamb and for nine years had been the centre of the lamb's existence. Cosette's childhood and adolescence, her growth to womanhood, had taken place in the shadow of that monstrous devotion. And this gave rise to endless riddles. Considering Jean Valjean, Marius felt his mind reel. What was one to make of that extraordinary man?

The two symbolic figures in the Book of Genesis are eternal. Until some deeper comprehension throws a new light upon our understanding of these things, human society will always be divided into two types of men, Abel and Cain, the higher and the lower. But what was one to make of this gentle-hearted Cain, the ruffian who had watched over Cosette, cherished her, protected her, seen to her education? What was it but a figure of darkness whose sole care had been to safeguard the rising of a star. And that was Jean Valjean's secret. It was also the secret of God.

At this twofold secret Marius recoiled, although the one half in some sort reassured him as to the other. God forges his own instruments, using what tools he needs. He is not responsible to Man. Jean Valjean had formed Cosette; in some degree he had shaped her soul. This was undeniable. Very well then, the craftsman might be deplorable but the result was admirable. God worked his miracle in his own way. He had created the exquisite Cosette and for the purpose had employed Jean Valjean, a strange collaboration. Are we to reproach him for this? Is it the first time dung has helped the spring to give birth to a rose?

Marius himself supplied the answers to these questions and he told himself that the answers were good. They were all points which he had not ventured to put to Valjean. But what further explanation did he need? Cosette was his; he adored her and she was utterly unsullied. What else mattered? The personal affairs of Jean Valjean were no concern of his. He concentrated on the words the unhappy man had spoken: 'I am not related to Cosette. Ten years ago I did not know that she existed'. As he said, he had been no more than an episode in her life, and now his part in it was over. It was for Marius henceforth to take care of her. Cosette had found her lover and husband, and, growing wings, had soared upward into Heaven, leaving the ugly, earthbound Jean Valjean behind.

Wherever Marius's thoughts led him, he always returned with a kind of horror to Valjean. Whatever the extenuating circumstances might be, there could be no escaping the fact that the man was a felon, a creature, that is to say, rejected by society, below the lowest rung of the social ladder, the lowest and the least of men. The law deprived men of his kind of all rights; and Marius, democrat though he was, was in this matter implacably on the side of the law. He was not, let us say, wholly progressive, able to distinguish between what has been written by Man and what was written by God, between what is law and what is right. He had not fully weighed these matters and was not repelled by the idea of revenge. He thought it natural that certain infractions of the law should be subject to lifelong punishment, and he accepted total ostracism as a normal social procedure. Until then, that was as far as he had gone, although it was certain that he would go further, being by nature well-disposed and instinctively progressive. But in the present state of his thinking he was bound to find Jean Valjean repulsive. A felon! The very word was like the voice of judgement. His reaction was to turn away his head. 'Get thee behind me . . .'

As to the questions which Marius had not put to Valjean, although they had all occurred to him—the Jondrette attic, the barricade, Javert—who can say where they might have led? The truth is that he had been afraid to ask them. It can happen to any of us, in a critical moment, that we may ask a question and then try not to hear the reply; and this is particularly so when love enters into the matter. It is not always wise to probe too deeply, most especially when we ourselves are affected. Who could say what the consequences to Cosette would have been of the answers to those questions, what infernal light would have been shed on her innocent life? The purest natures may be tainted by such revelations. So, rightly or wrongly, Marius had been afraid. He knew too much already. Desolated, he clasped Cosette in his arms and closed his eyes to Jean Valjean.

But, this being his attitude, it was agonizing to him that Cosette would still be in contact with the man. And thus he came near to reproaching himself for not having pressed his questions, which might have led him to a more drastic decision. He had been too magnanimous—in a word, too weak. He began to think that he had been wrong. He should have turned Valjean out of the house. He blamed himself for the wave of sentiment that had momentarily carried him away against his better judgement. He was displeased with himself.

And now what was he to do? The thought of Valjean's visits was repugnant; but here he checked himself, not wishing to probe too deeply into his own thoughts. He had made a promise, or been led into making a promise, and a promise must be kept, even, and indeed especially, a promise to a felon. In any event, his first duty was to Cosette.

This confusion of thought caused him to be greatly troubled in spirit, which was not easily hidden from Cosette. But love has its own cunning, and he managed. He asked her apparently casual questions, to which with innocent candour she unhesitatingly replied. Talking to her about her childhood and upbringing, he became more and more convinced that where she was concerned this one-time convict had been everything that was good, fatherly, and honourable. His first impulse had been the true one. The rank weed had cherished and protected the lily.

BOOK EIGHT

THE FADING LIGHT

I. *The Downstairs Room*

AT NIGHTFALL on the following day Jean Valjean knocked at the door of Monsieur Gillenormand's house and was received by Basque, who had evidently been told to expect him.

'Monsieur le Baron requested me to ask Monsieur whether he wished to go upstairs or would rather stay down here,' said Basque.

'I'll stay down here,' said Valjean.

Basque accordingly, treating the visitor with every sign of respect, showed him into the downstairs room. 'I will inform Madame,' he said.

The room on the ground floor was small and damp, with a low, arched ceiling, and was occasionally used as a cellar. It looked on to the street and was dimly lighted by a single barred window. Nor was it a room much visited by cleaners. Dust lay undisturbed and the spiders were untroubled. A large, blackened web, hung with the bodies of dead flies, covered one of the window-panes. A pile of empty bottles occupied one corner. Plaster was peeling off the yellow-painted wall. A fire had been lighted in the wooden fireplace at the far end, and two armchairs, placed on either side of a worn bedside rug which served as a carpet, were an indication that Valjean's preference for staying downstairs had been foreseen. The fire and the dingy window supplied the only light.

Jean Valjean was tired, having neither eaten nor slept for several days. He sank into one of the armchairs. Basque returned with a lighted candle and again withdrew. Valjean, seated with his chin sunk on his chest, gave no sign of having seen him. But suddenly he started to his feet, knowing that Cosette was standing behind him. He had not seen her enter, but he felt her presence. He turned and looked at her. She was enchantingly pretty. But it was not her beauty that he contemplated with that deeply penetrating gaze, but her soul.

'Well, of all things!' Cosette exclaimed. 'Father, I knew that you were a strange person, but I never expected this! Marius tells me that it is at your request that we're meeting down here.'

'That's quite true.'

'As I expected. Well, I warn you, there's going to be a scene. But let us start properly. Give me a kiss.' And she offered her cheek.

Valjean stayed motionless.

'So you don't move. The posture of a guilty man! Well, never mind, you're forgiven. The Lord told us to turn the other cheek, and here it is.'

She offered him her other cheek, but still he did not move. His feet seemed nailed to the floor.

'But this is serious,' said Cosette. 'What have I done to you? I'm at my wits' end. You owe it to me to make amends. You must dine with us.'

'I've dined already.'

'I don't believe you. I shall ask Monsieur Gillenormand to give you a good scolding. Grandfathers are the right people to keep fathers in order. So you're to come up to the salon with me this instant.'

'That's impossible.'

Cosette felt that she was losing ground. She stopped giving orders and resorted to questions.

'But why? And you have chosen the ugliest room in the house for us to meet in. This place is horrible.'

'Tu sais . . .' But then, having addressed her with the familiar 'tu', Valjean corrected himself. 'Vous savez, madame, that I'm peculiar. I have my whims.'

Cosette clapped her hands together.

' "Madame" and "vous"! Is this another whim? What in the world does it mean?'

Valjean bestowed on her a heartrending smile.

'You wanted to be "madame" and now you are.'

'But not to you, father.'

'You mustn't call me "father" any more.'

'What!'

'You must call me Monsieur Jean, or plain Jean, if you'd rather.'

'You mean that you're no longer my father? You'll be telling me next that I'm not Cosette! What in the world does it mean? What has happened? You won't live with us and you won't even come up to my sitting-room! It's like a revolution! But what have I done to you? What have I done wrong? There must be something.'

'There's nothing.'

'Well, then?'

'Everything is as it should be.'

'Why have you changed your name?'

'You've changed your own.' He gave her the same smile. 'Now that you're Madame Pontmercy surely I can be Monsieur Jean.'

'I simply don't understand. I think it's ridiculous. I shall ask my husband if you can be allowed to call yourself Monsieur Jean, and I hope he'll say no. You're upsetting me very much. It's all very well to have whims, but they mustn't hurt other people. You've no right to be cruel when you're really so kind.'

He made no reply. She seized his two hands and pressed them to her throat beneath her chin in a gesture of profound tenderness.

'Please, please be kind!' And she went on: 'And by that I mean, be nice and come here to live with us, and then we can go for walks together—there are birds here just as there are in the Rue Plumet. Don't set us guessing games but be like everyone else—live with us, have luncheon and dinner with us, be my father.'

He released his hands.

'You don't need a father any more. You have a husband.'

'What a thing to say,' Cosette exclaimed angrily. 'I don't need a father indeed! There's no sense in it!'

'If Toussaint were here,' said Jean Valjean, as though he were groping for any support, 'she'd be the first to agree that I've always had my peculiarities. There's nothing new in this. I have always liked my shady nook.'

'But it's cold in here and one can't see properly. And it's abominable of you to want to be Monsieur Jean, and I don't like you addressing me as "vous".'

'On my way here,' said Valjean, 'I saw a piece of furniture in a shop in the Rue Saint-Louis. It was something I'd buy for myself if I were a pretty woman—a very nice dressing-table in the modern style, what is called rosewood, I think, with an inlay and drawers and a big mirror. It was very pretty.'

'You great bear!' said Cosette; and with the utmost fondness, with closed teeth and parted lips, she made a face at Valjean. 'I'm furious,' she said. 'Since yesterday you've all been making me cross. You won't take my side against Marius, and Marius won't take my side against you. I arrange a delightful room for you and it stays empty. I order a delicious dinner and you won't eat it. And my father, who is Monsieur Fauchelevent, wants to be called Monsieur Jean and insists on seeing me in a horrible damp cellar full of spiders and empty bottles. I know you're a peculiar person, but you should be indulgent to a newly married pair. You shouldn't start being peculiar at the very beginning. And you think you'll be happy in that horrible Rue de l'Homme-Armé, which I simply hated. What have you got against me? You're hurting me very much!' Then, becoming suddenly serious, she looked hard at him and asked: 'Are you cross with me because I'm happy?'

Unwitting innocence is sometimes more penetrating than cunning.

The question, a simple one to Cosette, was a profound one to Jean Valjean. Thinking to administer a pinprick, she plucked at his heart. Valjean turned pale and for a moment said nothing. Then he murmured to himself:

'Her happiness was the sole object of my life. God can now give me leave of absence . . . Cosette, you are happy, and so my work is done.'

'You called me "tu"!' cried Cosette, and flung her arms round his neck.

He clasped her despairingly to his breast, and it was almost as though he had got her back again. The temptation was too great. Gently loosening her arms, he picked up his hat.

'Well?' said Cosette.

'I am leaving you, Madame. You are wanted elsewhere.' And from the doorway he said: 'I addressed you as "tu". Please accept my apologies and assure your husband that it will not occur again.'

He went out, leaving her stupefied.

II. *Further Backslidings*

Jean Valjean returned at the same time on the following evening. On this occasion Cosette asked no questions and did not complain about the room. She avoided addressing him either as 'father' or as 'Monsieur Jean', and she submitted to being addressed as 'Madame'. But she was less light-hearted than she had been. Indeed, she would have been sad, if sadness had been possible to her. Most probably she had had one of those conversations with Marius in which the man who is loved tells the beloved woman what he wants and she is content to obey. The curiosity of lovers does not extend far beyond their state of love.

The downstairs room had been put somewhat to rights. Basque had removed the bottles and Nicolette had dealt with the spiders. Valjean called every evening at the same time. He came every day, lacking the strength to take Marius's words otherwise than literally, and Marius arranged to be out when he came. The household accustomed itself to these novel proceedings on the part of Monsieur Fauchelevent, being encouraged to do so by Toussaint, who said, 'Monsieur has always been like this'. Monsieur Gillenormand summed the matter up by describing him as 'an original'. Besides, new arrangements are not easily accepted when one is in one's nineties; one has one's habits, and newcomers are not welcome. Monsieur Gillenormand was not sorry to be rid of Monsieur

Fauchelevent. 'These originals are really quite common,' he said. 'They do the most extraordinary things for no reason at all. The Marquis de Canaples was even worse. He bought himself a palace and lived in the attic. Human beings are strange creatures.'

No one knew of the sinister background, and how could anyone have guessed it? There are marshes in India which behave in an extraordinary fashion, the waters becoming turbulent when there is no wind to stir them. The troubled surface is all one sees, not the hydra lurking beneath. Many men possess a secret monster, a despair that haunts their nights. They live ordinary lives, coming and going like other men. No one suspects the existence of a sharp-toothed parasite gnawing at their vitals which kills them in the end. The man is like a stagnant but deep pond, only an occasional unaccountable ripple troubles the surface. A bubble rises and bursts, a small thing but terrible: it is the breathing of the monster in the depths. The strange behaviour of some men, their habit of arriving when others are leaving, of haunting unfrequented places, seeking solitude, coming in by the side door, living poorly when they have money to spare—all such idiosyncrasies are baffling.

Several weeks went by in this fashion. By degrees Cosette grew accustomed to a new way of life, new acquaintances brought to her by marriage, visits, household responsibilities, important matters of this kind. But her real happiness was not expensive, consisting as it did of one thing only, to be alone with Marius. Whether she went out with him or stayed at home with him, this was her main preoccupation; and to walk out together, arm in arm in the sunshine, without concealment, openly facing the world in their own private solitude, this was a joy to both of them that never grew stale. Cosette had only one cause for vexation. Toussaint could not get on with Nicolette, and finally when it became clear that the two old maids had nothing in common, she left. Monsieur Gillenormand was in good health; Marius did occasional legal work; Aunt Gillenormand settled down with the newly married couple to live the unobtrusive life that sufficed her. Jean Valjean paid his daily visit.

The use of 'vous' and 'Madame', and the fact that he was now Monsieur Jean, made him a different person to Cosette. The means he had used to detach her from him had proved successful. She was increasingly light-hearted but less tender. And still he felt that she loved him dearly. On one occasion she said abruptly to him: 'You used to be my father, but you aren't any more; you used to be my uncle, but you aren't any more; you used to be Monsieur Fauchelevent and now you're just plain Jean. Who are you really? I don't like this state of affairs. If I didn't know how good you are I should be afraid of you.'

He still lived in the Rue de l'Homme-Armé, being unable to bring himself to leave the quarter in which Cosette also lived. At first, when he came to see her, he stayed only a few minutes, but by degrees his visits grew longer. One day, she addressed him unthinkingly as 'father' and his sombre countenance was suddenly radiant. Then he said, 'You must call me Jean . . .' 'Of course,' she said, laughing, 'Monsieur Jean . . .' 'That's better,' he said and turned away his head so that she should not see the tears in his eyes.

III. *They Remember the Garden in the Rue Plumet*

That was the last time. From that moment all demonstrations of affection were banished between them—no more familiarities, no kiss of greeting, no use of that profoundly moving word, 'father'. Of his own free will he had relinquished all his happiness, and this was his final torment, that having in a single day lost Cosette as a whole, he had to go on losing her in detail. But the eye accustoms itself to a cellar-light. All in all, his daily glimpse of Cosette sufficed him. Those visits were the mainstay of his life. He would sit looking at her in silence, or would talk of incidents in the past, her childhood days and her little friends in the convent.

One afternoon (it was early in April, a warm day when the sun was bringing the world to life and there was a stir of awakening—budding leaves on the trees, primroses and dandelions beginning to show themselves in the grass of the garden outside their window) Marius said to Cosette, 'We said we would go back to our garden in the Rue Plumet. We mustn't be ungrateful,'—and off they went like swallows flying into the spring. That garden in the Rue Plumet had been for them the beginning of everything; it had harboured the springtime of their love. Since Jean Valjean had acquired the lease it was now the property of Cosette. They went there and, being there, forgot all else. When Valjean called at his accustomed hour Basque told him that Madame had gone out with Monsieur and they had not yet returned. Valjean sat down and waited, but when after another hour she still had not come he bowed his head and went away.

Cosette had so enjoyed their visit to the garden and reliving the past that the next day she could talk of nothing else. It did not occur to her that she had missed seeing Valjean.

'How did you go there?' Valjean asked her.

'We walked.'

'And how did you come back?'

'In a fiacre.'

For some time Valjean had been conscious of the rigidly economical fashion in which the young couple lived, and it perturbed him. He ventured upon a question.

'Why don't you have a carriage of your own? A coupé would cost you five hundred francs a month. You could easily afford it.'

'I don't know,' said Cosette.

'And then, Toussaint,' Valjean continued. 'She's gone but you haven't got any one in her place. Why not?'

'Nicolette is quite enough.'

'But you ought to have your own maid.'

'I've got Marius.'

'And you ought to have a house of your own, with servants of your own and a carriage and a box at the opera. Nothing is too good for you. Why not take advantage of the fact that you're rich? Wealth can be a great source of happiness.'

Cosette made no reply.

Jean Valjean's visits did not grow shorter. On the contrary. When it is the heart that fails we do not pause on the downward path. In order to stay longer he talked about Marius, praising his many excellent qualities. It was a subject that never failed to enthral Cosette, and so time was forgotten, and he could allay the aching of his heart with more of her company. It happened more than once that Basque entered with the words, 'Monsieur Gillenormand has sent me to remind Madame la Baronne that dinner is served.'

On these occasions Valjean went thoughtfully home, wondering if there might be truth in the thought that had occurred to Marius, that he was a sort of chrysalis obstinately returning to visit its butterfly.

One evening he stayed even later than usual, and the next day he found that there was no fire burning in the hearth. 'Well, after all,' he thought, 'it's April and the weather is no longer cold.'

'Heavens, how cold it is in here,' Cosette exclaimed when she entered.

'Not at all,' said Valjean.

'Was it you who told Basque not to light the fire?'

'Yes. It will soon be May.'

'But we keep fires going until June, and in this cellar one wants one all the year round.'

'I didn't think a fire was necessary.'

'Another of your absurd ideas,' said Cosette.

The next evening there was a fire, but the two armchairs had been placed at the other end of the room, near the door. 'Now what does that mean?' Valjean wondered, and he restored the chairs to their original place.

But the lighting of the fire encouraged him, and that evening he stayed even longer than usual. When at length he rose to leave Cosette said:

'My husband said a queer thing to me yesterday.'

'What was that?'

'He said, "Cosette, we have an income of thirty thousand *livres*, twenty-seven thousand of yours and the three thousand my grandfather allows me." . . . "Yes" I said, "that adds up to thirty." . . . "Would you be brave enough to live on the three thousand?" he asked. I said I was ready to live on nothing at all provided I was with him; and then I asked, "Why do you say that?" . . . "I just wanted to know," he said.'

Jean Valjean found nothing to say. Cosette had probably hoped for some sort of explanation, but he maintained a gloomy silence. He was so lost in thought that when he returned to the Rue de l'Homme-Armé he entered the house next door by mistake and did not realize what he had done until he had climbed two flights of stairs. His mind was filled with conjecture. It was evident that Marius had his doubts about the origin of those six hundred thousand francs and perhaps feared that they had come from some discreditable source—perhaps he had discovered that they had come from Valjean himself—and that he would sooner be poor with Cosette than live on tainted money.

In general Valjean had a vague sense that he was being rebuffed, and on the following evening this was brought forcibly home to him. The two armchairs had vanished. There was not a chair in the room.

'Why, what has happened?' Cosette exclaimed when she came in. 'Where have they got to?'

'I told Basque he could take them away,' Valjean replied, stammering slightly as he spoke.

'But why?'

'I shall only be staying a few minutes this evening.'

'Even so, there's no reason why we should stand up.'

'I think Basque needed the chairs for the salon.'

'What for?'

'Because you're expecting company, I suppose.'

'Nobody's coming.'

Valjean could think of nothing else to say. Cosette shrugged her shoulders.

'You told Basque to take the chairs away. And the other day you told him not to light the fire. You really are very peculiar.'

'Goodbye,' said Valjean. He did not say 'Goodbye, Cosette' but he had not the strength to say, 'Goodbye, Madame'.

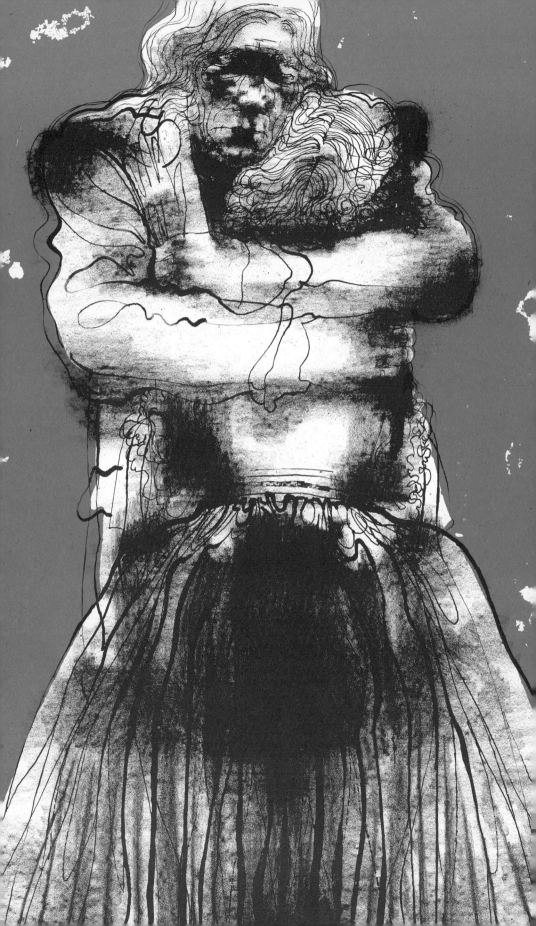

He went off in despair, having now understood exactly what was happening, and the next evening he did not come at all.

Cosette did not notice this until the hour was past, and when she remarked upon it her thoughts were quickly distracted by a kiss from Marius.

On the following evening Jean Valjean again did not come.

Cosette was unperturbed. She slept soundly and scarcely gave the matter a thought until the next morning. She was so bathed in happiness! But then she sent Nicolette round to the Rue de l'Homme-Armé to inquire if 'Monsieur Jean' was well. Nicolette returned with the message that Monsieur Jean was quite well but was busy with his affairs. Madame would remember that he had sometimes had to go away for a few days. He would be doing so shortly, and would come to see her as soon as possible after he got back. In the meantime there was nothing to worry about.

Nicolette, when she called upon Monsieur Jean, had repeated her mistress's words, that 'Madame wished to know why Monsieur Jean had not come to see her the previous evening'.

'I have not been to see her for two evenings,' Jean Valjean said gently.

But Nicolette failed to notice this and did not report the remark to Cosette.

IV. *Attraction and Extinction*

During the late spring and early summer of 1833 persons in the streets of the Marais, shopkeepers and loiterers in house doorways, noticed an elderly man decently clad in black who at about the same time every evening, when it was beginning to grow dark, left the Rue de l'Homme-Armé and walked to the Rue Saint-Louis. Having reached it he proceeded very slowly, seeming to see and hear nothing, his head thrust forward and his eyes intent upon a single object, which was the corner of the Rue des Filles-du-Calvaire. As he approached this point his eyes brightened with a glow of inward happiness, his lips moved as though he were talking to some unseen person and he smiled uncertainly. It was as though, while longing to reach his objective, he dreaded the moment when he would do so. When he was within a few houses of it his pace slowed to the point that he seemed scarcely to be moving at all; the swaying of his head and the intentness of his gaze put one in mind of a compass-needle searching for the pole. But however slow his progress, he had to get there in the end. Having reached the Rue des Filles-du-Calvaire, he stopped and trembled, and peered timidly round the corner into the street with the tragic expression of one who gazes into a forbidden paradise. Then the tear which had been slowly gathering in his eye became large enough to fall and roll down his cheek, sometimes reaching his mouth so that he tasted its bitterness. He would stay there for some minutes like a figure carved in stone and then slowly return by the way he had come, with the light in his eyes growing dimmer as the distance lengthened.

As time went on the elderly gentleman ceased to go as far as the corner of the Rue des Filles-du-Calvaire, and would stop and turn back half way along the Rue Saint-Louis; and one day he went only as far as the Rue Culture-Sainte-Catherine, from which point he had a distant view of the Rue des Filles-du-Calvaire. Then he shook his head, as though rejecting something, and turned back. Before long he did not go even as far as the Rue Saint-Louis, but stopped at the Rue Pavée. Then it was the Rue des Trois-Pavillons, and then the Rue des Blancs-Manteaux. His daily walk grew steadily shorter, like the pendulum of a clock that has not been re-wound and gradually ceases to swing. Every day he set out upon the same walk and perhaps was unaware of the fact that he constantly shortened it. His expression seemed to say, 'What is the use?' There was no longer any light in his eyes, nor did the tears gather as formerly. But his head was still thrust forward, painfully revealing the folds in his thin neck. Sometimes in bad weather he carried an umbrella, but he never opened it. The goodwives of the quarter said, 'He's simple', and the children laughed as they followed him.

BOOK NINE

SUPREME SHADOW, SUPREME DAWN

I. *Pity for the Unhappy, but Indulgence for the Happy*

To BE happy is a terrible thing. How complacent we are, how self-sufficing. How easy it is, being possessed of the false side of life, which is happiness, to forget the real side, which is duty.

Yet it would be wrong to blame Marius. As we have said, before his marriage Marius asked no questions of Monsieur Fauchelevent, and since then he had been afraid to question Jean Valjean. He had regretted the promise which he had been induced to make and had said to himself more than once that he should not have made that concession to despair. And so he had by degrees excluded Valjean from his house and effaced him as far as possible from the thoughts of Cosette, deliberately intervening between them, but in such a way as to ensure that she would not realize what was happening. It was more than effacement; it was eclipse.

Marius was doing what he held to be right and necessary. He believed that in keeping Valjean at a distance, without harshness but also without weakness, he was acting upon serious grounds, some of which we already know and others of which we have still to learn. In the course of a law-suit in which he had been professionally involved he had met a former clerk in the Laffitte banking-house and had received from him certain information which he was unable to investigate further because of his promise of secrecy and Valjean's perilous situation. At the same time he believed that he had a serious duty to perform, namely, the restitution of six hundred thousand francs to some person whose identity he was seeking to discover as discreetly as possible. In the meantime he did not touch the money.

As for Cosette, she knew nothing of all these secrets; but she, too, was scarcely to be blamed. Marius's power over her was such that instinctively and almost automatically she did what he wanted. She sensed a 'feeling' on the part of Marius where Valjean was concerned, and without his having to say anything she blindly acquiesced in it. Her obedience in this respect consisted in not remembering things that Marius had forgotten. It cost her no effort. Without her knowing why, or being in any way to blame, her spirit had become so merged in that of her husband that what was expunged from Marius's mind was also expunged from her own.

But we must not carry this too far. In the case of Jean Valjean her forgetfulness was only superficial. She was bemused rather than forgetful. In her heart she still loved the man whom for so long she had called father. But she loved her husband even more, and it was this that had somewhat disturbed the balance of her affections, causing her to lean to one side.

Occasionally she spoke of Jean Valjean, expressing astonishment at his absence. Marius reminded her that he had said he was going away. And this was true. He was in the habit of going away from time to time, although never for so long as this. Several times she sent Nicolette to the Rue de l'Homme-Armé to ask if 'Monsieur Jean' had returned. The answer, sent by Valjean himself, was always no. Cosette was not unduly perturbed, having only one need in life, and that was for Marius.

We may mention that Marius and Cosette had themselves been away. They had been to Vernon, where Marius had taken Cosette to his father's grave. Little by little Marius had detached Cosette from Jean Valjean, and she had allowed it to happen.

For the rest, what is sometimes over-severely described as the ingratitude of the young is not always so reprehensible as one may suppose. It is the ingratitude of Nature herself. Nature, as we have said elsewhere, always 'looks ahead'; she divides living creatures into those who are arriving and those who are leaving. Those leaving look towards darkness, and those arriving look towards light. Hence the gulf between them, fateful to the old, involuntary on the part of the young. The gulf, at first imperceptible, grows gradually wider, like the spreading branches of a tree. It is not the fault of the branches that, without detaching themselves from the trunk, they grow remote from it. Youth goes in search of joy and festivity, bright light and love. Age moves towards the end. They do not lose sight of one another, but there is no longer any closeness between them. Young folk feel the cooling of life; old people feel the chill of the grave. Let us not be too hard on the young.

II. *Last Flickers of a Lamp without Oil*

One day Jean Valjean walked downstairs and a few paces along the street, then seated himself on a curbstone, the same one on which Gavroche had found him on the night of 5 June. He stayed there a few minutes, then went upstairs again. It was the last swing of the pendulum. The next day he did not leave his room, and on the following day he did not leave his bed.

The concierge, who prepared his meagre repast, consisting of cabbage or a few potatoes with a little bacon, looked at the brown earthenware plate and exclaimed:

'But you ate nothing yesterday, my poor man.'

'Yes I did,' said Valjean.

'The plate's still full.'

'If you look at the water-jug you'll see that it's empty.'

'Well, that proves that you've had a drink, but not that you've eaten anything.'

'So perhaps all I wanted was water.'

'If you don't eat as well as drink it means that you've got a fever.'

'I'll eat something tomorrow.'

'Or next week, perhaps. Why put it off till tomorrow? And those new potatoes were so good.'

Valjean took the old woman's hand.

'I'll promise to eat them,' he said in his kindly voice.

'I'm not at all pleased with you,' she said.

Valjean saw no one except this old woman. There are streets in Paris along which no one passes and houses which no one enters, and he lived in one of them. While he had been in the habit of going out he had bought a small copper cross which he nailed to the wall facing his bed. A cross is always good to look at.

During the week that followed Valjean did not get out of bed. The concierge said to her husband: 'He doesn't get up and he doesn't eat anything. He isn't going to last long. He's very unhappy about something. I can't help feeling that his daughter has made a bad marriage.'

Her husband replied with lordly indifference:

'If he's rich enough he'd better send for the doctor; if he's too poor he can't afford to, and in that case he'll die.'

'But if he does send for the doctor?'

'He'll probably die anyway.'

The concierge was pulling up the blades of grass that had sprouted between the stones of what she called her own strip of pavement. She saw a local doctor passing the end of the street and took it upon herself to ask him to go upstairs.

'It's the second floor,' she said. 'He never gets out of bed and so the key's always in the door.'

When he came down the doctor said:

'The man's very ill indeed.'

'What's the matter with him?'

'Everything and nothing. From the look of him I would say that he has lost someone very dear to him. One can die of that.'

'What did he say to you?'

'He said he was quite well.'

'Will you come again, doctor?'

'Yes,' said the doctor. 'But he needs someone other than myself.'

III. *The Weight of a Quill-pen*

One evening Jean Valjean had difficulty in raising himself on his elbow. His pulse was so weak that he could not feel it; his breath came in short, faint gasps. He realized that he was weaker than he had ever been. And so, no doubt because he was impelled to do so by some over-riding consideration, he sat up with a great effort and got dressed. He put on his old workman's clothes. Now that he had given up going out he preferred them to any other. He had to pause several times to rest, and the business of getting his arms into the sleeves of his jacket caused sweat to drip from his forehead.

Now that he was alone he had moved his bed into the living-room in order to occupy as little of the apartment as possible. He opened the valise and, getting out Cosette's trousseau of small garments, spread them on the bed. The bishop's candlesticks were in their usual place on the mantelpiece; he got two wax candles out of a drawer and, putting them in the candlesticks, lighted them, although it was broad daylight. One may see candles lighted in rooms occupied by the dead. Every step he took, moving from one room to the other, exhausted him, and he had frequently to sit down and rest. It was not just a case of ordinary fatigue which uses up energy and recovers it; it was the last effort of which he was capable, exhausted life spending itself in an effort which it will not be able to repeat.

One of the chairs into which he sank was opposite the mirror, so disastrous for him and so providential for Marius, in which he had read the blotted handwriting of Cosette. He looked at himself in the mirror and did not recognize what he saw. He was eighty years old. Before Cosette's marriage he might have been taken for fifty. The wrinkles on his forehead were not the wrinkles of age but the mysterious stamp of death; one could see the impress of that inexorable finger. His cheeks sagged, and the colour of his skin was such as to make one feel that there was earth beneath it. The corners of his mouth drooped as in the masks that the ancients carved for the tombs of the dead. He was staring blankly in front of him, but with an expression of reproach, like one of those great figures of tragedy who rise in condemnation of some other man.

He was at the point, the last stage of despair, when pain is no longer active; the soul, as it were, has grown numb. It was growing dark. With great labour he dragged a table and chair close to the mantelpiece, and arranged writing materials on the table. Having done this he fainted, and upon recovering consciousness found that he was thirsty. Not being able to lift the water-jug to his lips, he tilted it painfully towards him and sipped from it. Then he turned towards the bed, and, still seated, for he could no longer stand, looked at the little black frock and the other garments that were so dear to him. He stayed looking at them for a long time, until with a shiver he realized that he was cold; then, leaning forward over the table lit by the bishop's candlesticks, he picked up his pen.

Since neither pen nor ink had been used for a considerable time, the quill was warped and the ink had dried. He had to get up and pour a few drops of water into the ink-pot, which he only managed to do with several pauses for rest, and he had to write with the reverse side of the quill. Now and then he wiped his forehead. His hand was shaking. Slowly he wrote the following lines:

'Cosette, I bless you. There is something I must explain. Your husband was right to make me understand that I must go away. What he supposed was not altogether correct, but still he was right. He is a good man. You must go on loving him after I am dead. And you, Monsieur Pontmercy, you must go on loving my beloved child. Cosette, you will find figures on this paper if I have the strength to recall them. That is why I am writing to you, to assure you that the money is really yours. This is how it is. White jade comes from Norway, black jade from England, and black glass from Germany. Jade is lighter, more rare and more expensive. Imitations can be made in France as they can in Germany. You need a small mould two inches square and a spirit lamp to soften the wax. The wax used to be made of resin and lampblack, but I hit upon the idea of making it of lacquer and turpentine. It costs no more than thirty sous and it is much better. The buckles are made of purple glass fixed with wax in a black metal frame. The glass should be purple for metal frames and black for gold ornaments. A lot is sold in Spain, which is the country where . . .'

And here the pen slipped from his fingers and he sank down, sobbing from the depths of his heart, with his head clasped in his hands.

'Alas, alas,' he cried within himself (those dreadful lamentations that are heard only by God), 'it's all over. I shall not see her again. It was a smile that came into my life and departed. I shall go into darkness without seeing her. If I could hear her voice, touch her dress, look at her just once more! To die is nothing, but it is terrible to die without seeing her. She would smile at me, she would say a word, and what harm would it do to anyone? But it is all over and I am alone. God help me, I shall not see her again!'

At this moment there was a knock on the door.

IV. *Marius Receives a Letter*

That same day, or, more exactly, that same evening, Marius having withdrawn to his study after dinner to work on a brief, Basque brought him a letter, saying, 'The writer is waiting in the hall.' Cosette at the time was strolling with her grandfather-in-law in the garden.

A letter, like a person, can have a displeasing appearance—coarse paper, careless folding—the very sight of them can be unpleasant. This was such a letter. It smelt of tobacco. Nothing is more evocative than a smell. Marius remembered that tobacco, and looking at the superscription he read: 'To Monsieur le Baron Pontmerci, At his home.' The familiar smell of the tobacco reminded him of the handwriting, and in a sudden flash of divination he put certain things together: the smell of tobacco, the quality of the paper, the way it was folded, the pale watered ink—all this brought a picture to his mind, that of the Jondrette attic . . . By the strangest of chances, one of the two men for whom he had searched so diligently, thinking never to find him, had of his own accord come his way!

Eagerly unsealing the letter, he read:

Monsieur le baron,

If the Supreme Being had endowed me with talent I might be the Baron Thénard*, member of the Academy, but I am not. I simply bear the same name as his, and I shall be happy if this recommends me to your favor. Any kindness which you may do me will be resiprocated. I am in posession of a secret concerning a certain person. This person concerns you. I am keeping the secret for your ears alone, being desirus of being useful to you. I can provide you with the means of driving this person out of your house where he has no right to be, Madame la Baronne being a lady of noble birth. Virtue and crime cannot be allowed to go on living together any longer.

I await Monsieur le Baron's instructions,
Respectfully,

* Baron Thénard, a chemist, had been a member of the Académie des Sciences.

434

The letter was signed THÉNARD.

The signature was not wholly false, being merely a little abbreviated. But the style and orthography completed the picture. There could be no doubt whatever as to the writer's identity.

Marius's agitation was extreme. After his first surprise came a feeling of satisfaction. If he could now find the other man he sought, the one who had saved his life, all his troubles of conscience would be at an end. He went to his desk, got some banknotes out of a drawer, put them in his pocket, closed the drawer and then rang the bell. Basque appeared.

'Show the gentleman in,' said Marius.

'Monsieur Thénard,' Basque announced.

And now Marius had another surprise. The man who entered was completely unknown to him.

He was an elderly man with a big nose, his chin buried in his cravat, with green-tinted spectacles and grey hair smoothed and plastered down over his forehead like the wigs of coachmen to the English nobility. He was clad entirely in black, his garments being worn but clean, and a bunch of fobs hanging from his waistcoat pocket suggested that he possessed a watch. He was carrying an old hat in his hand. He walked with a stoop, and the curve of his back made his bow upon entering all the deeper.

The first thing that struck Marius was that the suit he was wearing, although carefully buttoned, was too large and seemed to have been made for someone else. And here a brief digression becomes necessary.

There existed in those days in Paris, in a hovel near the Arsenal, an ingenious Jew whose business in life was transforming rogues into respectable men. Not for too long, since this might have made them uncomfortable. The change, which was simply one of appearance, lasted one or two days, at the rate of thirty sous a day, and was based on a set of clothes conforming as far as possible to accepted notions of propriety. The practitioner in question was called 'the Changer', this being the only name by which he was known to the denizens of the Paris underworld. He possessed a large stock, and the garments he hired out to his customers were more or less presentable. They covered all categories. From every hook in his establishment there hung, used and worn, a social status, that of a magistrate, banker, priest, retired army man, man of letters or statesman. He was in short the costumier of the great repertory theatre of Paris rascality, and his shop was the place where every kind of crime emerged, and to which it returned. A ragged footpad went there, deposited his thirty sous, selected whatever clothes suited the particular project he had in mind, and came out looking like another

435

man. Next day the garments were faithfully returned; the Changer, who dealt exclusively with thieves, was himself never robbed. But the clothes he hired out had one drawback: they didn't fit. Anyone whose physical dimensions in any way departed from the normal was uncomfortable in them: he must not be too fat or too thin, the Changer catered only for the average. This created problems which his customers had to solve as best they could. The statesman's outfit, for example, would have been too large for Pitt and too small for Louis-Philippe. We may quote the note in the Changer's catalogue: 'Coat of black cloth, black knee-breeches, silk waistcoat, boots and linen'—to which was appended in the margin, 'former ambassador', together with an additional note which read: 'In a separate box a neatly frizzed wig, green-tinted spectacles, fobs and two quill-tubes an inch long wrapped in cotton-wool'. All this came from the same source, the 'former ambassador', and all was somewhat the worse for wear, with the seams whitening and a slit in one of the elbows. Moreover a button was missing from the breast of the jacket. This, however, was a detail, the statesman's hand being always laid upon his heart to cover the deficiency. Marius would at once have recognized this outfit had he been familiar with the seamy side of Paris life.

Marius's disappointment at finding himself confronted by a stranger turned to disgust as he examined the visitor more closely while the latter was exaggeratedly bowing.

'What do you want?' he asked sharply.

The visitor responded with a grimace which may be likened to the smile of a crocodile.

'I find it hard to believe that I have not already met Monsieur le Baron in society—at the house of Princess Bagration, perhaps, or of the Viscomte Dambray?' To pretend acquaintance with someone whom one has never met is always a shrewd move in the performance of a confidence trick.

Marius had listened attentively to the sound of the man's voice, and with a growing disappointment. He had a nasal intonation quite different from the thin, dry voice which Marius had expected.

'I know neither Madame Bagration nor Monsieur Dambray,' he said, frowning, 'and I have never visited either of them.'

Despite the terseness of his manner the visitor was not discouraged.

'Well, then, perhaps it was at the home of Chateaubriand. I am on the friendliest of terms with Chateaubriand. He quite often asks me in for a drink.'

Marius's frown grew darker.

'I don't know Monsieur de Chateaubriand either. Will you please come to the point. What can I do for you?'

The visitor bowed more deeply than ever.

'At least, Monsieur le Baron, do me the honour of listening to what I have to say. There is in America, in the region of Panama, a village called La Joya. It consists of a single house. A big, square, three-storey house built of bricks baked in the sun. Each side of the square is five hundred feet long, and each floor is set back twelve feet from the one below it, forming a sort of terrace which runs right round the building. There is an interior courtyard in which provisions and munitions are stored. There are no windows but only loopholes, no doors but only ladders—ladders leading from the ground to the first terrace, from the first to the second terrace and from the second to the third; ladders for climbing down into the courtyard. No doors to the rooms but only trap-doors; no stairways to the rooms but only ladders. At night the traps are closed and the ladders are drawn up, and loaded guns and carbines are installed at the loopholes. The place is a house by day and a fortress at night, with eight hundred inhabitants. That is the village. Why so many precautions, you may ask? Because it is situated in very dangerous country, full of cannibals. So why does anyone go there? Because it is a wonderful country in which gold is to be found.'

'Why are you telling me all this?' demanded Marius, who was becoming increasingly impatient.

'I am a wearied ex-diplomat, Monsieur le Baron. Our ancient civilization has become oppressive to me. I want to live among savage people.'

'And so?'

'Egotism, Monsieur le Baron, is the law of life. The day-labourer working in the fields looks round when the coach passes, but the peasant proprietor does not bother to do so. The poor man's dog barks at the rich and the rich man's dog barks at the poor. Everyone for himself. Self-interest is the object of all men and money is the loadstone.'

'I'm still waiting.'

'I want to settle in La Joya. There are three of us. I have a wife and a very beautiful daughter. It is a long journey and it costs a great deal. I need a little money.'

'What has that to do with me?'

Stretching his neck out of his cravat in a gesture proper to a vulture, the visitor smiled with redoubled ardour.

'Has Monsieur le Baron not read my letter?'

This was not far from the truth. The fact is that Marius had paid little attention to the contents of the letter, being more interested in the handwriting. In any case, a new thought had occurred to him. The man had mentioned a wife and daughter. Marius looked at him with a searching scrutiny that not even an examining magistrate could have bettered, but he only said, 'Go on.'

The visitor thrust his hands in his waistcoat pockets, raised his head, without, however, straightening his back, and returned Marius's gaze through the green-tinted spectacles.

'Very well, Monsieur le Baron, I will go on. I have a secret to sell you.'

'A secret which concerns me?'

'To some extent.'

'Well, what is it?'

'I will tell you the first part for nothing. You will, I think, be interested.'

'Well?'

'Monsieur le Baron, you have living with you a thief and an assassin.'

Marius started.

'Not living with me,' he said.

Smoothing his hat with his sleeve, the visitor imperturbably continued:

'A thief and an assassin. Please note, Monsieur le Baron, that I am not talking about bygone transgressions that may have been cancelled out by process of law and repentance in the eyes of God, but of recent events, present happenings not yet known to the law. A man has insinuated himself into your confidence, almost into your family, under a false name. I will tell you his real name and I will tell you for nothing.'

'I'm listening.'

'His name is Jean Valjean.'

'I know that.'

'I will also tell you, also for nothing, what he is.'

'Please do.'

'He is an ex-convict.'

'I know that too.'

'You know it now that I have told you.'

'No. I knew it already.'

Marius's cool tone of voice and his apparent indifference to the information had their effect upon the visitor. He gave Marius a sidelong glance of fury which was rapidly extinguished; but brief though it was, it was not lost on Marius. There are looks like flame that can only come from beings of a certain kind; tinted glasses cannot hide them; they are like a glimpse of hell.

The visitor smiled.

'I would not venture to contradict Monsieur le Baron. In any case you will see that I am well-informed. And what I now have to tell you is known to no one except myself. It concerns the fortune of Madame la Baronne. It is a remarkable secret and it is for sale. I am offering it to you first of all, and at a low price—twenty thousand francs.'

'I know this secret already, just as I knew the others,' said Marius.

The visitor thought it judicious to lower his price.

'Well, let us say ten thousand.'

'I repeat, you have nothing to tell me. I know what you're going to say.'

The visitor's expression changed.

'But I've got to eat, haven't I? Monsieur le Baron, this is an extraordinary secret. I will let you have it for twenty francs.'

'I tell you I know it already,' said Marius. 'Just as I knew the name of Jean Valjean and know your name.'

'Well, that's not difficult, seeing that I wrote it in my letter and have only just told you. It's Thénard.'

'You've left out the rest of it.'

'What's that?'

'Thénard*ier*.'

'Who might he be?'

In moments of peril the porcupine raises its quills, the beetle shams dead, and the infantry forms a square. This man laughed and airily flicked a speck of dust off his sleeve.

'You are also the workman Jondrette,' Marius went on, 'the actor Fabantou, the poet Genflot, the Spaniard Don Alvares, and the widow Balizard.'

'The widow what?'

'At one time you kept a tavern at Montfermeil.'

'A tavern? Never!'

'And your real name is Thénardier.'

'I deny it.'

'And you're a thorough rogue. Here, take this.'

Marius got a banknote out of his pocket and tossed it in his face.

'Thank you, thank you, Monsieur le Baron!' The man bowed while he examined the note. 'Five hundred francs!' He murmured in an undertone, 'That's real money!' Then he said briskly: 'Well, we might as well be at our ease.'

And with remarkable adroitness he removed his disguise—the false nose, the tinted glasses and the two small tubes of quill which we mentioned just now and which figured in an earlier part of this tale*—stripping them away like a man taking off his hat. His eyes brightened, his uneven, knobbly and hideously wrinkled forehead was disclosed, and his nose was again a beak; in short, the avaricious, cunning countenance of the man of prey reappeared.

'Monsieur le Baron is infallible,' he said in a clear voice from which all trace of a nasal intonation had disappeared. 'I am Thénardier.'

And he straightened his back.

Thénardier was considerably taken aback and might even have been put out of countenance had this been possible for him. He had come there intending to astonish, and had himself been astonished. The fact that his humiliation had been rewarded with the sum of five hundred francs, which he had made no bones about accepting, had put the finishing touch to his amazement.

He was seeing this Baron Pontmercy for the first time in his life; nevertheless the baron had recognized him in spite of his disguise and seemed to know all about him. He seemed also to know all about Jean Valjean. Who on earth could he be, this almost beardless young man who was at once so icy and so generous, who knew all about everybody and treated rogues like a judge while at the same time paying them like a dupe? It must be borne in mind that although at one time Thénardier had been Marius's neighbour, he had never set eyes on him, a thing that happens often enough in Paris. He had written the letter we have just seen without having the least idea who he was. There was no connection in Thénardier's mind between the Marius occasionally referred to by his daughters and the present Baron Pontmercy. Nor did the name of Pontmercy mean anything to him because of the episode on the field of Waterloo, when he had heard only the two last syllables, which had not interested him since he had not supposed them to have any cash value.

For the rest, thanks to his daughter Azelma, whom he had put on the track of the bridal pair on 16 February, and thanks also to his own researches and his underworld connexions, he had picked up a good many scraps of information. He had discovered, or perhaps guessed, who the man was whom he had encountered in the sewer, and from this it was a short step to finding out his name. He knew that the Baroness Pontmercy was Cosette; but as to this, he had decided upon discretion. Who, after all, was Cosette? He himself did not precisely know. Thoughts of illegitimacy had occurred to him, since he had always regarded Fantine's story with suspicion, but what good would it do him to mention this? To be paid to keep

* The encounter between Gavroche and Montparnasse, Book Six, Chap. 2. Trs.

silent? He had, or thought he had, something better than that to sell. It also occurred to him that to come to the Baron Pontmercy with the tale, unsupported by evidence, that his wife was a bastard would be to invite his boot on his backside.

To Thénardier's way of thinking his conversation with Marius had not yet really begun. He had been obliged to give a little ground, to modify his tactics, but nothing essential was lost and he was already the richer by five hundred francs. He had something important to say, and well-informed and well-equipped though the Baron Pontmercy was, he felt that he was in a strong position. To men of Thénardier's stamp, every conversation is a contest. How did he stand in the one which was now about to begin? He did not know whom he was talking to, but he knew what he was talking about. He rapidly surveyed his resources, and having admitted that he was Thénardier he waited.

Marius was also thinking. At last he had caught up with Thénardier. The man whom he had so long sought stood before him, and he could carry out the injunction laid upon him by his father. It was humiliating to know that the dead hero should have owed his life to a scoundrel and that the blank cheque he had left behind him had not hitherto been honoured. It seemed to Marius also, in his complex state of mind where Thénardier was concerned, that there were grounds for avenging his father for the misfortune of having been saved by such a man. In any event he was pleased. The time had at last come when he could rid his father's shade of this unworthy creditor, and it was as though he would be releasing his father's memory from a debtor's prison.

But apart from this he had another duty, namely, if possible to resolve the mystery of the source of Cosette's fortune. It was a matter in which Thénardier might be of some assistance.

Thénardier had carefully stowed the five-hundred-franc note in his pocket and was smiling almost tenderly at Marius. Marius broke the silence.

'Thénardier, I have told you your name. Do you want me also to tell you the secret you were proposing to sell to me? I, too, have sources of information, and you may find that I know rather more than you do. Jean Valjean, as you say, is a murderer and a thief. He is a thief because he robbed a wealthy manufacturer, Monsieur Madeleine, whom he ruined. And he murdered the policeman, Javert.'

'I don't understand, Monsieur le Baron,' said Thénardier.

'I will explain. Round about 1822 there was a man living in the Pas-de-Calais who had at one time been in trouble with the law, but who, under the name of Monsieur Madeleine, had fully rehabilitated himself. He had become a man of probity and honour, and he had established a factory making objects of black glass which had brought prosperity to a whole town. It had also made his personal fortune, but this was as it were a secondary consideration. He looked after the poor, founded schools and hospitals, cared for the widow and the orphan—became in some sort the guardian angel of the region. He was elected mayor. A released convict who knew his background denounced him and took advantage of his arrest to draw from the Paris banking house of Laffitte—I have this from the chief cashier in person—a sum of over half a million francs belonging to Monsieur Madeleine, whose signature he forged. The released convict was Jean Valjean. As for the murder, Jean Valjean murdered the police agent, Javert. I know because I was there at the time.'

Thénardier darted at Marius the triumphant glance of a beaten man who finds that after all he has regained the ground he lost and victory is in sight. But his meek smile promptly returned. Abjectness, the humility of the inferior confronted by his superior, was a better card to play. He merely said:

'Monsieur le Baron, I think you are mistaken.'

'What!' exclaimed Marius. 'Are you denying what I've said? But those are facts!'

'They are incorrect. Monsieur le Baron has so far honoured me with his confidence that I feel it is my duty to tell him the truth. Truth and justice should come before all else. I do not like to hear a man unjustly accused. Jean Valjean did not rob Monsieur Madeleine, nor did he kill Javert.'

'How on earth do you make that out?'

'For two reasons. In the first place he did not rob Monsieur Madeleine because he himself is, or was, Monsieur Madeleine.'

'What in the world . . .?'

'And secondly he did not kill Javert because Javert killed himself. He committed suicide.'

'What!' cried Marius, beside himself with amazement. 'But what proof have you of this?'

'The police agent Javert,' said Thénardier, intoning the words as though they were a classical alexandrine, 'was found drowned under a boat moored near the Pont-au-Change.'

'Prove it!'

Thénardier fished in an inside pocket and got out a large envelope containing folded papers of different sizes.

'Here is my dossier,' he said calmly. He went on: 'Acting in your interests, Monsieur le Baron, I wished to discover the whole truth about Jean Valjean. When I tell you that he and Madeleine are one and the same, and that Javert was the only murderer of Javert, I

can produce evidence to prove it, and not merely handwritten evidence—handwriting can be forged—but printed evidence.'

As he spoke Thénardier was getting copies of two newspapers out of the envelope, both faded and creased and smelling strongly of tobacco, but one of which seemed very much older than the other.

The reader knows of both these newspapers. The older of the two was the issue of the *Drapeau Blanc* dated 25 July 1823 in which Monsieur Madeleine and Jean Valjean were shown to be the same person. The more recent, the *Moniteur* of 15 June 1832, reported the suicide of Javert, adding that it followed Javert's verbal report to the Prefect of Police that, having been taken prisoner by the insurgents in the Rue de la Chanvrerie, he owed his life to the magnanimity of one of them, who had fired his pistol into the air.

There could be no doubting this evidence. The newspapers were unquestionably authentic. They had not been printed simply to support the testimony of Thénardier. Seeing how mistaken he had been, Marius uttered a cry of joy.

'Why, but then he's a splendid man! The fortune was really his! He's Madeleine, the benefactor of an entire region, and Jean Valjean, the saviour of Javert. He's a hero! He's a saint!'

'He's neither one nor the other,' said Thénardier. 'He's a murderer and a thief.' And he added in the tone of a man who begins to feel that he has the upper hand, 'Let us keep quite calm'.

The words murderer and thief, which Marius had thought disposed of, came like a cold douche.

'You mean there's more?' he said.

'Yes,' said Thénardier, 'there is more. Valjean did not rob Madeleine, but he is nonetheless a thief, and although he did not kill Javert he is nonetheless a murderer.'

'Are you talking about the wretched little crime he committed forty years ago, which, as your newspaper shows, has been fully expiated?' asked Marius.

'I'm talking about murder and theft, Monsieur le Baron, and I'm talking about facts. What I have now to tell you is something unpublished and quite unknown which may account for the fortune so cleverly bestowed on Madame la Baronne by Jean Valjean. I call it clever because it enabled him to buy his way into a respectable family, create a home for himself and obliterate his crime.'

'I might interrupt you at this point,' said Marius. 'But go on.'

'I shall tell you everything, Monsieur le Baron, and trust to your generosity for my reward. This secret is worth a large sum. You may ask why I have not gone to Valjean. The reason is very simple. There is nothing to be got out of him. He has handed all his money over to you, and since I need money for my voyage to La Joya, you are the person to whom I must apply. I am a little fatigued. Will you permit me to sit down?'

Marius nodded and sat down himself.

Thénardier seated himself in an upholstered armchair and replaced his papers in the envelope, remarking, as he re-folded the *Drapeau Blanc*, 'I had a job to get hold of this one.' He then sat back with his legs crossed, in the manner of a man sure of his facts, and embarked solemnly upon his narrative.

'On the sixth of June last year, Monsieur le Baron—that is to say, on the day of the uprising—a man was hiding in the Paris main sewer at the point between the Pont des Invalides and the Pont d'Iéna where it runs into the Seine.'

At this Marius drew his chair closer, and Thénardier proceeded with the assurance of an orator who feels that he has a firm hold on his audience.

'This man, who had a key to the sewer, had been obliged to go into hiding for reasons unconnected with politics. It was, I repeat, the day of the insurrection, and the time was about eight o'clock in the evening. Hearing the sound of approaching footsteps, the man took cover. Another man was in the sewer. This happened not far from the entrance, and there was sufficient light for the first man to recognize the second, who was walking bent double with a heavy burden on his back. The man was an ex-convict and his burden was a dead body. Clear proof of murder if ever there was one, and as for theft—well, one doesn't kill a man for nothing. He was going to drop the body in the river. A thing worth mentioning is that before reaching the sewer entrance he had to go through an appalling trough where he might have dumped the body; but if he had done so it would have been found by the sewage workers next day and that didn't suit him. He preferred to struggle through the pit with his burden, and it must have cost him an enormous effort. The risk he took was horrible and I am surprised that he came out of it alive.'

Marius's chair had drawn even closer. Thénardier paused for breath and went on:

'No need to tell you, Monsieur le Baron, that a sewer is not as wide as the Champs-Élysées. Two men occupying the same part of it are bound to meet. That is precisely what happened, and this second man said to the first: "You see what I'm carrying on my back? I've got to get out of here. You have a key. Hand it over." This ex-convict was a man of enormous strength. It was useless to refuse. Nevertheless the first man bargained, simply to gain time. He could see nothing of the dead man except that he was young and well-dressed, seemingly rich, and that his face was covered with blood. While they were talking the first contrived, without the murderer noticing, to rip off a small piece of the murdered man's coat. As evidence you understand, so as to be able to bring the crime home to the criminal. He then opened the sewer gate and let the man out with his burden on his back. After which he made himself scarce, not wanting to get mixed up in the affair, and in particular not wanting to be there when the murderer dropped his victim in the river. And now I think you will understand. The man carrying the corpse was Jean Valjean, and the man with the key was the person addressing you. As for the scrap of cloth—'

Thénardier concluded the sentence by pulling a muddy fragment from his pocket and holding it out, grasped between his two thumbs and forefingers.

Marius had risen to his feet, pale and scarcely able to breathe. He was staring at the scrap of cloth, and without taking his eyes off it he backed towards the wall and fumbled for the key in the door of a wardrobe. He opened the wardrobe and thrust in his arm without looking, still with his eyes fixed on the scrap of cloth which Thénardier was holding out.

'I have every reason to believe, Monsieur le Baron,' said Thénardier, 'that the murdered man was a wealthy foreigner who had fallen into a trap set by Valjean when he had an enormous sum of money on his person.'

'I was the man,' cried Marius, 'and here is the coat I was wearing!' And he flung the bloodstained garment on the floor. Then, snatching the fragment of cloth from Thénardier, he bent over the coat and found the place from which it had been torn. It fitted exactly. Thénardier stood petrified, thinking, 'I'm done for!'

Marius rose up, trembling but radiant. He put a hand in his pocket and going furiously to Thénardier thrust a fist into his face, clutching a bundle of five-hundred and thousand-franc notes.

'You are an abominable liar and a scoundrel! You came here to accuse this man and you have cleared him; you wanted to destroy him and you have done the opposite. It's you who are the thief and the murderer! I saw you, Thénardier-Jondrette, in that foul garret in the Boulevard de l'Hôpital. I know enough about you to have you sent to gaol and further, if I wanted to. Here's a thousand francs for you, villain that you are!' He threw a thousand-franc note at him. 'And here's another five hundred, and now get out of here! What happened at Waterloo protects you.'

'Waterloo?' grunted Thénardier, pocketing the notes.

'Yes, you devil. You saved a colonel's life.'

'He was a general,' said Thénardier, looking up.

'He was a colonel. I wouldn't give a halfpenny for any general.

And now get out and thank your lucky stars that I want to see no more of you. Here you are, here's another three thousand francs. Take them and go to America with your daughter, because your wife's dead, you lying rogue. What's more, I'll see to it that you get there, and when you do I'll see to it that you're credited with twenty thousand francs. Go and get yourself hanged somewhere else!'

'Monsieur le Baron,' said Thénardier, bowing to the ground, 'I am eternally grateful.'

And he left, having understood nothing, amazed and delighted by this manna from Heaven. We may briefly relate the end of his story. Two days after the scene we have described he set off for America under another name with his daughter Azelma and a letter of credit for twenty-thousand francs to be drawn upon in New York. But Thénardier was incurable. He used the money to go into the slave-trade.

Directly he had left the house Marius ran into the garden, where Cosette was still strolling.

'Cosette!' he cried. 'Hurry! We must go at once. Basque, fetch a fiacre! Oh, God, he was the man who saved my life! We mustn't waste a minute. Put on your shawl.'

Cosette thought he had gone mad, and obeyed.

Marius could scarcely breathe. He pressed a hand to his heart to calm its beating. He strode up and down. He embraced Cosette. 'I'm such a fool!' he said. He was beside himself, seeing in Jean Valjean a figure of indescribable stature, supremely great and gently humble in his immensity, the convict transformed into Christ. Marius was so dazed that he could not tell exactly what he saw, only that it was great.

The fiacre arrived. He followed Cosette into it and ordered the driver to go to Number Seven, Rue de l'Homme-Armé.

'Oh, what happiness!' cried Cosette. 'I have been afraid to speak to you of the Rue de l'Homme-Armé. We're going to see Monsieur Jean.'

'Your father, Cosette. More than ever your father. Cosette, I have guessed something. You told me that you never received the letter I sent you by Gavroche. I know what happened. It was delivered to him, your father, and he came to the barricade to save me. It's his nature to save people. He spared Javert. He rescued me from that inferno and carried me on his back through the sewers, to bring me to you. Oh, I have been a monster of ingratitude! There was a deep trough, Cosette, where we might both have been drowned, and he carried me through it. I was unconscious, you see, and I didn't know what was happening. We're going to take him back with us, whether he likes it or not, and we'll never let him go again. Provided he's at home! Provided we can find him! I'll spend the rest of my life honouring him. It must have happened like that —Gavroche gave the letter to him instead of to you. And that explains everything. You do understand, don't you?'

Cosette did not understand a word.

'I'm sure you're right,' she said.

The fiacre continued on its way.

V. *Night with Day to Follow*

Jean Valjean looked round on hearing the knock on his door and feebly called 'Come in!'

The door opened and Cosette and Marius appeared. Cosette rushed into the room while Marius stood in the doorway.

'Cosette!' said Jean Valjean and sat upright in his chair, his face white and haggard, his arms extended and a glow of immense happiness in his eyes. Cosette fell into his arms. 'Father!' she cried.

Valjean was stammering broken words of welcome. Then he said, 'So you have forgiven me?' and, turning to Marius, who was screwing up his eyes to prevent the tears from falling, he said: 'And you too, you forgive me?'

Marius could not speak. 'Thank you,' said Valjean.

Cosette tossed her hat and shawl on to the bed, and seating herself on the old man's knees, she tenderly parted the locks of hair and kissed him on the forehead. Valjean was in a state of great bewilderment. Cosette, who had only a confused notion of what it was all about, embraced him again. Valjean stammered:

'One can be so stupid! I thought I should never see her again. Do you know, Monsieur Pontmercy, that at the moment when you entered the room I was saying to myself, "It's all over". There's the little dress she wore, there on the bed. I was the most miserable of men. That's what I was saying to myself at the very moment when you came upstairs—"I shall never see her again!" How idiotic it was! One forgets to trust in God. But I was so unhappy.'

For a moment he was unable to speak, but then he went on:

'I really did need to see Cosette for a little while every now and then. The heart must have something to live on. But I felt that I was not wanted, and I said to myself, "They don't need you, so stay in your own place. No one has the right to inflict themselves on other people". And now I'm seeing her again! Cosette, this is a very pretty dress you're wearing. Did your husband choose it? You don't mind, do you, Monsieur Pontmercy, if I address her as "tu". It won't be for long.'

'Such a cruel father!' said Cosette. 'Where have you been? Why were you away so long? The other times it was only three or four days. I sent Nicolette, but they always told her you were away. When did you get back, and why didn't you let us know? Do you know, you've changed a great deal. How wicked of you! You've been ill and you never told us. Marius, take his hand and feel how cold it is.'

'Monsieur Pontmercy,' said Jean Valjean, 'have you really forgiven me?'

At the repetition of the words Marius broke down.

'Cosette, did you hear what he said? He asked me to forgive him! And do you know what he did? He saved my life and, even more, he gave me you! And then he sacrificed himself by withdrawing from our lives. He ran hideous risks for us and now he asks me to forgive him, graceless, pitiless clod that I have been! His courage, his saintliness, his selflessness are beyond all bounds. There is no price too high to pay for him.'

'You have no need to say all this,' murmured Jean Valjean.

'Why didn't you say it yourself?' demanded Marius, in a voice in which reproach was mingled with veneration. 'It's partly your fault. You save a man's life and then you don't tell him. Even worse, you pretended to confess to me and in doing so you defamed yourself.'

'I told you the truth,' said Valjean.

'No. The truth means the whole truth, not just part of it. Why didn't you tell me that you were Monsieur Madeleine and that you had spared Javert? Why didn't you tell me that I owed you my life?'

'Because I thought as you did. I thought you were right. It was better for me to break away. If you had known about the business of the sewer you might have made me stay with you. It would have upset everything.'

'What or whom would it have upset?' demanded Marius. 'Do you think we're going to allow you to stay here? We're going to take you with us. Good God, when I think that I only learnt all this by pure chance! You're coming with us. You're part of us. You're Cosette's father and mine. I won't allow you to spend another day in this horrible place.'

'Certainly I shan't be here tomorrow,' said Jean Valjean.

'And what does that mean? We shan't allow you to go on any more journeys. You aren't going to leave us again. You belong to us. We shan't let you go.'

'This time it's final,' said Cosette. 'We have a cab down below. I'm kidnapping you—if necessary, by force.'

Laughing, she went through the motions of picking up the old man in her arms.

'We've still kept your room for you. You can't think how pretty the garden is just now. The azaleas are coming on wonderfully, the paths are sanded with real sea sand, and there are little blue shells. You'll be able to eat my strawberries, I'm the one who waters them. And there won't be any more of this "Madame—Monsieur Jean" nonsense, we're a republic and we call each other "tu", don't we, Marius? Everything will be different now. And oh, father, a most dreadful thing happened. There was a redbreast that had built its nest in a hole in the wall, and a horrid cat went and ate it. My darling redbreast, that used to look in at my window! It made me cry. I could have killed that cat. But now nobody's going to cry any more. We're all going to be happy. Grandfather will be so delighted when we bring you back with us. You shall have your own corner of the garden where you can grow anything you like and we shall see if your strawberries are as good as mine. And I'll do everything you say, and of course you'll have to obey me as well.'

Jean Valjean had listened without hearing. He had listened to the music of her voice rather than to the words, and one of those great tears which are the deep pearls of the soul brimmed in his eye. He murmured:

'This is the proof that God is good.'

'Dear father!' said Cosette.

'It is true,' said Jean Valjean, 'that it would be delightful for us all to live together. Those trees are filled with birds. I would stroll with Cosette. To be one of the living, people who greet each other in the morning and call to each other in the garden, that is a great happiness. We should see each other every day and would each cultivate our own corner, and she would give me her strawberries to eat and I would cut my roses for her. Yes, it would be delightful, only——' he broke off and said softly, 'well, it's a shame.'

The tear did not fall but lingered in his eye and he replaced it with a smile. Cosette took his two hands in hers.

'Your hands are so cold,' she said. 'Are you ill? Are you in pain?'

'No,' said Valjean. 'I'm not in pain. Only——' he broke off again.

'Only what?'

'I'm going to die in a little while.'

Cosette and Marius shuddered.

'To die!' exclaimed Marius.

'Yes, but that is not important,' said Jean Valjean. He drew breath, smiled and said: 'Cosette, go on talking. Your redbreast died. Go on talking about it. I want to hear your voice.'

Marius was gazing at him in stupefaction and Cosette uttered a piercing cry.

'Father! Father! You're going to live! You must live! I want you to live, do you understand?'

Jean Valjean looked up at her with adoring eyes.

'Very well, forbid me to die. Who knows, perhaps I shall obey. I was in the act of dying when you arrived. That stopped me. It was as though I were being reborn.'

'You're full of strength and life,' cried Marius. 'Do you think people die just like that? You have suffered greatly, but now your sufferings are over. I am the one to ask your forgiveness, and I do so on my knees. You must live, and you must live with us, and you must live for a long, long time. We're taking you back. Henceforth our every thought will be for your happiness.'

'You see?' said Cosette, in tears. 'Marius says you aren't to die.'

Jean Valjean continued to smile.

'If you take me back, Monsieur Pontmercy, will that make me any different from the man I am? No. God thinks as you and I do, and he has not changed his mind. It is better for me to go. Death is a very sensible arrangement. God knows better than we do what is good for us. That you should be happy, Marius Pontmercy and Cosette, that youth should marry with the morning, that you two children should have lilac and nightingales around you, that your life should be like a lawn bathed in sunshine and glowing with enchantment; and that I, who am no longer good for anything, should now die, that is surely right. We must be reasonable. There is nothing more left for me. I am well persuaded that my life is over. I had a fainting fit not long ago, and last night I drank all the water in the jug. Your husband is so good, Cosette. It is far better for you to be with him than with me.'

There was again a knock on the door and the doctor entered.

'Good day and goodbye, doctor,' said Valjean. 'These are my two children.'

Marius went up to him and spoke a single word—'Monsieur? . . .'—but the tone in which he said it made it an entire question. The doctor replied with a meaningful glance.

'Because things do not always please us,' said Valjean, 'that is no reason for reproaching God.'

There was a pause in which all were oppressed. Jean Valjean turned to Cosette as though he wished to carry her image with him into eternity. Even amid the shadows into which he had now sunk the sight of her could still raise him to ecstasy. The glow of her sweet face was reflected in his own. Even in the act of death there may be enchantment.

The doctor was feeling his pulse. 'You were what he needed,' he said to Cosette and Marius; and then in a whispered aside to Marius: 'Too late, I fear.'

Scarcely taking his eyes off Cosette, Valjean glanced serenely at Marius and the doctor. A low murmur escaped his lips.

'To die is nothing; but it is terrible not to live.'

Suddenly he stood up. These returns of strength are sometimes a sign of the final death-throes. He walked steadily to the wall, brushing aside Marius and the doctor, who sought to help him, and took down the little copper crucifix which was hanging there. Then he returned to his chair, moving like a man in the fullness of health, and, putting the crucifix on the table, said in a clear voice:

'He is the great martyr.'

Then his head fell forward while his fingers clutched at the stuff of his trousers over his knees. Cosette ran sobbing to hold him up, murmuring distractedly, 'Father, father, have we found you only to lose you?'

One may say of dying that it goes by fits and starts, now moving towards the grave and now turning back towards life. After that half-seizure Valjean regained strength, passed a hand over his forehead as though to brush away the shadows, and was almost entirely lucid. He seized a fold of Cosette's sleeve and kissed it.

'He's reviving!' cried Marius. 'Doctor, he's reviving!'

'You are both so good,' said Jean Valjean. 'I will tell you what has grieved me. What has grieved me, Monsieur Pontmercy, is that you have made no use of the money. It is truly your wife's money. Let me explain it to you, my children. I am glad you are here, if only for that reason. Black jade comes from England and white jade comes from Norway. It's all in this letter here. And I invented a new kind of fastening for bracelets which is prettier, better and cheaper. It made a great deal of money. Cosette's fortune is really and truly hers. I tell you this to put your minds at rest.'

The concierge had come upstairs and was looking through the half-open door. The doctor told her to go away, but he could not prevent the zealous woman from calling to the dying man:

'Do you want a priest?'

'I have one,' Jean Valjean replied; and he pointed upwards as though there were some other being present whom he alone could see. Indeed it is not improbable that the bishop was present in those last moments of his life. Cosette slipped a pillow behind his back. Valjean said:

'I beseech you, Monsieur Pontmercy, to have no misgivings. My life will have been wasted if you do not make use of the money that is truly Cosette's. I can assure you that our products were very good, rivalling what are known as the jewels of Berlin.'

When a person dear to us is about to die we fix him with an intent gaze that seeks to hold him back. They stood beside him in silent anguish, having no words to speak, Cosette clasping Marius by the hand.

Jean Valjean was visibly declining, sinking down towards that dark horizon. His breath was coming in gasps, punctured by slight groans. He had difficulty in moving his arms, and his feet were now quite motionless. But as the weakness of his body increased so his spirit grew in splendour, and the light of the unknown world was already visible in his eyes. His face became paler as he smiled. There was something other than life in it. His breath failed but his gaze grew deeper. He was a dead body which seemed to possess wings.

He signed to Cosette to come closer to him, then signed to Marius. It was the last moment of the last hour, and when he spoke it was in a voice so faint that it seemed to come from a long way off, as though there were a wall between them.

'Come close to me, both of you. I love you dearly. How sweet it is to die like this. And you love me too, dear Cosette. You'll weep for me a little, but not too much, I want you to have no great sorrows. You must enjoy life, my children. A thing I forgot to mention is that the buckles without tongues are more profitable than any other kind. They cost ten francs the gross to manufacture and sell at sixty. Excellent business, as you see, so there is really no reason, Monsieur Pontmercy, why you should be astonished at that sum of six hundred thousand francs. It is honest money. You can be rich with an easy mind. You must have a carriage and now and then a box at the theatre, and you, Cosette, must have beautiful dresses to dance in, and when you invite your friends to dinner. You must be happy. I am leaving the two candlesticks on the mantelpiece to Cosette. They are made of silver, but to me they are pure gold. I don't know whether the person who gave them to me is pleased as he looks down on me from above. I have done my best. You must not forget, my children, that I am one of the poor. You must bury me in any plot of ground that comes handy and put a stone to mark the spot. That is my wish. No name on the stone. If Cosette cares to visit it sometimes I shall be glad. And you too, Monsieur Pontmercy. I must confess that I have not always liked you, and I ask your forgiveness. She and you are now one person to me and I am very grateful. I know you are making Cosette happy. The greatest joy in my life has been to see her with rosy cheeks, and I have been grieved when she has looked pale. You will find in the chest of drawers a five-hundred-franc note. I haven't touched it. It is for the poor. Cosette, do you see your little dress there on the bed? Do you remember it? That was ten years ago. How time passes! We have been happy together. Now it is over. You must not weep, dear children, I shall not be far away. I shall watch over you from where I am. You need only to look when night has fallen and you will see me smile. Do you remember Montfermeil, Cosette? You were in the woods, and you were frightened. I helped you carry the bucket, do you remember? That was the first time I touched your poor hand. It was so cold! Your hands were red in those days, Mademoiselle, and now they are white. And do you remember that big doll? You called her Catherine, and you wished you could have taken her with you to the convent. You made me laugh at times, angel that you were. When it rained you floated straws in the gutter and watched to see which would win. Once I gave you a battledore of willow and a shuttlecock with yellow, blue and green feathers. I expect you have forgotten that. You were so enchanting when you were small. You hung cherries over your ears. All those things are in the past—the woods we walked through, the convent where we took refuge, your child's eyes and laughter, all shadows now. I believed that it all belonged to me, and that is where I was foolish. Those Thénardiers were wicked people, but we must forgive them. Cosette, the time has come for me to tell you your mother's name. It was Fantine. You must not forget it, Fantine, and you must bow your head whenever you speak it. She loved you greatly and she suffered greatly. She was as rich in sorrow as you are in happiness. That is how God evens things out. He watches us all from above and knows what he is doing amid his splendid stars. And now I must leave you, my children. Love one another always. There is nothing else that matters in this world except love. You will think sometimes of the old man who died in this place. Dearest Cosette, it was not my fault if lately I have not come to see you. It wrung my heart. I used to go to the end of your street. I must have looked a strange sight to the people who saw me. They must have thought me mad. One day I went without my hat . . . Children, my sight is failing. I had more to say, but no matter. Think of me sometimes. You are fortunate. I don't know what is happening to me, I can see a light. Come closer. I die happy. Bow your dear heads so that I may lay my hands on them.'

Cosette and Marius fell on their knees on either side of him, stifling their tears. His hands rested on their heads, and did not move again. He lay back with his head turned to the sky, and the light from the two candlesticks fell upon his face.

VI. *The Hidden Grave*

In the cemetery of Père Lachaise, not far from the communal grave and remote from the elegant quarter of that city of sepulchres which parades in the presence of eternity the hideous fashions of death, is a deserted corner near an old wall, and here, beneath a big yew tree, surrounded by mosses and dandelions, there is a stone. It is black and green, no more exempt than other stones from the encroachment of time, lichen and bird-droppings. There is no path near it, and people are reluctant to go that way because the grass is long and they are sure to get their feet wet. In sunny weather lizards visit it, there is a stir of grasses all around it and birds sing in the tree.

The stone is quite unadorned. It was carved strictly to serve its purpose, long enough and wide enough to cover a man. It bears no name.

But many years ago someone chalked four lines of verse on it which became gradually illegible under the influence of wind and weather and have now, no doubt, vanished entirely.

> *He sleeps. Although so much he was denied,*
> *He lived; and when his dear love left him, died.*
> *It happened of itself, in the calm way*
> *That in the evening night-time follows day.*

PART FOUR: BOOK SEVEN: Argot

I. *Its Origin*

PIGRITIA is a terrible word. It encompasses a world: la pégre, for which read robbery, and the hell which is la pégrenne, for which read hunger.

Thus idleness is a mother with two children, a son, who is robbery, and a daughter, who is hunger.

Where have we now got to? To argot.

What is argot? It is at once a nation and an idiom, robbery in its two aspects, the people and the language.

When, thirty-four years ago, the narrator of this grave and sombre history introduced into a work written with the same intention a thief who spoke argot, it was greeted with outrage and indignation—'What! Argot! But that is the language of the underworld, of pickpockets and prisons, everything that is most abominable in society!' etc. etc. etc.

We have never understood this kind of objection.

Later two powerful novelists, the first a profound student of the human heart and the second a fearless friend of the common people, Balzac and Eugène Sue, having made criminals talk their natural language, as the author of *Le dernier jour d'un condamné* had done in 1828, were similarly castigated—'Why do these writers inflict this revolting patois on us? Argot is a disgusting thing!'

No one would deny this. But when it comes to the probing of a wound, an abyss or a social phenomenon, can it be wrong to lead the way and penetrate to the heart of the matter? We had always thought this to be an act of courage, or at least a useful act, worthy of the sympathy that any performance of duty deserves. Why should not everything be explored and studied? Why stop halfway? To stop is the action of the plummet, not of the leadsman who operates it.

Certainly it is not an easy or an attractive task to peer into the lowest depths of the social order, the region where earth ends and mire begins; to burrow into the muck and capture and expose to the public view that debased idiom, that diseased vocabulary of which every word is like a scale of some monster of darkness and the swamp. Nothing can be more depressing than to expose, naked to the light of thought, the hideous growth of argot. Indeed it is like a sort of repellent animal intended to dwell in darkness which has been dragged out of its cloaca. One seems to see a horned and living creature viciously struggling to be restored to the place where it belongs. One word is like a claw, another like a sightless and bleeding eye; and there are phrases which clutch like the pincers of a crab. And all of it is alive with the hideous vitality of things that have organized themselves amid disorganization.

But since when has a horror been debarred from study? When has sickness driven the doctor away? Can one imagine a naturalist refusing to study a scorpion, a bat or a tarantula on the grounds that these things are too ugly? The thinker who turns his back on argot is like a surgeon who shrinks from a suppurating wound; he is a philologist reluctant to examine an aspect of language, a philosopher reluctant to scrutinize an aspect of humanity. For this must be said to those who are unaware of the fact: argot is both a literary phenomenon and a social consequence. The proper definition of the word is this: it is the language of poverty.

At this point we must pause. It can be argued that every trade and profession, one might almost say every accident in the social hierarchy and all forms of intelligence, have their argot, from the lawyer who wraps up an agreement in jargon of his own, the house-agent who talks about 'extensive grounds' and 'modern conveniences', the butcher who talks about 'prime beef' to the actor who says, 'I was a flop'. The printer, the master-at-arms, the sportsman, the cobbler, the cavalry-officer all have their specialized language. At a pinch it can be claimed that the sailor who uses port and starboard for left and right is talking argot. There is an argot of the great and an argot of the little. That duchesses have their argot is proved by the following sentence from a letter written by a great lady at the time of the Restoration, 'Vous trouverez dans ces potains-là une foultitude de raisons pour que je me libertise'. ('You will gather from this tittle-tattle a multitude of reasons why I am setting myself free'.) Twenty years ago there was a school of criticism which asserted that, 'Half Shakespeare is word-play and punning,'—in other words, that he used argot. The poets and artists who label Monsieur de Montmorency a 'bourgeois' because he is not well versed in art and poetry are themselves talking argot. Classical scholars have their argot; mathematics, medicine, botany, all have their own language. The splendid language of the sea, resonance of the wind and the waves, the humming of the shrouds, the rolling of the ship, the roar of cannon, and the crash of the boarding-axe, all this is a superb and heroic argot that, compared with the barbaric argot of the underworld, is like a lion compared with a jackal.

All this is true, but whatever may be said in its favour this extension of the meaning of the word 'argot' is something that not everyone accepts. For our own part, we restrict the word to its old, precise meaning, and for us argot is simply argot. The true argot, argot par excellence (if those words may be used in this context), the immemorial argot which was a kingdom in itself, is, we must repeat, nothing but the ugly, restless, cunning, treacherous, profound and fatalistic language of the outcast and squalid underworld, the world of hunger and pauperism—*les misérables*. There exists, at the bottom of all abasement and misfortune, a last extreme which rebels and joins battle with the forces of law and respectability in a desperate struggle, waged partly by cunning and partly by violence, at once sick and ferocious, in which it attacks the prevailing social order with the pin-pricks of vice and the hammer-blows of crime. And for the purpose of this struggle the underworld has its own battle-language, which is argot.

To rescue from oblivion even a fragment of a language which men have used and which is in danger of being lost—that is to say, one of the elements, whether good or bad, which have shaped and complicated civilization—is to extend the scope of social observation and to serve civilization. It is a service rendered consciously or unconsciously by Plautus when he made a Phoenician talk to Carthaginian soldiers, and by Molière with his Levantine and the varieties of patois which he put into the mouths of so many of his characters. To this it may be replied that patois is a different thing—it is a language that has been used by a whole people or province. But what is argot? What purpose is served by 'rescuing' it? Our answer is simply that if there is one thing more deserving of study than the language spoken by a people or province it is the language spoken by misery; a language that has been spoken in France, for example, for more than four centuries: the language not merely of one particular misery, but of misery itself, all possible human misery.

Moreover we must insist upon the fact that the examination of social failings and deformities is ordained so that they may be recognized and cured, an inescapable task. The vocation of the historian of mores and ideas is no less strict than that of the historian of events. The latter deals with the surface of life, with battles and parliaments and the birth of princes, while the former is concerned with what goes on beneath the surface, among the people who work and wait upon the outcome of events, weary womenfolk and dying children, ignorance and prejudice, envy and secret rivalries between man and man, the vague tremors running through the mass of the impoverished, the unfortunate, and the infamous. He must descend

457

in a spirit of both charity and severity to that secret region where the destitute are huddled together, those who bleed and those who strike, those who weep and those who curse, those who go hungry and those who devour, those who endure evil and those who cause it. Are the duties of the historians of hearts and souls less exacting than those of the historians of external fact? Has Dante less to say than Machiavelli? Is the under side of civilization less important than the upper side because it is darker and goes deeper? Can one know the mountain without also knowing the cave?

From the foregoing it might be inferred that a gulf exists between these two kinds of historian, but we have no such thought in mind. One cannot be a good historian of the outward, visible world without giving some thought to the hidden, private life of ordinary people; and on the other hand one cannot be a good historian of this inner life without taking into account outward events where these are relevant. They are two orders of fact which reflect each other, which are always linked and which sometimes provoke each other. All the features traced by providence on the surface of a nation have their sombre but distinct counterpart in the depths, and every stirring in the depths produces a tremor on the surface. True history being a composite of all things, the true historian must concern himself with all things. Mankind is not a circle with a single centre but an ellipse with two focal points, of which facts are one and ideas the other.

Argot is nothing but a changing-room where language, having some evil end in view, adopts a disguise, reclothing itself with masked words and tattered metaphors, a process which renders it horrible.

It can scarcely be recognized. Is this really French, the great human language? It is ready to enter the stage, to put words into the mouth of crime, to act out the entire repertory of ill-doing. It no longer walks but shuffles, limps on a crutch that can be used as a club; it bears the name of vagrancy and has been daubed with make-up by ghostly dressers; it crawls and rears up its head, two characteristics of the reptile. It is prepared to play any part, made fraudulent by the forger, tainted by the poisoner, blackened by the soot of the incendiary; and the murderer has daubed it with red.

When, from the honest side of the fence, we listen on the fringe of society, we may hear the speech of those who are outside. We distinguish questions and answers. Without understanding it we catch a horrid murmur, resembling the human accent but nearer to growls than to words. That is argot. The words are misshapen, distorted by some kind of fantastic bestiality. We might be hearing the speech of hydras.

It is the unintelligible immersed in shadow; it grunts and whispers, adding enigma to the encircling gloom. Misfortune is dark and crime is darker still, and it is of these two darknesses put together that argot is composed. Obscurity is in the atmosphere, in the actions and in the voices: a dreadful toad-language which creeps and skips and monstrously moves in that vast fog of hunger, vice, lies, injustice, nakedness, asphyxia, and winter which is the bright noontide of the underworld.

Let us have compassion for those under chastisement. Alas, who are we ourselves? Who am I and who are you? Whence do we come, and is it quite certain that we did nothing before we were born? This earth is not without some resemblance to a gaol. Who knows but that man is a victim of divine justice? Look closely at life. It is so constituted that one senses punishment everywhere.

Are you what is known as a happy man? Yet you experience sadness every day. Every day brings its major grief or its minor care. Yesterday you trembled for the health of someone dear to you, today you fear for your own; tomorrow it will be money trouble, the next day the slander of a calumniator, and on the day after that the misfortune of a friend; then there is the weather, or some possession broken or lost, or some pleasure which leaves you with an uneasy conscience; and another time it is the progress of public affairs. All this without counting the griefs of the heart. And so it goes on; as one cloud is dispelled another forms. Scarcely one day in a hundred consists of unbroken delight and sunshine. Yet you are one of the small number who are called happy! As for the rest of mankind, it is lost in stagnant night.

Thoughtful persons seldom speak of happiness or unhappiness. In this world, which is so plainly the antechamber of another, there are no happy men. The true division of humanity is between those who live in light and those who live in darkness. Our aim must be to diminish the number of the latter and increase the number of the former. That is why we demand education and knowledge. To learn to read is to light a fire; every syllable that is spelled out is a spark.

But to talk of light is not necessarily to talk of joy. One may suffer in the light; its excess burns. The flame is the enemy of the wing. To burn without ceasing to fly, that is the achievement of genius. When you have reached the stage of knowing and loving you will still suffer. The day is born in tears. The enlightened weep, if only for those still in darkness.

Argot is the language of the shadows.

Thought moves to its most sombre depths, social philosophy leads to the most poignant conclusions, when confronted by this enigmatic dialect which is at once blighted and rebellious. It is here that chastisement is visible; every syllable bears the brand. The words of this language of the people seem seared and shrivelled, as though by a red-hot iron; some, indeed, seem to be still smoking, and there are phrases which put one in mind of the swiftly bared and branded shoulder of a thief. Ideas are almost inexpressible in the language of the outlaw, of which the metaphors are sometimes so outrageous that one feels that they have worn manacles. But despite all this, and because of it, this strange patois is entitled to its place in that vast, impartial assemblage which finds room for a worn halfpenny as well as for a gold medal and which is known as literature. Argot, whether we like it or not, has its own grammar and its own poetry. If there are words so distorted that they sound like the muttering of uncouth mouths, there are others in which we catch the voice of Villon.

'Mais où sont les neiges d'antan' is a line of argot. Antan—ante annum—belongs to the argot of Thunes and signifies 'last year' and, by extension, 'the past'. It was possible thirty-five years ago, at the time of the departure of the great chain-gang of 1827, to read the following words scratched with a nail on the wall of one of the cells in Bicêtre prison by a leader of the Thunes mob condemned to the galleys: 'Les dabs d'antan trimaient siempre pour le pierre du Coëscne,' which means, 'The old-time kings always had themselves consecrated'—consecration, in this case, being the galleys.

From the purely literary point of view few studies can be more interesting and fruitful than that of argot. It is a language within a language, a sort of sickly excrescence, an unhealthy graft producing a vegetation of its own, a parasite with roots in the old Gallic trunk whose sinister foliage covers half of the language. That is what one might term the first aspect, the vulgar aspect of argot. But for those who study the dialect as it should be studied, that is to say, in the way a geologist studies the earth, it is more like an alluvial deposit. Examining it one finds, buried beneath the old colloquial French, Provençal, Spanish, Italian, Levantine—that language of the Mediterranean ports—English, German, the French, Italian and Roman varieties of Romance, Latin and finally Basque and Celtic. A profound, weird conglomeration; a subterranean edifice erected by all outcasts. Each accursed race has contributed its layer, every heart and every suffering has added a stone. A host of souls, evil or low-born or rebellious, who have lived through life and passed on to eternity, are almost wholly present and in some sort still visible in the form of a monstrous word.

Do you wish for Spanish? The old Gothic argot is full of it: for example *boffette*, for which the French is *soufflet*, meaning a bellows, a puff of wind (blow) or a buffet, derived from *bofeton*; *vantarne* (later *vanterne*) meaning a window; *gat*, meaning cat, derived from *gato*; *acite*, oil, derived from *aceyte*. Or Italian? There is spade, sword, derived from *spada*; *carvel*, boat, derived from *caravella*. English? There is *bichot*, bishop; *raille*, a spy, derived from rascal; *pilche*, a case, derived from pilcher, a sheath. German? There is *caleur*, from the German *Kellner*, a waiter; *herr*, the master, from *Herzog*, the duke. Latin? *Franjir*, to break (Latin frangere); *affurer*, to steal (fur); *cadène*, a chain (catena). There is a word which appears in all the continental dialects with a sort of magical power and authority. It is the word *magnus* (great). In Scotland it becomes *mac*, meaning the head of the clan*, such as Macfarlane or Macdonald; French argot turns it into *meck*, later *meg*, meaning God. Do you look for Basque? There is *gahisto*, the devil, derived from *gaiztoa*, evil; *sorgabon*, goodnight, derived from *gabon*, good-evening. Celtic? There is *blavin*, handkerchief, derived from *blavet*, a spurt of water; *menesse*, woman (derogatory) derived from *meinec*, full of stones; *barant*, a stream, from *baranton*, fountain; *goffeur*, locksmith from *goff*, a smith; *guedouze*, death, which is derived from *guenn-du*, white-black. Finally, do you want history? Argot calls a crown-piece a *maltaise*, recalling the money which circulated in the Maltese galleys.

Apart from its philological origins, of which a few examples have been given, argot has other, more natural roots, emerging, so to speak, from the very spirit of man. First there is the actual creation of words, which is the mystery of all language—the depiction of objects by the use of words which, no one can say why or how, bear a countenance of their own. This is the primal basis of all language, what one might call the bedrock. Argot teems with such words, spontaneous words, created all of a piece no one can say where or by whom, words without etymology, analogy or derivation, solitary, barbaric, sometimes hideous words, which are nevertheless singularly expressive and which live. *Le taule*, the gaoler; *le sabri*, the forest; *taf*, meaning fear or flight; *le larbin*, the lackey; *pharos*, the general, prefect or minister; *le rabouin*, the devil. Nothing can be more strange than these words which both conceal and reveal. Some, such as *rabouin*, are at once grotesque and terrible, conveying the effect of a Cyclopean grimace.

* It should be noted, however, that 'mac' in Celtic means 'son'. (Note by Victor Hugo.)

461

Secondly, there is metaphor. The characteristic of a language that seeks both to say everything and to conceal everything is its abundance of imagery. Metaphor is a riddle behind which lurks the thief planning a robbery and the prisoner plotting an escape. No dialect is more rich in metaphor than argot—*devisser le coco*, to twist the neck; *tortiller*, to eat; *être gerbé*, to be judged; *un rat*, a stealer of bread; *il lansquine*, it is raining, an ancient, striking image which in some sort reveals its own date, relating the long, oblique lines of rainfall to the couched weapons of 16th-century pikemen, and also encompasses the popular saying, 'it's raining halberds'. Sometimes, as argot progresses from its first stage to the second, words also pass from the savage, primitive stage to the metaphorical. The devil ceases to be *le rabouin* and becomes *le boulanger* (baker), 'he who puts in the oven'. It is more amusing but less impressive, something like Racine after Corneille, or Euripides after Aeschylus. And there are certain sentences of argot, belonging to both stages, which have a phantasmagoric quality. *Les sorgueurs vont sollicer des gails à la lune* (rustlers are going to steal horses tonight). This presents itself to the mind like a company of ghosts. One does not know what one is looking at.

Thirdly, there is expediency. Argot lives on the language, drawing upon it and making use of it as fancy directs, and sometimes, in case of need, arbitrarily and coarsely changing it. Sometimes, with ordinary words distorted in this fashion and interlarded with words of pure argot, it produces picturesque figures of speech in which one may find both original invention and metaphor. *Le cab jaspine, je marronne que la roulotte de Pantin trime dans le sabin*—'The dog is barking, I suspect that the Paris coach is passing through the wood.' *Le dab est sinve, la dabuge est merloussière, la fée est bative*—'The man (gentleman) is stupid, the wife is sly, the daughter is pretty'. Most frequently, in order to baffle any eavesdropper, argot simply adds an uncouth tail to the word, some such suffix as *aille, orgue, iergue* or *uche*. For example, *Vousiergue trouvaille bonorgue ce gigotmuche?* 'Do you think this mutton's good?' A phrase addressed to a prison warder by a prisoner offering a sum of money for his escape. *Mar* is another suffix that has been recently added.

Argot, being the dialect of corruption, is itself soon corrupted. Moreover, as its purpose is always concealment, it changes as soon as it feels that it is being understood. Unlike every other form of vegetation, it is killed by any ray of light that falls upon it. So it is in a state of constant flux, evolving more in ten years than the everyday language does in ten centuries. *Larton* (bread) becomes *lartif*, *gail* (horse) becomes *gaye*, *fertanche* (straw) becomes *fertille*, *momignard* (child) becomes *momacque*, *les siques* (clothes) become *les frusques*, *la chique* (church) becomes *l'égrugeoir*, *le colabre* (neck) becomes *le colas*. The devil is first *gabisto*, then *le rabouin* and then *le boulanger*; the priest is *le ratichon* and then *le sanglier*; the dagger is *le vingt-deux*, then *le surin* and then *le lingre*; the police are in turn *railles*, *rousses*, *marchands de lacets*, *coqueurs* and *cognes*; the gaoler is *le taule*, *Charlot*, *l'atigeur*, and *le becquillard*. To fight in the seventeenth century was *se donner du tabac*; in the nineteenth it was *se chiquer la gueule*—and there have been twenty different variants between those two. The words of argot are constantly in flight, like the men who use them.

But at the same time, and indeed because of this constant movement, old argot constantly re-emerges and becomes new. There are centres in which it survives. The Temple preserved the argot of the seventeenth century, and the argot of Thunes was preserved in Bicêtre when it was a prison. The old Thunes suffix of *anche* was heard in, for example, *Boyanches-tu*? (Want a drink?) and *il croyanche* (he believes). But constant change is nonetheless the rule.

If the philosopher decides to spare the time to examine this language that ceaselessly evaporates, he is led to painful but useful reflections. No study is more efficacious or fruitful in instruction. There is not a metaphor or etymological derivation of argot that does not contain a lesson.

Among those people *battre* (to fight) means to sham—*on bat une maladie* (one shams an illness), for tricking is their strength. The idea of 'man' is inseparable from the idea of darkness. Night is *la sorgue*, and man is *l'orgue*: man is a derivation of night. They are accustomed to think of society as a climate that destroys them, and they talk of their freedom as other people talk of their health. A man who has been arrested is *un malade* (sick), and a man under sentence is *un mort* (dead).

What is most dreadful for the man enclosed within the walls of a prison is a sort of icy chastity: he calls the prison *le castus*. It is always the gayer side of life outside that he recalls when he is in that dismal place. He wears leg-irons but does not think of walking on his feet: he thinks of dancing; and if he manages to saw through his irons, dancing is his first thought and he calls the saw a *bastringue* (cheap dance-hall). A noun is *un centre*—a profound assimilation. A criminal has two heads, the one which thinks and plans, and the one which he loses on the block: he calls the first *la sorbonne* and the second *la tronche**. When a man has nothing left but rags on his body and viciousness in his heart, when he has sunk to that state of material and moral degradation which is summed up in the word *gueux*, he is then ripe for crime; he is like a well-sharpened, double-edged knife,

* La Sorbonne—the university of Paris. Tronche—commonplace slang, as it might be, 'nut'. Trs.

463

one edge being his state of need and the other his depravity. Argot in this case does not call him *un gueux* but *un reguise* (re-shaped). What is a gaol but a furnace of damnation, a Hell? The inmate calls himself *un fagot* (faggot). Finally, they call the prison *le collège*, a word which sums up the whole penitentiary system. And to the thief his prospective victims—you or I or any passer-by—are *le pantre*, from the Greek *pan*, meaning *everyone*.

Should you wish to know where the greater number of the prison-songs were born, those ditties which prison argot calls *lirlonfa*, the following is for your enlightenment.

There existed in the Châtelet in Paris a large, long cellar some eight feet below the level of the Seine. It possessed neither windows nor ventilators, its only outlet being by way of the door: men could enter it, but air could not. It had a vaulted stone ceiling and for floor ten inches of mud, the original tiling having disintegrated under the seeping of water. A massive beam ran from end to end of the cellar, eight feet above floor level, and from it, at regular intervals, hung chains three feet long ending in iron collars. It was here that men condemned to the galleys were housed before being sent on to Toulon. They hung here in darkness chained by the neck, unable to lie down because of the shortness of the chains, up to their knees in mud, legs soiled with their own excrement, unable to rest except by hanging on to the chains and, if they dozed off, constantly awakened by the stranglehold of the collar—and there were some who did not wake. In order to eat they had to use their feet to retrieve their portion of bread, which was dropped on to the mud in front of them. How long were they left like this? One or two months, sometimes six months, in one case a year. They had been sentenced to the galleys for as little as poaching one of the king's hares. And what did they do in that hellish tomb? They did what can be done in a tomb—they died—and what can be done in Hell—they sang. Where there is no hope there is still song. In the sea round Malta when a galley was approaching one heard the sound of singing before one heard the sound of oars. The poacher Survincent, who survived that Châtelet cellar, said, 'It was the rhymes that kept me going.' Here it was that nearly all the argot ditties were born, including the melancholy refrain that was particular to the Montgomery galley—*Timaloumisaine, timoulamison*. Most of these songs were sad, but some were gay and one was tender:

Icicaille est le théâtre
*Du petit dardant.**

* This is the theatre
of the little archer.

Do what you will, you cannot destroy that eternal remnant of the heart of man which is love.

In that world of dark deeds one keeps one's secrets. Secrecy is the privilege of everyman, the faith held in common which serves as the basis of union. To break secrecy is to rob every member of that savage community of something of himself. To inform is to *manger le morceau* (eat the piece) as though the informer had stolen something of the substance of his fellows and fed on the flesh of all of them.

What is *recevoir un soufflet* (to get your ears boxed)? The commonplace French expression is *voir trent-six chandelles* (to see thirty-six candles; English equivalent 'to see stars'). Argot here makes use of the word *camoufle*, which also means 'candle' and adds the 'et' from the word *soufflet*, establishing a new word on the academic level, and Ponlailler, saying, 'J'allume ma camoufle' causes Voltaire to write, '*Langleviel la Baumelle mérite cent camouflets*' (Langleviel la Baumelle deserves to have his ears boxed a hundred times).

Burrowing into argot leads to countless discoveries. It leads us to the point of contact between respectable society and that of the outcasts; it is speech become a felon, and it is dismaying to find that the obscure workings of fate can so distort men's minds and bring them so low. The meagre thinking of the outcast! Will no one come to the rescue of the human souls lost in that darkness? Must they wait for ever for the liberating spirit, the rider upon the winds, the radiant champion of the future? Are they condemned for all time to listen in terror to the approach of the Monster of Evil, the dragon with foaming lips, while they remain without light or hope, a defenceless Andromeda, white and naked in the murk?

III. *Argot that Weeps and Argots that Laughs*

As we see, argot as a whole, whether it is the dialect of four hundred years ago or that of today, is pervaded by a sombre symbolism which is at once an expression of grieving and of threatening. One may catch something of the old, wild sadness of those outlaws of the Cour des Miracles who played card-games of their own devising, some of which have come down to us. The eight of clubs, for example, was a big tree with eight large clover-leaves, a sort of fanciful representation of the forest; at the foot of the tree was a fire over which a hunter was roasting three hares on a spit, while behind, suspended over another fire, was a steaming pot from which a dog's head protruded. One may picture smugglers and counterfeiters seated round this idyllic and melancholy conception of their world as depicted on playing-cards. All the diverse expressions of thought in the kingdom of argot, whether song or jest or threat, had this quality of helpless despair. All the songs, of which some of the tunes have been retrieved, were heartrendingly piteous and humble. The thieving rabble, *le pègre*, was always *le pauvre pègre*, always the hare which hides, the mouse which scuttles, the bird which takes flight. It utters few but simple sighs, and one of its sighs has been preserved —'*Je n'entrave que le dail comment meck, le daron des orgues, peut atiger ses mômes et ses momignards et les locher criblant sans être atigé lui-meme*' (I don't understand how God, the father of men, can torture his children and grandchildren and hear them cry without being tortured himself). The outcast, whenever he has a moment to think, makes himself small in the eye of the law and puny in the eye of society; he goes on his knees and begs for pity. One feels that he knows the fault is his own.

Towards the middle of the last century there was a change. Prison songs and thieves' refrains acquired as it were a flavour of jovial insolence. In nearly all the galley and prison songs of the eighteenth century there is a diabolical, enigmatic spirit of gaiety which puts one in mind of the dancing light cast by a will-o'-the-wisp in the forest.

> *Mirlababi, surlababo,*
> *Mirliton ribon ribette,*
> *Surlababi, mirlababo,*
> *Mirliton ribon ribo.*

This was sung while a man's throat was being cut in a cellar or a corner of the woods.

It was symptomatic. In the eighteenth century the ancient melancholy of this oppressed class was dispelled. They began to laugh, mocking the powers that be. Louis XV was known as the 'Marquis de Pantin'. They were almost cheerful, glowing with a kind of lightness as though conscience no longer weighed upon them. Not merely did they perform acts of desperate daring, but they did so with a heedless audacity of spirit. It was an indication that they were losing the sense of their own criminality, finding among the thinkers of the day a kind of unwitting moral support, an indication that theft and robbery were beginning to infiltrate doctrine and current dogma, and thereby losing something of their ugliness while adding greatly to the ugliness of the latter. Finally it was an indication that, if nothing happened to prevent it, some tremendous event was on the way.

Let us pause for a moment. What are we now accusing—the eighteenth century?—its philosophy? By no means. The work of

466

the eighteenth century was healthy and good. The encyclopaedists, led by Diderot, the physiocrats, led by Turgot, the philosophers, led by Voltaire, and the Utopians, led by Rousseau, these are four noble bodies. The immense advance of mankind towards enlightenment was due to them. They were the advance-guards of the human race moving towards the four cardinal points of progress, Diderot towards beauty, Turgot towards utility, Voltaire towards truth, and Rousseau towards justice. But at the side of the philosophers and below them came the sophists, a poisonous plant intertwined with healthy youth, hemlock in the virgin forest. While authority burned the great liberating books of the century on the steps of the Palais de Justice, writers now forgotten were publishing, with the king's sanction, books of a strangely subversive kind, avidly read by the outcasts. Some of these publications—patronized, astonishingly enough, by a prince—are to be found in the *Bibliothèque secrète*, the Secret Library. These facts, profoundly significant though they were, passed unperceived. Sometimes it is the very obscurity of a fact that renders it dangerous. It is obscure because it is underground. Of all those writers, the one perhaps who had the most harmful effect on the masses was Restif de la Bretonne. Work of this kind, which was being produced all over Europe, did more damage in Germany than anywhere else. During a certain period, which is summarized by Schiller in his play, *Die Räuber*, theft and robbery were paraded under the guise of protest against property and work. They embraced certain specious, elementary notions, correct in appearance but absurd in reality, and, thus dissimulated and invested with names denoting abstract theories, permeated the mass of hard-working, honest people, without the knowledge of the rash chemists who had concocted the mixture and even of the masses who absorbed it. Hardship engenders anger; and while the well-to-do classes close their eyes—or slumber, which comes to the same thing —the less fortunate, taking their inspiration from any spirit of grievance or ill-will that happens to be lurking in the background, proceed to examine the social system. Examination in a spirit of hatred is a terrible thing!

From this, if the times are sufficiently awry, emerge those ferocious upheavals at one time known as *jacqueries*, compared with which purely political agitation is child's play, and which are not the struggle of the oppressed against the oppressor but rather the revolt of the deprived against the comfortably off. Everything then collapses, for *jacqueries* are the tremors of the people. This peril, which was perhaps imminent in Europe towards the end of the eighteenth century, was harshly averted by the French Revolution, that immense act of probity. The French Revolution, which was nothing but idealism in arms, broke out and with a single decisive gesture slammed the door on evil and opened the door to good. It posed the question, promulgated the truth, dispelled the fogs, cleansed the century, and crowned the people.

The nineteenth century has inherited and profited by its work, and today the social disaster which seemed to be foreshadowed is quite simply impossible. Only the blind still rage against it, and only fools are afraid of it. Revolution is the antidote to *jacquerie*!

Thanks to the Revolution, social conditions have changed and we have got the feudal and monarchic sicknesses out of our system. There is no longer anything mediaeval in our constitution. We have come past the time when those ugly interior convulsions burst into daylight, when we heard the muffled sound of stirring beneath our feet, when the surface of civilization was littered with molehills, when crevasses suddenly yawned and monstrous heads emerged from the earth.

Revolutionary feeling is a moral feeling. The feeling for what is right, once it has matured, develops a sense of duty. The law for every man is liberty, which ends, in Robespierre's admirable definition, where the liberty of others begins. Since 1789 the populace as a whole is expressed in the sublimated individual; no man is so poor that, having rights, he has not his place. The starving man feels in himself the honesty of France; the dignity of the citizen is an inner armour; the man who is free is scrupulous; he who votes rules. Hence the incorruptibility, the suppression of unhealthy aspirations, the eyes heroically averted from temptation. Revolutionary cleansing is such that on a day of liberation, a 14 July or a 10 August, there is no longer a populace. The first cry of the enlightened crowds as they grow in stature is, 'Death to thieves!' Progress is honourable; the Ideal and the Absolute do not pick pockets. It was the scavengers of the Faubourg Saint-Antoine who in 1848 escorted the carts filled with the treasures of the Tuileries; rags and tatters mounted guard over riches. In those carts there were chests, some half-open, containing among a hundred dazzling adornments the ancient, diamond-studded crown of France surmounted by the royal carbuncle of regency, worth thirty millions. Those barefoot men preserved it.

So *jacquerie* is at an end. I am sorry for the clever men, haunted by an age-old fear which has found its last expression and now can only be serviceable in politics. The mainspring of the red spectre is broken, and everyone knows it. The scarecrow scares no longer. Birds perch on it, beetles nest in it and the bourgeois laughs at it.

Does this mean then, that all social dangers are over? Certainly not. There will be no more *jacqueries*, of this society can be assured; the blood will no longer rush to its head. But it has got to consider the way in which it breathes. Apoplexy is no longer a threat, but there is still consumption. Social consumption is simply poverty. One can die from wasting away as well as from being struck by lightning.

We never weary of repeating that we must before all else think of the disinherited, suffering masses, care for them, comfort and enlighten them, widen their horizon by bringing to them all forms of education. We must set them the example of toil, never of idleness, lessen the burden on the individual by increasing that borne by society as a whole, reduce poverty without reducing wealth, create great new fields of public activity, possess, like Briareus, a hundred hands to reach out to those who are in distress, use our collective power to set up workshops, schools, and laboratories open to men of all kinds, increase wages and decrease working hours, effect a balance between rights and possessions, that is to say, make the reward proportionate to the effort and the fulfilment to the need— in a word, derive more light and well-being from the social system for the benefit of the ignorant and oppressed. This is the first of fraternal obligations and of political necessities.

But all of this, we must emphasize, is no more than a beginning. The real question is, can work be the law without also being a right? We shall not pursue the matter, since this is not the place for it. But if the name for Nature is Providence, then the name for Society must be Provision.

Intellectual and moral growth is no less essential than material betterment. Knowledge is a viaticum; thought is a primary necessity; truth is as much a source of nourishment as corn. Argument lacking knowledge and wisdom grows thin. We must pity minds, no less than stomachs, that go unfilled. If there is anything more poignant than a body dying for lack of food it is a mind dying for lack of light.

All progress points in this direction, and the day is coming when we shall be amazed. As the state of the human race improves, its lowest layers will rise quite naturally above the zone of distress. The abolition of poverty will be achieved by a simple raising of the level. This is a blessed solution, and we shall be wrong to doubt it.

Certainly the influence of the past is very strong at the present time; it is reviving, and this rejuvenation of a corpse is surprising. It is on the march, and it seems to be winning—a dead thing yet a conqueror! It comes with its army of superstitions, its sword, which is despotism, its banner, which is ignorance, and in recent years it has won ten battles. It advances, laughs, and threatens; it is at our door. But we do not despair. Let us sell the field on which Hannibal is encamped. We who believe, what have we to fear? Ideas can no more flow backwards than can a river.

But those who do not welcome the future should consider this: in denying progress it is not the future that they condemn, but themselves. They are inoculating themselves with a fatal disease, the past. There is only one way of denying tomorrow, and that is to die.

The riddle will disclose its answer, the Sphinx will speak, the problem will be solved. The People, having burst their bonds in the eighteenth century, will complete their triumph in the nineteenth. Only a fool can doubt it. The coming achievement, the imminent achievement of universal well-being, is a phenomenon divinely pre-ordained.

The immense pressure of events indicates that within a given time human society will be brought to its logical condition, that is to say, into equilibrium, which is the same as equity. A power comprising earth and Heaven emanates from humanity and directs it; it is a power that can work miracles, to which miraculous accomplishments are no more difficult than extraordinary deviations. Aided by the knowledge which comes from man, and the event which comes from another source, this power is undismayed by contradictions arising out of the problem it poses, which to the common mind seem impossibilities. It is no less adroit in producing solutions out of the conjunction of ideas than it is in producing lessons out of the juxtaposition of facts. One may expect anything of this mysterious power of progress which on one occasion caused East and West to meet in a sepulchre, and the Imams to treat with Bonaparte in the interior of the Great Pyramid.

Meanwhile there must be no pause, no hesitation, in the forward march of minds. Social philosophy is essentially the science of peace. Its purpose is, and its outcome should be, to dissipate anger by studying the reason for antagonism. It scrutinizes and analyses, then reshapes. It proceeds by a process of reduction, eliminating the element of hatred.

That a society should be destroyed by the winds that assail human affairs is by no means unknown; history is filled with the shipwreck of nations and empires. The day comes when the hurricane, that unknown factor, bears custom, law, religion, everything away. One after another, the civilizations of India, the Chaldees, Persia, Assyria, and Egypt have perished, and we do not know why. We do not know the cause of these disasters. Could those societies have been saved? Were they at fault? Did they persist in some fatal vice which destroyed them? How great is the element of suicide in the death of a nation or a race? They are questions without answer. The condemned civilizations are lost in darkness. They were not seaworthy and so they sank, and there is nothing more to be said. It is with a sort of horror that we peer into the depths of that sea which is the past, through the great waves of the centuries, at the huge wrecks which are Babylon, Nineveh, Tarsus, Thebes, and Rome. But if they are buried, we exist in the light of day. We are ignorant of the sickness of ancient civilizations, but we know the infirmities of our own. We are able everywhere to throw light upon it, to admire its beauties and lay bare its deformities. We probe it to see where it hurts, and when we have found the pain-centre our examination of the cause leads to the discovery of the remedy. Our civilization, the work of twenty centuries, is at once their monster and their prodigy; it is worth saving. And it will be saved. To doctor it is to do a great deal; to enlighten it is to do still more. All the work of modern social philosophy should bear this end in mind. To auscultate civilization is the supreme duty of the thinker of today.

Let us repeat it, this auscultation is encouraging; and it is with emphasis on the note of encouragement that we wish to end these few pages of austere digression from our sombre narrative. Beneath social mortality we are conscious of human imperishability. The earth does not die because there are lesions on its body, craters and volcanoes out of which it pours its pus. The sickness of a nation does not kill Man.

Nevertheless, those who study the health of society must now and then shake their heads. Even the strongest-minded and most clear-thinking must have their moments of misgiving. Will the future ever arrive? The question seems almost justified when one considers the shadows looming ahead, the sombre confrontation of egoists and outcasts. On the side of the egoists, prejudice—that darkness of a rich education—appetite that grows with intoxication, the bemusement of prosperity which blunts the sense, the fear of suffering which in some cases goes so far as to hate all sufferers, and unshakeable complacency, the ego so inflated that it stifles the soul; and on the side of the outcasts, greed and envy, resentment at the happiness of others, the turmoil of the human animal in search of personal fulfilment, hearts filled with fog, misery, needs, and fatalism, and simple, impure ignorance.

Should we continue to look upwards? Is the light we can see in the sky one of those which will presently be extinguished? The ideal is terrifying to behold, lost as it is in the depths, small, isolated, a pin-point, brilliant but threatened on all sides by the dark forces that surround it: nevertheless, no more in danger than a star in the jaws of the clouds.

Set in 11 point Garamond type leaded 1 point
and printed by Fletcher & Son Ltd, Norwich
on Book Wove paper.
Illustrations lithographed by
W & J Mackay Ltd, Chatham.
Bound by W & J Mackay Ltd
using Tego Buckram and Halflinnen Cloth
blocked with a design by
Jeff Clements.